STEEL CITY MAGIC

BOOKS BY WEN SPENCER

Alien Taste
Bitter Waters
A Brother's Price
Dog Warrior
Tainted Trail

STEEL CITY MAGIC

Tinker
Wolf Who Rules

Wen Spencer

FANTASY

ISBN-10: 0-7394-6687-9
ISBN-13: 978-0-7394-6687-2

Published by arrangement with
Baen Publishing Enterprises
P.O. Box 1403
Riverdale, NY 10471

Visit the SFBC online at www.sfbc.com
Visit Baen Books online at www.baen.com

PRINTED IN THE UNITED STATES OF AMERICA

STEEL CITY MAGIC

CONTENTS

TINKER   1

WOLF WHO RULES   317

TINKER

Instant Message conversation dated
February 24, 2003, 7:00 p.m.

WS: To Don, who always helped me grow.

DK: Wow! Thanks. But that's kind of lame. How about: To Don, cute, but prickly like a hedgehog.

WS: . . . *

DK: Um, don't use that. . . .

WS: To Don, who will someday get his hedgehog. To Don, the hedgehog is just for you.

DK: To Don Kosak, King of hedgehogs.

WS: To Don, I will never look at hedgehogs the same way again? To Don, Champion of the hedgehogs! To Don, "What, no, it's not a hedgehog. It's his head!" To Don, it's hedgehogs the whole way down. To Don, who is forever seeing hedgehogs.

DK: To Don, How do you know that Don doesn't know that the hedgehogs are enjoying themselves in the spring.

WS: To zen Don, who may or may not be there.

DK: Hee hee. Okay.

*footnote: . . . is the Japanese way to indicate stunned or annoyed silence.

Many thanks for the people who have helped me with this novel: *Sherry Briggs, George Corcoran, Kevin Hayes, Deanna Hoak, W. Randy Hoffman, Kendall Jung, Don Kosak, Linn Prentis, Dr. Hope Erica Ring, June Drexler Robertson, John Schmid, Diane Turnshek, Aaron Wollerton, and all the Baen Barflies.*

Special thanks to: Ann Cecil

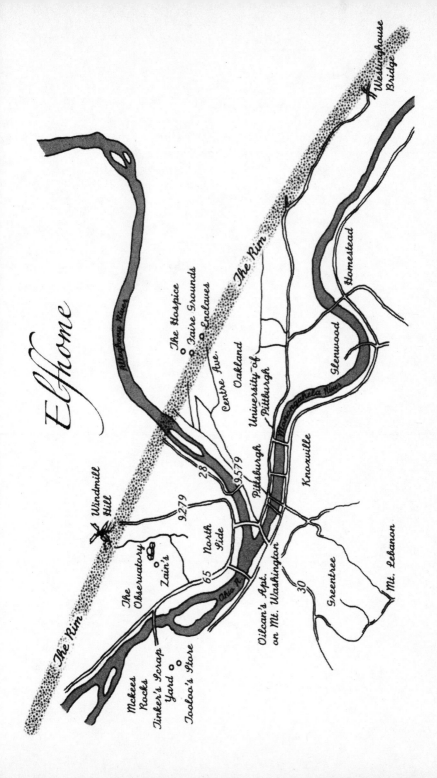

1: LIFE DEBT

The wargs chased the elf over Pittsburgh Scrap and Salvage's tall chain-link fence shortly after the hyperphase gate powered down.

Tinker had been high up in the crane tower, shuffling cars around the dark sprawling maze of her scrap yard, trying to make room for the influx of wrecks Shutdown Day always brought in. Her cousin, Oilcan, was out with the flatbed wrecker, clearing their third call of the night, and it wasn't Shutdown proper yet.

Normally, clearing space was an interesting puzzle game, played on a gigantic scale. Move this stripped car to the crusher. Consolidate two piles of engine blocks. Lightly place a new acquisition onto the tower of to-be-stripped vehicles. She had waited until too late, though, tinkering in her workshop with her newest invention. Shuffling the scrap around at night was proving nearly impossible. Starting with the crane's usual clumsy handling—its ancient fishing pole design and manual controls often translated the lightest tap into a several-foot movement of the large electromagnet strung off the boom—she also had to factor in the distorted shadows thrown by the crane's twin floodlights, the deep pools of darkness, and the urge to rush, since Shutdown was quickly approaching.

Worse yet, the powerful electromagnet was accumulating a dangerous level of magic. A strong ley line ran through the scrap yard, so using the crane always attracted some amount of magic. She had invented a siphon to drain off the power to a storage unit also of her own design. The prolonged periods of running the crane were overwhelming the siphon's capacity. Even with taking short breaks with the magnet turned off, the accumulated magic writhed a deep purple about the disc and boom.

At ten minutes to midnight, she gave up and shut down the electromagnet. The electric company changed over from the local Pittsburgh power grid to the national grid to protect Pittsburgh's limited resources from the spike in usage that Shutdown brought. She had no reason to risk dropping a car sixty feet onto something valuable because some yutz flipped a switch early.

So she sat and waited for Shutdown, idly kicking her steel-tipped boots against the side of the crane's control booth. Her scrap yard sat on a hill overlooking the Ohio River. From the crane, she could see the barges choking the waterway, the West End Bridge snarled with traffic, and ten or more miles of rolling hills in all directions. She also had an unobstructed view of the full Elfhome moon, rising up through the veil effect on the Eastern horizon. The distortion came from the hyperphase lightly holding its kidnapping victim, a fifty-mile-diameter chunk of Earth complete with parts of downtown Pittsburgh, prisoner in the foreign dimension of Elfhome. The veil shimmered like heat waves over the pale moon face, nearly identical to that of Earth's own moon. Ribbons of red and blue danced in the sky along the Rim's curve, the collision of realities mimicking the borealis effect. Where the Rim cut through the heart of Pittsburgh, just a few miles southeast, the colors gleamed brilliantly. They paled as the Rim arced off, defining the displaced land mass. Beyond the Rim, the dark forest of Elfhome joined the night sky, black meeting black, the blaze of stars the only indication where the first ended and the second began.

So much beauty! Part of her hated going back to Earth, even for a day. Pittsburgh, however, needed the influx of goods that Shutdown Day brought; the North American counterpart of Elfhome was lightly populated and couldn't support a city of sixty thousand humans.

Off in the west, somewhere near the idle airport, a firework streaked skyward and boomed into bright flowers of color—the advent of Shutdown providing the grounded airplane crews with an excuse to party. Another firework followed.

Between the whistle and thunder of the fireworks, the impatient hum of distant traffic, the echoing blare of tugboat horns, the shushing of the siphon still draining magic off the electromagnet, and the thumping of her boots, she nearly didn't hear the wargs approaching. A howl rose, harsh and wild, from somewhere toward the airport. She stilled her foot, then reached out with an oil-stained finger to snap off the siphon. The shushing died away, and the large disc at the end of the crane boom started to gleam violet again.

In a moment of relative silence, she heard a full pack in voice, their prey in sight. While the elfin rangers killed the packs of wargs that strayed too close to Pittsburgh, one heard their howling echoing up the river valleys quite often. This sound was deeper, though, than any wargs she'd heard before, closer to the deep-chest roar of a saurus. As she tried to judge how close the wargs were—and more important, if they were heading in her direction—St. Paul started to ring midnight.

"Oh no, not now," she whispered as the church bells drowned out the hoarse baying. Impatiently, she counted out the peals. Ten. Eleven. Twelve.

In another dimension infinitesimally close and mind-bogglingly far, the Chinese powered down their hyperphase gate in geosynchronous orbit, and yanked Pittsburgh back off the world of Elfhome. Returning to Earth reminded Tinker of being on the edge of sleep and having a sensation of falling so real that she would jerk back awake, flat in bed so she couldn't actually have fallen anywhere. The gate turned off, the universe went black and fell away, and then, snap, she was sitting in the crane's operating chair, eyes wide open, and nothing had moved.

But everything had changed.

A hush came with Shutdown. The world went silent and held its breath. All the city lights were out; the Pittsburgh power grid shut down. The aurora dancing along the Rim dissipated, replaced by the horizon-hugging gleam of light pollution, as if a million bonfires had been lit. A storm wind whispered through the silent darkness, stirred up as the weather fronts coming across Ohio collided with the returning Pittsburgh air. On the wind came a haze that smudged what had been crystalline sky.

"Oh, goddamn it. You would think that after twenty years they would figure out a saner way of doing this. Let's get the power back on! Come on."

The wargs took voice again, only a block away and closing fast.

Was she safe in the crane? If the oncoming menace had been a saurus, she'd say she was safe on the high tower, for while the saurus was a nightmarish cousin of the dinosaur, it was a natural creature. Apparently designed as weapons of mass destruction in some ancient magical war, wargs were far more than pony-sized wolves; it was quite possible they could climb.

But could she make it to her workshop trailer, the walls and windows reinforced against such a possible attack?

Tinker dug into the big side pocket of her carpenter pants, took out her night goggles, and pulled them on. In the green wash of the goggles' vision, she then saw the elf. He was coming at her over the burned-out booster rockets, dead cars, and obsolete computers. Behind him, the wargs checked at the high chain-link fence of the scrap yard. She got the impression of five or six of the huge, wolflike creatures as they milled there, probably balking more at the metal content of the fence than at its twelve-foot height or the additional three-foot razor-wire crown. Magic and metal didn't mix. Even as she whispered, "Just leave! Give up!" the first warg backed up, took a running start at the fence, and leaped it, clearing it by an easy three or four feet.

"Oh, shit!" Tinker yanked on her gloves, swung out of the open control cage, and slid down the ladder.

"Sparks?" she whispered, hoping the backup power had kicked in on her computer network. "Is the phone online?"

"No, Boss," came the reply on her headset, the AI annoyingly chipper.

Her fuel cell batteries kept her computer system operational. Unfortunately, the phone company wasn't as reliable. That her security programs needed a dial tone to call the police was a weakness she'd have to fix, but until then, she was screwed. Shit, they could build a hyperphase gate in geostationary orbit and put a man in the seas of Europa, but they couldn't get the damn phones to work on Shutdown Day!

"Sparks, open a channel to the wrecker."

"Done, Boss."

"Oilcan? Can you hear me? Oilcan?" Damn, her cousin was out of the wrecker's cab. She paused, waiting to see if he would answer, then gave up. "Sparks, at two-minute intervals repeat following message: 'Oilcan, this is Tinker. I've got trouble. Big trouble. Get back here. Bring cops. Send cops. I'll probably need an ambulance too. Get me help! Hurry.' End message."

"Okay, Boss."

She landed at the foot of the ladder. A noise to her left made her look up. The elf was on one of the tarp-covered shuttle booster rockets, pausing to draw his long thin sword, apparently deciding to stop and fight. Six to one—it would be more a slaughter than a fight. That fact alone would normally make her sick.

Worse, though, she recognized the elf: Windwolf. She didn't know him in any personal sense. Their interaction had been limited to an ironically similar situation five years ago. A saurus had broken out of its cage during the Mayday Faire, chewing its way through the frightened crowd. In a moment of childish stupidity, she'd attacked it, wielding a tire iron. She had nearly gotten herself killed. A furious Windwolf had saved her and cast a spell on her, placing a life debt on her essence, linking her fate with his. If her actions got him killed, she would die too.

Or at least, that's what Tooloo said the spell would do.

Sane logic made her question the old half-elf. Why would Windwolf save her only to doom her? But Windwolf was an elf noble—thus one of the arrogant *domana* caste—and one had to keep in mind that elves were alien creatures, despite their human appearance. Just look at loony old Tooloo.

And according to crazy Tooloo, the life debt had never been canceled.

Of all the elves in Pittsburgh, why did it have to be Windwolf?

"Oh, Tinker, you're screwed with all capital letters," she muttered to herself.

Her scrap yard ran six city blocks, a virtual maze of exotic junk. She had the advantage of knowing the yard intimately. The first warg charged across the top of a PAT bus sitting next to the booster rockets. The polymer roof dimpled under its weight; the beast left hubcap-sized footprints in its wake. Windwolf swung his sword, catching the huge creature in its midsection. Tinker flinched, expecting blood and viscera; despite their magical origin, wargs were living creatures.

Along the savage cut, however, there was a crackling brilliance like electrical discharge. For a second, the warg's body flashed from solid flesh to the violet, intricate, circuitlike pattern of a spell. That gleaming, rune-covered shell hung in mid-air, outlining the mass of the warg. She could recognize various subsections: expansion, increase vector, artificial inertia. Inside the artificial construct hung a small dark mass—an animal acting like the hand inside of a puppet. She couldn't identify the controlling beast, shrouded as it was by the shifting lines of spell, but it looked only slightly larger than a house cat.

What the hell?

Then the spell vanished back to illusionary flesh, reforming the appearance of a great dog. The monster rammed Windwolf in a collision of bodies, and they went tumbling down off the rocket.

These creatures weren't wargs, nor were they totally real. They weren't flesh-and-blood animals, at least not on the surface. Someone had done a weird illusionary enhancement, something along the lines of a solid hologram. If she disrupted the spell, the monsters should be reduced back to the much smaller, and hopefully less dangerous, animal providing the intelligence and movement to the construct.

And she had to try something quick, before the pseudo-warg killed Windwolf.

She ran twenty feet to a pile of sucker poles brought in last year from a well salvage job. They were fifteen feet long, but only two inches thick, making them light but awkward. More importantly, they were at hand. She snatched one up, worked her hands down it until she had a stiff spear of five feet fed out in front of her, and then ran toward the fight.

The monster had Windwolf pinned to the ground. Up close, there was no mistaking the weird-looking thing for a standard wolfish warg. While equally massive, the vaguely doglike creature was square-jawed and pug-nosed with a mane and stub tail of thick, short, curly hair. The monster dog had Windwolf by the shoulder and was shaking him hard. The elf had lost his sword and was trying to draw his dagger.

Tinker put all her speed and weight into punching the pole tip through the dog's chest. She hoped that even if the pole failed to penetrate, she might be able to knock the monster back off of Windwolf. As she closed, she wondered at the wisdom of her plan. The thing was huge. She never could remember that she was a small person; she had unconsciously used Windwolf as a scale, and had forgotten that he was nearly a foot taller than she.

This is going to hurt me more than it, she thought, and slammed the pole home.

Amazingly, there was only a moment of resistance, as if she had struck true flesh, and then the spell parted under the solid metal, and the pole sank up to her clenched hands. The beast shifted form, back to the gleaming spell. Both the spell form and the creature within reeled in pain; luckily someone had been careless in the sensory feedback limit. She reached down the pole, grabbed hold at the eight-foot mark, and shoved hard. The pole speared through the massive spell form, bursting out through the heavily muscled back, near the rear haunch.

The dog shrieked, breath blasting hot over her, smelling of smoke and sandalwood. It lifted a front foot to bat at her. She saw—too late to react—that the paw had five-inch claws. Before it could hit her, though, Windwolf's legs scissored around her waist, and she found herself airborne, sailing toward the side of the booster rocket.

I was right. This is going to hurt.

But then Windwolf plucked her out of the air on his way up to the top of the rocket. The crane's floodlights snapped on—the transfer of Pittsburgh to the national power grid apparently now complete—

and spotlighted them where they landed. Beyond the fence, the rest of the city lights flickered on.

"Fool," Windwolf growled, dropping her to her feet. "It would have killed you."

They were nearly the exact words he had said during their battle with the saurus. Were they fated to replay this drama again and again? If so, his next words would be for her to leave.

Windwolf grunted, pushing her behind him. "Run."

There was her cue. Coming across the booster rocket were three of the monstrous dogs, the poly–coated tarp insulating their charge. Enter monsters, stage right. Exit brave heroine, stage left, in a dash and jump for the crane ladder.

What disrupted magic better than a length of steel was magnetism! With the power back on, the crane was operational. If she could get up to it and switch on the electromagnet, the dogs were toast. Through the bars of the ladder, she could see a fourth monster coming across the scrap yard, leaping from nonconductive pile to nonconductive pile like a cat transversing a creek via stepping stones.

She was twenty feet from the cage when it landed on the crane trusses and started up after her. And she had thought herself so clever in using ironwood instead of steel to build the crane tower.

"Oh damn, my stupid luck." She frantically scrambled up the rungs, fighting panic now. She was forty feet up; falling would be bad.

The dog was being equally cautious, taking the time to judge its jump before making it. She climbed fifteen feet before it took its first leap, landing nearly where she had been when it first reached the crane. It reared and stretched out its front legs, claws extended, trying to fish her down off the steel ladder without actually touching metal. She climbed frantically up and into the crane's mostly wood cage. She slapped on the power button and fumbled wildly through the dark interior for a weapon, tipping toward panic.

With the scrabble of claws on wood, the monster landed on the window ledge.

Her hand closed on the portable radio. *No. Well, maybe.* She flung it at the massive head. The tool kit followed. She snatched up the fire extinguisher as the monster growled and reached out for her like a cat with a cornered mouse. Cat? Dog? What the hell were these things? She'd have to figure it out later; it would bug her until she knew.

She started to throw the fire extinguisher and then caught herself. These things seemed to have full sensory feedback! Flipping the fire extinguisher, she yanked out the pin, pressed the lever, and unloaded the foam into the monster's face. The creature jerked back, teetering on the edge as it rubbed a paw at its foam-covered eyes. She changed her grip on the extinguisher, hauled back, and then nailed the dog with a full roundhouse swing to the head.

There was a nice satisfying *clang*, a wail of terror, a brief fast scramble of claws, and then it fell.

With luck, it wouldn't land on its feet.

She jumped to the crane controls. She had to lean way out to see Windwolf at the foot of the crane as she swung the boom around. Three of the monster dogs had him down, tearing at him like a rag doll. Was she too late? "Oh, gods, let this work!"

She activated the electromagnet, hit the siphon to drain off magic to the magic sink, and dropped the disc as fast and close as she dared onto the tight knot of bodies.

Luckily Windwolf and the dogs were on the booster rocket, which was far too big to be lifted by the electromagnet. The illusionary flesh of the dogs shifted to semitransparent shells. The spells unraveled, their power sucked away by the magnet, dropping the small animals controlling the monsters onto the rocket.

Dogs. Small, ugly, pug-nosed dogs, not much bigger than alley cats. Still, they launched themselves at Windwolf, barking and growling. She swore, swung out of the crane's cage, and slid down the ladder. As she landed, she saw a huge dark figure coming at her.

Shit, the monster dog she'd smacked out the window!

She raced for the booster rocket with the electromagnet still hovering over it, magic wreathing the black disc. She could smell the dog's smoky breath, feel it blasting furnace hot against her back. With a strange clinical detachment, she remembered that cats killed their prey by biting down and breaking their necks. What did dogs do?

The dog hit her. She flung her hands back to protect her neck, and the massive jaws closed on her left hand. She screamed as they tumbled onto the ground. Gunshots cracked and echoed over the scrap yard as the dog shook its head, ravaging her hand.

"Help!" she screamed to the unknown shooter. "Help me!"

With a sharp crack, a bullet caught the dog in the center of its forehead, snapping its head backward. The flesh vanished to spell form, flaring deep violet, as the steel blasted through it. The dog released her hand, and she dropped to the ground. Immediately, she half crawled, half stumbled for the booster rocket. The shooter fired, again and again. She glanced back as she ran. The bullets struck the dog in a quick sharp hail, punching it backward. The runes flared with each shot, giving lightning flashes of the dog within, a vulnerable heart to the monstrous construct. The spell form, however, was robbing the bullets of their velocity and diverting them from a straight path. The monster came on, the dog within unharmed.

Sobbing in pain and fear, she hit the side of the booster rocket and clawed desperately for a handhold, leaving bloody smears with her savaged hand.

The monster launched itself at her—and hit the electromagnet's radius of influence. The spell flashed brilliantly, and then unraveled, the magic fraying upward in momentarily visible violet particles.

The small ugly dog within landed at Tinker's feet, growling.

"Oh, you're so dead!" she told it, and kicked it hard with her steel-toe boot. The dog landed a dozen feet away, struggled to its feet, and fled, yelping. "And it's good!" Tinker held her hands up like a referee judging a field goal. "And the fans go wild! Tink-ker! Tink-ker! Tink-ker!"

Elation lasted only a minute. The numbness in her hand gave way to pain. The wound bled at an alarming rate, though she suspected any rate would be frightening. Blood just had a way of being upsetting.

And there was still Windwolf to save.

"Sparks?"

"Yeah, Boss?"

"Is the phone working yet?"

"No dial tone, Boss."

Her luck, the phone company would only get the phones online an hour before Startup.

She struggled through cutting up her oversized shirt with her Swiss Army knife, reducing it down to a midriff. She had an individually wrapped feminine hygiene pad in her pants pocket. (They made good sterile bandages in such emergencies, and held twice their weight in motor oil.) She cut the pad in half and used her shirt to tie the two halves tight to either side of her bleeding hand. Not a great job, but it would have to do.

She walked around to the front of the booster rocket and clambered up the twelve feet to its top. Windwolf lay sprawled in a pool of blood. The ugly pug-faced dogs lay around him, dead. As she checked Windwolf's pulse, his almond eyes opened, recognized her, and closed.

The wounds that the dogs had inflicted on him were hideous. She needed to swallow hard to keep her stomach down. She noticed an empty shoulder holster tucked under his arm.

Oh, yeah, someone had shot the dog before it could kill her!

She glanced about for his gun, and finally thought to look up. An automatic pistol and a dozen shell cases were tacked to the bottom of the magnet. Windwolf was the shooter who'd saved her.

By the time she got Windwolf to the multiple trailers that served as the scrap yard's office and her workshop, she knew why vids always had men saving women and rarely the other way around. There just wasn't any way a woman—well, a five-foot-nothing woman—could carry around an unconscious, bleeding man in any *artistic* manner. In the end, she rigged a sling and used the crane to swing him across the scrap yard and down onto the front doorstep. She kept the electromagnet on until it was so close to the steel-shell trailers that they were shuddering. When she shut the magnet down, Windwolf's pistol dropped down into his lap.

She nearly fell climbing back down out of the crane and banged her head. She felt blood trickling down her face as she walked back to the trailers. She stuck Windwolf's pistol into her waistband. Getting the elf up into a firefighter's carry, she staggered through the office and into the trailer attached to it that she used as a workshop. Somehow, she got Windwolf laid out on her worktable without dropping or seriously banging him.

"Sparks." She sighed, head on Windwolf's chest, listening to his heart race.

Her computer churned slightly as the AI answered. "Yeah, Boss?"

"Are the phones online yet?"

"No, Boss."

"Oilcan check in yet?"

"No, Boss."

"What's the time?"

"Twelve fifteen a.m."

Fifteen minutes since Windwolf came over the fence. The longest fifteen minutes of her life.

Leaving Windwolf in her workshop, she staggered back into the office. It was a two-bedroom mobile home, complete with kitchen and full bathroom, forty years old and showing all of its age. She bolted shut the front door, got an Iron City beer out of the fridge, and then staggered back to the bathroom to wash her right hand well. Lava cleanser first, to scour off the day's layer of oil and grease, and then a rare soak in antibacterial soap for the upcoming messing with wounds. She cleaned around the bandage on her left hand, trying not to notice that it was blood-soaked.

The only clean place on her face was what the night goggles covered, giving her a weird inverse raccoon look. Her bottom lip was swollen, making her mouth seem even more full than normal. From somewhere within her haphazard hairline—a product of Oilcan's haircuts and her own occasional impromptu trims with whatever sharp object was at hand—blood trickled down. She hunted through her dark hair, looking for the source of the blood, and found a small cut. She wet down a washcloth and stood a few minutes holding it to her scalp, sipping her beer, and trying to figure out what to do next.

She had a weakness for strays. It was like someone early on had written "sucker" on her in magic ink. The weak and the helpless saw it, swarmed to her, and thrived under her care. Well, not all of them. Not plants. Her thumbs were black from motor grease and engine oil. She killed any plant she tried to doctor. Not the terribly fragile either. Baby birds and suicidal wrecks, she had found, all dropped dead in her care. They seemed to need more mothering than she could muster. Perhaps her lack came from never seeing the real thing in action.

The tough ones, though, survived. Perhaps more despite her care, she realized now, instead of because of it. When it came to healing, she knew enough to be dangerous. She could recognize that Windwolf was close to death. If he did die, she would find out if Tooloo was right about the life-debt spell. Except for throwing a few pressure bandages onto him, though, she didn't know how to deal with him. Usually elves healed at a phenomenal rate, but only in the presence of magic. The elves had mastered bio magic back when humans were doing flint weapons. Their dependence on magic to heal made Tinker theorize that their healing factor might mirror nanotechnology, that the elves had some type of spell interwoven into their genes that endlessly corrected their bodies, thus healing any damage and keeping them from aging.

She caught herself about to drift off into speculation on the type of spells they might be employing, and returned to the problem at hand.

Someone else would have to patch Windwolf up. Until she figured out who this mythical person might be and got Windwolf into his or her care, she had to keep the elf alive. It was Shutdown Day. They were on Earth. There was no ambient magic for his healing.

But she did have the power sink that collected the magic drained off the crane. She used a modified magnetic containment field to store magical energy—one of her more successful experiments. She couldn't use the stored magic directly on Windwolf's body—it would be like trying to link someone with an artificial heart up to a 110 outlet. She could, though, link the sink's energy to a healing spell.

"Sparks!"

"Yeah, Boss?"

"Search the codex for healing spells. Put the results up on the workshop screen."

"Okay, Boss!"

She got the first-aid kit out of the back storage room and went back to her workshop. She ran out of pressure bandages long before she covered all of Windwolf's wounds, so she raided the bathroom for feminine hygiene pads and affixed them with lots of Scotch tape.

Sparks had cued up twenty healing spells. Some were quite specific: broken bones, kidney failure, heart attack, and so on. She culled those out and looked at the more general ones. One was labeled "will not work on humans."

She had Sparks call up the spell schematics, wishing she understood bio magic better. It seemed to do what she wanted, which was focus energy into the body's existing healing abilities. She cut and pasted in a power distributor as a secondary ring. She made sure the printer was loaded with transferable circuit paper, sent the spell to the printer, and finished her beer as it printed.

Windwolf had worsened. Blood soaked the bandages. All color had drained out with his blood, and he breathed hard and shallow. She let the bandages be, but washed his chest. Peeling the protective sheet from the circuit paper, she pressed the spell to his clean flesh. She checked the spell's hertz cycle, hooked leads through a converter box, and tapped the power cords into the power distributor.

"Here goes everything." She checked one last time to make sure all stray metal bits were clear of the magic's path, and flipped the switch. She checked her database, and winced at the activation word phonetically spelled out. Oh great, one of those ancient Elvish words where you try to swallow your tongue. A footnote gave the translation: Be healed.

The outer ring powered up first and cast a glowing sphere over the rest of the spell. Then the healing spell itself kicked in, the timing cycle ring clicking quickly clockwise as the magic flowed through the spell in a steady rhythm.

Windwolf took five shallow breaths. Then a long, deep breath. Another. And another. He fell into a clean, easy breathing rhythm, color washing into his face.

"Yes! Be healed!" Tinker cried. "I am your magic god! Say Amen to me! Woohoo!" She danced around the room. "Oh yes, I am a god! The one! The only! Tinker!"

Still pleased to giggles, she went to look at Windwolf—really look at him—for the first time in years.

He was beautiful, but then again, he was an elf. They were all beautiful. (And unfortunately all snobs too.) A blue silk ribbon gathered his glossy black hair into a thick, loose ponytail that came nearly to his waist. She tangled her fingers in the curly tips of the ponytail and felt the smooth silkiness of his hair.

Deceptively delicate, his face held just enough strength in it to be masculine. All the fey features: full lips, sharp high cheekbones, perfect nose, pointed ears, almond-shaped eyes, and thick long eyelashes.

She couldn't remember the color of his eyes. They were the first elf eyes she had seen up close, within inches of her own, and they had been so stunningly vivid, she remembered that they left her breathless. But what color? Green? Purple?

She wrapped the lock of black around her finger and rubbed it against her cheek. So soft. It smelled wonderful—a musky spice. She held it to her nose, trying to identify the scent. Mid-sniff, she realized he'd opened his eyes and was looking at her with silent suspicion. His irises were the color of sapphires with the biggest price tags locked in jeweler's cases—the stunning deep blue that neared black.

She gasped with surprise, and then cried as he shifted, "*Nae-tanyau!* I've got a healing spell jury-rigged on you. If you move, it would be bad. Do you understand? *Kankau?*"

He studied the spell hovering over his chest, the power leads to the siphon, and then the bulky containment unit itself. "I understand," he said finally in English. He looked back at her.

She was still holding the lock of his hair. "Oh, sorry. You smell nice," she said, carefully dropping his hair.

"Who are you?"

He didn't remember her. Not that she was totally surprised—their minutes together, prior to today, could be counted on the fingers of both hands and had been shared with one nasty monster. She had been thirteen then, and still hadn't grown enough of a figure to distinguish her from the boys she played with. It seemed slightly unfair though; her imagination had decided that he stood as some kind of symbol and featured him often in her dreams.

"They call me Tinker." Tooloo had cautioned her against telling people her true name so often that using her nickname became habit. "You're in my scrap yard."

"Your eyes." He carefully lifted his right hand to make an odd gesture over his eyes. "They were different."

She frowned, and then realized what he meant. "Oh, yeah, I had my night goggles on." She fished them out of her pocket, demonstrated how they fit on. "They let me see in the dark."

"Ah." He studied her silently for several minutes. "I would have died."

"You still might. You're badly hurt. It's Shutdown Day, and we're on Earth. I'm afraid if I don't take some drastic actions, you're not going to make it."

"Then drastic actions it must be."

Tinker was trying to figure out what "drastic" might entail when a squad car screamed up the street and slewed in through the open gate.

The cop was Nathan Czernowski, shotgun in hand. "Tinker? Oilcan? Tink!"

"I'm in here!" she called to him, working the dead bolts. "A pack of warglike things attacked me. I think I got them all, but I wasn't taking a chance."

Nathan crossed the parking lot cautiously, scanning the yard, shotgun at his shoulder. "Someone stopped Cordwater out by the pike and said you were yelling for help over your radio line. There's an ambulance on its way. Are you okay? Where's your cousin?"

"One got my hand." She threw open the door, stepped back to let him in, and then bolted the door shut again. "It hurts like shit, but it's stopped bleeding. Otherwise, I'm fine. Oilcan is out with the wrecker. Sparks, edit the message to the wrecker: 'Oilcan, Nathan's here, the monsters are dead, and I'm fine. If I'm not here when you get home, I'll be at Mercy.' "

"Sure, Boss!"

"Can you wait for the ambulance?" Nathan pushed up his goggles and gazed down at her with dark concerned eyes. "I can take you to the hospital."

"I'm fine, but the—umm—the wargs were chasing down an elf." Normally she was a stickler for accuracy, but lacking a name for the monsters, it seemed easier just to say wargs. "He's in my workshop. They chewed him over good."

"He's still alive?"

"Barely. I jury-rigged up a healing spell, so he's stable."

"You've got a spell running now?" Nathan asked. "During Shutdown? Where's the magic coming from?"

"I'm running off of a power sink that I invented. I siphon magic into it while I'm running the crane."

Nathan grinned. "Only you, Tinker. Is he conscious?"

"He was. I'm not sure about right now."

"Did he tell you his name?" Nathan moved into "just the facts" mode, taking out a PDA and stylus.

"It's Windwolf. You know, the one with the saurus?" She traced a symbol in the air over her forehead. Nathan had been a rookie when he took her to the hospital that day, bleeding and crying.

"The one who marked you?" He noted it into his PDA. "The elves have a word for this."

"Shitty luck."

"It's like karma or something. Entanglement?"

"Entanglement is a quantum theory between photons. The polarization of one entangled photon is always the opposite of the other."

He worked his jaw as he thought. "Yeah. Once they're entangled, they stay that way, right?"

She looked at him, one eyebrow upraised.

"Well there's you, him, me, and a monster."

"Yeah, right." Strange, even after five years and with the monster dogs still fresh in her mind, it was the image of the saurus's mouth and the all-too-many ragged teeth that made her shudder. "Look, this has been pretty cranked. I talked to Tooloo about that symbol that Windwolf put on me. She said that's how elves mark life debts. Tooloo says that if Windwolf dies before I cancel the life debt, then some really nasty things will happen to me." Exactly what would happen changed every time she asked Tooloo about it. Once Tooloo had said that as Windwolf's body decayed, Tinker's would too. Another time, Tooloo had insisted that Tinker would simply vanish. She tried not to believe the old halfie, but she still had nightmares after every conversation.

Nathan looked troubled. "Tooloo is a superstitious fool. I saw the mark. You told me how long Windwolf took making the mark. That wasn't a full spell, whatever it was. It was quick and dirty, and is not going to turn you into a walking zombie five years later. Why would he do that to you, anyhow? You were just a kid."

"He was angry with me. I got in his way while he was trying to kill the saurus and pissed him off. You know what they say about elves."

"What they say and what is true isn't necessarily the same thing. It was nothing."

"It will be nothing. I'm going to save his life. I'm going to cancel the debt. We'll be even."

"Good."

An ambulance came up the street, wailing, and pulled into the yard. Nathan went out to escort the EMT and Tinker swore when she saw who followed Nathan through the front door. "You? Damn, my luck is all bad today."

Jonnie Be Good was an elf wannabe; tall and slender, he wore his blond hair elf-long and had had his ears pointed back in the States. Why anyone would want to be an elf was beyond Tinker. True, the living forever came in handy, but their society sucked; the lower castes seemed practically enslaved by the castes above them, and they were all elegant nose-in-the-air snobs.

Odd, she usually thought of Jonnie Be Good as a good-looking slimewad—apparently after a few minutes' exposure to Windwolf's level of beauty, Jonnie seemed ugly as wood-grain, self-stick wallpaper.

Jonnie smirked and grabbed his crotch. "Oh, bite me."

Add stupid to ugly. Tinker sidestepped quickly to block Nathan; she didn't want Jonnie squashed before he had a chance to treat Windwolf. "I've got a chewed-up hand, and there's a guy really messed up in my workshop. Don't touch the spell I've got set up—it's keeping him stable."

"I like the shirt," Jonnie murmured, squeezing between her and Nathan instead of going around, and made it an excuse to slide his hand over her bare stomach.

"Watch the hands," Nathan rumbled, continuing his big-brother routine. Between him and Oilcan, it was no wonder she didn't date— not that there was anyone she wanted *to* date. Pittsburgh had a stunning lack of young male humans who weren't buttheads. And while elves were pretty, she had yet to meet one that didn't treat her like a subspecies.

Nathan glowered at Jonnie until the paramedic had disappeared into her workshop. "I'll take a look around. Make sure the wargs are all dead."

"That shotgun will only piss them off," she said, and pulled the dent-mender magnet off the wall. "Here, take this."

Because she spent most of her time at the scrap yard, either working or tinkering, she had her laundry machines hooked up in the small, second bedroom. She kept her clean clothes split roughly in half between her loft and a dresser in her workshop. She was annoyed, but not surprised, to find Jonnie pawing through her panties when she walked in.

He had the balls to act like nothing was wrong. He held up a pair of black silk panties. "Very nice."

She snatched it back and stuffed it into the open drawer, trying to pretend her face wasn't burning. "Do you mind?"

"Not at all." He grinned lazily, gazing at her groin. "Wouldn't mind seeing them on, either. Or off."

"Dream on."

"Let me see your hand." For a few minutes he managed to be professional, undoing her bandaging, washing out the wound with peroxide, applying an antibiotic, and rebandaging it. "It's too deep for artificial flesh. You're going to want to go to the hospital with this. You could take nerve damage if it heals wrong, and there's a good chance it can go septic."

"Okay." She mentally took back some of the things she had been thinking of him, until he got up and made motions of packing. Slowly, though, as if he wanted her to notice. "Aren't you going to do something about Windwolf?"

He stopped and shrugged. "Mercy won't take him. According to the peace treaty, elves are to be taken to the hospice beyond the Rim. The elves don't want us messing around with them. Nothing says I have to treat him."

At one time Pittsburgh was home to dozens of world-class hospitals. Amazing what being transported to an alien world can do to health care. Mercy was the only hospital left open, doing only emergency work. Apparently, only *human* emergency work. All elective surgery took place on Earth. There were other hospitals, beyond the Rim, but Tinker neither knew where they were, nor wanted to be stuck at one when Startup hit.

"It's Shutdown Day. The hospice is on Elfhome."

"So? He's stable; wait it out."

"I don't know if I have enough magic to last twenty-four hours. I want him patched up."

"Well, I could be persuaded to treat him."

She clenched her jaw on a few choice names. She'd let him know what she thought of him after Windwolf was patched up. "What do you want?"

"Your name appears on a very short list of women who have never put out."

She clenched her fists. "So, what of it?"

"Well, there's money riding on who gets the first dip in your pool."

"I can pay you anything that's riding on the bet." She sneered.

"Oh, the prestige is more important than the money, although the money has a good bit to do with it. And then there's the thrill of conquest, going where no man has gone before."

"Yeah, right, with Nathan Czernowski poking around outside, and Windwolf bleeding to death in here, you think I'm going to let you do me?"

"Your word is good for me. I do the elf, and later I come back, and do you."

Some sounds, she decided, are fated to be huge no matter how quiet they are. The sound of Windwolf's knife coming out of its sheath was only a whisper of silver on leather, and yet it rang out in the room like a shout. She supposed Jonnie's eyes bugging wide and his sudden frozen attention to the blade pressed to his groin helped to make the noise seem louder.

"You do her," Windwolf whispered, "and you will never do another woman."

"It was a joke." Jonnie swallowed hard.

"Get out," Windwolf commanded.

Tinker glared at Windwolf as Jonnie scuttled out. Why did Windwolf have to wake up now? "Great. That was the only man in the tristate area who could help you."

"I would rather die than stain my honor in that way."

"Your honor? What the hell does it have to do with your honor? It was my decision to make, not yours. I would have been the one to screw him."

"And you think this would not reflect on my honor?"

"Look, I didn't really even have to sleep with him. I could have *lied* to him, got him to treat you, and then backed out later. No one would blame me. He's a complete slimewad."

"Would you really break your word of honor?"

"We'll never know."

He caught her hand. "Would you?"

How could he be so close to death and still be so strong? She finally gave up trying to get free and answered him, anger making her truthful. She considered her honor much more valuable than her virginity, which was a temporary thing to start with. "No." But that didn't mean she couldn't think rings around Jonnie Be Good any day; tricking him without lying would have been easy, probably would even have been fun.

Nathan returned from checking the scrap yard, his head tilted as he listened intently to his headset. "I hate Shutdown Day. People just turn into raging idiots on the road. They've got like twenty cars piled up on the Veterans Bridge. There's possible deaths involved, and apparently a fight has broken out. I've got to go. I've checked around.

There's no wargs skulking around." He frowned, noticing the lack of the third person. "What happened to Jonnie?"

"Oh, he opened his mouth, the normal sewage came out, and Windwolf pulled a knife on him. Says his honor would be damaged."

Nathan's eyes narrowed, and he muttered darkly, "I'm going to bust Jonnie's ass if he can't keep his mouth shut and his hands to himself."

"I can handle him myself." Men. All their posturing, yet she was going to have to pick up the pieces anyhow. She guessed it didn't hurt to ask. "What am I supposed to do with Windwolf?"

Nathan gazed at the battered elf bleakly. "I don't know, Tink. Just ride it out, if you can. I don't know anyone more qualified to take care of him than you."

"Damn it, Nathan." She followed him out to the front door. "I don't know anything about healing an elf."

"Nobody does. Take care of yourself, Tink!"

"Yeah!" She watched him get into his squad car and pull away. "Nobody else is going to do it."

She bolted the front door and glanced at the office clock: 1:20. Only a little more than an hour since Windwolf came over the fence, and another twenty-three before Pittsburgh returned to Elfhome and its magic.

Already there was a tiny slice off the top of the sink's power meter. She marked the one-hour's usage, feeling a growing sense of despair. The sink would last approximately another twenty hours. Alone she couldn't move the heavy sink, and if she disconnected Windwolf from it to get him to help, he would die. And according to Tooloo, if he died without the spell being canceled, so did she.

She remembered with a start that Tooloo had at one time given her a cancel spell. Tinker had transcribed it into her computer as an appendix to her family's spell codex. Windwolf seemed to be asleep; still, she did the search by hand, using the keywords of "cancel, life debt." Since the workshop screen was viewable from the table, she quickly sent the spell to the printer and closed the file. The printer hummed as it spit out a page of circuit paper.

Tinker picked up the paper and stared at it. Tooloo had scribed the single complex glyph out, and Tinker had copied it carefully; but the blunt truth was, she had no idea what the spell would do. The thought of using it smacked of putting an alien device to Windwolf's head, pulling the trigger, and *hoping* it didn't blow his brains out. Even if the spell didn't kill him outright, what if it disrupted his healing ability? At this moment, the result would be deadly.

And she only had Tooloo's often changing assertions that what Windwolf had done to her was harmful. Because Tooloo had taught her Elvish, and the fundamentals of magic, Tinker's scientific psyche allotted the half-elf the same basic faith she had in her other teachers. (If her grandfather had ever lied to her, he had done it with a mathematician's consistency and had taken all of his secrets to his grave.) Oilcan warned Tinker often that she was too trusting in general, so she forced herself to consider that Tooloo could be lying.

She sat in her still workshop, Windwolf's ragged, uneven breathing the only sound, painfully aware of the empty streets for miles in all directions, trying to decide. Did she risk killing Windwolf to save herself?

Throughout Tinker's childhood, Tooloo took odd perversity at being impenetrable; there was no knowing if what she told Tinker was anything more than attempts to frighten her. Windwolf, though, had saved her twice this evening, and once five years ago. Simple, cold, rational logic dictated that she owed Windwolf the benefit of the doubt. She put down the spell, but she found no comfort in her decision. Why was the unknown so much more frightening than the known?

A half hour later, with a rumble of the big Caterpillar engine and the rattle of chains, Oilcan returned to the yard. He had his tow lights on and a small shrub stuck in the flatbed's ram-prow.

"Tinker?" he bellowed as he swung out of the cab, a crowbar in hand. "Coz?"

"Here am I." She came out into the yard, the dent mender in hand.

Tinker and Oilcan favored one another, which sometimes made Tinker wonder about her egg donor. She knew that her grandfather had selected her mother mostly on intelligence—he could be quite vocal about his scheme to raise a genius grandchild—but she wondered occasionally if he had also tried to make it so that she and Oilcan looked like brother and sister too. Oilcan was just shy of average height for a man, slender built as she was, with the same nut-brown coloring. When they were little, Tooloo had called them her wood sprites. Tinker always thought the overall effect worked better on Oilcan; he had a spry puckish kind of look—what people used to think of as fey before they met the real elves.

Oilcan stopped at the sight of the blood on her, his dark eyes going wide and solemn with concern. "Oh, shit, Tinker—are you okay?"

"Fine, fine. Most of it isn't mine. Windwolf is chewed to hell. Someone cooked up a pack of monster dogs that—" She stopped as implications finally seeped in. While created for a war waged millennia ago, the wargs now ranged wild, for all purposes a natural creature despite their magical enhancements. Simple bad luck could account for a warg attack. Windwolf's mauling, though, was clearly an attempt of premeditated murder. Someone had made the monster dogs, taking days to set up the original spell and then copy it onto the five pug dogs. "Someone sicced a pack of killer dogs on Windwolf."

"Windwolf? Not the elf that marked you? That's bad, isn't it? Is he still alive?"

"Barely. We have to make sure he stays that way. Jonnie was here. He wouldn't do anything for him, and he says that Mercy won't touch him."

"The hell they won't. Not everyone is a self-serving bastard like Jonnie. We can take him over and someone will take care of him. It's not like they're going to let him bleed to death in front of them. Is it?"

For a moment, she thought she could let him take charge. Then she realized that he was waiting for her to say yes or no. The problem was that Oilcan knew she was smarter than he was. He had a lot going on upstairs, but he always deferred to her. She was never sure if it was because she'd played too many head games with him while they were growing up, or if it was some crippling fear of failure. He had been ten before falling into her grandfather's care and can-do style of child raising, and it showed. He was four years her senior, but still he was more than willing for her to be the boss.

Of course, that had drawbacks.

"I don't know!" She retreated back to the workshop to check on Windwolf, finding him unchanged. Oilcan trailed behind her, waiting for her to think of something. "Certainly if we can't think of anyone else to help with Windwolf, we can take him to Mercy. Can't hurt. Might help."

"Who the hell else is there? Tooloo?"

"She stays on Elfhome during Shutdown. Let me think." Tinker bounced in place. Weird as it seemed, sometimes bouncing helped, like her brain just needed to be jostled around so a good idea could surface to the top. "Elf. Heal an elf. Elf healing. Elf biology. Xenobiologist! Lain!"

Oilcan studied the setup around Windwolf. "How are we going to move him? You need to take the power sink, and that's nearly five hundred pounds there alone. I don't know if the two of us can move it."

She considered the sink, the pale battered elf, and all the blood. "We'll just take the workshop trailer, load it onto the flatbed."

"You've got to be joking."

"That's how we got it here in the first place."

"Shit, but up to the Observatory? And we don't know if she's even home. The phones are still out."

"She's usually home on Shutdown Day," Tinker said. "She transmits data from her home computer. If she's not, well, we'll just drive on to Mercy Hospital. If they won't take him, I don't know, maybe we'll drive out to Monroeville and see if we can find a vet."

"Monroeville? You mean drive to Earth?"

"We are on Earth."

"We're in Pittsburgh," Oilcan said. "Pittsburgh hasn't really been part of Earth for a long time."

"Yeah, we'll go to Earth if we have to."

It took longer than she thought to fill up the flatbed's gas tanks, jury-rig a power supply for the trailer, disconnect the city's power connections, rig a sling under the trailer, and use the crane (magnet turned off) to lift the trailer carefully onto the flatbed and secure it. She made sure that they had Windwolf's sword and pistol; if he lived until Startup, they'd deliver him and his weapons to the nearest hospice. Tinker found the abandoned cancel spell, folded the paper carefully so the rune itself wasn't creased, and tucked it into her front shirt pocket. If things went wrong, perhaps the spell could still work after Windwolf died, severing any magical bond between them.

The trailer's now-empty air-conditioning slot conveniently fit up against the flatbed's back window, allowing her to crawl between the trailer and the truck's cabin. Oilcan would drive, being the more cautious of the two of them, and certainly also the more patient. Tinker made sure everything was green with Oilcan, then slithered through the hole to ride beside Windwolf.

"What is happening?" Windwolf peered through slit eyes, his voice paper-thin.

"We're moving the trailer to someone that can help you."

"The house is moving?"

"Yes."

He closed his eyes and exhaled a very slight laugh. "And you humans used to think of us as gods."

*　　*　　*

The Allegheny Observatory sat high on a hill, deep in an old city park. A steep and twisty road wound up to it. In the winter, the road made an excellent bobsled course. In the middle of the rainy night, in a teetering trailer, with a dying elf, it was nightmarish. The Rim, however, cut through on the other side of the park, taking out one vital bridge to a saner route.

At the turn of the millennium, the district of Observatory Hill had apparently been struggling; the gate effect, and the loss of the bridge, had killed it completely. Whereas in other parts of Pittsburgh, the Rim remained a sharply marked borderline between Elfhome and transported Earth, here a young forest of Elfhome trees, a mile in from the Rim, stood in testament to how much of the neighborhood had been lost. None of the houses had actually been torn down; a scattered number still stood, lurking like undead under the trees. Some of the buildings had caught fire, whole blocks burning to rubble before the fire department could check the blaze's progress. The rest had just been whittled away: the windows, the doors, the sinks, the toilets, the copper pipes, and finally the nails. Little by little, they'd been looted by those desperate for finished building materials. Soon only sodden white piles of plaster would be left.

Now Observatory Hill was just a commune of scientists huddled around the Allegheny Observatory bulkhead. A hundred years ago, the area had been moneyed, and stately Victorian homes remained, refurbished to act as dorms for the transient scientists. Mean age hovered at twenty-seven, postdoctorate but still under the authority of older, well-established scientists on Earth. Every thirty days the population changed. Because of the Observatory, lights were low, but always on. The astronomers studied the parallel star system during the night. Xenobiologists studied the alien life during the day. They shared resources of backup generators, kitchen facilities, cooking and cleaning staff, and computers.

Lain Skanske's home sat near but apart from the dorms. A pristine white fence guarded a lush garden of roses, hosta, *laleafrin*, and *tulilium*. Lain called the garden her consolation prize for giving up a life in space after being crippled in a near-fatal shuttle accident.

Oilcan pulled the flatbed to a stop, headlights aimed at the front door of Lain's grand Victorian home, and called back, "Tink, we're here!"

Tinker slid into the cab beside him. "He's still alive." She had spent the ride wishing she had asked Windwolf about the cancel spell in his few moments of awareness. There seemed no polite way to say, "What does this do? Do you mind if I cast this on you before you die?" to a man mauled while protecting you. She had kept her silence. Besides, there was still hope. "I'll go see if Lain's home."

"It's four in the morning, Tink."

"Well, if she's in town, she's here, then."

Lain's house had a massive front door with leaded glass sidelights extending the entrance out another two feet on either side. The doorbell was an ancient device—one turned a key located in the center of the door, and the key spun a metal spring coiled inside a domed bell bolted to the other side. Tinker had broken it as a child; last year, she had fixed it in an act of adult penitence. She spun and spun the key now, making the bell ring unendingly.

Lights came on, starting from the lab in the back of the house. Lain came up the hall, her figure distorted by the lead glass and the shuttle accident. The xenobiologist had trained to study the life in the seas of Europa. Crippled, she'd found a second chance studying the alien life of Elfhome.

"Who is it?" Lain called as she came.

Tinker stopped ringing the bell. "It's Tinker!"

Lain opened the door, blinking in the flatbed's headlights, leaning heavily on her crutch. "Tink, what in the world? This better not be another tengu you're bringing me."

"A what?"

"A Japanese elf. Related to the oni. Sometimes it looks like a crow."

"I've never brought you a crow."

"In the dream I had last week, you brought me a tengu, and wanted me to bandage it. I kept on telling you that it was dangerous, but you wouldn't listen to me. We bandaged it up, and it turned you into a diamond and flew away with you in its beak."

"I'm not going to be responsible for dreams you had."

This was the way conversations tended to go with Lain. Tinker was never sure if she liked talking with Lain. They were never direct, easy-to-understand conversations, and were thus an annoyance and a treasure at the same time.

Lain pulled an umbrella out of a stand by the door and stepped out into the wet to thumb it open. "Well, the phones haven't started working yet, so I might as well deal with this emergency now. You couldn't have picked a worse day to bring me something to treat."

"If this weren't Shutdown Day, I wouldn't be coming to you with this."

At the flatbed, Lain collapsed the umbrella, set it inside the chest-high door, unlatched her crutch, put it beside the umbrella, and then reached up and swung gracefully into the trailer. Lacking Lain's height and reach, and with one hand nearly useless, Tinker scrambled up in a less dignified manner.

Running off the flatbed's electric, Tinker had only managed to set up two lights. The dimness hid the worst of Windwolf's condition. Still, the sight of the bandaged elf seemed to shock Lain.

"Oh, my," Lain said. "It is a tengu."

"I am not a tengu," Windwolf whispered.

"Close enough." Lain shrugged, picking up her crutch. "What happened?"

"He was attacked by dogs," Tinker said. "A pack of them—really ugly and bigger than wargs. They were magical constructs."

"They were Foo dogs," Windwolf whispered.

Lain limped to Windwolf and eyed his many wounds. "Foo dogs. Can tengu be far behind?"

"A good question." Windwolf sighed. "Do you understand the strictures of the treaty between our people?"

"Yes," Lain said.

"Do I have your pledge that you'll abide by it?"

"You'll trust my word?"

"Tinker has vouched for you."

Lain threw Tinker a concerned look. "I see. Yes, you have my word."

"Word about what?" Tinker asked.

"The treaty allows for simple first aid." Lain scanned the equipment connected to Windwolf. "It theorized that since we can interbreed, humans and elves must be ninety-eight percent to ninety-nine percent genetically identical. But then, we're ninety percent identical to earthworms, so it's not that amazing, except that this is an alien world."

"We're that close to earthworms?"

"Yes. Frightening isn't it?"

"How close are Earth earthworms and Elfhome earthworms?"

"Do you know how many species of earthworms are on Earth?" Lain eyed the power sink. "Of course primates are also ninety-eight percent identical to us, and we can't interbreed."

"Has anyone tried?"

"Knowing humans," Windwolf murmured. "Yes."

Lain laughed, looking amused and yet insulted. "As a scientifically controlled experiment or a sexual perversion?"

"Both." Windwolf earned a dark look from Lain.

"What does that have to do with anything now?" Tinker asked to distract the two.

"The point is that the elves want to keep it all theory," Lain said. "It's against the treaty to cull any genetic samples from an accident victim. It's why Mercy won't treat elves." She shook her head. "This is going to be tricky. I'll need him in my operating room to properly treat him."

Tinker considered. "I have longer leads. We could leave the sink in the trailer and run the magic into your OR with the longer leads. There might be a drop in power, though."

Oilcan peered through the AC slot from the truck cab. "If I take down a section of the fence, we can back up almost to the OR's window."

"Oh, we can't," Tinker said. "We'll drive over the flowers and ruin them."

"A man's life is more important than flowers." Lain brushed the objection aside. "Will the spell let you disconnect and reconnect?"

"I am not a man," Windwolf whispered.

"Elf. Man. Close enough for horseshoes," Tinker said, shaking her head in answer to Lain's question. "I can print a second spell and activate it in the OR. We'll have to scrub his chest to get all traces of the old spell off."

"Horseshoes?" Windwolf asked.

"It's a game," Tinker told him. "Oilcan and I play it at the scrap yard. When you're better, I'll teach it to you."

"Okay." Lain limped to the door. "Let's make this happen."

Tinker printed off another copy of the spell and found longer leads. Oilcan found help at the Observatory in the form of astronomers. They took down much of the picket fence and eased the truck to the porch. Luckily Lain had a hospital gurney in her lab, and they wheeled it over a ramp into the trailer. After Oilcan and two of the postdocs slid Windwolf onto the gurney, they wheeled it as far as the present leads allowed, which took them inside the foyer of Lain's grand Victorian home.

There they let him sit, while Tink threaded the longer leads out the lab window. Then came the mad scramble of disconnecting leads, pushing Windwolf to the lab, moving the truck, cleaning Windwolf's chest, applying the spell, and reconnecting the leads. Windwolf lay still as death on the gurney even after Tink activated the spell.

"Is he dead?" Tinker had been entertaining herself with thoughts of Windwolf's aristocratic reaction to flinging large metal horseshoes at a metal peg. Would he even come see how the game would be played, she had wondered, or would he vanish out of her life like he had done last time? The thought of him dead and unable to do either sickened her. *Oh please, no.*

And then after that, an even more horrible thought. *Oh, no, the life debt!* She patted her shirt pocket, and the cancel spell crinkled reassuringly. There was even magic left in the sink to power the spell.

Lain pulled on latex gloves and then pressed a hand to his neck. "No. He's hanging in there. Barely."

Tinker sniffed as blinked-away tears made her nose start to run.

Lain looked at her strangely.

"If he dies," Tinker offered as an excuse for the sniffling, "I'm screwed."

Lain frowned at her, then swung the brilliant light over to shine on the elf's face. "Wolf Who Rules Wind." She used his full true name in Elvish, seemingly stunned to immobility.

"You know him? Lain?"

Lain looked at her. "When are you going to start taking notice of things beyond that scrap yard of yours? There are two very large worlds out there, and you are in an uncommon position of being part of both of them. Speaking of which, Oilcan, can you see if the phones are working? I have several hours of data to upload while we're on Earth. These Foo dogs—they have fangs, like a cat?"

"Yes."

"These puncture wounds must have been made by the fangs. There is crushing damage from the teeth between them. I'm going to treat all this with peroxide, or they'll go septic."

"They weren't genetic constructs—more like a solid hologram. When I hit them with the electromagnet, they unraveled back down to the original creature. Their breath smelled like—" Tinker searched her memory now that she didn't have one of the beasts breathing down her neck "—like incense."

"Foo dogs are actually Foo lions—protectors of sacred buildings," Lain said. "Temples and suchlike. They're supposed to scare demons—oni."

"I thought you said oni were elves, related to the tengu."

"Elves, demons, spirits. Two cultures rarely have one-to-one translations. So, you're saying that these bites were made by holograms? You're guessing there's no bacteria involved because they weren't eating, breathing, real creatures?"

"Solid illusions, possibly. Oh, who the hell knows?"

"I'd rather be safe than sorry. We have another"—Lain glanced at the lab clock, which read 6:10—"eighteen hours. The thing about animal bites is that they will go septic if you don't stay on top of them."

It took hours. News of Windwolf's condition spread through the commune. Despite the frantic shuffle of leaving and incoming post-docs, many of the scientists stopped by to lend a hand. Hot food was carried from the kitchens. Biologists came to help with the first-aid efforts. When the phones came back online at eight in the morning, the biologists fielded phone calls from Earth-bound scientists looking for specimens and data forgotten during the callers' last trip to Elfhome. They even ran Lain's data transfer.

At ten, a van arrived to pick up botanical specimens that Lain had collected and quarantined over the last thirty days. Lain had to supervise, making sure that only the most harmless of Elfhome's biological flora were loaded, even though the most deadly, like the strangle vines and black willows, probably wouldn't flourish without magic. The drivers complained about the ten hours to travel the ten miles in from the Rim, unloaded the truck of food and supplies, stared at the improving Windwolf in open curiosity, and then hurried off, hoping aloud that the twelve hours of Shutdown remaining would be enough time to reach the Rim again. They prompted an exodus among the scientists who were returning to Earth.

Finally the house emptied, and Tinker sprawled on a white wicker chaise stolen from Lain's sunporch. Lain found her nearly asleep and tap-tapped her on the cheek with a printout. Tinker slit open her eyes, took the paper, and closed her eyes again. "What's this?"

"Carnegie Mellon University reviewed your application. Apparently they've been able to confirm your father's alumni-slash-faculty history prior to their hasty move out of Oakland. They were impressed by your placement tests and they've accepted you. They're offering you a scholarship, and your living costs would be handled by the displaced citizen fund. They're trying to decide if you qualify for the in-state tuition scale. If we get your reply out today, you can start in the fall."

"Lain!" Tinker kept her eyes shut, not wanting to see Lain's excitement. *They were impressed by my placement tests? How? I know I didn't get any of the questions right.* "I applied just to make you happy. I didn't think they would accept me." *I thought I made sure they wouldn't accept me.* "I don't want to go."

Frosty silence. Tinker could imagine the disapproving look. Even with her eyes closed, it had Medusa-like powers.

"Tinker," Lain said, apparently realizing the magic of her gaze alone wasn't working, "I didn't push this last year because you weren't legal yet, but now you can come and go without worry. You're wasting your life in that scrap yard. You are the most brilliant person I've ever met, and you're twiddling with junked cars."

Oh, the dreaded scrap yard attack! "The scrap yard pays the bills, gives me parts to work with and all the spare time I could want. It lets me do what makes me happy. If I want to spend three weeks inventing hovercycles, I make hovercycles."

"Any university or corporation would outfit you with a state-of-the-art lab."

Tinker made a noise of disgust. "No, they wouldn't." She cracked her eye, glanced over the paper, double-checking her facts before finishing. "See, I would be a freshman, whatever the hell that is, on probationary status *due to the unusual nature of my schooling and lack of exposure to normal human society*. They're not offering me a lab."

"They will. As soon as they see your full capabilities. Besides, a term or two of liberal arts classes could only help you. There's so much you don't know."

"Maybe about oni, but not about quantum mechanics."

"There's more to life than just physics. Shakespeare. Mozart. Picasso. You'll be exposed to the entire range of human culture, and meet intelligent people your own age."

"People my age are immature." She sat up, scrubbing at her hair and wincing as she hit a sore spot. "What's the bloody rush? Can't I think about this until next Shutdown?"

Lain pressed her mouth into a tight line, meaning she didn't want to answer the question, but her basic honesty forced her to. "You should go before you start to date." Lain held up a hand to check a protest. "I know you're not interested in any of the local guys yet, but it's only a matter of time before your curiosity overcomes repulsion, and once you get entangled with a man, it's so much harder to walk away."

With Jonnie Be Good fresh in her mind, Tinker said, "Oh, ick. I don't think that's really a danger, Lain."

"At CMU, there will be hundreds of intelligent boys your age who are more interested in graduating than getting married and having kids."

"Okay! Okay!" she cried to stop the flow. "Give me a little while to think about it. It was the last thing on my mind." Speaking of what was mostly on her mind, she asked, "How is Windwolf?"

"Stable. I'd like to think he's stronger than when I first saw him. I think he's out of immediate danger."

Rain still smeared the windows, graying the world beyond. The flatbed sat deep in Lain's prize flower beds. Rain-filled tire ruts ran across the yard and through the crushed flowers and the dismantled fence: six deep channels of torn-up earth zigzagging through the perfect lawn until it was more mud than grass.

Lain had spent hours, and days, and years working on her garden, crippled leg and all. It was going to take ages to right all the damage.

Tinker stared guiltily at the mess, and then looked at the paper in her hand. Lain had never asked, over the years, for any repayment for all the things she had done for Tinker. From comforting Tinker when her grandfather died, to advice on her menses, Lain had only given.

Classes would start in September and run until before Christmas. Three Shutdowns. Just ninety days, and she could always bail early if she hated it.

"Okay. I'll attend one set of classes and give it a try."

Lain went round-eyed in amazement. "Really?"

"Yes." Tinker cringed before her excitement. "One semester. Nothing more. I'll try it. I know I won't like it. And that will be that. We'll be square."

Lain gave her a sharp look, which probably meant she wasn't happy with the idea that Tinker viewed college as a prison sentence, but didn't debate it. She leaned forward and kissed Tinker on the forehead. "Good. I'll e-mail them your acceptance."

Tinker hunched in the chair, watching the rain sheet down the glass, feeling as if she herself were sliding down a slippery plane, gray and formless. There was no doubting she'd pleased Lain. The xenobiologist had always expected Tinker's best, and in doing so, usually got it. Tinker had learned all the levels of Lain's praise, from the scathing backhanded compliment for a job sloppily done, to the Mona Lisa smile and swat for a clever but naughty act. Lain had bestowed her ultimate seal of approval with the kiss.

Perhaps it was good that she was going to give Earth a try. Tinker had carefully avoided Earth her whole life, afraid that if she left Pittsburgh she wouldn't be able to return to Elfhome. Tinker grudgingly admitted to herself that it was childish to cling to the old and familiar, rebuking the new just because it was new. Didn't she pride herself at being extremely mature for her age?

And yet, with her whole heart and soul, she didn't want to leave home.

Tinker fell asleep sometime after that. Her sleeping mind twisted the day's worries and events and shaped them into her recurring "maze nightmare." As a new twist, Jonnie Be Good starred as a tengu, transforming into a crow's form to steal her diamond-shaped purity. Tooloo knew where Jonnie had hidden the gem inside the maze, but only spouted nonsense for directions. Windwolf did his typical "failing your potential" speeches—why him and not her grandfather or Lain, she never could fathom—and suddenly the dream went off in a new, erotic direction. Asserting that he knew what was best for her, Windwolf held her down and kissed his way down to her groin. His soft hair pooled over her bare legs as his insistent tongue caressed at a point of pleasure she barely knew existed. She woke with her abdomen rippling with the strength of her orgasm.

What the hell was that? She lay in the same position as in her dream, legs parted and hips cocked up. Her pose merged with the dream memory so strongly that for a moment she wasn't sure if she hadn't truly experienced the sex act. Common sense seeped in as she became more fully awake. No, it had just been a dream. Too bad. She squeezed her eyes shut, stealing a hand down the front of her pants, trying to recapture that roiling bliss.

Oilcan clunked into the room, rain darkening his shirt. "Hey."

Burning with embarrassment, Tinker yanked her hand out of her pants and tried to sound nonchalant. "Hey."

Oilcan shoved his damp hair back out of his eyes. "I went out to the trailer. The level indicators on the power sink are showing that we've only got a few more hours and then it's gone."

Tinker looked at the darkening sky, seeing that dusk was coming on. "What time is it?"

"Almost seven."

"Five more hours until Startup."

Oilcan shook his head. "The sink only has about two hours of power left."

"How's Windwolf?"

"At the moment, holding steady. Lain says that he's likely to worsen, though, once the power gives out."

Then they couldn't stay at Lain's. Magic wasn't like electricity; you didn't flip a switch and get current flooding the power lines. Instead, like a gentle rain after a drought, magic would need to saturate the area and soak in deep until the depleted earth couldn't hold any more and then form useable runoff. Even after Startup, it would take hours before the ambient level of magic in Pittsburgh would be where anyone could do a healing spell and expect it to work.

Tinker checked to see if she still had the cancel spell printout and then levered herself out of the chair. "We should be sitting at the Rim nearest to the hospice at Startup."

Windwolf woke as they prepared to move him back to the truck, blinking in confusion.

"Lie still." Tinker said to him, and repeated it in Low Elvish.

"Ah, my little savage," Windwolf murmured, lifting his good hand to her. "What now?"

"We're running out of time, which is unfortunately common for us humans." Tinker squeezed his hand in what she hoped was a reassuring manner.

"Does life go by so quickly, then?"

"Yes," Tinker said, thinking of leaving Pittsburgh in a few months and already regretting her promise to Lain. "It must be nice, having all the time to do all the things you want to do."

He turned his head and looked out the window. "There is a graveyard on that hill. I see them all the time here in your city. We do not have them. We do not die in such numbers. But it never truly struck me as to what these graveyards meant until now; all around you, the churches and the graveyards—death constantly stands beside you. I don't know how you tolerate the horror."

It scared her to hear him talking about death. "I'll get you to a hospice at Startup," she promised. "But you'll have to hang in there until then."

"Hang in?" He looked mystified by the English slang.

"Keep fighting."

"Life is a marvelous adventure," he whispered. "And I wish not to end it now. Especially now that things have gotten even more interesting."

They eased back down Riverview Road and through the maze of side streets to Ohio River Boulevard. There, the traffic snarled into knots as people fleeing the city collided with those trying to get back in. It took them an hour to travel the two or three miles to the first major split in the road. The night was sweltering, as only July in Pittsburgh could be. They rode with the windows down, and in the mostly stopped traffic, those without air-conditioning got out and stood waiting outside their cars for the chance to crawl ahead.

"There's Nathan's twenty-car accident." Oilcan indicated a score of wrecked cars and trucks sitting under the floodlights of the stadium parking lot. It wasn't difficult to guess which vehicle had been involved in the fatality. A red vehicle, make unrecognizable, sat to one side, smashed into an accordion two feet tall. "How do you suppose they managed that in this type of traffic?"

"One of the semis lost its load." Tinker pointed out the haphazardly loaded trailer. "It must have landed on the—minivan?—beside it." The parking lot's entrances, she noticed, had Earth Interdimensional Agency barricades up, and police tape strung at chest height about the cars created an imaginary fence. "Looks like someone got caught smuggling in the deal."

Judging by the amount of police tape and number of armed men, the EIA, the international agency in charge of almost everything in Pittsburgh even vaguely related to the elves, had stumbled onto a large illegal shipment. There were three tractor-trailer trucks, a dozen large Ryder and U-Haul box trucks, four pickup trucks, and the squashed car—any of which could have been the smuggler's vehicle. Unless they had been part of a convoy, it seemed strange that the EIA had impounded the whole lot.

"That Peterbilt is nearly new." The traffic opened up for a few hundred feet. Oilcan grunted slightly as he put in the clutch in order to shift out of first gear into second gear. The clutch in the flatbed, an ancient 2010 Ford F750, was stiff; Tinker nearly had to stand on it to shift when she drove. "It wouldn't take much to get it back to running."

Tinker drooled at it for a minute. "Yeah, but unless it's *the* smuggling vehicle and thus no one is willing to claim it, someone will have already made arrangements to get their truck back next Shutdown."

"One can dream." Oilcan grunted through another shift back down to first as they dropped to a crawl.

Speaking of next Shutdown . . . "I told Lain that I'd go to CMU for a term."

"You're kidding." He looked at her as if she had suddenly transformed into something slightly repulsive and totally unexpected, like one of those ugly pug dogs.

"It'll only be ninety days, and I'd get a chance to see what Earth is like."

"I've lived there," Oilcan pointed out. "Everything is too big. You can spend all day looking at thousands of people and not see a single person that you know."

They eased up onto the Fort Duquesne Bridge. Below them, barges choked the Ohio, the Allegheny, and the Monongahela rivers. It seemed possible to walk from one shore to the other without touching water. It happened every time Pittsburgh returned to Earth; trade goods coming and going by land, water, and air. She didn't want to think about living someplace this crowded all the time.

"You're not helping," she said.

"It's another world, Tinker. If you don't like it, you'll be stuck and miserable."

"Maybe I'll like it."

He shrugged. "Maybe. I don't think so. You hate having someone telling you what to do. *Think* about it. You're going for classes. You've never been to a regular school. Classes start exactly at eight a.m. Bang. A bell rings and you have to be sitting in your seat, quiet, facing forward. And you sit there, without talking, for hours, while you study what the teacher wants you to learn."

"Maybe college is different. Lain seems to think it's a good idea."

"And Lain likes to putter around in the garden, planting flowers. You tried that once. Remember how crazy it drove you."

"I already told Lain yes."

He scowled at her, and then focused on getting through the city. Downtown, despite it being almost ten o'clock, was filled with activity. Stores were sorting hastily delivered goods, preparing for the Startup rush. Once the stores sold out, there would be no more until next Shutdown. Fall fashions were appearing in the windows; anyone who didn't buy early might be facing the Pittsburgh winter without gloves and sweaters.

The delivery drivers who were still trying to get home to Earth were few, and easily identified. They leaned on their horns, they cursed out their windows, and they disobeyed all laws of man, elf, and common sense in their rush.

"Watch, watch, watch!" Tinker shouted, bracing herself as one such idiot cut them off. It was a small rabid pickup truck, streaking through a recently changed red light with horn blasting. At the last moment, it recognized that the flatbed outweighed it by three times, and veered sharply to avoid them.

Only a motorcyclist was in the way.

A normal man would have died. The motorcyclist responded with inhuman speed and strength, wrenching his bike out of the pickup's way.

"Is he an elf?" Oilcan asked as he responded to the blare of horns behind him and drove on through the intersection.

Tinker leaned out to look back. Strangely, instead of focusing on the pickup truck that nearly hit him, the motorcyclist was watching the flatbed drive away. He was far too homely to be one of the fey; under a wild thatch of black hair, he was long-nosed and sharp-featured.

"Nah. Just lucky," Tinker said, and scrambled through the back window to check on Windwolf.

The power sink read empty, and the spell had collapsed. Windwolf was cool to the touch, and for a moment she was afraid he had died. She stared at him for what seemed to be eternity before he took a long deep breath.

During the day, Lain had kept dryer-warm blankets on Windwolf. The current blanket was cool to the touch. Tinker called Lain. "The magic's out. Windwolf's cold. Is there anything I can do?"

"Lie down beside him, under the blankets with him."

"*What?*"

"Is he even conscious, Tinker?"

"I don't know." Lain was right, though. Tinker was letting the memory of her dream make her self-conscious. A moment ago she'd been afraid the elf was dead; how aware was he going to be of her? "Okay. I'll call you later, let you know how we're doing."

Tinker turned off the lights, took off her boots, and crawled onto the worktable with Windwolf. Sometime during the day, his hair had come unbound; it spread into a pool of blackness on the table. To keep from pinning his hair under her, she gathered it into her good hand and carefully moved it all to his right side. It felt as silky as in her dream. She stroked the long soft strands into order and then carefully cuddled up to Windwolf, trying not to press against any of his wounds. Lying in enforced idleness beside him, however, made her mind churn through possibilities at a feverish speed. Maybe, her brain suggested, she had dreamed so vividly of Windwolf because of the life debt, coupled with his proximity. Possibly he had shared the memory. Perhaps he had actually instigated the sex, since it was beyond her normal ken of experience.

She peered at his still face in the shifting beams of the passing headlights. *Come on, Tinker, a male this beautiful—and in this much pain—doesn't dream about getting it on with scruffy little things like you.*

Which left her solely responsible. Wow.

"Tinker. Tinker!"

"What is it?" She blinked awake and realized she was in Windwolf's arms, his head on her shoulder and his scent on her lips.

"It's the EIA," Oilcan whispered through the window. "They're checking citizen papers. Do you have yours?"

"Yeah. Hold on." She slid out of Windwolf's loose hold to the floor. Someone banged on the trailer door, hard, making the whole back wall rattle. "Who the hell is out there? The Jolly Green Giant?"

"All three are big guys." Oilcan's face was visible only from his eyes up, but it was a portrait of fear. Border guards spooking Oilcan?

"What time is it? Where are we?"

"Six blocks from the Rim. It's five minutes to Startup."

"And they're EIA border guards?" Something didn't ring true, and she glanced about for a weapon. "Give me a minute!" she shouted. "I'm—I'm getting dressed!"

Windwolf's shoulder holster and pistol sat by the worktable. She reloaded the pistol quickly, looped the holster into place, and pulled on a jacket over it.

She unbolted the door and swung it open. "Here." She held out her citizen papers.

Some estimated the elfin population to be a billion for the entire planet. Others thought there might be as few as a few hundred million. No human knew and the elves guarded the information closely. Regardless, the elves had allowed displaced humans to remain only on certain conditions specified in the peace treaty. All humans judged criminal or insane in nature were banished, and immigration was to be by elf approval only. While many people fled living on an alien planet under control of an alien race, the benefits outweighed the negatives for some people. Nonexistent unemployment, cheap housing, and a blissfully unspoiled planet proved too much of a lure for others. A brisk trade of smuggling immigrants existed. The responsibility of controlling it fell to the Earth Interdimensional Agency, EIA.

The border guards usually hugged the border, since anyone a foot within the Rim made the trip to Elfhome. This close to midnight, they should be at the fence, catching the last desperate few and then calling it a night as Startup made all things moot. Six blocks away from the Rim, with only five minutes left, was setting off alarms. They were big men, all three Nathan Czernowski's size, which was odd in humans.

The largest one seemed to be the leader. He took her ID but dismissed it and her in a glance. Nor did he hand it back. She noticed that he also had Oilcan's papers.

"Check the trailer," the leader told the smallest guard, although that was a relative "small." "See if the little bird was right. Get the car," he ordered the remaining guard, who moved off into the night. "I want to be gone when this is done."

The smallest guard grabbed the door frame and levered himself up into the trailer, barely squeezing through the door. His nose worked like a dog's. "It smells like a slaughterhouse in here."

"We're transporting a wounded elf." Tinker backed away from him, keeping out of range of an easy grab. "We're taking him to the hospice as soon as Startup happens. Wargs chewed him up. He got blood everywhere. That's what you smell." She sniffed to see if it was really that noticeable, and caught his scent.

Smoke and sandalwood.

The guard saw Windwolf. His eyes narrowed, and he grinned savagely. "He is here," he rumbled to the leader. "Laid out like the dead. Easy prey."

"Do them all," the leader ordered. "Quietly."

Tinker yanked out the pistol, sliding between the guard and Windwolf. "Don't touch him! Touch him and I'll shoot you! Get back! Get out!"

"Tinnnker?" Oilcan asked quietly in the startled silence that followed, and then started the flatbed's engine. "I don't know what you're doing, but you'd better do it quick! The one outside just waved down some kind of backup in an unmarked car."

The smallest guard started to move toward her and she fired a warning shot over his shoulder. He jerked backward like it had hit him.

"Get out!" She fought to keep her voice firm. "This is your last chance! Go!"

Amazingly, the small guard tumbled out of the trailer, almost onto the leader, and they both scrambled away. She'd never felt so huge before. She slammed the door, bolted it, and raced back across the trailer, yelling, "Drive! Drive! Drive!"

The flatbed lurched forward, roaring up through first. "Tinker, I don't think I'm going to be able to make it! The car is cutting me off! Oh shit!"

A black sedan had raced past them on the left and was swinging right to cut them off. Oilcan was already slowing down when Tinker hit the window. She slid through the window, down into his lap, and jammed her foot down on top of his.

"Just go!" she shouted. "Shift!"

Swearing, Oilcan stomped down on the clutch, threw the truck into second, and let up on the clutch. "Watch the car!"

"I am watching it!" she shouted, nailing the gas pedal to the floor. The big truck leapt forward, caught the sedan at the front bumper, and smashed it aside. The flatbed shuddered at the impact and then shrugged it off, roaring forward.

They had been driving down a side street, and needed to turn onto Centre Avenue to reach the border. They were going too fast, though, for her to turn the truck alone. "Help me turn!"

Together they cranked the steering wheel through the sharp right turn onto Centre Avenue. There was a stop sign on the other side of the intersection. They mounted the curb, flattened the sign, and swung through the rest of the turn.

"That was a stop sign, Tink!" Oilcan complained.

"Yes! It was!" she growled. "Will you shut up? I'm thoroughly pissed off, and I don't need you complaining to me!"

They hadn't hit the sedan hard enough. It came sweeping up behind them, front panel gone and showing undercarriage.

The flatbed topped second gear.

"Shift!" Tink called, easing minutely up on the gas. Oilcan clutched and shifted up to third.

The sedan took the moment to leap ahead, veering into their path again.

"Fuck them!" Tink growled and elbowed Oilcan in the stomach as he started to turn the wheel. She stomped on the gas, and the flatbed roared straight at the sedan. "Eat this!"

She hadn't grown up in the scrap yard without knowing the strength of the vehicle under her. Built heavy enough to carry over ten tons, backed with a 250-horsepower engine, it was a close cousin to a bulldozer. She aimed at the sedan's back panel, knowing that the car would pivot on its engine block. The sedan spun like a child's toy as they hit.

The narrow strip of no-man's-land of the Rim was now only a block before them. Beyond it was a tall chain-link fence and the Oakland of Earth rising up in full glory.

"Oh shit, it's not Startup yet!" Tinker cried.

"Two more minutes," Oilcan said.

"Damn!" Tinker slammed the brakes. The big truck fought her more than when she'd hit the car, the wheels locking up, slewing them sideways. She sent up a quick prayer that the bolts on the trailer held.

Oilcan yelped and caught the clutch before the engine stalled out. "What are we going to do?"

The guards were swarming forward to intercept her the moment they stopped. Behind them, the sedan was gamely straightening out.

"Shift!" Tinker said.

"Shift to what?"

"Reverse." She shoved his hand aside and worked the gear shift into reverse. "Hold on."

They started backward, gathering speed. She watched her side mirrors as the sedan this time scrambled out of the way. The flatbed shot past its bumper by inches. Would they chase? No, they seemed confused.

"A minute," Oilcan intoned.

A block. Two. Four blocks, and she said, "Okay, let's stop."

They shifted back to first and sat, their feet arrayed across all the pedals. Far off, so faint Tinker barely heard it over the rumble of the flatbed engine, came the ringing of St. Paul's bells.

"This is it," Oilcan breathed.

"One hopes," Tinker said.

Void. The odd sense of falling without moving. All the streetlights flickered out, and only their headlights cut the sudden darkness. The chain-link fence and Oakland vanished. The primal forests of Elfhome and the elfin enclaves lining the border took their place. The aurora effect gleamed directly overhead, dancing along the gate's curving veil.

"Let's go!" Tinker nailed the gas pedal.

The gate remained closed. The guards, gathered to watch her wild driving, scattered, except one fool waving like he thought she'd stop. Tinker reached up, caught the pull on the air horn, and blared her intention to barrel through. Said fool took the warning.

The gate was wood, and it sheared off with a sharp crack. The enclaves on either side of the road formed a chute of tall stone walls, three hundred feet in length, and then they plunged into the dark woods.

She had driven the road before, knew it to be a straight path. Roads on Elfhome were mostly fitted stone, following ley lines, acting as both road and power source. Unlike the wide-berm, multi-lane highways of Earth, they were more like paths. Branches scraped along the roof of the trailer and threatened to take out her mirrors.

Tinker leaned up. "See if you can check Windwolf. I don't have him strapped down back there."

Oilcan slid out from under her, squeezed through the window, and called, "He's fine. There are cars coming."

Reaally? Imagine that!

The side mirrors polarized to keep the car's headlights from blinding her completely. "I see them."

"We're in shit trouble, Tink."

"I know." She was determined not to be sidetracked into being upset. "We get through this, and then I'll worry about the mess."

The hospice was two miles in. Luckily the road remained too narrow for the EIA cars to try cutting them off. She geared down to make the turn into the hospice parking lot, swung the flatbed around, and backed up to the hospice's door as the EIA cars swarmed about her like gnats, hemming the truck in on the sides and front.

A moment later, and EIA men clung to every surface of the truck, pointing guns at her through the windows. Tinker raised her hands.

They hit the truck with a police override, and the door locks thunked up. They jerked the door open.

"I've got a wounded elf in—" she started to say, but finished with a yelp of surprise as they plucked her out of the seat.

"Tinker!" Oilcan shouted from the back.

"There's a wounded elf in back!" she said.

They pushed her up against the flatbed's hot hood, face down, and twisted her hands behind her back. Pain flared from her wounded hand. She couldn't bite back the cry of hurt.

"Tinker!" Oilcan threw open the back door and was yanked down himself. A moment later he was slammed up against the hood beside her. "She's hurt!" he growled. "Be careful with her!"

There were elves among the men. She could hear the rapid bark of Elvish. A man was leaning his weight into her back, while frisking her.

"She's got a shoulder holster on!" the man shouted in warning. "They've got a pistol someplace."

The gun! Where had she dropped it? It was lost in a blur of events.

He reached her pants pockets and started to unload them onto the high hood. "Damn, she's carrying a household."

"We haven't done anything except protect our patient," Tinker said, trying to turn to face him.

"Shut up, punk." He pulled her backwards and then slammed her against the hood again.

"Leave her alone!" Oilcan shouted.

The guard turned, nightstick upraised. Tinker shouted wordlessly in protest.

Then everything went silent and still. An elf had hold of the nightstick, and there were others, armed and hard-eyed, ringing them.

"They are not to be harmed," the elf said in Low Elvish. "Wolf Who Rules has placed them under his protection."

"*Naekanain,*" Mr. Nightstick said, slurring the word as if he'd learned the phrase by rote. *I do not understand.*

"They have brought Wolf Who Rules here to be cared for," the elf clarified in Low Elvish. "He asked me to protect the young humans. I will not let them be harmed."

"What's he saying?" Mr. Nightstick asked the woman beside him.

"He's saying, 'Hands off the kids or we'll break your face.' "

* * *

It quickly became apparent that there were two types of armed elves present. Hospice security appeared to be *laedin* caste, in camouflage green and browns done with elfin flare for fashion. They carried bows and spell-arrows and interceded between the humans of the EIA and Windwolf's personal security—which was all higher-born *sekasha* caste, armed to the teeth and thoroughly peeved. Even the hospice healers seemed intimidated by the *sekasha*, taking care to make no threatening moves as Windwolf was shifted off the worktable onto a stretcher and then handed out the trailer. The cousins were kept back, out of the way, as the healers and the *sekasha* carried the injured elf into the hospice.

By then, news of the cousins' arrival with Windwolf must have reached the enclaves that lined Elfhome's side of the Rim; elves drifted out of the darkness to gather in the parking lot. They were largely ignored by everyone, but seemed satisfied with swapping information among themselves. Only one rated attention from the guards; she drifted out of the woods like a will-o'-the-wisp, a gleaming beauty who made Tinker extremely aware of how short, dirty, and scruffy she herself really was in comparison. Obviously one of the high caste, the female crossed the parking lot and stopped one of the hospice guards with a touch of her luminous hand. The two made an effective roadblock, preventing the cousins and their joint elf/human guard from entering the hospice.

"Wolf Who Rules has been found?" the female asked in High Elvish. The guard bowed low and answered in a rapid flow of high tongue that Tinker couldn't follow. (Tinker had always found the more formal language to be too tedious and pretentious to become fluent in it.) She did catch, however, the female's name: Saetato-fohaili-ba-taeli. Roughly, it meant "Sparrow Lifted By Wind" though the "Saetato" could indicate soaring rather than lifted. While the female did not seem the type to take a human nickname, she would probably be called Sparrow.

As if collateral damage from Sparrow's beauty were not enough, the guard indicated the cousins, and Sparrow turned her stunning regard their way. From ankle-length hair, so pale blond it was nearly silver, with ribbons and flowers worked through it, to her tall lithe body encased in softly gleaming fairy silk of pale green, she was perfection taking humanoid form.

"These two wood sprites?" A soft musical laugh as eyes of deep emerald studied the cousins.

The guard clicked his tongue, the elfin way of shrugging, and added something about Windwolf putting them under his protection.

"Yes, of course." Sparrow clicked her tongue against straight pearly teeth and drifted away.

Minutes later the cousins were alone, under joint human/elf guard, in a waiting room, holding mugs of hot chai. Oilcan was quietly shaking off the adrenaline, which left Tinker plenty of time to think. They had done it—kept Windwolf alive all of Shutdown Day and delivered him to safety. With all of Pittsburgh, why though, had he ended up in her scrap yard? Just stupid luck, or had the life debt between them somehow guided him to her? And now what? Did he disappear out of her life again, until the next monster and the next life-or-death fight?

She touched her breast pocket to feel the spell within. If she got a moment alone with Windwolf, it might be the last time she could ever cast the spell. Even if she was sure the spell wouldn't harm him, did she want to sever the link? She scoffed at herself; what did she know of him except that he was arrogant? Strong. Brave. Altruistic. Honorable. Beautiful. That he was capable of wit and patience even while enduring great pain, facing probable death. And he was possibly a great lover.

The door swung open, and a man came in as if he ruled the place. He could nearly pass as an elf. He was tall, sleek, had blond hair drawn back into a braid, and was stylishly dressed from painted silk duster to tall, polished boots. He checked himself at the sight of the cousins huddled on the couch. Finally, the man let out his breath loudly and glanced at his PDA. "Which one of you is Oilcan, and which is Tinker?"

"I'm Tinker," she answered. "He's Oilcan."

He crossed the room to tower over them. "Brother and sister?"

"We're cousins," Tinker said.

"I'm Maynard." He didn't need to say more. Everyone knew Director Derek Maynard, head of EIA. In Pittsburgh, it was just short of saying "I'm God."

Oilcan moaned softly and sank deeper into the couch.

"You are in luck that elves believe that the ends justify the means, as long as it's done with honor. We've been told that the court would be most displeased with us if we press charges." He said it almost like the royal "we." "So the question is, what all do we need to pardon you of? Are you citizens, or do we have to draw you up papers? Is that truck yours, or did you steal it?"

"We're citizens," Oilcan said. "But we need our papers back. Your men never gave them back."

"We didn't do anything wrong until your men attacked us," Tinker said.

Maynard looked at her, eyes narrowing. "Was this before or after you destroyed the checkpoint?"

"We were waiting for Startup about a mile from the checkpoint when they forced their way into the trailer," Tinker said. "They were going to kill Windwolf. I had Windwolf's gun, so I pulled it on them. I made them get out. Then we rammed the gate."

Maynard studied her, all expression going from his face until he was unreadable. "What made you think they would kill Windwolf?"

"The one who got into the trailer called Windwolf 'sitting duck' or something like that."

" 'Easy prey.' " Oilcan mimicked their thick rough voices. "He said 'He is here—easy prey.' Then the other said, 'Do them all. Quietly.' They were going to kill all of us."

"Yeah, no witnesses," Tinker said.

"What makes you think they were EIA men?"

"They had on the border guard uniforms and asked to see our papers."

"It is important for you to understand this." Maynard dropped to one knee so he was level with them. *The EIA did not try to kill Lord Windwolf.*"

"They were too big to be wearing stolen uniforms," Tinker said. "They were taller than you, with lots more muscle."

"Whether they were truly EIA or not is yet to be seen. I doubt very much that they were my men. If they were, *they were not acting under my orders.* It is *very* important that no rumors to the contrary start. Me sanctioning a murder of Lord Windwolf would mean war. Perhaps war isn't a strong enough word. It would be genocide. The elves would rid Elfhome of humans."

Had he ordered it? Tinker considered what she knew of the man. Everyone had something different to say about Maynard—some of it insulting. No one called him stupid, though, and sending men in uniform would be the height of stupidity.

"Okay," Tinker said. "You had nothing to do with it. So, I guess this means we won't get our papers back."

"I will see you are issued replacements," Maynard said. "We had reports that Windwolf and his guard had been attacked by wargs just before Shutdown. His guard had been killed, and he disappeared.

We had no idea if he was in the city or still on Elfhome. We were hoping he made Elfhome. Apparently he didn't. How did he end up with you?"

"The wargs chased him into our scrap yard at midnight last night. I was there alone. They were temporary constructs, so I was able to disrupt them with our electromagnet. They reverted to dogs, and Windwolf shot them."

"And you've been sitting on him the last twenty-four hours?"

Tinker explained about Jonnie refusing to treat Windwolf and about taking the elf noble to the Observatory.

Maynard cursed softly. "None of them thought to call the EIA?"

"No," Tinker admitted. "What could you have done?"

"The hospitals don't treat the elves because the elves are worried we'll take blood samples in order to study their genetics and use it to tailor spells and germ warfare. You took a member of the royal family to a conclave of scientists while he was helpless. Do you have any idea what this might mean to our peace treaty?"

"We told him the choices. He agreed to it," Tinker said. "Besides, we gave him our word of honor. No one took samples."

"You know that for certain? You were with him every second?"

"When I wasn't with him, Oilcan or Lain was with him. We didn't leave him alone."

"Who is Lain?"

"Doctor Lain Skanske; she's a xenobiologist. She did the first aid on Windwolf. He asked her first if she understood the treaty and would swear to abide by it."

Oilcan nodded. "Tinker vouched that Lain could be trusted, and Windwolf said that was good enough for him."

Maynard looked at her in surprise. "He trusted you to vouch for someone?"

Tinker shrugged. "I suppose. I saved his life. He saved mine. He defended my honor. I helped stitch him together. I got into bed with him. It was one hell of a twenty-four hours, okay?"

"I see." Maynard continued looking at her, but she couldn't read his expression.

"Are we all free and clear with the EIA?" Tinker asked.

Maynard sighed. "We need you to describe the men who attacked you the best you can. We'll get someone in with a composite sketch program. I know you've been through a lot, but we need to nail these men."

He gave them no chance to say no. Standing, Maynard motioned to one of the human guards to go make his wishes reality.

"If Windwolf is out of danger, can I see him to say good-bye?" Tinker asked.

"I'll let his staff know," Maynard said. "They'll decide."

With that, he swept out of the room, apparently to start the search for the mysterious assassins. The cousins were left, once again, under the joint guard.

A police officer with a datapad showed up. They worked through sketches for the three big men. Oilcan proved to have a better memory for their faces, despite the fact that Tinker had interacted with them longer. The cousins were provided with forms to fill out and turn in later to replace their lost citizen papers.

As they finished up, an elf came and announced something in fast High Elvish.

"Windwolf is sleeping," Oilcan translated for Tinker. He had had the patience to learn high tongue where Tinker had not. "He left word that our desires be met."

"Can I see him?" Tinker struggled through the request in High Elvish, earning a surprised look from Oilcan over the top of his chai.

"*Batya?*" The elf asked. *Now?*

Tinker stood and did a formal bow. "*Shya. Aum gaeyato.*"

The elf returned her bow and led her to a door flanked by two stunningly beautiful elves elegantly carrying swords and automatic rifles. She ducked between them, feeling as scruffy as a junkyard dog.

They had worked serious healing magic on Windwolf. All his wounds were mere puckered scars. While he slept deeply, his breathing was regular and easy. All in all, he looked better than she did.

She took out the circuit paper, unfolded it, and looked at the glyph. *Now or never.*

Could she really lean over his battered body and place the glyph on his forehead? Cast the spell and hope for the best? Play magical Russian roulette with his life? She flashed suddenly to the weight and shape of his pistol in her hands, and shuddered at the thought of pressing that steel barrel to Windwolf's temple.

Never.

She dropped the paper into a wastebasket next to the bed. Bad as her luck was, she'd rather trust that Windwolf would outlive her by centuries than risk killing him by accident. Standing on tiptoe, she kissed Windwolf good-bye lightly on his bruised perfect lips. Perhaps in another five years, some monster would chase him into her life again. Strangely enough, she would miss him this time.

2: IN THE EYE OF GOD

Time seemed to crawl by. The cousins went outside and found it was dawn. Someone had pulled the flatbed out of the way and locked it up. The keys needed to be found. Once they managed to get into the truck, they discovered that they'd made the break across the border on fumes. Oilcan dug out a fuel can and went off in search of gasoline.

Exhausted, Tinker bolted the trailer door, then stripped out of her day-old clothes and pulled on clean panties and her hoverbike team shirt. Curling up on her worktable where Windwolf had recently lain, she tried to sleep. Her torn left hand hurt, but she was too tired to check under the bandages that Jonnie had put on her. It wouldn't help to look anyhow; she'd killed all her first-aid supplies dealing with Windwolf. Jonnie had said that she would need to check into a hospital, she thought as she drifted off. When Oilcan came back, she'd have him drop her at Mercy.

A banging on the trailer door woke her. She felt cold and weak as she half fell off the worktable. She put out her left hand to catch herself, and the pain made her cry out; she curled tight around her hand, cursing. Whoever was at the door stopped beating on it.

The flatbed jostled oddly. Tinker squeaked in surprise as she suddenly found herself being hauled up and backward. Windwolf swung her up and sat her on the worktable.

"Windwolf!" She blinked at him, confused by his appearance, until she realized that he had opened the flatbed's cab door and crawled through the AC vent. "What are you doing here?"

"What is this for?" He held up the spell she had abandoned in the trash.

"Tooloo told me that's what I should cast when I paid the debt."

"Debt?"

"You put a life debt on me, during a fight with a saurus—five years ago."

He cocked his head and looked at her for a long minute. "You're the fearless little savage with the crooked metal bar? The one that put the saurus's eye out while I was dazed?"

When had he been dazed? "Um, yes. I had a tire iron."

"You were a boy."

She shook her head. "I've always been a girl. I was only thirteen. I was a child."

He gave a cold hard laugh. "And you're not a child now?" He crumpled up the circuit paper and flung it away. "And who told you about this debt?"

"Tooloo. I showed her the spell you put on me and asked her what it was. She said if you died, as your body rotted, so would mine."

He went still. "So that's the only reason you saved me?"

She waved his question away with her good hand. "It just made things scarier, that's all. As if the Foo dogs weren't enough to scare the shit out of me, I had this added little creepiness to deal with. I wouldn't have done anything different, but now we're even."

"We are not even."

"What? Look, I saved you! I risked my life, got my hand screwed up." She held up her hand to show the bound wound. "I tore my place into pieces so I could crate you around! We drove all over Lain's flower beds and yard, making big ruts and killing the plants, and I told her I would go to college to make it up to her! I pulled a gun on the border patrol—who weren't even border patrol, but that's another story. All to save your life! And you would have been dead! If I hadn't helped you fight those Foo dogs, and then hauled your skinny elf ass out here to the Rim, you would have died a couple times over."

He pulled his knife, making her yelp and flinch back. He caught hold of her wounded hand. A glint of light from the silver blade, and he cut off the bandage.

Don't argue with the elf! Yes, sir. No, sir. Then get the hell away from him!

He gazed at her hand, and then caught hold of her head, pulled her to him. His lips touched her forehead where he had once painted the symbol.

What the hell does that mean?

Windwolf reached over and unlocked the trailer door. He picked her up then, like she was a child.

Tinker squirmed in his hold. "What the hell do you think you're doing? Put me down!"

"No." He carried her out of the trailer and across the street. Various elves scurried toward them, bowing and speaking quickly in High Elvish. Windwolf gave curt commands that were instantly obeyed with a fluid bow and *"Shya, ze domou."*

Windwolf carried her into the hospice, through a maze of hallways. A storm of High Elvish continued all around her, all too fast for her to understand.

"Please speak slower, please!" She hated High Elvish because it was so extremely polite. Yet no matter how many times she asked, no one seemed to take notice of her.

Windwolf stopped finally in a small room, typical of the hospice. The floor was a dark, warm blue color, the walls the color of honey, and the lighting came from the soft glow of the ceiling. Windwolf laid her on a high bed. Its pale birch headboard was more ornate than any human-style hospital bed, but otherwise it seemed to serve the same purpose.

Tinker sat up, swearing in a mix of Low Elvish and English. "Answer me, damn it! What do you think you are doing?"

A silver-haired female elf took a clear jar down from a birch cabinet. She handed it to Windwolf. He carried it back across the room, unscrewing the wide lid. Inside was a large golden flower.

"What's that for?" Tinker didn't bother with Elvish this time.

Putting the jar on the table beside the bed, Windwolf lifted the flower out and held it so close in front of Tinker's face that she nearly went cross-eyed looking at it.

"Smell it!" Windwolf commanded.

Tinker sniffed it cautiously. It reminded her of honeysuckle, a warm drowsy smell, with the soft drone of bees, the sway of green boughs, summer wind, blue skies, white clouds blistering white, softness piled and billowed upwards, wispy here, knife-edged sharp . . .

Tinker realized that she was going under, and jerked back. She tried to push the flower away with her wounded hand, too sleepy to remember it was hurt, and whimpered at the sudden flare of pain.

Windwolf caught the back of her head, holding her still, pressing the flower to her nose. "Just breathe it."

Tinker fought instead, not sure what was happening, only determined not to be helpless before him. She punched him as he bruised the sweet silken petals against her. She had aimed for his groin, but he turned and she caught him in the hip.

"Do not fight, little savage." He caught her chin between thumb and pinkie, holding her face as if in a vise, the flower cradled by his other fingers. He let go of her head and caught her wrists, forcing her back, pinning her down. "You are only going to hurt yourself."

She held her breath and squirmed under him, trying to kick him. He had his weight against her thighs and hips. Then she couldn't hold her breath any longer, and gasped. Sweetness, warm and sleepy as clean sheets on a feather-soft bed full in the early morning sun, white light through sheer curtains, open window to wind from a garden . . .

The female elf came across the room, laughing musically as only elves could, a silver knife in hand. The air went shimmering white, closing in around them, warm and liquid as honey, and sweet . . .

The Foo dogs chased her in her nightmares. Only they kept changing. One moment, they were great cats. Another moment—huge dogs. Other times—Chinese dragons, coiling through the scrap like giant poisonous snakes. She ran, her legs heavy as if she waded through mud. Suddenly the dream changed; Windwolf rocked her, warm and gentle as her grandfather's arms. His voice rumbled soft comfort into her ear.

"The Foo dogs!" she gasped, looking about wildly. The dream room held nothing more dangerous than shadows, a chair beside the bed, a low table with a pitcher of water and glasses.

"They are all dead," he murmured, stroking her back.

She clung to him as the dream wanted to slide back to the monsters in the scrap yard, the edges of the room blurring into heaps of metal. "Don't let go!"

"I will not."

She worked at forcing her dreaming to focus on him. She thought she heard the slither of scales over steel and whimpered, burrowing into his hair.

"Easy. You are safe," Windwolf stated calmly. "I will let nothing harm you."

Think of Windwolf. She ran fingers through his hair, found his ears and traced their outline. She investigated their shape and texture, the slight give of the cartilage, the softness of the lobe, and the intricate coil of inner part versus the firm, stiff points of the ear tip. After a few minutes, he gave a soft moan and caught her exploring hand. He moved it to his mouth, kissed her fingertips, the palm of her hand, and then ran his tongue feather light over the pulse point on her wrist.

Who would have guessed that would feel so good? She would have to try it awake some time. She gazed at him, stunned again by the beauty of his eyes.

"I don't think I've ever seen anything so blue. Cobalt maybe."

"My eyes?"

"Yes."

He studied her solemnly and then said, "Your eyes are the color of polished walnut."

"Is that good?"

This dream Windwolf looked at her with gentleness that she wasn't accustomed to from him. "Your eyes are warm and earthy and yet strong enough to face any adversity."

"Oh, wow, you like my eyes?"

"I like all of you. You are pleasing to look at."

Now she knew she was dreaming. "Yeah, right, with my hair and my nose." She twanged her nose a couple of times. It was numb, just like when she was drunk. Windwolf's nose, of course, was perfect; she traced her fingers over the bridge of his nose. Just right.

"I find your hair appealing," perfectly dreamy Windwolf said.

"You do?"

"It is very pure."

"I thought elves liked long hair." She tugged on a short lock to illustrate that hers was anything but long.

"There is beauty in functionality that makes fashionable seem jaded. In our case, fashionable has passed traditional and become something nearly geological."

She pondered this for several minutes before realizing that he meant that the length of hair in elves was set in stone. "Sounds boring."

"I am not sure if it is lack of courage or lack of creativity that dictates the length of elfin hair; unlike you, there is a notable shortage of both in our females."

"Me?"

"You are the bravest female I have ever met, as well as the most intelligent."

"I'm brave?" *When?*

"Fearless."

Tinker blew a raspberry. "Hell, no, I was scared a lot in the past"—how long had it been since Windwolf came over the fence, disrupting her well-ordered life?—"days." At least it seemed like days. She could remember at least two nights, but the number of meals and periods of sleeping didn't add to anything reasonable. "I only did what had to be done."

"And that is true courage. As you pointed out, without you, I would have died many times over. Indeed, I hazard a guess that of all the people of Pittsburgh, humans and elves, you alone had the intelligence and fortitude to keep me safe."

It was such a weird dream. The edges of the room slipped in and out of focus, and she felt too light and bold. It was like she was drunk, only usually then her limbs felt huge and needed effort to move them about. Her hands now kept adventuring off on their own, exploring Windwolf.

His fingers proved to be long and slender, with the cleanest fingernails she'd ever seen. Of course, everyone she knew spent a good amount of time with their hands in dirt or engine grease. Under a loose silk shirt of moss green, only faint silvery scars remained where the Foo dogs mauled him.

"Why did the wargs attack you? Who wanted you dead?"

"I do not know. I have many enemies. Other clans are envious of the Wind Clan's monopoly on the Westernlands, and within my own clan, many consider me a dangerous radical. This, though, was not a simple political assassination. This was pure madness, to loose monsters that kill everything in their path. I can not imagine any of my enemies attacking me in such a cowardly method."

"Someone has."

"Yes. Who remains a mystery."

There seemed to be some barrier that she had breached. Normally she would not think of touching someone, nor did she need to rebuff most people. A quick hug. A handshake. A pat on the shoulder. It was like they all walked around with invisible shields, deflecting even thoughts of reaching out to another person. She had never noticed before, but now, snuggling against Windwolf, she noticed the lack of them. Like antimatter and matter meeting, their protection shields had collided and annihilated one another.

Windwolf allowed her to explore his scarred shoulder. She found herself nuzzling into his neck, once again tracing the outline of his ear. She drew back slightly in surprise of herself.

"I'm sorry."

"Why?"

She tried to form an answer and lapsed into confused silence until she forgot what she had been thinking about. He took her hand from his ear tip again.

"Does it hurt?" she asked as he lifted her hand away.

"It feels far too good to let you continue." He nibbled on her wrist, delighting her. "You are too pure to follow that course. You are not yourself right now."

"Who am I?"

"You are Tinker without her normal defenses. You are on the edge of sleep, still full of *saijin*."

"I'm drugged?"

"Very much so."

She considered her body. Yup. That would explain things. "Why?"

"I did not want you to lose your hand."

She peered at her right hand. Windwolf took hold of her left, opening it to expose a network of pink scars, and anti-infection spells inked onto both the palm and the back. She flexed the hand, discovering it hurt faintly, deep inside. Thinking back now, she vaguely remembered he had carried her into the hospice.

"Oh. Thank you." She kissed him. She meant it to be a chaste kiss, but it became something more. Suddenly it dawned on her that she was half drugged, half naked, and alone with a male in a bed. Her heart started to hammer in her chest like an engine about to throw a rod.

"Do you think you can sleep now?" he asked, stroking her cheek lightly.

What did he mean by that? "Sleep sleep" or "sleep?" Luckily, the Elvish was a much more concise language. "*Saijiata?*" The act of sleeping?

He nodded, looking inquiringly at her, as if the other possibilities had never occurred to him.

Interestingly, the moment of panic had burned out all thoughts of monsters. "Yes. I think I can."

Tinker woke with a start. Her head seemed big, and full of air. The pain in her left hand had deepened into a constant dull ache. Turning her head, she saw the empty chair beside the bed. Windwolf.

A vase of flowers sat on the nightstand next to the pitcher of water. The vase was elfin, a deceptively simple twist of glass, a thick base sweeping up to an impossibly thin rim, elegant beyond words. The flowers were black-eyed Susans. She guessed that the flowers were from her cousin and that the hospice staff had provided the vase. As usual, the bright wildflowers made her smile. A note card leaned against the vase, printed in Oilcan's neat, over-careful hand and smudged with engine grease.

> When I got back with the gas, they told me that your hand
> was going septic and that you were in surgery. I'm sorry I didn't

check it before I left. I looked in just now, but you were still
sleeping. If we want food and fuel for the next thirty days, I've
got to go make sure to get it now. I hate leaving you alone. I'll be
back as soon as I can. Get well soon. Love, Orville.

Orville. He must truly be rattled if he was using his real name.

There was a light tap on the door, and Maynard, God himself,
opened it up.

"You're awake."

"Yes." Tinker wondered what God wanted with little her.

"I didn't make the connection between you and *the* Tinker until
Windwolf told me about some of what you did to keep him alive."

She shrugged. "Happens all the time. No one expects the legendary Tinker to be a little snot-nosed girl."

No smile. Maybe God didn't have a sense of humor. She often
suspected that.

"How old are you?" Maynard asked. "Sixteen? Seventeen?"

"Eighteen, as of last month."

"Parents?"

Little alarms were going off. "Where's this going?"

"I like to know who I'm working with."

Make that big alarms. "Since when am I working with you?"

"Since today. I've got a bit of a mystery I need solved, and maybe
you can help. They say you're fit to leave."

He left it nebulous as to whether this was a declinable personal
request or an official demand. Maynard certainly wasn't someone she
wanted to alienate; as god of Pittsburgh, he could make her life hell.
Now that she was a legal adult, she had nothing to hide. At least, she
didn't think she did.

"Okay. Let me figure out what they did with my clothes, and you
can show me this mystery."

Clothes found, and Maynard carefully shooed off, she got up to
change.

Under the cotton gown she was naked. She put on her panties
and bra without taking off the gown, eyeing the door—which had no
lock. Luckily no one burst in to catch her dressing. She pulled on her
carpenter's pants, and then in one quick motion pulled off the gown
and slipped into her team shirt. With her back to the door, she took
her time buttoning it up.

The hospice had cleaned her clothes, managing to get all of

Windwolf's blood off her carpenter's pants and to find a replacement for the bottom button of her team shirt. It had gone missing weeks ago, and she'd been at a loss as to how to replace it. Cleaning clothes she could do. Repairing was something she could only do to machines.

She stepped into her steel-toed boots, sealed them, and clonked about the room, feeling more able to take on Maynard.

The contents of her pockets sat elegantly arranged in an elegant rosewood box. Elves stunned her sometimes. Most humans probably would have gone through her pockets and tossed most of her treasures. The hospice staff, however, had not only cleaned all the old grease-coated nuts and bolts, but had properly mated them together, and then arranged them by size on green velvet. They looked like bits of silver jewelry. Her spare handmade power lead (extremely crude looking but actually poly-coated gold) had been coiled and tied off with a strand of blue silk. They'd even kept the interesting-looking twig she'd pocketed the day before Shutdown, which now seemed weeks ago, instead of two days. It pleased her (she would have been unable to rebuild three separate projects without the various bolts), but still it weirded her out. When one was immortal, apparently, one had time to waste on other people's little details of life.

She pocketed her eclectic collection and went out into the hall to find Maynard waiting. He led the way out to the sun-blasted parking lot, towering over her. The flatbed was gone; Oilcan must have driven it back to the yard. Looking at the empty parking space where the tow truck had sat made her feel horribly alone and vulnerable. Stripped of her powerful toys and standing beside Maynard, she felt all of her five feet nothing. Nathan was as tall as Maynard, but he was a friend, so she never felt particularly small around him. Maynard was EIA. Her grandfather had viewed all forms of government with deep suspicion, which she of course had inherited in some part. After her grandfather had died, and she had been left an orphan in a town that exiled stray human children, the EIA had grown to bogeyman proportions.

I have nothing to fear from the EIA now. She and Oilcan had coasted a year, staying low, until Oilcan hit eighteen. At that time he could stand as head of household, and they were legal again, barely. There was the little matter that they were living in separate houses by that time. Last month, though, she had finally turned eighteen herself.

Maynard traveled in style; a big, black, armored limo rolled up to the curb, stopping so that the back passenger door could swing open without hitting them, and not an inch farther away. Maynard indicated that she was to slide into the air-conditioned comfort first.

"Parents?" Maynard asked after they pulled out of the hospice's parking lot.

"I'm eighteen—a legal adult." She tried dodging around the whole parent thing. Gods knew it was far too complex to go into. "I'm also a legal citizen: I was born and raised in Pittsburgh. I'm sole owner of Pittsburgh Scrap and Salvage. I did a quarter million dollars in business last year, and all my taxes are paid."

"Your cousin works for you?"

"Yeah."

"Any other family?"

She tried to bluff him off. "Should I save us both the effort and just dump a whole family history on you?"

"Like I said, I like to know who I'm working with."

She considered him and decided that meant "yes." She made a note not to bluff with Maynard again. "My grandfather had two kids: my father, Leonardo, and Oilcan's mom, Aunt Ada. That's all the family that I know of."

"Oilcan?" Maynard lifted one eyebrow. "Surely that's not his real name."

Apparently the loss of their ID cards had slowed down the EIA network. "No, it isn't. Aunt Ada was married to a man named John Wright. Oilcan's real name is Orville John Wright. I'm sure it was Grandpa's idea; he had a thing about inventors."

"Orville Wright." Maynard proved he had some sense of humor and smiled. "I can see why he goes by Oilcan. How did you and Orville end up here in Pittsburgh? You're too young to immigrate."

"Grandpa immigrated during the first year. I was born here. Oilcan came to live with us when I was six."

"What about your parents? Both yours and Orville's?"

"Both my dad and Aunt Ada were murdered."

"I'm sorry." Maynard thought for a moment, and then cocked his head. "Not here in Pittsburgh, or I would have known about it."

"My father was killed in Oakland before the first Startup. John Wright was a man with a temper; he killed Aunt Ada in Boston. I stayed with Lain when Grandpa went to Boston to get Oilcan; I've never been on Earth."

Maynard looked at her for several minutes through narrowed eyes. "Your father was killed—what—ten years before you were born?"

So, one couldn't slip things easily past this man. "Yes. My grandfather never got over my father's death. Grandpa used cryogenically stored sperm to have my ovum inseminated in vitro ten years after my father died."

"But your mother is still alive?"

"Technically, no." Tinker sighed—so much for trying to avoid complexity. "My birth mother wasn't the donor of the egg that my grandfather had inseminated. He also used a cryogenically stored egg. My real mother was also dead before I was born."

Maynard stared at her for several minutes before asking, "Did your parents, your real parents, even know one another?"

"I don't think so."

"Your parents, who had never met, were dead when you were conceived?"

"Yeah."

"Doesn't that bother you?"

"Mr. Maynard, if we're going to work together, can we just stick to scientific facts, and not go jaunting off through history and psychology?"

Maynard exhaled what might have been a laugh. "You hold your own."

Tinker wasn't sure what he meant by that. Sick of the whole inquisition, she forced the conversation off onto another track. "So what the hell do you want me to do?"

"Someone smuggled a large shipment of illegal goods in during Shutdown. Lucky for us, though, they were involved in a multiple-vehicle accident on the Veterans Bridge. Their vehicle was disabled, and they panicked in spectacular fashion, which makes us worried about what all they might have brought into Pittsburgh."

"You didn't catch them?"

"No," Maynard said. "They unloaded their truck, sorted through the shipment, and carried away what they deemed most important. The driver had been pinned by the accident; they shot him so we couldn't question him."

"Ouch." That earned her a dark look from Maynard. "So far it doesn't sound like a panic."

"Well, throw in a carjacking, assault on the other accident victims, picking up and throwing a Volkswagen Beetle over the side of the bridge in a fit of rage, engaging in a gunfight with police, and trying to blow up with C-4 what they couldn't carry away, and you start to get the idea."

Tinker gasped. *Nathan!* "Were any of the police hurt?"

Maynard looked surprised at the question. "Luckily, no. Not for the want of trying, though."

"And how do I fit in? I was in McKees Rocks fighting wargs when that accident happened."

"How do you know *when* it happened?"

"My friend Nathan Czernowski is a cop. He was with me at the scrap yard when the call came in. I'm assuming that there was only one multiple-vehicle pileup and fistfight on the Veterans Bridge."

"Yes." Maynard relaxed slightly, apparently accepting her alibi. "Well, you'll be interested to know that the description of the smugglers match that of your attackers at the Rim."

Tinker swore. "Smuggle in contraband one night, attack Windwolf the next?"

"Very busy people," Maynard said. "It denotes a large organization, of which these men are merely disposable muscle. So far, EIA has been able to keep such crime rings out of Pittsburgh. I want to pull this one up by its roots."

"Sounds like a plan. What does this have to do with me?"

"Some of the load wasn't contraband, just extremely expensive high-tech parts. The question is, what could they be used to make?"

"Oh, I see."

The impounded goods had been unloaded in a warehouse in the Strip District. Basically just one low room a block long, the place fairly crawled with armed EIA. While security for the building ran high, lighting and climate control left much to be desired. Natural light came in from windows lining an upper walkway. Work lamps tacked to support columns provided additional light, plugged into jury-rigged electrical boxes on newly strung Romex line.

Because of the virgin forests occupying most of the western continent, Elfhome usually ran several degrees cooler than Earth. Since Pittsburgh suffered from high humidity, the lower temperatures were a blessing. The rain storms of Shutdown and Startup over, a rare summer heat, however, had moved in. The warehouse's only nod toward climate control was ceiling fans, cloaked in the shadows high overhead, that barely moved the ovenlike heat of the building.

Tinker found herself wishing for shorts and a midriff shirt. In Maynard's company, she didn't even feel like unbuttoning her shirt. Sweat trickled down her back as she followed Maynard through trestle tables set up and loaded with smuggled goods.

What she discovered made her forget the heat.

There were digital boards, stripping kits, and connector kits. For

fiber-optics work, they had a full run of splice trays, hot-melt connector systems, and a curing oven. She found a spool of gold wire.
Fault finders, microscanners, and status activity monitors. There
were tech kits that set her mouth drooling. Punch boxes. Wire crimp
tools. Small precision mirrors. There were even new digital markers
that laid out a metal-based ink held in a buckyball matrix. Tinker
poked through the stuff, wishing she could take the lot back to her
place. Lain had told her tales about the world beyond the Rim where
such stuff was plentiful. Much as Tinker loved Pittsburgh, she had to
admit that there was a true shortage of goods.

Maynard interrupted her trolling to hand her a length of cable
with a box at the end. "Do you know what this is?"

Tinker took it. She turned it in her hands, studying it. The box
was molded plastic with two power ports. She tried the various
screwdrivers she had tucked into her pockets, the third being the
charm, and undid the screws. "Oh my, this is sexy."

"What is it?"

"It's a power transformer."

"You recognize it?"

"What's to recognize? This is a male 220 line, meaning you plug it
into a 220 outlet. It would have a pull on par with an electric clothes
dryer or an electric range. The female leads are typical magic connectors. It takes electrical power and transforms it to magic. The
question is—what type of spell is it keyed to?"

"It would have to be keyed to only one spell?"

"There isn't any way to change the output frequency. It's preset.
Although, if you knew the frequency it was outputting, then you
could probably set up a secondary translation spell anytime you
wanted to use it for a different spell. You'll see a loss in power effi-
ciency on the order of eleven percent, but at this amperage, such a
power loss would be negligent. Shit, I could have used something like
this on Windwolf. I'll have to build one."

"You could build one of these?"

"Yeah. It wouldn't be too hard. Of course, there's the whole question of why bother. Here on Elfhome, there's enough magical power
to fuel any spell without the cost of electrical energy. And on Earth,
except for healing elves, there are already mechanical solutions for almost everything."

"Magic doesn't work on Earth."

"Does too." Tinker replaced the screws and tightened them
down. "The laws of the universe don't change just because you hop
dimensions. The difference is the amount of magical power in the di-

mension. Think of magic as a waveform passing through multiple realities. Elfhome exists at the top of the wave: Magic is plentiful. Earth
exists at the bottom of the wave: Magic is rare. Magic follows the laws
of physics just like light, gravity, and time. I could show you the
math, but it's fairly complex. There are types of radiation more common in one reality than the other, but lucky for us, the generation
waveform seems larger, so we fall close enough on the curve that it
doesn't affect either species adversely."

"So you can do magic on Earth?"

"It's how I kept Windwolf alive," Tinker said. "I had magic stored
in a power sink and used it to feed a healing spell."

"Can you tell what the smugglers might have been trying to build
with all this?"

Tinker shrugged. "Not a clue. I'm afraid I don't have a criminal
mind."

"Make a wild guess."

She sighed, glancing around. "Well, unless they scooted off with
all the uncommon stuff, they're not going to make a wide range of
items. I'm guessing all those power transformers are set to the same
frequency, or else they would be labeled somehow. There's a lack of
moveable parts, so it's not like a car or a bike or a printing press. It's
magic-based, either many scattered copies of one spell, or one massive spell."

"Can you tell what spell?"

"You'd better check with the elves for that. The best I can do is to
match the frequency to a known spell, but my knowledge of magic is
fairly limited. For all I know, they're going to change the population
of Pittsburgh into frogs."

Maynard sighed slightly, perhaps not looking forward to trying
to pry information from the always-obtuse elves. "Anything else?"

"Well . . ." Tinker held out the power transformer. "You could let
me take this home and play with it. I can figure out the cycle on the
magic output and search through my spell database for a match. It
would at least start eliminating possibilities."

"Take it then."

She lifted up the markers. "I don't suppose I could have these as
part of my payment?"

Was that a smile that tugged his mouth slightly sideways for one
second? "You can have them." Maynard produced a business card and
presented it. "This is my direct number. If you figure anything out,
give me a call. It is always answered."

Of course it was—he was god of Pittsburgh. There was no

name on the card, only a phone number. Wow, God's private phone number.

Tinker pocketed it. "I'll let you know what I find out."

"I'll take you home."

She wasn't comfortable with the idea of God knowing where she lived, although, he certainly could find out easily enough. "I've got some shopping to do, before everything's gone. Could you just drop me at Market Square?"

3: ACCIDENTAL LOLITA

It wasn't until Maynard's armored limo rolled away that Tinker realized she had just stranded herself downtown.

She had taken her headset off in the trailer, and thus Windwolf had carried her into the hospice without it. Pay telephones had started disappearing from Earth cities at the turn of the century as cell phones eliminated the need for them. Luckily, Pittsburgh had moved to Elfhome before the last wave of dismantling pay phones. Supposedly to maintain the lines of communication between Shutdown and Startup, the governments of Earth heavily subsidized Pittsburgh's phone system. Thus Tinker was able to find a phone, and with her lone rumpled dollar changed into dimes at the *okonomiyaki* cart, could afford ten calls.

The afternoon sun had heated the plastic of the pay phone to nearly blistering. Tinker winced at the pain it lanced through her newly healed hand, and juggled the hot receiver around while she called Oilcan. He didn't pick up, which was odd. She tried his home number, but he wasn't at his condo. She didn't bother leaving a message; most likely by the time he checked his home machine, she would be someplace other than Market Square.

Oilcan wasn't at the scrap yard either. Because she'd yanked her workshop to ferry Windwolf around, her office AI was offline at the scrap yard. After a dozen rings, she hung up, and called her loft.

Her home AI Skippy answered. "Hello, this is Tinker's residence. Tinker isn't in. Please leave an audio message, video clip, or data file."

"It's me. Let me have the audio messages." She used her voice code. "Tesla titillates treacle."

"There were sixty-seven calls," Skippy reported, and started into replaying the messages. "Message one."

Sixty-seven? Who the hell is calling me? Tinker frowned as Nathan's voice came on.

"I was wondering what happened after I left," Nathan said. "Call me. I'm worried about you."

Skippy time-stamped the message from the morning of Shutdown and gave the number. She recognized it as the pay phone at the McKees Rocks gas station; Nathan might have stopped there after checking the scrap yard. She made a mental note to call him.

"Message two," Skippy queued into the next call, which was from Oilcan.

"Hey, I got gas for the shop, tracked down a load of fresh batteries, and even managed to snag you a new clutch system for your bike. I swung past again to pick you up, but you had gone already. I'm heading out to buy food now. I don't know about you, but all I have in my cupboard is instant oatmeal and brown sugar. I'll see you tonight at Lain's."

Lain's?

Skippy time-stamped the call at two hours earlier, meaning Oilcan must have been on Maynard's heels in his attempt to pick her up at the hospice. The phone number was a South Hills number, so Oilcan must have gone straight out to the food warehouses.

"There are no more audio messages," Skippy reported.

"Wait, what about the other sixty-five calls?"

"No other messages were left."

The phone company's automated system hijacked the connection and demanded more money. Tinker fed two of her dimes into the coin slot. Satisfied, the phone company's AI released the line.

"Give me a report on all calls."

Nathan's was indecently early, meaning he had probably left it as he came off shift. The second call hit at the ungodly time of 5:15 A.M. The third was at 5:30 A.M., and then the calls settled into an every-half-hour event. The first thirty-eight originated from an Earth phone number with an area code that she didn't recognize, and came with no ID flag. At midnight, when Pittsburgh returned to Elfhome, the Earth phone number dropped off the list.

At six the next morning, the calls started again, only this time the phone numbers were all local pay phones at systematic half-hour intervals. They moved in a widening circle around the scrap yard, starting at the gas station on the corner. She had just missed the most recent call.

Just out of curiosity, she had Skippy compare call times for all calls, Earth-based and local. All of them listened to the full outgoing message, as if checking to make sure nothing had been changed.

The phone company's automated system hijacked the line again, demanding more money if she was going to stay on. She hung up instead, not sure what to make of the mysterious phone calls. Obviously someone, apparently from Earth, was looking for her, but who?

Perhaps Lain knew, as all of Tinker's contacts with Earth came through the xenobiologist. Tinker used her fifth dime to call the xenobiologist, and got Lain's AI.

"It's Tinker," she told Lain's simple, unnamed AI.

"Tinker," Lain's recorded voice came on. "Oilcan called early this morning. He said there's nothing to eat out at your place. We're doing the traditional summer Startup cookout here at the Observatory. I'm probably outside, so just come on up. You can spend the night if you want."

Tinker's mouth drooled at the thought. Huge and crowded as Earth was, the scientific community of Earth remained small enough that the incoming scientists knew to bring food for a social gathering, each trying to outdo the rest. Since Pittsburgh pulled in people from all across Earth, the cookout was held the day after Startup, so those coming in at the last minute wouldn't miss out on the festivities.

Getting to the Observatory, however, might be tricky. Maybe she should have taken Maynard up on the offer of a ride. While South Hills still had a light-rail public transportation system, only taxis went to Observatory Hill. She now had only five dimes to her name.

She considered her dimes, then dropped one into the coin slot and called Nathan.

He picked up on the first ring.

"Czernowski."

"It's Tinker."

"Tink! What happened after I left? Where have you been? Are you okay? Where are you?"

"I—um . . ." She paused, not sure which question to answer first. The last two days' events seemed impossible to explain. "I'm fine. I'm downtown. Market Square. I'm kind of stuck. I need a ride out to the Observatory. I'm going to crash with Lain tonight."

"I'll be right there."

Which was what she had hoped he would say.

Nathan double-parked his Buick by the pay phone, twenty minutes later. "I've been worried sick about you," he called as he climbed out. "I'm sorry I had to leave you with that mess. The accident was unreal, and I was stuck there all night. By the time I got free, you had yanked your trailer and were gone."

"It's okay." She waved it away. "I had Oilcan and Lain to help me. You're here now."

"Lain! Of course." He surprised her by hugging her. What, was everyone suddenly touchy-feely? "How's your hand?"

She showed it to him, flexing it. "It got infected."

He dwarfed her left hand in his and eyed it with deep sorrow. "Oh, Tinker, I'm so sorry."

"It's fine now. They fixed it at the hospice." She wiggled her fingers in a show of health. She pulled her hand free. "I heard about your accident. You okay?"

"My accident?"

"Veterans Bridge," she prompted, heading for his car and its air-conditioned interior.

"Oh, yeah."

Nathan needed more coolant in his Buick. The air-conditioner struggled against the sticky summer heat. Tinker redirected the passenger vents to blow on her and unbuttoned her shirt above and below her bra line in an attempt to cool down.

"So, what happened?" she asked.

"Mass chaos is what happened." Nathan shook his head. "Shutdown traffic is usually so bumper to bumper you don't get much more than fender benders. This crew in a Ryder truck misses their turn, and they miss it big time, getting like halfway across the Veterans Bridge before realizing that they either wanted the Fort Duquesne Bridge to the Fort Pitt tunnels, or simply to get off at the North Shore. Who knows? Either one they could have gotten to by cutting through downtown. Instead, they try to back up. Of course they can't, everything is bumper to bumper for ten miles. They block traffic for like half an hour trying to bully the drivers for a couple hundred feet behind them into backing up—but those people don't have anywhere to go. Meanwhile, all the traffic in front of them clears out."

"Let me guess. Once they stop blocking traffic, everyone races across the bridge trying to get in front of the jerks."

"Oh, yeah," Nathan said. "Only the Ryder truck is still lost. He's in the left-hand lane, and realizes either he's going to end up back at the Rim and a border-patrol check, or through the Liberty Tunnel and into the South Hills."

"And they're sitting on a truckful of illegal goods, so the Rim is out."

Nathan glanced at her sharply. "How do you know they were smuggling?"

"Maynard wanted me to look over their stuff; he told me a little about the accident. I was worried about you."

"Really?" The info seemed to please him greatly. "I'm fine. I was the first unit called, but by the time I worked my way around to the accident, the EIA and most of the cops in Pittsburgh were there."

"Good. So, go on. They tried to take the Sixth Avenue exit and cut through town."

"Yeah, only they did it at the last minute and cut off a Peterbilt fully loaded with steel girders and just getting up to full speed."

"Bad move."

"The Peterbilt tries, but he can't stop, not with the load he's carrying. He catches the Ryder in the back driver corner and rams them into the support beams for the overpass. His load comes off and crushes a minivan beside him, killing the two people inside instantly."

She recalled the flattened car. "Oh my."

"There's a pileup, cars everywhere, and of course police are called, and things start to escalate. The goons from the Ryder truck discovered that they couldn't free their driver and that their truck was totaled. They carjack a pickup truck, and unload the Ryder into it. While they're doing that, I start working my way across the Veterans Bridge, and that's when they get their guns out."

"Maynard says they shot their own driver, flung a Volkswagen off the bridge, and tried to blow things up with C-4."

Nathan nodded. "Even with the traffic snarled they managed to get away just by the sheer mess they left behind; it blocked everyone from chasing after them."

Tinker told Nathan of her run-in with the fake EIA agents.

He swore softly. "It certainly sounds like them. If I'd known there was any chance you'd get mixed up with them, I would have tracked you down yesterday."

"Ah, I dealt with them." Knowing that they had coldly killed one of their own made her encounter, in hindsight, more chilling.

Nathan shook his head. "That's my Tink."

The cookouts were held in the wooded grove next to the Observatory, handy to the dormitory kitchen. True to form, the picnic tables looked overcrowded with food, and the smoke from the charcoal grills, scented with the smell of cooking meat, drifted out into the parking lot. Oilcan's hoverbike sat on the grass beside the lot, almost as comforting a sight as Oilcan himself.

Nathan parked his Buick, and they got out.

"I'm going to have to go soon." Nathan scanned over the picnicking scientists, as if making sure none of them were the missing smugglers. "My shift starts in half an hour. Make sure Lain locks her doors tonight. If you need a ride home tomorrow, call me."

"Sure." Tinker was never sure how to take Nathan's protective streak. "Thanks for the ride."

"Any time." He turned to her with the start of a smile, which vanished with a look of surprise. "Tink!" He reached out to button the bottom of her shirt closed. "Please, try to stay decent."

"What?" She brushed away his hand and gave her middle button a slight tug. "You can't see anything important with this one done. Besides, I've got a bra on."

"I know," he said in an oddly husky voice. "It's a very sexy bra."

"You checked it out?" She would have been embarrassed except for the fact that he beat her to the blush. Weird seeing such a big guy turn red and knowing she had done it to him. Empowering. She tugged on the middle button again, flashing a bit of her bra's black lace. "Like what you saw?"

"Tink." He caught her hand with his. "Don't tease guys like that. The wrong guy will get the wrong idea."

"It's just you."

"I'll take that as a compliment." He surprised her by running his finger across her bare skin, just above the middle button—a glide of rough fingertip over the upper swell of her right breast. "And yes, I liked what I saw."

Her turn to burn. "You're just being nice." She frowned when he laughed. "What?"

"It's just you're so smart, and yet you're so naïve, innocent."

"What do you mean by that?"

He looked up at the sky for a minute, and then gave her a look like a boy caught stealing candy: guilty, but wanting so badly to get away with it. "You were just this skinny little kid until you turned about fifteen, and then, one day, I turned around and you were suddenly so drop-dead sexy."

She laughed out of total surprise. "Me?"

"You bloomed that year."

In plain English, she got breasts that year. "Well, yeah, but sexy?"

"Yes. I've been quietly obsessed with you since then."

"You've got a funny way of showing it. You've never laid a hand on me."

"You were fifteen, and I was twenty-five. I kept my hands to myself. I would bust any guy for doing what I was thinking."

"Big brother" Nathan thought she was sexy? She couldn't believe it. "Yeah, sure."

"That's always been the worst of it. You've never been aware of how sexy you are. Like the way you eat strawberries."

"What's wrong with the way I eat strawberries?"

He opened his mouth, and then thought better of explaining. "Nothing. Just forget it."

"Come on; tell me."

"You don't eat them; you make love to them. It's such a turn-on, I need a cold shower afterward."

"You get off watching me eat?"

"See!" He shook a finger at her. "You're innocent. You don't understand. And I do. I'm older, and—"

"If you say wiser, I'm going to smack you."

He held up his hands to ward off any blow. "Hey, when it comes to brains, you're clearly way ahead of me. I've never minded. This isn't about you; it's about me. I wouldn't be able to live with myself if I thought I was taking advantage of a kid."

"So? I'm a legal adult now."

"Hell, you just turned eighteen and never been kissed. And you still look young enough to be sixteen. I'm twenty-eight."

Tinker studied him, trying to reevaluate the last three years. How had she missed his obsession? Certainly he spent an inordinate amount of time with her and Oilcan—but he'd also had two or three girlfriends that she could remember. "Yeah, you're twenty-eight and definitely more experienced than me. That doesn't seem fair. You get to screw around while I stay a virgin."

He kicked at a weed growing up in a crack in the parking lot's cement. "I thought if I found someone else, I'd stop having a thing for you. It really hasn't been fun, wanting you and feeling like a filthy old man at the same time."

"You know, you are always going to be ten years older than me. There's nothing I can do about it."

"I figured that when you hit nineteen, if I was still hooked on you, that was old enough."

Was he serious about this? It was weird to think he had waited three years already for her to grow up, and planned to wait another year. Certainly at fifteen she could have cared less about men, but in the last three years she had developed definite interest. Most guys she knew were like Jonnie, too slimy to consider. But Nathan Czernowski? She trusted him.

Everything inside her went suddenly, nervously aquiver. She looked at his mouth and wondered what it would be like to kiss him. "What am I supposed to do for the next eleven months? Sit and twiddle my thumbs until you feel righteous?"

He glanced at her, squinting in speculation. "You'll probably hit me if I say that would be nice."

"Yes," she growled. Eleven months of wondering would kill her. She was too used to satisfying her curiosity to wait that long. "Why don't we compromise? It would be stupid to spend the next eleven months, waiting, only to find out we can't stand each other in more than a good-friend way. We should try a date."

"A date?"

"You know. Go out to eat. See a movie. Go to the Faire. Date. That is, if your ego can stand being seen with me, and whatever people might think of you."

"Ouch."

"That's really it, isn't it? You're afraid that people will think you're as nasty as the guys you bust for molesting little kids."

"Okay, yes. You look younger than you are, and anyone who doesn't know how much you've got going on upstairs will see me as some kind of pervert. And that bugs me."

"I *can* look older. If I put some makeup on and some nice clothes, I can look twenty." Or at least Lain said so. "Especially in a dark restaurant."

A pleased grin spread across his face. "You really want to go out to eat with me?"

"I've watched you eat. What I actually want is to find out what it's like to kiss you, but I figured I'd scare you off if I told you that."

The smile vanished to a look of such intensity it seemed to solidify the air between them, making it impossible to breathe.

Oh my, he's totally serious about being gaga about me.

With infinite slowness, he leaned down and kissed her. His big hands caught her hips, pulled her to him, and then held her tightly. Her hands were momentarily pinned between them, and then they slid up, searching for someplace to go. She'd never realized how tall he was, or imagined how solid he would feel.

He nuzzled down her neck and kissed her where her shirt gaped open, exposing the top curve of her breasts. She clung to him, feeling suddenly small in his embrace, unsure if she wanted him to stop or go on.

He stopped, though, kissing her more chastely on the cheek, and then just held her. "I think anyplace we go," he whispered huskily, "should be brightly lit, with very little privacy."

"Possibly, that would be a good idea."

"Possibly." He sighed. "I need to work tomorrow night. Want to say Friday? We could do the Faire."

"Friday at the Faire would be good."

They kissed again, and she discovered that by knowing what to expect, the experience was even more enjoyable.

She waved as he drove away, feeling slightly silly doing so. Kids waved. What she really wanted was to pull him back and explore further—only more slowly. After he was out of sight, she pressed her hand to her mouth, capturing again the warmth and pressure.

Nathan Czernowski is in love with me!

Would wonders never end?

4: BEWARE ELVES BEARING GIFTS

Wargs, Windwolf, Maynard, interdimensional smugglers, and Nathan Czernowski were all pushed out of her mind at the sight of the loaded picnic tables. The competitive spirit of the scientists had produced amazing culinary feats. On the slim excuse of alerting people to possible food allergies each dish had the maker's name and the list of ingredients. The most elaborate dishes had the name first. The very simple donations had the makers listed last.

Even Lain was not immune to the competitive nature of the cookout. Her dish of fresh strawberries, spinach, walnuts, and homemade vinaigrette managed to be simple yet elegant.

Tinker loaded her plate with Lain's salad, dill potato salad, German coleslaw, three-bean salad, a linguine salad, a tortellini salad, baked beans, a sweet bean bun, a brownie, something made with pine nuts, and a cream cheese pineapple Jell-O salad.

She found Oilcan playing grill master, trying to smoke out his forming harem. Something about being stranded on a strange world combined with Oilcan's spry, puckish good looks seemed to make her cousin irresistible as a safe elf substitute to Earth women wanting to experience Elfhome to the fullest. Oilcan dodged the more aggressive attention, especially from the married women; he tended to be very moral in that regard. Still, Oilcan liked people, clever conversation, and playful flirting, so he went through something close to juggling fire sticks to attend any party at the Observatory. Already two women hung at the edge of the smoke, laughing at his witty remarks.

"Hey." Tinker braved the smoke to eye the meat on the grill.

"Hey!" Oilcan hugged her soundly. What had happened that suddenly everyone was hugging her? The harem eyed her with slight dismay. Oilcan chose not to introduce her, probably as a tactic to get rid of the women. He edged some of the food threatening to topple over the edge back onto her plate. "Think you got enough food?"

"I haven't had food since dinner yesterday." Tinker pointed out the largest hamburger on the grill. "Can I have that one cooked to medium?"

"Okeydokey." Oilcan patted it with a spatula. Red juices welled up in the slots. "It will be done in a couple of minutes. I came back to get you, and they said you'd left with Maynard. I tried calling you. Is everything okay?"

"I left my headset in the trailer." She balanced her plate in her left hand and ate with her fingers. "Where's the forks? Have you tried Lain's salad? Boy, is it good!"

"Here you are, little savage." Oilcan handed her a dormitory fork, unknowingly echoing Windwolf. "Try the stuff with the corn, if there's any left."

"I don't think I have room for more." Still, Tinker turned to scan the picnic table for the "stuff with the corn." "What about you? I couldn't get through to you."

Oilcan looked embarrassed. "I busted my headset on Shutdown. I had taken it off after it started to rain and put it on the seat next to me."

"We sat on it?" she guessed.

"No!" He laughed. "That would have been too simple. It fell out onto the ground at the yard sometime, and it got run over. I found it pressed into the mud, but in a thousand little pieces."

"Oh, crap, Oilcan, do you know how hard it is to get those things in Pittsburgh?"

"I know. I know. I knew you would be pissed, so I tracked down another one. You'll need to integrate it into my system for me."

"What? Where'd you find it?"

He glanced to the women still hovering on the edge of their conversation and dropped into Elvish. "It was probably stolen merchandise. Someone was selling headsets out of the trunk of their car down in the Strip District. The box was beat up, like it had been drop-kicked. I do not even know if the thing will work, but I only paid ten dollars for it."

Tinker pondered the possibility that the headset was part of Maynard's mystery shipment, wondering whether she was obliged to tell the EIA or not.

One of the harem women took advantage of Tinker's silence and pointed out that Tinker's burger needed to be flipped. Having recaptured Oilcan's attention, the women laughed with him as he flipped the burger and pressed it down onto the blackened grill, the dripping grease making flame leap up. Tinker ate and thought.

The Veterans Bridge crossed over the top of the Strip District; a box dropped over the edge of the bridge would land on a rooftop or street. Depending on the packing, the box and contents could survive fairly intact. Oilcan had seen all of the men dressed as EIA guards, so he would have recognized any of them; thus the person who'd sold Oilcan the headset most likely found the box. Telling Maynard would probably result in having the headsets seized and the unlucky finder questioned and possibly jailed.

The important piece of information was that the smugglers had brought a box of headsets to Elfhome. Headsets themselves were useless without some kind of service plan, but once you had air connection they could tie together anything from a home/work/user tri-base to a multiuser network like the police ran to link together their officers.

Tinker heard her name spoken and looked up.

Oilcan had lost one of his harem girls and was finally introducing her to the remaining woman. "I told you about my cousin, the mad scientist."

"I am not a mad scientist."

"Yes, you are. You like to make big machines that make lots of noise, move real fast, or reduce other objects down to little pieces."

"You're only saying that because you know I can't hit you at the moment." Tinker considered throwing food instead, and then decided it was a waste of good food.

Oilcan grinned smugly at her as if he had guessed that she would decide against throwing food.

Recognition of Tinker's matching nut-brown coloring and slight frame dawned in the woman's eyes. She put a hand over her mouth to catch a laugh. "Oh, I'm sorry, I was expecting someone—"

"Older," Tinker guessed.

"Male." The woman winced. "I, of all people, should know better." She gave an honest smile. Not only was her left ring finger unadorned, there wasn't even a slight band of pale skin—honestly single then. "Hi, I'm Ryan MacDonald. Glad to meet you."

"Glad to meet you." Tinker bobbed a slight bow over her full plate. "Sorry for butting in earlier, but life has been a little insane for the last few days."

"Speaking of which," Oilcan said, "we really left the yard wide open. I bolted two metal plates over the workshop doorway, locked up, and padlocked the gate as we went out, but we *took* the whole security system with us. Someone broke in during Shutdown."

"Oh, shit." Tinker tried not to think of everything scattered haphazardly through the offices. At least her most expensive equipment was in her workshop trailer. "Were we robbed?"

"No. Whoever it was broke all the way in, and then walked back out without taking anything. They might have been looking for Windwolf." Was that supposed to make her feel better? "I went over to Roach's and picked up Bruno and Pete to keep an eye on the place until you get the security system back online."

Bruno and Pete were two elfhounds, on par in size with the Foo dog wargs, bred for intelligence, courage, and loyalty.

"Oh, that's horrible," Ryan said. "They said that Pittsburgh was safe."

The cousins looked at her and after a moment of silence said in unison, "If you don't count the man-eating animals, yes."

Ryan looked startled. "Are there a lot of those?"

"The elves patrol the woods around here." Oilcan waved his spatula at the Earth scrub trees slowly being overrun by elfin forest. "But you shouldn't go into the woods without a weapon."

Tinker ate a mouthful of the Jell-O salad before adding, "And if you hear an animal moving around outside, don't leave the building you're in, even during the day. Call nine-one-one, and they'll send someone to make sure it isn't a dangerous animal."

"Don't leave doors ajar," Oilcan said. "Always shut them firmly."

Tinker considered which of the other common safety practices Ryan should know as she polished off the Jell-O salad. "Stay out of the swampy areas unless you have a xenobiologist with you who can spot the black willows and the other flesh-eating plants."

"Oh!" Oilcan waved his spatula at Ryan. "And the rivers aren't safe for swimming. The water is clean enough, but some big river sharks come up the Ohio."

"River sharks? Flesh-eating plants? You two are teasing me, right?"

"No," the cousins both said.

"There's a list of safety procedures that they usually hand out," Tinker said. "If you didn't get one, it's posted on the dorm's bulletin board. You really should read it; this isn't Earth."

Ryan glanced about the picnic grove with the red-checkered tablecloths on the picnic tables, the teams of scientists playing volley-ball, and a portable stereo playing neon rock music. "Actually, things don't seem any different."

"Give it time." Oilcan cut Tinker's hamburger, peered at the center, and lifted it off the grill. "Here you go. Medium cooked."

"Are there buns?"

"Picky, picky, picky." Oilcan went off in search of a bun for her.

Ryan watched him go with a look that made Tinker view her cousin with a new eye. One had to admit he had mighty fine assets.

"Can I ask you," Ryan said hesitantly, her eyes still following Oilcan, "if your cousin has a girlfriend?"

"Look, you seem nice, but you're not staying. It might seem fun to you, to go to Elfhome and date a cute local, but it's not fair to Oilcan. Thirty days is just long enough to break his heart."

Ryan turned to consider her. "You've given this speech before."

"Every thirty days."

"Sorry," Ryan said. "They said that the elves don't socialize much with humans; I suppose it would seem like the same thing to them— here today and gone tomorrow."

Tinker winced. Did Windwolf view her the same way Oilcan saw the astronomers?

Oilcan came back with a bun lying open on a paper plate. "There. Tomato, lettuce, spicy brown mustard, chopped red onion, and real Heinz ketchup—the stuff made on Elfhome, not that new plant on the other side of the Rim on Earth."

"Oh, you know me so well it's scary." Tinker paused, considering the bun and her still overflowing plate. "Excuse me." She took the second plate. "I'm going to have to sit down to finish."

Lain slid onto the bench beside Tinker as she finished the hamburger. "How's your hand?"

"Good." Tinker licked her fingers clean and showed Lain her palm.

Lain examined it quietly, nodding at the pale scars. She closed up Tinker's hand, ending the examination, but continued to hold it. "I want to warn you about elves bearing gifts."

"Huh?"

"Windwolf gifted me with a new garden."

Tinker looked without thought in the direction of Lain's house, but the swell of Observatory Hill was in the way. "Is that a good thing or a bad thing?"

"Yes, that is the question, isn't it?"

Tinker winced at her carefully neutral tone. "What did they do?"

"They were very considerate in putting everything they dug up into pots. And I have to say that the specimens they planted are stunning. I dare to guess that I have a garden to rival the queen's now."

They'd dug up Lain's flowers? Lain's work made it almost impossible for Lain to return to Earth. In Pittsburgh, she was as much an exile as she would be on Europa. And more importantly, the garden of Earth flowers she loved was a salve for not being in space.

"Oh, Lain, I'm sorry."

Lain hid away some of the pain in her eyes. "I can't say I'm completely displeased. Much of the garden would not have survived the root damage that the truck did. It would have taken me weeks just to fill the ruts. The new plants are all extremely valuable; it would have taken me years of wheedling to get any one."

"But it's not your garden of Earth flowers."

"No," Lain admitted. "It's not."

"I'm sorry. I'm really sorry."

Lain gave her a small, sad smile that vanished away before a look of true worry. "I'm nervous about what Windwolf might gift on you."

"Me?"

"There's no telling what he might decide to give you."

"I doubt he'll give me anything. There's still the matter of the life debt. Windwolf said that we weren't even." Tinker choked to a halt. *We drove all over Lain's flower beds . . . I told her I would go to college to make it up to her . . .*

Oh, gods, he didn't replace the flowers because of what I said—or did he?

"Tinker?"

What else did I say? But she couldn't even remember exactly what she had said. The conversation was a feverish blur. Had she asked for anything for herself? Old fairy tales cautioning against badly worded wishes loomed suddenly large.

Lain watched her, worry growing.

"Can I turn it down?" Tinker asked. "Anything he might give me, if I don't like it?"

"Windwolf might not give you a chance to say no."

Tinker thought about it. What could he possibly give her that would be bad? "What do you think he might give me?"

"I'm not a superstitious woman, but our legends never have good to say about gifts from the fey."

"I'm not sure he's going to give me anything, Lain. He says we're not even."

Lain's eyes narrowed. "Did he say it in Elvish or English?"

Tinker paused to think. Windwolf had woken her up in the trailer, and they'd shouted at each other. But in what language? "English."

"Then it might not mean what you think it means, Tinker."

She thought it had been fairly straightforward, but Lain had much more experience dealing with elves. She recounted the conversation the best she could remember and ended with, "So, what do you think he means?"

"I'm not going to hazard a guess," Lain said. "But be careful around him. He meant well with my garden, but it was done with the arrogance of an adult catering to a child. He believes he knows what is better for us."

"Oh, great. I've got enough of that type of people in my life already."

"Tinker." Lain gripped her hand tightly. "I know I've pushed you into this college thing; I did it in the name of your own good. I've had a taste of my own bullying, and I'm sorry. Of all people, I should have realized that I was asking you to go alone to another world. If you don't want to go, you don't have to. I release you of all pledges."

The elves said that: I release you of all pledges. The irony of it kept Tinker from cheering. Knowing Lain, though, it might have been her reason for using the phrase. So Tinker said, "I'll think about it."

Dusk fell slowly. As the sky darkened and the stars started to peek out, the conversation turned from the world left behind, the experience of Startup, and the rustic amenities that the scientists found in the dormitories, and focused on the sky itself.

First Night was always fun; it was like watching children discover Christmas. Since it always rained during Startup—the warmer returning Earth air colliding with the chillier Elfhome climate—this was the scientists' first real sight of Elfhome's stars. Their faces were turned upward at the winking lights, and they murmured reverently, "Oh, wow!" Once Tinker's eyes adjusted, she could see the upraised hands, pointing out sights. As always, the cry of "Look at Arcturus!" went up. The elves called it the Wolf's Heart, on the shoulder of the constellation they called the First Wolf. One of the brightest stars in the sky, Arcturus was also the fastest moving; there was a fifteen-degree difference between the star of Elfhome and Earth.

"I can't believe this is the same sky we were looking at two days ago," someone close at hand said with awe. "A twenty-mile drive south, and all the constellations shift. Look at Corona Borealis! It doesn't look anything like a C anymore."

"Twenty miles south, and a side step into another dimension," another voice corrected the first speaker.

Because they would need to share the big telescopes, they all had personal telescopes set up. After minutes of fiddling, they excitedly swapped views.

"There are new stars in the star formation region of the Eagle Nebula—"

"Where?"

"M16—in Serpens."

"Look at the alignment of the planets. They'll be in full conjunction on Friday."

They ohhhed, and ahhhed, and talked about constellations that up to that point had only been textbook learning.

Tinker spent the night at Lain's. Oilcan picked her up in the morning and they headed over to the scrap yard. He went over the schedule he'd planned for the day. As usual, he was spending the days after Startup doing running, tracking down supplies and goods they needed. Tinker gave him a full report on her meeting with Maynard, Lain's garden, and finally the mystery calls on her home system.

Oilcan stopped at a red light at Route 65 and looked at her sharply. "I think I should leave Bruno and Pete with you."

"Please, no. I think it will be a while before I can deal with large dogs again."

"I don't like you being alone when everything is so weird."

"The weirdness is over," Tinker asserted.

"Someone is trying real hard to find you, Tinker. They're searching the neighborhood for you. Someone tried to kill Windwolf."

"Can't be the same people." She wished he wouldn't dwell on it—it was scary enough without him talking about it. "Windwolf was attacked on Elfhome before the Shutdown, and the calls started from Earth after Shutdown."

"So? Whoever's trying to find you is still *on* Elfhome."

"Whoever it is has nothing to do with Windwolf being attacked." Tinker could see where this was heading, and stopped it. "I'll arm the office security system first thing. My home security system is still running. I'll be okay."

Oilcan grumped a while longer but gave in, promising to check in with her often. No doubt he'd also find a way to let Nathan know.

Tinker tried to detour the conversation. "Can you do me a favor and see if you can track down some peroxide this morning? Lain says it's best for cleaning up large amounts of blood. We need to replace all the first-aid supplies, and I need pads."

"I restocked the first-aid kit," Oilcan said. "I also got you groceries. They're at my place. But you've got to get your own female stuff."

"It's not like they bite, Oilcan, and everybody knows they're not for you."

"It's embarrassing. Besides, I didn't know what type to buy."

"I used most of them to bandage wounds. Any kind will do."

"You get your own," he stated firmly. "Do you want me to bring the rest of the stuff over to your place tonight?"

A bid to make sure she was okay. Once there, he'd probably stay late.

"Nah. I'll eat out—get a pizza and some beer. Just bring it with you tomorrow."

He looked unhappy, but he let it go at that.

Windwolf came to the scrap yard late in the morning. One moment he wasn't there, and the next he stood watching her.

She stood looking back. She had been running in tight circles all morning—not wanting him to show, eager to see him, terrified of him appearing, cautioning herself that he might not come, and as the day wore on, nearly sick with the thought that she had read more into the situation and he wasn't coming. Now that he was here, she had no clue to her heart. That tight circle just spun faster, emotions whirling too quickly to latch on to.

Pick one, idiot, she growled at herself. *Happy. I'll be happy to see him.* Her happiness welled up so quickly and strongly that she suspected it was the truest of her emotions. She walked out to greet him then, a smile taking control of her face and refusing to give it up. "Hi!"

Elegantly dressed in elfin splendor, he looked out of place in the grimy scrap yard of rusting broken metal and shattered glass. He seemed a creature woven out of the glitter of sunlight on the river. Behind him, and well back, were armed elves—his bodyguard.

Windwolf nodded in greeting, an inclining of the head and shoulders that stopped just short of a bow. He presented a small silk bag to her. "For you. *Pavuanai wuan huliroulae.*"

It was High Elvish, something about talking together—at least that was what she thought *pavuanai* meant. She didn't recognize the word *huliroulae.*

Tinker eyed the bag suspiciously, thinking of Lain's garden and the xenobiologist's warning, but it didn't look dangerous. "What is it?"

"Keva."

"Oh." Tinker took the bag, opened it, and found indeed the golden cousin to soybeans. Genetically altered for millennia, keva beans were the elfin wonder food. Raw, roasted, fried, ground for flour, or even candied, keva beans were at the base of all celebrations. These were roasted with honey, one of her favorites. Still, this was her reward for saving his life? She noticed then that one of the guards held a fabric-wrapped bundle that looked for all the world like a present. Maybe this was a weird gift-giving appetizer. "Thanks."

Windwolf smiled as she popped one of the mild nutty beans into her mouth. "You said you would teach me horseshoes."

She laughed in surprise. "You really want to play?"

"Do you enjoy playing?"

She nodded slowly. "Yeah, it's fun."

"Then I wish to learn."

"Well, okay. Let me grab the shoes and the keys."

The keys were for the gate between the scrap yard and the small wood lot next to the scrap yard. Pittsburgh had many such pockets of wildness, places too steep to build on, full of scrub trees and wild grapevines. The lot was a series of level steps between steep drops, stairs cut into the hillside leading from level to level. There she and Oilcan had set up regulation-sized horseshoe pits.

"It's a simple game. You stand on one end, here, and throw the horseshoes at the stake. Like so." Tinker made sure she wasn't going to hit him with her swing, and tossed the horseshoe with a well-practiced underhand pitch. The horseshoe sailed the nearly forty feet and clanged against the stake in a single clear ringing note. "A ringer! That's what you're trying for." Her second shoe hit and rebounded. "But that's what normally happens."

He took the second set of horseshoes from her. He eyed the large U-shaped pieces of metal. "Are the horses on Earth really this big?"

"I don't know. I've never left Pittsburgh."

"So Elfhome is your home?"

"I suppose. I think of Pittsburgh as my home, but only when it's on Elfhome."

"That's good to know," Windwolf said.

And while she tried to decide what that meant, he copied her underhanded throw. He gracefully missed the stake by several feet. "This is harder than it appears."

"Simple doesn't necessarily mean easy," Tinker said.

They crossed the playing field to the pit to gather the shoes.

"Are you and your cousin orphans in this place?"

"Well, close. Oilcan's father is alive, but he's in prison. When he gets out, he won't be able to immigrate."

"Will Oilcan want to see his father?"

Tinker shook her head and concentrated on throwing the horseshoes. "His father killed his mother; not on purpose—he just hit her too hard in anger—but dead is dead." Not surprisingly, Tinker missed the stake. "Oilcan works hard at being the antithesis of his father. He never drinks to the point of being drunk. He doesn't yell or fight, and he'd cut off his hand before he'd hit someone he loved."

"He is a noble soul."

Tinker beamed at Windwolf, inordinately pleased that he approved of her cousin. "Yes, he is."

"My family is unusual among elves." Windwolf's horseshoe landed closer to the stake this round. "We elves do not life bond as readily as you humans, and I think sometimes it is because of the manner in which we are raised. Siblings are usually centuries apart, fully grown and moved on before the next becomes the focus of their parents' attention. We are basically a race of only children and tend to be selfish brats as a result."

"You're blowing my preconceived notion that you're a wise and patient race."

"We appear patient only because our conception of time is different. Amassing oceans of knowledge does not make you wise."

They collected horseshoes with oddly musical clangs of metal on metal.

"But your family is different?" Tinker prompted Windwolf.

"My mother loves children, so she had many, and she did not pace them centuries apart. She thought that when a child was old enough to seek out playmates on his or her own, it was time for another. Amazingly, my father put up with it, mostly. Perhaps their marriage would not have survived if we were not a noble house with wealth and Beholden." Tinker knew that Beholden were the lower castes that acted as servants to the noble caste, but she wasn't sure how it all worked. "The Beholden gave my father the distance he needed from so many children."

Given that his mother could have spent centuries raising children, Tinker blinked at the sudden image of the old woman who lived in a shoe, children bursting out at the seams. "How many kids are in your family?"

"Ten."

"Only ten?"

Windwolf laughed. "Only?"

"I thought maybe a hundred, or a thousand."

Windwolf laughed again. "No, no. Father would never submit to that. He finds ten an embarrassment he suffers only for Mother's sake. Most nobles do not have any children." Windwolf's voice went bitter. "There is no need for propagation when you live forever."

"Well, it keeps your population from growing quickly."

"The elfin population has only declined in the last two millennia. Between war, accidental death, and occasional suicide, we are half the number we once were."

That did put a different spin on things. "That's not good."

"Yes, so I try to tell people. I had great hope that with this new land would come a new way of seeing the world."

"Had?"

"The arrival of Pittsburgh was unexpected."

Tinker winced. "Sorry."

"It has actually been beneficial," Windwolf said. "Enticing people to an utter wilderness was difficult; few wanted to suffer the ocean crossing for so few comforts. Human culture, though, is attracting the young and the curious—the ones most likely to see things my way."

"Good." Tinker focused back on throwing the horseshoes. That's what she liked about the game. It encouraged a flow of conversation.

"What about you?"

"What do you mean?"

"Do you desire children?"

She missed the stake completely, only the chainlink fence keeping the horseshoe from vanishing into the weeds. "Me?"

"You. Or would you rather be childless?"

"No." She blurted out the gut reaction to the question. "It's just I've never thought about kids. Sure, someday I'd like to have one or two, maybe as many as three, but hell, I've never even—" She was going to say kissed a man, but she supposed that wasn't true anymore. "You know."

"Yes, I do know," he purred, looking far too pleased, and it put a flash of heat through her. Her and Windwolf? Like her dream? Suddenly she felt the need to sit down. As if he were reading her mind—gods, she hoped not—Windwolf indicated the battered picnic table beyond the horseshoe pit.

As she clambered up to sit on the tabletop of the picnic table, she wondered what it would be like to be with him, as they had been in her dream. "How old are you?"

"For an elf, barely adult. For a human, I am ancient. I'm two hundred and ten."

Or 11.6 times older than she was. Nathan suddenly seemed close to her age.

"Is that too old?" Windwolf asked.

"No, no, not at all." Tinker struggled for perspective. Elves were considered adults at a hundred, but until they reached a thousand, they were still young. Triples were what the elves called them, or those that could count their age in three digits. Windwolf could be compared to a man that just turned twenty; only he'd been born in the 1820s.

And she was like one of Oilcan's astronomers to him, staying only long enough to break his heart.

First Nathan and now Windwolf. Well, didn't her choice of men suck?

"Have you ever played ninepins?" Windwolf asked, breaking the silence.

"Bowling? Yeah. But only with humans."

"I am much better at ninepins."

"Tooloo says humans should never play ninepins with elves. It always ends badly for humans."

"This Tooloo is a font of misinformation. She was completely wrong about the life debt."

"How so?"

"The debt between us is not yours. It is mine," Windwolf said.

"Yours?"

"How could the count be any other way?"

"During the fight with the saurus . . ."

"You saved my life. I was dazed, and you distracted the saurus by putting out its eye at great risk to yourself."

She blinked at him, stunned as the events now rearranged themselves in her mind. "But the spell you placed on me?"

"If I did not survive the rest of the fight, I wanted others to know you had acted with courage. You were to be adopted into my household and cared for."

"Oh." She didn't know what else to say.

"We looked for you after the fight, but we thought you were a boy. We asked about 'the boy,' and no one knew who we were asking about."

How could Tooloo have gotten it so wrong? Or had Tooloo been lying all this time? But why? Tinker struggled to keep faith in the crazy old half-elf; Windwolf could be lying to her now. But why would he? His version of the events certainly matched what she remembered better, and made more sense.

"I must go. There are days when, even for elves, there is not enough time." Windwolf waved the guard with the present forward, took it, and banished both guards back to the scrapyard. "When I last saw you, you were a child, and now you are an adult. I want to grasp this moment before it too slips away."

He held out the present.

The keva beans had been harmless enough, and this gift looked no larger than the last. "Is this for me?"

"If you desire it."

Why did elves make everything seem so dangerous? It was just a small fabric-wrapped bundle. "What is it?"

"I thought it best to stay with the traditional gift for the occasion."

Trust elves to have a traditional gift for saving one's life. She unwrapped it tentatively. She was glad he had told her it was a traditional gift. Certainly it wasn't what she expected. She wasn't even sure *what* it was. It seemed to be a metal bowl, intricately worked as one expected of an elfin work, yet it stood on three legs anchored to a disc of marble. It had quite a heft to it, and what impressed her most was that Windwolf had made it seem so lightweight. She tried not to compare it with Lain's entire garden. The child in her, though, wanted to cry, *That's it?*

"Do you accept?"

"Yes."

He smiled. It was like the sun coming out. He spoke a word in High Elvish and kissed her on the forehead. The touch of his lips seemed to sizzle on her skin.

Tinker called Lain from her scrap yard. "He brought me a bowl."

"A bowl?"

"Well, I think it's a bowl." She described it at length to Lain, who identified the gift, after some thought, as a brazier, and explained that one burned incense or charcoal in the bowl, and the legs anchored into the marble made it stable and protected whatever it was sitting on from the heat.

A brazier? "Well, it's certainly not what I expected." Tinker eyed her gift. "I'm trying to figure out what the catch is."

A click of keys came from Lain's side of the connection. " 'Braziers are a symbolic gift.' " Lain read from something. " 'Great importance is made of the wrapping of the gift, which must be extravagant, and the presentation, which must be subtle.' Yes, but what does it stand for?"

"I don't know. He just said it was traditional for the occasion."

"Not you. Barron. He released his anthropology paper on the elves this spring, but don't ever repeat that. The elves don't study themselves and certainly don't want us studying them either."

"I was never sure why we compulsively study ourselves."

"How else are we going to learn and grow?"

"If the elves don't study themselves, does that mean they don't change?"

"Possibly. We certainly haven't been able to pry any information out to indicate that they have." There was a pause, and Lain murmured softly, skimming the info in front of her. "Tinker, what did you talk about with Windwolf?"

"I'm not sure. You know how it is to talk to them. It's worse than talking to you. Why?"

"The brazier is a customary gift for what Barron only terms as 'delicate arrangements.' I don't know what the hell that's supposed to mean. Apparently, accepting the gift implies agreement to the arrangements."

Tinker yelped, as the only delicate arrangement that sprang to mind was sex. "W-w-we didn't talk about any arrangements. At least not that I can remember. Doesn't this Barron list anything?"

"He says that this information was told to him in passing, and that when pressed, the elves stated that it wasn't a ritual that would occur between elf and human."

Tinker made a rude sound of negation. "Maybe Barron has it completely wrong."

"What did you talk about?"

"Horseshoes. Oilcan. His family." Tinker glanced in the mirror and yipped in surprise at her reflection.

"Tinker?"

"What the—" A triangle of blue marked where Windwolf had kissed her on her forehead. The spot wouldn't rub off, even with spit. "He marked me—somehow—after I accepted."

There was a long silence from Lain's side, and then, "I think you should come over."

Tinker and Oilcan had laid claim to an old parking garage between her loft and the scrap yard, thus convenient and inconvenient to them both. It easily held the flatbed, her hoverbike, and whatever miscellaneous vehicles they'd picked up and refurbished.

Tinker went round to the first bay and coded open the door. Her honey baby waited inside, gleaming red. She'd traded a custom-built

Delta model hoverbike for a custom paint, detail, and chrome job at Czerneda's. Oilcan bitched that she was ripped off, because the detail job was so simple—gold pin striping—on a redshift paint job, but hell, it was perfection. She suspected that he bitched mostly because her own custom Deltas were the only serious competition she had on the racecourses, and every custom job she did chipped away at her odds of winning. Oilcan's loyalty wouldn't let him bet against her, but he liked to win.

Well, he'd have to get used to it. The Gamma models were being mass-produced by a machine shop on the South Side, kicking back a royalty to her for the design. At the moment, she was the only one who seemed able to grasp all the physics involved to make modifications. Sooner or later, someone would be able to bend his or her mind around the whole concept and beat Tinker at her own game. It was how humans worked.

She swung her leg over the saddle, thumbprinted the lock, and hit the ignition button. Ah, bliss—the rumble of a big engine between one's legs. She eased down on the throttle to activate the lift drive. Once the Delta actually lifted off of the parking studs, she retracted them and walked the Delta out of the garage. Once past the door sensors, she clicked the door shut.

She opened up the throttle. The Delta soared up and forward, the lift drive providing altitude while the spell chain provided the actual forward torque. Simple physics. Sooner or later, someone would twig to what she'd done.

Tinker set the dish of whipped cream beside her bowl of strawberries. Lain was the only person who seemed to understand the correct ratio of topping to fruit, which was three to one. "Have you found out anything more about the brazier or the mark?"

"Well, there's this." Lain put a slickie down in front of Tinker. "These are photos taken during the signing of the treaty. Look closely at the elves."

Tinker thumbed through the slickie's photos, dipping the strawberries into the whipped cream and idly licking it off. Despite the president's acting career, the humans looked positively dowdy next to the elfin delegation. It did not help that the humans kept to the stately solids of navy, black, and gray, while the royal party dressed in a brilliant riot of colors and sparkled with gems and gold. So vivid was the elvish beauty that it crossed the line of believability and became surreal, as if the images next to the drab humans were computer-generated art. It was a cheap slickie, so most of the photos were two-d, allowing no panning or rotation. The centerfold, however, was full three-d, and she rotated through the photo, zooming in on the faces of the elves.

Four of the thirty elves wore the same style of forehead marks. All four were female. Tinker frowned; the sample size was too small to use as a base for any good conclusion, but the marks certainly seemed to be a female thing only. Put there by males?

All four marks were of different colors—red, black, blue, and white—and shape. As she studied the one in blue, she recognized the female as the high-caste elf at the hospice, the one who had called her and Oilcan wood sprites. In the shadows of the parking lot, Tinker had missed the mark. What had her name been? Sparrow something or other.

Tinker dipped her current strawberry for the second time and studied the blue mark on Sparrow. Was it the same mark, or just the same color? "Do you have a mirror?"

Lain went off to her downstairs bathroom and returned with a small hand mirror. They carefully compared marks.

"No, they're not quite the same," Lain announced after several minutes.

Tinker grunted. "What do you suppose it means?"

"I don't know," Lain said. "But you seem to be in good company. This is the royal majesty herself and her court. They're the world leaders of Elfhome."

Good company or not, she didn't want to be part of it. In her book, elves made colorful neighbors but she was glad not to be one of the family. She'd seen enough of their stiff formality and casual cruelty between castes to know it would drive her nuts.

Tinker started at another familiar face. "This is Windwolf."

Lain leaned over to check the photo. "Yes, it is."

Tinker realized that despite a growing awareness that Windwolf was important in the local politics, she didn't know exactly what his title was. "This might be a silly question, but who exactly is Windwolf?"

"Lord Windwolf is the viceroy of the Westernlands."

Viceroy? Before Tinker could ask what that meant, the doorbell rang.

"Looks like I have company," Lain said, reaching for her crutch.

"What am I? Sauerkraut and kielbasa?" Tinker muttered.

"Hush, my little pierogi," Lain called back as she limped up the hallway to the front door.

Tinker considered the photo of Windwolf as Lain answered her front door. Tinker had thought him stunning the few times she had seen him, but now she knew she hadn't yet seen him at his best. The creature in the photo seemed as untouchable as a god.

Lain's visitor, in a deep raspy male voice, introduced himself as the son of her fellow crew member who had died in the training exercise that crippled Lain. "I don't know if you remember me at the memorial. I was about five at the time."

That drew Tinker out of the kitchen. Lain stood, apparently rendered speechless by the sudden appearance.

The man was in his early twenties, tall with a shock of black hair and a long sharp nose. He was in biking leathers, wore a pair of sunglasses, and had a helmet tucked under his arm.

Tinker recognized him with a start. He was the motorcyclist she and Oilcan had seen nearly hit on Shutdown Day. "I thought you might be a half-elf."

He looked at her, frowning, and the frown deepened. "No. I'm not, lady. You're mistaken."

"Tinker!" Lain admonished with a single word, then turned her attention back to the man. "I remember you. My, how you've grown, but children do that, I suppose. You were such a grieving little boy; I don't think I heard you say a single word that day."

"It was long ago. I've moved past that," he said.

"Riki was your name, wasn't it?"

He nodded. "Yes, you do remember me. I was afraid that you wouldn't."

"Your mother spoke a lot about you before the accident." Lain indicated Tinker. "This is Tinker, who is very worth knowing."

Riki turned to look at Tinker. She reflected in his sunglasses. He nodded and turned back to Lain. "I was hoping you could tell me about my mother."

"You stranded yourself on Elfhome just for that?"

"No. I'm going to be attending the University of Pittsburgh once fall classes start. I've got a grant from Caltech as part of my graduate studies. I showed up a little early so I'd have a chance to experience Elfhome fully. It would be exploring an alien world, just like my mother hoped to."

Lain clicked her tongue over what she certainly considered the folly of youth. Tinker had heard the sound often enough to recognize the thought behind it. "Pitt is a shadow of what it was; it's barely more than a community college right now. Well, there's not much to be done about that now. You're here. The question is, what is to be done with you now? Do you have a place to stay? Money enough to last?"

"I have the grant money." Riki tapped a breast pocket, making paper inside wrinkle loudly. "It's supposed to last me six months, but I've got to make it stretch to nine. I'm hoping to find a job, and a cheap place to stay."

"Housing shouldn't be too hard; it's summer—just find someplace that looks empty and squat," Lain said, and limped back to the kitchen. "Come have something to eat and drink, and we'll consider work."

Riki followed Lain, glancing around with vivid interest, pausing at the doorway of the living room to scan it fully. "It's a nice place you have here. I expected something more rustic. They talk about how backward Pittsburgh has become, cut off as it is. I half expected log cabins or something."

Lain laughed from the kitchen.

Tinker had stayed in the foyer. She picked up her helmet and called, "Lain, I'm going to go."

Lain came to the kitchen doorway. "You! Stay! Into the kitchen."

Tinker put down the helmet and obediently went into the kitchen. One didn't argue with Lain when she used that voice. "Why?"

"All the positions up here on the hill are government funded; all hiring has to be written out in triplicate and approved in advance. You have more contacts than I do down in the city."

Tinker winced. "Lain, I'm not an employment agency."

Riki regarded Tinker with what seemed slight unease. It was hard to tell with the sunglasses. "You seem too young to be anything but a high school student."

Tinker stuck her tongue out at him and got smacked in the back of the head by Lain.

"Behave." Lain filled the teakettle and set it onto the gas range. "Tinker is much more than she seems. She's probably the most intelligent person in Pittsburgh. Now if she could learn a bit of common sense and get a more rounded education . . ."

"Lain," Tinker growled. "I don't want to beat that horse right now."

"Then be nice to my guest. Offer him a job."

"I doubt if he wants to do demo work at the yard," Tinker said. "He certainly doesn't know anything about magic, and it's nearly as unlikely that he knows anything about quantum physics."

"I've got a master's degree in quantum physics," Riki said.

"Eat crow, little girl!" Lain cried, laughing at the look on Tinker's face.

Riki startled at Lain's reaction.

"You're kidding," Tinker said.

"I'm going to do my doctorate on the quantum nature of magic. No one has done research on magic in its natural state. That's why I'm studying at Pitt."

"If you want to learn about magic, you need to work with Tinker. She's the expert."

"No, I'm not; elves are."

"True, true, their whole society seems to be based on the ability to cast spells." Lain laughed, putting out cups. "But that does him no good, not as closed mouthed as they are."

"What do you mean? Anyone can cast spells."

Lain looked at her with surprise. "Tooloo has never explained why the nobles rule over the other castes?"

"I'm never sure when Tooloo is telling me the truth," Tinker said. "She's told me that nobles can feel ley lines and can cast certain spells with gestures and words instead of written patterns . . . which might be true. Certainly the spoken component of spells is merely setting up certain subtle resonance frequencies. I'm not sure about the hand gestures. Written spells follow a logic system similar to the and/or gates of computer circuitry, creating paths for energy to follow toward a desired effect. The only way I could see it working was if somehow the noble's body replaces the circuitry. . . ." She fell silent, thinking of energy following fingertips while the hands moved through the pattern of a spell. The ability to feel ley lines could result by simply bioengineering an organ like the inner ear that was sensitive to magic. How would you manipulate magic with your hands? She looked at her own oil-stained hands, the left one with its new patchwork of pink scars. With what she knew of biology, it was unlikely that they fitted new organs into their fingertips, unless it was on the tip of the bone, or perhaps their fingernails. She flexed her fingers as if typing. She supposed fingernails would work, although if one could engineer it so each finger bone had a separate function, then each finger could perform three functions instead of just the one. . . .

"Tinker. Tinker." Lain interrupted her thought process.

"It might work that way," Tinker conceded. She added, "Tooloo also tells me stories about elves making gems or frogs falling out of people's mouths when they talk, and unless you have an N-dimensional space filled with frogs, it couldn't work. Besides, what would the frogs eat? How would you deal with the heat they generated packed together like that? I suppose you could use that energy to move a frog into our dimension."

A smile spread across Riki's face. "I like how your mind works."

That startled Tinker into silence. No one had ever said that to her.

"If you hire him," Lain said, pouring tea out, "every minute he frees up, you will have for fiddling around with your inventions."

Tinker opened her mouth and shut it on a protest. She remembered the condition of the offices—her workshop still on the back of the flatbed and thoroughly splattered with blood. Suddenly the idea of having help, and thus more time, was seductive—and Lain knew it. "That's not playing fair."

"I don't like wasting time."

Tinker frowned. The words "sucker for strays" on her forehead were coming into play. "Well, I could offer part-time at minimum wage, but nothing more than that. Tooloo might have some work."

He looked at her for a minute, and finally said, "I don't know if this is rude—I don't know elf customs—but what's the mark for?"

Speaking of casting spells with just a gesture. Tinker rubbed at her forehead, wondering how exactly Windwolf had marked her. "I don't know. We were just trying to figure that out."

Lain looked troubled. "That worries me. Why don't you see Maynard about that? You should find out why Lord Windwolf marked you."

"The viceroy?" Riki asked.

Tinker got up, annoyed that this newcomer knew more about Windwolf than she did. "Look, if you want the job, show up at my scrap yard tomorrow morning. Lain can tell you how to get there. And I'll need to see your papers. I'm not getting into trouble with the EIA for hiring an illegal immigrant."

Lain gave her a look of disapproval, but Tinker clumped out. She'd had enough motherly scolding for the day.

5: VARIABLE SUBSTITUTIONS

Tinker's grandfather had often told her that moving Pittsburgh to Elfhome raised the intelligence of human bureaucrats. He commonly cited the Housing Act as proof. People fleeing Elfhome registered their property with the EIA in return for displacement vouchers. The United Nations redeemed the vouchers for a house of equal value (prior to the gate of course) anywhere on Earth, doling out the Chinese Compensation money to those most affected by the gate. The EIA resold the Pittsburgh real estate for a dollar to anyone who pledged to make the home his or her permanent primary residence. The system encouraged squatters to maintain property that would otherwise stand empty. Housing, which had always been affordable and easy to find in Pittsburgh, became basically free.

Her grandfather, Oilcan, and she had lived in an old hotel looking out over the river on Neville Island. It was a four-story palace bought for a dollar.

The locks and dams that controlled the Allegheny, Monongahela, and the Ohio rivers, however, stayed mostly on Earth. Every spring, the muddy river water would creep up the steep bank and swirl into the hotel's downstairs. The basement had slowly filled with river silt, as they only pumped out the water. The first floor they shoveled out and sprayed down with fire hoses. All the wallpaper had long peeled off, leaving stained plaster behind. They left the windows open all summer to dry out the wood. When Tinker and Oilcan rode their bikes through the large empty first-floor rooms, or played street hockey using the old fireplaces as goals, they would kick up clouds of fine dust. Come fall, they would loot empty buildings for window glass, and patch the plaster anywhere the winter winds would be able to blow through.

Her grandfather had converted the second floor to the kitchen, workshop, and classroom. The third floor contained the library, away from the lower-level floods and the fourth story's dripping roof. They slept on the fourth floor, drips and all, as it was the safest place in case of flash flood.

Oilcan moved out the winter of his sixteenth birthday to Mount Washington, claiming he wasn't going to spend another spring worrying if the river would wash into their bedrooms. When their grandfather died the next year, Oilcan offered to take Tinker in with him. Nothing could make him move back to the river's edge. Nor would he let her stay at the hotel alone when she refused his offer. Showing surprising strength of character, he insisted she find someplace above the floodplain.

Tinker had scoured the hill around the scrap yard. After the high ceilings, long halls, and sprawling first floor of the hotel, everywhere else had seemed small and cramped. Finally she'd found a large loft. The living room was thirty by sixty, and the one bedroom was a roomy fourteen by twenty.

Now she went up the steps to her loft wearily, unlocked the door, mumbled her security code to her security system, and slammed the door behind her. She was at the fridge, opening the door to get a cold beer, before she realized her security system hadn't acknowledged her. She jerked around, hand still on the refrigerator door handle, and found she wasn't alone.

A woman—tall, leggy, with dark spiky hair and armed with a stocky handgun leveled at her—drifted out of the shadows to block the front door. "Durrack?"

A man appeared at the bedroom door. He quirked up one eyebrow. "Well, what do we have here?"

"She let herself in, and gave a security code," the woman said. Her taste in clothing ran to black, and very tight fitting. If she had any weapons other than the handgun, they were small, or strapped to her back. Tinker couldn't tell how lethal the handgun was. It seemed too large to be loaded with something as mundane as bullets.

"Who are you?" Tinker asked, and was somewhat pleased she didn't sound as scared and angry as she was. When was her life going to go back to normal? "What are you doing here?"

"We're going to ask the questions," the man said. "We're looking for Alexander Graham Bell. He goes by the name of Tinker. This is his residence."

He? Hell, they were confused. They had her name right, but certainly not her sex. Not that she was about to point out the error in their thinking. "And I take it that he's not here."

"No," Durrack said, closing the distance between them. "What's your name? Let me see some ID."

Tinker backed away. "Look, I don't want any trouble. My name is Lain. My ID was stolen two days ago by some big goons. I've had a really shitty week, and I haven't seen Tinker for days. Skippy, activate emergency system!"

"We turned the AI off." He checked his forward motion. "Cooperate with us, and you're not going to get hurt."

"You break into my house, wave guns at me, and expect me to turn over my boyfriend?" It was weird talking like this, keeping pronouns straight. It was like a math problem, substituting in values.

"You live here with him?" Durrack asked.

"Yeah."

The woman made a disgusted noise. "How long have you two been together?"

What would the right answer be? A few weeks or months? It didn't seem long enough. "Three years."

Durrack and the woman exchanged dark looks. Perhaps three years was too much.

"I hate this assignment more and more," the woman muttered.

"Patience, Briggs. It's a whole new world."

"Doesn't mean I have to like it."

And while they murmured together, Tinker said quietly, "Tripwire."

Briggs jerked her head up, and then swore. "She's activated a backup defense system!"

Durrack caught Tinker under the arm and hustled her out of the house. Out on the street, he pushed her up against the wall. Not as hard as he could, but still she found herself dangling a foot from the ground.

"Look, you little twit. We've been down to your boyfriend's scrap yard, and there's blood everywhere. We've been to Mercy. We checked with all the Earth-based hospitals. He wasn't checked in at any of them. If your boyfriend is still alive, he's running on borrowed time. If someone finds him before we do, he'll end up roadkill just like his father did. Do you understand?" She didn't understand any of that, but she wanted him to let go of her, so she nodded. "Now, where is Tinker?"

Oilcan's? No, he probably wasn't home. Lain's? No, keep her out of this, whatever it was. Nathan's? He was most likely on duty. She thought of a dozen more places and rejected them. Tinker needed someplace with lots of people where, if these folks really turned out to be American agents, the U.S. government carried little weight. "He's at a hospice just beyond the Rim."

"What's he doing there?"

"Wargs attacked the scrap yard at Shutdown. They downed a high-ranking elf. Tinker took him out to the hospice after Startup."

"That was two days ago."

"Tinker was hurt. One of the wargs messed him up, and the wound got infected."

Durrack swore and took hold of her. "Come on. I'm not letting you out of my sight until I have your boyfriend under my thumb."

Tinker hunted for signs of squad cars responding to the tripwire distress call, but the police weren't showing. Pittsburgh police were spread too thin.

Their car was tucked out of sight, half a block down. A sleek late-model sedan, it looked out of place in Pittsburgh and especially in Tinker's neighborhood. It didn't need the D.C. plates to identify it as out of town. Briggs unlocked the car with a remote.

Durrack opened the back passenger door but held Tinker in check. "Search her."

Briggs moved Tinker so her hands were on the car roof and her legs were slightly spread. The woman combed fingers through Tinker's short, dark hair. The search went down the back of Tinker's neck, up under her shirt and into her bra. Durrack averted his gaze. Briggs' hands stayed impassive, but Tinker clenched her hands into fists on the car roof, until her knuckles showed white, as the search moved to her groin.

"You have no right to do this." Tinker blinked to keep tears out of her eyes. "I haven't done anything."

"Sorry, kid, them's the breaks." Durrack actually sounded like he was sorry.

Finally Briggs moved down to the less personal territory of Tinker's pants pockets. There the search slowed to a crawl. Tinker's pants had a half dozen pockets, and all of them held something. After the first handful, Briggs dumped the items onto the floor of the backseat.

"Please don't lose the nuts and bolts," Tinker said. "They're irreplaceable."

The pockets empty, and double-checked, Briggs stepped back away from Tinker. "If she kicks you with those boots, you're going to know it."

"Take them off," Durrack ordered Tinker.

Briggs sorted through the pile on the car floor, confiscating "dangerous" items: three different-sized screwdrivers, a pocket acetylene torch, and her Swiss Army knife. They went with her boots into the trunk.

"Can I have the rest of my stuff back?" Tinker asked, nearly whispering in an effort to keep from showing how much she wanted her possessions.

"Just get in. You can pick it up while we drive."

Tinker scrambled into the backseat. There was no lock switch, door handle, or com device.

Durrack slid into the passenger seat, letting Briggs drive. "Where's the hospice?"

"You cut through downtown and go up past where the Hill District used to be." Tinker stuffed away her things.

"Where?"

"Centre Avenue out of town. Corner of Old Center and Old Penn."

"New roads named after old roads that don't exist anymore." He programmed it into the nav system. It must have been tied to one of the few government satellites, because it actually seemed to be working.

Distantly a police siren rose, but they were already turning off her street. Tinker slumped back in the seat. If the police arrived at her place now, she wouldn't be there to be rescued.

"Who are you two, anyhow?" She contented herself with kicking the back of the front seat.

"I'm Corg Durrack. My associate is Hannah Briggs. We're with NSA."

"What's that?"

"National Security Agency."

It just didn't make sense. What had she done to bring these guys down on her? "What do you want with Tinker? He's never been in the United States."

Durrack made a negation sound. "He was born in the United States—someplace. He would have been five when the gate first moved Pittsburgh to Elfhome."

Oh, this made sense why they didn't suspect her of being Alexander Bell. They were looking for someone nearly ten years older than her. They hadn't considered that Tinker was anything but a naturally inseminated child. Add in her male name, and they were obviously completely lost. Still, that didn't explain why they were *looking*.

"We want to protect Tinker," Hannah Briggs said. "He's in a lot of danger."

"So you keep on saying." It was a good line to have someone betray a loved one. "Why would anyone want to hurt Tinker? He runs a scrap yard. He keeps his nose clean. He's a good guy."

Briggs gave a flat laugh and murmured, "Yeah, right."

Durrack gave Briggs a hard look. "He's an extremely intelligent young man who apparently understands the working of the phase gate and in all possibility could build one."

Understood it, yes. Build one? She'd never considered doing that, mostly because the parts were too exotic to find as scrap in Pittsburgh. "So?"

Durrack threw her a surprised look. "Do you have any idea how rare that is?"

"Apparently not."

"People like that can be counted on one finger. No one has been able to develop a hyperphase device since Leonardo Dufae's death. The Chinese figured out how to build it off the designs they stole, but they can't change it or improve it. If they could, we wouldn't have this little weirdness called Pittsburgh. Then up pops Tinker, son of the gate's inventor, trained by the same man, and one assumes privy to any family secrets."

"Yeah. Energy equals mass times constant squared."

Durrack turned in his seat now to consider her in a silent study. They crossed the heavy McKees Rocks Bridge, all stone and steel, hopping parts of the riverbank before crossing the Ohio River proper, still choked with barges. It would be a week before river traffic returned to normal. The roads, though, were clear, and minutes later they were crossing the Allegheny River on the Fort Duquesne Bridge.

"Tinker applied to Carnegie Mellon University last Shutdown. It took them a while to put all the pieces together and notify NSA. We've blacked it out, except letting them issue an acceptance letter. Hopefully, no one else put the pieces together either."

"What pieces?"

"That Alexander Bell listed Leonardo Dufae as his father, and that according to the testing AI, he understood all the questions, even though he answered them wrong. That includes the filter questions on hyperphase that no one is supposed to be able to answer."

Shit. She hadn't considered that they would have an AI filtering the placement testing. Lain had explained that the test was just to see what courses she would need to attend: *You can test out of the basics and only take advanced courses.* By tracking eye movement, key-strokes, length of time per question—and correct answers changed to wrong ones—a good AI would easily have determined that she had comprehended all the questions and just chose to get them wrong. "What an idiot."

"If he meant to confuse people, he's succeeded. Why did Tinker bother to apply to Carnegie Mellon University?"

"He only applied to humor a friend. He doesn't want to leave Pittsburgh, so he tried to keep them from accepting him."

Durrack made a slight noise of discovery. "Why doesn't he want to leave?"

Tinker snorted. Durrack had said it with faint disbelief that any-one would want to stay. "Earth has nothing that interests Tinker."

Durrack's eyes narrowed, and he exchanged glances with Briggs. "What about you?"

"Me?" Tinker squeaked. *Oh, please, don't pay any attention to lit-tle old me.*

"Would you like to go to Earth?"

Tinker laughed. "No!"

"We can set you up at a nice house. All new furniture. Cleaning robots. Two new cars. Basically replace everything you might lose in a move. You could go to school if you wanted. Earth has malls, the net, cable television, first-class restaurants, and Disney World."

"Disney World? I'm supposed to give up my family and friends and everything I know for Disney World?"

"Offer her candy and ice cream," Hannah murmured. "At her age, that might still work."

They were coming up to the Rim. There were long-standing jokes about the slowness it took to move across the border. One joke was that the border was an event horizon of a black hole, something that you could spend a lifetime trying to reach. Another sarcastic prod was that elfin magic made any event last longer than a human lifetime, which was why they'd bioengineered themselves to be immortal.

Hannah, apparently feeling the need for privacy, slid up the sound barrier behind the front seat.

Tinker took out the digital marker that Maynard had given her from the smuggler's loot and traced a quick eavesdropping spell on the back of the seat.

". . . so chances are, Tinker isn't going to want to come with us."

"That's a possibility," Durrack said. "I say that if we don't find the boyfriend at this hospice, we tuck the girl away for safekeeping."

"Durrack, sometimes you scare me. The Pittsburghers are still American citizens—"

"Whose willingness to live on a foreign planet makes their loyalty to the United States suspect."

"Don't feed me that line. You don't give a shit about that."

"Yes, but it looks good on a report when you bend the hell out of the rules."

"Making the girl disappear would do more than bend rules."

"Protective custody. If we've thought to use her to get to Tinker, then she's fair game to anyone looking for him. Do you want the kid in the middle of this? You want to deal with that again? I sure as hell don't."

"It isn't all black and white. There's a lot of gray out there, Durrack."

"It's not the black, white, or gray that I'm worrying about. It's the blood red. I say if Tinker is out here, we stick them both away until next Shutdown and then smuggle them out to the States."

"We should make sure they actually like one another first. She might be lying about their relationship."

More than you can guess. Tinker watched as the second car in front of them got waved through. Tinker or Tinker's lover, she was slated to disappear after the hospice search, which meant she had to get away from them at the hospice. She mostly needed to get out of the car. She considered the tactics she could try, from asking to go pee to stating that she wanted to stay in the car. Just because they'd made the one mistake on her identity didn't mean they were truly stupid. Her real name was misleading, and she didn't remember the application asking for gender or age.

She considered the hazards of being locked in the car, in case her ploy failed. Could she get out? Unlikely. Trying the reverse-psychology ploy of refusing to leave the car was too risky.

Might as well start working on the bathroom ploy. She tapped on the divider.

It was their turn through the security checkpoint. Hannah slid down the window and handed out her NSA ID. Durrack handed his across via Hannah.

"We're looking for a human male," Hannah said in rough, slow Low Elvish. "The girl has no ID. She is our prisoner. We are responsible for her."

While they talked, Tinker pieced together a plea for help in High Elvish.

The elfin border guard glanced in the window at her. She mouthed the plea, just in case she didn't get the chance to talk to an elf at the hospice.

"Where do you seek this human male?" the elf asked Hannah, gazing intently at Tinker.

"The hospice."

The guard went off with their papers into the guardhouse. Tinker whispered, "Come on, come on," crossing the fingers on both hands. That simple magic didn't work, if it ever really worked. The guard returned and waved them through.

Hannah drove to the hospice and parked. Tinker's stomach churned nervously as they walked in. She needed to do this quickly, because the NSA were about to find out that she had been the only human ever treated here.

She picked the brawniest-looking of the elves in the foyer as the NSA agents checked stride, apparently scanning about for an equivalent of a reception desk. She locked eyes with the elf and said quickly, "Please, help me. I am in grave danger. Wolf Who Rules . . ."

Durrack jerked her back and slapped a hand over her mouth. "What the hell did you say?"

Hannah produced her ID and was saying carefully, "This one is in our care and might be charged with crimes. She is young and foolish."

Tinker hadn't thought of what the elves might *do* in response to her plea. She expected demands for identification and long legal proceedings. She was stunned as the elf unsheathed his sword in a ring of metal.

Durrack reacted instantly, shoving her aside to pull his own weapon. Hannah shouted, "Drop it! Drop it!"

Tinker scrambled to one side, swearing. This wasn't what she'd planned! Still, she'd be an idiot not to take advantage of the opportunity. She darted through the door and into the maze of hallways.

What had happened to her life?

One minute it was all so sane and orderly, and now look at her! They say that the elves really couldn't curse anyone. Elves could use their magic to turn a person into a toad, cause someone to become incredibly uncoordinated, or drop one's inhibitions like a six-pack of Iron City Beer, but really rotten, everything-turns-against-you-bad luck they couldn't do.

So why did it seem that someone had cursed her?

Tinker skittered on the slick stone to round the corner; then yelped as she came face-to-face with armed men in EIA uniforms. EIA? How did they get here so fast? Were they real EIA? She tried to turn, her stocking feet went out from under her, and she went sliding directly into them. *In a frictionless universe, objects in motion stay in motion.*

Durrack and Briggs came around the corner, and there was sudden excited shouting. She looked up to find the EIA and the NSA pointing guns at one another.

"NSA!" Durrack shouted. "Put down your weapons!"

"EIA!" the others yelled back. "Drop it!"

Tinker edged toward the closest doorway. No one really seemed to be paying attention to her, but then, she didn't have a gun.

"This girl is in our protective custody," Briggs growled.

"Drop the guns!" the EIA or EIA look-a-likes shouted. "You're not doing anything until we see proper identification and clearance papers."

Tinker bolted through the door.

Behind her, Durrack didn't seem to notice she had fled. "This is code black!"

Nor had the EIA. "I don't give diddly what color it is. This is Elfhome!"

After thoroughly losing herself, she slid through a door and discovered she was at a dead end in an empty patient room. She could hear booted feet echoing through the halls, rapidly approaching her, cutting off other possible exits.

Hiding looked like her only course. Other than the bed, nightstand, and guest chair, the only piece of furniture was a large wardrobe. She opened the door and found that the bottom was taken up with drawers. What kind of wardrobe was this? The upper part was one tall shelf, about the size of a dress shirt. Oh well! She scrambled up onto the shelf and closed the door with her fingernails.

The pounding of her heart covered all sound until someone entered the room in long booted strides. The footsteps continued straight to the wardrobe. The door opened, and Derek Maynard studied her. Hovering over his shoulder was a locate spell.

"There are times I hate magic," Tinker sulked, remaining tucked on the top shelf.

"You are a hard girl to keep pinned down." Maynard motioned her out.

"Unfortunately, not hard enough." She reluctantly unfolded and swung down off the shelf.

Maynard reached into his pocket and produced a bright yellow rectangle. "Gum?"

"I've been told not to take candy from strangers."

He raised one eyebrow, as if saying "Get real" or "How wise" or something truly witty. Tinker supposed that was one of the benefits of keeping one's mouth shut—people made up better dialogue for you than you yourself could imagine. Then again, the trick would never work for her; she couldn't stay quiet. She scowled at him and took the offered piece.

The gum filled her mouth with sweetness, and ran counter to her banging heart.

"Juicy Fruit," She identified the brand. "They say that elves love this stuff."

"Juicy Fruit and peanut butter." Maynard unwrapped a piece for himself. "I have always wondered if it's a cultural thing or something more genetically based. Gods know there are human cultures that have weirder tastes."

She shrugged, not knowing or caring. Why were they standing there trading inane remarks? If Maynard had tracked her down, did it mean that he was going to turn her over to the NSA and correct all their misconceptions? Maynard had been studying her while making what seemed to be a deliberate show of chewing the gum. He reached out now to rub the triangular mark between her eyebrows.

"Where did this come from?"

"Windwolf." She jerked her head away. It occurred to her that if any human knew what it was, Maynard would. "What does it mean?"

"The elves run a rigid caste system, but sometimes a high-ranked elf can elevate a lower-rank elf. He marks them with a *dau*." Maynard tapped her forehead again. "And they become part of his caste, with all rights and privileges."

"Why'd Windwolf do it to me?"

"Why didn't you ask him at the time?"

"I didn't notice the mark until after he left. I haven't seen him since."

"Ah," Maynard murmured, and said nothing more.

He had been dealing with elves too long. Maynard was nearly as obscure as they were. It seemed as if they would spend all day simply chewing gum.

"So, are you going to turn me over to the NSA?"

"Can't," Maynard said.

"Can't? Won't? Shan't?"

"By the rules of the treaty, no elf of any caste can be moved to Earth by any human agency for any reason."

"Rights and privileges?"

Maynard nodded.

Well, the day was suddenly looking up, but it seemed too good to be true. Tinker tested her luck. "I don't think the NSA will see it that way."

"I don't give a fuck," Maynard said. "Lord Windwolf will not allow it, and that's all I care about. I'm walking a delicate line with the elves. I'm not going to piss the viceroy off to make two gun-happy American agents' jobs easy."

"What the hell is a viceroy?"

"You, girl, need a lesson in politics."

6: A DATE WHICH WILL LIVE IN INFAMY

A viceroy turned out to be a very high position in the elfin government. The word *viceroy* was a weird smash-together of the words *vice* and *royal*, kind of like vice president, but with the idea that the president was somewhere else. In Windwolf's case, it was the queen of the elves, who lived in an area that corresponded with Europe. Windwolf apparently was the youngest elf ever appointed to be a viceroy, but Tinker got the impression it was by default. Windwolf had researched human explorations of the Americas and then led the first elfin landing in the Westernlands once he reached majority. As a colony, it hadn't rated a viceroy, but with Pittsburgh's arrival and the sudden boom in trade, Windwolf had been elevated solely because he was the principal landowner.

This made him a target both inside and outside his clan. Elders in his clan thought someone older with less radical ideas should replace him. The other clans were split—half wanted control of the trade with the humans and the rest wanted to break off contact totally. The queen, though, favored Windwolf, so he remained viceroy.

All things considered, girl genius or not, Windwolf was depressingly out of reach for a human teenager that ran a scrap yard.

Maynard tried to explain the elfin politics to Tinker while escorting her out to his limo. He was hampered by the fact that her grandfather had taught her nothing about human government and very little world geography. (*No use cluttering up one's mind with things that change*, as he'd put it. What she did know came from Lain, who believed in a rounded education: *insects specialize, not humans.*)

"It's in humans' best interest that Windwolf stay viceroy," Maynard finished. "He's an intelligent, honorable being with an open mind. It's also in our best interest to stay on his good side. Letting two minor human agents kidnap his newest family member would surely infuriate him."

"Family member?" Tinker squeaked.

"I'm keeping things simple," Maynard said cryptically. "The elfin guard at the border saw a member of Windwolf's family with two humans, and the humans claimed that person—you—as their prisoner. That's a basic violation of the treaty—I'll have to finesse things to calm the waters. If Windwolf doesn't know about this already, he will shortly. Luckily the border guard called the EIA to help extract you safely."

"You mean I did all that running around for no reason?"

Maynard slanted a look in her direction. "It did keep the NSA from learning the truth about your identity and the whereabouts of Alexander Graham Bell. And it delayed their attempts to remove you from the hospice until I had a chance to arrive. It wasn't a waste of time."

"Where are they now?" Tinker glanced out of the limo's back window at the hospice.

"They've been arrested for violating the treaty. If they're lucky, they won't be summarily executed."

"You're joking."

"I'm not," Maynard said. "The NSA has committed a serious breach of protocol out of ignorance. They're making it worse by refusing to discuss why. Did they explain anything to you?"

She considered him. He currently was the only thing standing between her and the NSA, but that was for Windwolf's sake, not hers. She was only important because of Windwolf. She hedged. "I told you my father was murdered. The NSA think I could be in danger from the same people."

"The NSA doesn't usually commit two agents for thirty days to protect a little girl."

She glared at him. "I'm not a little girl; I'm a woman."

"Or a woman."

She supposed that keeping the truth from him when he was bound to discover it from the NSA agents sooner or later would only serve to annoy him. "My father was Leonardo Da Vinci Dufae."

She hadn't expected him to recognize her father's name, and was thus surprised when he did.

"Leonardo Dufae? The man who invented the hyperphase gate? Where did the name 'Bell' come from? Is that your egg mother's name?"

Tinker winced. "It's complicated. On the night Leonardo was killed, his office was ransacked and all his notes and computer equipment stolen. About a month later, someone tried to kidnap my grandfather. Grandpa always claimed it was Leonardo's murderers, who realized that what they stole off Leo wasn't complete and thought Grandpa could fill in the missing information. The government stepped in and gave Grandpa a new identity and relocated him out of Pittsburgh. When the Chinese started to build the gate, Grandpa left protective custody and disappeared totally. I'm not sure what he did during the next five years, and what names he went by, but when Pittsburgh was first transported to Elfhome, he was living here under the name of Timothy Bell."

"And to stay in Pittsburgh, he couldn't change it," Maynard guessed. The hasty peace treaty had allowed only residents listed on the census to remain after the first Shutdown, a ruling carried out by armed forces.

"Even when I was born, he was still too afraid to give me the name Dufae. He kept his inventions hidden. Lain always said he was a little loony in that regard."

"Then how did the NSA suddenly find you?"

"I applied to CMU. Since I'm basically homeschooled, and didn't want to be stuck on Earth for a month in order to take the standardized tests, Lain thought I should use my father's legacy to get in. After all these years, with Grandpa dead and all, I didn't think anyone would care who my father was."

Maynard gazed out of the window of his limo, considering what she'd told him. After a moment of silence, he said, "You said the stolen information wasn't complete."

"No. It wasn't." She'd never thought it important, but now maybe it was, and so she tried to piece it all together in her own mind. "If I had just lived with my grandfather, I probably wouldn't know the whole of this, but Oilcan lived with his mother until he was ten, so there are family things he knows that Grandpa never told me. The founder of the Dufae line, hundreds of years ago in France, was an elf. Dufae was a physician to the nobility, and was beheaded in the French Revolution; his wife and son fled to America. When my father and aunt were children, my great-great-"—she paused to count it out—"-great-aunt lived with them. She was over a century old, and she recounted stories that her great-grandmother had told her about the first Dufae.

"What made my father's work so groundbreaking was that much of it wasn't an extension of someone else's work, but was extrapolated from anecdotal information handed down through my family for generations. Apparently Dufae had traveled from Elfhome to Earth, but couldn't get back. If you believe the stories, then Dufae was proof of parallel dimensions."

"The elves had gates?"

"No, not really. It seemed to be a natural phenomenon in certain cave systems, most likely an iron ore embedded in quartz with a great deal of ambient magic present. In human legends, elves were a race that lived 'under a hill.' By all accounts, including Dufae's, elves and humans crossed back and forth between the two dimensions quite freely. Then something happened, and Dufae became stranded on Earth."

"Something happened?" Maynard echoed, puzzled. "Like the 'gates' stopped working?"

"From the stories, yes. Dufae traveled Europe, trying all the gates he knew about, and none of them worked, but he didn't know why."

Maynard frowned over this news for a minute, then turned his mind back to Tinker's father. "I'm not sure I follow. What does this Dufae have to do with Leonardo's plans being incomplete?"

She considered telling Maynard about Dufae's Codex, but decided not to. Let that remain a long-kept family secret. "Because of the great-aunt's stories about Dufae, my father started work on his theories as early as ten, writing down the tales and trying to conduct scientific analyses of them. This was the 1980s and 1990s, when computers were still limited in processing power. When he upgraded to a new computer, he would only move his most recent files across and continue work from there. After Leo's death, my grandfather consolidated everything into one system, but on the night of Leo's murder, his work was spread across half a dozen machines. The thieves only took the one at his offices without realizing there were five more at home. They got information on how to build the gate, but not why it was designed the way it was in the first place."

Maynard groaned at the stupidity of the thieves. "I've seen the intelligence reports showing that the gate was definitely your father's work, but there have always been things that puzzled me about the whole thing. Most inventions have been a footrace to see who could make the breakthrough first. With the gate, your father's work came out of the blue, and it's been a scramble to work backward to see how he designed it. This explains why there were no small-scale experiments, but it leaves the biggest question."

"Which is?"

"Why in the world did the Chinese steal the design and sink so much money into building the gate when there was no proof that it would work? It's stunning that it does work."

"Mostly works. The little problem of Pittsburgh swapped to Elfhome is because the plans were flawed, but the Chinese haven't been able to fix the problem."

Maynard turned his focus on Tinker. "NSA thinks that you can build a gate from scratch, without the design flaws of your father's."

"It's a possibility that they're seriously entertaining."

"Can you?"

It would be safer to say no. Straight-out lie. There was the matter of the placement-test questions, but there were levels to understanding. One has to know enough to answer rote questions. The higher level was understanding to the point of creation. It was an invisible barrier that divided the likes of Newton and Einstein from the rest of the scientific world. Could a test question expose that level of understanding? Did she even have it? She thought she understood her father's theories, but she could be wrong. Certainly she'd never played with them, attempting to create or correct.

"You can," Maynard said while she wavered.

"I might." She tempered it. "There's a profound lack of parts for such items in Pittsburgh."

"And there's the matter of getting into space," Maynard quipped.

"It doesn't have to be in space. My family's stories are filled with foreboding as to what might have caused the gates to fail. My father thought that space was just the safest place to put a doorway between worlds."

"So he wasn't predicting the veil effect?"

Tinker looked out the side window, past the river to the elfin forest. "No. To be quite frank, I think he would be horrified."

She had Maynard take her to the yard, and as she hoped, Oilcan was there. Her cousin hugged her and held on—he had heard about her kidnapping. His obvious source of information, Nathan, was there, glaring at Maynard as if he were responsible for dragging her away instead of returning her.

Tinker kicked him. "Act nice. He's one of the good guys. This is Nathan Czernowski. He's a close friend of the family. Nathan, this is Derek Maynard."

"I recognize him," Nathan stated, barely civil, but extended his hand.

"Officer Czernowski." Maynard shook hands.

It struck Tinker that they were the same height and coloring.

Nathan, though, was nearly twice the width, all muscle, and had a steady plainness to him, like a piece of stone.

"What the hell happened?" Nathan asked. "Your front door was wide open, your tripwire was activated, but your home system was shut down."

Tinker sighed and tried to explain, keeping the facts bare. She didn't bother to mention the NSA misgivings that her life was in danger. Maynard, however, added them in.

"I need to get back and deal with the NSA agents," Maynard finished. "There's a slim chance they'll be freed by morning, but I'll let you know before they are."

"Thanks."

After Maynard left, Nathan hugged her, lifting her off the ground.

"Hey!" she complained, tired of being manhandled for the day.

"I was worried about you." He put her down.

"I can take care of myself," she said, more for Oilcan's sake than Nathan's.

"What's this?" Nathan rubbed the mark between her eyes.

"Oh, that." She sighed. "Windwolf has elevated me to elf status or something like that. Maynard says it's kind of like he adopted me into his family."

Nathan frowned and rubbed the mark harder. "You let him tattoo you?"

"No!" She jerked her head back. "He had the spell initialized and coded to a word and a kiss. Apparently the mark is a big deal, so it could have some authorization coding in it so someone with a temporary tattoo kit can't duplicate it."

"He kissed you?"

She had never seen jealousy on Nathan before, but still she recognized it on his face. "Oh, cut it out. It was a little peck on the forehead." She turned away from him as she recalled cuddling with Windwolf at the hospice. Had that actually happened, or was it some drug dream? "Look, it's a good thing. The NSA tried to kidnap me, and Windwolf's mark kept them from doing it."

It was hard to tell what annoyed Nathan more—that the NSA had grabbed her or that Windwolf had permanently marked her. She hadn't suspected that Nathan would react with such primal male chest beating. "He's the viceroy, Nathan, get over it!"

And even Nathan could see the unlikelihood that an elf noble would be interested in a little junkyard dog. "I'm sorry, Tink."

He turned her toward him and leaned down to kiss her, cautiously at first, and then hungrily. She was too tired and annoyed with life to enjoy it completely.

When he broke the kiss, he leaned his forehead against hers and asked huskily, "Do you want me to take you home?"

That put a thrill through her. Nathan. Her place. Her big bed. No. That was too scary a thought, despite the sudden wanting throb inside of her. The couch? Yes, she could deal with the couch, but still, the bed was frighteningly close by.

"No," she said once she swallowed down her heart. "I've got some things I want to do here," she lied. Then, because she knew Nathan wouldn't allow her to go home alone, not after today, she said, "Oilcan can take me home."

Oilcan looked struck dumb. When he realized that they were talking about him, he nodded. "Yeah! Sure!"

"Okay." Nathan stepped away reluctantly. "If you need anything, just call me."

"I will," she promised.

"See you tomorrow night." Nathan went to his squad car and drove away.

It wasn't until after he left that she realized he meant for their date.

"What the hell was that all about?" Oilcan broke the silence. "What's tomorrow night?"

"We're going to the Faire tomorrow night."

"You're dating Nathan? Since when?"

"Friday! You've got a problem with that?"

"I don't know. It just seems weird. You two kissing?" He squirmed. "It's like you're dating me."

"What the hell does that mean?"

"Well, you know Nathan's like family."

"So?" She kicked a dead headlight sitting on the ground. It sailed off to smash with crystal clarity. "You want me to date a complete stranger like . . . like"—she couldn't say Windwolf because that would hurt—"Maynard?"

"No! Well, maybe." Oilcan rubbed at the back of his neck. "I don't know. Nathan knows you're smart, but I don't think he knows how smart."

"What does that have to do with anything?" She didn't want to point out that she and Oilcan got along fine, even though they both knew she was smarter than he was.

"You're only going to get smarter. You're not happy unless you're learning something. Nathan, he's at the top of his game right now. He sees you and thinks he can handle it, but he doesn't realize things aren't going to stay the same."

"Could you at least let us get one date in before you doom the whole relationship?"

"As long as you keep in mind that it's probably not going to work out."

"Why not? You said yourself that Nathan already knows what I am."

"I don't know if Nathan has ever really *listened* to you. I mean, when you're talking about racing, or bowling, or horseshoes, he's listening to you. But when you talk about what's really in your soul, the real you, he's tuning you out. His eyes glaze over, and he does all sorts of fiddly things, and if you go on too long, he tries to shut you up."

He does? Embarrassingly enough, she had never noticed. She shrugged it away. If she didn't notice, it couldn't be something hugely important. "I'm going to have to date someone, sometime."

"Have you told Nathan about CMU?"

"Actually, Lain released me from that. She said I only had to go to college if I really wanted to."

"And?" Oilcan asked, as if it was still a possibility.

She opened her mouth to say no, but for some reason it came out, "I don't know!"

Nor did she know later as Oilcan dropped her off at her loft. She cleaned up the mess that the NSA agents had made of her place, trying to wrap her mind around the sudden changes in her life. Too much had hit at once. If it had just been Windwolf, or the EIA, or CMU, or the NSA, or Nathan, maybe she could have dealt with any one. She finally drew decision trees to map out her possible actions.

Windwolf yielded no branches; there was nothing for her to actually do, so she tried to delete him from her mind. Unfortunately, sometimes a mind wasn't as obedient as a piece of hardware.

Nor did the NSA tree provide actions; they were dealt with for the time being. EIA worked out to be a simple "help Maynard or annoy Maynard." While Windwolf's adoption obviously provided her with protection from the EIA, it seemed wiser to help the EIA.

Nathan broke down to the simple "go on the date or cancel." Because of her age and Nathan's reticence, neither would lead to massive changes in her life.

The tree for going to college, however, disturbed her greatly. The branch for attending splintered into multitudes of possibilities. Staying in Pittsburgh yielded unending sameness. For the first time she wondered if Lain was right; was she in danger of stagnating if she stayed in Pittsburgh?

She glanced at Nathan's tree. If she dated him, at least that was some change. She circled the "go on the date." She had promised him to try to look older. That required better clothes and makeup, of which she had neither. She made a note to get both in the morning.

Maynard called and told her that the NSA agents would be released in the morning. "Unfortunately the elves don't deal with gray very well. We either had to execute Durrack and Briggs or let them go. While killing them would keep them safely out of our hair, it was a little excessive."

Tinker made sure the door was triple bolted, and she armed her security system before going to bed. The events of the last few days combined oddly in her mind until she was dreaming of Foo dogs, crows, Riki, the NSA agents, and Windwolf all jumping through magic hula hoops. Despite the teleporting abilities of the hula hoops, the dream played out entirely at the EIA warehouse. At some point, the Foo dogs ran off with the magical toys, reducing her to tears.

"Do not cry." Windwolf produced a ring. "This works just as well. The gates can be quite small, if you understand the quantum effect of magic."

"What about the veil effect?" Tinker breathed as he slid the ring onto her oil-stained finger.

"Here it is." He placed a bridal veil on her head. The shimmering fabric was at once invisible and a glistening black caught full of stars.

Proving that she had paid attention to the handful of weddings she'd attended, Maynard married them in what seemed a fairly accurate though amazingly short ceremony.

"Do you take this woman to be your lawfully wedded wife?"

"She is already mine." Windwolf parted the veil to touch the spell mark on Tinker's forehead.

"Do you take this man to be your husband?" Maynard asked.

"I really just want to mess around," Tinker said.

"Oh, okay." Maynard stepped back out of the room, saying, "You can kiss the bride."

Windwolf did more than kiss her. She was riding a wave of orgasm when her doorbell woke her. She opened her eyes, the morning sun spilling across her bed, an echo of the pleasure still washing through her. The doorbell rang again, and she stirred in her nest of rumpled white linens to find her bedside clock.

It was seven in the morning.

Who the hell was ringing her doorbell at seven in the freaking morning?

She fumbled with her spyhole display and discovered the NSA agents actually standing on her doorstep and ringing the doorbell like real people instead of breaking in.

She thumbed the display to two-way sound. "What do you want?"

Briggs located the camera and microphone first and pointed it out to Durrack while saying, "We want to talk to you, Ms. Bell."

Durrack ducked slightly to look earnestly into the camera, as if trying to make eye-to-eye contact with her. In an apologetic mood, he actually had a boyish face with dark eyes and thick eyelashes. "We're sorry about yesterday; we let our concern for your safety carry us away. We really crossed the line, and we're very, very sorry. We promise it won't happen again."

"You sound like you get a lot of practice at groveling, Durrack."

Hannah laughed at her partner while he rubbed an embarrassed look off his face.

"Well, actually, being a federal agent is hard on relationships," Durrack confessed. "Chicks really dig the spy thing, but they really get pissed off when you miss their birthday because you were off saving the world."

Tinker laughed despite being annoyed at the NSA agents. "So you save the world a lot?"

"Small American slices of it, yes."

Briggs pushed Durrack impatiently aside and leaned close to the camera. "Ms. Bell, we believe you're in a great deal of danger."

Tinker sighed, resting her forehead on her nightstand. Let them in or chase them away? Neither seemed like a good idea.

"We promise to behave," Durrack added.

Yeah, right. She didn't believe them totally, but she suspected they weren't going away—at least not without talking to her face-to-face. She crawled out of bed, pulled on some clean clothes, and padded out to her front door, rubbing sleep out of her eyes. She supposed it was a good sign that they didn't rush her when she unbolted the door and swung it open.

Why was everyone suddenly coming in jumbo sizes? Both NSA agents towered over Tinker. Corg Durrack was broad-shouldered with deep chest and lean waist, giving him the proportions of a comic book hero. He fairly bristled with weapons and carried a white wax paper bag that he held out as a peace offering. "We brought donuts."

Briggs scoffed quietly at this. The female agent wore a long-sleeve shirt and pants that looked like black wet paint. Apparently the shirt doubled as a sports bra, and if she wore panties, they were thong. Still, Briggs was a stunning example of what strength training could do to the female body. As she stalked through the loft like a caged cat, the outfit showed off muscles on her long legs that Tinker didn't know women could develop.

"Do you want to start over from the top?" Tinker accepted the bag and swung up onto her countertop in an effort to keep a level playing field. "My life is in danger, oh ah, and you want to drag me back to Earth in order to lock me up in protective custody."

"Well, I'm glad you're taking this seriously." Briggs matched Tinker's sarcastic tone.

"I know all about protective custody." Tinker peered cautiously into the wax paper bag. Inside were four large coffee rolls of pure decadence. "My grandfather did some time in it, and he had choice stories to tell of the victim, rather than the criminal, being the prisoner."

Durrack sighed. "The sad truth is that we can't arrest all the bad guys."

" 'Sorry, madam, I couldn't get your rapist, but I did lock up the baby girl next door just in case.' " Oops, judging by the look Durrack gave Briggs, there was only so far Tinker could push the NSA agents—or at least Briggs—and she had just hit it. "Come on; let's do a history update. Twenty-five years ago, a quarter of a century, someone killed my father. They've got their gate. They don't know that I exist, unless someone leaked the CMU information, but even then, there's no proof I can *build* a gate. Hell, even I don't know if I can build one. There's a big jump between knowing something well enough to answer elementary questions and being able to create a working prototype. Oilcan does as well as I do on just about any test, and can understand what I create, but he can't develop things on his own. The spark isn't there."

"But you have the spark, and anyone who puts Alexander Bell together with Tinker is going to know it too."

Tinker picked up a dog-eared copy of *Scientific American* off the counter. "In the last quarter century, scientists have been working feverishly to understand what Leo did. This magazine is two years old, but there's an article in here from some Norwegian who's doing field manipulation using quantum particles."

"Torbjörn Pettersen," Durrack said.

"Pardon?" Tinker said.

Durrack tapped the magazine. "The Norwegian was Torbjörn Pettersen, and he's been missing since that article hit the streets."

"Oh." She dug out the most recent issue—although the mailing lag made it the December issue and not the May one. She noted with a sudden relief that even though she paid the exorbitant subscription, it was still addressed to *Timothy Bell, Neville Island, Pittsburgh on Elfhome.* "What about"—she checked the table of contents—"Lisa Satterlund?"

"Dead," Briggs said simply.

Durrack expanded the single word: "Satterlund was killed during a kidnapping attempt in December."

"Marcus Shipman? Harry Russell?" Tinker named the two scientists she could remember who had published important advances in gate theory.

"Missing," Briggs said.

Durrack sighed. "Harry Russell had a GPS chip on him after a DWI arrest. We found the chip in the stomach of a catfish in St. Louis. The forensic scientists are trying to determine when he died. The thing is that, for at least four months, the chip wasn't in North America."

"You think he was here in Pittsburgh?"

"Yes."

"It's a possibility," Durrack allowed. "It's possible that the kidnappers just managed to block the signal while holding him in the United States. It seems more likely that they brought him to Elfhome."

"To kill him and dump his body into the river?"

"These people use excessive force," Briggs snapped. "His death was probably accidental."

"How he died isn't as important as the fact that you're still in peril," Durrack said. "At the moment, we have an advantage. You're a complete blank: no fingerprints, no retina scans. The other side is going to be looking for a guy about to hit middle age. With just a name change, you could vanish into the general populace. Hell, you could go to MIT or Caltech and live in the dorms. That's assuming you want to attend college. If you don't, we could set you up with a lab."

"Like I want to turn my life over to you." Tinker shook her head as her stomach growled. "I have a life here. There's my cousin, and all my friends. Besides, I thought you couldn't take me off Elfhome since technically I'm an elf now."

"We can't *take* you off, but you can request permission to leave," Briggs said. "Elves have traveled to Earth in the past, but they usually only stay thirty days, until the next transfer. They don't like living without magic."

"Neither do I," Tinker said, and gave in to the temptation of the donuts, taking out one of the still-warm pastries. "There's lots of cool possibilities with magic I haven't explored yet. If I go back to Earth, I'd lose that ability."

"The U.S. government would be willing to make it worth your while," Durrack said. "Everything we offered before and then some. A house. Someone to cook and clean so all you have to do is invent. A fully equipped lab. A law firm to file your patents."

"What does the government get out of this?" Tinker unrolled the spiral coffee roll, tearing off bite-sized pieces. "I know there's a price hidden in there somewhere."

"The U.S. gets insurance that the Chinese don't get a land-based gate first."

"Why does the U.S. want a gate?"

"Part of it is that they're used to being the ones with the new toy, and it annoys them to no end that the Chinese have something that they don't. But there's also a fear of what a land-based gate can and can't do. What if it lets you travel through time, or to several dimensions? If the Chinese get it first, they're not going to share information any more than they've shared details on the gate."

"I'm not going to leave my cousin," Tinker said.

"He could come with you," Durrack said. "We set him up a new identity. He could pick out a name nicer than Orville or Oilcan. He could go to college too. I hear he's an intelligent young man—it seems a waste for him to spend his life as a tow truck driver when he's got the smarts to be anything he wants. It could be a great opportunity for him."

Durrack would say anything to manipulate her, but it didn't make it any less true. While Oilcan occasionally stated that Earth had been too big and crowded, he complained about the lack of people their own age and temperament. He hovered around the Observatory, drawn to the women postdocs, but was never able to do more than watch them come and go.

The NSA agents waited for her response.

"Let me talk to my cousin. See what he says."

"We can take you over to his place."

"Oh, stop pushing," Tinker said. "I'm going to take a shower, and then go shopping for clothes. I've got a date tonight." And Nathan wasn't going to be happy about any possibility of her leaving town; his whole family clung to Pittsburgh, refusing to leave. "And I've got lots of hard decisions to make. So just go away; leave me alone to figure out what I want in life."

Tinker took the well-worn path down through the steep hillside orchard, carefully avoiding the beehives, to Tooloo's store at the bottom of the hill. The store itself was a rambling set of rooms filled with unlikely items, many ancient beyond belief. One section was secondhand clothes, where Tinker often found shirts, pants, and winter coats. Some of the clothes were elfin formal wear that Tinker drooled over from time to time but never found any reason to buy. Even secondhand they were pricey.

There was an odd collection of general goods, but the main focus of the store was food—often the rarest items to find in Pittsburgh. In an area behind the store, Tooloo had an extensive garden and various outbuildings: a barn, a henhouse, and a dove coop. She had fresh milk, butter, eggs, freshwater fish, and doves all year. During the summer, she also sold honey, fruit, and vegetables.

Tooloo herself seemed to be an eclectic collection. Locals referred to her as a half-breed, left over from the last time elves visited Earth. Tooloo certainly had the elfin ears, spoke fluent Low and High Elvish, and could be counted on as having in-depth knowledge on matters arcane. Unlike any full elf, she looked old, a face filled with wrinkles and silver hair that reached her ankles. Her elfin silks were faded and nearly threadbare, and she wore battered high-top tennis shoes.

Whereas Lain was a known quantity, comforting in her familiarity, Tooloo refused to be known. Asked her favorite color, it would be different each time. Her birthday ranged the year, if she would admit to having one. Even her name was unknown, Tooloo being only a nickname. In eighteen years, Tinker had never heard Tooloo mention anything about her own parentage.

If Tinker's grandfather was the source of Tinker's scientific thinking, and Lain the source of all common sense, then Tooloo was her font of superstition. Despite everything, Tinker found herself believing a found penny meant good luck, spilt salt required a pinch thrown over the shoulder to ward off bad luck, and that she should never give an elf her true name.

Thinking about what she'd say to Oilcan about the NSA proposal and her date with Nathan, Tinker wasn't prepared for Tooloo's reaction to recent events.

"You little monkey!" Tooloo swept out of the back room that

served as her home, shaking a finger at Tinker. "You've seen Wind-wolf again, haven't you? I told you to stay away from him."

Tinker turned her back so she didn't have to look at the scolding finger. "You've told me lies."

"No, I haven't. Only bad will come of this. He'll swallow you up, and nothing will be left."

"You said he marked me with a life debt." And as Tinker said it, she realized that Tooloo had told the truth, only the half-elf had twisted it somehow. "You didn't tell me that he was in debt to me."

"It's a curse, either way." Tooloo came to rub the mark between Tinker's eyebrows. "Oh, he's got his hands on you now. The end be-gins."

"What do you mean?"

"What I've said all along—but then you've never listened. You come asking again and again for the same story and go away not lis-tening despite how many different ways I tell you."

"It can't be the same and different at the same time."

"Windwolf is dangerous to you," Tooloo used the scolding fin-ger again. "Is that simple enough for you? I've tried to keep you hid-den all these years from him, but he's found you now, and marked you as his."

Tinker realized suddenly that as one of the few people in Pitts-burgh who spoke High Elvish, Tooloo would have certainly been the one asked about Tinker's identity after the saurus attack. "I don't understand."

"Obviously." Tooloo snorted and moved off to rearrange stock.

From years of dealing with Tooloo, Tinker recognized that the conversation had come to an impasse. She changed the subject to the reason she was at the store. "I have a date with Nathan Czernowski. We're going to the Faire."

"Ah, what is with you and fire?"

"What does that mean?"

"It's dangerous to offer a man something he wants but that can't be his."

"Why can't it be his?"

Tooloo caught her chin. "When you look at Czernowski, do you see your heart's desire?"

"Maybe."

"You know your heart so little? I don't think so. You do this to satisfy that little monkey brain of yours. Curiosity is a beast best starved."

"Nathan wouldn't hurt me."

"If only the same could be said of you."

Tinker stomped to the clothes, trying to puzzle that warning out. Was it something in the water that made older women impossible to understand?

At Tooloo's she found an elfin jacket. Or at least, on an elf it was a jacket. On her it was a duster, coming down nearly to her ankles. The sleeves were slightly long, but she could fold them back. A mottled gold silk, it had a purple iris hand painted on the back. She fell in love with it but could find nothing to complement it, so she took her hoverbike into Pittsburgh in search of an older self.

Kaufmann's was a Pittsburgh tradition, the oldest department store located downtown. It had withstood flood, suburbia, the invasion of foreign department stores, and being transported into the fey realms.

"I need some clothes to make me look more mature," she told the saleswoman in an area marked "Women's," who pointed her firmly toward "Petites." She found a push-up bra that made the most of her chest, a clingy black slip dress, and high-heeled shoes.

"I need a cut that makes me look older," she told the hairstylist, who eyed her hacked hair with slight dismay.

"Did you tattoo yourself, sweetheart?" the stylist asked, gingerly touching Windwolf's mark on Tinker's forehead.

"Umm, ah, it's a long story." Remembering Nathan's reaction to the mark, Tinker raked her hair forward with her fingers. "Is there any way I can cover this with my bangs?"

"What bangs?" The stylist found the longest lock and pulled it forward to show that it fell short of the mark. "Sweetheart, at this point all you can do is wear it proudly."

In the end, the stylist could do little more than even out the length of her hair and then rub a gel into it so it stood up in little spikes. "It's retro chic," the stylist chanted. "Very elegant."

The makeover woman eyed Windwolf's mark and pronounced it extremely cool.

"Is there anything that will cover it up?"

The woman laughed again. "Not without an inch or two of concealer. Why would you want to? It becomes you; it makes you very exotic looking."

"The guy I'm dating tonight doesn't like it."

The woman swabbed the mark with cleanser and shook her head. "He better learn to like it; it's there to stay."

"Can you make me look older then, like I was in my twenties?"

"Why does every woman under twenty want to look over it, and every other woman in the world wants to look under it?" She resoaked the cotton ball, took Tinker's face in one hand, and started to clean her face gently. "Men, that's why. Honey, don't be in a rush to change for a man. You might make him happy, but most likely only at the cost of making yourself miserable. . . . You've got wonderful skin," she cooed.

"I've got freckles."

The makeup woman tsked. "Here's the secret, honey; you've got what men want. You're young, and pretty, and nicely padded in all the right places. You might be saying, 'Oh, my hair isn't down to my ankles, I have freckles, and my ears aren't pointed,' but men see the chest, the hips, the butt, and the pretty face—in that order—and little else. You can have any man in this city, so take your time and be picky. Make *him* work to get you."

Perched on a bar stool, Tinker spent nearly two hours and nearly a hundred dollars learning the arcane skill of applying makeup and dealing with men.

To some degree, she managed to achieve looking older than her real self. How much older, she wasn't sure, but she felt a little wiser in the ways of the world. She detoured on her way back to her bike for condoms and a can of mace for "protection, just in case of any emergencies."

It wasn't until then that she remembered Riki.

Someone had been busy while she was gone. Her workshop trailer was back into place, square and level as if it had never been moved. All the various power links were reconnected, and the air conditioner was even back in its slot. Someone had also gathered up all the blood-soaked bandages into a plastic garbage bag and then scrubbed the floor and worktable clean of blood until the air smelled sweetly of peroxide.

She would have suspected Oilcan of the progress, except that the flatbed was missing and Riki's motorcycle sat next to the office door. When she found the offices empty, she wandered through the scrap yard, wondering where the grad student was. Had he gone with Oilcan on some errand, or just taken a walk?

Finally something drew her eye toward the crane, and she found him at last, perched on the boom, sixty feet straight up. Still dressed in the black leather pants and jacket of yesterday, he sat on the end of the boom, a black dot on the blue sky.

"What the hell?" Tink scrambled up the ladder to the crane's cage.

What was he doing out there? Was he planning on jumping? How had he even gotten out there? She leaned out the window and saw that with the boom level, it was basically a straight walk out from the cage.

"Riki? Riki?" she called in a low pitch, trying to get his attention without startling him.

He glanced over his shoulder at her, the wind ruffling his black hair. "Oh, there you are."

"Sorry that I was late. I got busy and forgot about you." She winced. Maybe that wasn't the right thing to say at a time like now.

"Your cousin was here." Riki stood up and casually picked his way back along the narrow boom. He had her datapad with him, and it caught the sun and reflected it in blazes of sheer white. Blackness and brilliance, he moved through seemingly open sky. "Oilcan called Lain, and she let him know I was legit."

She drew back from the window, gripping the operator's chair. Just watching him made her suddenly afraid of falling. "What the hell are you doing out there?"

"I have a thing about heights." He leaned in the window. Unlike yesterday, he seemed relaxed and pleased, a lazy smile on his face. "They clear my head. I think better when I'm high up."

"Get in here; you're making me nervous."

He laughed and swung his long thin legs in and sat framed in the window. "Sorry. I forget how much it bugs people. The sky was too perfect, though."

She looked out the other window. The sky was a stunning deep blue, with massive stray clouds dotting it, huge and fluffy as lost sheep; only when you gazed at them, you saw how complex they were, with lines so crisp they were surreal. A cool wind scented with the endless elfin forest just beyond the Rim moved through the blueness, herding the sheep. It was the kind of sky she had sat and stared at as a child. "Yeah, it's perfect." When she turned back to him, he was watching her, head cocked to one side. "What?"

"Just that you gave that thought before you passed judgment."

"Thanks. I think."

He held out her datapad. "I was reading over your notes. They're brilliant."

She blushed as she snatched it back. "I really didn't mean for other people to see them." She glanced down at the pad. He had her theory for magic's waveform pulled up. In the scratch space, he'd worked through her equations, double-checking her work. "You followed this?"

"Mostly." He held out his hand for the pad.

She reluctantly surrendered it back.

He closed her documents and enlarged the scratch space, clearing out his work. "If I'm understanding this right, the multiple universes can be represented by a stack of paper." He drew several parallel lines. "Earth is at the bottom of the stack, and Elfhome is somewhere higher up." He labeled two of the lines appropriately. "Now magic is coming through the entire stack as a waveform." He drew a series of waves through the stack. "Since both the stack and the waveform are uniform, the point where the wave intersects the individual universe is constant; it always hits Earth at N and Elfhome at N + 1."

"In a nutshell, yes." Tinker looked at him in surprise. She had tried to explain her theory several times, but never using this model. It seemed so clear and simple. Of course, one of the reasons it was easy to understand was that Riki had ignored the fact that the universes weren't stacked like paper, but were overlapping in a manner that boggled the mind. To reach out and touch a point meant that your finger would almost be touching a zillion identical points across countless dimensions, separated only by that weird sideways step that made it another reality. Of course, only in the nearby realities were you touching that same spot. Farther away you were touching another position, and farther away, like on Elfhome, you never existed because at some extremely distant time life took a different path and elves came about instead of humans.

"This is what I don't follow." Riki pulled up her notes again, scrolled through them, and found what he was looking for. "I came here to see if I could wrap my brain around it."

"It's not fully formed." She sighed unhappily at it. "I hate it when there are things in the universe that I don't understand."

"It looks like you're trying to figure out how to reach other dimensions."

"Well, the real question is: Why do we always return to the same Elfhome? At least, we seem to. All indications are that we return to the exact dimension."

"Well, the gate generates the same field."

"Consider all the universal changes. We start on Earth, which is spinning with the gate in orbit over China, so the veil effect has to travel through the Earth's core. Then the planet is slowly wobbling through the precession of equinoxes. We've got the Moon's effect on Earth, and then the Earth moving around the Sun, which is moving around the center of the Milky Way galaxy.

"We're talking about numerous vectors that we're traveling in at any one time. That Pittsburgh returns to the same Elfhome, again and again, indicates something other than just dumb luck."

Riki grasped what she was talking about. "Like we're dealing with a universal constant. If you can travel from one dimension to a second dimension once, you'll always be able to?"

"Yeah, some commonality between the two dimensions."

"So how do you make a gate to a third dimension?"

"A third dimension?"

"Well, with countless dimensions available, why only travel to just one?"

"Two seems to be plenty for us to handle right now."

"Well, surely there are more than just two dimensions with the same commonality. You'd expect something more like a string of pearls, linked together on a silk thread."

"Oh, that's elegant." Tinker gazed out at the perfect sky, but she was looking at a strand of planets strung together in a black universe. Earth. Elfhome. Worlds unknown. "But what's the thread?"

"The gate traverses the thread."

"Yes."

"Do you understand how the gate works?"

"Oh, not you too!"

"What?"

"All of a sudden, that's all anyone seems to care about," Tinker snapped. "Gates and babies."

"Babies?" Riki cocked his head at her. "What did you do to your hair? I like it that way."

She frowned at him. Her hair? She put a hand to her hair, touched the gelled tips and suddenly recalled Nathan's date. "Oh, no, what time is it?"

Riki tugged up his leather jacket's sleeve to show his watch. It read 4:38.

"Oh shit, I'm going to be late!"

"Where are you going?"

"On a date! To the Faire! Hey, you should go. It's Midsummer Eve's Faire tonight, so it's extra special. The Faire grounds are out just beyond the Rim." She leaned out the window but the Hill blocked any sign of the Faire. She pointed out the Hill, explaining that the Faire grounds lay behind it. "Just ask anyone for directions. On any old map, its off of where Centre Avenue used to be."

"Will there be a lot of humans there?"

"Yeah, sure, don't worry; you won't stand out."

"Okay then, I'll be there."

*   *   *

There was a note tacked on her front door. By the style of paper—thick, creamy, handmade linen—and the elegant script, she guessed that it was from Windwolf. A single piece of paper trifolded, the note was sealed shut with a wafer of wax and a spell that would notify the writer that the note had been opened, and perhaps by whom. The outside had her name written so fancy that she didn't recognize it at first:

The inside gleamed softly as she unfolded, a second spell being triggered, but it faded before she could tell what it did. Unfortunately the writing was in a language that she could only guess to be High Elvish.

She considered driving to Tooloo's to get it translated, but the old half-elf would probably only lie to her. Maynard? She glanced at the clock—after five. Nathan would be here within an hour, which didn't give her time to go downtown and back. If she took it with her to the Faire, though, surely someone would be able to read it to her.

Nathan knocked at exactly six o'clock, and looked slightly dazed when she opened the door. "Wow, you look wonderful."

"Thanks!" She stepped out onto the sloop, armed her security system, and locked the door. Her outfit had no pockets, and it had taken an hour to pare things-to-be-carried down to a single key and Windwolf's note; she stood a moment, unsure what to do with the key. The note was fairly simple to carry, but she couldn't hold the key all night. Her bra presented a natural pocket, so she tucked the key under her breast. Would it stay there? She jiggled a moment. Yes. "Are we going to eat first? I forgot to eat all day."

Embarrassingly enough, Nathan had watched the whole key thing and now stammered, "Y-y-yeah, I've made reservations at one of the Rim's enclaves, Poppymeadow."

She tried to ignore the burn on her face. "I didn't think you liked elfin food."

"Well, it's like eating at my mom's; you get what's being served, and if you don't like it, they still make you eat it."

"They do not."

"Okay, they make you pay for it, and they don't give out doggie bags."

He wasn't being logical. "So why are we going?"

"Because I know you like it."

She thought of the makeover woman's advice and nodded slowly. "Okay."

In the car, Nathan became oddly silent as he headed for the Rim.

"What do people normally talk about on dates?" Tinker asked to break the silence.

Nathan shifted uncomfortably, as if this stressed that he was older and more experienced than she was. "Well, normally you get to know each other. Where you're from, who your parents are, if you have brothers and sisters. You know. Background info."

"We know all that."

"Yeah," Nathan said unhappily. "Common interests and if nothing else, the weather."

Common interests? Bowling? That made her think of Windwolf. No, no, not a good idea.

"It sure was hot this Shutdown." She started the inane conversation about the weather.

As the steelworkers had at one time divided themselves into richly ethnic neighborhoods, so did the current inhabitants. The UN workers, which made up the bulk of the EIA, lived within downtown's triangle of land, using the rivers to shield them on two sides against packs of wargs, the occasional saurus, and other Elfhome creatures with big mouths and sharp teeth. On the South Side, sheltered less so by the Monongahela River and the bulk of Mount Washington, was a set of Americans whose expertise was the freight trains that did the East Coast run. Mixed in with them were the oil workers who kept a steady supply of natural gas flowing throughout the region, supplied by gas wells long since tapped on Earth. On the sliver of the North Side remaining, a Chinatown had grown up, part of the treaty with China when their gate triggered the whole mess. Native Pittsburghers were sprinkled everywhere, refusing to move despite everything.

Lastly, in Oakland, were the elves.

The elfin businesses sat just beyond the part of old Oakland that had been razed by the Rim. The southern side of the street was graveled parking lots with large warning signs that the lot fell into the Rim's influence during Shutdown and Startup. The northern side of the street was elfin enclaves, half a block wide, high-walled and gated, built firmly on Elfhome. Once through the gates, one was into lush private gardens filled with exotic flowers, songbirds, and glowing cousins to fireflies.

Since it was Midsummer Eve, the traffic was heavy for Pittsburgh, and Nathan had to cruise the parking lot for several minutes to find a space. Most of the crowd, however, were heading several blocks to the east where the Earth street ended abruptly in the Faire grounds.

There was a group of mostly elves waiting to be seated as Tinker and Nathan came down the garden path of the Poppymeadow enclave. A female elf with long silvery hair that nearly reached her ankles glanced toward Tinker. Her eyes went wide in surprised recognition. "Tinker *ze domi*!"

Tinker startled; of the handful of elves she knew, this wasn't one. She glanced behind her to see if maybe an elf noble named Tinker was standing behind her. The garden path was empty.

The other waiting diners turned, saw Tinker, and bowed low, murmuring, "Tinker *ze domi*!"

She didn't recognize any of them. To cover her confusion, Tinker bobbed a shallow bow to the crowd and gave a semi-informal greeting. "*Nasadae!*"

The *domo* of Poppymeadow pushed through the diners, bowed low, and gushed out High Elvish faster than Tinker could hope to follow.

"Please, please, *Taunte*," she begged him to use the low tongue.

"You honor me!" the *domo* cried, taking hold of her hands. "Come. Come. You must have the finest seat in the house."

He guided the bewildered Tinker through the waiting diners, into the public eating areas, and to an elegant table set into a small alcove. Nathan followed, looking as mystified as Tinker felt. "Here! Let me be the first to wish you merry!"

"Thank you, but . . ." Tinker started to ask why they were fussing over her, but the *domo* was already gone.

"What was that all about?" Nathan asked.

"I'm not sure," Tinker said slowly.

"What were they saying?"

"You don't speak Elvish?"

"Not really. Just enough to do a traffic stop. What did they say?"

Tinker flashed to the patrol guard who had roughed her up at the hospice on Startup. She pushed the ugly comparison away; no, Nathan wasn't like that. Wait. The hospice.

"Tinker?"

"Um, they recognized me somehow, but I don't know them." Or did she? Was the silver-haired female the one who had helped with the surgery on her hand? Startup had been a blur, but that would be a whole crop of elves who would know her.

"Maybe they know you from the hoverbike racing," Nathan suggested.

Elves called her Tinker-*tiki* at the races, which was a friendly informal condescending address, on the order of "baby Tinker." This had been Tinker *ze domi*, an address of extreme politeness. More likely these *were* elves who knew her from the hospice. Certainly between her arrival with the flatbed at Startup, and Windwolf carrying her through the hospice yelling the next morning, and this morning's fight with the NSA, she had made herself memorable enough. All the elves at the hospice most likely knew that she had saved . . .

Realization hit her. She barely kept her hand from reaching up and touching her forehead. The elves had to be reacting to Windwolf's mark! She glanced worriedly at Nathan. If he thought this weirdness meant that Windwolf did have some claim on her . . . She winced; she didn't want to deal with a jealous Nathan again. What a mess.

The *domo* returned with a bottle labeled in Elvish, two drinking bowls, and a small silver dish of something white. While she was trying to decide if it was sugar or salt or something more exotic, the *domo* flicked it onto her, exclaiming, "*Linsa tanlita lintou!*" He continued in Low Elvish, saying. "May you be merry!"

What the hell? Tinker blinked in surprise, too confused even to form a reaction.

The *domo* pushed one of the small drinking bowls into her hands, saying, "Praise be to the gods."

She at least knew how to react to that. "Praise be," she said, and drank the wine. What was in the glass was clear, sweet as candy, and burned the whole way down. While she gasped for breath, the *domo* vanished again.

"You okay?" Nathan asked, and she nodded. "What did he throw on you?"

"I think it was salt."

"Why?"

"I don't know." Nor could she guess. What had the *domo* said? *Linsa* and *lintou* were both forms of the same word—purity. *Tanlita* was the word *tanta* meaning "will make" in its female form. Pure into purity? Purity into cleanliness?

The food began to arrive on tiny delicate handpainted dishes. At an enclave, you ate what you were served. Tinker usually liked it because there were no choices to be made, and you weren't stuck with a large portion of something that was only so-so, or in envy of what another person ordered. Sure, you never knew what you were about to be served, or sometimes had already eaten, but it made the entire meal an adventure.

She could really do without adventure and mystery in her life right about now.

Like most businesses in Pittsburgh, the enclaves relied heavily on local produce to supplement the supplies brought in during Shutdown. Thus the dishes appearing before Tinker and Nathan featured woodland mushrooms, walnuts, trout, venison, hare, keva beans, and raspberries. Luckily the dishes came with built-in conversation: *What do you suppose this is? Oh, this is good. Is there more? Are you going to eat that?*

It made it easy for Tinker to ponder what the *domo* meant by "wish you merry." Had she translated that right? Merry what? Merry dinner? Merry Midsummer's Eve? Merry Christmas? Why did languages have to be so vague? This is why she loved math!

During the third round of dishes, the other diners started to appear at the table. They would slip up, eye Nathan doubtfully as he grew more and more surly, then smile warmly at Tinker and press something into her hand, saying, "I wish you merry!" The first was the silver-haired female, with a flower plucked from the enclave garden, which seemed innocent enough. It wasn't until the second diner pressed a silver dime into Tinker's hands that she realized she should have refused the flower. Now she couldn't refuse following gifts without grave insult, something you didn't do with elves. So she smiled and accepted the dime and prayed that Nathan wouldn't blow a gasket. Flowers, coins, note paper folded into packets containing salt, and slender vines woven into a small wicker cage holding a firefly followed.

"What's with the bug?" Nathan asked.

"I don't know." She winced as she realized that she was whining. "It is kind of cute, in a weird kind of way."

"Why are they doing this?"

"If I told you, you'd get all bent out of shape, and I don't want to deal with that."

He frowned at her and pushed his latest dish away. "Look, why don't we just go to the Faire? I don't feel like eating any more."

The *domo* saved her from having to abandon all the gifts behind. He came forward with a basket while Nathan went off to settle up the bill.

Under all the gifts, she found Windwolf's note. "Please, can you read this—and translate it to low tongue for me?"

"Yes, certainly." He glanced over the note. "It is from Wolf Who

Rules. He—" a pause as the *domo* worked through translation from formal to informal "—will see you at the Faire."

Oh wonderful.

"What is it you say: I wish you merry?" she asked awkwardly. "Merry what?"

"Life. I wish you a merry life. May all good things come to you."

That seemed harmless enough. Nathan appeared, waiting, so she didn't ask about the salt or the gifts.

They stopped at the Buick and dropped off the basket. Night had fallen, and the Faire had awakened a gleam of multicolored lights and the beat of exotic music. There by the car, they seemed to be in their own envelope of space-time. Nathan pulled her close, kissing her while slipping his hands under her silk duster and running his hands down the back of her dress. For a little while, it was very nice; his strong warm body holding her, the smell of his musky cologne, and the excitement of kissing in the open darkness. It felt similar to when she raced her bike fast down Observatory Hill, exhilarated by the speed, heart leaping to her throat every time she slid out of control toward the edge of the tree-lined road.

At some point, though, Nathan realized that the duster shielded his hands from any chance passersby, and he slipped them down and then back up, this time under her dress. He straightened slightly, pulling her off her feet, at the same time kissing down her neck to nuzzle into her breasts.

"Nathan." It was getting too scary, and she was a little angry that he was taking it so fast, out in the open, as if he wanted to be seen, so that everyone would think that she belonged to him. It was as if this was his way of marking her.

"No one's here." He was strong enough that he could support her easily with one hand. Their joint focus became his free hand, rough fingertips on her inner thigh, exploring higher.

"Nathan!" she hissed, wriggling in his hold. "Someone might come. Put me down."

"We could get into the car," he groaned into her hair.

Into the car and what? Did he think the car afforded shadows deep enough to disguise what he wanted to do? Or in the car, they could go to someplace more appropriate? His place? Her place?

"No." She squirmed more, tempted now to use elbows, knees, and the practically sharpened tip of her shoes. "I want to go to the Faire."

He gave a long-suffering sigh. "Are you sure?"

"Yes!"

"All right." He set her back onto her feet. "Let's go to the Faire."

*   *   *

The first booth beyond the gate was a portable shrine to Redoeya; she paused to clap and bow to the statue and drop a dime into his silver-strewn hands. She considered, eyes closed, hands clasped. What was it that she wanted? In earlier years she had prayed for things as simple as winning something from one of the booths. Searching her heart, she found only conflicting desires. Finally she prayed simply: *May I figure out what it is I want in life.*

"Why do you do that?" Nathan had hung back, looking a mix of annoyed and bewildered.

"I always do that." She headed for the sweet bun stands as Faire custom number two; one needed to get them fresh and hot. "Tooloo said that if Grandpa wasn't going to put me in the protection of human gods, then she'd see me protected by the elfin ones."

He made a face.

"What?"

"Oh, I was fairly sure you weren't Catholic, but I expected you to be at least Christian."

"And?"

"Nothing."

Nathan bought sweet buns for both of them, and they drifted on, pulled by the tidal force of moving bodies.

There was more of everything at the Faire than she'd ever seen before. Another row had been added to the basic grid to accommodate the additional booths. Despite the extra space, more people strolled through the aisles: elves dressed in human fashions, humans dressed in elfin fashion, parents with infants, couples of mixed races, and most surprisingly of all, armed guards of both races. Tinker had never seen on-duty guards at the Faire before. She wasn't sure if the tension she felt came from the armed presence, or her own sudden unease with Nathan.

"I can't believe there are armed guards here," she said to Nathan as they passed the third guard, her dark EIA uniform and flat black gun a black hole for attention.

"The viceroy was nearly murdered twice," Nathan said. "And then there's the whole thing with the smuggling ring. With this many people in one place, it's the smart thing to do."

"I don't like it."

"You wouldn't have ended up tangling with that saurus if there'd been more than Windwolf and his bodyguard at the Faire."

Tinker flashed to that day, the saurus standing with a foot pinning the lower half of Windwolf's bodyguard to the ground and his upper half in its mouth. In an image that haunted her nightmares, the saurus pulled upward, stretching the guard's body obscenely long before shaking its head, tearing the male in half. She shuddered. "Let's not talk about that."

But once called up, she couldn't stop thinking about the day. Strange how she couldn't recall Windwolf's location until he was yelling in her face to run, and how, even now, she didn't remember him as wounded, only angry.

In a sudden rewrite of history that was almost dizzying, she realized that Windwolf had lost a friend that day, not only torn to shreds but also eaten. How long had they known each other? A hundred years? Poor Windwolf! No wonder he had been so angry.

"Guess." Nathan interrupted her thoughts.

"What?"

"So guess what they named the baby."

Baby? She glanced around and spotted a human woman showing off her baby to curious elves. She had always thought it odd that elves seemed fascinated by babies, but considering what Windwolf had said, a young adult elf may have never seen an infant in his or her life. She had to admit there was something intriguing about the miniaturization of a being that babies represented, but they were, on a whole, too fragile for her to deal with. She supposed that if someday she had "kids" she would have to deal with "babies"—an utterly frightening thought.

Nathan was still waiting for her to guess the baby's name and was growing impatient.

"I don't know the mother. Who is she?"

"What?" A frown quirked at the corner of Nathan's mouth as he scanned the brightly dressed crowd. "No. Not her," he said, spotting the baby being passed around the knot of adults. "My sister's baby. Guess what they called my niece."

Oh, yes, his sister Ginny lived in Bethel Park. She had been waiting for Shutdown to go to Earth in order to have her second child, but the baby came a week early, and she delivered at Mercy Hospital. When Tinker had talked to Nathan before Shutdown his sister hadn't named the baby yet.

"Oh. Um. After you?" Was there a female version of "Nathan"?

"No. Mercy. Mercy Anne."

Yuk! Tinker tried to keep her face neutral and made polite noises. Luckily they'd collided with the mass of people listening to the musicians onstage at the edge of the Faire ground. She didn't recognize the group's name, but they were a common mixed-race band, blending the raw American rock beat and guitars with traditional elfin instruments and melodies. They featured an *olianuni,* and an obvious master playing it, his mallets a blur as he hammered. The guitars snarled around the rich deep bell-like melody beat out by the *olianuni* player. The lead singer was human, growling out a song about the shortness of human life and the reckless abandonment with which the race embraced its fate. In a high pure counter, the elfin backup singer chanted out the thousand blessings of patience.

"Want to dance?" Tinker shouted to Nathan, bobbing in place to the beat of the music.

"Actually, I was working my way to something. Can we find someplace quieter to talk?"

"Okay." Still moving with the beat of the song, she threaded her way through the crowd, trusting him to find a way to follow.

"You know"—he caught up with her beside a fishing booth, where people were trying to fish brightly gleaming *pesantiki* out of a pool with small paper nets—"if you let me go first, I'd open up a path for you to follow."

"Then all I could see would be your back. You can see over me. Here, let's sit."

The next booth down was the *okonomiyaki* cart that usually sat in Market Square. Side benches folded down from it, and there were banners hanging down from the bamboo awning to give the deception of privacy.

"You're still hungry?" Nathan asked.

"I didn't get to eat a lot at the enclave." She felt a little guilty. Enclaves charged a set price that was rather steep. She held up the bag of silver dimes. "Let me pay."

"No, I'll pay." Nathan thumbed out some coins to the Asian man on the other side of the griddle.

They ordered their toppings, and the chef started to mix up the eggs, water, flour, and cabbage for the pancake.

"So?"

"The family across the street from my sister decided to emigrate back to the States, and they signed over their house to the EIA. They had a nice place: a four-bedroom Cape Cod with a two-car garage, and a natural-gas furnace with a wood burner backup system."

"Your point being?"

"Well, it got me thinking," Nathan said. "The house would be a nice starter place for you and me."

"What?" Her cry startled the chef.

"It's a nice place, well maintained. We could nab it now and move in later."

She could only stare at him in surprise.

"We put up curtains," Nathan said. "Buy a few pieces of furniture, and no one would know the difference. It needs sprucing up, so we take our time painting and such."

"You want to live together?"

Nathan took her hand. "I want to marry you."

"Whoa, whoa, whoa. What happened to waiting until I'm nineteen? I thought this was just a date."

"I don't mean right away. I don't want to rush you."

"I don't know—talking about marriage on a first date sounds like rushing."

Nathan winced. "Sorry, I suppose it is. It's just that this house is so perfect. My brother-in-law took me through the place. The rooms are large and sunny, the woodwork is all natural, there's this marvelous stone fireplace in the living room, and there's a level backyard for kids."

Kids?

Her face must have reflected her shock. He laughed.

"It's only eleven months until you're nineteen. In less than two years you'll be twenty." Nathan sounded like he was trying to convince himself. "We've got to look ahead. Sure there are lots of houses out there. Most of them have been standing empty for years; the pipes and windows are broken and roofs need to be replaced. This place is cherry."

"Nathan, I really meant it when I said we should date to see if we liked one another as more than friends. I don't know if I want to marry you."

There was a moment of hurt hidden quickly away. "I'm sorry, Tink; I shouldn't be pushing. I'm the one, after all, who wanted to wait until you're nineteen."

"Yeah." Tinker shook her head vigorously and then looked down, embarrassed to be suddenly so eager to wait. "Is this about the mark? You're rushing because Windwolf made me part of his family?"

"That has nothing to do with it," Nathan said, so surlily that she figured it had everything to do with it.

"Oh, come on, Nathan, he's the viceroy. He's rich and powerful and could have any woman, elf or human, that he wants."

"Exactly."

"Look at me!"

"You're beautiful."

"Not when you compare me to high-caste elf females. You've

seen them; everyone on the street stops and stares until they're out of sight."

"Maybe he has a thing for human women," Nathan said.

The possibility that Windwolf might like human women made her insides go weird, like someone had dropped them through hyperspace to some point billions of miles from where she stood. She tried to root herself back to reality and ignore the possible "delicate arrangements" that the brazier might indicate. "I saved his life, twice now. He feels indebted to me. I'm an orphan. He's an elf; he's nearly twelve times my age. He's probably just acting like a father figure to me."

"This has nothing to do with Windwolf." Nathan reached out and took her hand. "It's just made me think, that's all. You're a legal adult. There's no *real* reason to wait."

Having just compared herself to elfin females, Tinker felt a stab of sympathy and guilt for Nathan. How could he compete for her attention when just the idea of Windwolf kept making her feel all goofy? Nathan's interest in her had been intriguing until he started to talk about marriage. All of Windwolf, from his thoughts to his interest, did weird things to her emotions.

Nathan was waiting for an answer, and she didn't know what to say. She scrambled for something, and came up with, "I've got to go pee."

Nathan let go of her hand, and she fled. Why did he have to go all serious on her? Why couldn't he just take it slow and let her get used to the idea? And what was that scene at the parking lot? Was he going to try that again the moment they were alone in his car? Did he think they were going to have sex tonight?

Suddenly she just wanted to be home in her own bed, alone.

She headed for the Faire entrance, but her tight skirt and high heels were making it difficult to run away. And how was she going to get home? Like a fool, she hadn't brought money enough for a taxi. She could call Oilcan, but how would he react? He might think something worse had happened between her and Nathan—and that would be bad.

She hit a patch of soft dirt, and her heels sunk deep, making her trip. Hands caught her before she fell, righting her.

"Thank y—oh." Her words dried in her mouth as she realized it was Windwolf holding her lightly.

What was it about him that inspired so many emotions all at once? She peered up at the viceroy for all of the Westernlands. Gosh, what did she even call him? Your Majesty? All she managed was a faint, "Hey."

"I am glad to see with my own eyes," Windwolf said as quietly, "that you are well."

"I'm okay." She balanced against him while she took off her shoes. High heels in dirt being mistake number ten or eleven for her tonight. "Maynard took care of me."

"Ah, good." Windwolf relieved her of her shoes, handing them off to one of his guards. "Come with me. My car is waiting."

"Great!" She took a step forward and then stopped. "Oh, wait. I told Nathan I was just going to—um—going to the rest room. He'd worry if I just disappeared." He'd also probably call out a manhunt for her, and that might get the NSA involved.

"Describe this Nathan. I will send someone with a message."

Oh, that was tempting. Whatever had caused her to bolt suddenly—it wasn't quite fear, she told herself, just huge anxiety—receded in Windwolf's presence. "No." She held his hand tightly, drawing strength. "I should go back and tell him myself." Tell Nathan what, she wasn't sure. Oh, gods, what a mess. "It would be proper."

Windwolf bowed his head, and they started to retrace her route. Now, what was she going to say? *Nathan, I'm going home with Windwolf.* No. *Windwolf is taking me home.* No. *Windwolf is dropping me at my loft.* That sounded innocent enough. Nathan was going to ask why. *Because—because—because you're scaring the shit out of me.* "Oh, be real, this is Nathan after all."

"Pardon?" Windwolf leaned closer to hear her mumbled comment.

"Nothing. I'm just trying out apologies."

The crowd had been parting like waves when Nathan appeared before them, a rock to smash up against.

"What's going on here?" Nathan stared at Tinker's right hand holding Windwolf's.

Tinker hadn't even been aware that she still held tight to Windwolf. She fought the urge to snatch her hand free. She wasn't doing anything wrong. "I—I—I need to go home. Windwolf is dropping me at my loft."

"I'll take you home." Nathan took her left hand.

"Nathan!" she whined. Why did he have to be so dense? "Things went too fast tonight. I just want to go home."

"So I'll take you home." Nathan gave her hand a gentle tug.

Windwolf stepped in front of Tinker and caught Nathan's wrist. "No. She is coming with me."

"Look, you stay out of this." Nathan dropped into cop mode, and his voice went hard. "This is between me and her. Elves have no say in this."

"You did not listen to her. She is saying no. Now let her go."

The two males locked angry gazes at one another, ignoring her completely, while each holding on to one of her hands. She felt like a bone between two dogs.

"Nathan!" She tried pulling free of him. "Look, I just need some time to think about things. Give me time."

Nathan finally looked at her, and there was a world of pain in his eyes. "I'm sorry if things went too fast. Just don't go away with him."

Things went too fast? No, you went too fast! But she didn't say it aloud because she'd used the phrase first: It bothered her that he didn't own up to his actions, though. "Please, Nathan, let me go."

Nathan glanced hard at Windwolf, but then sighed and dropped her hand.

"I'll see you later," she promised. "We'll talk. Okay?"

"Yeah. We'll talk."

Having done the proper thing, she fled with Windwolf.

7: CARBON-BASED TRANSFORMATION

Windwolf's car was a silver Rolls-Royce. Buttery-soft leather covered the seats. The privacy shield between the front and back sections turned opaque. The door shut, enclosing them in a womb of darkness, and Tinker discovered that the barriers between her and Windwolf remained down. Despite the couch-sized backseat, Windwolf sat close beside her, their bodies touching in the dark.

"You look lovely," Windwolf murmured into her ear.

She breathed in his warm scent, of sandalwood and leather. "How did you find me?"

"I had notes delivered to every place you might be today. You opened one and triggered the tracking spell on it. I would have found you anywhere tonight."

"Oh."

He cradled her left hand in his. "I would have come for you sooner, but there was much to prepare." He bowed his head over her hand, and kissed her palm, soft as butterflies alighting. "I wish there was more time, but that is something that you, as a human, do not have. Just yesterday, it seems, you were a child. I lost that chance to protect you. Now that I have found you, and come to know you, I do not wish to lose you again."

He ran his tongue feather light over the pulse point on her wrist, just as he had done at the hospice. Gods, it felt even better when she was fully awake.

Her fingers curved and touched the supple pearl of his ear lobe. She found herself exploring the alien beauty of his ear, so different from her own. "You don't mind me touching you?"

"Tonight it is you, not the *saijin*," he said huskily.

She took that as permission to explore. No stubble marred the line of his jaw, as elves did not have facial hair. He kissed her fingers as she glided them over his full mouth. In the strong column of his neck, she found his pulse just over his high shirt collar. Hard muscles played under the warm silk. By touch she found the structure of his shoulders, the solidness of bone. She came to the line of his buttons, and he undid them before her curious fingers. His skin under the shirt was soft and smooth as the silk, sculptured into taut muscles.

"Do you lift weights?" she whispered as he shifted them, lifting up her knee as he settled back against the seat, pulling her after him. In one graceful motion, she found herself straddling his lap, facing him.

"It is the sword play, it is hard work."

Her exploration peeled back his shirt, laying bare his upper torso. The cloth lay draped across his back and over his forearms. His nipples were dark coins and his abdomen a stack of well-defined muscles. His shirttails were still tucked into his pants; white silk cut off by black suede. Her dress had ridden up where she straddled Windwolf, and they pressed together with anatomical correctness, only leather and silk separating them.

What was she doing? She just bolted from Nathan, afraid of going too fast, and here she was, stripping the clothes off of Windwolf.

But being with Nathan had been like losing the brakes on a big truck—careening out of control. He had scared her. He picked her up, and overwhelmed her with his strength. What's more, there had been none of this gentle exploration; Nathan had zeroed in on her private zones, ignoring the tiny erotic places that Windwolf exploited. Windwolf had yet to touch her beyond her arms and back.

If she had gone home with Nathan, what they would have had was sex.

What she was doing with Windwolf—it felt like making love. She rested her hand on his chest, and felt the beat of his heart, and knew that she trusted him. She leaned forward and kissed him tentatively. He opened his mouth to her, and he tasted of plums.

"Can the driver see us?" she whispered, her heart hammering in her chest at her own boldness.

"No. Nor can he hear. We are in our own private space here."

"Make love to me. I want you to be my first."

"Gladly." He touched her cheek. "But not here. We're nearly at the lodge."

Lodge? The landscape beyond the windows was dark, and she suddenly realized that they hadn't gone through downtown, that they weren't heading for her loft. Pittsburgh was far behind them, and they traveled now through the primal forests of Elfhome.

"Where are we going?"

"When I'm in Pittsburgh, I use this hunting lodge." Windwolf looked out into the passing darkness. "It was the only structure here before Pittsburgh arrived. I've had it enlarged, but it is not very convenient. We're just arriving."

She got the impression of the forest growing only slightly less dense before the Rolls came to a stop. For a moment she was annoyed that they hadn't gone to her place, and then she thought of all the dirty dishes piled in her kitchen sink, and her dirty clothes strewn on her bedroom floor. Okay, so Windwolf's place would be classier than hers.

"Come." Windwolf slid out from under her. "There is not much time. We must hurry."

The driver opened their door. Windwolf got out without bothering to button his shirt.

She scrambled after him, puzzled and frustrated. She thought things were working up to them making love. "Why are we hurrying?"

"There are times when a spell is more likely to succeed than others." Windwolf took her hand and led her through a row of tall trees, branches interwoven, their pale bark gleaming in the candlelight. Moss-covered boulders lurked like giants in the shadows beyond the trees. "It has to do with the alignment of stars and planets, the Sun and Moon, the nature of the magic. A blessing should be done at noon, when the Moon is full and in the day's sky. A curse should be done at night, after the set of the new Moon, when none of the planets are on the horizon."

Windwolf chose a path down into a steep ravine, across a stream on an arched wooden bridge, and up steps cut into living rock. "Sometimes there is leeway. An optimal effect comes when the conditions are right, but still, the spell can be cast even if the time is wrong. A blessing can be placed at night, but it will not be as strong."

"Perhaps it has to do with gravity." *Where were they going?*

On the summit sat a lone structure; an open shelter with fairy silk hung from the eaves. It glowed softly like a Chinese lantern, surrounded by dark, silent forest. Tinker paused, glancing back the way they'd come, and found they'd climbed up above the treetops. Pittsburgh was nowhere to be seen on the night horizon. The moon was rising, bright as a spotlight, already washing out the brilliance of Jupiter, Saturn, Mars, and Venus' conjunction.

"This spell should be done now." Windwolf kissed her brow, his breath warm on her face. "The conditions will never be this perfect again, not in a human's lifetimes."

"What spell?"

"Come," he urged her to the shelter.

One of the silk panels had been tied back, and looking inside, she recognized the building for what it was.

One heard of such places, where elves did powerful spells. Secluded away from anything that could affect a spell, the sites rested on the intersection of strong ley lines, tapping directly into an incredible amount of power. Those ley lines were permanently carved into a floor of white marble. White to show the tracings of a spell. Stone to act as a natural insulator. The marble sat on a bedrock limestone, and the wooden shelter was constructed with no nails, containing not a single scrap of metal.

"Wow!" Tinker whispered.

A massively complex spell was inked out onto the shelter's stone floor. Even without knowing the spell, Tinker recognized it as a major enchantment. She studied the design, trying to find any components she knew. She could pick out that they built in an error-testing loop, and a slight blur on the tracings indicated that they had done a debugging run already.

"Take this off." Windwolf slid her jacket off her shoulders. "There is metal woven into it."

Tinker shuddered at the thought of wearing metal near an active spell. She stepped out of her high heels, balancing with one hand on Windwolf's arm; her shoes might have a steel shank worked into them. Jacket and high heels went onto a wooden table beside them, well outside the shelter. Tinker fished through her bra until she found the key to her loft. The key joined the others on the table.

"So, what is this?" Tinker asked. "I thought we were going to make love."

"We will." He kissed a line up her bare shoulder to the nape of her neck.

"Oh, good." She reached for him and found his shirt still unbuttoned, all that wonderful, warm skin to explore.

He unzipped her dress and eased it off her, murmuring, "This too must go."

She pressed against him, using him as a shield against prying eyes. "What if someone comes?"

"No one will come." He held her close as he dropped her dress onto the table. "They know we wish privacy. You have more metal on. Once we remove it, the curtains will shield us."

She glanced downward at her bra and panties. "More metal? Where?"

"This." He indicated the bra's wire under her breasts and then the tiny hooks clasping the fabric tight.

"Remove my bra?" *Yes, Einstein, you have to take off your clothes to make love.* She swallowed down the jolt of fear, and, turning her back to him, she fumbled with the hooks.

"Let me." Windwolf undid the clasps—his knuckles brushing her back—and her bra went loose. She trapped the fabric to her chest, as the straps slid down over her shoulders, making her feel suddenly naked.

"Do not be afraid." He kissed her on her spine. "Nothing will happen that you do not allow."

You want this. You want him. Stop being a coward. She tossed her bra toward the table and turned to face Windwolf.

Amazingly, a moment later, in his loose hold, skin touching skin, she no longer knew why she'd been so scared. It seemed that the more nerve endings were involved, the better kissing became.

"Much as I wish there was more time, we must start." Windwolf stepped away from her, voice husky, and unbuttoned his pants.

Tinker turned away from him, blushing furiously. She had just gotten used to the concept of being half-naked in front of him. Despite being raised by men, she had never seen a male nude outside of Lain's anatomy books. "What's the rush?"

"The spell must start while the moon is high."

The spell? She'd forgotten all about the mysterious design inked out onto the white marble. "Wha-wha-what exactly—"

He eased her back to settle against him, only the thin silk of her panties separating them. Naked and aroused, he felt like a shaft of polished wood. Awareness of him forced the air out of her lungs.

"We are at a branching." He held her, letting her grow accustomed to his presence. "To the left, every path leads to death. No matter which way you go, you will die."

"Me?"

"Yes, you." He nibbled lightly on her ear lobe. "And I do not wish to lose you. You have become very dear to me."

"I'm going to die?"

"If we do this spell, no. It is the path on the right, which leads to life. I wish there was more time for you to decide, but the full moon rises, and the planets align tonight. This is the perfect time, which will quickly pass."

She huddled in his arms, stunned by her mortality. She was going to die? Her stay at the hospice must have revealed something. She shuddered, remembering how quickly her grandfather died once he fell ill.

"Trust me, my little, savage Tink." He kissed her neck, finding some pleasure zone that she didn't know existed.

Trust him? Wasn't that the line that men always used? But she did trust him, perhaps more than she knew, perhaps more than she should.

"Shall we do the spell?" Windwolf asked.

She nodded her head, mute with shock.

He hooked his thumbs into the band of her panties and slid them down. With gentle pressure, he pushed her out across the spell to its center. She could feel the power shimmering through the spell tracing through her bare feet, the marble warm with resistance-generated heat.

"This isn't exactly what I expected when I asked you to make love to me."

"I will make it good for you." He stopped her at the center of the stone, the spell radiating out around them. "And because of tonight, there will be other times, at our leisure."

Other times.

He pulled her close, his right hand following the curve of her body, slipping down to caress her with shocking intimacy. He was at once hard as stone, and soft as petals. She could do nothing more than squirm in his grasp as he gently touched her. Electric shocks of pleasure shot through her with every caress.

She felt like a rag doll in his arms. He handled her with his incredible elfin strength. She seemed to weigh nothing. She had no form, bent supply to give him access to her pleasure points. He lit a golden ember of sexual pleasure in her, and then stoked it to a molten heat. He would not let her touch him, returning her hands to her own body until she realized that all of her focus must remain on herself.

As she started to moan, he spoke a word of power, activating the spell. The outer shell of the spell took form and rose up to rotate clockwise. When her first tremors of impending release hit her, changing her moans to cries of joy, he spoke a second word. A second and third shell shimmered into being, canting up to spin counterclockwise at 45- and 135-degree angles. The magic grew dense, a visible shimmer.

Windwolf muffled her then with his mouth, and shifted himself so that he moved now between her parted legs, a hardness sliding through her wetness. She wanted him with a sudden wanton desperation. She wanted him inside of her, wanted to be taken. The force of it frightened her, and if she had been less a captive, she would have wriggled away, fled her own desires. He held her in his iron grasp, muffling anything she might have said, so she could neither plead with him to stop nor urge him on.

When she trembled on the peak, he slid into her to her maidenhead.

She bucked and cried out at the intrusion, the sense of being filled spilling her over the edge into release.

He lifted his mouth, spoke a word, and muffled her again.

The fourth shell rose, and it reflected that moment back at her, intensifying it, and then reflecting the next level back. She barely noticed the pain as he broke through and thrust into complete union. She was aware only of the golden tide of pleasure. He spent himself, uncoupled, and then turned her in his arms. Cautiously, he released her, touching her briefly on the mouth to remind her of silence. She clasped her hand over her mouth, unable to keep silent in any other way.

The pleasure continued, rolling like the tide, over and over her, each wave stronger than the last. Her skin gleamed with its essence, and she drifted in midair, suspended by magic.

He dipped his fingers into her, and then traced symbols on her skin, dropping words of power like stones.

"Nesfa." Seed. *"Nota."* Blood. *"Kira."* Mirror. *"Kirat."* Reflect. *"Dashavat."* Transform.

He stepped away from her, made a motion, and leaped out of the shell. Turning her head, she saw him land at the part in the curtain. He gazed into her eyes, raised his hand, and spoke the final word.

Her universe became brilliant, blissful oblivion.

The elfin ceiling was quite amazing. Arched somewhere high above her, it had been dark when she awoke, but phased slowly to a pale rose color like the morning sky would as the sun crept to the horizon. After that, it blushed slowly to a pale white, then deepened into a delicate blue.

She felt hollow, and fragile, an eggshell, broken and empty, the life released and flown away. Her mind seemed to come online as gradually as the ceiling. In a calm, detached way she reasoned out that the ceiling looked odd because it was unknown, and then guessed it was the one at Windwolf's hunting lodge, and finally figured out what she was doing under it. *Oh yeah, we made love. So that's sex? Oh, hoo-chee mama! I definitely want to do that again.*

Windwolf said there would be other times. That thought made her squirm with delighted anticipation. She lolled in a nest of soft, white linens recalling all the sensations of being with him, the feel of his hard muscles, strong hands, and warm mouth. She tried not to think how pissed Nathan would be at what she'd done—and failed. She'd bullied him into a date, dropped him in public, and went off to make love to another male. And the worst thing about it, everyone else seemed to see it coming but her, so she was going to get the "young and inexperienced" speech from everyone.

Groping about, she found a pillow and screamed into it. Oh, why did Nathan have to be such a jealous butthead? If he hadn't started talking about marriage and kids, she wouldn't have gone off with Windwolf—or would she? Certainly it had been Windwolf she had been having kinky dreams about and the one that made her heart do silly things.

But Nathan would be the one waiting for her back at the scrap yard. She groaned but forced herself to sit up. While Oilcan could run the business short-term, and now had Riki to help, she still had to get back to work. Between saving Windwolf, her stay at the hospice, the NSA's kidnapping, and a day wasted getting ready for Nathan's aborted date she'd lost four days out of the week already.

Tinker crawled from the bed. Her clothes, cleaned, pressed, and folded, sat at the foot of the bed. Something was odd about her body, but she couldn't figure out what. Everything looked the same. Her underwear, at least, fit comfortably. For some reason her dress seemed stiff and uncomfortable. No matter, she'd need to change before heading to the yard. Her house key had been strung on a silk cord; she slipped it over her head, and it lay ice cold on her chest.

The stone floor was warm underfoot, so she carried her high heels to the door and slid it open. The hallway beyond opened directly to woods idealized; surely no random lot of trees could be so beautiful without careful, invisible work.

There was an elf in the hall too, of the heavily armed guard variety. His hair and eyes were black as engine grease, and he had a build that imparted a sense of sturdiness, which was rare in elves.

"Tinker *ze domi*," he said in careful Low Elvish, and bowed deeply to her, which creeped her out. "*Domou* is not here. He and

Sparrow Lifted By Wind were summoned away. He left word that you were to be given anything you wanted."

"Who? Windwolf?" And getting no reaction, Tinker struggled the full mouthful of Elvish that was Windwolf's real name. "Windwolf?"

"Yes. Windwolf." Obviously the elf had never used Windwolf's English name. He pronounced it as if he didn't speak English, or didn't recognize the two words that made up Windwolf's name. "Windwolf is not here."

"I want to go home."

"Do-do-domi," the elf stammered out, "Aum Renau is very far away."

Huh? "I want to go to Pittsburgh." She tried again, slower. *"Pitsubaug."*

He looked to his right and left, seemingly seeking someone to translate. Surely her Low Elvish wasn't that bad. "Pittsburgh? Now?"

"Yes, now."

He considered her for a silent minute, a foot taller and a foot wider than she, and then bowed again. "As you wish, *domi.*"

She'd missed quite a bit during the trip north while making out with Windwolf in the Rolls' backseat. They traveled half an hour just on elfin roads cut through dense forest until they reached the Rim, coming out near what was left of Sewickley. They went directly to the scrap yard gate, and from there she gave directions to her loft.

"Stop here," Tinker said as they pulled up to her building. She got out, and then put out a hand to block the elf, who showed every sign of following her into her loft. She knew her nerves wouldn't take someone underfoot. "Um, thanks for the ride. Let Windwolf know I got home safe."

"I'm not sure if—"

"I want to be left alone."

The elf nodded, and she closed the door.

There were messages from Nathan on her home system, the scrap yard's line, and at her workshop. She let them play while she showered, piloting on automatic. The hollow feeling persisted, and it was hard to concentrate, as if her thoughts wanted to float around the empty space.

What had Windwolf done to her? What had been wrong with her? She hadn't felt sick.

There was a banging at her door, and Nathan's voice. She wrapped a towel around her and went to answer the door.

The Rolls was still at the curb when she opened the door. Nathan took in that she was naked except for the towel, and pushed into her loft. By the smell of him, he'd been at a bar; there was beer on his breath, and smoke clinging to his clothes.

"Where in the world have you been? You've been gone for three days." He roved the loft like a SWAT team looking for snipers.

"Three days?" No wonder she felt empty and dull-witted. When was the last time she'd eaten?

"I tagged my later messages so I'd be notified when you picked them—" He had turned to her and froze. "Oh, God, what did he do to you?"

"A major enchantment of some sort," she said, toweling her hair. "I'm starved. Want to go out for something to eat?"

He closed on her, staring. "Why did you let him do this to you?"

"I don't want to argue about this right now. I'm hungry. Let's just go get something to eat."

He caught her wrist as she started to turn. "You don't want to talk about it? Jesus Christ, Tink. I thought we had a future together and you pull this."

She was missing something here. Something visible, that he was staring at with dismay. She yanked her hand free and rushed to the bathroom. The mirror she had ignored earlier was partially fogged, but there was enough to show her what Nathan saw. For several minutes, she could only stare in silent shock. Nathan came to the bathroom door, filling up the frame.

It was *her* in the mirror—but it wasn't. It was an elf that looked like her. Her damp brown hair. Elfshaped eyes—that slightly almond-shaped, almost Asian look. Had her eyes always been that color? They *were* brown, but hers couldn't have been that vivid. Right? Those brown eyes widened on a fearful thought, and she pushed her hair back.

Elf ears.

"All the gods in heaven!" she swore. "I'm going to kill him!"

"He didn't tell you that he was going to change you? He just took you out to the woods and changed you?"

"Yes!" Tinker answered without thinking, and then caught the dangerously hard look on his face. "No. No. He didn't. He asked me, but I didn't understand. You know how he is. How they all are. I didn't understand."

"What did he say?" Nathan asked.

"He said I was going to die, and that he cared too much about me to let that happen, so if I let him do the spell, then I wouldn't . . ." She wouldn't die, because elves were immortal. "Damn him. Why couldn't he say it in plain English?"

"So you're," he stumbled on the words, sounding physically sick, "you're immortal?"

"I don't know. I think that was what he was trying to do. He wasn't there when I woke up, so I just came home."

"It's taken three days for the spell to run?"

Three days. Three days to work through her entire body and transform every cell into elf. Tinker stared intently at herself. Her skin had the creamy perfection of elves. Her nose—not even being an elf fixed that. Her lips seemed fuller, a red of subtle lipstick. "I can't believe he did this! I'm not human anymore! Of course I was going to die. All humans die!" She noticed that her teeth had that unreal look of elves and Hollywood actors. She grimaced, pulling back her lips to bare teeth and gums to examine them closer. "I think even my one filling is gone. It was one of those white poly-cement ones. It was this tooth, I think."

She stared now at her fingers. All her fingernails were long and hard like she'd had them done at a salon. They seemed longer and more graceful. Were they? Would she be able to do the fine work that she was used to with a stranger's hands? Her hands started to tremble, and she found she was shaking all over.

Nathan's officer training took over. He guided her out of the bathroom, saying, "Why don't you sit down? I'll get you something to drink. You've had a shock."

A bark of laughter slipped out and threatened to explode into something longer, completely uncontrolled. She clasped her hand over her mouth, those delicate elfin hands over those full, cherry red lips. Oh gods, she wasn't human anymore. The bastard had turned her into an elf without even asking.

Nathan got two beers from the fridge, opened them, and came back. He handed her one. "I didn't think it was possible to turn a human into an elf."

"They can change a little Shih-Tzu into something the size of a pony, why not a human into an elf?" She took a large drink and nearly choked on the taste. "What the hell? This beer is bad."

He took it and handed her the one he had been drinking. She took a drink and choked it down. "This one is bad too."

"It tasted okay." He took it back and sipped it cautiously. "Tink, its not the beer. It's fine. It must be you. The change did something to your taste."

He gave her back her original beer and finished his own. She tried to drink the vile-tasting stuff, but after the second swallow, handed it to him, saying, "I can't drink it."

So he drank it also. "What was the spell like? Did it hurt? What do you remember? Can he undo it?"

She flopped back, pressing hands to eyes. What a mess! There was no way she could tell *him* everything Windwolf had done. What she had *let* Windwolf do.

What she had *enjoyed* having Windwolf do to her. "He had a big enchantment room set up with the spell inscribed and everything. I remember him activating it, but nothing afterward until I woke up about two hours ago."

"So he could have raped you while you were unconscious and you won't know."

She turned and kicked him, partly because he focused on sex, partly because Windwolf had gotten into her without having to rape her. "I would know."

Nathan put down the empty beer bottle next to his first, leaned over, and pulled open her towel.

"Nathan!" She tried to keep the towel closed. "What do you think you're doing?"

"I want to see what you look like now."

"No!" Surprisingly, a blush can start at the tips of one's toes and go all the way up. At least, it can when you're an elf.

"Let me see!" He pulled away the towel.

"Nathan!" she cried, trying to tug the towel out of his hands, but it was like trying to move a mountain. Then the mountain moved of its own will, lowering itself to kiss her bared skin. When Windwolf had kissed her in the same way, it had been like plugging straight into a 220 line. This hurt in a way that had only a little to do with bruising flesh. "Nathan! Don't! Stop!"

He did, only to kiss his way up her body. "Don't you see, Tink?" He supported himself with one hand, his other undoing his pants. "There's no reason to wait now. There's no getting older for you."

He was up against her, hard as steel, large as the rest of him. His weight was on her thighs and hips and chest, pinning her down so she couldn't even kick at him.

"No!"

"You're going to look this way for the rest of my life." He moved, seeking her entrance. "But the beauty of it is that with you being an elf, no one will think anything of you being young."

"Get the hell off me!" She got her hands to his face, thumbs pressing in warning at the edges of his eyes. "I said no! You of all people should understand that no is no."

"I love you, Tink."

"Then get off me. We're not doing this, not now, not this way. Be nice, and there's still a chance for us. Force me, and I'll press charges."

He stilled, hurt and guilt warring for control of his face. "Tink."

Was it a plea for forgiveness, or permission to continue? She couldn't tell, and it was rendered moot by a sword blade suddenly appearing at Nathan's neck.

"*Naetanyau!*" The elf from the Rolls growled, pressing the sword tip until it cut Nathan's skin and Nathan's blood dripped onto Tinker's breasts. "*Batya!*"

Nathan jerked back, shoving Tinker up and over the back of the couch like a rag doll as he moved. While she found herself deposited behind the sofa, Nathan tumbled back, coming up with his pistol. "Put down the weapon!"

"What the hell are you doing?" she shouted at the elf in Low Elvish. "I told you to leave me alone!"

Both males moved toward her, and checked as it brought them closer together.

"Put down the weapon!" Nathan commanded again.

"*Ze domou ani* said that I was to watch over you," the elf said to Tinker in Low Elvish. "This man was forcing himself on you. I couldn't allow that."

"Put down the weapon!" Nathan cocked his pistol. "Drop it or I'll shoot!"

And he would. Tinker edged between the males, facing Nathan, holding out her hand in warding. "Nathan! Nathan! Don't. He's just protecting me. He thought you were going to rape me."

Nathan flinched at that. "Tell him to put the sword away."

God, what was the word for policeman? "He's—he's a law enforcer," she said to the elf. "Put the sword away, or he'll kill you." That just got a look of stubbornness from him. "I command you to put your sword away."

That got a startled look. The elf obeyed grudgingly.

"Put your gun away, Nathan."

"Who the hell is he?"

"He works for Windwolf. Put the gun away."

Nathan holstered his pistol and zipped his pants. Tinker picked up her towel and wrapped it around her again; it seemed to have shrunk in size over the last few minutes and was woefully inadequate at covering her.

"What's his name?" Nathan asked.

Tinker looked to the elf, expecting him to answer, since the question had been fairly basic English. He gave no indication of understanding. "Do you know any *Pitsupavute*?" The human language spoken in Pittsburgh, or in other words, English.

The elf nodded stiffly and said in English, "No. Stop. Don't. Water. Rest room. Please. Thank you. Yes. Go." Had he listed them purposely in order, to indicate he understood her refusing Nathan? His English used up, he switched back to Elvish. "Windwolf did not expect you to leave home, so my lack of *Pitsupavute* seemed unimportant."

"What's your name?" Tinker asked the elf.

"Galloping Storm Horse On Wind." He gave it in Elvish, which was *Waetata-watarou-tukaenrou-bo-taeli*, which made her grimace. "My family calls me Little Horse, so *domi zae* says I would be *Po-nie*." Po-nie? Pony! "If you find that easier, I would be pleased for you to call me that."

"Yes. Thank you," she said. She switched to English. "His name is Stormhorse, but he says I'm to call him Pony."

Nathan snorted at the name, then sighed deeply. "I'm sorry, Tinker. I had no right to do that."

"Damn right you didn't." She had trusted him more than almost anyone else on the planet. She wished Stormhorse had waited, given Nathan a chance to back off and apologize. She wanted desperately to believe he would have, that her trust in him could remain intact. That things could go back to the way they were.

He raked a hand through his hair, and then stood tugging at it, as if he wanted to yank the whole handful out. "It's just I spent all those years, wanting you so badly, and I finally had you. You were going to be mine. There was nothing stopping the whole marriage and kids and growing old together thing. Then Windwolf walked up, waltzed you away, and I let him. I fucking let him take you to do anything he damn well pleased to you. I've been going nuts the last three days, trying to find you, and now . . ." He held out his hand to her, tears coming to his eyes. "It's like he killed you, and all I have left is an elfin shadow. I just wanted to claim you, before he took that too."

"Your timing sucks. If—if—if . . ." If what? She didn't know what to say to make things right. Could anything make things right after he'd almost raped her? After Windwolf had made her into an elf? After she'd gone molten in Windwolf's arms? Would she have said no to Nathan if Windwolf's smell and touch weren't still lingering in her mind?

"If things were different?" Nathan asked. "The shitty thing is, they were different until Windwolf did this to you without even asking."

"I know," she whispered. "Look, things are too screwed up right now. I'm hungry, and confused, and hurt, and scared. Don't ask me to make decisions like this. You're just hurting me."

"I know. I'm sorry."

"Go home."

"Tinker—Tink—please . . ."

The front door opened, and Oilcan walked in.

8: REDEFINING SELF

Oilcan called out, "Tinker? Are you here?" as he came through the door and then checked at the sight of angry Stormhorse, flustered Nathan, and Tinker in a towel.

The sight of Oilcan destroyed all control Tinker had, and she went to him, suddenly crying. Her cousin held her without asking questions, and the males regarded each other in tense silence.

"I think it's time for you to go," Oilcan said quietly, and Nathan left without another word.

Stormhorse's hand rode his hilt, and he eyed Oilcan with open suspicion.

"*Nagarou.*" Oilcan identified himself as a sister's son of Tinker's father. His Elvish had always been better than hers. He and Stormhorse launched into a High Elvish discussion, faster than she could follow, which ended with Stormhorse bowing and letting himself out of the loft. And then Oilcan held her until she wept herself out. Then, in fits and starts, mostly from editing out what she didn't want him to know, she told him about Windwolf and Nathan.

"Look at me; I'm shaking so bad."

"If you haven't eaten anything for three days, then you're probably weaker than you think. Stormhorse went to get you something to eat."

"He did?" She got up. "Where would he get anything this time of night?"

"I don't know. Why don't you get dressed before he comes back?"

So she went back to her bedroom to dress. She found herself pawing through her underwear drawer, looking for the plainest pair of panties she owned. She stopped herself, picked a pair randomly off the top, and pulled them on. Clean jeans, a T-shirt, socks, and then her boots. She stomped around, feeling more like herself.

Oilcan had cleared her kitchen table, wiped it clean, and was washing her few pots and dishes. She got a clean towel and started to dry.

"How long do you think it will take him to get back?"

The sweep of headlights through her loft announced Pony's return.

"Not long," Oilcan said dryly.

She smacked him with the towel and went to open the door.

Pony came in carrying stacked wicker baskets, wreathed in the perfume of heavenly smelling food. Setting the baskets lightly on her table, he undid the lid and lifted it off to reveal noodle soup in the hand–painted bowl of an enclave restaurant.

"I didn't think enclaves did takeout." Tinker sat down on the footstool, leaving her two battered and mismatched chairs for the males.

"I persuaded them to do so this one time." Pony sat the noodle soup in front of her. "It would be best if you eat this first."

"Why this?" The noodles were long as spaghetti but nearly as thick as her pinkie and had a slightly waxy appearance. After her experience with the beer, she eyed the soup with suspicion.

"Rich foods on an empty system might upset your stomach, and you need to eat as much as possible. This has very little fat."

Oilcan found her a spoon, and she tried the stock. It was keva bean paste mixed with hot water, simple but delicious. She had to fight to get the noodles into her mouth. Despite their looks, they were mild but good.

"I told them of your *nagarou*, and they sent enough to share." Pony unlocked the top basket and lifted it off, exposing the next level of food: steamed meat dumplings.

"*Mauzouan!* You can count me in." Oilcan fetched plates and silverware, got himself a beer from the refrigerator, and settled at one of the chairs. Pony unloaded the rest of the baskets, but remained standing.

"Why don't you sit?" Oilcan paused in sharing out the *mauzouan* to three plates.

"I am Tinker *domi*'s guard. I should stand."

"Sit," Tinker snapped.

Pony wavered a moment, then pulled out a chair and sat unhappily. "This isn't proper."

"Currently I'm too peeved to care," Tinker snapped.

Wise man that he was, Oilcan set a dish of *mauzouan* in front of Pony without comment.

With Pony on the other side of the table, and food in her hands, Tinker could study him now at leisure. While pretty as all elves tended to be, he was by far the most solid of elves she'd ever seen. He wore wyvern armor, harvested from a beast that ran to the dark blues, with an underlining of black leather to keep the sharp edges of the overlapping scales from cutting him since they themselves couldn't be dulled. The armor left his arms bare from the shoulders. Permanent protection spells were tattooed down his arms like Celtic knots. For reasons she thought were no more than artistic, the spells were done in graded shades of cobalt; they shifted with the play of his muscles. Unlike most elves she knew, who wore dazzling jewelry, from complex dangling earrings to rings, Pony's only decoration was dark blue beads woven into his black hair.

While previously it had seemed to Tinker impossible to judge an elf's age, Pony struck her as young, but she couldn't tell if that was from some hint in his face or just his manner. He fairly bristled with weapons: a long sword strapped to his back, a pistol riding his hip, and knife hilts peeking out of various locations. Still, he met her gaze with a look that shifted from open honesty, to slight embarrassment, to bewildered confusion, and back around again.

"Where is Windwolf?" Oilcan asked as Tinker ate her soup and studied Pony.

"A message came from Aum Renau." Pony glanced at them to see if they understood. *Aum Renau* was the name of the palace on Elfhome in roughly the same place as the Palisades were on Earth—overlooking the Hudson River, near New York City. "His presence was requested by Queen Soulful Ember. He couldn't refuse the summons. He had to go. He wished to leave Sparrow to care for you. She's quite fluent in *Taniananté*"—the Elvish for "those many human languages"—"and *Pitsupavute*. The queen, however, requested her appearance specifically along with Windwolf's."

"The queen is in the Westernlands?" Oilcan asked.

"It is very unexpected. She has not been here since the treaty signing," Pony said. "He wished to bring Tinker *domi* with him, but he didn't want to take her so far away without consulting her first."

That would have pissed her off proper, but at least it would have saved her from Nathan being a jerk.

"How did Windwolf change me?"

"I-I do not really know, honestly." Pony screwed up his face, and Tinker suddenly liked the sturdy dark elf. "I am only of the *sekasha* caste, and still considered young. The *domana* understand the great transformation spells. Windwolf took blood samples while you slept; by the old reckoning, you're genetically *domana* caste now."

She shivered. "What do you mean 'by the old reckoning'?"

"There was a time when clan leaders often transformed their most trusted followers to *domana* caste. They were then considered full equals by the rest of the caste."

"And now?"

Pony touched his own forehead where Tinker bore Windwolf's mark. "There is the *dau*."

Which Maynard said elevated her to Windwolf's caste.

"When is Windwolf coming back?" Oilcan asked.

"He couldn't say," Pony said. "But if he can't return soon, he might choose to send for Tinker *domi*." Seeing the look on her face, Pony added, "If she wishes to join him."

Unfortunately, all the wonderful food meant lots of delicate dishes to be cleaned. Still, with all three of them washing and drying, the work went quickly. Pony, however, made no sign of leaving.

"Shouldn't you go back to the lodge?"

"Windwolf told me to guard over you. I can't do that at the lodge."

"So, you plan to stay with me until Windwolf comes back to say otherwise?"

"Yes."

Oh, great.

Tinker saw the look on Oilcan's face. "What?"

"You're sleeping at my place tonight," Oilcan said in English. "I wasn't crazy about you being alone, but him here too—I'd feel better being close."

"Then stay the night."

"You only have your bed and the couch."

"Oh, yes. Okay." She sighed and yawned. "Your place."

Oilcan had lucked into a place on Mount Washington, a sprawling three-bedroom condo in a high-rise apartment building, on the sole condition that he keep the elevator, air-conditioning, and heat working. His balcony looked out over downtown Pittsburgh and the endless canopy of elfin forest.

Pony worked to make himself invisible to them, keeping still and quiet. As Oilcan went to check on his rarely used guest beds, Tinker strolled out onto the balcony and looked down at the city.

Why had Windwolf changed her? Was it a gift for saving his life—a life for a life? Or was it more, as the sex implied? Did he love her? And what exactly did she feel about his gift? It was too frighteningly huge to handle. She was an elf.

"You okay?" Oilcan padded out onto the balcony with her.

"I'm fine—just a little rattled. What about you?"

"You mean, how am I with this?" Oilcan flicked his hand up and down to indicate her new body. "I'm cool. So you've got dorky ears." He leaned out and fingered one tip, and it felt embarrassingly good.

"Hey, don't mess with the ears."

Oilcan jerked his hand back and looked hurt. "Sorry."

"It's just—they're erogenous zones."

"Oh. *Oh!*"

"Exactly."

"Are we still cousins? At least in the genetic sense?"

"Would it matter if I'm not?"

"No, but it would be comforting if you were." Oilcan took her hand. "After my mother died, Grandpa said something to me. He said that as long as I and my children after me lived, my mother would be alive, living on through her bloodline. It's how humans reach immortality. It's why he made sure you were born, even after your father had died so long ago."

They lapsed into silence.

"Lain could check and see," Tinker whispered. "We could go see her tomorrow."

"But what if she says we're not?" She wondered how much it meant to him. If it meant a lot, she wouldn't give up Oilcan for Windwolf; she'd find some way of getting back to her real self.

"Whatever Lain finds, you'll always be my best friend and little sister."

"Little sister?"

"Based on love, not blood," Oilcan said. "Nobody can touch that if we don't let them."

She hugged him hard and wondered if he wasn't the smarter of the two of them.

They made an odd threesome on Lain's porch. Oilcan with his blatant humanity, Pony unmistakably elfin, and Tinker caught somewhere between the two. Latin answered the door, went pale at the sight of Tinker, and murmured, "Oh dear. Oh dear."

"It's really not that bad." Tinker tried for a brave front, and then failed. "Is it?"

Lain gazed at her for another minute before saying, "No, love, no. It's fine. Come in. I'd ask what in the world happened, but it's obvious that Windwolf happened."

"Pony, this is Lain." Tinker introduced the warrior. "Lain, this is Galloping Storm Horse On Wind, but he goes by Pony. He's one of Windwolf's bodyguards, but he's been told to guard over me. He doesn't speak English."

The two bowed to each other.

Lain led the trio back to her sprawling kitchen. Pony ranged through it and the connecting rooms, looking for danger.

"Where's his master?" Lain asked quietly in English, avoiding Windwolf's name.

Tinker followed suit as she explained about the queen's summons as Lain put the teakettle on. "Oilcan and I want you to test us to see how much *he* changed me—are we still cousins?"

"Of course you are!" Lain cried, then saw the looks on their faces. "There's a good chance you'll only be disappointed. He's obviously done something quite radical."

"But I'm still me. I feel the same. I think the same way. I have all my memories." Tinker had woken in a blind panic the night before, searched through old memories, factored out several large numbers, and considered a fix to one of her newer inventions before satisfying herself at that level. "The only thing different seems to be my sense of taste. Beer tastes awful, and I couldn't stand the instant hot chocolate this morning. Pony wouldn't drink it either."

"Well, beer is bitter because of the hops." Lain shooed Pony out of her path to the fridge with her crutch. "Elves seem to have evolved an intolerance to alkaloids. That's why they avoid coffee, tea, and nicotine in addition to the many toxic alkaloid-containing plants we stay away from as well."

"Well, that kills most of my favorite drinks," Tinker said.

"I have some herbal tea you can drink, but I think you'll have to be careful. A strong allergic reaction can be quite deadly." Lain took out a bowl of strawberries. "I've also found that elves are sensitive to certain types of fats we put in commercial food products. They love natural peanut butter, but the brands with trans-fat cause them trouble."

Tinker named her favorite brand of peanut butter.

"Sorry, love." Lain sat the strawberries in front of Tinker. "Luckily I make my own whipped cream, or that would be out too. Depending on the brand of instant you're using, it might be why you couldn't stand the hot chocolate."

Tinker considered her well-stocked kitchen at her loft. "I don't have any food I can eat, then."

"You'll have to rely on Tooloo more for fresh foods, then." Lain fetched the whipped cream. "Vegetables, meat, eggs, butter, and even the bread she bakes is most likely safer. Can I get you anything, Oilcan? Coffee? Tea?"

"I'll take coffee." Oilcan settled near to Tinker, fidgeting. "How long will the tests take?"

Lain shot a glance toward Pony standing guard by the door. "It's against the treaty to do gene scans of elves."

"I'm not an elf," Tinker growled, and dunked one of the strawberries.

"I know," Lain murmured. "But we can't let your guard know what we're doing."

Tinker controlled the urge to glance toward Pony. "Ah. Yes." She nibbled at the strawberry, considering. "Well, he seems to do what I tell him to do."

Oilcan also studiously avoided looking at Pony. "If we station him at the front door, then we can be in the lab unwatched."

So Tinker finished her strawberries, moved Pony to the foyer, and went back to the lab to have her blood drawn.

"When we're done, I'm going to destroy the samples and the results." Lain tied a tourniquet around Tinker's arm and swabbed down a patch of skin inside her elbow with alcohol. "It's a whole little Pandora's box we're peeking into. You will not tell anyone—not humans or elves—about this."

"We won't," Tinker promised.

Oilcan echoed it, and then added, "It's just for us to know."

Lain not only took a blood sample from Tinker, but also swabbed the inside of Tinker's mouth, plunked out a hair, and then asked for a stool sample.

"What?" Tinker cried. "Why?"

"Please, Tinker, don't be squeamish." Lain motioned Oilcan to sit in the chair Tinker just vacated. "The cells of the intestinal lining are excreted with the stool and are a source of DNA. I want to see how invasive this change is."

Lain was just untying the tourniquet on Oilcan's arm when the doorbell rang.

"Oh, who can that be?" Lain grumbled. She put the vials containing the blood out of sight, and stuck a bandage on Oilcan's arm. "Pull your sleeve down, Tink."

The woman on the front porch looked familiar. She brightened at the sight of Tinker and said to Oilcan, "Oh, wow, you found your cousin!"

"Yeah." Oilcan actually looked sheepish under Tinker's puzzled stare. "You remember Ryan. She's one of the astronomers?"

Oh yes, the one she'd tried to warn off the night of the cookout.

"I came over to see if there was any news." Ryan waved toward the Observatory. "I'm just getting done for the night, and I thought I'd check in before hitting . . ." She stopped and cocked her head. "You weren't always an elf, were you?"

"I've got work to do," Lain announced into the sudden silence.

"No, no! She—she—" Oilcan looked to Tinker for help.

"Don't look at me," Tinker snapped, then picked up on Lain's cue. "I want to go to Tooloo's to stock up on some food I can actually eat. Do you want anything, Lain?"

"Actually, yes. See what she has in the way of fish. A dozen eggs." Lain listed her needs as she crutched to the kitchen and returned with her shopping basket and a glass milk bottle that she held out to Tinker. "A pint of whipping cream. And some fresh bread would be nice."

Tinker took the empty return and wicker basket. "I'll be back in . . . two hours?"

Lain nodded. "That would be good."

That left Ryan to be kept out from under Lain's feet. Oilcan blushed slightly at his assignment, but indicated the dorms with a jerk of his head. "Let me walk you back to the dorms, Ryan, and I'll explain."

So they split up, each to their own task.

Pony insisted that Tinker sit in the back of the Rolls, so she hung over the front seat to give him directions to Tooloo's store. She noticed that he handled the car smoothly as he took it down the sharply curving hill of the Observatory.

"How long have you been *driving*?" Driving was an English word, since the nearest Elvish words implied horses and reins.

"*Nae hae.*" No years. The full saying was *Kaetat nae hae*, literally "Count no years" but actually meant "too many years to count"—a common expression among elves; it could mean as few as ten years or as many as a thousand. After a thousand, it changed to *Nae hou*, or roughly, "too many millennia to count." In this case, however, *Nae hae* had to be less than twenty years, since that was when the elves were introduced to modern technology with Pittsburgh's arrival.

"The Rolls were part of the treaty," Pony explained. "It required that the EIA provide quality cars for *ze domou ani*'s use. All of his guard learned, as did *husepavua* and *ze domou ani*, though not all enjoy doing it."

"Do you?"

"Very much. *Domou* lets me race, although *husepavua* says it is reckless."

She directed him onto the McKees Rocks Bridge. The morning sun was dazzling on the river below. "Who is *husepavua*?"

"Sparrow Lifted By Wind."

The name sounded familiar, but it took her a moment to place it; Sparrow had been the stunningly beautiful high-caste elf at the hospice. Pony had mentioned her once or twice the night before, calling her just Sparrow.

"Is Sparrow . . . Windwolf's wife?"

He looked at her with utter surprise on his face, reinforcing her impression that he was fairly young. "No, *domi*! They are not even lovers."

Oh, good. Pony was giving her amazingly direct answers, something she hadn't thought possible for elves. Perhaps it had to do with his willingness to obey her—had Windwolf told him to do so? Or was it an offshoot of being young? "How old are you, Pony?"

"I turned a hundred this year."

While that seemed really old to her, she knew that elves didn't start into puberty until their late twenties and weren't considered adults until their hundredth birthday. In a weird, twisted way, she and Pony were age-equals, although she suspected that he was much more experienced than she could hope to be.

"Is this the place?" Pony asked, pulling to a stop beside Tooloo's seedy storefront. To conserve heat in the winter, the old half-elf had replaced the plate glass with salvaged glass blocks. Somehow, though, she'd tinted the blocks, so the wall of glass became a stained-glass mosaic on a six-inch-square scale. Typical of elfin artwork, the picture was too large for a human to easily grasp. If one stood in the kitchenette and looked through the entire length of the shop, one could see that the squares formed a tree branch, sun shafting through the leaves, with the swell of a ripe apple dangling underneath. From the outside, though, one only saw the salvaged block and the muted colors in a seemingly random pattern—keeping the store's secrets just as the storekeeper kept hers.

The only nod toward advertising the store's function was painted under the length of the windows: Bread, Butter, Eggs, Fish, Fowl, Honey, Pittsburgh Internet Access, Milk, Spellcasting, Telephone,

Translations, Video Rentals. Of the words that could be translated into Elvish, the rune followed the English word. It mattered much to Tinker that she could remember standing in hot summer sun as the cicadas droned loudly, carefully painting in the English traced onto the wall by Tooloo's graceful hand.

"Yes, this is it." Tinker slid out.

She hadn't considered Tooloo's reaction to her transformation. When the old half-elf saw her, Tooloo let out a banshee cry and caught Tinker by both ears. "Look at what that monster did to my dear little wee one! He's killed you."

"Ow! Ow! Stop that!" Tinker smacked Tooloo's hands away. "That hurt! And I'm not dead."

"My wee one was human, growing up in a flash of quicksilver. Dirty Skin Clan scum." Tooloo spat.

"Windwolf is Wind Clan." Tinker rubbed the soreness from her ears.

"All *domana* are Skin Clan bastards," Tooloo snapped.

Tinker winced and glanced to Pony. Thankfully, the exchange had been in English, but Pony obviously had picked up Windwolf's name and was listening intently. "Don't insult him, Tooloo. Besides, if you'd just warned me, I might have been able to avoid this."

"I told you the fire was hot! I told you that it burns! I told you to be careful. So don't cry that I never told you it could burn down the house. I warned you that Windwolf would be the end of you, and see, I told you and there it is."

"You have told me nothing." She went and got a basket, angry now but determined to keep her calm. "Knowledge is not cryptic warnings, indistinguishable from utter nonsense. 'All *domana* are Skin Clan bastards.' What the hell does that mean? I've never heard of the Skin Clan."

"There wasn't a need for you to know if you'd just stayed away from Windwolf. I know humans; if it's ancient history, it doesn't pertain, so I would have been wasting breath to explain a war that happened before the fall of Babylon."

Tinker picked up a crock of honey, intending to put it into her basket. "Well, tell me now."

"Too late now." Tooloo stalked away, flapping her hands over her head as if to swat away questions. "Done is done!"

Tinker barely refrained from flinging the crock at Tooloo's retreating backside. "Tooloo, for once just tell me, damn it! Who knows what mess I might get into because you've kept me ignorant?"

Tooloo scowled at her. "I have things to do. Cows to milk. Chickens to feed. Eggs to gather."

"Well, you don't feed chickens with your mouth. I'll help you, and you can tell me what I need to know." Besides, Tinker had to keep Pony out from under Lain's feet for a full two hours.

Tooloo sulked but went to the store's front door, flipped the "Open" sign to "Closed" and threw the dead bolt, muttering all the while.

Tooloo lived in the one big back room of the store, a house done at miniature scale with changes in the flooring to indicate where walls should be. Mosaic tile delineated the kitchenette. The two wing chairs of the living room sat on gleaming cherry-wood planks. The floor around Tooloo's fantastically odd bed was strewn with warg skins. Tinker had spent countless hours on the floor, from studying the dragon shown coiled on the kitchenette's tile to building forts under the bed. She thought she knew it well.

Entering the room, Tinker discovered she didn't know it completely.

It felt like stepping into a pool of invisible warmth. No. There was movement, a slow current to it, heading east to west. She stopped, surprised, looking down at the wood. It did more than gleam. It shimmered as if heat roiled the air between her toes and her eyes. As she studied the floor, an odd, pleasant sensation crept up her legs until her whole body felt strangely light.

Even odder was the change in Tooloo's bed. The pale yellow wood seemed at once sharper and brighter, almost surreal, like someone had overlain computer graphics onto reality.

Pony followed Tinker's gaze, and grunted in surprise. "Dragon bones."

"Yes, dragon bones," Tooloo snapped, wrapping her braid loosely around her neck like a scarf of thick, silver cording. "That's how I survived on Earth all these centuries. Silly beast died without the magic, but its very bones stored massive amounts that slowly leaked off. Every night I slept in that bed, *nae hou*, aging only when I strayed away from it. I was tempted to burn it after the Pathway reopened, but waste not, want not, as the humans say. There were times I grew so depressed that I wouldn't stir out of it for months on end."

"Why is the floor so weird?" Tinker asked Tooloo, but the half-elf had stepped out the back, so she turned instead to Pony. "Can you feel that?"

"It must be a ley line."

"I can *see* it—I think."

"Yes, you should be able to." But he explained no further.

Deciding to focus on one mystery at a time, Tinker went out into the backyard after Tooloo. What used to be a small public park lay behind the store, but Tooloo had claimed every patch of green in the area plus several nearby buildings to use as barns, regardless of what their previous functions might have been. Fenced and warded, her small yard gave way to a sprawling barnyard.

Tooloo had already filled a pan with cracked corn from the feed room and now stood throwing out handfuls, calling, "Chick, chick, chick." All the barnyard fowl ran toward the falling kernels. She kept a mix of Rhode Island Reds (which were good egg layers), little bantams (which fared better on the edge of Elfhome's wilderness), and a mated pair of gray geese called Yin and Yang (that acted more like watchdogs than birds).

"Tell me about the Skin Clan." Tinker picked her way through the pecking and scratching birds. Pony hung back, staring in fascination at the chickens. She wondered if elves had chickens, or if they were one of the species that hadn't developed on Elfhome.

"Tens of thousands of years ago, in a time past reckoning, the first of our race discovered magic." Tooloo tossed out handfuls of corn. "It is said that we were tribes then, nomadic hunters. Our myths and legends claim that the gods gave magic first to the tribe that became the Fire Clan, and perhaps that is true. It is fairly simple to twist magic into flame.

"But one tribe rose up and enslaved all the rest—they were the ones who practiced skin magic. They learned how to use magic to warp flesh, and to remake creatures stronger and faster. They were the ones who discovered immortality, and they used the beginning of their long lives to make themselves godlike in beauty, grace, and form."

Tinker scooped out handfuls of corn and flung it at the chickens to speed up the feeding process. "I don't understand how they enslaved the others; surely not because they were pretty."

"Can you imagine the advances that your famous thinkers might have made if they had lived a thousand years? What would Einstein be creating if he were still alive today? Or what Aristotle, da Vinci, Newton, Einstein, and Hawking could create if they all worked together."

"Wow."

"As a race, we went from being bands of nomadic hunters to an empire with cities in a fraction of the time it took humans. As their realm expanded, the Skin Clan crafted fierce beasts to wage war and enforce their laws: the dragons, the wyverns, the wargs, and many other monstrous creatures. In time, they spanned the known world, which was roughly Europe, Asia, and Africa on Earth.

"All of this happened before humans dreamed of building their first mud hut." Tooloo dumped the last of the corn, tapping the fine dust and small bits of broken kernels out to be fought over by the chickens. "See, old news."

Exchanging the feed pail for wicker baskets, Tooloo headed for the one-car garage converted into a chicken coop. Long used to helping Tooloo with chores, Tinker took one of the baskets and worked the east wall of cubbyholes, lifting the day's eggs out of the still-warm nests. It was easy to tell which nest belonged to the bantams, as the eggs were much smaller. Pony stepped cautiously into the coop, peered into one of the cubbyholes near the door, and lifted out an egg, which he examined closely.

"Okay." Tinker carefully deposited her discoveries into her basket. "But there's some reason you're telling me about the Skin Clan."

"They are the seed of everything elfin." Tooloo systematically worked through the western cubbyholes. "Humans are like snowflakes; nothing about humans is the same. They've chopped their planet up into thousands of governments, cultures, traditions, religions, so forth and so on. At their dawn, though, the elves were all gathered together and forced into the same mold and then made immortal. As we were when the humans started to build the pyramids, we are still."

Windwolf had talked about the stagnation of his race, but Tinker hadn't realized that it was so profound.

"Why haven't I heard of the Skin Clan before?"

"Because they're all dead, except for their bastard children, the *domana*."

"What happened? How did they die?"

"They didn't die, silly thing; they were killed. Hunted down. Killed to the last one—in theory."

With that Tooloo ducked out of the coop and swung around to her back door to set her basket in the store before heading for the small milk barn.

"Wait!" Tinker snatched up the last of the eggs, including the one Pony still held, and scurried after Tooloo. She caught up to her at the pasture where Tooloo's four milk cows waited to be let out. "Tooloo!"

"What?" Tooloo opened the pasture gate and the cows ambled to their stalls without guidance. "I'm trying to compress twenty thousand years of history into a teaspoon, and you complain? History isn't easy stuff. It's a tangled web full of lies and deceit. There's no easy way of pouring it out."

"Okay, fine, the *domana* are the Skin Clan's children?"

Tooloo scoffed loudly as she poured grain out to the cows. "The Skin Clan was the first of the castes, for they raised themselves up to perfection. Then they created the other castes. The *filintau* born for a clean breeding stock. The *sekasha*." Tooloo thumped Pony in the chest. "Sound and strong, able to withstand massive damage, but not necessarily smart. It's the same that humans did with dogs, chickens, and cows." She gave one of the cows a similar pat. "Breed a bloodline for certain properties until they're nearly a different species—and when they no longer suit, let them die off. When I lived in Ireland, I had this lovely herd of small, hardy Kerry cows that nearly went the way of the quagga."

"The what?"

"It was like a zebra. It went extinct in the days of Queen Victoria. Ah, there was a woman!"

"So, the Skin Clan set up the castes and fathered the *domana*?" Tinker tried to steer the conversation back to elfin history.

"As you will no doubt learn, you don't wake up and fully realize you're immortal. It takes a few hundred years." Tooloo washed her hands, took down a clean milk bucket, and moved the milk stool beside the first cow. "Once the genetic tinkering started, the Skin Clan grew increasingly infertile, so they originally accepted all their offspring into the caste. About a thousand years into their immortality, they realized that they were diluting their power by sharing it with their 'half-breed' children, so they ruled that only those born to a Skin Clan female could be accepted into the caste. It did not keep the males, however, from fathering children among the lower castes, and that's where the *domana* came from."

Tinker leaned against the stall side, watching Tooloo wipe the udder clean and position the milk bucket. Tinker drew a line at milking the cows, as she'd been swatted in the face with a tail once too often. Pony watched in complete mystification. Head tucked against the cow's flank, Tooloo settled into a fast milking rhythm, shooting alternating streams of milk into the bucket. "This happened a long time ago; Windwolf wasn't even born. And even if his father is a Skin Clan bastard, so what? Oilcan's father killed his mother, and that doesn't make Oilcan a bad person."

"Nah, nah, Longwind—Windwolf's father—is just a young buck too. Politics does what time can't; Windwolf's grandfather, Howling, was murdered and Longwind took his place as clan head. Howling, though, he was ten thousand years old when the blade found him, and he had been part of the Skin Clan downfall. But to be precise, he wasn't the bastard—it was his father, Quick Blade, before him, who was the bastard, but Quick Blade died in battle during the war."

"How do you know all this?"

"How do you know about George Washington and Thomas Jefferson? These were the 'heroes' of the war and the leaders of our people afterward." Tooloo said it with such bitterness that both Tinker and the cow flinched. "It was, though, a simple trading of masters. Perhaps more benign than the Skin Clan, but ironfisted all the same."

That Windwolf was one of "them" made Tinker uncomfortable with the conversation. Tooloo said whatever suited her with little regard to truth, and Tinker hated the concept of being poisoned against Windwolf with lies. Still, it was fairly obvious from the caste system that the *domana* ruled and the others served.

"I don't understand," Tinker said. "If Quick Blade was Skin Clan, how did Howling get to be Wind clan?"

Tooloo sighed into the cow's flank. "The Skin Clan tried to wipe out the use of other magic, but they only drove it underground. And exactly what they were afraid of happened—the seeds of power became great trees. The ignorant but physically strong—like your strapping young *sekasha* there—pledged their services to those with arcane knowledge. Over time the castes linked together into the current clans, but they were slowly losing during the Years of Resistance."

"Until the *domana* joined the clans against their fathers."

"There's still hope for you, my bright wee one. Yes. The Skin Clan had added the ability to wield magic to their blood, and then fathered bastards among their rebel slaves." Tooloo stilled for a moment, considering the past. "There is, I suppose, an inevitability to it all."

Tooloo finished with the first cow and carried the milk to the scales to be weighed. "Thirty pounds. Nothing to piffle at, though Holsteins have been bred to output twice that amount. Here, take this back to the cooler."

Tinker reached for the bucket, but Pony stepped forward and took it.

"What are you doing?"

"It will be heavy for you, but nothing for me to carry."

Tinker snorted but let it go because, unfortunately, he was right. She found it disgusting that, while Oilcan wasn't much taller or more muscled, he was proportionally stronger than she was.

Pony eyed the bucket of milk as they walked to Tooloo's large walk-in cooler. "Ah, they are cows."

Tinker considered that the elves had a word for cows and chickens. "Yes. You seem . . . surprised."

"They don't look like our cows," he said. "And I have never seen any of ours milked before. *Kuetaun* caste handles livestock, not *sekasha.*"

"Oh, I see." That would explain his reactions to the chickens too. "Not in a hundred years?"

"I devoted a great amount of time to training. Only the best are chosen to be bodyguards, and that is what I wanted."

"Why?"

"It is what I'm good at. I enjoy it."

"But, doesn't it mean you're setting yourself up as a sacrifice to someone else's life?"

"If I do my job right, no. But if I must, yes."

"I don't understand how you can make yourself anyone's disposable servant."

"I choose who I guard, that is the only way it can be. Windwolf values my life as much as I value his; he protects me as I protect him."

They had stopped in front of Tooloo's ten-foot-square walk-in cooler. Tinker unlatched the heavy door, frowning at what Pony had said; it seemed to defeat the whole concept of bodyguard.

"Windwolf protects you?"

Pony cocked his head. "Why do you find that so hard to believe? You put yourself between me and harm, do you think that Windwolf would do anything less than that?"

She what? When did she protect Pony? Oh, when Nathan was being a butthead. "That was nothing."

She yanked open the door and cool moist air misted out into the sunshine.

"You put yourself in harm's way to save Windwolf." Pony let her take back the bucket and watched with interest as she poured the warm milk into wide-mouth crocks. "Not only against the EIA imposters at the Rim, but against the wargs at the salvage yard."

"I don't plan to make a living out of it." From another crock that had already separated, she skimmed off the cream with a clean ladle, filling a pint bottle for Lain. "Grab me one of those glass jars."

"In all things, there must be those who are willing to guard and protect." Pony picked up the bottle of milk. "It is the way of nature. You humans have *police* and *firefighters* and *EIA*. It is not that I do not value my life, but if I risk it, it is for a worthy cause."

Tinker supposed that Pony's job was not much different from

Nathan's. Stepping back out of the cooler, she latched the door and headed back into the store. Drat Tooloo, the half-elf had her seeing everything in a bad light already. And the comparison to Nathan dragged that whole mess up. Damn him, why had Nathan betrayed her that way? Beyond Lain and Oilcan, there wasn't another person in the city she would have opened the door for dressed only in a towel. The more she thought on it, the more she realized how much she misjudged Nathan. She had been looking at the cop, not the man. She expected him to stay the nice big brother type, only with kissing thrown in. In one giant step, they'd moved into new roles, and Nathan, the boyfriend, was a different person. That Nathan was possessive and overpowering. Perhaps her instinct to flee him at the Faire was for the best; perhaps no matter when or how they'd ended up on her couch, it would have led to Nathan trying to force her into something she didn't want.

And if that was the case, what did she do now? She'd opened the door and let the warg in; how did she get it back out?

Tinker tried, but she couldn't stretch the shopping out to the full two hours without alerting Tooloo or Pony that she was stalling. She and Pony returned to Observatory Hill a full forty minutes early, but Lain had already finished up and sat in the kitchen with a cup of tea and a stunned look on her face. The expression set off alarms in Tinker. She quickly stashed away the perishables from Tooloo's store and banished Pony to the foyer so she could safely discuss the results of the DNA tests with Lain.

"It's bad, isn't it?"

Lain raised an eyebrow. "What? Oh, no, I'm still stunned at the amount of change Windwolf accomplished in an adult seemingly without fear that it would kill you. You look so much like yourself that it didn't really click until I started working with your DNA. I-I-I'm in awe."

"Lain, please, you're freaking me out."

"You have no idea of the enormity of this. It changes everything we know about the elves' ability. We've considered the concept of elves being able to turn people into frogs with magic just folklore and urban legend."

"So you're saying I'm lucky not to be a frog?"

The stunned look vanished before annoyance. "Oh, Tinker!"

"Where did scientists think the gossamers and wyverns came from?"

"Humans have made amazing changes in animals over thousands of years of breeding. One only has to look at the extreme phenotypic variation of the canine genotype."

"What?"

"Dogs. From Chihuahuas to Irish Wolfhounds, they're all thought to be descendants from a species of small Northern European wolf."

"Lain, can we focus on me. What did you find out?"

"Don't you want to wait for Oilcan?"

"No. I think—if it's bad—he'll take it a lot worse than me. I want to deal with it so I can be strong for him."

"I wish I had thought to analyze your original DNA." Lain limped to her lab with Tinker following her. "This was a stunning chance to learn so much about the difference between our two races."

"Lain!"

"I'm sorry, but it's like watching someone destroy the Rosetta stone."

"The what?"

Lain sighed, picking up a thermometer. "You need a more rounded education."

"I am not in a mood to have my inadequacies discussed."

"Fine." Lain poked the thermometer into Tinker's ear, made it beep, and then took it out to look at the readout. "Ah, that's what I was afraid of." Lain limped to her medicine drawer and picked out several bottles. "Here, I want you to take these."

"Why?"

"Your white blood cell count is extremely high. Elves seem more resistant to disease, which suggests an aggressive immune system, so it's possible that an elevated count is normal. But you're running a low-grade fever, which isn't surprising considering all the cells of your body have been radically altered."

"They have?"

"All four of your samples were identical, which indicates the change was global."

"Oh. What are these?" Tinker eyed the pills that Lain shook out into her hand from several different bottles.

"Tylenol to control the fever." Lain recapped the bottles. "Calcium, folic acid, iron, zinc, and a multivitamin. I have no idea what Windwolf has done to you, but it might be viral in nature, so trying to stop the process might be disastrous. Those will help keep you strong through this; you probably should take a nap after this afternoon. Pushing yourself now could be very bad."

"So, all of my DNA samples were the same. What about mine compared to Oilcan's?"

"I separated the DNA out of all the samples, and used a restriction enzyme to cut the DNA into a defined set of fragments." Lain opened up a window on her workstation. "Those I stained with a fluorescent dye and passed it through the flow cytometer. As the laser strikes the fluorescent dye molecules that are bound to the DNA fragment, a photon 'burst' occurs. Because the number of photons in each burst is directly proportional to the fragment's size, the cytometer counts the photons in a burst to obtain an accurate fragment-size measurement."

Lain clicked open an image file showing a line of smudgy dots in a vertical row. "The resulting distribution of fragment sizes in the sample shows the raw DNA fingerprints. It's rough, but it's enough for our purposes. Basically, the more closely related two people are, the more gene sequences they will share."

"The smudgy dots?"

"Yes, those are gene sequences. This is the fingerprint of your blood."

"Okay." Tinker braced herself. "And Oilcan's?"

Lain reduced Tinker's sample and clicked open a second scan. "This is his."

At first glance, they didn't match. As Lain made them the same size, and placed them side-by-side, the differences only seemed greater.

"Oh." Tinker sat down, amazed at how much it hurt. She didn't think it would matter so much to her.

"It isn't as bad as it looks." Lain pointed to a cluster of dots in the center of Tinker's fingerprint. "These spots are from DNA on the telomere."

"The what?"

"Telomeres are segments of DNA at the ends of chromosomes. Each time a cell divides to make a copy of itself, the telomere gets shorter. Once it gets too short, the cell can't copy itself and dies. That's how we age. We've theorized that the elves would have longer telomeres than humans and thus age much slower; this is evidence that we're right."

"And the extra DNA is muddying the fingerprint, so to speak."

"Yes." Lain pointed to a second cluster. "This is from telomeres, and here too." Lain tapped a third section. "If you ignore these three regions, you'll see that the rest of the fingerprint is very similar."

Tinker squinted, trying to see "around" the smudges, wanting desperately to see the similarities. "I don't see it."

"Here." Lain opened up a third image. "This is my DNA."

"This is supposed to help?"

"Wait. I'm now isolating telomere DNA on your sample."

Red shot through Tinker's sample as the sections that Lain had pointed out as telomeres shifted color.

"Okay, let's find matching probe locus points in lane one and two." Lain flicked through another menu. Green flooded through Tinker and Oilcan's samples as ranks of black smudges turned to jade.

"That's what we share?"

"Yes." Lain pulled up a fresh copy of Tinker's DNA, isolated out the telomere, and placed it next to Lain's sample at the bottom of the screen. "As a control, let's compare your sample and mine."

Only a trace of green appeared.

Tinker looked back to the top of the screen, and all the lovely jade in the first two samples blurred slightly until she blinked away the tears. "So we're still cousins?"

"In my professional opinion, yes."

Tinker clapped, making the gods aware of her, and said, "Thank you."

"That settled, I have questions. How did Windwolf do this? Did he inject you with anything? Did he give you something to ingest?"

They spent the next ten minutes with Lain asking detailed questions and taking notes.

"You don't have to put down that we made love, do you?"

"Obviously it was vital to the spell. Sperm is made by nature to be a perfect carrier of DNA."

"Lain!"

"No one will know. This is just for me to know." Lain saved the notes, making them disappear into her computer system under heavy encryption. "So, Windwolf was the tengu of my dream after all."

Tinker paused, trying to remember exactly what Lain was talking about. "Oh, the raven elf."

Lain looked out her window at the garden Windwolf gifted on her. "You brought the tengu to me to bandage up. It turned you into a diamond and flew away with you in its beak."

"Lain, I'd rather not talk about prophetic nightmares and Chinese legends."

"Japanese," Lain corrected absently. "Just as the Europeans had brownies, and pixies, and elves, the Japanese have tengu, oni, and kitsune, and so forth."

"And Foo dogs."

"Well, the Foo dogs are Chinese, but they were imported along with Buddhism. The original religion of the Japanese is Shinto, a worship of nature spirits."

"If the tengu are the elves that can become crows, what are oni and kitsune?"

"Kitsune are the fox spirits. They usually appear to be beautiful women, but they really are just foxes that can throw illusions into their victim's mind."

Tinker made a face; silly nonsense was what she hated about fairy tales.

Lain tapped her on the head to stop Tinker from making faces. "Oni are fearsome ogres usually depicted as seven feet tall with red hair and horns. I've heard a theory that the oni are actually lost Vikings with horned helmets."

Now that sounded familiar. It all clicked together in her mind. "The three men who attacked us were very tall, with red hair. Windwolf called the pseudowargs Foo dogs. He also recognized your references to tengu. If we have legends of elves, and they are real, by simple logic then, the oni are real too."

Lain admitted Tinker's theory might be true with a thoughtful nod of her head, and then poked holes into it. "The world doesn't always follow simple logic. The cultures of the ancient worlds were highly contaminated by each other. The Chinese interacted with the Japanese, and then traded on the Silk Road to the Middle East, which spread into Europe. You can find the same children's story of Cinderella with the evil stepmother and the magical fairy godmother in almost every culture now. The oni could be just the Japanese version of our elves."

"But someone used Foo dogs and onilike people to try to kill Windwolf."

"There's so little we know about the elves, even after twenty years. For all we know, these attacks are part of elfin political infighting."

Tinker considered it, and shook her head. "No. Tooloo just gave me a history lesson and—provided it's all true—the elves are quite homogeneous."

"Ah." Lain murmured and thought for several minutes. "Then maybe there's something about oni that the elves aren't telling us."

Tinker glanced toward the foyer where Pony stood guard. "Weren't telling us. Windwolf has changed the game by swapping one of the players to the other team."

"Well," Lain locked up her workstation. "You crack that nut, and I'll make lunch."

* * *

Tinker felt guilty when she walked into the foyer and realized that Pony had been standing there since they returned from Tooloo's. "Why don't you sit down?"

"It's not proper—"

"Oh, sit down!" She pointed at the chair beside the door.

Pony sat, unhappy but obedient.

Tinker settled on the fourth step of the staircase, which put her level with Pony. "What do you know about oni?"

"Oni?" Pony lifted his hands to his head and made his index fingers into horns.

"Yes, oni."

"They are cruel and ruthless people with no sense of honor. Their weapons are crude, for they are a younger race than either elves or humans, but they spawn like mice and would crush us with sheer numbers."

So much for oni being mythical. "They live on Elfhome?"

Pony looked puzzled at this. "No, then they would have been elves. They live on Onihida."

"So, where is Onihida?"

Pony screwed up his face in the way that Tinker recognized as him reaching the limit of his ability to explain something. Finally he held out his left hand, palm down. "Elfhome." He waved his right hand under it. "Earth." Then, holding his right hand still, he moved his left hand under his right and waved it. "Onihida."

She pointed at his left hand. "How did you get to Onihida? Or did the oni come to Elfhome?"

"We found them." Pony looked daunted. He sat silent for several minutes, thinking. "There were at one time certain caves and rock formations that formed Pathways to walk from one world to the next. They were perilous, for the movement of the Moon and the planets made them inconstant."

It confirmed her family legend of caves being gates. Tinker suspected that a mineral deposit running through quartz next to a strong ley line could mimic the hyperphase field of a man-made gate. Like the gate in space, the power needed to be supplied to only one side to create two-way travel. Based on what Windwolf told her about gravity affecting magic, then perhaps ley lines had "tides" which would cause the gates to occasionally fail.

Pony plunged on. "While we bent our minds to shaping magic, humans learned to forge bronze and then steel. For goods we could not make ourselves, we walked the Pathways to Earth. We kept close to the Pathways and traveled heavily cloaked and mostly at night, for without magic we lived a breath away from death. But the risks were always well rewarded with rich trade goods."

Obviously Pony was using the historic "we" since the Pathways had mysteriously failed prior to the 1700s, and he had just hit his majority.

"But some of these Pathways led to Onihida," Tinker guessed.

"In a manner, yes." Pony scratched at the back of his head, pondering how to—as Tooloo put it—compress history into a teaspoon. "Where a Pathway opened on Earth, magic would flow out. While humans would only find a Pathway through blind luck, a *domana* could sense it from a distance. Still maps were made to keep careful track of the Pathways. One day on Earth, a *domana* found a Pathway that was not on our maps. Nor, when the matching location was investigated on Elfhome, could it be found where it opened. A group adventurous in spirit decided to investigate where the Pathway led. Twenty journeyed out, only two returned."

"The oni killed them?"

Pony nodded. "At first, the explorers had thought they'd somehow traveled to Elfhome, for Onihida—unlike Earth—flows rich with magic. Then they realized that the plants and the animals were unknown to them, and showed signs of being spell-worked." The elfin way of saying the object had been bioengineered. "Whereas on Earth, they would have easily traveled undetected, wards revealed their presence, and they were surrounded before they could flee back to Earth. The oni lords 'invited' them to a nearby fortress. The explorers were treated well, served rich foods, and offered beautiful whores. The oni called them their brothers and tried to deceive them, but a dragon always shows his teeth when he smiles."

"The oni wanted to know where the gate to Earth was?"

"Natural gates apparently were usually quite small." Pony measured out four feet with his hand. "Many only wide enough to take a pack horse through, and sometimes much smaller." He reduced the width to only two feet. "They were within dark caves, and like the veil effect," he waved his hand about to take in the house around him, shoved from Earth into Elfhome, "invisible. Anyone without the ability to detect a ley line could search closely, even to the point of stepping in and out of worlds, and never find it. Like the elves prior to the birth of *domana*, no oni passing through a gate to Earth had ever returned."

So that the oni didn't realize a gate wasn't just a deathtrap to be avoided until the elves showed up. "Obviously the explorers didn't reveal its location."

"At first, they easily evaded the questions, for they did not know the oni language, and deliberately misunderstood their gestures and the demands for maps to be drawn. But they were forcibly detained, taught the tongue, and asked more directly. Then they were tortured, then healed, and tortured again until their minds broke."

"That's horrible!" Tinker shuddered. "But the gate only led to Earth. The elves could have given it up to the oni without risking Elfhome."

Pony stood to pace. "The oni had spell-worked their warriors to be far stronger than the average man. What's more, they had discovered the secrets of self-healing and immortality, yet continued to breed like mice. With their numbers and abilities, they would have flooded Earth unchecked."

"I'm surprised that the elves cared that much about Earth."

"The explorers had traveled Earth for centuries; some had taken human lovers and sired half-breed children." He leaned against the banister to give her a soulful look. She found herself suddenly aware of his eyes, dark and full of sincere concern. "We have always seen humans as our reflection, good and bad. Man was how gods made the elves before the Skin Clan remade them."

Pony spoke with the same bitterness as Tooloo used while explaining the origin of the *domana* as the ruling caste.

"If elves hate the Skin Clan so much, why hasn't spell-working been banned?"

"It was for a while. Blight struck our main grain crop, though, and a great famine followed, so one of our most holy ones, Tempered Steel, petitioned for reform. *Evil lies in the heart of elves, not in magic.*"

This was one bit of elfin history she knew—learned from puppet shows during the Harvest Faire—only she had never understood the full context. Much was made that Tempered Steel was a *sekasha* monk, which made sense now, since a *domana*'s motives for bringing back spell-working would have been questionable. The creation of keva beans was linked to Tempered Steel's reform, saving the elves from starvation.

"Two of the explorers survived?" She steered the conversation back to the oni.

"Two escaped, reached the gate and returned to Elfhome. Once their tale was told, *sekasha* were sent to destroy the gate from Oni-hida to Earth, and then systematically all gates from Earth to Elfhome were destroyed."

"That seems rather drastic."

Pony clicked his tongue. "They say an elfin carpenter is more thorough than a human one, for he has forever to hammer down nails."

"Did they warn travelers first?"

"We had no way of contacting all the far-flung traders."

Thus her elfin ancestor and Tooloo were trapped on Earth. While long lived, without a source of magic, even elves age and die.

Pony half-turned, head cocked. "Someone is coming."

There were footsteps on the porch, and the front door opened. Oilcan paused in the doorway, surprised to find Tinker and Pony in the foyer, focused on his arrival. He tried for nonchalant but Tinker could read the tension in him. "Hey."

"Hey." Tinker held out her hand to him. "I got back early too."

He lifted his arm to take her hand and allowed her to pull him warily into the room. "Is it good?"

He meant the news about the tests.

"It's good." Tinker gave his hand a squeeze before letting go. "Everything's cool."

The tension flooded out of him with a huge sigh, and he grinned hugely at her. "Ah, that's great."

"Lain's making lunch."

"And she's finished," Lain called from the kitchen. "Come eat while it's hot."

The EIA was located in the Pittsburgh Plate Glass corporate head-quarters, the Rim having cut it off from all of PPG's factories and most of its customers. The building was a fairy castle done as a mod-ern glass skyscraper. Pony parked the Rolls in the open courtyard, ig-noring all the "No Parking" signs. Tinker wasn't sure if he couldn't read English, or if such things didn't apply to the viceroy's car.

There seemed to be some protocol to walking together. Outside she hadn't noticed it, but as she wandered about the crowded lobby, looking for an office directory and gathering odd looks, Pony tried matching her step in awkward starts and stops.

"Do you know where Maynard's office is?" she snapped finally.

"This way, *ze domi*." Pony led her to the elevators, where she gath-ered a few more double takes before the elevator's doors closed them off from curious stares.

What tipped people off that she was now an elf? Her ears weren't really visible, and certainly her hair was in the same "pure" hairstyle as always. It had to be the eyes—the shape and vivid color. She made a mental note to get a pair of sunglasses.

They hit the top floor, the doors opened and Pony pushed back an EIA employee by mere presence. It was still startling to see Pony go from invisible to in-your-face in a blink of an eye. After assuring himself that the floor was clear of menace, he allowed Tinker off.

On second thought, it probably wasn't anything about her tipping people off, it was the six-foot-something elfin guard.

The space beyond the elevator was small, elegant, and tastefully decorated to elfin sensibilities. The only furniture was two chairs for waiting visitors, and a receptionist desk staffed with a woman pretty enough to be mistaken for a high-caste elfin female.

"I'd like to see Director Maynard, if I can."

The woman was definitely staring at Pony as she asked, "And you are?"

Tinker gave the receptionist her name—making the woman's eyes go wide as if this were some startling news—and added, "Tell him it's very important that I see him."

Maynard came out of his office, saying, "Where have you been—" He took in first Pony's presence and then her new eyes. "Tinker?"

"Tinker *ze domi*," Pony corrected Maynard.

Maynard flashed a look back to Pony and then bowed to Tinker. "Tinker *ze domi*. It is good to see you're safe."

Oh, this couldn't be good if Maynard was doing it too.

A few moments later Tinker was in Maynard's office and, with careful maneuvering, Pony was not.

"I need language lessons," Tinker complained, ranging his office nervously. The reason for the tiny foyer was Maynard's office seemed to take up a large portion of the top floor. Must be a bitch to heat in the winter, although the AC seemed to work fine. The wall of windows looked out over the North Shore to the elfin forest beyond.

"I thought you spoke Elvish." Maynard anchored the conversation to his desk by sitting down behind it.

"Tooloo taught me like any elf would, cryptically. I would like a more direct routine, like a dictionary! I want to know for sure I understand what the hell is going on, instead of walking around thinking I know but probably getting it all wrong."

"Such as?"

"What the hell is this whole *ze domi, ze domi, ze domou ani*? I thought it was like Mr. and Ms., only politer. And what exactly does *husepavua* mean?"

"*Husepavua* literally means 'loaned voice'; figuratively it means an assistant. Sparrow Lifted By Wind is Windwolf's *husepavua*. *Sedoma* is the word for 'one who leads.' *Domou* is 'lord.' *Domi* is 'lady.'

Ze denotes a level of formality. *Ani/Ana* indicates the tie between the speaker and the noble. When it's *Ana* it means the speaker doesn't share a tie with that lord or lady. *Ani* means the speaker and the person he or she is addressing shares a tie with the noble. Basically 'my lord' or 'our lord.' "

My Lady Tinker. That's what Pony had been calling her. And the elves at the enclave. All the little presents. She'd nearly forgotten that. *May I wish you merry, my lady.*

Her knees went, and luckily there was a chair close enough to collapse into. "Am I—am I—*married* to Windwolf?"

"It seems a very strong possibility." Maynard spoke with what seemed like exaggerated care. "What exactly has happened since you left the Faire with Windwolf?"

She was surprised for a moment that he knew her movements and then remembered that he was the head of the EIA. "We went north to his hunting lodge and . . . and"—she swept a hand down over herself to indicate the transformation—"he cast this spell on me and I woke up yesterday like this. Pony says that Windwolf was called back to Aum Renau, and that he ordered Pony to guard me, so Pony hasn't left my side since yesterday. He slept on the floor of my bedroom last night. I think he slept."

Maynard winced slightly. "Yes, a very strong possibility that you're married to Windwolf."

She sat there stunned for a few minutes. Maynard got up, opened a cabinet to expose a small bar, and poured out a drink for her. She eyed the clear liquid, dubious after the beer, but it was strong and sweet and burned its way down. After she drank it, she realized it was the same stuff that the elves at the enclaves had used to toast her during Nathan's date—only it tasted much better now. "What was that?"

"Ouzo. Anisette liqueur. The elves love it."

She groaned as she realized that the elves had toasted her marriage in front of Nathan. Oh, thank goodness he hadn't understood what was going on—a pity she hadn't known either. "I just want to know when I supposedly agreed to all this. I didn't ask him to do this." She meant making her an elf. "At least I don't think I did. And I *know* there wasn't any wedding."

"You probably accepted a gift from him?" Maynard made it a question, clueing her.

"Well, there was this weird brazier that he gave me. That's when he marked me."

Maynard pinched the bridge of his nose as if to ward off a headache. "I'm guessing that the brazier was a betrothal gift. Windwolf offered marriage—and everything it entails—and you accepted. When he put the *dau* mark on you, you were, in essence, married."

"You're kidding."

"In elfin culture, it is offering and acceptance that are important. Everything else, as we humans are wont to say, is icing on the cake."

"That's it? No priest? No church? No vows? No blood test?" Well, strike that. Pony had said that Windwolf gave her a blood test.

"That your word of honor is binding is the keystone of elfin society."

"I don't know if I want to be married to him! What if I want to get out of it? Do elves have divorce?"

"Frankly, I don't know." He sighed. "I'm sorry, but the last thing I want to do is to disturb the marital bliss of the viceroy. That would be bad for relations between the two races."

"Are you saying that you can't help me?"

"No." Then he clarified himself. "I'm not saying that." He spoke slowly, obviously studying what he'd say before speaking, looking for traps. "This is a very delicate situation. On one hand I'm going to have humans, on Elfhome and Earth, see this in the worst possible light. And on the other side, any complaints might seem to be questioning Windwolf's honor."

"Big whoop-de-do!"

"Windwolf is acting head of the Wind Clan in the Westernlands."

It irritated Tinker that she had such an incomplete understanding of elfin society. She knew that there were clans and castes and households and families but, like most humans, could never get a clear picture of how they all worked. While she knew that major clans were named after the four elements, and that there were lesser clans, she'd only met elves from the Wind Clan. They had names like Sparrow Lifted By Wind, Galloping Storm Horse On Wind—and Wolf Who Rules Wind. As a child, she'd assumed that "Wind" meant they were part of the same family, until Tooloo explained that it denoted clan alliance, that most clan members were not related, and that a family usually shared the same clan, but not necessarily always. Clear as mud, as her grandfather would say.

What Tooloo had taught her thoroughly was the elfin code of honor. You kept your word, and you never implied that an elf's word wasn't as solid as cash. A single slur could pit you not only against the elf you insulted, but all the elves "beholden" to them. Implying that the head of a clan wasn't honorable would be slurring the entire clan, in this case, all the elves in the Westernlands.

"Let's start with the simple things first," Maynard said. "Are you in love with Windwolf? Do you want to be married to him?"

If those were the simple questions, then they were in trouble. Life as an elf was easier to imagine than being married. What did married people even do when not having sex?

Maynard sat, waiting for her to decide, saying nothing to sway her.

"I don't know," she finally admitted. "I've never been in love before; I don't know if I'd recognize it when I felt it."

"But it's a possibility?"

"It would be easier for you if I said yes."

"Yes, it would, but I'm not going to close my eyes to a rape, if that was what it was."

"No!" Tinker squirmed in her chair. "I can take care of myself. I wanted him. I just didn't expect this!"

"I've heard you speak low tongue; you're extremely fluent. Windwolf might have assumed that you knew his culture better than you do based on your fluency of his language."

"Well, I don't. I can't believe that there's nothing in the treaty to cover this." Tinker pushed back hair to expose her ear. "You made laws against this, didn't you?"

"We didn't know the elves could do this," Maynard said quietly, "in order to prevent it. Is that why you're here? Do you want charges pressed?"

"No. At least I don't think so. Depends. I haven't had a chance to talk to Windwolf yet."

"Why are you here?"

Tinker shifted in her chair. "It's weird. Before this, if I found something out, I'd consider things in a 'me versus the EIA' way. What do I get out of it? Will I get into trouble knowing this? Will this bring the EIA down on me? And now—maybe I'm afraid people will think I've changed loyalties as well as my ears."

"What did you learn?"

"There were, might still be, natural gates on Elfhome. It's a matter of getting magic to resonate on the right frequency, and you open up a wormhole to another dimension. Most of Westernlands is unexplored, so there might be gates here that the elves don't know about."

"Between Elfhome and Earth."

"Or someplace else," she said. "We have legends of more than just the elves. In Japan, the people from other worlds are known as the oni. Pony told me this morning that the oni are from Onihida, and they're the main reason that elves stopped trading with humans a millennium ago. The oni are very tall, and red haired, with a grudge against the elves."

"Windwolf's attackers."

"Somewhere, there's a gate to a third world open, and the oni are coming through. They're here, in Pittsburgh."

"Does Windwolf know?"

Tinker considered and nodded. "I think he might. Certainly, it might be the reason that the queen of the elves is in the Westernlands."

9: A GATHERING OF WYVERNS

◦←━━⊃ ⊂━━→◦

There, she had done her duty to the human race, and reported her suspicions to Maynard. Only it didn't make her feel better. She'd repeated Pony's story and Tooloo's history lesson and gone away feeling like an alarmist circulating dangerous rumors. Maynard had nothing he was willing to add to her news, so she left still in the dark and feeling grumpy.

On top of that, it felt ridiculous to ride into the scrap yard in the back of the Rolls-Royce: the elegance of the car rolling into the lot of wrecked machines, and her handed out like a fairy princess. She was tempted to kick Pony just to protect her junkyard-dog image. Checking the impulse, she unlocked the offices, disarmed the security system, and got gently put aside so Pony could check out the offices.

"My system was up and running, so no one is in here," she complained, following him in. She should have kicked him. The air was stale, smelling still of blood and peroxide. The offices suddenly struck her with their worn, cluttered ugliness. All the office equipment was second-hand, jarring in its mismatched, battered appearance. Despite her best efforts to stay paperless and organized, the paperwork sprouted out of every nook and cranny.

"Forgiveness," Pony murmured, but continued looking. In the small, crowded rooms, he seemed larger and more imposing.

She ignored the impulse to get out a beer. One, it was way too early to start drinking; secondly and more importantly, the beer would just taste like piss. She was going to have to find some ouzo somewhere.

Sparks had nearly a hundred messages cued up. She told her bot to skip past all messages from Nathan, and the number of waiting messages dropped by half. There were messages from Oilcan, Lain, Maynard, and the NSA from the time she had been with Windwolf, covering all bases as they tried to locate her. Those she had Sparks delete. The last two dozen messages were from actual customers, looking for parts and wanting to sell scrap.

"Sparks, make a list of wanted parts."

"Okay."

The door burst open, and Riki rushed in. "Where the hell have you—"

Pony had his sword out and to the grad student's neck, cutting off the words while almost cutting open his neck.

"Pony!" Tinker cried.

Riki had rebounded, hitting the door frame in an attempt to get back out the door, his hands up in a hopefully universal signal of un-armed surrender. "Hey! Watch it!"

"Put your sword away, Pony," Tinker commanded. "He works for me. This is Riki."

Pony eyed the tall gangly human suspiciously, even as he sheathed his sword. "Riki?"

"Yeah, dude, Riki."

"He doesn't speak English," Tinker told Riki. "Windwolf told him to guard me."

"I see." Riki continued to eye Pony, but Tinker could only stare at Riki. A cut split the skin of his cheek, his nose was clearly broken, and his sunglasses couldn't completely cover the fact that both eyes were blackened. Everything was purpling gloriously, which meant the damage had been done soon after she last saw him, three days ago.

"What the hell happened to you?"

"I got in a fight." He glanced at her for the first time and stared. "Oh, shit. What the hell did you do?"

"I didn't do anything."

"Oh, you did something! You're a fucking prissy elf!"

She was stunned at the venom that he put into the word and pro-jected at her. "What's your problem?"

"You sold yourself to them like a whore, only you did it body and soul. I didn't think you were such a slut. How many of them did you fuck until you found one that could remake you?"

"*What?*" It took a moment to actually get something else out. "You're one word away from being fired. You don't know anything about me, about what's happened to me. You have no right to talk to me that way."

He snapped his mouth shut and spent a moment or two choking on whatever he wanted to say. "I'm sorry," he finally managed to growl. "It's not you I'm mad at, but you're here and they're not."

"If you're pissed at someone else, go scream at them."

"Okay." He ducked his head down again. "I'm sorry."

She glanced to Pony, slightly surprised that he had let the shouting take place, even if he didn't understand the language. Pony stood tense, one hand gripped around his hilt. Okay, he was ready to shish kebab Riki. The danger of Pony actually doing just that helped cool Tinker's anger.

"Look, there was a misunderstanding between me and Windwolf. I didn't know he was going to do this to me, and I'm not sure how I feel about it. So can we just ignore it for a while and get some work done?"

"Fine," Riki snapped, much too fast to have really thought about it, but she'd deal with that if and when he brought it back up.

"Who did you get in a fight with?"

He blinked a moment at the sudden change of subject before saying, "Some elves at the Faire. I said the wrong thing. The jerks took it as an insult."

She'd never heard of elves ganging up on anyone before. Usually honor dictated that fights were one against one. "What did you say?"

Riki sucked his teeth a second before saying, "I'm not sure. I was really drunk, and I thought I was being friendly."

Well, if Riki was drunk, then anything could have happened, including him just tripping and falling flat on his face. It at least explained why he suddenly hated elves.

She searched the top of her desk, found her headset, and pulled it on. It fit oddly on her new ears and refused to stay in place. "Sparks, upload the list to my headset."

"Yes, Boss."

Now if she could get Riki to be as cheerful and helpful.

She fought with her headset long enough to scan the parts list, and then stuck it in her pocket to be modified later. The quickest order to fill was an alternator for a turn-of-the-century Dodge truck. She dragged Riki through the yard to where she knew a Dodge sat already partially stripped of door panels, back axle, and windshield. Pony made sure no one was hiding in among the salvaged cars, and then settled into a guard position a couple dozen feet back.

Tinker leaned into the cab to pop the hood latch. "Do you know anything about engines, Riki?"

"I know the basic parts. Why?"

"It would be nice to know what I can trust you to do. Lots of different jobs go into keeping this place profitable. If you can't buy your own food, keep clothes on your back, and heat your place in the wintertime, the EIA ships you back to Earth."

She found the latch, slipped it aside, and hoisted up the hood. As usual, she couldn't reach it up high enough to fit the brace into place. God, she hated being short. Why couldn't Windwolf have fixed that while he was turning her into an elf? Maybe she would start growing again. It would be nice to be taller.

Riki pushed the hood up and slipped the brace into its slot.

"Thanks." She spread out her catchall. "So, what's the alternator?"

"Here." He tapped on it.

"Good." She stepped up onto the bumper so she could lean over the engine to reach the fist-sized part. "Okay. Carburetor."

They played name-that-part while she used WD-40 and patience to loosen up nuts and bolts untouched for years.

"Nuts and bolts are important here." She coaxed one set after another off and tucked them into the catchall's pocket, where they couldn't fall to the ground and possibly be lost. "Don't strip them if you can help it, and don't lose them. If you find one on the ground, pick it up. I've got boxes of spares back in the offices. Lose a vital bolt, and you could wait two months for a simple repair to be done."

"Two months?"

"One Shutdown to order the lost piece, a second Shutdown for it to be delivered."

Riki grunted. He was looking at her oddly. With slow carefulness—as if he expected her to hit him if he moved too fast—he took out his handkerchief and wiped grease off her nose. "I can't figure you out. If you just went to Earth, you wouldn't have to be mucking around with junk like this."

"I like this," she growled. "What's so great about pure science? So what if the universe is expanding or contracting? What difference will it make?"

"What difference will a used alternator make?"

"It makes a hell of a difference to the poor schmo with his Dodge up on jacks, waiting for this part."

He grinned briefly, and then sobered. "I don't know what Windwolf offered you, but remember that everything has costs. Sometimes the price is out in the open, and sometimes it's hidden."

"One fight makes you an expert in elves?"

"I don't need to know about elves to know how the universe

works. There are always strings attached, and it's the hidden ones that are the real bitches."

Yeah, like suddenly being married. "I said I didn't want to talk about it. I'm pretty freaked out about it."

"I'd be more pissed than freaked, especially with a watchdog thrown into the deal." Riki jerked his head in the direction of Pony. "I would hate having to hide everything from a spy on top of dealing with the change. Or are you so naïve that you don't realize everything you say and do is going to be reported back to Windwolf?"

"Can we just drop this?" Tinker cried. "And I'm not naïve! I've been careful all morning about what I said and did around him." But all the juggling had been for Pony's sake alone. Having a total stranger invade her life had been intrusive enough without making him privy to all her personal conversations. It hadn't occurred to her that Pony might report her activities back to Windwolf, or that Windwolf might have arranged a guard just for that purpose. Had he? Her gut instincts said no, but what did she really know about Windwolf?

"I'm just trying to warn you. You do know it works two ways."

"What do you mean?"

"He can also keep you from doing anything Windwolf doesn't like."

"Like what?"

"I don't know." Riki raised his hands to show he was innocent of the knowledge. "I can only guess. I'm fairly sure that I can't take you out for a drink, just the two of us, on my bike. Which is a shame, because you seem like you could use a drink."

She shifted uneasily. "I've got a ton of work to do."

"You really amaze me. If I were you, the last thing I would want is to go through the motions with some watchdog keeping an eye on me. I'd take off, take a little *me* time to deal with being jerked out of the human race."

"That would be immature."

"News flash: You're still a kid. And here's another important announcement: You're now stuck that way."

"I'm an adult."

"As a human," Riki said. "As an elf, you're about sixty years shy. You're not going to be an adult for a long, long time."

She could only stare at him in horror. "Oh, no, no, no."

"Like I said, if I were you, I'd ditch the watchdog and fly."

She barely kept from looking toward Pony. "Yeah, with him watching every minute?"

"Duck around the car where he can't see you, and I'll stand here and keep talking. He'll probably assume you're working there."

"And what about you? When he figures out I'm gone?"

"Don't worry about me. I'm very good at pretending to be harmless."

It was blind panic that took her out of the scrap yard and halfway back to her loft. True to his word, Riki stood at the Dodge and talked to thin air as she crept to the back of the truck, around an old PT Cruiser and into the Fords. Then, before she knew it, she was walking faster and faster until she was running.

She started for her loft out of pure instinct, which became more rational as she grew nearer to home. Without thinking, she'd taken Pony to the three places she'd most likely lie low: Oilcan's condo, Lain's house, and Tooloo's store. That left the hotel on Neville Island. She'd need the keys to the front door, her shotgun and fishing pole, and some money. A change of clothes would be nice too, but if she delayed at her loft too long, Pony might catch up with her. Rounding the last corner, she glanced over her shoulder. No sign of her watch-dog yet.

Thus Tinker nearly collided with the stranger.

That the person was tall and redheaded impressed Tinker first. She jerked back away from the stranger, gaining an arm's distance to realize that the stranger was a female elf, not one of the tall male humans who had attacked her on Shutdown. The elf was slender and beautiful, with hair the color of fire, pulled back and braided into a thick cord. Like Pony, she wore a vest of wyvern-scale armor, and permanent spell tattoos scrolled down her arms; both were done in shades of red that matched her hair.

"Sorry, I didn't see you," Tinker said in English.

The elf's eyes went to the *dau* mark on Tinker's forehead. "Tinker *domi*?"

Oh, hell, the elf knew her name. At least the elf didn't have horns. Unfortunately, the female wasn't alone. She had two brothers or cousins: tall, elegant redheads loaded with weapons. The one farthest back actually stood on her doorstep—they had been coming from or going to her loft. Either way, they blocked her from the safety of her place and the gas station down the street. Everything behind her was abandoned until one hit the scrap yard.

"Who are you?" Tinker hedged away from the elf. "What do you want?"

"Kiviyau fom ani. Batya!"

Or at least that's what she thought the female said. The elf had an odd accent that made her hard to understand. The first and last words were fairly clear. *Kiviyau.* Come. *Batya.* Immediately. Tinker could also read the body language fairly easily. The female definitely wanted her to come with them.

"Chata?" Tinker tried for a stall by asking why while taking a step backward. Every muscle in her body had gone taut as a stretched elastic band, thrumming with the chorus of "run, run, run" so loud she was sure the elves could hear it.

"Kiviyau. Batya!"

"I don't understand. *Naekanat.*" She took another step backwards. *"Chata?"*

There was some weird universal law that stated, when faced with someone that didn't understand, humans spoke loud and slow, and elves talked polite and fast. The female went into a rapid tirade of High Elvish.

"I don't understand," Tinker said. "Please, explain in—"

"Kiviyau!" The female stepped forward, lifting a hand to catch hold of her. She might as well have pulled a trigger; Tinker bolted.

Later Tinker would realize that her brain had mapped out an escape route, but at the moment, she went blindly. She didn't expect to get anywhere; no one won footraces with elves. She ducked into the narrow space between two buildings and had reached the next street over before she knew that she was running. As she darted across the empty street, then through the obstacle course of the old school yard playground, she realized that she was running as fast as a startled rabbit. It dawned on her that she was an elf too, shorter of leg, but that she otherwise had all their advantages. Well, except the guns. And the fact that there were three of them. She would have to do something about that, but gently, just in case these were rude cousins of Windwolf's.

As she plunged down Tooloo's steep hill, she detoured off the path through the apple trees to cut through the beehives. As she flashed past the wooden boxes, she thumped the sides hard and was gone, leaving behind a growing angry buzz, and a moment later, shouts of surprise and pain. At the bottom of the hill, she dropped to the ground and rolled under the lowest strand of barbed wire, then scrambled on hands and knees through the barnyard muck. Yin and Yang came at her, hissing, wings half spread.

"Not me, you stupid things. Them! Them!" Tinker cried, risking a look back.

The female had discovered that the top wire was electrified and was backing up to vault the fencing.

Shit! Tinker picked up gravel and tossed it toward the fence, calling, "Chick, chick, chick!" Instantly, all the barnyard fowl ran toward the falling pebbles, pecking and scratching for corn.

She ducked into the barn while behind her Yin and Yang started to honk out warnings at the stranger landing in their midst. The warehouse Tooloo used as a haybarn had little in common with a real barn except the deep shadows, the scent of hay, and the drift of dust on the air. The female elf barked commands, and there were answering calls, spiraling in around the barn. Tinker had planned to just cut through the barn, but now she tucked herself into one of the smaller nooks, panting, scared. What now?

She shouldn't have ditched Pony, that's what. What the hell had she been thinking? Obviously she hadn't been thinking. Someone had tried to kill Windwolf, and someone had killed her father, and how did she know that these weren't the same someones?

She spied a pile of things and scrambled toward it, muttering, "Stupid, idiotic, moron, brain-dead ass"—which might have made her feel better if she hadn't been talking about herself. Tooloo must have traded someone for several yards of fishnet, a set of ninepins complete with two balls, a spring hinge, a length of cord, and a collection of hickory walking sticks. She grabbed the hinge, two of the sticks, and the fishnet.

Minutes later, the far door creaked open and one of the male elves slipped into the barn with her. She flung the first ninepin ball at him. The ball was weighted differently than a horseshoe, but she managed to nail him in the temple. As he went down, the female came through the near door and rushed her. Tinker tripped the spring hinge; it flung the netting—weighed down with the ninepins threaded through the holes of the net—over the female. Snatching up the hickory stick, Tinker swung as hard as she dared.

The elf shouted, throwing up her arm. Magic spilled out of the ruby on her earring, traced down the crimson tattoos on her arm, and flared into a shimmering red force.

It was like hitting a brick wall, inches from the elf's body.

A shield spell! Oh shit, I'm in trouble now!

The female flung off the net, the pale red aura of the shield pulsing around her arms. She balled up her fist, hauled back, and swung at Tinker.

Oh, this is going to hurt! Tinker flung up the stick, trying to block the blow.

But then, appearing like magic, Pony was there. *"Domi!"* He caught Tinker from behind, and jerked her backward out of range of the female.

The male she'd nailed with the ball was staggering to his feet, and the much stung and vastly annoyed second male was closing fast.

"Pony!" Tinker tried to run, but couldn't pull free of his grasp. "They're coming!"

Pony tucked her behind him, maintaining his grip on her. He held out his empty hand to the strangers. "Hold! Hold!"

"What are you doing?" Tinker cried, still trying to get free. Surely he wasn't going to fight all three unarmed.

"You must not fight them!" Pony said quietly. "They're Wyverns."

"Wyverns?" Tinker twisted in his hold to peek around him. What the hell did that mean? They looked like regular elves to her. The three halted, so perhaps there was the time for an explanation.

"Promise me, please, that you will not fight them," Pony pleaded.

"Okay." Tinker, who had been considering running, had no problem with not fighting.

Pony turned, keeping her tucked behind him, and spoke carefully in High Elvish. He went on at length. The looks cooled from anger to slight disgust and total annoyance.

The strangers finally replied, which generated another long elegance from Pony.

"I have explained that you are only recently transformed and that you do not know the high tongue nor recognize their uniforms. They understand the situation now, and while they are the Wyverns, they are also merely *sekasha* and do not wish to face the full anger of Windwolf."

Tinker grunted to keep in snide remarks. Annoyed as she was, even if it was one-on-one and without swords, they would probably still beat the snot out of her. It was so lowering and frightening to discover exactly how small you were in the world.

"Are you hurt?" Pony asked.

"I'm fine," Tinker said.

"I am sorry. I should have been here to forestall such a misunderstanding."

"Who the hell are these guys?"

Pony raised an eyebrow. "I told you. They are Wyverns."

"What the hell are Wyverns?"

"Oh," Pony said. "I see. They are the queen's guard. They bring a summons from the queen."

"Summons? Is that like being arrested?"

"No. Not completely. The Wyverns have come on the queen's personal airship to take you to Aum Renau. It is not a summons that we can refuse."

"You mean, we have to leave now?"

"Yes. The order indicates all speed must be taken."

"Why?"

Pony turned to the waiting elves and spoke with them. When he turned back, he was wincing slightly. "They did not ask; it is not in their manner to do so."

On the way back to the Rolls, she remembered she had her headset stuffed into her pocket. She guessed it was just as well; getting the police involved would have only complicated things. She called Oilcan and let him know that she was safe but being taken to Aum Renau.

"I want to come with you," Oilcan said.

"No, no, no. I'm fine." She didn't want to get him caught in the mess she was in. "Someone has to keep the yard going."

"There's Riki."

Yeah, Riki, who talked me into ditching Pony, she thought and then sighed, knowing that wasn't fair. Riki couldn't have known that the Wyverns were standing on her doorstep. "I went and saw Maynard. He says—well—that Windwolf probably thinks we're married. If that's the case, then the queen probably just wants to meet the viceroy's new wife."

"You're *what*?"

"Married. Please don't tell anyone yet, at least until I know for sure. Windwolf is at Aum Renau. He won't let anything happen to me."

There was long silence from Oilcan's side, and finally, "Okay, okay, okay. Don't get hurt."

"I won't." She folded away the headset.

"I've been thinking," Pony said quietly. "If we are going to court, it would be best that you did not have a guard, but have a guard."

She considered the sentence. He was using two different forms of have; she had thought the words were equal, but obviously they weren't. "What do you mean?"

"It would raise your esteem in court. Unless you do not wish me to be your guard."

The idea of being completely alone raised sudden panic in her. "No. I want you to be my guard. I don't want a stranger."

"I would be honored to be your guard." He paused to bow low. "I will not disappoint you."

10: BLIND SIGHT

A gossamer airship was moored over the Faire Ground's now-empty meadow. Tinker had seen many gossamers at a distance, but never one close enough to appreciate their true size. Something so huge, living, floating in mid-air challenged the mind to accept it as truth. The gondola alone was a hundred feet long and sixty feet wide; the gossamer rippled in the wind above it, dwarfing the teak structure. And that was the portion of the animal easily seen—the cell structure of the creature fractured the sunlight into a million prisms, giving substance to the nearly transparent form. The creature's countless frilled fins, extending far beyond the glittering mass, showed only as a distortion high overhead, like water running over a glass roof.

"How much tinkering did you have to do to get the gossamers that big?"

"I believe getting them large was not the problem," Pony said. "They occur in nature nearly that size. Probably making them float in air was the difficult part. Originally they were sea creatures."

"Why wouldn't they start with something that already floated in air?"

"You can grow wings on turtles, but they still crawl on the ground."

"What the hell does that mean?"

Pony struggled a moment to put it into words. "Those that float in air naturally go where the air takes them. They needed something that could choose its own course—a swimmer."

It took her a moment to realize he was talking of instinct. "You can give turtles wings—somehow—but not the understanding of flight."

"Yes!" Pony beamed a smile. "There are some side considerations. Redesigning a body structure to take the stresses of such a massive size in strong currents would have been difficult, so they selected an animal already quite large."

"Who are 'they'?"

"The *domana*."

On a signal from the Wyverns, there was a loud clank above their heads as safety locks disengaged. An ornately carved, wooden elevatorlike cage smoothly lowered from the gondola. The doors were handmade works of art, and they folded aside to reveal the stunningly beautiful Sparrow Lifted By Wind. Her shimmering white gown of Faire silk was cut so far off her shoulders—displaying her pearly skin, delicate bone structure, and full breasts to perfection— that Tinker wasn't sure what was keeping the dress on, except for the fact that it was too tight to otherwise slip down. What kept Sparrow from being the antithesis of Hannah Briggs' tight black was an overdress of cerulean that drifted around her like smoke and matched the blue of her *dau* mark. Sapphires, cerulean ribbons, and pale blue forget-me-not flowers weaved through her intricate pale blond braids, not a hair out of place.

Instantly Tinker realized that she was covered with motor grease, engine oil, dirt, and chicken shit. That she wore Oilcan's hand-me-down T-shirt, her worn carpenter pants, and boots large enough for Minnie Mouse didn't help either. "Oh, hell," she breathed.

"*Husepavua.*" Pony bowed in greeting.

Tinker started to bow too, but Pony checked her with a hand to her shoulder and a slight shake of his head.

Sparrow's eyes narrowed slightly at the gesture, and she flicked her hand dismissively at Pony. "You are released from this duty. Take the car and return to the enclave."

"I am *ze domi ani's*"—Pony stressed the plural—"guard. I will be going with her."

Pony startled Sparrow into showing cold deep anger that smoothed away a moment later.

"Come, then." Sparrow motioned toward the elevator cage. "I am needed at Aum Renau and can ill spare my attention for this babysitting run."

More than three would have crowded the elevator, so the Wyverns waited on the ground while Sparrow, Pony, and Tinker boarded. The doors had to be closed manually, and a bell rung to signal that all was ready for the cage to be raised. Still, the elevator rose as smoothly as it had descended.

Sparrow studied Tinker as they rode upward, and gave a slight sniff. "She smells so much of mud, one would think Wolf Who Rules fashioned her out of dirt."

Pony did not bother to hide his anger. "You fumbled badly, Sparrow. The Wyverns dealt with her in their normal heavy-handed manner and nearly hurt *ze domi ani*. You should have accompanied them."

"And you should remember I'm *domana* now, not *kuetaun*," Sparrow chided him. "As for the Wyverns . . ." She clicked her tongue in an elfin shrug. "The fault does not lie with me. No one would expect the Wyverns to be stupid enough to attack the viceroy's wife."

The cage slid up into the gondola and the safety locks reengaged with a thud under their feet, muffled now by wood and carpet.

Sparrow folded back the door to reveal that the cage was tucked into an alcove of a richly paneled hallway. "I have clothes for her; they'll need fitting. First, though, she'll have to have the barnyard washed off her. Go, clean her."

Tinker bristled. "I can speak low tongue quite well. And I'm fully capable of washing myself."

"Then do so. We have much to do before we arrive at Aum Renau. You must be fit to be brought before the queen." Sparrow bowed curtly and shot a hard look at Pony to collect a bow from him. Once Pony had paid his due to her, she flowed away, a shimmer of white and cerulean.

"This way, *domi*," Pony murmured to Tinker, indicating that they were to get out of the way of the arriving Wyverns. He led her down the hallway that cut through the center of the gondola. Behind them, the gossamer's crew prepared to cast off the moorings. There was an odd unpredictability to the floor that hadn't been that noticeable standing still; it shifted right and left, up and down minutely, so that each stride felt like a misstep.

Rooms were carefully balanced off either side of the hallway. The first door stood open, revealing an observation room, all done in creamy white and accents of red, with a bank of windows open to sky. Three elf females sat surrounded with bolts of Faire silk, laughing as they worked with the material. They looked up as Tinker paused to glance in at the view, and they went into stunned silence at her appearance.

"Pardon," Tinker stammered, and started to bow out of reflex. Again Pony caught her shoulder and shook his head. "Why do you keep doing that?" she whispered as she fled the doorway.

"You are higher caste than Sparrow and those females," Pony said. "There is no one on board that you should bow to."

"Oh." Tinker pointed to her forehead. "The *dau*?"

"Yes, the *dau*, and that you are now Windwolf's *domi*." Pony opened a door to a small room of hand–painted ceramic tiles. The motif was phoenix and flame flowers—a riot of reds and oranges on pristine white. "This is the bath. Do you wish to be attended? I can call a female . . ."

"No!" she cried, then eyed the room. Having been practically raised by Tooloo, she thought she knew how elves bathed—just like humans. The room certainly challenged her notion of this. She recognized the bathrobe hanging on a hook, but there were no faucets. There was what looked like a pull chain dangling next to a spout, but it was at knee level. "This is a bathroom?"

Pony considered the question carefully and then nodded. "Yes." He leaned into the room—he seemed loath to actually enter it—and lifted up a wooden disc sitting on a wide waist-high shelf. Beneath it was a large circular tank of steaming water. "This is the *pesh*." He replaced the lid. "*Bae.*" This was a wide shallow bowl. "*Giree.*" A dried hollow gourd. "*Safat.*" A sponge-looking . . . thing.

"Soap?" she said hopefully.

Thankfully there was soap, heavenly scented, in a paste form close enough to bar soap that she could wing it. Pony handed the soap crock down off its shelf, then stood there, distressed. "I can get an attendant to help you."

"I can wash myself." *Yeah. Sure.* "Just—what's the pull chain for?"

Pony winced. "The wash water." He pointed to the low spout. "You fill the basin and pour it over you, then use the soap and the *safat*, and rinse again, then into the *pesh* to soak."

"Ah, I see." Seemed a damn uncomfortable way to wash, but she supposed it saved water. No wonder Tooloo stuck to human showers. "I can handle it from here."

The cold-water scrub was bracing—she'd rather never do that again. The tub's water seemed hot enough to melt her into a careless puddle, but she found herself worrying about everything. Why did the queen want to see her? Was Windwolf in some type of trouble for using the Skin Clan magic? How was she going to stand being so short and plain in a herd of high-caste elves? And why did Sparrow have a *dau* mark? Had the female been human in some distant past?

Pony tapped on the door. "*Domi*, pardon, but Sparrow does need you to fit your clothes."

It took every ounce of courage to climb out of the tub, tie on the bathrobe, and unlatch the door.

Pony looked as unhappy as she felt.

"What's wrong?" she asked him, trying not to clench the bathrobe tight around her. It covered her neck to ankles and then some, but still she felt naked in front of him.

"There is much for you to know before you meet the queen, what is proper and what would be unspeakably rude. It is not my . . . place to tell you these things, for I am just *sekasha*—but there is only Sparrow, and I'm afraid she's taking a *kaet*."

"A *kaet*?" She giggled; it was a purposely rude way of saying Sparrow was throwing a snit. "Why?"

"I suspect she's jealous of you."

"Of me?"

"She had ambitions to become Windwolf's wife." Seeing the look on her face, Pony added quickly. "No, no, they are not old lovers. There are some who make alliances with marriages, where two work together well, and they agree to make it a partnership. But that would not suit Windwolf."

"Are you sure?"

"I have known Windwolf all my life, and I believe I see him with clarity, whereas Sparrow—age only makes you wiser if you stay honest with yourself."

"Why does she have a *dau*?"

"Windwolf's father marked her when she was young to raise her out of the *kuetaun* caste, otherwise the *sekasha* would have never listened to her orders."

Ah, yes, the snobbery of elves. Like it or not, she was stuck dealing with it now. "What does the queen want with me anyhow?"

"She wishes to see you."

"Me? Why? I'm just a snot-nosed Pittsburgh teenager with an interesting ear job."

Pony nodded several times, as if ticking off her words in an effort to parse them. "Yes," he finally said, still nodding. "Exactly."

"What?"

"You are a young elf. All things elfin fall under the queen's power. Now that you are elfin, so you are now her subject."

"Automatically? I don't get any say?"

"No more than when you were born in Pittsburgh and fell under Maynard's power."

She wanted to say that was different, but she couldn't decide how. The fact that her conception was far from normal—perhaps paralleling her transformation into an elf—gave her a very unstable base to argue from. "Does she do this with every elf?"

"No. You are, however, now her cousin."

"What!"

"You are now her cousin," Pony repeated, more slowly.

"How did that happen?"

"You married Windwolf."

"He's her cousin?"

"Yes, which, by law, makes you her cousin too."

It was such a sane reason that Tinker found it comforting.

"Please." Pony indicated that she was to head back to the observation room. "Sparrow has a gown ready for you."

Tinker winced. "Oh, I don't like the sound of that."

"Why not?"

"In my own clothes, I'm still me. I can't see the change, so I don't notice it."

"I am sorry, but it will be better if you look your best."

Fortunately—in a manner of speaking—only Sparrow was in the Observation Lounge. The other females had been banished to another part of the ship, most likely because of the limited space in the room. Pony took up a post by the door and practiced at being invisible.

"We only have a few hours before arriving at Aum Renau," Sparrow told her. "We'll be going straight from the airfield to an audience with the queen. You must be ready." She handed Tinker a mass of fabrics. "This is a court gown."

Tinker fumbled with it for several minutes trying to make sense of it, until Pony finally took pity on her and reorganized the layers. He held it out then, by the shoulders, for her to see. It was a deep, rich, mottled bronze that looked lovely against her dusky skin, a silk soft as rose petals. While the skirt flared out full, the bodice seemed to be skin-tight, with long sleeves that ended in a fingerless glove arrangement. It wasn't something she'd pick out for herself—to start, there was no way to roll up the sleeves to keep them out of grease. Tinker wasn't even sure how you would get it on; she supposed you pulled it over your head and wriggled a lot. Over the bronze silk was another layer of fine, nearly invisible fabric with a green leaf design, so that when the bronze silk moved, it seemed like sunlight shimmering through forest leaves.

Sparrow waved toward a folding screen set up in the corner. "Step behind there and put it on."

"Just pull it over my head?"

"There are small hooks here that we'll close after you slip it on." Sparrow flipped the material up to show tiny hooks and eyes, oddly enough made of cling vine and ironwood instead of metal.

Pull and wriggle. She tried not to think of Pony standing on the other side of the mostly fabric wall as she gyrated half-naked.

"Wolf Who Rules sent footwear." Sparrow fastened the tiny hooks in the back of the dress. It fit nearly as snugly as Sparrow's gown. The female elf clucked and pinched it tighter. "It needs to be taken in more."

Sparrow handed her slippers that matched the gown—tiny dainty things that Tinker loathed on first sight—but sitting on the floor were two pairs of stylish boots heavy enough to please her.

She tried one of the slippers on, hoping that they'd be too small, and found they fit perfectly. "How did you know my size?"

"Windwolf had your clothes measured," Pony said.

Tinker marveled at the slipper. "Truly? The high heels I was wearing were too wide."

Sparrow sniffed. "He asked me to measure your clothes, but I knew how humans make their clothes—standard sizes that fit no one well. I measured you while you were sleeping."

How utterly creepy.

"So, why is the queen here?" Tinker asked Sparrow to avoid thinking about it.

"I don't know." Sparrow smoothed away a hard, resentful look. "We no sooner arrived than the queen requested that you be sent for, and that triggered an argument over you—"

"Me?"

"You. Windwolf wanted to keep you in Pittsburgh until you adjusted, but Soulful Ember insisted that you be fetched, which resulted in my being sent back. I had to leave before learning why the queen has come to the Westernlands."

"Considering the speed at which the court moves," Pony said, "you may not have missed more than the formal greetings and exchange of gifts."

Sparrow fidgeted. "No, something has happened; I've never seen the court like this. The queen has her full guard with her and two dreadnoughts." She glanced sharply at Pony, as if she had said more than she intended. She picked up another gown. "Change into this one and give me that gown to have altered."

It was more difficult to wriggle out of the tight bronze silk than it had been putting it on. She handed it out to Sparrow and slipped the next one on. While she disliked the notion of *her* wearing a dress, she had to admit that the gown was a lovely mottled green. She came out from behind the screen, smoothing down the skirt, to find Sparrow gone.

"What are dreadnoughts?" Tinker asked Pony, glad she didn't have to look ignorant in front of Sparrow.

"Gunships," Pony told her. "Very big gunships."

"Here, hook me up in back."

He hesitated a moment before crossing the room to fasten the little hooks.

She found herself blushing as his fingers brushed her bare skin. In the full-length mirror, she could see their reflection, him leaning over her, the muscles of his arms rippling under his tattoos.

She looked away, for some reason embarrassed by the intimacy shown. She hunted for a safe subject to talk about. "The Wyvern female triggered her spell tattoo for some type of shielding. Do yours trigger defensive spells too?"

"Yes. The shield is to protect you from damage you can't avoid. They are a last resort; but they can not be taken away from us, short of removing the skin from our arms."

"The Wyverns' are red."

"Red is the Fire Clan's color."

"The queen is part of the Fire Clan?"

"She is head of the Fire Clan."

"And Windwolf is Wind Clan?" Getting a nod, she asked, "Does that make me Wind Clan too?"

Obviously this was a "why is the sky blue" question. Someone could tell her a reasonable answer, but it stumped Pony. "You were human, and humans don't have clans, so there was no other choice but for you to join the Wind Clan."

She looked down at her spill of mottled green silk and the tips of her bronze slippers peeking out from the edge of the skirt. "Why am I not wearing blue?"

Pony indicated her *dau* by touching his own forehead. "That speaks of your alliance. But it is not necessary for a *domana* to announce their clan; only the lesser castes do."

Tinker frowned, recalling all of the blue Sparrow was wearing, from the cerulean overdress to the ribbons woven in her hair.

"Why is Sparrow in blue then?"

Pony clicked his tongue in an elfin shrug. "Sparrow has issues of her own making."

* * *

They reached Aum Renau just before sunset, and the palace sprawled glorious in the shafts of deep gold sunlight. It crowned the steep hills along the river—white limestone with mullioned glass windows, partially obscured by towering trees and a riot of flowers.

"Aum Renau," Pony murmured beside Tinker as the gossamer closed on the palace.

"As viceroy, Windwolf usually stays here? Does the palace come with the appointment?"

Pony nodded to the first question, and then shook his head. "It is his, not the crown's."

Your boyfriend is rich, Tinker thought, and then winced as she remembered that—as far as the elves were concerned—Windwolf was her husband. *We're going to have a long talk about that.*

Typical of elfin design, the palace seemed to be a linked series of buildings incorporating the natural landscape. Beyond the structures that crowned the hill, more buildings stepped down the eastern exposure, tucked onto ledges and around a steep waterfall. In one wide flat area, jarring against the green and white, sat a courtyard filled with tall stark black stones.

"What are the stones?" Tinker asked, pointing them out.

"Nothing for you." Sparrow focused on storm clouds moving toward them. She made a slight hurt noise and headed toward the control cabin.

"They are the Wind Clan's spell stones," Pony told Tinker, glancing after Sparrow, and then he too focused on the storm clouds.

The dark forms converged in a manner not natural to clouds, although far too large and dark to be other gossamers.

"What are those?"

"Dreadnoughts," Pony said.

As the airships drew closer together, she saw that they were a product of elves' contact with man. Instead of a living ship like the gossamer, the dreadnoughts were fully mechanical, obviously a blend of airship and armored helicopter. The barrels of heavy guns bristled from the black hull, reminding Tinker of the spiked hide of a river shark. The two dreadnoughts blocked the airspace over the palace and flashed out a warning on a signal lamp. A few minutes later, having apparently received some communication back from the gossamer, the dreadnoughts pivoted and moved off.

"How odd," Pony murmured, his eyes narrowed in speculation. "I've never heard of the flagship being challenged before. Sparrow is right; something has happened."

* * *

The gossamer tethered at an airfield in a wide hilltop meadow, some distance from the palace. Horses and a coach waited. The Wyverns, still bruised and sulking, mounted the horses. The ground crew unrolled a carpet from the elevator to the carriage in order to save Tinker's hated slippers from harm. Pony had to help her mount the tall step up into the coach without entangling her long skirt. Inside one could hold a party; facing leather-upholstered bench seats allowed eight adults to sit comfortably.

"Slide over to the other side," Pony murmured as he made sure Tinker's gown didn't catch in the doorway.

Annoyance flickered over Sparrow's face as she stepped into the coach. She sat on the right side of the bench instead of making room for Pony. The bodyguard climbed in, latched the door, and settled on the bench opposite the females.

Minutes later, the reason for Pony's suggestion and Sparrow's annoyance became clear. They traveled along a wide avenue designed with views in mind. Around each curve was a new beautiful vista of the valley. The river ran wide as a lake, reflecting the sun. Stone walled enclaves sectioned up the west bank into orderly squares and rectangles. Virgin forest blanketed the far eastern bank. A ship was sailing upriver, the wind filling its sail colored Wind Clan blue, leaving a V-shaped wake behind it. A great white bird drifted over the water, giving desolate cries.

"What kind of bird is that?" Tinker asked.

Pony leaned forward to peer out the window. "A *chiipeshyosa.*" He then directed her attention to the wooden docks lining the river. "Those smaller boats were built in Pitsubaug," he used the Elvish word for Pittsburgh, "and taken down river to the ocean, then around to here. They are steel-hulled, and use *fuel-cell* engines."

But then the palace came into sight, and Tinker lost all joy of the experience. The last few hours of Sparrow's and Pony's frantic tutoring had done nothing but reveal her ignorance of formal elfin culture, making her feel like a junkyard dog about to go on parade.

The front entrance had a portico of stone arches heavy with climbing roses. From there, they walked through a series of hallways—wide, airy, filled with sunlight and polished marble. Elves stood talking in small groups, all dressed in elegant splendor. Recognizing Sparrow, they would fall silent and bow, but their eyes fixed with curiosity on Tinker.

"Am I that odd looking?" Tinker whispered to Pony.

"They are merely curious to see who has captured Windwolf's heart."

"Me?"

"Yes, you."

And that gave her the courage to walk into the great gathering room full of beautiful females and males.

The room had been designed on a large scale, meant to be impressive. A grove of ironwood had been cultured into a straight row. The thick tree trunks vaulted hundreds of feet straight up before branching into a canopy of green. Polished granite formed the floor, and whatever made up the ceiling was lost somewhere overhead. Elf shines drifted in the shadows, gleaming motes of living light.

Large as it was, the room hadn't been designed to hold the number crowded into it now. Thankfully they were focused on the other side of the room, where a heated debate ranged. As Sparrow murmured something to a male in the queen's colors waiting at the door, Tinker recognized Windwolf's voice, and she edged sideways to see through the crowd to spot him.

He stood near the front of the hall, his hair unbound in a shimmering black cascade down his back. He wore a bronze that matched her underdress and a duster of the leaf pattern of her overdress. The sheath of his long ceremonial sword cut a slash of deep blue across his back.

"Earth Son, your proposals are like setting a forest fire to bring down one black willow," he was saying in High Elvish, in carefully chosen words. Between his clear, deep enunciation and slow pacing, Tinker easily followed what he said.

Earth Son was a male in a rich green, taller than Windwolf, but more slender. He was flanked by *sekasha* tattooed in Stone Clan colors. "You deny the Seer's Sight?"

"I am not saying that." Windwolf's voice filled the space with a deep grandeur that was unmatched by his opposition. "Certainly I have seen shadows of the oni against the wall. Even the humans are dreaming of tengu." At least that's what Tinker thought he said, although she didn't understand it fully. "Obviously their spies have reached Elfhome."

"We must take steps to protect ourselves."

"Slashing about madly will only take out our allies."

The press of bodies shifted and Tinker lost sight of the two speakers.

"Allies?" Earth Son's voice filled with scorn. "The humans? All evidence points that they are in league with the oni!"

"What evidence? Do you have proof that you are keeping hidden from me? If so, I demand that you bring it forward now. I represent the Wind Clan here; I will not be kept ignorant."

"The human Pathway is punching a hole through our defenses, leaving us open to attack! They are acting in conjunction with the oni."

Tinker shifted sideways just as Windwolf paced into view, in profile to her now. *My husband.* Gods, that sounded so weird.

"You are conjecturing that creating a tool is the same as gifting it?" Windwolf rolled his hand lazily, indicating one unsound statement following another. "Do you blame a smith for the crimes of a thief?"

"Ah!" Earth Son cried as if he won some great victory. "So you at least admit that the oni are using the humans' Pathway?"

Windwolf sighed visibly and shook his head. "I do not deny that is possible, but I will also remind the court that the oni are as mythical to the humans as we were." He paced back out of sight. "It's undeniable that individuals or even groups of oni have reached Earth, why else the legends, but where are the screaming hordes? They are not on Earth."

"Do you think you've been told the truth? Do not be naïve in thinking humans understand honor."

Tinker shifted and caught sight of the two males again. They stood now only an arm reach apart, intent as duelists upon each other.

"I have found," Windwolf said with a dangerous rumble, "the percentage of honorable humans is the same as elves."

As Earth Son stood still, apparently considering whether he'd been insulted or not, Pony whispered to Tinker, "The Stone Clan have lost power since the Pathway to Pittsburgh opened. They have always advocated that the humans be forced to close the Pathway."

That helped clarify the situation! Now, why was she here?

Windwolf too took advantage of Earth Son's silence. "I have done all in my power to ensure that I know the truth. We of the Wind Clan have learned the human tongue and I have sent members of my household out to Earth proper to travel it extensively. If the oni are on Earth, they have concealed themselves well. They have passed out of the minds of humans, out of their nightmares, and nearly out of their language."

"But they are in Pittsburgh now."

Windwolf's face went bleak. "Yes. That is undeniable. How they came to be there, that is not known."

"The human Pathway opens to Onihida!" Earth Son cried.

"No!" Windwolf's denial rang through the hall. "If it opened to Onihida, the oni would have flooded out, unchecked, long ago. Look at this wilderness and think of their numbers. If they had clear passage, nothing would stop them! The only reason they would be using subversion would be because frontal attack is not possible."

"You speak as if you know this as truth."

"I know that the sun is hot, the stars are distant, and rules of warfare follow certain logic, regardless of the world."

"There is a door, open but not open." A female spoke in a cold, dispassionate tone, and all turned to look at her. In the shift of bodies, Tinker picked her out. She was willow-slender, dressed in pale moth white, with a glistening red ribbon tied over her eyes and trailing down over her gown like a trail of blood. "Darkness presses against the frame but can not pass through. The light beyond is too brilliant; it burns the beast."

"Can we keep the door from opening?" someone asked.

"No. It is only a matter of time. But if it is a time of our choosing, then the beast will be slain. If we do nothing and let the darkness come when it will, all will be lost to night."

The very lack of emotion was chilling. The room had stilled to utter silence, everyone straining to hear. Tinker caught Pony's shoulder and pulled him down to whisper in his ear, "Who is that?"

"The *intanyai seyosa*," Pony whispered. Literally it meant "one who sows and harvests the most favorable future of all," but what did that mean?

Sparrow hissed them to silence.

"How do we choose?" the same questioner asked.

"Bind the pivot," the *intanyai seyosa* said. "If the pivot be true, then the battle can be won. If the pivot proves false, all will be lost."

"Is the pivot here?" the questioner asked.

The female raised her hand and pointed. Elves parted like water, stepping back out of the way, and the finger did not waver. Where moments before Tinker could barely see the blindfolded elf, suddenly there was a clear path between them, and the female pointed straight at Tinker's chest.

Let there be someone behind me! Tinker shifted sideways as she glanced over her shoulder. No one stood behind her. When she looked back, the finger still pointed straight at her as if laser guided.

"Shit," she whispered.

Windwolf gave her a look of dismay and alarm. He turned back toward the front of the room. "What is the meaning of this?"

All other eyes remained on Tinker. The hard fixed interest was daunting. She wanted to hide, but there seemed to be no place to take cover. Pony must have sensed her fear; he stepped in front of Tinker to shield her with his body.

Gratefulness profound as love filled Tinker, and she reached out to lay her hand on Pony's back. He glanced over his shoulder at her touch and whispered, "Neither Windwolf nor I will let harm come to you."

"Calm yourself, cousin," the questioner commanded. "Let her come forth. We wish to see her for ourselves."

Pony gave Tinker a querying look, and she nodded, even though she still felt like bolting from the room. She couldn't hide behind him forever. He stepped smoothly to one side, and—as they practiced on the gossamer—they walked toward the queen. At least the seer had cleared them a path.

There was no mistaking Queen Soulful Ember. Not that one could truly mistake her, for she sat while everyone stood, crowned with a ruby-studded circlet. There seemed to be nearly visible power emanating off her, like the pulse of a heavy engine against the skin. Tinker expected her to be beautiful, but that was too meager a word for the queen. Soulful Ember was glorious: skin a radiant white, hair so gold it was metallic, eyes so blue they seemed neon.

Pony stopped and went down to one knee. Tinker carefully measured out the two extra steps beyond him that her rank allowed, and then gave a deep bow. Windwolf came to stand beside her, and she wished she could find his presence more comforting. He was at least a familiar face, but he obviously didn't know what he'd gotten her dragged into.

The queen studied Tinker for a moment, glanced to Windwolf as if puzzled by his choice, and asked, "How old are you?"

"Eighteen."

"You're only counting the days you've been an elf?"

Tinker frowned, trying to translate it, then shook her head. "I'm eighteen years old."

"You said nothing, cousin, as to how young she was. She's just a baby."

Tinker flushed with anger, and snapped, "I am not," out of habit, and then winced as she remembered to whom she was talking. "I'm an adult."

"Did you know she was the pivot when you had me summon her?" Windwolf growled.

"We suspected her," Queen Soulful Ember said without apology or anger in her voice. "The pivot would be marked with the Wind

Clan *dau.* That is why we demanded that Sparrow Lifted By Wind accompany you originally. It was not known that you'd taken a wife."

"I don't understand. What is a pivot?" Tinker said.

"As there are layers of worlds, there are layers of future," the queen said. "Paths can be taken to lead to very different outcomes or just the same conclusion via a different route. Usually it is the action that chooses the path, not the person acting; any messenger can deliver the important message, and any sailor can lose the vital ship in a storm. When only one person can guide the future, they are a pivot."

"Are you serious?" Tinker looked to Windwolf. "How can you know the future?"

"It is the nature of magic to splinter things down to possibilities," Windwolf explained. "Spells merely guide the outcome to the desired path. In the presence of magic, the ability of humans and elves to guess the future becomes the ability to see possible futures."

"Lain says fortune telling is mumble-jumble," Tinker said.

Windwolf looked pained. "Yet Lain sees the future in her dreams."

"You brought me a tengu, and wanted me to bandage it," Lain had said the night Tinker brought her the wounded Windwolf. *"I kept on telling you that it was dangerous, but you wouldn't listen to me. . . ."*

And Tooloo had known too. *"He'll swallow you up, and nothing will be left."*

They had seen, in some fearful way, that Windwolf would unmake the human Tinker, leaving an elf in her place.

Tinker turned to the blindfolded elf, suddenly trembling. "What do I need to do?"

"You weave the ropes to bind yourself. Be true, and the battle can be won. Be false, all will be lost."

"What the hell does that mean?" Tinker whispered fiercely to Windwolf in English. "They're not going to tie me up, are they?"

"Dreams are the forerunners of visions," Windwolf said. "She does not have to be asleep to see, but they are still . . . difficult to determine their true meaning."

"So she could be wrong about me?"

"No." Windwolf put out his hand to her. Tinker hesitated a moment, Tooloo's words ringing in her mind, but then took his hand, lacing her fingers through his. It helped to have something to cling to in this sea of beautiful, dispassionate strangers.

"Let me send her off to rest," Windwolf asked the queen. "She has been through much the last few days."

"Is there anything we can do to influence the pivot?" the queen asked the seer.

"No. All is in place. The rest is of her own making."

11: SPELL STONES

Tinker wasn't sure if she was annoyed or relieved to be hustled off center stage. Certainly she didn't like being the focus of attention, but she would have liked to know more about what was going on. She had a feeling, though, that there was no way she could stay and not be the focus.

Sparrow seemed to take the escort duty as badly, though she did try to hide the fact that she was seething.

The sprawling layout of the palace translated into a maze of hallways, open courtyards, and short flights of stairs. Armed warriors stood guard everywhere. At first they only passed Fire Clan warriors who watched their passage in still silence, but at one intersection of hallways, they apparently moved into Wind Clan territory. From that point on the warriors all wore Wind Clan blue, and bowed low, their gazes curious although their expressions were neutral.

Finally they entered a large beautiful room with heavy mahogany furniture. Sparrow paused to state, "This is the private living quarters of Wolf Who Rules. You will be sleeping here until we leave for Pittsburgh," and continued walking through the room.

"What?"

"These are the *domou*'s and *domi*'s private quarters," Sparrow answered without stopping. "This way!" She entered a bedroom the size of a baseball field. "You will be sleeping here until the queen gives us permission to leave for Pittsburgh."

Tinker paused at the door, her attention caught and fixed by the large bed turned down to show off satin sheets. Did Windwolf plan to sleep with her in it? Surely in a place this large, there was another place he could sleep. Had he just assumed she agreed to it? Or would

it be taken badly if she made him sleep elsewhere? How would anyone even know, if she did, in a place this big?

Did she want to sleep with him?

"Take off the gown," Sparrow stated briskly and Tinker realized
that the female had already repeated herself several times. "You only
wear that gown for formal occasions." Sparrow held out something
white and flowing. "This is your nightgown here."

Automatically Tinker started to consider how to get off the gown
before she found enough mental stability to realize that one, Pony
and an unknown female warrior stood behind her and two, she
didn't want to change into the diaphanous thing that Sparrow held.
She crossed her arms and glared at Sparrow.

"I want my own clothes back."

"They are being washed. This is all you have to wear other than
the gown."

Great. Tinker looked back at Pony.

He took that as permission to speak on a different matter entirely, "Forgiveness, *ze domi*. This female is Sun Lance; she is well
known to me as brave and able. I have chosen her to attend you in the
evening, and those places I can not join you."

Sun Lance bowed low. "I live to serve, *ze domi*."

Tinker felt like someone had kicked the legs out from under her.
"You're leaving me alone?"

"Even a *sekasha* must sleep," Sparrow snapped. "He's staggering
where he stands as it is."

Tinker realized guiltily that Pony was indeed exhausted. He must
never really have slept since they left Windwolf's hunting lodge. "Of
all the idiocy," she muttered in English, and then in Elvish said, "Go.
Sleep." Tinker shooed Pony away.

Sparrow waited, nightgown in hand.

Now that they were down to just females, Tinker considered how
to get out of her gown again, and decided that she couldn't do it
alone. "Can you help me undo the hooks?"

It was interesting to note that elves made the same aspirated
sounds when they were frustrated. Sparrow tossed the nightgown
onto the bed, and came to undo the hooks. Her pale graceful hands
were ice cold and trembling. Was she shaken by the news that she had
been considered the pivot, or jealous that Tinker took her place once
again? If she wanted the position, she could have it back.

Tinker carefully wriggled out of the gown and Sparrow took it to
hang up in a vast empty closet. While not quite as tight, the nightgown of white fairy silk matched the gown in cut: long sleeves, tight

bodice, and full flowing skirt. It slipped over her head too, like so much cool air, and spilled down over her body to swirl around her ankles. Despite being fully dressed, she felt naked. She glanced at herself in a mirror across the room and winced—the tight fabric left nothing to the imagination, looking like so much cream poured down over her.

"You don't have anything else for me to wear?"

"Nothing to lounge in." Sparrow came back with another pair of dainty slippers, these white to match the nightgown.

"Where're the boots you showed me earlier?" Tinker pulled off the bronze slippers and surrendered them to Sparrow's care.

"The boots are not appropriate to wear in the palace."

"Where are they?"

Sparrow looked at her levelly, whatever she felt carefully hidden away, but yet she seemed to radiate distaste. Were elves secretly psychic? After a minute of cold silence, Sparrow said, "They're in the closet with the other footwear."

Score one for the visiting team.

"Will that be all?" Sparrow asked.

"Yes," Tinker said, wanting rid of all elves, short-tempered Sparrow in particular.

Sparrow nodded, and Sun Lance bowed deeply, and at last, Tinker was alone.

Tinker went through the closet. Besides the gowns they fitted on the gossamer, there were several other elaborate gowns hanging—evidence that Windwolf must employ an army of seamstresses. What he didn't employ was common sense—she hated all of them. To be fair, the gowns were all very lovely; the only fault she found with them was that *she* was expected to wear them. Beside the dresses sat a rack of matching slippers. She found two pairs of boots, one of suede and the other of polished leather. Both had soles of hard leather, and a heel of ironwood. Not as hefty as her work boots, but they certainly were better than the slippers.

She also discovered a wonderful duster of painted silk that fit her perfectly. Made from a rich, mottled blue, subliminal images of wolves ran through wispy clouds of white.

Boots and duster made her feel dressed enough to take on the world. Avoiding the big bed and all its implications, she explored the bedroom. It seemed oddly sterile, like one of the Observatory dorm rooms, cleaned after the last scientist left and waiting for the next one to arrive. Just bigger with lots more doors. She worked clockwise from the walk-in closet: an updated toilet complete with imported toilet paper, a traditional bathing room done in Wind Clan blue tile, French doors that opened to a balcony.

Dusk had come and gone since the gossamer arrived at Aum Renau, and night covered the sky. The constellation of First Wolf was raising its bright shoulder star on the horizon. Roses, pine, and wood smoke scented the air. Below was another patio, nearly lost in the sea of darkness. Elf shines gathered like a living exit light around an open archway. Tinker glanced back to the big bed, the door to where Sun Lance stood guarding over her because she was Windwolf's *domi*, and the great hall filled with elves believing that the future pivoted around her.

It proved to be a quick scramble down off the balcony to the dark courtyard below.

So running away wasn't a bright idea. She could see that now. She really had to learn to plan three or four steps ahead instead of just one or two. Where the hell did she think she was going to go? Certainly she couldn't get back to Pittsburgh. One can't outrun the future. All she managed to do was get lost.

A figure stepped out of the darkness, barring her path. "Who are you?"

"I'm—I'm . . ." It grated to realize that her identity depended wholly on Windwolf's. "I'm Tinker *ze domi*."

He grunted in surprise and pulled out a spell light, activating it with a guttural keyword. The light flared to nearly painful white until he clasped the orb tightly, cutting down its intensity. A powerful ley line must run close by; now that she focused on it, she felt the invisible warmth running over her. Even in the darkness, squinting from the painful shafts of light escaping from between the elf's fingers, she could see the power roiling on the air around them, like moonlight on water.

The spell light revealed that the elf was a *sekasha* armed with longbow, pale feathered spell arrows, and a sword of ironwood. Considering the strength of the ley line, carrying steel weapons would be nearly impossible. His tattoos identified him as Wind Clan, which was oddly comforting. His shield spell was activated, though she hadn't heard him utter the spell; the intricate deep blue lines seemed to flow as magic followed the circuit, and an aura of dark blue outlined his body.

The warrior tilted the spell light to pick out her *dau* mark. "Ah, *ze domi!*" He flicked the light away from her eyes, but continued to block her way.

"Is something wrong?" she asked.

He hesitated and then whistled lowly. A moment later, a second warrior appeared silently out of the dark.

"What is it?" The newcomer eyed Tinker.

"It is Wolf Who Rules' new *domi*," the first said. It was interesting to note that he used the word "new" that denoted "first" instead of "newest." "I—I don't know—do I let her pass?"

The second one glanced back over his shoulder at whatever the darkness hid, and then clicked his tongue in a shrug. "She is Wind Clan *domana*." He bowed lowly to her. "Do you wish to continue this way, *domi*?"

Now they had her curious.

"Yes, please," Tinker said.

The first bowed too, and backed up to clear the path. "Forgiveness, *ze domi*."

"Forgiveness." She started forward slowly, in case they changed their minds. *I'm harmless. I'm harmless.*

"So that is her?" the second murmured lowly. "They said she was small, but I did not expect her to be that tiny."

"It certainly puts her fight with the oni warriors in new light."

"The courage of dragons, they say."

She blushed hotly, embarrassed but pleased by their words. After her dealings with Sparrow, she was afraid that everyone except Pony disliked her. Perhaps it was just Sparrow. Certainly they seemed to think that she had a right to the mysterious stones.

She came to an open plaza and the guards and Sparrow were forgotten.

Monoliths stood in a massive circle, like silent giants. Elf shines drifted through the dark shadows cast by the stones. The air roiled with magic; it flushed her fever hot and made her feel so light she worried about drifting away. She stepped forward, and something thrummed underfoot, making her jerk backwards.

A channel for a ley line had been chiseled into the paving stone, slashing across her path. As she looked at it, her eyes slowly registered the nearly invisible purple of potential magic. Outside of the buildup on her electromagnet, she'd never seen magic in enough quantity to be visible. She backed up another step and considered what she was wearing. Suddenly the wood and leather fasteners on her clothes made sense. What about her boots? Sparrow had made some remark about them not being appropriate for the palace. She backed up a little more and pulled off her boots. The paving stones were polished smooth and toasty warm under her stocking feet.

Her boots in hand, she stepped over the channel and went out into the plaza for a closer look. Attracted by her movement, elf shines drifted to her in order to light the way. Without scale, she had mistaken the size of the monoliths, thinking they were only nine or ten feet tall. As she hiked across the wide flat plaza, they loomed taller and taller as she neared them, until they towered nearly twenty feet above her. The monoliths were made of polished granite, with spells permanently inlaid in their surfaces. She peered at the elaborate arcane design as the shines floated around her, reflected in the polished stone.

The spells inscribed into the rock were unlike anything she had worked with before, so much so she couldn't even guess their function. She found a jumper point sunk deep into the stone and realized that the monoliths were layers of inlaid slabs, in essence huge macro chips. They could trigger complex spells fueled by the massive amount of magic represented by the ley line—but to do what? And why hadn't Sparrow wanted her to know about them?

Someone was walking toward her, footsteps loud on stone. She turned to find Windwolf coming across the plaza, still in the matching bronze. As usual, all her emotions went tumbling so she wasn't sure what she really felt. Relief. Desire. Anger.

"Tink."

And she remembered him kissing her neck, whispering, *"Trust me, my little savage Tink."*

With a snarl, she flung her boots at his head, and immediately regretted it. What if she actually hit him in the face? She didn't want to hurt him—well, yes, she did—but not that bad.

Windwolf flinched his head aside so her boots sailed past him, not even ruffling his hair. "Is something wrong?"

"Yes! Look at me!"

"You look beautiful."

"Why did you do this to me?"

"I did not want you to die. You did not want to die."

"I thought you meant I was sick! I thought you were going to heal me of something." She pointed to one of her now-pointed ears. "You didn't tell me that you were going to make me an elf!"

"I thought you understood." He slipped his hand through her hair to run his fingertips over her ear point. "At least as far as you could."

His touch sent electric sparks all through her body. She wanted him, wanted him so badly it terrified her. She pulled away, trembling with more than desire. "Play fair. I'm not stupid, you know; I would have understood."

"It will take you a human's lifetime, and perhaps more, to understand what it is to be an elf. Can a wildflower tucked in the roots of an ironwood understand what it is like to tower over everything, face to the bare sky? Can the wildflower understand facing winter instead of going dormant underground? Can it imagine surviving lightning strikes and forest fires?"

She punched him in the shoulder, hard enough to knock him back. "Oh, don't go metaphysical on me. *'Do you want to be an elf?'* That's all you had to ask so that I knew what decision I was really making. I feel like you tricked me. I feel like you betrayed my trust!"

"I am sorry that you feel like I tricked you," he said in a low, sincere voice. "The timing was important, and I rushed things to meet the window of opportunity. I thought you understood as much as possible and consented fully. I would never betray you."

Much as she didn't want to, she believed him. Without malice or arrogance on his part, it seemed pointless to argue blame. She had, after all, given her consent, stupid as it was in hindsight.

"Can you change me back?"

"Is it so bad that to die a human is better?"

"Not to die human, to live a human."

"Is being an elf so bad?"

"No. Yes. I don't know. I don't like having someone follow me around." She didn't name Pony, feeling like she'd be betraying him. "And I don't like strangers showing up with swords and demanding that I drop everything to come with them. I don't like wearing these stupid clothes, and being looked at as if I'm some rude, ignorant thing. And I hate that saying even this makes me sound whiny."

"Ah."

He stood silent and still as she stalked away to retrieve her footwear. Tinker was too angry to be motionless, too civilized to scream like she desperately wanted to. After throwing her boots at him, she was too shamed to shout without provocation. If he had said something, anything, to let her vent, she would have happily latched on to it. He remained quiet as she pulled her boots back on; if he could wear his boots, she wasn't going to stand around in stocking feet.

"Tinker, I am sorry," he said finally. "I did not want to make you miserable."

"Well, you succeeded in doing just that."

He opened his arms, offering comfort without asking her forgiveness. She glared at him but her anger had run out, and all that remained was lonely hurt. She leaned against him, letting him wrap his arms around her and kiss her temple.

They stood unmoving and silent for several minutes until all the hurt was soothed away and curiosity took over.

"What are these monoliths?"

"They are the Wind Clan Spell Stones," Windwolf said. "It is from these that the Wind Clan *domana* derive their power."

"What do they do?"

"In the same manner that magic can allow travel *through* worlds, it can allow power to *cross* worlds."

"I don't understand."

"One calls for power, and it comes."

She shook her head, still not understanding.

"I will show you."

Windwolf stepped away from her, and held out his right hand, thumb and index finger rigid, middle fingers cocked oddly. "Daaaaaaaaae."

Tinker felt the tremor in the air around Windwolf, like a pulse of a bass amplifier, first against a sense she hadn't been aware of before, and then against her skin. She realized that she had felt the magic triggering. Windwolf's hand apparently was taking the place of a written spell, and his voice starting the resonance that would focus the magic into the pattern set up by the spell. Once triggered, the spell would continue until canceled or all magic was sucked out of the area.

Even as she realized that, the spell stones reacted. With the same "magic sense" she felt the sudden vast structure around them come alive. The invisible sluggish current that she had noticed before began to move faster, surging toward the standing giants. When it reached the monoliths, the violet gleam of magic crawled up the spell tracings. So close to the end of the visible spectrum, the effect was at first barely noticeable, and slowly grew to unmistakable. As she stared, the air around the monoliths started to distort, not from heat or light, but some other potential that echoed back on her "magic sense."

Allow travel through worlds . . . allow power to cross worlds.

He was talking about the quantum effects on a hyperphase level. Windwolf had the ability to *jump* magic from this point to his location. Judging by what she just felt, Windwolf would perform a trigger and it would bridge the gap between him and the spell stones, allowing the power to jump back, along the quantum level resonance.

Triggered and waiting, the massive power pressed invisibly against her.

Windwolf gestured and intoned another guttural vowel, and the power slowly collapsed. He indicated that she should be silent and still and, afraid that she might trigger something, she held motionless.

"You will be taught how to use these." Windwolf broke the silence when he deemed it safe to speak again.

Tinker let out the "oh wow" she'd been holding in. "I had no idea that elves could control magic like this! I've never seen anyone do anything like that in Pittsburgh."

"Only *domana* can summon magic. Only Wind Clan *domana* can call on these stones."

Somehow the monoliths were keyed to a specific genome, so the *domana* of one clan alone could set up the correct resonance to match the stones.

"Do other clans have their own stones?"

"Yes. Each clan normally has several. There are four other sets of Wind Clan stones. There is a range limit of one *mei*."

A *mei* was an odd number, nearly a thousand miles in length, and yet only rough in estimate, as if the exact distance wasn't important. It never made sense as a measurement before now.

She looked at her hands, the remembrance of the power still lingering like the memory of pain. "You made it so I can call magic?"

"Yes, but it takes a great deal of learning."

"Can I do it by mistake?"

He shook his head. "The triggers are quite complex on purpose."

That was comforting. Nothing like accidentally frying oneself in the middle of a deep yawn. Still it was mind boggling that Windwolf had gifted her with this type of power. Why her? Every female she'd seen, while maybe not her mental equal, certainly was young and beautiful. Why hadn't Windwolf fallen in love with one of them in the last hundred and ten years? Hell, Sparrow was right under his nose, and already marked with a *dau*.

It occurred to Tinker that while Sparrow was as beautiful as one of the high caste females, she was in fact still low caste. "Sparrow can't access the spell stones?"

"No. Genetically she is not *domana*."

"Why not?"

"That is no longer done." Windwolf reached out his hand. When Tinker took it, he started them toward the gate. "At one time, yes, we freely shifted lesser castes up to *domana* ability. But that was during a time of war. We no longer do it."

"What about me?"

"You were human and extremely mortal. The two cases are completely different, dire need versus convenience."

At the gate, they picked up shadows in the form of two *sekasha*. She realized with some mortification that one was Sun Lance. Had the female come with Windwolf, or climbed down the balcony and followed her silently from the very start? What in the world did the female think of her, fleeing into the dark and throwing boots at Windwolf? Tinker winced and thought back through her conversation with Windwolf. What language had they been arguing in? English. Good.

"Will you please explain what you've done to me? Fully."

"Are you sure? It will be a very analytical discussion. You have been through so very much, it might be hard to hear."

"Yes, I want to know."

"Very well. I used a transformation spell, keyed via my sperm, with protections against any radical changes to the original. The spell is considered very safe; the base was developed by the Skin Clan millennia ago and improved since then. I took every precaution to make it failsafe."

"What precautions?"

"That you were a virgin was the ultimate insurance against possible contamination."

She blushed. "You're kidding!"

"No. When you do the spell, you use a source key. Sperm works best; it is, by its very nature, a template of life." What he said matched what Lain guessed. "However, having two sources could be dangerous."

"So I didn't need to be a virgin—just abstaining for a day or two would work."

Windwolf shook his head. "Human sperm stays active anywhere from three days to a week. Elfin sperm stays active up to a year."

"A year?"

"Half-elfin could range anywhere between the two."

"A year?"

"It is a sometimes problematic side effect of being immortal," Windwolf admitted. "It is one reason why we are not as promiscuous as humans."

"Yeah, that would do it."

"With you being a virgin, it wasn't a worry." He reached out and ran his finger lightly over her ear tip. "You are mine, and mine alone."

* * *

They had reached "their" living quarters.

She halted him before they could walk on to the bedroom. "Are you—we—there's just one bed."

He cocked his head. "In your bedroom, yes."

"And you have a bedroom too?"

Wordlessly, he showed her the second bedroom, undeniably Windwolf's. His scent hung in the air. A closet door stood open to show off his impressive wardrobe. All about the room were things to catch the eye, objects of beauty and interest, set down at the end of the day and not picked up again.

Two bedrooms? Didn't married people share one bedroom? Or was this whole marriage thing only a way for Windwolf to control the pivot? It certainly made more sense than him suddenly falling in love with her. Tooloo had been right; she didn't know her own heart. That he might not want her, hurt more than she could imagine. She sat on a bench at the end of Windwolf's bed, confounded by herself.

Windwolf had shut the door, giving them privacy from the *sekasha*, and came to sit beside her. "I know that all this is difficult. I wanted to give you time to think and to adjust."

What do I want? What do I want?

I want him.

She reached out to touch his hair. If he had looked at her, she probably would have lost courage, but he didn't, so she stroked its softness. She gently brushed his hair away from his ear, and explored its outline.

He shifted, and she jerked her hand away.

"I wish you to continue," he murmured.

"Really?"

"I desire it very much."

She leaned against him and buried her face in his hair. She'd never really looked at someone's ear before. Were human ears as delicate and mysterious, with their odd little turns and curls? She kissed his lobe, and the pulse point beating under his ear, and then the strong column of his neck. She realized she was trembling, and wasn't sure if it was with fear or excitement.

She buried her face into his shoulder, and whispered, "Take me."

His arms encircled her lightly. "There is no rush, beloved. Let us learn together what pleases us most."

"You seemed to know what pleased me before." His shirt was bronze silk, warmed by his body, his muscles moving under it. He filled her senses, and she seemed so small.

"And yet you're afraid of me now."

Was it possible to shrink to nothing in his arms? "I'm afraid you don't want me."

"You are all that I want," he breathed against her neck, and even that warmth sent shivers through her. "My universe resides within you."

She peeked at his face, and found him watching her with tender regard. "Does that mean that you love me?"

"Love is such a small word to carry what I feel."

She would have to take that for a yes.

She never noticed her duster coming off, or when the hooks of her nightgown came undone. The nightgown was slipped down over her breasts, and bunched up high on her waist before she realized how undressed she was. By then Windwolf was lightly kissing his way up her inner thigh, and she didn't want him to stop. She raised her hips so he could slide off her underwear. He held her cupped in his hands, his thumbs opening her to him, his breathing the most intimate of touches. She shook with the need of something more, and whispered to him, "Please." He dipped his head, and pleasure seemed to pour liquid out of him, spilling from his tongue and into her.

It was only later, with his soft hair pooled over her bare legs, she realized it had been just like her dream.

12: AUM RENAU

-*-=--o (---=-*-

They stayed at Aum Renau for three weeks.

Tinker tried to be happy there. Certainly it was a pleasant enough stay. She had the new universe of sex to explore. Outside of bed, Windwolf seemed genuinely in love with her, although why was as hard to fathom as how she felt about him. Her scientific mind wanted something to see and measure and quantify before she was willing to admit that she loved him.

Windwolf arranged things so she could avoid the queen, the court, and all things political—apparently needing only to cite her age and recent transformation to excuse her from those "duties." He, however, could not absent himself, and so needed to spend hours away. The first two days, she took apart everything remotely mechanical in the Wind Clan section of the palace: ten clocks, three music boxes, the kitchen dumbwaiter, and both master bathrooms. After that, Pony and a changing subset of the palace's twenty *sekasha* took her out exploring the countryside. They rode horses, sailed on a nearby lake, hiked in the mountains, visited the open market down by the river, practiced archery, and played a cutthroat, fast-paced cousin to lawn croquet. Eventually she tired of that, and nosed her way into the kitchen to carry on science experiments in the form of cooking, and spent a day in awe of the massive, steam-driven laundry facility, and finally talked her way onto the dreadnought (but only after promising that she'd take nothing apart).

The palace's staff took to her invasion well, their initial dismay and subservience thawing to open friendliness. At least she seemed to be meshing much better than Sparrow, especially among the *sekasha*, who treated Sparrow with quiet disdain.

"Sparrow is too self-centered," Pony explained. They were on the archery field, whiling away the long summer afternoon. "It is true that the *domana* rule the other castes, but it does not mean that it's more important. If the *seyosa* did not farm, and the *sepeshyosa* did not fish, and *selinsafa* did not do the laundry, or the *sefada* did not cook, where would we be?"

"Dirty and hungry." Tinker took aim at the warg target down field. (She refused to shoot at the disturbing humanoid targets.) The first arrow hit in the warg's hindquarters, but the next three grouped around the heart bull's-eye. The last actually landed in the red. *"Kiyau!"*

The *sekasha* laughed at her answer, and complimented her on her shots. One of the runners at the end of the field collected her arrows and ducked back to his shelter.

"Exactly. Pull!" Pony called, setting the warg whizzing around on its track in unpredictable starts and turns. "A body must have a brain, mouth, eyes, hands, bowels, and feet." He shot as he talked, loosing his five arrows nearly as fast as he could nock and pull, and yet they all grouped around the heart, three in the red.

"Oh, you flatter me so," Tinker said, meaning their compliments on her shots.

"You are doing well for someone who never handled a bow before," Pony said. "I've been practicing for nearly a century, the rest for millennia. Someday you'll be good as we are; your eye is good."

A century. That still put shivers through her. The *sekasha* seemed happy to spend an entire day on archery, but she was bored in an hour or two. Of course, they were honing their abilities while she saw it as a mere diversion, something to do while talking. She supposed that they didn't do math problems for fun. She wished she had been able to at least bring her datapad with her. Windwolf had given her several reams of fine paper and a score of pens, but it wasn't the same. He promised that he'd take her home soon, but needed the queen's permission. ("Is that elfin time or human?" she complained. "Elfin," he said sadly, "for I fear the human 'soon' has already passed.")

"Sparrow believes the brain to be all important." Pony drew her attention back to the conversation about Windwolf's assistant.

"Sparrow thinks nothing of making work for the rest of us," complained the female Stormsong—whose attitude toward clothes and boots delighted Tinker no end. "She demands fresh flowers in her quarters, special food from the *sefada*, and countless changes in her gowns. Pull!"

They fell silent the minute it took Stormsong to shoot. She carefully put all five arrows into the red, but Tinker had learned that the *sekasha* unofficially took points off for being too deliberate at aiming, and gave points for managing a discussion around one's shooting, as Pony had. It seemed a secret ego thing between them.

"Am I making extra work?" Tinker asked.

They laughed at Tinker's fear, belittling the idea that she was a nuisance.

"No, no, *domi*," Stormsong hurried to reassure her. "Pony's job is to guard you, and most of the time we merely include you on activities we normally do."

"Sparrow never says please or thank you." Skybolt made a sound of disgust as he shot, sending out his arrows in a show of graceful speed. "The other castes are beneath her politeness."

He too put all five arrows into the red; even Stormsong acknowledged his skill with *"Kiyau."*

Pony shook his head. "Sparrow does not see the clans' strength to be the cooperation of castes, but solely as the clan head in possession of spell stones. Since she can't access the stones, she grasps for other ways to show power: withholding politeness and pretty demands."

The others nodded to this.

"We should call you Hawkeye," Skybolt said, "for your clear-sightedness."

The next day, it rained, trapping Tinker indoors. The grayness seemed to invade her soul, so after a Windwolf-less lunch she curled in the sunroom and watched the rainfall, fighting to keep in tears. It would be stupid to cry; everyone had been bending over backward to make her happy.

All the little seeds of fear, doubt, and unease, though, were growing into a wild, dark tangle. What was going to happen that made her the pivot? Beyond the cryptic warnings, there had been nothing more from the seer. At some point, all would depend on her, and she had an unspoken terror that the decision would have to be made when she was completely alone against a horde of oni, without so much as a datapad.

And what if the queen never let her go back to Pittsburgh? Certainly if the queen wanted to keep control of the pivot, she could insist that Tinker stay at Aum Renau, or take her back East. Windwolf told her that he asked permission daily, but for all Tinker knew, he could be lying to her. Surrounded by beauty and luxury, it seemed stupid to be so homesick for the squalid, half-abandoned steel town. She wanted her computers, tools, and hoverbike. She wished she could call Oilcan, just to know he was okay and not worrying about her. She desperately wanted to talk to Lain; since her grandfather died, Lain had been her guide through life's confusion. Lain could tell her what to do, make it all right.

"*Domi.*" Pony crouched down beside her. "The *sefada* know you are unhappy and say that you can come help them make *falotiki*. They are very simple to make, and the *sefada* promise to watch carefully so they will not catch fire, and afterward you decorate them with icing in bright colors."

"Um," her voice cracked, and his face blurred, so she scrubbed at her eyes. "Yeah, sure." And then to make them all stop worrying about her, "It sounds like fun."

And through sheer determination on her part, it actually was.

Windwolf came into the kitchen while she was icing. The little square *falotiki* cakes reminded her of the periodic table, so she had arranged them into the classic chart and was making each cake a different element. She was working on radium, and after telling the kitchen staff its radioactive properties, was reciting the "Little Willie" poem that featured his grandmother's tea. "Now Grandpa thinks it quite a lark, To see her shining in the dark."

"*Dama!*" cried Lemonseed, the head cook.

Tinker looked up to find Windwolf leaning in the doorframe, watching her with a grin. "You look pleased about something."

"The queen says we can leave for Pittsburgh in the morning."

Tinker squealed and flung herself at Windwolf. He swept her up and she kissed him until she realized that she was covering him with flour and that tears were running down her face. "Oh gods, I screamed, didn't I? Oh, that's so stupid. I'm not the type to scream."

"No," he agreed, resting his forehead on hers. "You are not the type to scream."

"Is she really letting me go home?" She saw the hurt go through his eyes. "I mean, back to Pittsburgh?"

"Yes. With provisions."

"Provisions?" She didn't like the sound of that. "Here, let me down, so I can wash my hands."

"The queen is concerned." Windwolf paused, obviously picking out the most politic way of putting things. "She sees you as a child with a child's grasp of the universe. She's not saying you're immature," Windwolf hastened to explain as Tinker made a rude noise. "By the time an elf reaches adult, he has had a hundred years of being steeped in our culture—which isn't always a good thing—but it does teach him about living for millennia. You can barely speak the high tongue, and you're not going to learn it, or any of the skills you need, by living daily with humans."

She froze, hands in the water. "What—what does that mean? That I can't go home? But you just said—I'm staying in Pittsburgh— or is this just a visit?"

"It is not a visit, but it will be a change in your living arrangement."

"What the hell does that mean?"

"We closed our Pathways on a land as pastoral as our own. The Dutch were a superpower. Latin was the tongue of the learned man, and the laundry you term 'prehistoric' would be a marvel of advanced technology." Windwolf pulled her hands out of the water and toweled them dry. "Most of the elves here at Aum Renau were alive during your Dark Ages. Many saw the fall of the Romans. There are even ones that saw the rise of the Egyptians."

She squeaked, as the weight of the ages seemed to compress down on her. "Really?"

"Lemonseed here is over nine thousand years old."

Tinker glanced to the sweet-tempered *sefada* who seemed no older than Lain. "Nine thousand?"

"By the very nature of humans and elves, the gate *will* close while you're alive," Windwolf said. "Currently you have the queen's protection. No one can call insult on you, or challenge you to a duel. But that protection will not last forever. What is forgiven in a child will not be forgiven in an adult. You must know how to live with us— your people."

She became aware that everyone in the kitchen was trying hard to pretend that they weren't listening to the conversation. What language had they been arguing in this time? She winced as she realized that it had flowed almost seamlessly between English and Elvish, sometimes changing halfway through the sentence. Growling, she undid the mega apron protecting her dress, shoved it into the hamper for dirty linens, and stomped out of the kitchen.

Windwolf came after her, and a few steps behind him, were Pony and Stormsong. She headed to their living quarters as one of the few places they could talk without the bodyguards overhearing.

"What are the provisions?" she asked once the door shut between them and the *sekasha*.

"I must establish a residence at Pittsburgh and move my household there."

"Move? For how long?"

He clicked his tongue in a shrug. "A couple of decades, maybe a century."

She winced, thinking of the close-knit community she'd found at the palace. "How many of the clanspeople here at the palace are part of your household?"

Windwolf looked slightly confused. "All of them."

"All!" Hope turned to ash; there was no way the entire palace staff would be shifted just because she was homesick. "There's like sixty people here!"

"Seventy-four, not counting Pony."

"Why not count Pony?" Tinker cried. Of all the *sekasha*, Pony was her favorite.

"Pony is yours, not mine."

"Mine?"

Windwolf paused, apparently considering his English. "Yours," he repeated, this time in Elvish. "Not mine."

Oh, shit, now what had she done? "How did Pony get to be mine?"

"Pony's parents are beholden to my father and I watched him grow up, which makes me protective of him. As he neared his majority, he wanted a chance to make a real decision about whom he looked to, and not just take his parents' path. I gave him refuge in my house, although he hadn't yet come of age. I expected him to offer to me, for we are fond of one another, but he was free to offer to you."

She dropped onto the bench before her bed, remembering then the conversation just before they left Pittsburgh, under watch of the queen's Wyverns. Once again, someone offered, and she accepted without realizing what strings were attached. "Oh, no."

Something on her face made Windwolf kneel down in front of her and take her hands. "I am pleased. I thought you two would suit well, that's why I left him with you. He brings you honor, since not everyone can hold a *sekasha*."

"I didn't realize what he was saying."

Windwolf looked dismayed and then sighed. "It is done now. Once accepted, even by mistake, the contract can not be unmade. It means you find the person unacceptable. No matter what you said, everyone would believe the worst of Pony, that he had acted in some way inappropriately."

She pressed the heels of her hands tight against her eyes. "Oh, gods, what a mess."

"I don't understand why you're so upset. You obviously love Pony well, and we're returning to Pittsburgh."

She peeked at him through her fingers. "We are?"

"I told the queen that the provisions were acceptable."

The hands came off her face completely. "You did!"

"It is only for a short time."

Of course.

Yet, she felt guilty that so many people were having their life turned upside down because she didn't want to change. Windwolf, though, had volunteered knowing full well who would be affected and how. She hadn't known. She hadn't known when she saved him from the saurus and he marked her to be part of his household. She hadn't known when he offered his betrothal gift. Or when he asked if she wanted to be immortal. Or when Pony offered himself. Again and again, she was lost in ignorance, while others acted with full knowledge. Why should she feel guilty?

Because they thought she'd understood. Because she didn't admit to her ignorance. It was bad enough when it was just her suffering the consequences, but others were now being dragged in.

Tinker leaned against the glass, eager for her first sight of Pittsburgh. For hours they had sailed over the unending green of elfin forest, gently rocked as the gossamer swam against the headwind. The crew had said that it would take six hours, and now at noon, the time of arrival was nearing.

Beside her the navigator had been peering intently through a spyglass, picking out familiar landmarks. "We're here."

She scanned the horizon, finding the glitter of a river, guessed it to be the Monongahela and watched it unravel westward through the forest. There was a clearing in the forest with a cluster of enclaves and a wide field thick with colorful tents, and then more forest, and another river. "What's that?"

"Oakland," the navigator said. "Bring her to a slow speed!"

Oakland? Tinker frowned, studying the onrushing buildings. Faintly she could see the Rim, its barren strip of no-mans-land, arcing through the forest. Yes, it was the elfin Oakland, but Pittsburgh wasn't there. No human streets, half-empty buildings, skyscrapers, or bridges. Just unending forest. "Oh no, it's Shutdown!"

"Of course it is," Sparrow said. "We've always thought it an odd and awkward way of doing a Pathway, but that's humans for you."

Windwolf shot Sparrow a hard look, which gained a contrite half-bow and his assistant fleeing. "I am sorry. I had forgotten to check."

"It will be back tomorrow." Tinker shoved away her disappointment. They were all but home now. "The enclaves will be full tonight."

"Room will be found." Windwolf hugged her.

His presence distracted her from Pittsburgh's absence, to a realization of the date. "We met last Shutdown. Just twenty-eight days ago." Oh gods, the last three weeks had been the longest in her life. Immortality at this speed was going to drive her nuts.

"Time expands and contracts." Windwolf kissed her hair. "Sometimes a day can seem like a second, and sometimes it lasts forever. Certainly the hours that I lay helpless on Earth were the longest I've ever lived."

"Then we're even."

Prior to Shutdown, all the elves living in Pittsburgh shifted temporarily to either the enclaves or camps at the Faire Grounds, thus the collection of bright-colored tents crowding the meadow. Since the Faire Grounds doubled as the airfield for the massive airship, it took shouted negotiations, followed by careful maneuvering to accomplish a tethering.

While this was being accomplished, Tinker studied the flip side of Pittsburgh, the great circle of forest sent to Earth with Startup. Here on Elfhome there was nothing at the Rim but barren land. Back on Earth was a chain-link fence surrounding the forest—a great wall of China done in steel—to keep in dangerous elfin wildlife, and more importantly, keep out unwanted human immigrants. On Earth and in Pittsburgh, EIA patrolled the Rim. From the Observation lounge (having been politely scooted out for the already complicated tethering) Tinker could see elfin rangers moving through the trees, keeping close to the Rim but scouting for trespassers. The sole building within the forest was the legendary EIA lockup, an ugly squat cinderblock building whose only function was to hold prisoners until Startup returned them to Earth. At one time, Tinker lived in fear of it and its polar opposite, the glass castle of EIA headquarters in Pittsburgh.

Also from her high vantage point, Tinker could see that someone had managed to do some illegal logging of the virgin forest. The south shore of the Ohio, approximately where the West End Bridge crossed in Pittsburgh, had been stripped bare, although she couldn't imagine how anyone could cut down the trees and get them into the river without heavy equipment. Apparently the EIA's watch on Earth wasn't as legendary as she'd always heard.

Movement directly below caught her eye and she looked downward. Someone was waving at the gossamer, a short and plain figure among the tall, elegantly dressed elves.

"Oilcan!" she cried. "Oh gods, what is he doing here?"

After waving at her cousin to let him know she saw him, she went to beat on anyone who could get her down to the ground. Minutes later the elevator dropped her down, the door opened and he was there, waiting, and she pounced on him.

"What are you doing here?" She hugged him tightly.

"Waiting for you," he said. "Gods, look at you. You look wonderful."

"I still feel a little dorky in these clothes." She plucked at her skirt. "I had to be 'acceptable' at Aum Renau in case I ran into the queen in some dark hallway." She realized that she was rambling and hugged him again. "What are you doing here?"

He grinned. "I just had this feeling that you'd be coming back during Shutdown, and I'd been kicking myself for not going with you, so I asked Maynard to get me permission to ride out Shutdown on Elfhome." He glanced back at the wall of trees beyond the Rim. "It was weird watching Pittsburgh vanish, though. I've had this creepy feeling all morning, like it wasn't coming back and I'd be stuck here. I was starting to think I'd made a big mistake."

"By the very nature of humans and elves, the gate will close while you're alive."

She glanced around at the single cluster of enclaves and the handful of tents—no electricity, no computers, and no phones. Oh gods protect her, she'd go mad.

13: CROW BLACK SHROUD

"Tinker! Tinker!"

Tinker had learned to ignore her own name, since anyone not calling her "*domi*" only wanted to interrupt her with stupid questions. She wasn't listening: 546879 divided by 3 equaled 182293.

"Alexander Graham Bell!"

Tooloo was right; anyone knowing your real name gained power over you. Tinker flipped up her welding visor and looked down through the tower's trusses to the ground far below. Lain glared back up at her. A quick check showed Lain's hoverbike parked alongside Tinker's and Pony's, which explained how the xenobiologist got to the remote building site, but not why.

"What?" Tinker shouted down.

"Come down here." Lain tapped the ground with her right crutch.

"Why?"

"Young lady, get your butt down here now! I am not going to scream at you like a howler monkey."

Sighing, Tinker turned off the welder. "Pony, will you kill the generator?"

He paused, sword half-drawn. "Kill what?"

"Hit the big red switch." She pointed at the purring generator.

"Ah." He slid his sword back into its sheath. "Yes, *domi*."

She stripped off her welding visor, and pulled off the heavy gloves.

The carpenters' foreman realized that she was leaving, and hesitantly asked, "*Domi*, what should we do next?"

Good thing she'd planned for this. She searched her blue jean pockets until she found her printouts for the current phase of work. "Please, do as much as you can of this and then take a break. Thank you."

She climbed down the tower calling out instructions to work crews as she spotted problems.

The cutting crew waited for her at the foot of the ladder. "We cut to the survey marks, *domi.*"

"Good, good, thank you." She scanned the ten acres of cleared hilltop. "The stumps in the area of the foundation need to be removed. I'm not sure how that's done. I suppose we could blast them out."

"No, no, no." Strangely, they seemed anxious for her not to use explosives. Too bad—it would have been fun. "There is magic to excise roots. We'll see it done."

"Thank you, thank you."

Lain stood beside the board tacked heavy with technical drawings, floor plans, and concept pictures. "What do you think you're doing?"

Was that a trick question? "I'm creating infrastructure." Tinker drew Lain's attention to the board. "Phase One was to choose an appropriate building site. Phase Two was to commandeer a work crew. Phase Three is to clear the building site." She waved a hand at the denuded ridgeline. The topology maps were correct—this was one of the highest hills in the area. "Phase Four is to secure the building site." She paused to check off item one of the Phase Three schedule posted on the board. "Phase Five is to create an energy source. Based on an article I read once, I've designed a wind turbine using rear brake drums from Ford F250 trucks. See." She found the concept drawing. "This is really beauty in simplicity. I can adapt old electric motors into these 'inside out' alternators common on small wind turbines—which eliminates the need to build a complicated hub that attaches the blades to a small-diameter shaft. See, this simple plywood sandwich holds the blades tightly in the rotor and the entire assembly is mounted directly to the generator housing: the brake drum. It should churn out three hundred to five hundred watts per turbine."

"Per turbine?"

"Roughly." Tinker realized watt output wasn't Lain's question. "Oh, I'm hoping for at least five to start with along this ridge. I originally thought I could install them near the Faire Ground and then realized since it doubled as the airfield that wouldn't work."

"Tinker . . ."

Tinker held up her hand, as she hadn't really come to the heart of the plan. "Phase Six will be to create telecommunication abilities not relying on Pittsburgh resources. Phase Seven will be to develop the Tinker Computing Center. Scratch that. Tinker *domi* Computing and Research Center."

Tinker paused to note the name change and Lain snatched the pen from her hand. She eyed Lain, tapping her pen-less fingers. "What are you doing here?"

"It is the sad truth that anyone that knows you well also knows that I have some influence with you. I have had Oilcan, Nathan, Riki, Director Maynard, four human agencies, and five elfin household heads call me in the last hour. I even had my first ever telephone conversation with Tooloo, not something I ever want to repeat. Honestly Tinker, what in the world do you think you're doing?"

Tinker glanced at the plan-covered board and back to Lain. Strange. She thought Lain was fairly intelligent. "I told you. Creating infrastructure."

"You've commandeered workers from all the enclaves, and I'm sure you're working them without enclaves, and I'm sure you're working them without pay. The EIA director is in a froth about missing evidence, the department of transportation supervisor complained that you've hijacked one of their dump trucks, and the police say you've taken a Peterbilt truck from the impound."

"I needed a lot of stuff."

"Why are you doing this?"

Tinker jabbed a finger at her plans. "I'm creating *infrastructure*!"

Lain caught her hands, held them tight. "Why?"

"Because it's not there. Twenty years of Pittsburgh being on Elfhome, and everything is still in Pittsburgh. Elfhome has the train and some boats, and that's it."

"That is not why. Why are *you* doing it, in this manner?"

"Because obviously no one else is going to do it, or it would already be done."

"Have you considered that the reason why might be because the elves don't want it on Elfhome?"

"I don't care what they want. I want it. I'm not going to spend another day without a computer, let alone three weeks, or a century, or millennia. Maybe this is why I'm the damn pivot. I say 'enough already, get with the program' and when the oni comes, my Elfhome Internet saves the day."

"Tinker, you just can't do this."

"Actually, yes I can. See, I've learned something in the last three weeks. When the queen says 'you're dropping everything and flying to Aum Renau,' you go. And when the queen says 'you're staying at Aum Renau,' you stay. And when the head of household says 'we're all moving to Pittsburgh,' you move. And when the clan head says 'I need all the rooms in this enclave, please find other lodgings,' you do. Well, I'm Tinker *domi*! I can make a computing and research center."

"Where is your husband?"

"Oh gods, don't say that." Tinker fled her, ducking into the commandeered tent of Wind Clan blue.

Lain followed close behind, despite the deep ruts churned up by the heavy equipment. "Don't say what?"

"Husband." Tinker peeked into the wicker lunch boxes sent from the enclaves until she found some *mauzouan*. "You want something to eat?"

"No, thank you."

Tinker scowled at Pony until he got himself some food. "A male gives you a bowl and suddenly you're married? Please. Okay, the sex is fantastic, but is that any basis for a relationship?"

"Of course not." Lain sat down in one of the folding chairs purloined out of the gossamer. "But I can't imagine Windwolf committing himself to marriage solely for sex."

"He says he loves me." Tinker settled herself at the teak table, also from the airship. "I don't know why."

"Tinker!"

"I mean . . . he didn't know me. I still barely know him. We spent the twenty-four hours of Shutdown together. I saw him once the next morning—oh, wait, make that twice—and then he proposed to me. Elves don't fall in love that fast—do they?"

"I suppose it could be a case of transference."

"Mmm?" She mumbled around a hot *mauzouan*.

"It's not uncommon for patients to fall in love with their doctor."

"You stitched him up."

"Yes, but you moved houses and fought monsters to keep him alive."

"Is this supposed to make me feel better?"

"Tinker, we can't know other people's hearts. Humans fall in love at first sight, and only time tells if that love is true. There is no reason that elves can't do the same. Certainly while Shutdown was only twenty-four hours, they were quite intense ones."

"Yeah, I suppose," Tinker murmured, remembering what Windwolf had said to her. *"Certainly the hours that I lay helpless on Earth were the longest I've ever lived."*

"If nothing else," Lain continued, "you showed the depth of your intelligence and grit."

"Grit?" She popped another *mauzouan* into her mouth. "What does sand have to do with it?"

"It's a way of saying your strength of character; your courage under fire."

Tinker snorted at that. "Lain, how do you know when you're in love? How do you recognize it?"

"Sometimes you don't. Sometimes you mistake lust as love. And sometimes you only know after you've thrown love away."

Trust Lain to say anything but words of comfort. Tinker dropped her head on the table and considered banging it a couple of times. "Argh," she groaned into the wood.

"Give it time," Lain said.

"If someone says that one more time, I think I'll scream."

She hated this feeling of being out of control. Last night, they had sat up waiting for Startup. Elves had little need for wristwatches, so it was without warning that Pittsburgh had flashed into existence, a dark sprawl of buildings washed in moonlight. From the enclaves up and down the street had come shouts of approval, as the elves cheered the return like a magician's trick. And in that moment, Tinker had realized that she would probably never see Earth again; elves stayed on Elfhome during Shutdown.

Like a cascade, realizations spilled down on her. She wasn't going back to her loft—Windwolf and Pony wouldn't fit, let alone the rest of the household. There was no reason for the viceroy's wife to work. Leaving Pittsburgh now wasn't just a matter of convincing Oilcan to come with her, but also leaving Windwolf and Pony behind.

It wasn't that Windwolf had taken away *all* her choices, but the ones left were dubious. Insist on living alone? Continue to spend inventing time on the scrap yard when Windwolf had money to burn? Betray the elves who loved her to leave everyone and everything she knew?

Desperate to snatch control of her life back—and yet not totally wreck everyone's lives with stupid decisions—she came up with the computing center. So maybe she went a little overboard.

Tinker sighed. "Let's get it over with. Give me my lecture."

"I don't know what to say," Lain stated, getting up. "And I'm not sure it's my place to say anything. I suggest you go talk to Windwolf."

"Run to my husband and get permission for what to do with my life?"

"No, go discuss with the viceroy what future the two of you are going to build for your people."

"Ouch," Tinker said.

"I never said being an adult is easy." Lain squeezed Tinker's shoulder. "But I have faith in you. And I'm fairly sure Windwolf does too."

After Lain left, Tinker glumly finished her lunch. She had no idea how Windwolf might take this scheme of hers. Would he think she overstepped her bounds, as Lain obviously did? Or would he be pleased at her initiative? Oilcan had gifted her with her datapad the evening before and she'd spent the night communing with it, laying plans, and barely noticed when Windwolf left in the morning. She eyed the denuded hillside, the conscripted elves, and the commandeered equipment; wherever Windwolf was, it couldn't be nearby.

"Pony, where is Wolf Who Rules?"

"He and Sparrow are looking for oni. The queen wished verification that the oni are not using Pittsburgh to access Elfhome."

A jolt of fear went through her. "They went out alone?"

"No, they have the *sekasha*, the EIA, and the rangers with them."

It sounded like a small army. She had been more wrapped up in her own plans than she realized. If the EIA were with them, then finding them would only be a matter of a phone call. Of course there was the problem that she'd apparently ticked off Maynard by misappropriating the smugglers' high-tech goods.

Then again, a small army shouldn't be too hard to spot.

The road up to the work site was just raw dirt, already growing deep ruts. She'd have to get it properly graded and graveled before it turned into a mud slalom. There was no way they could drive the Rolls up and down it without fear of tearing out the undercarriage. She'd pulled her old Gamma out of storage early that morning and coaxed Pony into trying the hoverbike.

He'd been dubious at first, but he smiled now as she headed for the bikes. "Ah, good, we're going flying again."

"Yeah." She swung her leg over her Delta's saddle. "I want to find Wolf Who Rules. Do you have any idea where he might be?"

"Sparrow was to search between the Rim and the rivers." Pony pointed down the Ohio River. The Rim arced along the Ohio's bank, clipped above the confluence of the Allegheny and the Monongahela, and then ran roughly parallel to the Mon, leaving odd slices of Pittsburgh without bridges. "Wolf Who Rules chose to search the bulk of the area, beyond Mount Washington."

Yes, Windwolf had more land to cover, but Sparrow actually had the thankless job. Between the three major rivers, the numerous smaller rivers and larger streams, Sparrow's team would be back-tracking often to navigate over water or sheer hillsides. Pittsburgh had been the city of bridges—unfortunately, most stayed on Earth.

"You up to a long ride?"

"Very much so." Pony mounted up, thumbprinted the lock, and hit the ignition button of the Gamma. The bike's lift drive rumbled to life. Pony eased down on the throttle until he was at cruise level, and retracted his parking studs. "Come, *domi*, let's find Wolf Who Rules."

They went down the steep muddy road hacked through the forest until they hit the Rim. There, they crossed onto the abrupt start of I-279 North—six lanes heading into downtown with no traffic. There, to Pony's delight, she opened up the throttle and soared along the wide even pavement, gaining altitude. He was a good mix of fast learner and yet still cautious.

Confident that Pony could take care of himself, she focused on finding Windwolf. The South Hills continued the Pittsburgh tradition of houses clinging to steep hillsides, narrow valleys, and winding roads. She and Pony could miss Windwolf by a hundred feet and never realize it.

Maybe I should make nice with Maynard first, she thought, and bypassed the Veterans Bridge on-ramp to head for the Fort Duquesne Bridge; that would drop her closer to the EIA castle.

Two car-lengths behind her, Pony suddenly veered off onto the steep on-ramp, followed close behind by a blue sedan. Focused on Windwolf, Tinker had missed whatever caused him to swerve onto the ramp. Had the car cut Pony off? Tinker couldn't see how; it wasn't that close to Pony. Strangely, Pony wasn't watching to see what she was doing. She glanced up to check if she was cleared for pop-up onto the road, but there were signs and streetlamps in the way. A second later, she was under the sudden tangle of Route 28 crossing over 279, and the Veterans Bridge's on-ramps and exits vaulting over it all.

That neatly, a trap was sprung. Hoverbikes surged out from around bridge supports and down off of Route 28, converging on her. Even as she did a pop-up to miss the first one, she recognized at least three of the riders. The oni.

She nailed the throttle, ducking as the pop-up threatened to smack her into the I-beams of the Route 28 overpass. Even at maximum lift, she didn't have the clearance to make it up onto the Veterans Bridge, now two street levels above her. She shifted power into the torque spell chain, sacrificing height for speed.

She glanced in her mirrors, seeing the oni scramble to chase after her. *Nyah, nyah, eat my dust.*

But there were more combatants than she had counted on; a red Corvette came snarling down the on-ramp from Nash Street. There had to be an ancient V8 under the hood as the Corvette matched her speed, crowding her to the left side of the road, forcing her to take the lower deck of the Fort Duquesne Bridge. The bridge closed in around them like a tunnel, and the Corvette herded her across the river, with the other bikes following. They flashed across the bridge and down into the chute of the Tenth Street Bypass that ran along the river. The surface tension of water wasn't enough to support a bike, or she'd skip off across the river.

As they rushed toward the overpass of the Sixth Street Bridge, she popped up—slewing sideways in mid-air as she scraped over the railing—and landed hard on the overpass. She skidded across the road, momentum carrying her in a straight line toward the far railing. Sometimes she really hated the laws of physics. She leaned hard to redirect the lift drive to check her slide.

There were two hoverbikes coming across the bridge, the riders nearly dwarfing their machines. She had to keep moving. If she stopped, they would have her. The city was to their advantage—the short runs and sudden dead-ends would let them pen her in with sheer numbers. The long stretches gave her, on the faster bike, the advantage.

She nailed the throttle open—the torque spell shooting her forward—and threw her mass far out, nearly kissing pavement, as she muscled the bike through a sharp right turn onto Fort Duquesne Boulevard, heading back to the bridge. All three lanes of traffic were slowing for a red light, too tight for her to weave through. A single tractor-trailer truck occupied the rightmost lane. She popped up to race the trailer's length, skipping her lift drive off its roof. She shot out over its cab, lost lift, and smacked down hard on the pavement in a bone-jarring impact. The truck horn blasted behind her, a wall of metal filling her peripheral vision.

Cursing, she flung all power into the torque. The bike leaped forward and she ran it up the gears as she whipped back over the bridge, this time on the top deck. Mid-bridge, she took the fork toward 279. She didn't know what they'd done to Pony, but they'd gotten him away from her somehow. She had no idea what she was going to do when she caught up with them, but there was no way she was leaving Pony in their power.

She came to the snarl of on-ramps to the bridge. None actually connected the road she was on to the bridge, but she skipped over jersey barriers to catch the Route 28 on-ramp.

Veterans Bridge crossed the Allegheny in eight lanes of broad plainness, crossing first the Allegheny River and then the Strip District. At the far end it splintered into mad twistings, each exit heading in a radically different direction. She roared across the bridge, sick at the thought of reaching its end and not spotting Pony. Did they take him downtown, intending to hold him in whatever trap they had tried to maneuver her into? That didn't make sense. Why hadn't they caught her the same way they had caught Pony? Was it because she was *domana?*

Movement caught her eye, and she glanced into her mirrors. Oni were skipping up from the Strip District to land on the bridge behind her.

Shit. She ignored the first exit off the bridge that would have funneled her back into the city. Beyond it the roadway carved through the foot of the Hill, creating a cement canyon of pavement and bridge supports. She shot into the canyon, six hoverbikes trailing behind her, and the Corvette joining the fray from the downtown on-ramp. Straight would take her over the Liberty Bridge arching over the Monongahela River, through the tunnel to the South Hills maze and Windwolf somewhere searching for oni with a small army.

"Look what I found, sweetheart," Tinker muttered, but the Corvette was attempting to herd her that direction. No, if that was the way they *wanted* her to go, she'd better not.

As the Corvette crowded close, she popped up, and then kissed off his hood before he could correct, leaning hard to angle the lift into a sideways skip. She touched down on the exit ramp for the Boulevard, the scream of brakes behind her as the Corvette tried to stop, followed by the unmistakable thud of him hitting something.

Yeah, bring a car to a hoverbike chase. Loser!

She lost speed in the jump, though, and the pack of hoverbikes closed like a pack of wargs scenting blood. She put everything into torque, and whispered sweet things to her Delta. The ramp leaped from the canyon to the clifftop Boulevard of the Allies in one mid-air arc. Dropping down to the Parkway that ran parallel to the Boulevard at the foot of the cliff would be insane; even with the lift drive at max, she'd drop like a stone and—from that height—splatter.

If she could keep ahead of them, it was only a quick run to the Rim, and the EIA border patrol. She'd get them and the cops and find Pony.

The lead oni hoverbike, though, was one of her custom Deltas—

talk about a mistake coming back to haunt you. For an oni, the rider was a little shit, grinning viciously at her with a mouthful of sharpened teeth. He matched her speed, smacking her closer and closer to the edge of the cliff. She ground her teeth, fighting to control her bike, but he had the mass on her. A pop-up might lose him, but that would cost her speed, and put her in the middle of the pack. His bike looked like Czerneda's, done in aquamarine fish scales. He had to have stolen it, since Czerneda would rather sell his soul than give the bike up. She braced herself against the battering and risked a look down at the thumblock. In its place dangled a mass of wires, bypassing the bike security system. *Ha, well, bye-bye Mr. Oni.*

She reached to yank loose the wires. He realized what she was doing and swung away from her. She risked overextending herself in a desperate grab. He came back at her, grabbing for her outstretched arm.

Shit, she had forgotten that their goal was *her*! She jerked away, and the motion rode her bike up the retaining wall and left her teetering on the narrow lip. Before she could push her bike back down to safety, the oni hit her again. As her bike tipped over the edge, he realized what he'd done—eyes going wide in panic, he grabbed hold of her bike instead of her and yanked it hard.

Instantly she was airborne, screaming as she went over the cliff and rushed toward the ground with nothing, nothing, to grab.

And then something grabbed her.

Riki had her by the back of her shirt.

She flailed backward, got hold of him, and swarmed up his body to cling deathly tight to him. "Oh, gods, oh gods, thank you, thank you."

Far below their feet, her Delta struck the riverbank and was instantly reduced to a mass of twisted wreckage.

Feet?

She jerked her gaze upward.

Massive wings, crow black, sprouted from Riki's back. She could feel soft down on his back and the start of wing structure and the movement of muscle as the wings beat the air. She could only stare in amazement as feathers shrouded the sky with black.

"Don't thank me," he snarled, shifting his hold on her so he had her by the back of the neck.

"I would have been dead if you hadn't caught me," she said, for the first time in her life only able to think "what—what—what—?"

"I shouldn't have had to." He twisted her in his hold, bringing up something to her face. "They weren't supposed to hurt you."

It all sank in as she recognized the flower in his hand. He was one of them. He was a tengu. He was there to catch her because he'd helped to design the trap in the first place. She tried to twist away from the flower, but he tightened his hold on her neck until she thought he would snap it. He pressed the *Saijin* to her face, crushing soft fragrant petals to her nose. The heat and goldness of the sun filled her senses.

"No!" She struck out. Her fist slammed into his nose, snapping back his head and instantly bloodying him. He straightened out his arms, keeping out of her reach as he kept the flower tight against her.

She tried to squirm out of his hold, turn her head away.

He forced her still, watching her with furrowed brow. Without his sunglasses his eyes were a stunning blue—not the blue of Windwolf's, whose eyes were the dark, rich blue of expensive sapphires, but the cerulean blue of an electric spark. She could see that they weren't human eyes now, too vivid a color, the shape faintly almond, the lashes thick and long, viewing her with the same deadly detachment as electricity . . .

14: ONI MOON

Tinker woke with her head pounding and stared in confusion at the strange ceiling above her. For several minutes it seemed like a normal white plaster ceiling. Then she felt as if a long, thin-limbed spider was picking its way across her forehead. She bolted upright, swatting at her brow. Her fingers found nothing to kill, nor was there anything now on her lap except a spill of fine linen sheets. She sat on a futon mattress, level on the floor, with a nest of sheets, blankets, and pillows so comforting to look at that she nearly sank back into them. Things were wrong, though, and she dragged her eyes back to the ceiling. Same plain white ceiling, or was it? She got the vague impression that something had changed, only she couldn't put a finger on what.

A few feet from the end of the mattress was a stone wall with a deep-set window. Sitting on the floor, she could only see a slice of blue sky. She crawled to the wall, having difficulty controlling her overly light limbs. She looked out the window and gasped.

A city rolled out to the horizon, endless heavy stone buildings with red clay roof tiles. It reminded her of martial arts vids. As she stared hard at it, she finally made out the Allegheny and Monongahela rivers, converging to make the Ohio, meaning she was on Mount Washington, not far from Oilcan's apartment—only at least one reality removed. Whatever they called the city below, it wasn't Pittsburgh.

"Wondering where you are?"

She turned and discovered that a female dressed in a kimono, feet tucked under her, sat in the far corner of the room, watching her. Had she always been there? Tinker's mind was too drug-clouded for her to remember.

"No," Tinker said, not because it was the truth—she was dying to know—but mostly because it was the opposite of what the female wanted her to say.

"Obstinacy will get you nowhere," the female said.

"It's all I have at the moment, so I'll stick with it."

Tinker went back to staring out the window. This wasn't Earth, nor Elfhome, but something beyond Elfhome. Judging by the room she was in, the narrow twisting roads, and the lack of any outward sign of machinery, the technology level of the reality was on par with Elfhome. Unlike the elf world, though, it seemed as if this place staggered under Earth's population problems.

"You're on Onihida," the female said. "There is no escape."

No need for bars on the window; the whole world was a prison. Still Tinker examined the possibilities for escape. The building she was in continued the Oriental theme, only on fortress scale. The outside wall was of massive stones and was mortared tightly, presenting seriously scary rock-climbing potential. The drop down to the ground was thirty or forty feet. A misstep would put her down over the cliff edge too, adding two hundred feet to the fall.

All things considered, she should find another escape route.

Tinker turned her attention finally to the female. She seemed familiar. While lacking the elfin ears, she was beautiful in the way of elves, perfection in the small-pored, unblemished skin, symmetrical features, a cascade of red-gold hair, and eyes of a vivid reddish-brown. "Who are you?"

"I am Taji Chiyo."

"What did you do to Pony?"

"The little horsie betrayed you," Taji said casually, but her eyes sharpened with interest, as if she wanted to see the pain her words caused.

"No he didn't. Riki did."

"You will call me Lady Chiyo. And yes, he did, he drove off and left you. Ta ta."

"I don't know how you did it, but he didn't betray me," Tinker growled. "Pony wouldn't do that, and you have no reason to tell me the truth, Chewie."

"Chi-yo. Lady Chiyo."

"Look, bitch, you snared me this way because you needed to get around Pony." Tinker scrambled for facts to support her gut feeling. "If he was one of you, he could have delivered me up in the Rolls at any time. The first day Windwolf left me at the lodge, or all the next day while I was running all around Pittsburgh—hell, Riki talked me into ditching Pony at the scrap yard just before the Wyverns nabbed me. That probably pissed you all off—didn't it? You got me all by my-self and the Wyverns showed up unannounced." Chiyo's eyes went wide and the startled look fit another piece of the puzzle together. "You're Maynard's secretary."

"Was." Chiyo rose out of the awkward-looking sitting position with grace and poise. "Someone else does that petty work now. If you want to know what happened to your warrior, come with me."

Chiyo glided to the door with little delicate footsteps nearly com-pletely masked by her flowing kimono. Tinker thumped after her, annoyed with the way her feet seemed enormous. Had they always been that big, or was it a side effect of the drug that Riki had given her, making them look bigger?

Chiyo had paused at the door; she noticed Tinker's inspection of her feet and gave a small smug smile. Tinker decided at the first pos-sible point to step on those delicate lady points with her steel-shod feet, hard. Lady Chiyo frowned slightly, slid open the door, and hur-ried down the hall in tiny little steps.

There were two burly armed guards outside the door, bracketing it. Tinker slipped between them, trying blithely to ignore them. *I'm not scared of you. I'm not scared.*

Oh, gods, she wished she and Pony were home safe.

Lady Chiyo led, and a step behind Tinker, the guards followed.

Tinker forced herself to amble, trying to stay oriented despite the drug. Except for occasional windows looking out over the sprawling city, the stone passages were maddeningly the same, like a computer-generated video screen with a limited algorithm. Abruptly they were in a garden courtyard, all done in Oriental style. A stream meandered through the heart of it, through a bed of mossy rocks. A ribbon of sil-ver here, murmuring over a slight falls. A widening and deepening there, to make a still dark pool full of darting fish. Chimes rang in the wind with stunningly clear tones, and yet, yet, there was something hazy about the whole thing, like a dream.

It's the drugs, isn't it? Tinker wasn't sure.

Lady Chiyo led her to a gazebo overlooking one of the still ponds.

Riki sat in the gazebo, wearing an over-large muscle shirt and loose black pants, with bare feet. Despite the casual clothes, he perched in the gazebo window, looking as unhappy as a caged bird. He wore earbuds trailing wires down to an old MP3 player. Surpris-ingly, he was smoking, something an elf could never do.

He was alone.

"Where's Pony?" Tinker said.

Riki sighed, and pulled the earbud from his right ear, letting the

music play on in his left. "Hopefully, your guard is even now report-
ing your untimely death, a mid-air stunt resulting in a fall into the
river. Of course the river will be dredged, but that will prove nothing."

"You're lying. Pony wouldn't betray me."

"He's not betraying you; we've deceived him." Riki took a deep
drag on his cigarette, and breathed it out his nose in a twin column of
smoke. "We have magic that the elves do not, the bending of light and
sound to make illusions."

Chiyo complained in a foreign language made harsh by her sharp
tones.

Riki gazed at Chiyo unrepentant. "Stop your barking. I'm in
charge. I tell her what I want."

"Lord Tomtom gave orders for . . ."

"He wants her to work. She won't work if she thinks we killed her
warrior." Riki stared Chiyo into silence. "The magic works on the
lesser elves, but not on you greater bloods," he explained, meaning
the *domana*. "We didn't want to expose the people we have in Pittsburgh. If the elves knew you were kidnapped, they would tear the city
apart looking for you. They're already searching; the fewer clues we
give them the better. So we split your guard away and fed him what
we wanted him to see. You got increasingly daring with your flying
until you fell and the hoverbike crashed. Oh so tragic, but accidents
happen, and your warrior provides the incontestable witness."

Strange how she could be relieved and increasingly terrified at the
same time. Pony was utterly loyal, and safe and oh so far away. Windwolf would never question her "death" with Pony witnessing it. She
clung to hope. "What about all the people that saw me being chased?"

"We oni know that what is seen is not always correctly perceived." Riki took one last drag of his cigarette, and ground the tiny
ember out. "Think of the difference of being in a race and watching it
from the pits. To you, it was clear that you were being chased. What
did the average person see? You going fast and dangerous—that
matches Pony's story. A hoverbike chasing you? That would be Pony.
Did they even see a second or third hoverbike? If they looked away
for an instant, probably not. And what if they did? If Pony says no
one was chasing you, they must have been mistaken—that must have
been another group of hoverbikes racing."

She tried to resist the logic, but it was too sound. There would be
no rescue.

Chiyo murmured something to Riki in the foreign language.

He nodded, flicking the dead butt out into the garden. "So, you
understand your situation."

"I've been knifed in the back by a man I thought was my friend."

"I am not a man, nor, regrettably, have I ever been free to be your friend," Riki corrected her almost gently. "I was under orders, penalty for failure greater than you can imagine, although you will soon be educated in that regard."

It hurt to think she had been so wrong. "You're a tengu."

"Yes."

The wings she remembered were massive, but there were no signs of them now, as he sat in the window, even as he flicked away the cigarette butt.

"Where are your wings?"

Wordlessly, he turned around. The muscle shirt covered only his front, leaving his muscled back exposed. An elaborate spell had been tattooed onto his skin, from shoulder to waistline, in black. He whispered a word, and magic poured through the tracings, making them shimmer like fresh ink. The air hazed around him, and the wings unfolded out of the distortion, at first holographic in appearance, ghosts of crow wings hovering behind him, fully extended. Then they solidified into reality, skin and bone merged into the musculature of his back, glistening black feathers longer than her arm.

She couldn't help herself. She reached out and touched one of the primary feathers. It was stiff and unyielding under her fingers. The wings were real, down to the tiny barbs of the feather's web. "How—how can they come and go and yet be part of you?"

"They aren't truly real, but solid illusions, crafted out of magic."

"You should not be telling her this," Chiyo snapped.

"Go play with the dogs," Riki said.

"Shut up," Chiyo cried.

Riki spoke another word, and the wings vanished, and only the tattoo remained as evidence.

This close to him—and without the distraction of the wings—she could now recognize the song leaking out of the one earbud; it was one of Oilcan's favorite elf rock groups. With a jolt, she recognized the MP3 player as Oilcan's old system.

"Where did you get that?"

"Your cousin gave it to me when I told him that I had nothing to play music on." Riki gazed at the thumb-sized player. "It was kind of him."

"Have you hurt him?" she asked fearfully.

"No, of course not." Riki glanced toward Chiyo and added, "It would endanger my cover."

Chiyo said something that earned her a glare of disgust from Riki.

"What did she say?" Tinker asked.

"Something stupid. It's stunning that her kind is considered clever. She must be a throwback to the original bitch."

Chiyo curled back her lip in a snarl. "At least I'm not from blood stock of scavengers easily distracted by bright and shiny toys."

"Yes." Riki seemed only amused by Chiyo's retort. He gave a suddenly birdlike cock of his head, and another verbal poke. "But your blood stock has a tendency to run mad, frothing at the mouth."

Tinker took a step back in sudden horror. "Your people interbred with animals?"

No wonder the elves fled back across the worlds, closing gates behind them; the oni had crossed moral lines that even the Skin Clan hadn't. The two oni turned to look at her as if they'd forgotten she was listening.

"Shut up!" Chiyo snapped and sulked to the other side of the gazebo.

"The greater bloods are still pure." Bitterness tainted Riki's expression. "They mixed their servants with animals at the genetic level to create us lesser bloods. We tengu have the crow's ability to fly at an instinctual level."

Chiyo responded to Tinker's questioning gaze with, "Don't look at me that way, little fake elf. You're a dirty little human girl in a fancy skin."

"Thank you, you don't know how good that makes me feel."

Riki gave a squawk of surprised laughter.

"So why did you kidnap me?" Tinker asked.

Riki sobered. "Lord Tomawaritomo wants you to build him a gate."

"Who?"

"To-ma-wa-ri-to-mo." Riki sounded out the syllables. "He is Windwolf's counterpart among the oni."

Remembering Chiyo's comment earlier, Tinker asked, "Lord Tomtom?"

Riki gave a very human shrug. "That's what those of us born on Earth tend to call him."

No wonder he passed so easily for human if he grew up around them. "That's why you speak English so well?"

"Yes. I was born in Berkeley, California."

"Hatched! Hatched!" Chiyo barked. "If you're going to go all truthful with her, then tell it all. Your mother popped out an egg." Chiyo measured out a stunningly large sphere with her fingers. "And brooded on it to keep it warm, and when the time came, listened all so close so she could break you out of your shell, and as a child they kept jesses on your feet to keep you from picking your nose with your toes."

Tinker glanced downwards and noticed for the first time that Riki's toes were stunningly long, thin, agile-looking and only three in number. "Your mother wasn't the woman killed when Lain was crippled; she couldn't have passed the physicals as human."

Riki looked at Chiyo in cold rage, and said, "I hope you are keeping your focus. You know how angry Lord Tomtom would be if this failed."

Chiyo went white and silent. For a minute only the tinny music from Riki's earbud could be heard, and then like a bubble breaking, the background noise from the garden started again. Chiyo stared at the ground, panting like a frightened animal.

"I don't understand," Tinker said. "If you can get to Earth, Elfhome, and back again, why does he need me to build a gate?"

Chiyo giggled and murmured something in their own tongue.

Riki shot her an irritated look and explained, "When the elves destroyed the door from our world to Earth, they stranded a large group of tengu and others in China. We've lived in secret among humans, hiding our differences."

He lifted his foot up, flexing his toes to demonstrate what differences he meant. "Like the elves, we're immortal on our own world, and long lived on Earth. We waited for our chance to return to our own land, our own people. When the gate opened the door between Earth and Elfhome, it also opened a door to Onihida, but it's inconveniently placed. We don't have the ability to move an army through it."

The seer's words went through her mind. *There is a door, open but not open . . . darkness presses against the frame but can not pass through.* The seer must have been talking about the unusable door. But what the hell did the rest mean? *The light beyond is too brilliant; it burns the beast.*

Chiyo murmured something to Riki which surprised him.

Tinker was tempted to kick her. "I don't like it when people talk about me in front of me."

"It's better you don't understand her poison," Riki said.

So, the seer was right. She was going to be the pivot. "You want me to betray Elfhome?"

"I know what they've done to you. They took you and changed you to make you loyal to them. All the while they held you at the palace, I was with your cousin, watching him go quietly insane with worry whether they'd bring you back or just decide that you were too dangerous to allow to live."

"Windwolf would never—" She bit off the retort. Riki had no reason to tell her the truth and every reason to lie. "Oilcan didn't say anything to me last night."

"He's a fair man. He wouldn't try to poison you against your husband, not even if what he had to say was the truth."

Tinker backed away from him, shaking her head. "You've lied to me since the first moment I met you. You're probably lying to me now. You'll say anything to get me to help you."

Riki lunged and caught hold of her tightly. "Yes, I would!" he cried, looking pained. "I'd say anything because I know what Lord Tomtom will do to get his way—and I'd rather not see you go through that."

"I believe Lord Tomawaritomo has arranged a demonstration." Chiyo turned to speak to one of the guards.

With a thin shriek of terror, the little oni who had knocked her over the cliff was brought forward between two of the massive guards. He begged in the oni tongue, sobbing.

"They're going to remove the bones from his left arm," Chiyo told Tinker in a casual tone, as if what was about to happen had no more import than picking wildflowers. Tinker had a sudden sympathy for black-eyed susans. "All of them. While he's awake."

While the guards pinned the oni down, a third, wizened-dwarf of an oni with a bloodstained leather apron and bright sharp knives started to cut.

After putting the earbud back in his ear, Riki held her still, made her watch.

Tinker curled her arms up tight against her chest, trying hard not to cry. If she had still been on Elfhome, she might have been able to defy them, clinging to the hope that Windwolf and Oilcan would be there to rescue her, or even that she could escape. All alone on this strange world, every hand upraised against her, she couldn't find the courage.

When it was done, Riki said, "Lord Tomtom expects results."

Tinker was still numb as they escorted her to the workshop. Riki tried to guide her with a hand to her elbow. The touch made her aware of the bones within her arm, and she jerked away from him. Something in her face—either her initial fear or the anger that followed it—made him look unhappy. Good. She stomped after Chiyo, who minced down the hallways at a surprising speed.

Riki noticed it too. "Why are you going so fast, Taji?"

A sharp retort in the oni tongue from the female made Riki laugh.

"What?" Tinker demanded, angry now. Angry that they were talking in a language she couldn't understand. Angry that Riki could laugh after watching *that*. Angry that she had been too scared to tell them no.

Riki grinned but would not say.

After all she had seen since she woke up—the castle they were in and the city outside it—Tinker was surprised by the workshop. It was a vast Earthlike warehouse, not much different from the one that the EIA had used to store the smugglers' goods. The one massive room was five hundred feet long, three hundred wide, and perhaps three stories tall. High above were sunlit windows, but the lower windows were all painted black; great floodlights fought the resulting gloom. What was it that they didn't want her to see? All the windows up to this point had looked out over the cliff with the oni city far below. Perhaps the painted windows were at ground level.

The only outside door was padlocked shut and wired with an alarm.

The floor was an oil-treated wood, swept spotless. Workbenches lined the outside walls, leaving the center of the huge room open for large equipment to be assembled. As she toured through the various workstations, she found that all the tools were human-made.

She picked up a cordless screwdriver. "This stuff is all from Earth."

"Unfortunately, your technology is far in advance of ours."

"How did you get it here?"

"One piece at a time," Riki said. "We've had twenty years to put together this workshop."

"All assuming that you'd find a genius to put it all together?"

"We're patient; humans are creative. Sooner or later, we'd find someone to suit our needs."

Tinker flipped the on switch on the drill press, and it roared to life. She glanced behind the machine to see that it was plugged into a standard 220 outlet. "Where is the power coming from?"

"We've got a power plant," Riki said after a moment. "It runs everything in here. Lord Tomtom is quite thorough and gets results. Everything has been well tested, and that's all you need to know."

"So I'm supposed to build a gate out of scratch, something I've never tried, that no one else on the planet has managed. Am I to spin straw into gold too?"

"According to the CMU entrance test, you understand the gate theory well enough to create a functioning gate."

So much for the NSA keeping that news from leaking out. "Theoretical design and actual working prototype can be years apart."

"You don't understand. Lord Tomtom is immortal, and now, so are you."

So she could be here forever, building until she got it right, or Lord Tomtom got impatient.

At the back of the shop, a skylight threw a shaft of sunshine down into an office area, complete with drafting table, desk, and computer equipment. There were designs already laid out on the table: blueprints for the orbital gate. She glanced to the legend. Her father's name was printed there in neat drafting print. "Your people killed my father and gave his work to the Chinese."

"He wasn't supposed to be killed," Riki said. "They were just trying to kidnap him. The car was truly an accident."

"Were you there?"

"No. I was in high school, being a geek: playing on the Internet, learning basic physics, and sitting out gym class on a doctor's excuse."

"So you don't know what really happened."

"Lord Tomtom wanted him alive. You've seen how he punished the oni that merely put you at risk. I won't upset you with the details of what he does to those who utterly fail him."

"Your people killed my father while trying to kidnap him—just to get back to a world you'd never seen which is ruled by immortal sadistic madmen?"

"That's about the size of it."

"You're all insane."

"Perhaps," Riki said.

She was hoping for a less unsettling answer. On the desk was a datapad with a complete download from her pad. She glanced at the computer system, identical to her own, down to style of printer, scanner, and holo projector. "Sparks?"

"Yes, Boss?"

"Fuck." She whirled on Riki. "You copied everything while I was gone! I trusted you. Oilcan trusted you! But you just used him to break into my security and steal my thoughts."

"I had to," Riki said.

She hit him, a stupid girlie smack the first time, and then, realizing that he wouldn't dare hurt her, she hauled back and punched him right. Then did it again, and again. All her fear became rage and she funneled it at him. He grabbed her right wrist, so she stomped down on his bare foot, and jerked out of his hold as he fell. There were tools lying on the table beside her; she snatched up a heavy monkey wrench and laid into him. He managed to block most of her hits, so she flung the wrench away and grabbed a crowbar off the table.

Riki scrambled backward, holding out his hand. "Tinker, I'm sorry! I'm sorry! I really am. But the moment I came to Pittsburgh, it was do it, or die horribly."

Tinker stopped, crowbar cocked back over her shoulder, panting. His words hadn't checked her—it was the sudden knowledge that she wanted to kill him, and had the means tight in her hands. Already he was bleeding from his nose and mouth and a cut along his cheek. She'd caught him in one eye with something, and the white was now a shocking red. There were bruises on his arms from fending her off. From the odd look of his foot, she'd broken at least one of the bones. She could beat him to death—but what would that gain her? Certainly not her freedom. And she was in his shoes now; do or be tortured, with an entire world staked on the outcome of her intelligence.

Think, you idiot, don't react.

"Okay, I forgive you." Tinker lowered the crowbar, but didn't put it down.

The NSA agents Durrack and Briggs said that someone had kidnapped several scientists. Obviously it was the oni. Obviously the scientists refused to work on the gate, or tried to escape, or just hit the end of Tomtom's patience. She was just the most recent victim. The seer said that there was no stopping the door from being opened. Tinker was the pivot. If she said "fuck off" then they'd just kill her and get someone else. She had the means, somehow, to stop them cold. Why hadn't the damn bitch just told her how?

Chiyo was talking to Riki in Oni again. Tinker glanced at her, irritated, and considered whacking the female a couple of times with the crowbar instead. She might even be able to get the guards to hold the little bitch down for her, just like they'd done with the tortured oni. Tinker's look was enough to make Chiyo yelp in fear and dart out of range, crying, "No, no, I'll stop!"

"Good." Tinker put aside the crowbar. "We all understand each other now."

"Yes." Riki wiped the blood from his mouth. "I think we do."

* * *

"Don't you ever sleep?" Chiyo asked peevishly.

"Sometimes, I do." Tinker squirmed around on her futon bed to put her feet on the wall without taking her eyes from her datapad. "Sometimes, I don't."

Chiyo whimpered.

With the exception of the skylight, the warehouse office hadn't been set up with comfort in mind. After a few hours on the padded stool that was the office's only seat, Tinker moved back to her bedroom. Annoyingly, everything that the oni missed when they killed her father, Riki had copied off her home system. He had made notes in a separate file, obviously trying to design a land-based gate himself. He'd gotten far enough to confirm that he had a degree in physics from Caltech, and that while gifted, was seriously out of his league.

Riki had also added everything ever published on the gate since the Chinese received her father's plans from the oni. Some of them were in original Chinese, and others had been translated, hopefully accurately. There was an entire folder on as-built drawings for the space station, the hyperphase gate, and the power systems for both. Reading over the files, it became obvious that some of her father's obscure notes relating to the Dufae Codex had been translated by an oni familiar with both physics and magic.

She was familiar with everything published after the gate was built, as Western scientists scrambled to reverse engineer the device that the Chinese seemed to produce out of thin air. She skipped them, reading only papers published in the last three months and making notes in a scratch file.

Of the missing scientists, there was frighteningly little. She checked to see if maybe Riki loaded files and then deleted them without doing a deep scrub. She found Harry Russell's journal of his captivity. In a stunning display of iron will, he'd resisted the oni while they whittled him down, first finger by finger of his left hand, then the hand itself, and finally his arm. They broke him too completely, and after a brief stuttering dictation as Russell fell into shock from pain, the journal ended abruptly. She scrubbed the file completely off her datapad.

All the while, she pondered the seer's words, or lack of them. For the first time she saw a certain Heisenbergian logic to the seer's silence: the act of seeing the future—thus able to avoid it—made it more unlikely that path would be taken. The seer didn't want her to deviate from some path she'd naturally take—perhaps. It would be nice, if she had some clue as to what she was supposed to be doing. Just as a straight "no" to the oni wasn't the answer—as Harry Russell found out—fully cooperating with them surely couldn't be either.

Finally sick of the whole mess, she dropped her pad onto the futon and went to the window to stargaze. The moon was out and full, looking the same as Earth's or Elfhome's. She looked for the planets that had been in conjunction the month before on Elfhome.

"Stop looking out there," Chiyo moaned from her corner.

"Why?"

"Because it gives me a headache."

"Why does my looking out a window make your head hurt?"

"Because you are a stupid little fake elf, and this is a stupid waste of my abilities. I was meant for greater things than being your jailer. You'll never figure out this gate, and all my time and effort will be wasted."

"Well, then let me go."

Chiyo gave her a dark look. "They should just shackle you in a dank little hole and be done with it. Throw in scraps of moldy bread and let you eat cockroaches for protein. There is no reason you need to live like a princess."

"Except the whole plan depends on her," Riki said, standing at the door, his arms full of clothing. Chiyo barked something in Oni, which got a sputtering laugh from Riki. "Dream on, little kitsune. It's not going to happen. We're never going to be more to them than what we were created to be: tools. You don't turn a hammer into a noble just because it hammered down a stubborn but vital nail. You either whack another nail with it, or shove it away and enjoy what you've made using it."

"A noble?" Tinker asked. So the whole "Lady Chiyo" was the female's desired reward for spying on Maynard and guarding her.

"Onihida is mostly feudal, with a few small bright sparks." Riki had healing spells inked over his foot, and it looked normal—for him—but he limped as he walked, wincing in pain. "We seem forever stuck in the dark ages. Nobles are usually greater blood, but occasionally a lesser blood can work its way up to a minor lord by being brutal and meticulous. Lord Tomtom is one. Mostly, though, lesser are tools made by the greater bloods, just like Windwolf made you."

"Windwolf changed me, but he didn't make me."

"Make, change, twist, mold; it's all the same. Here are your clothes."

He handed her the clothing. The stack contained five changes of panties, socks, shirts, and jeans. The underwear were silk, and the jeans were Levi's, all in her size. Behind a mask of vivid bruises, Riki's eyes were dilated into wide cerulean blue discs. If she hadn't read Russell's journal, she might have felt guilty.

"I'd tell Windwolf to piss off before I'd betray a friend."

"Sometimes you get stuck in a trap of your own design." He limped to the window to collapse onto the deep sill. "I didn't know what Tomtom had done to the other scientists, just that they were dead, and they needed someone that could pass to find Dufae's son."

"Why the hell did you even get involved with them? You nearly have a doctorate of physics, why the hell would you give it all up to be a tool on some backass world?"

"You wouldn't understand." Riki fumbled through his pockets, found the MP3 player, gazed at it sadly, and put it away to pull out cigarettes.

"No, I don't. Nothing could make me do what you're doing."

"Really?" He tapped out a cigarette, his motions slow, like he was moving through deep water. "What if someone sealed away your intelligence? Made you an idiot but left the memories of your brilliance? At night you'd dream that you were smart again, creating clever gadgets, having that wildfire of creativity, and wake up to find it all ashes. What would you do to get it back?"

She swallowed down sudden terror. "I wouldn't do this."

"Liar," Riki whispered. He clicked his tongue and the cigarette lit.

"What is it that you get out of this deal?"

"I'm a tengu." He took a deep drag off the cigarette, and languidly raised the hand to rest against his temple. "Hard wired in this brain is the instinct of flight. Millions of years of evolution focused on that one thing, tightly packed away," he held out his hand, showing it innocent of feathers, "in a body that can't fly. You can't imagine—even with your marvelous brain—what an endless torture it is. Tengu don't die of old age on Earth—sooner or later, they just climb the tallest mountain and throw themselves off, just to feel that oneness with the sky."

"There's hang gliding."

Riki's shoulder shook with a short, silent laugh. "Hang gliding, parachuting, high diving . . . I could name them all, but the thing is, you only go down, you never come back up."

"You could have just gone to Elfhome. Obviously the spell works there."

"When people throw themselves off mountains, normally there's not much left to salvage." He took another long drag on his cigarette. "But we tried. We skinned the bodies of the old ones who had the tattoo, preserving them for centuries, waiting for a chance to have our wings and our freedom at the same time, slowly going mad."

"But it didn't work, so you sold yourself back into slavery."

"Yes," he murmured and then looked sharply at Chiyo. "Hey! Chiyo! You can't go to sleep!"

"I'm so tired," Chiyo moaned.

Riki sighed, and gave a sharp whistle. The guard from the hall opened the door and looked in. Riki flicked the hand with the cigarette, giving a command in rapid Oni. The guard glanced at Chiyo, then to Tinker, nodded and went out.

"What?" Tinker asked.

"We have a slight personnel problem. One of Chiyo's cousins was killed in a car accident the Shutdown we missed our kill on Windwolf. It leaves us shorthanded."

Things suddenly clicked for Tinker. The oni were the smugglers; the high-tech goods were for building the gate. Chiyo's cousin must have been the pinned driver who had been shot by the other oni, rather than let him fall into EIA hands and be questioned. Tinker looked sharply at the female; if someone had killed Oilcan, she would—she would . . . She couldn't finish the thought, the possibilities of Oilcan being caught and hurt in all this was all too real for idle speculation.

"So." Tinker distracted herself with details. "We're missing materials for the gate?"

"No. Lord Tomtom is quite methodical. We have a surplus of everything."

The door opened and the guard came back, carrying a *saijin* flower.

"What's that for?" Tinker scrambled backward, away from the guard.

"It's time for you to sleep." Riki took another drag on his cigarette, and breathed the smoke out his long sharp nose.

"I don't need that. I'll sleep without it."

"We have to be sure. Please, just take it nicely. With what I'm buzzing on for the pain—" he lifted his foot that she had broken "—I don't trust myself not to hurt you."

Sullenly, she held her hand for the flower, and with everyone watching closely, breathed deeply of its false comfort.

Tinker drifted out of the white fog of drugged slumber, opening her eyes to an unfamiliar ceiling. Where was she? Sleep still clung to her with pulled taffy strength, making it hard to think. She dragged her hand free of the blankets to rub at her eyes, trying to force herself awake. As she moved, she felt the spider again, picking its way carefully across her forehead. She smeared her hand up, over her brow, and combed her fingers on through her hair, finding nothing. *What the hell?*

The ceiling had changed.

She frowned at the expanse of white, now recognizable as the one above her futon on Onihida. Wait, the ceiling hadn't changed—or had it? Both ceilings had been featureless white; she couldn't say how one was strange and the other familiar. And why would anyone swap ceilings? That didn't make sense. Maybe it had been a trick of lighting. She sat up, knowing that something was wrong, but still not sure what.

Chiyo sat in her corner wearing a fresh kimono and a smug smile.

Tinker fumbled her way into the clothes Riki had brought her the night before, trying to think past the fog banks rolling through her mind. The Levi jeans distracted her from the ceiling mystery. The blue jeans were men's thirty-by-thirty carpenters, which she usually wore, but brand-new. She puzzled over them a moment—wondering how they had gotten the correct size and type—before realizing that Riki probably had just checked the dresser in her workshop. Oilcan might have noticed missing clothes, so the oni bought her a new wardrobe. The oni's thoroughness depressed her.

Riki arrived as she was putting on her boots. Annoyingly, his bruises had faded during the night to almost nothing.

"It wasn't an elf," Tinker said to him.

"What?"

"You said it was an elf that beat you up at the Faire the night Windwolf changed me. It couldn't have been—you would have been healed by the time I got back three days later."

"Tomtom had me beaten," Riki admitted. "He didn't think you were coming back. I convinced him that you'd come back eventually for your cousin's sake, so he let me off lightly."

Tinker grunted at the oni's idea of "lightly." "I want something to eat, and then we can talk about this gate you want me to build."

At least they had good food: smoked trout, eggs poached in heavily salted water, and a sweet, orange-yellow, soft fruit peeled and sliced, all dumped on top of a huge bowl of nutty-flavored, dark brown rice. The only thing she didn't like were oddly pickled vegetables. Chiyo and Riki ate them in a resigned manner.

Riki explained that they were traditional staples from Lord Tomtom's region; apparently in the warmer climates, pickling was the easiest way to preserve food. "And the cook is a seven-foot-tall *shankpa* whose family died in a famine. He takes wasted food personally."

Shankpa? Tinker refused to ask on the grounds that at some point ignorance started to sound like idiocy. She'd find out later.

"You don't send plates back with food on them." Chiyo tipped her bowl to show it was empty.

"I see." Tinker picked up her pickles and dumped them into Chiyo's bowl.

Chiyo looked laughably stunned for a moment, and then her lip curled back into a snarl. The look vanished away with one murmured word from Riki.

"What's the magic word?" Tinker asked him as they walked the maze of identical stone hallways.

"Which one?"

She attempted to reproduce the word; apparently she didn't come close because Riki puzzled a moment.

"Ah," he said. "That's the act of being deboned."

At the workshop, she found a distance measurer and a piece of chalk. She walked around the vast room, pointing the instrument at the distant walls.

"What are you doing?" Riki perched on a workbench. He'd sent Chiyo off on some errand, much to everyone's relief.

"I'm measuring the room to find its exact size so we can model it on the computer." Tinker tapped the button, called the measurement to Sparks, marked the floor and moved down roughly a foot. "If we're building the gate in this room, then we need to know the maximum size it can be." She paused. "You do want it built in here, don't you?"

"Yes."

"I thought so, judging by your notes and what you told Russell."

"You found that?"

"Yes."

Riki winced but said nothing.

"The gate in orbit is just over twenty-six hundred feet in diameter, basically half a mile." She finished the width measurement and started on length. "The ceiling is going to be the prime determiner. Depending on the slope of the ceiling and the various support beams, it's going to be somewhere between twenty and thirty feet in diameter."

"Russell maintained that it couldn't be scaled down."

"It was only designed that size to allow for spaceships to pass through it. Didn't you show him my father's notes?"

"There's nothing on how Dufae decided on its size."

Gods save her from idiots. "What do you think all the technical specs on the space shuttle were about? He was trying to plot out the minimum size of a colony ship. At minimum, a colony would need something that could safely land people on a planet. He thought that anything going out should be able to have a shuttle riding piggyback on it and still fit through the gate."

"Doh!" Riki said, sounding very human.

Scaling it down presented a host of problems. With the large surface to play with, her father hadn't bothered to economize his design, and the Chinese apparently hadn't dared to deviate from the stolen plans. She'd have to use every trick she knew to compact the circuits. "Where is the ceramic coming from? You said we have surplus of everything."

"We've been stockpiling ceramic tiles for nearly fifteen years. They decided early on, though, that the shield material wasn't needed."

"Yeah, that's just to protect the gate from micrometeor impacts and solar wind." Tinker finished up her measurements by taking the ceiling readings at every grid point that she had chalked on the floor. "Sparks, render that for me."

"Okay, Boss."

While she waited she considered the scale ratio. The easiest might be a simple one to a hundred ratio: 2640 feet shrinking to 26.4.

"Done, Boss." The AI projected it onto the screen.

She snapped out a circle to represent the scaled down gate and moved it around the workshop. Gods, manufacturing the damn framework was going to be a bitch. The nonconductive material used in space wouldn't stand up to gravity. While steel could take the stress load, the amount of metal needed to make the gate would play havoc with the system.

A good fit on the model drew her attention back to it. She locked the circle down. "Let's see if this works."

As Sparks read off the gird coordinates, she found the matching points on the workshop floor and circled them in chalk.

"Is that it?" Riki asked with quiet awe.

She snorted in disgust. "That's the easy part. Of course if I make a mistake now, we might not know until the last moment. Let me think on this for a while. Get me a list of supplies that we have, and see if you can find some more comfortable chairs."

She'd shifted the locations three times including rotating the gate half a turn as she considered factors from height clearance, use of the overhead crane during construction, the ease of getting large materials into place, and finally the local ley lines, faint as they might be. Riki reappeared with the materials list and a surprising array of office chairs just as she was spray-painting the final location onto the workshop floor. He also had a lunch of steamed fish, brown rice, and more pickles.

She took the list and studied it as she ate. Again, she found the oni depressingly efficient, though noncreative; they had slavishly gathered what had been used to build the orbital gate and nothing else. "We need something for the superstructure of the gate, something inert and nonmetallic. If we were on Elfhome, I'd use ironwood. I don't suppose you have something similar?"

"Ironwood?"

"Yeah."

"You want to use ironwood?"

She flicked her pickles at him. "Hello! That's what I said. I know you understand English, Mr. Born-and-raised in Berkeley."

"It's just using wood is so low tech."

"To quote you—doh! From little minds come no solutions. Ironwood is stunningly strong, renewable, non-toxic, recyclable, and easy to work with. Do the oni have anything like it or not?"

"We can get ironwood."

She waited for explanations but they weren't forthcoming.

"I'm talking massive timbers." She held out her hands to show the beam size.

Riki nodded. "Just tell me how much, and I'll get it."

"Okay. We're in business then."

Time blurred for the rest of the day, as she designed the wood framework. Riki came and went, searching out samples of the ceramic tiles and other materials stockpiled elsewhere. Each item fired new ideas, and she branched out to how to affix the tiles, a ramp over the threshold to protect the gate, and a preliminary sketch of the power supply grid.

Night fell, and shadows in the warehouse grew deeper. Chiyo brought dinner and almost instantly the female and Riki started bickering in Oni. Tinker sighed, leaning back in her chair to look up through the skylight. She expected the stars to be strange and unfamiliar, like the sky of Earth. First Wolf, though, was right overhead, his shoulder star the brightest thing in the sky as always. It was comforting to see it, so very familiar. Then it struck her—it was too familiar. She leaned from side to side to see more through the overhead rectangle of Plexiglas, studying the constellations. The moon spinners. The dark-eyed widow.

It was the sky of Elfhome overhead.

And suddenly it was all clear to her.

You have a prisoner, extremely intelligent, to whom you need to give great freedom and entrust with a great deal of material that could easily be twisted into weapons. Wouldn't the simplest method of holding said prisoner be simply to convince her that she is in another dimension? Even if she fled the building, the whole world would act as a prison. Escape would seem impossible.

She had to still be on Elfhome. Why else would they paint the warehouse windows to keep her from seeing outside? How else could Riki be on Elfhome prior to Shutdown and after Startup and yet have a copy of her computer system up and running? How he had access to office chairs and ironwood? How he got her to the "castle?" If Riki could pop back and forth freely between Elfhome and Onihida, carrying kidnapped girls, ergonomic workstations, and large trees, the oni had no need of a gate.

And yet, she couldn't completely explain away the city outside the windows. How had they tricked her so completely?

"Kitsune are the fox spirits," Lain had told her. *"They usually appear to be beautiful women, but they really are just foxes that can throw illusions into their victim's mind."*

Was the spider she felt every morning Chiyo stepping into her mind, reading it and planting illusions? When she considered it, she could find a dozen times Chiyo had reacted to her thoughts.

Chiyo could read her mind.

Tinker glanced over at Chiyo, who was still arguing with Riki. Her greatest weapon was her enemies' ignorance. As long as they didn't realize she had discovered the truth, they would continue to allow her the freedom of the workshop. And with the workshop, she could build tools to escape. But Chiyo mustn't discover that she knew . . .

The fight finished up when an oni guard came into the warehouse to fetch Riki away, leaving behind Chiyo to guard Tinker. To distract herself, Tinker started to factor out large numbers, looking for primes.

Chiyo winced at her. "What are you doing?"

"Factoring numbers," Tinker said truthfully.

Chiyo rubbed her forehead. "You're a hideously ugly little creation."

Tinker gathered together all the cordless screwdrivers and started to remove the battery packs. The joy of being a genius was that you could do complex math in your head while assembling simple but effective weapons almost thoughtlessly.

Trying not to grin, Tinker switched to determining escape velocities, which reduced Chiyo to quiet whimpers of pain.

Tinker would have liked to create more of a plan, but she didn't dare plan anything with Chiyo prying into her mind. She finished the simple stun baton and tested it by pressing it against Chiyo. The kitsune collapsed into a satisfying heap of silk. Tinker bound and gagged her quickly, surprised to discover Chiyo had very sharp canine teeth, small furry dog-ears, and a foxtail hidden under the kimono.

Tinker swapped fresh batteries into the stun baton, glancing around. The warehouse had changed little, but that would almost be expected. The low windows had been painted black so Chiyo wouldn't have to disguise anything outside.

She bypassed the alarm on the outside door, cut off the padlock with a welding torch, and opened the door.

She expected to be on Mount Washington—it was the view out her bedroom window, only from the Onihida perspective. Looking at the moonlit hills rising all around her, she realized that the view had been a complete sham. They were in a river valley someplace far from downtown. As she scurried down the alley, she decided that it was logical. The oni would want to be as far out of the public eye as possible. Mount Washington, being far above the floodplain and yet close to downtown and the Rim, was still heavily populated.

She paused at the mouth of the alley, trying to get her bearings. She was in an industrial park of some sort, the long tall warehouses standing dark all around her. Nothing looked like a stone castle, so her bedroom and the rest of the living spaces were probably in one of the warehouses, hidden from prying eyes.

Fake, all of it.

She peered around the corner. Surely there would be guards—unless they were afraid of advertising their presence. She dashed across the street to the cover of the next alley. It took her to the water's edge.

Only twenty feet across with high cement retaining walls for banks, the waterway was too narrow to be a river. Most streams in the area, though, flowed into the Ohio River eventually. A silvery leaf tossed down to the dark water pointed out which direction the creek flowed. Following the creek would take longer than striking off across country, but heading in a random direction might only take her deep into Elfhome wilderness. Hopefully Riki wouldn't be back soon.

After five minutes of walking with the warehouse to her right, she realized how large the oni complex was. The long building was easily a quarter mile or more long. There was a wide break, and then another long warehouse running alongside the creek. At the end of the second warehouse, a thick column of white limestone lit by moonlight drew her eyes upwards. A massive bridge spanned the valley in several graceful arches, totaling sixteen hundred feet long with a deck two hundred feet above the creek. Even in the city of bridges, it was quite singular, and she recognized it.

The bridge was the Westinghouse Bridge, which meant the oni base was the old Westinghouse Electric Airbrake plant. By blind luck she had gone in the right direction, because the Rim cut through just feet north of the plant. The erratic path of the Monongahela River and the Rim effectively isolated this small slice of Pittsburgh. The elfin forest deeply encroached on the area, slowly whittling it down. Last she'd heard, something had killed and eaten the last human inhabitants; now she wondered how much the oni had had to do with that.

No matter; now she knew where she was, she knew where to go for help. She sold scrap to the converted USX steel mill just downriver. The mini mill operated twenty-four hours a day, melting down old steel to reforge it to slabs which were sent upriver via barge to the rolling mill at Dravosburg. It was less than three miles. Unfortunately, most of the steelworkers now lived across the river, where miles of transplanted Pittsburgh buffered them from Elfhome wilderness, but there were plenty of bars.

Sticking to the water's edge would be slow, and considering the black willows and jumpfishes, far from safe. She decided to take a risk and follow the street.

She heard the car engine and saw the headlights running on the power lines overhead moments before the car swept into view. She had ducked back into the shadows, and then recognized the car. It was one of Windwolf's Rolls-Royces.

"Hey!" she cried, stepping into the light. "Stop!"

The car squealed to a stop and the driver's door flung open. Surprisingly, it was Sparrow who got out. The female was in mourning black, with her pale hair simply braided. It was the most unadorned that Tinker had ever seen her. "Tinker? What are you doing here?"

"Escaping!" Tinker laughed, crossing to touch the marvelous, beautiful car. "Is Windwolf with you? Pony?"

"It's in the middle of night," Sparrow said. "They were searching the river for the last two days. I believe they're sleeping now. How did you get away?"

"With this!" Tinker proudly held out her homemade stun baton.

"That tiny thing?" Sparrow held out her hand. "What is it?"

Without thinking, Tinker handed the weapon to Sparrow. "It's a stun baton. You just press against someone, hit the trigger and the person is stunned."

"Like this?" Sparrow pointed the baton toward her, thumb on the trigger.

"Careful." Tinker reached to take it back.

Sparrow pressed the tip into Tinker's outreached hand.

The pain was instant and intense, and she started to fall as all her muscles spasmed.

Sparrow caught her. "Ah, yes, how clever of you. I must tell Tomtom to keep a closer eye on you."

By the time she recovered, Sparrow had her bound and inside the car.

"Are you mad? Why are you working with them?"

"Sometimes the best tool is a very big stick."

"What the hell does that mean?"

"I'm using the oni to fix what is wrong," Sparrow said. "I'm going to take things back to the way they should be."

"How should they be?"

"If you repeat a lie long enough it doesn't become a truth, but everyone will act like it has. I'm sure you've been told how evil the Skin Clan was and how the *domana* nobly dispatched them. The truth is that the Skin Clan took our race from one step above apes and made them one step below gods. As we were when the Skin Clan toppled, we still are. Under the *domana* we're stagnating. It's time to go back to the old ways."

"How could you do this to your honor?"

Sparrow gave a slight laugh. "Honor is nothing but convenient ropes that the *domana* use to bind the lower castes helpless. They are slave lords with invisible chains."

"How can you say that? They made you one of them."

"They've made a mockery of the *dau*. I should have undergone the same transformation as you, to be wholly *domana*, but that would have weakened their power base. So they call me *domana*, and expect the lower castes to bow to me, but everyone knows the truth. I'm no more *domana* than I was at birth."

"You're going to destroy your people because the lower castes never groveled to you? The *domana* are evil because they wouldn't make you one of them?"

Sparrow stopped the car to look down at her. "I can kill you. Doing this now is convenient, but if it proves too annoying, I can easily wait another hundred years for my chance. And so can the oni."

Tinker shrank away from the cold, impartial stare, barely able to breathe.

"Good." Sparrow started the car. "You really must start thinking like an elf. Look at the long-term future."

Like I have one.

Tinker found no comfort that Sparrow, after several minutes of silence, felt the need to justify her actions with, "My case only illustrated the hypocrisy of the *domana*; even when they lift up one of the lower castes, they still suppress us."

15: WHIPPING BOY

The back door of the Rolls opened and an oni warrior, face painted for war, gazed down at her—bound hand and foot—as Sparrow murmured something in the Oni tongue. The warrior grunted, took out a whistle, and blew a single long note that jumped from shrill to inaudible. Somewhere close by, small dogs broke into excited barking.

Sparrow said something about Tomawaritomo, and the warrior pointed off into the darkness. She walked away without looking back.

The warrior reached into the Rolls with huge gnarled hands and lifted Tinker out, passing her like a hissing kitten to another guard. Oni warriors were emerging out of the night, faces painted and heavily armed. Apparently her escape had been noticed, and the oni had been on the hunt, now called back by the silent whistle.

Without the kitsune's deception, the airbrake plant was a collection of massive, old buildings, heavy with the sense of otherworldliness where men did the works of gods and sneered at the concept of magic. Yet rising up in the moonlight beyond the great buildings was the wild primal forest of Elfhome, and all around Tinker, smelling like wet dogs, were the brutish oni warriors.

Tinker was carried into one of the mile-long buildings. The first section was a garage, holding a host of hoverbikes and cars; Riki's motorcycle sat to one side, as singular as the tengu. The second section was a kennel, filled with steel cages. Many of the cages held yapping little pug dogs. In one cage was a muzzled warg, its glowing eyes lighting its corner with icy rage, its bulk filling the cage.

Beyond was empty warehouse. A shallow, narrow channel cut down the center of the vast room; oily water flowed in the cement drain. On one side was the bare skeleton of a freight elevator. There was something disturbingly familiar about the space. They passed a dark stain of old blood on the floor, and there, in the dust on the floor, were her bootprints and Riki's footprints, where he had held her still and made her watch the deboning that first morning. This was the true appearance of the courtyard garden with the gazebo.

At the far end, they caught up with Sparrow. The elf female was coming to a stop beside an oni male. Riki knelt on the ground in front of the male, head bowed until his forehead nearly touched the dusty floor. To one side, the wizened-dwarf torturer sharpened his boning knives.

"I caught her before she could do harm," Sparrow was saying to the oni. The guard dropped Tinker onto the ground, knocking the breath out of her. "Really, Lord Tomawaritomo, I had hoped you could contain her more than three days."

"The kitsune let her slip away." The oni male reached down to catch Tinker by a handful of shirt and bra and lifted her up to dangle in mid-air as he inspected her.

So this was Lord Tomawaritomo. Tall and lean, he towered over Tinker; even the long thin sword strapped to his side was taller than her. He was striking in appearance, but not beautiful; his cheekbones and chin were too sharp, and his nose too flat. The gold of his pupil filled his eyes, with an iris a dark vertical slit. He had a mane of white that spilled down over his back. His ears were more than just pointed: they were white-furred, and cupped forward, like a cat's. He wore a kimono of vivid purples and greens, and a fur of pristine white that matched his snow-white hair. The pelt was wrapped over one shoulder and pinned in place by his shoulder guard of ridged bone. The fur looked to be white wolf or warg, though larger than either species. The origin of the bone, however, Tinker couldn't guess, except that the body part involved was the jawbone, hinged midpoint at the oni's chest.

After inspecting Tinker closely, Tomtom grunted. "Such trouble in a little package."

"It seems to be a universal constant that keys to doorways are usually small." Sparrow smiled at her own wit.

Tomtom grunted again. "Perhaps I should put this one on a chain to keep it from being lost."

"Whatever it takes," Sparrow said.

Perhaps it was just as well that Tinker didn't have breath to talk; she had a feeling that she would be saying things that she'd regret later. She comforted herself by thinking choice insults.

Tomtom clicked his tongue and Riki looked up. "Take this." The oni lord held Tinker out to Riki. "See that it doesn't slip away again."

So Tinker found herself handed off again like a child's doll. Annoyingly, she couldn't help but feel somewhat safer with Riki, perhaps just because he was familiar. He, at least, balanced her upright and stooped to undo the ties around her ankles. "Stay still. Stay silent," he whispered to her without meeting her eyes. *Yeah, right.*

Tomtom's cat ears flickered from Riki to a distant wail. "Ah, my warriors have found the vixen."

"You'll have the kitsune killed." Sparrow said it as a disinterested statement, not a question.

"One normally has to be diplomatic with the kitsune," Tomtom said. "This presents possibilities . . ."

A moment later frantic cries became audible, growing louder. Chiyo was dragged into the vast room, struggling in the hold of two oni warriors. Her fox tail stuck out of a tear in her kimono, and her doglike ears were laid back in distress. At a signal from Lord Tomtom, the warriors released Chiyo and she flung herself at Tomtom's feet. As the kitsune begged in frantic Oni, the corners of the oni lord's mouth curled up into a grin.

"Her Oni is worse than mine," Sparrow said. "What is she saying?"

"She says she'll do anything to avoid the knives." Lord Tomtom motioned to one of the waiting oni. "This will interest you."

Sparrow gave an exasperated sigh. "My time is limited."

Tomtom gazed at Sparrow hard. "Stay and be instructed."

He put out his hand and one of the warriors gave him a leather lead and slipknot collar. Tomtom dangled out the lead, clucking as one would to a dog. Chiyo cringed but sat up, canting back her head to lay bare her throat.

"Many of the lesser bloods have the spells to manipulate them threaded through their genetic pattern," Tomtom explained to Sparrow as he slipped the collar over Chiyo's head. He pulled the slipknot tight, winding the lead around his fist. "I could reduce her back to fox if I wanted."

Chiyo whimpered in fear.

"What use would a fox be to me, little kitsune?" Tomtom purred, wiping away Chiyo's tears. "I've decided to breed you. No, no, no." He murmured as Chiyo glanced at the surrounding warriors. "Your mate will have to be fetched. Now hold still."

He growled out a word, and strange runes gleamed to life on Chiyo's skin. In a low dull drone, Tomtom chanted out a spell, and her very skin began to glow. After a minute, he fell silent and the light vanished, and Chiyo panted quietly.

"I've put her into season." He loosened the lead and handed it to one of his warriors, pointing back across the warehouse and saying something in Oni.

Chiyo cried out as if struck. "Warg?"

Sparrow made a face of distaste. "Oh, beat her and be done with it."

"The lesser bloods are socketed so they can breed with anything," Tomtom said. "I want to introduce the warg abilities into the kitsune line."

Sparrow scoffed at this. "You don't change the genome directly?"

"Breeding for pups is a simpler method," Tomtom said.

"This is a waste of my time," Sparrow said. "I must be gone before I'm missed."

"Speak then," Tomtom said absently, watching the kitsune be stripped of her kimono, bent over a bale of bedding, and tied into position.

Tinker turned away as warriors took advantage of Chiyo's helplessness; the males laughed as their manipulations made the kitsune in heat moan wantonly. *Remember what she's done to me. I hate her. I should be glad she's being punished.*

Sparrow took no notice of the events with the kitsune. "I told you at the start of this that Wolf Who Rules needs to be eliminated."

Riki caught Tinker before she could launch herself at Sparrow, muffling her stream of curses at the elf.

Tomtom glanced at Tinker struggling in Riki's arms and a smile quirked at his mouth. "I have done all I will do in that regard."

"You failed miserably," Sparrow said.

Damn right, bitch, Tinker thought fiercely, still muted by Riki's hand.

"Exactly," Tomtom said. "I will not endanger my position by fruitlessly striking at him. The dogs were expendable, but I will not risk my warriors."

"He suspects that his *domi*'s disappearance is not an untimely accident," Sparrow said. "He plans to return to the citywide search."

"And you will take the river edge as before," Tomtom waved aside her concern. "Avoid this valley as planned. If you can not, call your contact first and we'll trigger the greater cloaking spells."

"Wolf Who Rules loves this little piece of trash!" Sparrow cried, making Tinker's heart do a strange little flip in her chest. "He's not being swayed from the truth. He knows we took her, he just doesn't know how or where we're hiding her."

Tomtom turned to look at Sparrow full on, wordlessly.

Sparrow visibly needed to steel herself against his cold look. "You are failing to see how dangerous he is."

"And you are overestimating him," Tomtom said flatly.

"Your people have never dealt with a *domana* lord on his own land," Sparrow said.

"A knife in the spine," Tomtom said. "An arrow through the eye, or a sword through the heart, and he will die like everything else in this universe."

"No!" Tinker cried into Riki's palm, and the tengu held her tighter still.

Tomtom turned away dismissively as the massive warg was brought in, muzzled, on a stout stick lead. The beast strained against the handler, heading for Chiyo.

"So arrange the knife!" Sparrow refused to be ignored. "Or the arrow or the sword! Kill him!"

Tinker wriggled in Riki's hold. *Shut up, bitch! Shut up!*

Tomtom's tone grew flatter, colder. "I will not stand here, repeating myself, or do you wish to go after the kitsune?"

Sparrow looked then, as did Tinker. The warg loomed over the kitsune, erect, proportionally wrong for the female, seeking an entrance in her slight body. Tinker looked away, desperately concentrating on anything but Chiyo and her sharpening whimpers. Sparrow watched, not even flinching as the kitsune gave a scream of agony. Tinker hunched against the sound of the big animal laboring, and Chiyo's now endless, shrill barks of terror and pain. She wanted to cover her ears, but Riki wasn't loosening his hold.

Sparrow tore her gaze away from the godless union. "So be it then. Let Wolf Who Rules be the *domana* you cut your teeth on. If you're to take this land, you'll need to face them eventually."

"Ah, good, he's tied with her." Tomtom ignored Sparrow in favor of the breeding. "If she brings a litter to term in two months, I'll breed her again next season." Tomtom glanced down at Tinker. "This one has the *domana* genome? Perhaps I'll get my own litter on her. She's tiny, but I suppose that gives her a certain childlike allure."

Tinker shrank away from his clinical gaze.

"You can breed her later," Sparrow said. "The queen's seer says she's the key to our plans regarding the gate."

"So it was reported to me." Tomtom knowing obviously threw

Sparrow; Chiyo must have told him earlier, after reading Tinker's mind.

"The seer said," Sparrow continued, "that the only way to bind her was with ties of her own making."

"Which means?" Tomtom asked.

"You'll only be able to hold her with promises freely given," Sparrow explained. "How you'll manage that, I do not know, nor do I care. Torture her if you must, but bind her. Obviously she'll slip away if you do not."

Sparrow nodded then and swept away, leaving Tinker with her enemies without so much as a glance. Tinker had thought she hated Riki and Chiyo; she understood now what a shadow of hate that had been.

With a look from Lord Tomawaritomo, Riki released his hold on Tinker.

"You were human, the weakest of us." Tomtom studied her with his cat eyes. "If the elves had left the gate between our worlds open, we would have long since enslaved the humans. Weaklings, all."

"You don't need muscles when you have brains," Tinker snapped.

"The question is, how elfin are you now?" Lord Tomawaritomo said. "If I have you punished as you should be, will you survive it? The human didn't."

He meant Russell, whittled down by inches. Her arms tucked tight to her chest, and he laughed. She tried not to think of those bright sharp knives, the blood, and the white of bone.

"The risk would be great that she wouldn't survive," Riki murmured.

Lord Tomawaritomo glanced at Riki, eyes narrowing in speculation. "If you helped it escape, death would be preferable. You are being spared right now only because I myself called you away."

It took Tinker a moment to realize that Tomtom was referring to her as "it" as if she was a thing, not an intelligent being. Only a warning look from Riki kept her silent.

"Chiyo doesn't have the brain to keep her deluded," Riki explained.

"See that this is secure," Tomawaritomo growled softly, pointing at Tinker. "Then get me a whipping boy to use against it."

Riki bowed low, caught Tinker, and hurried her from the room, while Tomtom turned back to supervise the end of Chiyo's breeding.

* * *

They locked Tinker in a broom closet. It was only wide enough for her to sit down, knees tucked under her chin. No air ducts or even electrical outlets. After Riki untied her, four of the oni warriors, the shortest clearing seven feet, put her firmly into it, shut the door, and locked it, leaving her in darkness.

Hours crawled by.

A whipping boy. Who would they bring to torture in her place? Oilcan? *No, no, please not him!* Lain? That would be unbearable too. Windwolf? Unlikely—for all the reasons why Tomtom was refusing to kill him—Windwolf was too visible, too well guarded. Nathan? It would be the ultimate irony if he died for her.

Oilcan made the most sense, though, and the realization made her start crying. Damn it, she hated to cry. She rocked in place as tears burned in her eyes. Oh, please, please, anyone but Oilcan.

She heard footsteps approach the door and an exchange in Oni. One of the guards unlocked the door in a jangle of keys, and they opened it up, all poised to grab her if she tried to put up a fight. Ha! She was tempted to snarl at them, and make them flinch, but something about coming only to mid-stomach on them kept her from taunting them.

They took her to Tomtom's suite. Whereas most of the place was run-down offices and warehouses, the suite had been remodeled to opulence. The ceiling was a design of blocks within blocks, the walls a deep rich red, and the polished wood floor strewn with the pelts of large white animals.

Tomtom, Riki, and the torturer waited there with a host of armed, tense, and bloody warriors. Their focus had been on a body lying still on the floor in front of Tomtom. They shifted their feral interest to her as her guard checked her just inside the door. The body lay curled into a fetal position so that she could see only the curve of the spine.

Tinker trembled. Who was it? What had Tomtom's people done to the person to make him or her lie so still? Please, not Oilcan.

The body shifted, revealing the spill of long elfin hair, and she felt a wave of relief. Not Oilcan. Oh, thank God. And then she recognized the elf: Pony.

On the slight wave of Tomtom's hand, the guard let go of her, and she went to Pony without thinking. They had stripped him down to his loose black pants and beat him soundly. He flinched violently when she touched him.

"Easy. It's me, Pony."

He slit open his blackened eyes, and looked at her in first confusion and then in dismay. He groaned and tried to get up, to get her behind him, to protect her. He only managed to sit up, and she caught him before he collapsed.

Lord Tomawaritomo came and stood over them, gazing down at her with his cat eyes. "Good. You care for this whipping boy."

She realized then that she had made a mistake. She shouldn't have put her arms around Pony. She should have ignored his presence, refusing to acknowledge him. Lord Tomawaritomo knew now that he could affect her by hurting Pony.

"You didn't have to beat him," she snapped.

"One does not lightly take a warrior prisoner," Tomtom said. "They are sturdily made. One can cut them down to almost nothing before their life force gives out."

Tomtom lifted his hand and the squat torturer scurried forward wearing its bloodstained leather apron, boning knife glittering in his hand.

"You don't have to hurt him," Tinker cried, tightening her hold on Pony. "I'll make a gate."

"I am not afraid." Pony pulled out of her arms and managed to get to his feet. "Go ahead. Torture me. Kill me. She will not do what you ask of her."

Tomtom stepped back. "We will take only his sword arm first."

"No!" Tinker shouted, stepping between the oni and Pony, spreading wide her arms to shield him. "Don't hurt him! I'll do it! Just don't hurt him."

"Tinker *domi*!" Pony caught hold of her, pulled her back. "Do not do what they ask of you."

Tinker wriggled in his hold. "I can't watch them kill you little by little."

"I do not care what they do to me," Pony said.

"Pony, I can't." She swung around to focus on him. "I know myself too well. I can't sit and watch you scream your life away. I'll break. Maybe I can last until you've been tortured to death. But then they'll go find someone else to hold against me, and I won't be able to say no again, especially not after watching them cut you to pieces. I *will* break. I would rather break *now*, without having to take your screams to my grave, than after you're dead."

"I see," Pony said quietly. "Forgive me my selfishness."

"You do not understand." Tomtom's voice was a dangerous low rumble. "They will take his bones just so you know how serious I am. For any disobedience, the punishment will be worse."

Tinker could not imagine worse, but she was sure that Tomtom could. "No. No. Don't hurt him. I'll do what you want."

"Yes. You will." Tomtom gave an order. One of the warriors bent down and caught her by the waist, lifting her off the ground, while the other two caught hold of Pony.

"No! No!" Tinker cried. "If he's hurt, I will do nothing!"

"If torturing him does not work, we'll get another. One that works better."

Oilcan! She cried out as if struck, and then thought quickly. Did she have any leverage point beyond her ability? "Leave him alone, and I'll finish in a month!"

Tomtom whipped around and had her by the throat before she could react. "A month? That is twenty-eight days?"

He was going by the moon cycle, instead of Earth's calendar, but she wasn't going to argue schematics with him.

"Yes, twenty-eight days," she whispered. "Hurt him, and I'll do nothing! No matter who you get to replace him."

"You're lying," Tomtom said, making her stomach turn to lead and sink. "You cannot do it in a month."

"Yes, I can!" she cried. "The process is easier than I thought. I'll make a gate in a month, but only if you torture no one—I'd rather die than reward those who harmed ones I love."

Tomtom cocked his head, considering her. "Twenty-one days."

"What? Three weeks?"

"Twenty-one days or I'll have the bones removed."

She glanced at Pony, and wet her mouth. "Fine, I'll do it in twenty-one. But I'll need work crews: carpenters, electricians, and Riki."

"So be it." Tomtom gave an order, and the guards started to separate them again.

"Wait!" Tinker cried. "No! We had a deal!"

"He is spell-marked," Tomtom said. "The skin will have to be flayed."

"No!" Tinker said. "He's not to be hurt in any way."

"I'd be a fool to let him keep the spells," Tomtom said. "You could use them to escape."

"I promise I won't!" She beat on the massive arms holding her, trying to get to Pony. "On my honor, and the honor of my house, I will stay here without escaping and build your gate. Harm him, and I will do nothing."

Tomtom shook his head. "What is it with you *domana* and your sentimentalism for your underlings? It must be genetic. It makes you weak."

"Fine. I'm weak." She kicked her feet, dangling as she was in the guard's hold, emphasizing that she was small and scrawny. "I'll give my word and stay without trying to escape and build your gate within twenty-one days *only* if he's completely unharmed."

Tomtom came to grip her chin and gaze deep into her eyes. "Say it again."

So she repeated it. Carefully.

"Sparrow said that we'll only be able to hold her with promises freely given," Riki said. "If she can hold a warrior, then her word must be binding: she can't lie when giving her word."

"Very well." Tomtom released Tinker's chin and growled a command. She found herself on her feet, Pony supporting her. "Take them back to her room. She'll start working tomorrow at first light."

Riki helped her support Pony on the long walk to her bedroom, through dusty warehouses and barren offices. The *sekasha* concentrated on putting one foot in front of the other, only flinches of pain on his face showing how badly he was hurt. Tinker wanted to scream accusations at Riki, but Chiyo's punishment was still stark in her mind. Even the kitsune thought that the breeding had been considered the kindest of the possible punishments.

"I'm sorry," Riki said as he delivered them to the bedroom that proved—without Chiyo's presence—to be windowless.

"Why?"

He took her to mean "why Pony," although she wasn't sure herself which of the many whys she meant. Why did he continue serving such a monster? Why had he kept her silent—thus, and in hindsight, safe from Tomtom's anger? Why hadn't he chosen one of the many humans she loved? "I find that I actually think of myself as human more than I thought," Riki said. "It was easier to pick an elf; I was taught to hate them."

"I'm an elf."

"You'll always be a human to me."

Only humans said things like that, so maybe he was telling the truth. Still, she couldn't find any room to forgive him.

"Go away," she said, and shut the door on his face.

She wanted to press Pony for details about what Windwolf was doing, how Oilcan was coping with her supposed death, if work had continued on her research center . . . but Pony looked like hell. She cleaned the blood from Pony's face, and nearly cried over the heel print bruised into the back of his right hand, his fingers swollen and broken.

"It is nothing," he mumbled. "I heal quickly. I will be better in no time."

Unfortunately, until he was functioning better, there would be no escaping.

She fingered where the power beads had been worked into his hair; the oni had cut his braids off, leaving little tufts of hair. Spell-marked or not, without the stored magical power, Pony's shields would quickly fail. The oni's ability to create "permanent" constructs—like Riki's wings and the Foo dogs—outclassed the elves' magic that normally required a ley line or it exhausted local ambient magic.

Pony took the lack of weapons and shields personally. "I'm sorry that I have failed you."

"Don't be an idiot. You haven't failed me." And then, because he didn't seem to believe her, she added truthfully, "I'm glad not to be all alone."

"Ah. I see. Then I'm glad to be here."

She couldn't bring herself to scorn him, despite it being silly for him to be happy to be stuck in such a situation. "What are you doing?"

Pony had started to stretch cautiously out on the floor. "I am going to sleep."

"Oh, get in the bed."

"You should sleep in the bed. I can sleep on the floor."

"Don't make me hit you." Tinker pushed him toward the bed. "The bed is huge, and I'm quite small, as everyone keeps pointing out. We can both share it without even noticing the other is in it."

"It wouldn't be proper."

"Get in the bed or I'll sleep on the floor too."

He actually agonized over it before giving in.

What the hell had she been thinking?

Fully awake in the darkened room, Tinker listened to the whisper of Pony's breathing. He lay so close she could feel the warmth from his body. His well-defined, muscled body. If she put out her hand, she could touch his hard stomach. Run her hand down his lean flank.

Why had she thought sharing a bed would be a good idea?

She had been scared and angry and frustrated when she went to bed. Now, for some inexplicable reason, she wanted to be held. No, more than held. All too easily, she could imagine being cradled naked in Pony's arms, his mouth on the nape of her neck, his strong hands cupping her breasts, their bodies thrusting together as his . . .

That was a truly dangerous line of thought. *You're a married woman, idiot!* She loved Windwolf, so why was she suddenly lusting for Pony?

Even pretending to be asleep became impossible. She opened her eyes and found that she could make out Pony's face: the shape of his mouth, the line of his nose, and the soft curve of his brow. Among the elves, she had taken his good looks for granted. After being surrounded by the oni and their alien ideals of beauty, she saw him with new eyes. Looking at him shot something akin to a low-voltage current down through her body to her groin. What would it be like to kiss him? Would he taste like Windwolf? She turned over to resist the temptation to find out.

Why was she feeling this way? She loved Windwolf. Didn't she? Certainly, if she could choose, she would want Windwolf beside her. Did she desire Pony only as a stand in for her husband? Did she only want someone bigger and stronger to make her feel safe and protected? Or did she love Windwolf only because of the sex? Would any sexy elf male do?

What a stupid time to be worrying about it. Pony's honor would never allow anything to happen, and besides, she'd probably never see Windwolf again. The oni were going to kill both of them as soon as the gate was done. There was no point pretending that Tomtom wouldn't dispose of them in some cruel yet offhandedly casual method. The white of exposed bone flashed into her mind. She curled against the flare of fear and misery.

I got away once, she reminded herself. *I can do it again.*

What was the point of being a genius, if she couldn't outthink her enemies?

Pony was doing exercises when Tinker woke the next morning. Stripped to the waist, he worked through a series of lightning-fast moves that would end suddenly in a perfect pose. Movement. Stillness. An attack. A block. A kick. A parry. Fluid. Precise. Soundless. Muscles upon muscles shifting under sleek skin, he was beautiful to watch. She felt the ache of desire flare up again. She moaned, rolling over to bury her head under pillows. Could this get any more embarrassing?

She realized then that she needed to pee.

She sat up and discovered that in that position, the need was greater.

"Good morning." Pony pressed his fist against his palm and bowed.

"Morning." She eyed the chamber pot in the corner. There was a real toilet off the workshop—could she reach that? No. She felt like she was about to burst. "Could you, um, turn around?"

She tried to pee quietly, but failed due to the acoustic properties of ceramic and the amplifying curvature of the bowl. Horses pissed quieter. Was it possible to die of humiliation? Mark up another difference between Pony and Windwolf—she hadn't been self-conscious the first time she used the toilet in front of Windwolf. She tried to act nonchalant, but she could feel the burn of embarrassment on her face as she washed her hands.

"Do you train every morning like that?" she asked to distract both of them.

"Yes. The *sekasha* were made to be living weapons. We hone our bodies to perfection."

"You embrace being a weapon?"

"I take joy in my strength." He high-kicked and locked into place, balanced on one foot. "And I like to fight."

He grinned, and suddenly he didn't seem like the mild Pony she knew, but someone wilder, and fiercer, more aptly named Storm-horse. She tried to study him clinically, taking note only of his injuries. His bruises looked days old, mottled purple and faded yellow.

"How do you feel?"

"Whole, except for my hand." He held it out for her inspection. The middle and ring fingers were still swollen and stiff. He flexed them carefully, wincing. "It will be another day or two before I'll be able to hold a sword, perhaps as much as four before I can strike with this hand without fear of causing more pain to myself than my opponent."

"Good. We have to get out of here."

"Out?"

"We need to escape."

Pony looked at her with utter surprise. "But you gave your word."

Tinker winced: She had suspected that this was how the conversation would go, but she hated to have her fears confirmed. "Pony, these are bad, nasty people with not a fleck of honor among them."

"In giving your word, it is only your honor that matters, not the receiver. If you think the person is not worth your honor, you don't extend it."

She checked the impulse to stick her tongue out at him. "Would you rather I break my word or let these monsters take over our world?"

"I would rather die than be the reason you broke your word."

Elves! "This is not about you, this is about them doing whatever they could to break me."

"That's because you are the pivot."

"Yeah, yeah, so everyone keeps reminding me." But, actually, she had kind of forgotten all that between Sparrow's betrayal, Chiyo's breeding, and Pony's capture. Tinker thought she understood the mess until Sparrow waltzed in and clued the oni. How did their knowledge and her promise change things? The seer had said that it was only a matter of time before the oni opened a gate—certainly if Tinker refused to cooperate, they could bide their time; they were immortal and humans made advances in technology daily. That equation had a zero sum—which was why she was cooperating until she could escape. But the seer also indicated that they could only defeat the oni by choosing when the gate was opened, and indicated that the pivot picked the time. If she was in the oni's control, did it mean that the oni controlled the choice?

She decided to bounce her questions off of Pony, who probably had more experience in these seer-type of things. "Sparrow told the oni that the only way to bind me was with ties of my own making . . ."

"Sparrow?"

Oops, she forgot Pony didn't know that little piece of nastiness. "She's working with them. They had me fooled into thinking I was on Onihida, but I figured it out and got away last night. Sparrow recaptured me and brought me back to them."

Pony darkened with anger, and he stalked about the room as if looking for something to vent his rage on. He growled out Elvish she didn't recognize, but they sounded like obscenities.

"Pony, I'm trying to figure out what the seer meant."

"Forgiveness." He fell silent, but he continued to stalk about the room.

"Do you know if the seer said anything more about me being the pivot?"

"She did not, although closely pressed by all. *'Bind the pivot,'* was all she said. *'If the pivot be true, then the battle can be won. If the pivot proves false, all will be lost.'* "

Tinker tried to wrap her mind around it, but Sparrow's translation was making it difficult. "Sparrow told the oni that they'll only be able to hold me with promises freely given. Has the oni won merely by making me promise? Is it just the words, or . . ."

"Sparrow often hears what she wants to hear," Pony interrupted her. "The seer isn't saying that getting you to make promises will win the battle. The seer said 'if the pivot be *true*' which means you must keep all your promises, no matter to whom."

"Oh, you must be kidding."

"No."

"I can't make them a gate."

"You must. You promised."

"Th-that doesn't follow logic," Tinker protested.

"Seeing into the future is like having a gleaming thread appear in the darkness. You must walk that path, no matter how treacherous, to reach the foreseen outcome. If you step off it, you're lost from sight, and both you and your goal become unknown again."

"So, although it flies into the face of everything sensible, the only way to stop the oni . . . is to do . . . what they want."

"What they forced you to promise."

She shook her head. No. It didn't make any more sense out loud or stood on its head. "What if being 'true,' is just 'loyal'? I can't be 'loyal' to the elves if I'm making a gate for the oni."

"No. You're confusing words. Those don't mean the same thing."

She winced. "They're synonyms, right? Close to the same meaning."

"True only means that one keeps their word of honor. It is a word applied to head of households and clan leaders as they interact with equals or enemies."

If she got out of this, she had to smack Tooloo a good one. Obviously when the half-elf taught her Elvish, any approximate English word would work, to hell with confusion that other meanings of the English word might cause.

"*Domi*, you swore not only on your honor but on the honor of your house. For an elf, there is no stronger oath."

Yeah, that was why she used it. She wanted to scream. What an irrational mess. "I'm not really an elf! I'm a human with funny ears. I didn't know what Windwolf intended with the spell. I'm not even sure why Windwolf made me this way. If you love someone, don't you take them as they are?"

"*Domi*, I am young for an elf, but I am over a hundred. I grew up in a large city in the Easternlands. Many elves live there, but in a hundred years, one meets most of them. And in all that time, I have never met anyone like you. Not a single person, having met you, has questioned Windwolf's desire to prolong your life. You blaze like a star. You don't seem to see that, but then you surround yourself with people nearly as bright as yourself. You raise people up to your heights. Even if Windwolf did not love you, he would not want to see your brilliance put out."

She burned in embarrassment. "Me? Blaze?"

"From your wit to your confidence to your compassion, you are an amazing person."

"Windwolf barely knew me when he proposed."

"After living so many years, if you're wise, you learn your own heart. You know when you meet someone that 'this person I can be friends with,' or 'this person I can build a friendship with—it will be difficult work—but it *may be* very sound,' or 'this person I will never be friends with.' There are times, though, where it seems like magic; you look at a person and your soul opens up and recognizes a true love. Windwolf looked at you and believed you are one he could live forever with. And in some ways, I am the same."

She looked at him. "What?"

He dropped to one knee and took her hand. "*Domi*, do you think I would pledge my life to you, be willing to die for you, if I did not in some way, love you?"

"You love me?" she repeated, stunned.

"You are my *domi*. And in all ways, you have proved the worth of my decision. You have protected me, as I have protected you. A holding is like a marriage, where trust runs deep. And in only a few days, I knew that to be beholden to you would be a good thing."

That threw her into a whirlwind of emotions, but the door opened behind Pony, saving her from discovering what dangerous thing might arise from that chaos. A gale force of alarm blasted through her, scouring away everything else.

There was an entire squad of oni warriors with Riki to escort her and Pony back to the workshop. Ironwood timbers sat stacked just inside the side door, which was padlocked shut again. A crew of humans sat waiting. They were Asians in blue jeans, T-shirts, and work boots.

Tinker checked in confusion. "Who are they?"

"They're the carpenters to make the frame out of the ironwood," Riki explained. "I thought since you designed the framework yesterday, that you'd want to get started on building it. We've got a tight deadline."

"Wait, isn't this like your ultra-secret hideout? What the fuck are they doing here? Did you kidnap them all? Are you going to kill them when they're done?"

Riki blinked and glanced again at the carpenters. "Oh, no, they're not humans. They're oni permanently disguised as humans, sort of like how the yap dogs were those big monster things. We had to immigrate them into Pittsburgh under Chinese visas."

Tinker thought of the sprawling Chinatown on the Northside. "Oh shit, don't tell me all the Chinese are oni."

"Okay." Riki walked away.

* * *

She was growing sure that Riki had told her one truth—a gate had only recently opened from Earth to Onihida. Too many little things were pointing at it: the throwaway comments about Earth-born oni, the carpenter's obvious awkwardness with the most basic of power tools, the famine-obsessed cook, the brown rice which turned out to be a luxury item not served to the carpenters, to their dismay. The list grew the entire morning. When she believed she was on Onihida, she hadn't paid attention—that she was no longer on Elfhome had been proof enough for her. Now she couldn't stop wondering about it.

She had delegated building the framework to Riki so she could concentrate on limiting the veil effect and making it the primary function of the new gate. Her biggest fear was she'd only swap the dimensional side effect with the jump capabilities of the gate and accidentally send Pittsburgh to Alpha Centauri. An hour of running models reassured her that if she did, it would be a very small chunk, most likely only the oni compound itself. Small loss there.

Her mind, however, kept trotting back to the oni's door to Onihida. Riki had said it was in an inconvenient spot; obviously it was located outside of the U.S., or the Chinese visas wouldn't be needed. Certainly, if the two doors were on opposite sides of the planet, it could be called inconvenient.

She jerked to a halt. Luckily only Pony noticed.

"What is it?"

"I think I know where their stupid door is," she murmured, wheeling her chair away from the drafting table to her desktop screen and calling up a world map. "I just can't believe no one's noticed before now."

Like all the information on the gate, she had the location where the gate was in geosynchronous orbit over the Earth's equator. She found the point and zoomed in. "It's so simple. Pittsburgh is on Elfhome because the gate projects the veil effect down through the Earth, where the magnetic core bends it, kind of like a prism bends light, thus hitting Pittsburgh on the other side of the planet."

Only partially under the gate was a tiny island surrounded by ocean. She laughed. "Of all the dumb luck, a few more feet and their gate would have been totally in open water."

Pony peered at the island for several minutes before saying, "I don't understand. How can this open to Onihida, and this," he pointed to the other side of the world, "open to Elfhome?"

"That's the simple part. The Earth core is acting as a lens."

"Pardon?"

She closed the incriminating map and opened a scratch file. "Look, here's Earth with the core in the center. This side is the China Sea, and the other side, up here, is Pittsburgh. The gate orbits over the sea. The veil effect comes down a cylindrical shape, but the core acts like a lens. That means the veil is 'flipped.'" Seeing Pony's blank look, "You see things because light comes down and reflects off it. So if you have a tree, the light comes from the sun, hits the trees, and reflects to your eye."

He nodded. "Yes, I know this."

"But if you hold a glass lens up between you and the tree, the light is bent by the lens. The top of the tree is bent to the bottom, and the bottom is bent to the top, so the image is flipped."

Pony pointed to the tree. "Onihida." And tapped the upside-down image. "Elfhome."

"Yes. That simple. For twenty years, every Shutdown and Startup, that tropical island has been going to Onihida and back, and no one has noticed."

"Or noticed and the oni killed them."

"Yes, that too."

Pony pointed then to the gate in orbit. "Whatever you do—build the oni a gate or not—means little while that exists. That is the true prison door hanging open."

The carpenters tried to quit after dinner, but she tracked Riki down in the ocean of sawdust with shoals of massive timbers and littered with the flotsam of cut ends.

"Tell them that they can't leave," she said.

"They've been working for like ten hours."

"They can work until they drop," Tinker growled. "Tell them to get back to work."

"They're tired."

"I don't care! If I'm going to meet Tomtom's deadline, then *everyone* is going to have to work until they drop."

"Be reasonable."

"Your people started this. I'm just going to finish it. Tell them to go back to work or I'll take a crowbar to them."

Riki winced. "Okay, okay, I'll get them back to work."

Only Tomtom's appearance at midnight kept the carpenters from revolting. The carpenters would jerk to a stop, bow low, and get waved back to work, which they did with stunning enthusiasm. No, no—no slackers here. Tinker shut files on her desktop as he closed in on her office.

"It looks nearly complete." Tomtom motioned to the massive circle of wood taking form.

"The frame work is getting there," Tinker said. "It's still a long way to go on this gate. Once we finish here, the carpenters can start work on the second gate. The frame itself will be identical, so the crew will need less guidance—I need Riki here with me."

"*Hanno.*" Tomtom cocked his head. "Second gate?"

Tinker picked up evidence A. "Well, you've got enough material here for two gates, maybe three. I just assumed that you were building more than one—since the gate size is limited by the roof."

"A second gate," Tomtom said slowly.

"I haven't had a chance to look over the area." Tinker indicated the buildings around them. "I recommend you keep the two gates as far apart as possible; there might be possible interference between the two. Besides, it would prevent bottleneck."

"Bottleneck?"

"Traffic jams." Tinker turned to Riki as he arrived from the other side of the warehouse. "Riki, can you explain 'bottleneck' to him?"

Riki looked puzzled, but launched into Oni, pushing his hands together to illustrate two forces colliding together. Tomtom's reply made Riki jerk around to stare at her. "A second gate?"

"Doh!" she said.

Riki looked at her in blank confusion.

"The framework for a second gate might go faster." She ignored Riki to focus on Tomtom. "But the rest of it will take the same amount of time, and I won't be able to start it until after this one is done. The schematics will need to be tailored to the location and orientation and various other deciding factors."

"Riki can not do them?" Tomtom said.

Tinker shook her head. "No more than he can do this one."

Tomtom turned to Riki for verification.

Riki looked at her strangely. "No. I can't. I'm still not grasping how the gate works. I have no clue what the next step will even be."

Tomtom accepted the truth. "Fine, we will have a second gate, on the other side of the compound."

The carpenter foreman came up to grovel and beg.

Tomtom laughed, showing sharp cat teeth. "As eager as you are, I can not have you slave-driving my people. It would reflect poorly on me. Everyone quits for the night. Even you."

*   *   *

Twenty days left.

Just stay focused, Tinker told herself but found she eyed the clock often as the numbers jumped through the hours of the day at despairing speed.

Chiyo appeared at the workshop late in the morning, with head high and hard stares at anyone glancing at her. Of the mating, there was no outward sign. The kitsune, however, radiated hostility like a steel blast furnace. The looks she gave Tinker shifted Pony from nearly invisible behind Tinker to between the two females. Unfortunately, he could do nothing about Chiyo's illusions; since the kitsune no longer needed to keep her mental abilities secret, she began torturing Tinker with them.

"Does she have to be here?" Tinker asked Riki later after reacting to the third giant illusionary spider.

"She's the only one besides me and Tomtom that speaks English, Elvish, and Oni."

"Fine." Tinker resolved herself to factoring numbers, and occasional remembrances of a nasty brush with a steel spinner—anyone that could do spiders that creepy had to be scared of them. "I've done some research. Normally you'd lay down ceramic tiles onto a backer board, but we can't do this here. In space they used these brackets. We're going to have to modify the brackets, since they were designed to connect to the framing with these connectors." Tinker showed him the hooks, and then tossed them over her shoulder. "Can't use those."

There was a yelp behind her, which she ignored.

"I want a wooden mounting plate made, then holes drilled into the brackets here, here, and here." Tinker marked the points. "Then we got these cool plastic bolts here, which were actually part of the shielding. Fasten the brackets to the mounting plate, but first, have the carpenters figure out how to attach the plate to the framing. I'm thinking to cut grooves—" she did a quick sketch to illustrate "—and slide them in and attach a piece of molding to lock them in. We can't use nails, but they should be used to that. The end result needs to have the tiles separated by no more than an eighth of an inch, but not much less since we have to allow for heat expansion."

Riki took out a handheld and jotted down notes. "Okay."

"Once we get the mounting plate designed, we need to run the power cables, so have them moved into the workshop. Remind the carpenters that we're going to be running power to the tiles up through this point in the bracket."

Riki made a face and scribbled more notes.

"Also we need the station for the tiles set up eventually." Tinker picked up the specially made ceramic tile. "Once I get the circuits designed, we can start masking them. You know, if your goons had held off just five or six years, my father would have done all this work himself on a Home Chip Lab."

If she had more than twenty days she could translate the entire thing down to integrated circuit level, shrinking the whole process down to something the size of . . . a wedding ring. That thought put shivers down her spine.

"Things were right for us to make a move," Riki said simply.

"Keep riding herd on the carpenters," Tinker turned back to her computer, trying to ignore the end of the conversation. *Twenty days. Focus.* "I want the framework done today and the mounting plates ready to go by tomorrow."

Ten days.

Tinker was growing frightened that she wasn't going to make the deadline.

True, the carpentry finished the first week, and the carpenters moved to the second gate to leisurely work there. After a week of hammering, the silence had seemed a blessing, but now the quiet seemed only to make the approaching deadline more ominous.

She hadn't counted on the fact that the oni had no electricians, and that those oni working with her were so unfamiliar with electricity that they were clueless. What could be so hard about running cables? She thought monkeys could do it. She had been interrupted time and time again to check their work. Wiring out of phase. Miswiring the grounds. Hooking the grounds in sequence into the main 240 line. The oni didn't miss a single way to screw up something so simple. More than once she had them rip several hours of work out. At least the confusion allowed her to slip in modifications unnoticed by Riki or Chiyo.

Speaking of the kitsune, she was going to kill Chiyo soon.

After a battle of spiders—which she won with the steel spinner incident—snakes began to infest her thoughts. Unfortunately, all the bits of cable littering the warehouse lent themselves to Chiyo's illusions. The kitsune apparently couldn't find room in Tinker's head while she was locked on circuit design, but the moment she was called away, she'd find the nearest cable suddenly slithering around. Annoying as it was—Tinker was more frightened that Chiyo would report Tinker's concerns of missing the deadline.

Only ten days remained. She had carefully reshaped the original gate's specs so that her gate opened a dimensional door only within its limits. She was still struggling with compressing the design down to the hundred-to-one ratio. There was still the masking, dipping, fitting . . . the list went on and on. And that assumed everything worked the first time. In danger of losing track of details, she'd sacrificed an hour to creating a schedule, copied it to her datapad, and printed up a copy for the wall. She found herself, however, now glancing at the schedule instead of the clock. Ten heavily loaded days.

"Stay focused," she murmured, and jumped slightly as Pony set a bowl down in front of her.

"Forgiveness."

"Oh, it's just Chiyo with her damn snakes and prying thoughts keeping me on edge on top of everything else. Rice and fish again? Bleah."

Pony grunted slightly. She looked up, and noticed that he was focused across the warehouse. A patrolling oni warrior had come into the warehouse, strolling around the massive wooden ring.

"A new one?" she asked, returning to her food and diagrams. Non-workers wanting to see the imposing gate were an annoyance she suffered for Pony's sake; he used the opportunity to track the onis' numbers.

"Sixty-one," Pony whispered. "Small, rifle and sword, no pistol."

Tinker winced at the number, which climbed daily. Already the oni warriors outnumbered Windwolf's *sekasha* three to one. Pony was of the opinion, though, that oni weren't as skilled fighters. *"The ones in charge are always the biggest and loudest, they run toward fat, and I haven't seen any sign of weapon practice."*

Riki came up, checking things off his datapad. "I think we finally nailed down the wiring. How's the circuit coming?"

"I'm just finishing—I think. I want to run them through a simulator before committing them to tile."

Riki nodded to the wisdom of this.

Tinker sensed Pony tensing, which probably meant Chiyo was closing on them. She spared a glance to check. The kitsune had paused, standing in profile to them to talk to one of the oni doing the wiring. Already the kitsune looked like she had a small pumpkin under her kimono. Riki had mentioned that a kitsune gestation was only fifty days; at ten days she was nearly the equivalent of three months in human pregnancy.

I can't let the oni into my world, Tinker thought for the thousandth time, and then firmly locked away her thoughts. "What is your plan? Do you have an army sitting on the other side of this gate?"

"Yes," Riki said.

"It started to amass last year." Chiyo joined the conversation. "I'm told it numbers in the tens of thousands."

"This gate is only good while Pittsburgh is on Elfhome," Tinker pointed out. "Even if you wait until after Shutdown to start bringing over your army—to maximize your time before the humans can react—you only have twenty-eight days until the next Shutdown. Then Pittsburgh goes back to Earth, either fully loaded with oni, or a war-torn ghost town. What little I know of the United States, they usually don't take kindly to that kind of shit."

"We'll ride this Shutdown out," Riki said, unconsciously echoing Oilcan's phrase. "And after that, there won't be another Shutdown."

"What?" Tinker yelped. "How can you stop Shutdown?"

"Shutdown is just flipping a switch," Riki said.

Chiyo laughed. "Oh, stupid fake elf, if we had the station built, don't you think we can control when it turns on and off?"

"The oni are working *with* the Chinese?" Somehow Tinker thought the oni had merely been feeding the Chinese information. But even as she said it, she realized that the cooperation would have to go deeper than that.

"I told you that some of us were stranded on Earth for hundreds of years," Riki said quietly. "Many of the kitsune's mental powers, like the mind reading, do not need magic to work. They have infiltrated the Chinese government to the highest levels. They're the ones that pushed through the building of the gate."

Tinker frowned. "The gate was wholly an oni's project? What about the colony at Alpha Centauri?"

"There is no colony," Riki said. "It's an elaborate sham that the tengu and the kitsune dreamed up. The gate is nothing more than a huge magician's box that we pull rabbits out of."

The problem with liars was knowing when they were telling the truth. Tinker couldn't believe that the entire twenty-year colonization program had been a sham. "Where the hell are the colony ships going?"

"Don't know," Riki shrugged. "We were hoping that they would go to Elfhome, or, failing that, Onihida, but they didn't go to either. We don't know what star system your father calibrated the gate for, so we picked one for the media. As far as we know, the ships could be on the other side of the galaxy, or a fourth dimension of Earth. Wherever they are, they've got a lot of empty cargo pods—we had to keep pushing stuff through the gate to justify leaving it on."

"They've been without supplies for twenty years?" Tinker stared at him, stunned. Lain and the astronomers had filled her life with information on the colonists until they were intimate strangers. "How could you do that?"

"We don't even know if they've survived the jump. If they came out next to a black hole, or any exotic star system—like a red nova or white dwarf—all the supplies in the world couldn't keep them alive."

"But—but—but all the progress reports from the colony?"

"We didn't have to worry about reports immediately, as Alpha Centauri is light years away. Eventually we put up a satellite in an extreme orbit with correctors to fake a signal from the colony. Beijing beams the feed up to the satellite that bounces it back in a wide enough spread that you can pick it up anywhere on Earth."

She noticed Chiyo's gaze fixated on her, like a hunter seeing prey, and concentrated on factoring numbers. "Stay out of my mind, you little bitch."

Riki picked up the dirty dishes and handed them to the kitsune. "Make yourself useful." They watched Chiyo carry the plates away. "If it makes you feel any better, all the first colonists were tengu and kitsune. They knew the risks. And we did send supplies for the first few years—they were our family—but Tomtom decided it was a waste of food and goods. He diverted the cargo to Onihida, where starvation is common."

"There's been ships full of people every five years since then!"

Riki nodded, bleak. "Yes. There have."

16: END GAME

Tinker was sick of keeping Chiyo out of her head. Working on the various mathematical and mechanical problems of the gate had provided automatic protection for the first two weeks, but the last few days—as much of the work resolved down to grunt work, little fiddles and small fixes—she had to switch to solving random math problems. More annoying was that she hadn't been able to share with Pony anything she didn't want Chiyo to pick out of his head. The level of trust that her bodyguard had in her was unnerving; if their places were swapped, she'd be climbing the wall to know "the plan." Pony, however, seemed content to wait and see what she pulled out of the hat.

The first step of "the plan" was simply to finish early. Tomtom would be on hand during the twenty-first day, so she slaved everyone unmercifully to hit the twentieth. Stunningly, they actually managed to finish early in the morning, but she dawdled, going so far as creating minor glitches. She wanted the cover of night—and confusion on both ends of the gate—when they activated it.

But what if it didn't work?

She tried to ignore that worry. Dusk grayed the sky as the dinner bowls arrived. As usual, afterward it fell to Chiyo to clear the dishes. Sexism, got to love it sometimes. Tinker gave Riki the chore to start moving the heavier tools and equipment to the second gate site.

For a few spare seconds, she and Pony were alone with a handful of guards that didn't speak Elvish.

"I've finished the gate, and I think it works," she murmured to Pony. "We'll see in a few minutes. I kept my promise. We go as soon as I turn it on and we can slip away."

"The other gate?" He nodded his head in the direction of the second gate, currently being wired without her guidance.

"If we don't get away, it's what will keep us alive." *But not intact.* She shoved the thought away, and pulled him over to the rack that used to hold the wiring spools. "These." She twisted and pulled the middle pole far enough out to show that it wasn't attached. "They're a weapon for you. It's the best I could do."

The poles lacked the magically sharp edge of the *sekasha*'s ironwood swords, but they matched the blades in size and weight.

Pony's eyes widened at the long stout poles of ironwood. "They will do nicely. Very clever."

"We'll see how clever I really am."

With her stomach squirming like a nest of snakes, she walked to the huge red-painted switch and threw it. It started the sound and light show on the gate, drawing the guards' eyes while she moved back and kicked the secret power switch on. If she was right, the gate would exist *between* both dimensions while operating, and thus be impossible to damage. Hopefully no one would discover how to turn off the power until too late.

Oh merciful gods in heaven, and the five spirits of the world, let this work.

The air around the gate shimmered and distorted, a massive confusion of particles as space was folded. Almost immediately she could feel the feedback pulses, but still so slight that she hoped no one would be able to notice them. Visibly, the area *through* the center of the ring looked no different, just oddly distorted, like water over glass, with the back of the workshop still discernible. No wonder natural gates were so hard to find. One might think the gate wasn't working, except the entire structure—including the ironwood framework but luckily not the ramp—had also phased out, becoming ghostlike.

The sudden blaze of lights brought Riki and the guards with him back.

"You turned it on?" Riki cried.

"It's the only way to see if it works." Tinker stood with her hand on the big red button, hoping to implant the wrong impression in the tengu's mind.

"Does it work?" Riki peered at the shimmering area inside the gate, keeping well back of it.

"I merely build these things, I don't test them." Tinker raised her hands, warding off any attempt to send her through. That would totally mess up her plans. "But it looks like it works to me. Why don't you get one of the guards to test it?"

That triggered the debate she hoped for. Trying to be all-so-unnoticeable, she walked back to the wire rack, took down the dinner-plate-sized spool of lead wire, and pulled free the pole. That she handed Pony, and removed another for herself. *Us? Just moving wire. Nothing to see here.*

The smallest of the construction workers was drafted to be first through the gate. Every eye was on him as he crept nervously up the ramp. The poor thing was trembling violently as he scanned the entire gate, arching around him. The others shouted at him in Oni, encouragements, commands, and curses.

As the oni stepped forward, vanishing into another world, Tinker and Pony slipped out the side door into the darkness.

The oni warriors were too well trained to let the gate totally distract them. The four assigned to Tinker tore themselves away, and the one who spoke crude English said, "Where go you?"

"The other door." Tinker motioned with the spool of wire. *See, harmless.* "Build next door?"

He glanced back to the brightly lit workshop, where everyone waited for the vanished worker.

Tinker didn't wait for him to decide, but headed slowly into the darkness.

Twenty days of playing construction demon goddess paid off; the guard followed without trying to stop her.

She had made only one trip to the second site, early last week, learning its location under the disguise of having to sign off on the exact orientation of the gate. Tomtom had taken her at her word and placed it at the complete opposite end of the mile-long warehouse, where the garage had once been. They passed through the gazebo room, and then through the kennel. The little dogs instantly launched into barking fits, but the warg merely eyed them as they passed.

Oh, gods, let this work.

The second workshop was empty of oni; the work crews had already left for the night. A handful of low-wattage bulbs threw pools of light down into the cave dark. Their footsteps echoed as they walked toward the gate; wrapped in shadows, it loomed over them—their insurance plan in ironwood.

"This part of the plan is nebulous," Tinker whispered to Pony in High Elvish, while pretending to examine work done. Without her slave driving, only the wood framing had been completed. Table-sized and smaller spools of wire—like the one she carried—sat waiting for the wiring to begin. "Do you think you can kill our escort?"

"Yes, *domi zae*," Pony said, paused, considered, and then asked, "Now?"

"Yes." She stepped behind him to give him room to work. "Now."

Pony took out the first two oni before the guards even realized he was attacking. One moment he was standing with the pole in his right hand, and the next he was driving the pole through the eye of the oni to the left with a motion that had his full body strength behind it. He shifted his grip, and swung the pole back to the right, like a baseball player hitting a line drive. The pole hit the oni's nose with a crack of shattering bone; the guard crumpled to the ground and lay still as death.

The third oni actually managed to dodge Pony's lightning swing, as the fourth pulled out his sword.

"Shit!" Tinker flung her spool of wire underhand—like a horseshoe—at the dodging oni. The spool hit him mid-chest, knocking him off balance, and Pony's pole struck him hard. The oni continued to move, though, while the last oni charged Pony with his sword ready. "Get the sword warrior, Pony, I'll deal with that one."

Yeah, right. But Pony was already engaging the last oni, meaning she'd better act. She gave the two fighters a wide berth as she dashed toward the crawling oni. She'd kicked a lot of people, and punched, and hit, but she never struck to kill. It'd been so easy to tell Pony to do it. The oni looked up, read her intent, and lunged at her—and she stopped being afraid to hurt him. She jerked backward, out of his reach, and swung at him as hard as she could. He threw up his arm, caught her pole and, laughing, wrenched it out of her hands. Cursing, she stomped down on his foot. He backhanded her and it was like being hit by a truck. The blow knocked her across the floor and up against the tanks of the acetylene torch. The taste of blood filled her mouth. Growling something in Oni, the guard flung aside the wood pole and came after her.

She twisted both gas lines wide open, snagged the torch, aimed it at the oni, and hit the igniter button. A foot-long lance of white-hot flame shot out in a deep "woof" of rapidly expanding air. It struck the oni full in the face.

He screamed in agony, stumbling back—and then went suddenly quiet as Pony cut his throat.

"*Domi*, are you hurt?" Pony asked, dropping the oni's body.

She shook her head, panting, staring at the blood rushing out of the still body. *This was soooo not her.*

"We should go." Pony came to lift her up, making sure for himself that she wasn't hurt. "Can you shoot a gun?"

"I've done it once." To save Windwolf from the oni to be exact. "It's not that hard. Point and pull the trigger."

He held out one of the onis' guns. "This is an Uzi. This is the fire selector switch. This is a single shot. This is a three-bullet burst. This is rapid fire. This is the safety position." He left the gun set on safety. He demonstrated holding it while firing it. "Brace yourself, it jumps in your hand and you quickly find yourself shooting into the sky. The bullets go until they hit something, so never fire with someone you don't want to hit standing anywhere in front of you."

"Good safety tip." Especially since it would most likely be Pony.

"It eats bullets fast." He showed her that the ammo clip slid out and another could be locked into place. "It takes about three seconds of continuous fire to go through a clip, so be selective."

He let her pocket the three extra clips before handing her the gun. It was cold and heavy. It felt like death in her hands, and she didn't like it, but there was no way she was going to stay helpless.

Pony took one of every weapon available; tucking away knives and guns, here and there, making them vanish on his solid frame.

Still shaky, she crossed to the windows and peered out. During her visit the week before to select the building site, the oni hoverbikes and cars were still parked in this section of the warehouse. She had hoped that the oni hadn't moved them, but the vehicles were gone. Damn, they weren't even outside. Much as she'd love to steal a pair of hoverbikes, they didn't have time to search blindly for them. Change of plans.

"Where might Windwolf and the other *sekasha* be at this time of night?" Tinker headed for the door. "At the hunting lodge?"

"Unlikely." Pony followed, her second shadow. "We were staying at one of the enclaves while the site for the new palace was cleared, and then we were to move into tents at the work site until temporary housing could be made."

"Where is that?"

"Between here and the enclaves, but much closer to the enclaves."

The steel mills were closer, but it didn't make sense to bring the oni down on unarmed humans. She'd love to call the EIA, but the oni had infiltrated it. A call for help might only bring disguised oni down on them. Windwolf and his bodyguards were the only ones that probably could deal with the oni.

"Let's head there." She bypassed the security alarm on the door and cracked it open. One would think that the oni would have gotten a better security system after the last time. Oh well, their loss, her gain.

There were no guards in sight. Quietly, they slipped out into the night. They moved cautiously through the compound, listening carefully and moving slowly to keep quiet. In the stillness, she could once again feel the feedback from the gate. Good, her gate was still on. Perhaps the oni couldn't feel the faint pulse; maybe she could only feel it because she was *domana*.

Minutes later, they made the safety of the forest and started to run.

"*Domi*, what is wrong with the air?" Pony matched her stride despite the fact he probably could outrun her.

Okay, it wasn't just her then. "I realized that the veil effect would link this gate with the one in orbit. By designing this one to be on the same proportions, I set it up to be a harmonic, in order to amplify the resonance."

"I don't understand."

"Every object has a frequency at which it will vibrate if disturbed. When an outside force with the same frequency as the natural frequency of the object causes the object to vibrate, it's called resonance, or sympathetic vibration. I can't believe Riki didn't realize what I was doing—although I kept him as busy as I could."

"I still don't understand."

Tinker had to check the impulse to stop and explain—with little pictures and lots of hand waving. "Oh, sweet lords, Pony, it's not easy to give physics lessons at a full run! When you have resonance, a small force can increase the amplitude of the object's vibration substantially."

"Talk plain Elvish," Pony groaned.

"Do you know that if a singer hits a certain note loud enough it can break a crystal goblet?"

"Yes."

"That's resonance. The note the singer is singing is the same frequency as the glass, which makes it literally vibrate itself apart. The gate I made is on the same frequency as the orbital one."

"The orbital gate will shake itself apart?"

"It should, as long as the as-built drawings are correct. Structurally, the one on the ground is much sturdier. Either my father wasn't much of a structural engineer, or he never had time to go back and add supports—and the oni never corrected the design weaknesses."

Pony checked at that point.

"What?" Tinker glanced back into the valley. The second workshop was now lit up as brightly as the first—someone had found the dead guards.

"We should go back," Pony said. "Make sure that they don't turn off the land-based gate."

"I rigged it so it's not easy to turn off, and we're now escaping, which hopefully—I think—will distract them long enough."

"Ah, yes. I see. We should hurry then."

Minutes later, a flare of magic behind Tinker made her stop and look back. The valley was now out of sight; there was nothing but trees and moonlight. For the first time she realized that, while the woods were dark, she was seeing quite well. Ah, built-in night vision—how handy.

"What is it?" Pony stopped beside her. He wasn't even breathing hard to her panting.

"I don't know. I felt something. Magic, I think."

"A powerful spell then."

"There it is again."

"We've got another mile to go. Come."

She was starting to wonder if everything she'd experienced at the palace had been by design. Certainly if the oni had captured her three weeks earlier, then she wouldn't have risked everything to save Pony, who was nearly a stranger at that point. Obviously she needed someone of his abilities to make an escape attempt feasible. And the exercise—all the hiking, jogging, and horseback riding she did keeping up with the bodyguards—was the only reason she was able to run as far as she had. But she was slowing down, and she didn't think she could run for more than another mile.

Oh, Windwolf, please be there.

"Run," Pony commanded suddenly, although he dropped a step behind her.

"I *am* running."

"Something is coming."

"What?" She risked looking back, but there was only forest behind her.

"Something large. Run."

She could hear it then, something big, coming through the forest; padded feet beat a fast cadence, and the harsh breathing of a big animal grew louder as it closed.

Oh god, not a saurus, was her first thought, *not now.* And then she realized what it had to be—the Foo dogs. Riki had told her that they kept the dogs small to make them easier to hide and to handle. He also mentioned that they could be expanded as easily as his wings.

"Shit! We should have killed the dogs."

"We didn't have time," Pony said.

"You have to hit the dog inside the construct." What else should she tell him? How did her Uzi work again? "The spell form protects them from sword swings; it will also affect the speed and path of bullets."

The forest ended and they were suddenly in a clearing of torn earth. Thirty acres had been thinned down to a scattering of trees on a wide hilltop. The trees left seemed to be all elfin oak, squat toadstools against the tall ironwoods, but still the lowest branches were at least twenty feet up. Stacked logs, survey markers, foundation stones, and large tents of white canvas cluttered the building site, but it was without activity or light. No one seemed to be there.

She stumbled to a stop, panting. "Oh shit."

There were two roads cut into the surrounding forest, but she was too disoriented by the shortcut through the trees to know where the roads might lead.

"Here it comes," Pony warned.

She whirled to face the oncoming animal. It was twice as massive as the constructs she had fought with Windwolf. Somehow the flattened face and mane were more recognizable as a lion's, although the body still seemed built on a bulldog design with the same odd poof tail arched over its back. As big as a horse, the Foo dog—no, make that Foo lion—rushed toward them.

She yanked up her Uzi, flicked the safety off with her thumb, and braced herself against the reported kick. When she pulled the trigger, it seemed like she was suddenly holding a living thing, intent on getting out of her hands, spitting smoke and fire. The noise of each bullet firing blurred into a prolonged rolling thunder. If the damn Foo lion hadn't been nearly on top of her, she might have missed the beast completely. As it was, though, hitting a barn would have been as easy.

As the first bullet struck the lion, its appearance transformed to the deep violet spell form, a polygon rendering of a lion done in magic. The runes flared with each rapid hit, flashing like a strobe light, the small dog writhing inside the monster puppet. The spell form slowed the bullets until she could actually see them flying through the magic like a swarm of angry bees. The first bullets missed the important dog core, but they acted like tracers for her aim, even with the kicking gun. The construct was smashed backward, and at least three bullets struck home. Once dead, she expected the lion to revert back down to lap dog, but the massive body remained, showing no sign of what killed it.

Three seconds. Her gun was empty, her ears were ringing, and the beast was dead.

Then the second Foo lion hit her from behind, bowling her over.

Its massive jaws closed on her shoulder and she was jerked upward, off her feet. She screamed in surprise and fear. With her dangling in its mouth, the lion bounded back toward the oni compound. Shit, it was *fetching* her like some rubber play toy!

"Pony!" she cried as she thrashed, trying to squirm free. The teeth didn't seem to be piercing her skin, but it had a firm hold on her. She clawed at its face, but it didn't seem to be feeling pain from her flailing at it. How was it seeing, she wondered, and clamped both hands over its eyes.

The Foo lion stumbled to a stop and shook her hard; its teeth sank into her shoulder, and she screamed in pain and sudden fear of being mauled.

The construct's pause, though, had given Pony a chance to catch up. He slammed the oni sword deep into the lion's side. The length of steel shifted the lion into spell form and revealed the dog within. The blade struck not where the real heart of a lion would lie, but farther back, to unerringly pierce the dog. The lion roared with pain, dropping her, and then collapsed.

"*Domi*, are you hurt?" Pony crouched beside her as she crabbed backward away from the unmoving lion.

"No." With him between her and the beast, she felt safe enough to stop crawling and actually consider if she was hurt. "At least not badly, but I'm getting tired of hearing that question."

"Forgiveness," Pony murmured, and lifted up her shirt to examine the puncture wounds.

"Pony!" she whined.

"Sometimes one is wounded more than one knows." Pony eyed the puncture wounds, then glanced about, as if looking for a light source. "I can not tell how deep they are. We need to stop the bleeding. Come, there will be supplies in one of the tents."

"I'm fine." She stood by herself to prove it. "I just want to get someplace safe. And I want my gun." She swayed as she looked down, trying to see the matte black Uzi on the ground, but the dark was making it impossible to see.

"I'll look, you just walk to the tents."

So she teetered off ahead of him as he went slowly, searching the ground that the Foo lion had covered while carrying her. It was a surprising amount. If she'd been feeling up to a faster pace, she would have told him to forget the gun. As she reached the tents, delayed reaction was setting in and she came to a complete, trembling halt. Why couldn't she get her breath? Was her lung collapsing? Oh, no, that's right, she'd just run like three miles.

Oh gods, oh gods. She desperately wanted Windwolf, a hot shower, and a comfy bed with him in it.

"Here it is, *domi*." Pony handed her the Uzi, considered her, took it back, searched her pockets for a fresh clip, reloaded the gun, put the safety back on, and slung its strap over her head, settling it on her back. "I'll find a first-aid kit. Sit down."

She sat on a pile of massive foundation stones between two tents, panting and shaking, as he went off. Now that she was still, she could feel the feedback again. It seemed stronger.

Okay, get a grip. Two roads. Which one should we take?

When built, the palace was going to have a great view of Pittsburgh. From where she sat, she could see out over the top of the surrounding elfin forest to the barren cut of the Rim and the bright human city beyond it. Both roads, however, led downhill into dark unknown. The left road would be the more direct way—but in Pittsburgh, that usually meant a need for a bridge. She doubted that three weeks had been enough time for something as ambitious as a bridge to be built—but hey, she built a gate that folded dimensions during that period. Still, if said bridge was unfinished, they'd lose valuable time backtracking.

On the left-most road, a shadow moved against the blackness, perceivable only as motion. Tinker froze in sudden fear that it was another Foo lion, and then realized it was humanoid. Friend or foe? Human, elf, or oni? Tinker got the impression of tall, slender, and graceful, realized it was an elf, and had started forward to greet the elf when she suddenly recognized the female. By then it was too late. Suddenly the tents and stones became sides of a trap.

Sparrow was in black leather pants and a black shirt, only her white skin and long pale braid glinting in the moonlight. The elf pointed a pistol at Tinker, the barrel hole seeming massive. "They must be complete twits not to be able to keep track of one little girl. Where is Stormhorse?"

"The oni sent Foo lions after me." Tinker indicated the nearest dead lion and the dark forest beyond. She could feel the Uzi heavy on her back. Could she get it swung forward and the safety off before Sparrow shot her? She let all the weariness and heartache of the last three weeks bleed into her voice. "He told me to run . . ."

"How convenient. Tomtom wants you back. Make no mistake, you're too dangerous for me to let wander back to Windwolf. One false move, and I will kill you."

"You've already lost, Sparrow. I'm the pivot. I've made my choice. There's nothing anyone can do about it."

"You're still thinking like a human," Sparrow tsked. "I've got the rest of time to figure out another way of doing this. The beauty of all this is that I only lose if you live to tell Windwolf what I've done."

Guessing what was coming next, Tinker threw herself sideways, but still Sparrow's bullet smashed into her side, knocking her off her feet in a violent half turn. Pony was suddenly there, catching Tinker before she fell against the stone. He shouted something and Tinker felt magic surge up, rushing like hot floodwaters. The blueness of his magical shields flared around them.

Sparrow's gun thundered again and again, the muzzle spitting flame and smoke.

Tinker felt the bullets strike Pony's shields—expending energy into the system with a hard kick that transmitted through the spell and Pony's body to her—and then ricochet harmlessly away.

When Sparrow hit the end of her clip, Pony drew his oni sword—the steel blade disrupting his shields—and thrust the sword deep into Sparrow's chest. "Die, you traitorous bitch," he growled and shoved it on through her.

Sparrow had cried out when the sword first penetrated her. She looked surprised at the blade buried in her own body, and then concerned as she tried to gasp for breath that wouldn't come. Sparrow slumped backwards against the tent wall even as Pony yanked the sword back out of her chest, her eyes going unfocused. The canvas cradled Sparrow gently, bowing under her falling weight so she slid elegantly downward, leaving a smear of blood on the white canvas.

Tinker stared at the dead elf. She thought she'd be happy to see Sparrow dead, but she could feel no joy in the killing. Maybe she hadn't hated the female as much as she thought.

"Tinker *domi*! Where did she hit you?"

"In the side." Tinker realized she was holding her side. She lifted up her hand and found it covered with blood. "Oh shit."

Pony sat her back on the stones, activated a light sphere, and examined the wound. "It is not bad. The bullet merely grazed you. I feared the worst; I thought she had killed you."

"I'm still alive and kicking."

"We must stop the bleeding. Then we must get out of here." He took his hands away as if he expected her to topple without his support. When he saw she could actually sit by herself, he went to fetch the abandoned first-aid kit.

"Sparrow came up the left road," Tinker told him when he'd returned. "She probably left the Rolls somewhere close by."

Pony sprayed the wound with a cool antibiotic and then pressed three large artificial skin patches into place. "You need a healing spell."

The kit was human-made, so there would be no spells in it. She was surprised he knew how to use the skin patches, but she supposed that knowing all sorts of first aid would be handy in a bodyguard.

"That looks good," Tinker lied. "Let's go."

Pony raided Sparrow's body for weapons, coming away with a pistol, two clips, a light bow, a quiver of white fletched spell arrows, and a sword and dagger of ironwood, which would allow him to keep his shields up. He left the oni sword where it lay, covered with Sparrow's blood.

Tinker felt light-headed and odd as Pony guided her to the road, saying, "We need to get to the enclaves or the hospice."

The road cut a narrow path through the forest, only twelve feet or so wide. It went straight down to a gorge; wooden scaffolding provided a temporary footbridge across while stone buttresses indicated that the future bridge would be built on an impressive scale. On the other side of the bridge were the enclaves and human civilization gleaming just beyond.

Pony, however, pulled her to a halt, and drew his sword. The shadows moved all around them, and oni warriors merged out of the darkness.

"Oh, fuck," Tinker whispered.

Magic surged in around them as Pony activated his shields, a scant comfort in the face of so many guns pointed their way. How much could the spell stop? Five bullets? Ten?

"I have played lightly with you." Tomtom's voice came out of the night, and he shifted into view directly in front of them, flanked by two of his largest warriors. Gone were the kimono and any pretense of being anything but a large dangerous animal. Spell tattoos covered his skin, starting at his collarbone and flowing downward over muscled thighs and calves. He wore only a loincloth of black silk hung on a diagonal cut from right hip to left shin and a sword belt. Like Chiyo, he had a tail to match the inhuman ears; it flickered behind him in agitation. "My claws are out." He lifted his left hand to show that indeed his claws were extended, showing off three inches of needle-sharp points. "One false step, and I'll content myself with whatever the tengu can do to salvage your work. This is not your battle, female—you are truly human under that skin. You owe them no alliance. My people are crowded and starving while the elves greedily hoard this vast wilderness. We only want what they do not use."

"I'm not going back with you. I'm not going to betray them."

"Submit now, and I will show mercy."

"I've seen your mercy with Chiyo." She was surprised that he was even bothering to talk to her. By oni mentality, she needed to be punished, something she was highly resistant to submitting to. There was no way she'd agree—so why wasn't he just ordering an attack? She glanced to the right at Pony, sword ready, his shields gleaming softly blue like an aura around him.

Of course. Pony's shields sucked down large amounts of ambient magic. On a ley line, he could maintain them indefinitely. Where they stood now, though, it was only a matter of time before the shields drained the area and failed. Tomtom was stalling.

"I gave the kitsune a choice of punishments," Tomtom was saying. "Drop your weapons, surrender yourself, and I will go lightly on you too."

Screw this. Tinker leveled her Uzi, flicked off the safety, and emptied the machine gun at Tomtom. Even as she pulled the trigger, though, the oni lord flicked up his left palm, growling out a spell, and the tattoos along his left arm flared and a haze appeared between them. The bullets spat out of the muzzle of the machine gun, struck the magic barrier, making it flare and, weirdly enough, gleam brighter. She actually felt it sparking up levels with each bullet hit. The bullets didn't pass through, nor ricochet, but instead dropped to the ground, inert. Damn, somehow the oni shield translated the kinetic energy of bullet back into the spell, fueling it.

Too late she thought to spray the warriors to either side of Tomtom; she'd already run through the clip and now worked the trigger to be rewarded only with a series of clicks.

Tomtom pointed at Pony and uttered a word, and then indicated Tinker, and gave a longer command. Tinker didn't need to know Oni to know what he'd said. *Kill him, take her alive.*

"No!" she shouted as the oni warriors surged forward, some with swords and others with hands outreached.

She tried to reload the Uzi only to have clip and gun wrenched from her hands, and then her arms held and she was lifted off the ground. She screamed wordlessly this time, kicking at the oni holding her, and her legs were caught. Hoisted upwards by the four oni, she saw Pony, shields blazing blue, desperately fending off eight oni warriors with sword and knife.

He was never going to be able to hold them off. They were going to kill him.

"No! No!" she cried, trying to wriggle free of the warriors' hold, but it was like being held by steel bands.

With a deep roaring sound—like an oncoming train—the wind suddenly blasted across the bridge and up the road, pouring over them, strangely hot. Her skin seemed to crawl as all her hair stood on end. She recognized the massive influx of active magic, but there was more—something like static electricity—that rode piggyback upon the magic. Judging by the startled outcries around her, the oni felt it too.

"To me! To me!" Pony shouted and went down to his knees, crossing sword and dagger over his head.

"Pony!" she screamed as he dropped his guard.

With blinding whiteness, lightning struck.

She'd never been this close to lightning before. It split the air with a deafening crack, and the boom of thunder was instantaneous in a wave of heat and pressure that vibrated clear through her bones. It was there, and then not there, but its brilliance remained burned into her sight. The bolt had splintered, forking all around Pony, striking the eight oni attacking him. The warriors flew backward to land dead—blackened and smoking from the lightning.

It seemed an impossible miracle, and then she realized the truth.

Windwolf had arrived, summoning the magic of the Wind Clan spell stones to call down lightning.

Pony came off the ground now, blades flashing, and launched himself at the oni holding Tinker. Tinker struggled harder to get free, cursing at her captors. Tomtom shouted in Oni, pointing toward the bridge, correctly identifying which of the three elves was the most dangerous. Another lightning bolt hit close at hand, striking into a knot of oni warriors attempting to attack Pony from the rear.

Two of the oni holding her decided to face Pony rather than die keeping her captive—and a hard kick into the face of the third left her dangling in one warrior's hold. There was a knife in his belt; she yanked it free and stabbed him in the stomach with it. The blade slid in to the hilt with stunning ease, and blood poured hot over her hand. The oni howled and punched her in the face.

Darkness washed in, and when it retreated Pony had her over his shoulder and was running for the bridge.

Had they won?

The crack of rifles and whine of bullets verified that no, they hadn't.

Lightning struck—and as it flashed all vision to white—Pony

stumbled and fell. It seemed as if he'd tripped over something. He started to fall to the left, which would have smashed Tinker under him. He dropped his sword, tucked her close, and rolled in mid-air to hit his right shoulder first. They tumbled through the mud of the road, Pony taking the brunt of the damage, as he protected her with his own body. They stopped when Pony slammed against the stone abutment at the end of the bridge.

As Pony lay unmoving, Tinker glanced back toward the pursuing oni.

She had one glimpse of Tomtom standing approximately where Pony had stumbled, a vicious grin on his face, before the oni lord stepped back into the shadows, completely vanishing from sight. She flashed to his first appearance on the road, he and his guard suddenly appearing as if teleporting. How was he doing it? Was he actually teleporting? Was he going invisible? Or like Chiyo, was he projecting what he wanted them to see into their minds?

Maybe the reason Chiyo had been so sure she could become a noble was because Tomtom had the same talents.

"Tinker?"

Windwolf still had his great sword sheathed, and he moved down the bridge in a stylistic stalk, like dancing in slow motion. She could feel the power he had gathered around him, the wind thrumming in his hold. He wore black leather pants, and a white silk shirt that blazed in the moonlight like a target. His long black hair was unbound, and it flowed out on the wind.

Of the *sekasha*, there was no sign. He was all alone.

"Is Pony alive?" His voice was quiet but loud, like a whisper over a microphone.

Pony was breathing, so Tinker said, "He's unconscious."

"Get him up," Windwolf commanded. "Get him to the other end of the bridge. The others are coming."

Tinker glanced down at the still unmoving Pony, a foot taller and easily fifty pounds heavier than her. How the hell did she move him? And where was Tomtom? What could the oni lord do—especially if he could throw illusions into Windwolf's mind?

Pony had dropped his sword, but he had other weapons on him. The guns were useless; the bullets would only feed energy into Tomtom's shield—assuming that wasn't an illusion. The knives placed her too near the much larger and better-trained oni. That left Sparrow's light bow and spell arrows. The arrows were all fletched white, which meant the same spell was marked onto the shaft and activated by the sound of the arrows' flight.

As Tomtom surely planned, Windwolf moved to the end of the bridge to cover her and Pony. He spoke a word, shifting his right hand with fingers cocked in stiff positions, and his shield extended out to cover the full end of the bridge.

"Go! Leave Pony if you have to." Windwolf commanded as the oni opened fire from the cover of the trees. The bullets deflected off his shield, but Tomtom could walk through it.

She didn't spend the last three weeks protecting Pony to leave him now, not even to save Windwolf. Tinker nocked an arrow—and looked for the factors of 73931. She could keep Chiyo from reading her mind by doing math, but that hadn't kept Chiyo from deluding her. She'd foiled Chiyo by noticing something that the kitsune had forgotten to disguise. Surely if Tomtom had two people to affect, there would be something he'd overlook, but what? The darkness itself would erase most of his errors. She lifted the bow, drew back the arrow, and tried to find a target.

"Tinker, what are you doing?" Windwolf growled.

"Trust me."

I can outthink him. I know I can.

Tomtom could fool her eyes. The gunfire covered his footsteps. What would he miss? His shadow? His smell?

Then it came to her—Tomtom would never think of hiding magic from a *domana*, since he couldn't feel magic himself—and she focused on the active magic in the area. There, passing through Windwolf's shields and nearly on him, was Tomtom's own shield spell.

She guessed the location of Tomtom's heart and loosed the arrow. As the arrow leapt from her bow, its whistling passage through the wind activated the spell written down its shaft; the kinetic energy of its physical form was transmuted into coherent light—a bolt of pure energy. There was a faint ripple as it passed through Tomtom's shield spell—apparently designed only for solid projectiles. Then it lanced its way through the oni lord, and he appeared with a gurgling scream. He was only six feet from Windwolf, sword upraised and ready to strike—with a neat hole burned through the right side of his chest.

Windwolf shouted, lifted his arm straight out, fingers splayed. The wind slammed Tomtom backwards thirty feet. Windwolf growled a spell to summon another bolt of lightning, moving his hands in interweaving circles, his fingers flicking through complex patterns. The brilliance struck Tomtom as the oni lord started to rise.

He didn't get up again.

There was a sweep of headlights on the far side of the bridge, and the *sekasha* spilled out of two of the Rolls and charged across the bridge.

Windwolf flinging lightning bolts, the arrival of the *sekasha*, and their own lord dead made the oni flee into the forest. The *sekasha* met no resistance as they passed beyond Windwolf's protection. Only when the *sekasha* had set up a line of defense did Windwolf loose his hold on the magic, letting it drain away.

He triggered a light orb as he walked to her, bathing them in light. People surrounded them, but he seemed to be the only one in focus.

"You're alive! My most wonderful, clever, little savage!" He lightly traced her face. She'd never seen him smile so widely. He blinked away a threat of tears, and glanced toward the waiting *sekasha*. "I must go and fight, but I will be back."

"Kiss me at least once," she complained.

"If I start, I will not be able to stop."

"Bullshit." She grabbed hold of his collar and pulled him down to her level.

He hadn't been exaggerating. Someone had to catch the light orb—he let it fall in order to crush her to him—and she had to finally push him breathlessly away after the third "*dame zae*, the oni" from the *sekasha*.

"Go," she said. "Deal with oni. Come back to me."

He kissed her fingertips and reluctantly left to chase after oni. Tinker slumped down beside Pony, quite willing to let them fight without her.

"*Domi?*" Pony croaked.

"Oh good." She took his hand. "You're awake."

"Yes." He frowned as she checked his attempt to get up. "Is it over? Did we win?"

"Yes, we've won."

Hospice elves arrived, first-aid kits in hand. "*Domi*, are you hurt?"

"No, no, see to him first," Tinker lied, motioning to Pony.

There were, however, more than enough healers to treat them both. One inked a healing spell onto her side and triggered it while the rest dealt with Pony. In the desperate fight, he'd been hit more times than she realized. As the healers stabilized him, enclave elves moved into the forest to deal with the oni dead.

Sparrow's body was found and carried to the enclaves, along with news of her betrayal. Apparently in an effort to keep searchers from the Turtle Creek area, the female had planted evidence in the South

Hills: articles of Tinker's clothing, items from Tinker's pockets, Pony's beads, scraps of paper with Tinker's handwriting. Windwolf and his forces had been at the farthest point in Pittsburgh from Tinker when she escaped, but the reports of gunfire at the construction site had brought Windwolf literally flying back, out ahead of his bodyguard, to save her.

The fighting had now moved far off, heading back toward Turtle Creek; Tinker could track it from the sound of gunfire and the occasional bright strokes of lightning.

That is so cool. "I'm really going to have to learn how to do that."

Or did she? Now that she was once again still, she could feel the feedback, definitely stronger. According to the models she ran, the orbital gate would soon shake itself to pieces, permanently returning Pittsburgh to Earth.

Which world did she want to be in?

Earth? With Oilcan, Lain, all the neat gadgets, the Internet, colleges full of like-minded people, and the possibility of returning to Elfhome anytime she decided to build a gate back?

Or Elfhome? With Windwolf and Pony, but no humans or techno toys, and the grim possibility that even if she could find the supplies, she might be denied the permission to build a gate back to Earth?

On the surface, all logic seemed to say that she should get up and walk into Pittsburgh proper before Shutdown. Go back to Earth.

But it wasn't that simple. In truth, she'd never been to Earth. Every Shutdown, she'd clung to her scrap yard and waited for Startup. She disliked the dirty air, the noise, the confusion, and the crush of people that Shutdown brought to Pittsburgh. Oilcan—who knew her best—predicted she'd hate Earth for those very reasons. It was a foreign other place she always resisted visiting.

Becoming an elf didn't make Elfhome her home—it only strengthened her tie to it. She grew up praying to elfin gods, practicing elfin morals, and celebrating elfin holidays. What did she know about being human besides beer, bowling, junked cars, and advanced science? On Earth, she wouldn't be a human with fancy ears; she'd be a displaced elf—just like Tooloo had been.

What's more, Pittsburgh was filled with oni disguised as humans, and by now, all of them knew she could build a gate. She'd never be able to trust anyone again; every new friendship would have to be endlessly questioned. Oilcan and Lain would be in danger of being used as leverage against her.

"Oh this sucks." Much to the healer's dismay, Tinker started to pace.

The feedback was becoming a hard pulse, as if the ground and the sky beat out the word "decide, decide, decide."

There was another crack of lightning, and she looked in that direction, but it was already gone and all there was to see was the dark primal forest of Elfhome. Trees. Magic. *Sekasha*. Windwolf. That kind of summed it up. The world she considered home, the people she trusted, and the male she loved.

But Oilcan, Lain, her datapad, the hoverbikes, people that understood physics, clever little gadgets, pizza, and pierogies . . .

She found herself at the far end of the bridge, a city block from the Rim.

Was she so shallow that she'd give up everything she loved for stuff?

Without the stuff, though, she'd been bored to tears at Aum Renau.

But she could have spent her time learning the complex magic of the spell stones. Windwolf had said that he'd teach it to her. She'd ignored it—in what now seemed like childish spite. In hindsight, she certainly could have used the power in the last twenty days. And the oni magic opened up a new realm of possibilities—creating solid temporary matter.

She paced back to Pony, the feedback beating on her even harder. Any minute now, she'd lose the chance to decide. She wanted to stay on Elfhome, right? It felt more like her home than Earth, with or without Pittsburgh.

Except there was still the problem of Oilcan—if she stayed, she'd lose him forever.

The hospice elves had moved Pony onto a stretcher. They piled all the various guns and knives on beside him, and then checked at the light bow, obviously not a *sekasha* weapon.

"*Domi*, your bow and arrows."

It was simpler just to take the bow and quiver than to explain they were Sparrow's.

She trailed slowly behind Pony's stretcher as they started for the enclaves, trying to decide. Go or stay. She got as far as mid-bridge before coming to a complete stop.

She didn't know what to do, and she was running out of time.

"You're still thinking like a human."

She hated to admit it, but Sparrow had been right. She was thinking of tomorrow, next month, or next year. If she stayed, she wasn't going to lose Oilcan forever. Humans knew Elfhome was here. They had all the technology needed to build a gate. They had the oni desperately cluing them in. Sooner, more probably than later, another land-based gate would be built.

She'd stay.

Only after she decided did she realize Sun Lance had been trailing back and forth after her.

"*Domi*," the female *sekasha* said, "I don't think it's safe to stay on the bridge with the air shaking so."

There had been no sign of fighting for the last few minutes, so she went back to the new palace construction site. From there, she had a panoramic view of Pittsburgh. She should have only minutes left. The feedback had become a low roar, and everything shook with its vibration. She found a couch-sized stack of canvas tarps to sit on and drink in her last sight of her hometown.

"Tinker? What's happening?" Windwolf called to her as he and the *sekasha* came out of the forest. "The oni tried to retreat to Turtle Creek, but there was something very wrong with the valley."

"What do you mean 'wrong'?"

"It was—fluid."

She considered a moment. "The veil effect must be extending the area of the gate, so there's several layers of overlapping realities all being disturbed by the feedback."

"What do you mean?"

"The gate I built for the oni is creating a resonance effect with the orbital gate. The veil effect of the orbital gate is pulsing the local gate." She made a fist and flared her other hand out over it to show the radius effect. She pulsed her top hand in time with the feedback. "It's doing Elfhome, Earth, Onihida, Elfhome, Earth, Onihida."

"The area affected wouldn't grow?"

"No. The local gate doesn't have the power to affect more than a few"—she considered the possible range—"hundred feet. I think a mile from the gate would be the maximum range."

"You planned it this way?"

"Actually, I planned for it to tear the orbital gate apart—which it should do any second now—with Pittsburgh going back to Earth permanently."

He glanced to the city below and then to her. "Then you're staying with me?"

"Yes, this is my home."

Silence fell while he was kissing her. Being in his arms, knowing that they had forever together, made the pain bearable. Still, she didn't want to turn and see the city gone, so she kept her eyes closed tight, and thought of only how much she loved him. The kissing led to other things, and he eased her back onto the tarps, and careful of her cuts and bruises, made gentle love to her.

Sometime later, he grew still and silent. "Love, I do not think it worked."

"Hmmm?" She rolled over to follow his gaze. Pittsburgh was still there. "*Shit!*" She rolled on her back to look at the stars instead. "Oh damn. What could have gone wrong?"

"Perhaps your gate failed first."

"Oh, I was so sure it wouldn't. It didn't on any of the model programs I ran."

"It is no matter. We will settle it with politics."

Tinker made a rude noise. "The governments of Earth are not going to want to destroy it—it represents too much money."

"We can compromise. If they destroy the orbital gate, we'll fund land-based gates to replace it."

It sounded like a long, drawn-out mess with the oni interfering at every step.

A streak of light caught Tinker's eye. "A falling star," she pointed out. "Humans think they grant wishes."

Windwolf shook his head. "I will never understand why a race without magic can believe that so many random things are magical."

"Wishful thinking."

"What do you wish for?"

"That we can get rid of the orbital gate without triggering a war between dimensions."

"A wise wish. There is another falling star."

Tinker blinked at the night sky. "Is it my imagination, or is that one much larger than the first?"

"Look!" Windwolf said and pointed to a fireball. "And there too."

"For us to see anything falling, though, there must have been an explosion that kicked large parts of the orbital gate into the atmosphere. I'm surprised they didn't just bounce off."

"Bounce off what?"

"It's, um, all orbital mechanics and velocities." Tinker waved it aside. "Oh, oh, that's not good. We shouldn't be able to see the gate— if that is the gate. It's in orbit around Earth—oh shit, I think I might have yanked it into Elfhome space by accident."

"If it is broken, then it is off," Windwolf said. "Shutdown. Right?"

Tinker eyed the city lights spread out down over the hills to the rivers. "Oh, this is really not good. I-I-I think, I think Pittsburgh is permanently on Elfhome. I'll have to run some models, but I think I changed a constant by shoving too hard, or maybe it was the resonance between the two gates. . . ."

"Without the gate in orbit, we will not be able to return Pittsburgh to Earth," Windwolf pointed out.

"Oh, this is so bad."

"I thought you wanted to stay."

"Yes, me, but the city? Without the supplies from Earth, Pittsburgh will be starving within weeks."

"Ah, yes. Not to worry, love. We will work it out."

End

"<evil> Eh heh heh! </evil> Finish the gate in 21.54 days or the HEDGEHOG GETS IT!!!"

WOLF WHO RULES

To Ann Cecil,
In many ways, elf-like.

Thanks to
Greg Armstrong, David Brukman,
Ann Cecil, Gail Brookhart, Kevin Hayes,
W. Randy Hoffman
Nancy Janda, Kendall Jung,
Don Kosak, June Drexler Robertson,
John Schmid, Linda Sprinkle,
Diane Turnshek, Andi Ward,
Joy Whitfield and
Thorne Scratch, who let me steal
her lock, stock and barrel

PROLOGUE: CUP OF TEARS

Elves may live forever, but their memories do not. Every elfin child is taught that any special memory has to be polished bright and carefully stored away at the end of a day, else it will slip away and soon be forgotten.

Wolf Who Rules Wind, viceroy of the Westernlands and the human city of Pittsburgh, thought about this as he settled before the altar of Nheoya, god of longevity. It was one more thing he would have to teach his new *domi*, Tinker. While clever beyond measure, she had spent her childhood as a human. He had only transformed her genetically into an elf; she lacked the hundred years of experience that all other adult elves lived through.

Wolf lit the candle of memory, clapped to call the god's attention to him, and bestowed his gift of silver on the altar. Normally he would wait to reach perfect calmness before starting the ceremony, but he didn't have time. He'd spent most of the last two days rescuing his *domi*, fighting her oni captors, and discovering how and why they had kidnapped her away. In truth, he should be focusing on his many responsibilities, but the fact that his *domi* had been restored to him on the eve of Memory made him feel it was important to observe the ritual.

He picked up the cup of tears. As a child, he couldn't understand why anyone would want to cling to bad memories. It had taken the royal court, with all its petty betrayals, to teach him the importance of bitterness; you needed to remember your mistakes to learn from them. For the first time, however, he did not dwell on those affairs of the heart. They all seemed minor now. His assistant, Sparrow Lifted by Wind, had taught him the true meaning of treachery.

He replayed now all her betrayals, slowly drinking down the warm saltwater. He did not know when she had started working with the oni, perhaps as early as the first day the human's orbital hyperphase gate had shifted Pittsburgh to Elfhome. He knew for sure that she'd spent the last few weeks subtly detouring him away from the oni compound. She had arranged for his blade brother Little Horse to be alone, so the oni could kidnap him and use him as a whipping boy. So many lies and deceptions! Wolf remembered the blank look on her face as she talked on her cell phone on that last day. He knew now the call was from the oni noble, Lord Tomtom, alerting her that Tinker and Little Horse had escaped. What excuse had she used to slip away in order to intercept them? Oh yes, a member of the clan needed someone to mediate between them and the Pittsburgh police. He had thanked her for sparing him from such small responsibilities so he could focus on finding the two people most important to him. Too bad Little Horse gave her such a clean death.

Dawn was breaking, and the cup of tears was drained, so he set aside his bitter memories. As light spilled into the temple, he lifted the cup of joys.

Normally he would dwell for hours on his happy childhood in his parents' household, and then, with a few exceptions, skip over all the lonely years he spent at court, and start again as he built his own household and settled the Westernlands. He did not have time today. In celebration of their safety, he thought only of Tinker and Little Horse.

Sipping his honeyed tea, he remembered Little Horse's birth and childhood, how he grew in leaps and bounds between Wolf's visits back home, until he was old enough to be part of Wolf's household. He brought with him the quiet affection that Wolf missed from his parents' home. Bitterness at Sparrow tried to crowd in, but Wolf ignored the temptation to dwell on those thoughts. He had only a short time left, and he wasn't going to waste it on her.

He turned his thoughts to Tinker. A human, raised on Elfhome, she was a delightful mix of human sensibility steeped in elfin culture. They had met once years ago, when she had saved him from a saurus. She had saved him again from a recent oni assassination attempt. The days afterward, as she struggled to keep him alive, she proved her intelligence, leadership, compassion, and fortitude. Once he realized that she was everything that he wanted in a *domi*, it was as if floodgates had opened in his heart, letting loose a tide of emotions he hadn't suspected himself capable of. Never had he wanted so much to protect another person. The very humanity that he loved in her made her butterfly fragile. The only way to keep her brightness shining was to make her an elf. At the time, he had regretted the necessity, but no longer. As a human, Tinker would have either been taken away from the home she loved by the NSA, or she wouldn't have survived Sparrow's betrayal. If he had any regrets it was trusting Sparrow and underestimating the oni.

Much as he'd have liked to continue dwelling on the good memories of his beloved, there was too much to do. Reluctantly, Wolf Who Rules blew out the candle, stood, and bowed to the god. The oni had forced his *domi* into building a gateway between their world and the neighborhood of Turtle Creek. Since the oni were gaining access to Earth (and ultimately Elfhome) via the orbital hyperphase gate, Tinker had used her gate to destroy the one in orbit. Unfortunately there were side effects not even his beloved could explain. Pittsburgh was now stuck on Elfhome. Turtle Creek had melted into liquid confusion. And something, most likely the orbital gate, had fallen from the sky like shooting stars. It left them with no way to return the humans to Earth, and an unknown number of oni among them.

1: GHOST LANDS

There were some mistakes that "Oops" just didn't cover.

Tinker stood on the George Westinghouse Bridge. Behind her was Pittsburgh and its sixty thousand humans now permanently stranded on Elfhome. Below her lay the mystery that at one time had been Turtle Creek. A blue haze filled the valley; the air shimmered with odd distortions. The land itself was a kaleidoscope of possibilities—elfin forest, oni houses, the Westinghouse Air Brake Plant—fractured pieces of various dimensions all jumbled together. And it was all her fault.

Color had been leached from the valley, except for the faint blue taint, making the features seem insubstantial. Perhaps the area was too unstable to reflect all wavelengths of light—or maybe the full spectrum of light wasn't able to pass through—the—the—she lacked a name for it.

Discontinuity?

Tinker decided that was as good a name as any.

"What are these *Ghostlands*?" asked her elfin bodyguard, Pony. He'd spoken in Low Elvish. *Ghostlands* had been in English, though, meaning a human had coined the term. Certainly the phrase fit the ghostly look of the valley.

So maybe Discontinuity wasn't the best name for it.

A foot taller than Tinker, Pony was a comforting wall of heavily armed and magically shielded muscle. His real name in Elvish was *Waetata-watarou-tukaenrou-bo-taeli*, which meant roughly Galloping Storm Horse on Wind. His elfin friends and family called him Little Horse, or *tukaenrou-tiki*, which still was a mouthful. He'd given her his English nickname to use when they met; it wasn't until recently that she had realized it had been his first act of friendship.

"I don't know what's happening here." Tinker ran a hand through her short brown hair, grabbed a handful and tugged, temptation to pull it out running high. "I set up a resonance between the gate I built and the one in orbit. They were supposed to shake each other apart. They did."

At least, she was fairly sure that they had. Something had fallen out of the sky that night in a fiery display. Since there were only a handful of small satellites in Elfhome's orbit, it was a fairly safe bet that she had somehow yanked the hyperphase gate out of Earth's orbit.

"This was—unexpected." She meant all of it. The orbital gate reduced to so much space debris and burnt ash on the ground. Turtle Creek turned into Ghostlands. Pittsburgh stuck on Elfhome.
Even "sorry" didn't seem adequate.

And what had happened to the oni army on Onihida, waiting to invade Elfhome through her gate? To the oni disguised as humans worked on the gate with her? And Riki, the tengu who had betrayed her?

"Is it going to—get better?" Pony asked.

"I think so." Tinker sighed, releasing her hair. "I can't imagine it staying in this unstable state." At least she hoped so. "The second law of thermodynamics and all that."

Pony grunted a slight optimistic sound, as if he was full of confidence in her intelligence and problem solving. Sometimes his trust in her was intimidating.

"I want to get closer." Tinker scanned the neighboring hillsides, looking for a safe way down to the valley's floor. In Pittsburgh, nothing was as straightforward as it appeared. This area was mostly abandoned—probably with help from the oni to keep people away from their secret compound. The arcing line of the Rim, marking where Pittsburgh ended and Elfhome proper began, was diffused by advancing elfin forest. Ironwood saplings mixed with jagger bushes— elfin trees colliding with Earth weed—to form a dense impenetrable thicket. "Let's find a way down."

"Is that wise, *domi*?"

"We'll be careful."

She expected more of an argument, but he clicked his tongue, the elfin equivalent of a shrug.

Pony leaned out over the bridge's railing; the spells tattooed down his arms in designs like Celtic knots—done in Wind Clan blue—rippled as muscle moved under skin. The hot wind played with tendrils of glossy black hair that had come loose from his braid. Dressed in his usual wyvern-scaled chest armor, black leather pants, and gleaming knee boots, Pony seemed oblivious to the mid-August heat. He looked as strong and healthy as ever. During their escape, the oni had nearly killed him. She took some comfort that he was the one thing that she hadn't totally messed up.

As they had recuperated, she'd endured an endless parade of visitors between bouts of drugged sleep, which gave the entire experience a surreal nightmare feel. Everyone had brought gifts and stories of Turtle Creek, until her hospice room and curiosity overflowed.

Thanks to her new elfin regenerative abilities, she'd healed far faster than when she was a human; she'd awakened this morning feeling good enough to explore. Much to her dismay, Pony insisted on bringing four more *sekasha* for a full Hand.

Yeah, yeah, it was wise, considering they had no clue how many oni survived the meltdown of Turtle Creek. She was getting claustrophobic, though, from always having hordes of people keeping watch over her; first the elves, then the oni, and now back to the elves. When she ran her scrap yard—months ago—a lifetime ago—she used to go days without seeing anyone but her cousin Oilcan.

As viceroy, her husband, Wolf Who Rules Wind, or Windwolf, held twenty *sekasha*; Pony picked her favorite four out of that twenty to make up a Hand. The outlandish Stormsong—her rebel short hair currently dyed blue—was acting as a Shield with Pony. Annoyingly, though, there seemed to be some secret *sekasha* rule—only one Shield could have a personality at any time. Stormsong stood a few feet off, silent and watching, in full bodyguard mode while Pony talked to Tinker. It would have been easier to pretend that the *sekasha* weren't guarding over her if they weren't so obviously "working."

The bridge secured, the other three *sekasha* were being Blades and scouting the area. Pony signaled them now using the *sekasha's* hand gestures called blade talk. Rainlily, senior of the Blades, acknowledged—Tinker recognized that much by now—and signaled something more.

"What did she say?" Tinker really had to get these guys radios. She hated having to ask what was going on; until recently, she had always known more than everyone else.

"They found something you should see."

⤙═◉═⤚

The police had strung yellow tape across the street in an attempt to cordon off the valley; it rustled ominously in a stiff breeze. Ducking under the tape, Tinker and her Shields joined the others. The one personality rule extended to the Blades; only Rainlily got to talk. Cloudwalker and Little Egret moved off, searching the area for possible threats.

"We found this in the middle of the road." Rainlily held out a bulky white, waterproof envelope. "Forgiveness, we had to check it for traps."

The envelope was addressed with all possible renditions of her name: Alexander Graham Bell, "Tinker" written in English, and finally Elvish runes of "Tinker of the Wind Clan." The *sekasha* had already slit it open to examine the contents and replaced them. Tinker tented open the envelope and peered inside; it held an old MP3 player and a note written in English.

I have great remorse for what I did. I'm sorry for hurting you both. I wish there had been another way. Riki Shoji.

"Yeah, right." Tinker scoffed and crumpled up the note and flung it away. "Like that makes everything okay, you damn crow."

She wanted to throw the MP3 player too, but it wasn't hers. Oilcan had loaned it to Riki. The month she'd been at Aum Renau, Oilcan and Riki had become friends. Or at least, Oilcan thought they were friends, just the same as he thought they were both human. Riki, though, was a lying oni spy, complete with bird-feet and magically retractable crow wings. He'd wormed his way into their lives just to kidnap Tinker. She doubted that Oilcan would want the player back now that he knew the truth; it would be a permanent reminder that Oilcan's trust nearly cost Tinker her life. But it wasn't her right to decide for him.

She jammed the player into the back pocket of her shorts. "Let's go."

Rage smoldered inside her until they had worked their way down to the Discontinuity. The mystery of the Ghostlands deepened, drowning out her anger. The edge of the blue seemed uneven at first, but then, as she crouched down to eye it closely, she realized that the effect "pooled" like water, and that the ragged edge was due to the elevation of the land—like the edge of a pond. Despite the August heat, ice gathered in the shadows. This close, she could hear a weird white noise, not unlike the gurgle of a river.

She found a long stick and prodded at the blue-shaded earth; it slowly gave like thick mud. She moved along the "shore" testing the shattered pieces of three worlds within reach of her stick. Earth fire hydrant. Onihida building. Elfhome ironwood tree. While they looked solid, everything within the zone of destruction was actually insubstantial, giving under the firm poke of her stick.

Pony stiffened with alarm when—after examining the stick for damage done to it and finding it as sound as before—she reached her hand out over the line.

Oddly, there was a resistance in the air over the land—as if Tinker was holding her hand out the window of a moving car. The air grew cooler as she lowered her hand. It was so very creepy that she had to steel herself to actually touch the dirt.

It was like plunging her bare hand into snow. Bitterly cold, the dirt gave under her fingertips. Within seconds, the chill was painful. She jerked her hand back.

"*Domi?*" Pony moved closer to her.

"I'm fine." Tinker cupped her left hand around her right. As she stood, blowing warmth onto her cold-reddened fingers, she gazed out onto the Ghostlands. She could feel magic on her new *domana* senses, but normally—like strong electrical currents—heat accompanied magic. Was the "shift" responsible for the cold? The presence of magic, however, would explain why the area was still unstable—sustaining whatever reaction the gate's destruction created. If her theory was right, once the ambient magic was depleted, the effect would collapse and the area would revert back to solid land. The only question was the rate of decay.

Pony picked up a stone and skipped it out across the disturbance. Faint ripples formed where the stone struck. After kissing "dirt" three times, the stone stopped about thirty feet in. For a minute it sat on the surface and then, slowly but perceivably, it started to sink.

Pony made a small puzzled noise. "Why isn't everything sinking?"

"I think—because they're all in the same space—which isn't quite here but isn't really someplace else—or maybe they're everywhere at once. The trees are stable, because to them, the earth underneath them is as stable as they are."

"Like ice on water?"

"Hmm." The analogy would serve, since she wasn't sure if she was right. They worked their way around the edge, the hilly terrain making it difficult. At first they found sections of paved road or cut through abandoned buildings, which made the going easier. Eventually, though, they'd worked their way out of the transferred Pittsburgh area and into Elfhome proper.

On the bank of a creek, frozen solid where it overlapped the affected area, they found a dead black willow tree, lying on its side, and a wide track of churned dirt where another willow had stalked northward.

Pony scanned the dim elfin woods for the carnivorous tree. "We must take care. It is probably still nearby; they don't move fast."

"I wonder what killed it." Tinker poked at the splayed root legs still partly inside the Discontinuity. Frost like freezer burn dusted the wide, sturdy trunk. Otherwise it seemed undamaged; the soft mud and thick brush of the creek bank had cushioned its fall so none of its branches or tangle arms had been broken. "Lain would love an intact tree." The xenobiologist often complained that the only specimens she ever could examine were the nonambulatory seedlings or mature trees blown to pieces to render them harmless. "I wish I could get it to her somehow."

The tracks of both trees, Tinker noticed, started in the Ghost-lands. Had the willow been clear of the Discontinuity at the time of the explosion—or had the tree died after reaching stable ground?

"Let me borrow one of your knives." Tinker used the knife Pony handed her to score an ironwood sapling. "I want to be able to track the rate of decay. Maybe there's a way I could accelerate it."

"A slash for every one of your feet the sapling stands from the Ghostlands?" Pony guessed her system.

"Yeah." She was going to move on to the next tree but he held out his hand for his knife. "What?"

"I would rather you stay back as much as possible from the edge." He waited with the grinding power of glaciers for her to hand back his knife. "How do you feel, *domi*?"

Ah, the source of his sudden protectiveness. It was going to be a while before she could live down overestimating herself the night of the fighting. Instead of going quietly to the hospice, she'd roamed about, made love, and did all sorts of silliness—and of course, fell flat on her face later. It probably occurred to him that if she nose-dived again, she would end up in the Ghostlands.

"I'm fine," she reassured him.

"You look tired." He slashed the next sapling, and she had to admit he actually made cleaner, easier-to-see marks than she did, robbing her of all chance to quibble with him.

She made a rude noise. Actually, she was exhausted—nightmares had disrupted her sleep for the last two days. But she didn't want to admit that; the *sekasha* might gang up on her and drag her back to the hospice. That was the problem with bringing five of them—it was much harder to bully them en masse—especially since they were all a foot taller than her. Sometimes she really hated being five foot nothing. Standing with them was like being surrounded by heavily armed trees. Even now Stormsong was eyeing her closely.

"I'm just—thinking." She mimed what she hoped looked like deep thought. "This is very perplexing."

Pony bought it, but he trusted her, perhaps more than he should. Stormsong seemed unconvinced, but said nothing. They moved on, marking saplings.

With an unknown number of oni scattered through the forest and hidden disguised among the human population of Pittsburgh, Wolf did not want to be dealing with the invasion of his *domi's* privacy, but it had to be stopped before the queen's representative arrived in Pittsburgh. Since all requests through human channels had failed, it was time to take the matter into his own hands.

Wolf stalked through the broken front door of the photographer's house, his annoyance growing into anger. Unfortunately, the photographer—paparazzi was the correct English word for his kind, but Wolf was not sure how to decline the word out—in question was determined to make things as difficult as possible.

Over the last two weeks, Wolf's people had worked through a series of false names and addresses to arrive at a narrow row house close to the Rim in Oakland. The houses to either side had been converted into businesses, due to their proximity to the enclaves. While the racial mix of the street was varied, the next door neighbors were Chinese. The owners had watched nervously as Windwolf broke down the photographer's door, but made no move to interfere. Judging by their remarks to each other in Mandarin, neither did they know that Wolf could speak Mandarin in addition to English, nor were they surprised by his presence—they seemed to think the photographer was receiving his due.

Inside the house, Wolf was starting to understand why.

One long narrow room took up most of the first floor beyond the shattered door. Filth dulled the wood floors and smudged the once white walls to an uneven gray. On the right wall, at odds with the grubby state of the house, was video wallpaper showing recorded images of Wolf's *domi*, Tinker. The film loop had been taken a month ago, showing a carefree Tinker laughing with the five female *sekasha* of Wolf's household. The image had been carefully doctored and scaled so that it gave the illusion that one gazed out a large window overlooking the private garden courtyard of Poppymeadow's enclave. Obviously feeling safe from prying eyes, Tinker lounged in her nightgown, revealing all her natural sexuality.

Wolf had seen the still pictures of Tinker in a digital magazine but hadn't realized that there was more. Judging by the stacks of cardboard boxes, there was much more. He flicked open the nearest box and found DVDs titled *Princess Gone Wild, Uncensored.*

"Where is he?" Wolf growled to his First, Wraith Arrow.

Wraith tilted his head slightly upward to indicate upstairs. "There's more."

At the top of the creaking wooden stairs, there was a large room empty of furniture. A camouflage screen covered the lone window, projecting a blank brick wall to the outside world. A camera on a tripod peered through a slit in the screen, trained down at the enclaves. This room's video wallpaper replayed images captured this morning, a somber Tinker sitting alone under the peach trees, dappled sunlight moving over her.

Wolf moved the camera, and the device's artificial intelligence shrank Tinker's image into one corner and went to live images as the zoom lens played over Poppymeadow's enclave where Wolf's household was living. Not only did the balcony provide a clear view over the high stone demesne wall but into the windows of all the buildings, from the main hall to the coach house. One of Poppymeadow's staff was changing linens in a guest wing bedroom; the camera automatically recognized the humanoid form and adjusted the focus until she filled the wall. The window was open, and a microphone picked up her humming.

"I haven't done anything illegal," a man was saying in the next room in English. "I know my rights! I'm protected by the treaty."

Wolf stalked into the last room. His *sekasha* had broken down the door to get in. The only piece of furniture was an unmade bed that reeked of old sweat and spent sex. His *sekasha* had a small rat of a man pinned against the far wall.

On the wall, images of Wolf's *domi* moved through their bedroom at Poppymeadow's, languidly stripping out of her clothes. "You want to do it?" she asked huskily. Wolf could remember the day, had replayed it in his mind again and again as his last memory of her when he thought he had lost her. "Come on, we have time."

She dropped the last piece of clothing on the floor, and the camera zoomed in tighter to play down over her body. Wolf snarled out the command for the winds and slammed its power into the wall. The wall boomed, the house shuddering at the impact, and the wallpaper went black. Tinker's voice, however, continued with a soft moan of delight.

"Hey! Hey!" the man cried in English. "Do you have any idea

how expensive that is? You can't just smash in here and break my stuff. I have rights."

"You had rights. They've been revoked." Wolf returned to the balcony and knocked the camera from its tripod. The wallpaper showed a somersault of confusion as the camera flipped end over end. When it struck pavement, it shattered into small unrecognizable pieces, and the wallpaper flickered back to the previously recorded loop of Tinker sitting in the garden.

"Evacuate the area," Wolf ordered in low Elvish. "I'm razing these buildings."

Apparently the man understood Elvish, because he yelped out, "What? You can't do that! I've called the police! You can't do this! This is Pittsburgh! I have rights!"

As if summoned by his words, a commotion downstairs announced the arrival of the Pittsburgh police.

"Police, freeze," a male voice barked in English. "Put down the weapons."

Wolf felt the *sekasha* downstairs activate their shields, blooms of magic against his awareness. Bladebite was saying something low and fast in High Elvish.

"*Naekanain*," someone cried in badly accented Elvish—*I do not understand*—while the first speaker repeated in English, "Put down the weapons!"

Wolf cursed. Apparently the police officers didn't speak Elvish, and his *sekasha* didn't speak English. Wolf called the winds and wrapped them about him before going to the top of the stairs.

There were two dark-blue-uniformed policemen crouched in the front door, keeping pistols leveled at the *sekasha* who had their *ejae* drawn. The officers looked human but, with oni, appearances could be deceiving. Both were tall enough to be oni warriors. The disguised warriors favored red hair while one policeman was pale blond and the other dark brown. The blond motioned with his left hand, as if trying to keep both his partner and the elves from acting.

"*Naekanain*," the blond repeated, and then added. "*Pavuyau Ruve*. Czernowski, just chill. They're the viceroy's personal guard."

"I know who the fuck they are, Bowman."

"If you know that," Wolf said, "then you know that they have the right to go where I want them to go, and do what I want them to do."

Bowman flicked a look up at him and then returned his focus on the *sekasha*. "Viceroy, have them put down their weapons."

"They will only when you do," Wolf said. "If you have not forgotten, we are at war."

"But not with us," Bowman growled.

Czernowski scoffed, and it saddened Wolf that he was closer to the mark.

"The oni have been living in Pittsburgh as disguised humans for years," Wolf said. "Until we're sure you're not oni, we must treat you as if you were. Lower your weapons."

Bowman hesitated, eyeing the *sekasha* as if he was considering how likely it was that he and his partner could overwhelm Wolf's guard. Wolf wasn't sure if Bowman's hesitation was born from overestimating his own abilities, or total ignorance of the *sekasha's*.

Finally, Bowman made a show of cautiously holstering his pistol. "Come on, Czernowski. Put it away."

The other policeman seemed familiar, although Wolf wasn't sure how; he rarely interacted with the Pittsburgh police. Wolf studied the two men. Unlike elves, where one could normally guess a person's clan, humans needed badges and patches to tell themselves apart. The officers' dark blue uniforms had shoulder patches and gold badges identifying them as Pittsburgh police. Bowman's brass nameplate read *B. Pedersen*. Czernowski's nameplate was unhelpful, giving only a first initial of *N*.

"I know you," Wolf said to Czernowski.

"I would hope so," the officer said. "You took the woman who was going to be my wife away from me. You ripped her right out of her species. You might think you've won, but I'm getting her back."

Wolf recognized him then—this was Tinker's Nathan, who bristled at him when Wolf collected his *domi* from the Faire. The uniform had thrown Wolf; he hadn't realized the man was a police officer. At the Faire, Czernowski had acted like a dog guarding a bone. Even though Tinker had stated over and over again that she was leaving with Wolf, Czernowski had clung to her, refusing to let her leave.

"Tinker is not a thing to be stolen away," Wolf told the man. "I did not *take* her. She chose me, not you. She is my *domi* now."

"I've seen the videotape." Nathan indicated the open box of DVDs. "I know what she is, but I don't care. I still love her, and I'm going to get her back."

"Who gives a fuck?" the thrice-damned photographer shouted behind Wolf. "It doesn't give these pointed-ear royalist freaks the right to break down my door and trash my stuff. I'm a tax-paying American! They can't—"

There was a loud thud as he was slammed up against his broken wall to silence him.

"Sir, can you step aside?" Bowman started cautiously upstairs before Wolf answered.

Wolf stepped back to make way for the two policemen.

The policemen took in the open window, the recording of Tinker in the garden, the smashed-down door, the broken wallpaper now stained with blood, and the broken-nosed paparazzi in Dark Harvest's hold.

"It's about time," the photographer cried. "Get these goons off me!"

"Please step away from him," Bowman told Dark, his hand dropping down to rest on his pistol. He repeated the order in bad Elvish. "*Naeba Kiyau.*"

"He's to be detained." Wolf wanted it clear what was to be done with the photographer before relinquishing control of him. "And these buildings evacuated so I can demolish them."

"You can't do that." Bowman pulled out a pair of handcuffs. "According to the treaty—"

"The treaty is now null and void. I am now the law in Pittsburgh, and I say that this man is to be detained indefinitely and these buildings will be demolished."

"The fuck you are." Czernowski spat the words. "In Pittsburgh we're the law and you're guilty of breaking and entering, assault and battery, and I'm sure I can think of a few more."

Czernowski reached for Wolf's arm and instantly had three swords at his throat.

"No," Wolf shouted to keep the policeman from being killed. Into the silence that suddenly filled the house, Tinker's recorded voice groaned, "Oh gods, yes, right there, oh, that's so good."

Bowman caught Czernowski as the policeman started to surge forward with a growl. "Czernowski!" Bowman slammed him against the wall. "Just deal with it! He's rich and powerful and she's fucking him. What part of this does not make sense to you? He drives a Rolls Royce and all the elves in Pittsburgh grovel at his feet. You think any bitch would pick a stupid Pole like you when she could have him?"

"He could have had anyone. She was mine."

"The fuck she was," Bowman growled. "If you'd scored once with her, all the bookies in Pittsburgh would know. You were always a long shot in the betting pool, Nathan. You were too stupid for her— and too dumb to realize that."

Czernowski glared at his partner, face darkening, but he stopped struggling to stand panting with his anger.

Bowman watched his partner for a minute before asking, "Are we good now?"

Czernowski nodded and flinched as Tinker's recorded voice gave a soft wordless moan of delight.

Bowman crossed to a section of the broken wall and pressed something and the sound stopped. "Viceroy, none of us like this any more than you do, but under international law, as of five years ago, this scumbag is within his rights to make this video."

"He's under elfin law now, and what he has done is unforgivable."

"Your people don't have technology capable of this." Bowman waved a hand at the wallpaper. "So you don't have laws to govern capturing digital images."

Wolf scoffed at the typical human sidestepping. "Why do humans nitpick justice to pieces? Can't you see that you've frayed it apart until it doesn't hold anything? There is right and then there is wrong. This is wrong."

"This isn't my place to decide, Viceroy. I'm just a cop. I only know human law, and as far as I last heard, human law still applies."

"The treaty says that any human left on Elfhome during Shutdown falls under elfin rule. The gate in orbit has failed; it is currently and always will be, Shutdown."

Bowman wiped the expression off his face. "Until my superiors confirm this, I have to continue to function with standard protocol and I can't arrest this man."

"Then I'll have him executed."

"I *can* put him in protective custody," Bowman said.

"As long as protective custody means a small cell without a window, I'll agree to that," Wolf said.

"We'll see what we can do." Bowman moved to handcuff the photographer.

Wolf felt a deep yet oddly distanced vibration, as if a bowstring had been drawn and released to thrum against his awareness. He recognized it—someone nearby was tapping the power of the Wind Clan Spell Stone. Wolf thought that he and Tinker were the only Wind Clan *domana* in Pittsburgh—and he hadn't taught Tinker even the most basic spells . . .

As the vibration continued, an endless drawing of power from the stones, cold certainty filled him. It could only be Tinker.

--≈◎═⊷--

Tinker and her *sekasha* had neared the far side of the Ghostlands, crossing once again into Pittsburgh but on the opposite side of the valley. The road climbed the steep hill in a series of sharp curves. As they crossed the cracked pavement, Stormsong laughed and pointed out a yellow warning street sign. It depicted a truck about to tip over as it made the sharp turn—a common sight in Pittsburgh—but someone had added words to the pictograph.

"What does it say?" Pony asked.

"Watch for Acrobatic Trucks," Stormsong translated the English words to Elvish.

The others laughed and moved on, scanning the mixed woods.

"You speak English?" Tinker fell into step with Stormsong.

"Fuckin' A!" Stormsong said with the correct scornful tone that such a stupid question would be posed.

Tinker tripped and nearly fell in surprise. Stormsong caught Tinker by the arm and warned her to be careful with a look. Most of Tinker's time with Windwolf's *sekasha* had been spent practicing her High Elvish, a stunningly polite language. Stormsong had just dropped a mask woven out of words.

"For the last twenty-some years, I pulled every shift I could to stay in Pittsburgh—" Stormsong continued. "—even if it meant bowing to that stuck-up bitch, Sparrow."

"Why?" Tinker was still reeling. Many elves first learned English in England when Shakespeare still lived and kept the lilting accent even if they modernized their sentence structure and word choice. Stormsong spoke true *Pitsupavute*, sounding like a native.

"I like humans." Stormsong stepped over a fallen tree in one long stride and paused to offer a hand to Tinker; the automatic politeness now seemed jarringly out of place. "They don't give a fuck what everyone else thinks. If they want something that's right for them, they don't worry about what the rest of the fucking world thinks."

The warrior's bitterness surprised Tinker. "What do you want?"

"I had doubts about being a *sekasha*." She shrugged like a human, lifting one shoulder, instead of clicking her tongue like an elf would. "Not anymore. Windwolf gave me a year to get my head screwed on right. I like being *sekasha*. I do have—as the humans say—issues."

That explained the short blue hair and the slight rebel air about her.

Stormsong suddenly spun to the left, pushing Tinker behind her even as she shouted the guttural command to activate her magical shields. Magic surged through the blue tattoos on her arms and flared into a shimmering blue that encompassed her body. Stormsong drew her ironwood sword and crouched into readiness. Instantly other *sekasha* activated their shields and drew their swords as they pulled in tight around Tinker. They scanned the area but there was nothing to see.

They were in the no-man's-land of the Rim, where tall young ironwoods mixed with Earth woods and jagger bushes in a thick, nearly impassable tangle. They stood on a deer trail, a path only one person wide, meandering through the dense underbrush. For a moment no one moved or spoke. Tinker realized that the birds had gone silent; even they didn't want to draw the attention of whatever had spooked Stormsong.

Pony made a gesture with his left hand in blade talk.

"Something is going to attack," Stormsong whispered in Elvish, once again becoming the *sekasha*. "Something large. I'm not sure how soon."

"*Yatanyai?*" Pony whispered a word that Tinker didn't recognize. Stormsong nodded.

"What does she see?" Tinker whispered.

"What will be." Pony indicated that they should start back the way they had come. "We're in a position of weakness. We should retreat to—"

Something huge and sinuous as a snake flashed out of the shadows. Tinker got the impression of scales, a wedge-shaped head, and a mouth full of teeth before Pony leaped between her and the monster. The creature struck Pony with a blow that smashed him aside, his shields flashing as they absorbed the brunt of the damage. It whipped toward Tinker, but Stormsong was already in the way.

"Oh, no, you don't!" The female *sekasha* blocked a savage bite at Tinker. "Get back, *domi*—you're attracting it!"

A blur of motion, the beast knocked Stormsong down, biting at her leg, her shield gleaming brilliant blue between its teeth. The Blades swung their swords, shouting to distract the creature. Releasing Stormsong, the creature leapt to perch high up the trunk of an oak. As it paused there, Tinker saw it fully for the first time.

It was long and lean, twelve feet from nose to tip of whipping tail. Despite a shaggy mane, its hide looked like blood red snake scales. Long-necked and short-legged, it was weirdly proportioned; its head seemed almost too large for its body, with a heavy jawed mouth filled with countless jagged teeth. Clinging to the side of the tree with massive claws, it hissed at them, showing the teeth.

Its mane lifted like a dog's hackles, and a haze shimmered to life over the beast, like heat waves coming off hot asphalt. Tinker could feel the presence of magic on her *domana* senses, like static electricity prickling against the skin. The second Blade, Cloudwalker, fired his pistol. The bullets struck the haze—making it flare at the point of impact—and dropped to the ground, inert. Tinker felt the magic strengthen as the kinetic energy of the bullet fed into the spell, fueling it.

"It's an oni shield!" Tinker cried out in warning. "Hitting it will only make it stronger."

Stormsong got to her feet, biting back a cry of pain. "Go, run, I'll hold it!"

Pony caught Tinker by her upper arm, and half carried her, half dragged her through the thicket.

"No!" Tinker cried, knowing that if it weren't for her safety, the others wouldn't abandon one of their own.

"*Domi.*" Pony urged her to run faster. "If we cannot hit it, then we have no hope of killing it."

Tinker thought furiously. How do you hurt something you can't hit but could bite you? Wait—maybe that was it! She snatched the pistol from the holster at Pony's side and jerked out of his hold. Here, under the tall ironwoods, the jagger brushes had grown high, and animals had made low tunnel-like trails through them. Ducking down, Tinker ran down a path, the gun seeming huge in her hands, heading back toward the wounded *sekasha*. The thorns tore at her bare arms and hair.

"Tinker *domi!*" Pony cried behind her.

"Its shield doesn't cover its mouth!" she shouted back.

She burst into the clearing to find Stormsong backed to a tree, desperately parrying the animal's teeth and claws. It smashed aside her sword and leapt, mouth open.

Tinker shouted for its attention, and pulled the gun's trigger. She hadn't aimed at all, and the bullet whined into the underbrush, missing everything.

As the beast turned to face her, and Stormsong shouted warning—a wordless cry of anger, pain, and dismay—Tinker realized the flaw in her plan. She would need to shove the pistol into the creature's mouth before shooting. "Oh fuck."

It was like being hit by a freight train. One moment the beast was running at her and then everything become a wild tumble of darkness and light, dead leaves, sharp teeth, and blood. Everything stopped moving with the creature pinning her to the ground with one massive claw. Then it *pulled*—not on her skin or muscle, but something deeper inside her, something intangible, that she didn't even know existed. Magic flooded through her—hot and powerful as electricity—a seemingly endless torrent from someplace unknown to the monster—and she was just the hapless conduit.

She had lost the gun in the wild tumble. She punched at its head, trying to get it off her as the magic poured through her. The massive jaws snapped down on her fist, and suddenly the creature froze—teeth holding firm her hand, not yet breaking skin. Its eyes widened, as if surprised to see her under it, her hand in its mouth. She panted, scared now beyond words, as the magic continued to thrum through her bones and skin. Her hand seemed so very small inside the mouthful of teeth.

A sword blade appeared over her, the tip pressing up against the creature's shields, aimed at its right eye. The tip slid forward slowly as if it was being pressed through concrete.

"Get off her," Pony growled, leaning his full weight onto his sword, little by little driving the point through the shields. "Now!"

For a moment, they seemed stuck in amber—the monster, Pony, her—caught in place and motionless. There came a high thrilling whistle from way up high, bursting the amber. The creature released her hand and leapt backward. She scrambled wildly in the other direction. Pony caught hold of her, hugging her tight with his free hand, his shields spilling down over her, encompassing her.

"Got her!" he cried, and backed away, the others closing ranks around them.

The whistle blew again, so sharp and piercing a sound that even the monster checked to look upward.

Someone stood on the Westinghouse Bridge that spanned the valley, doll-small by the distance. Against the summer-blue sky, the person was only a dark silhouette—too far away to see if he was man, elf, or oni. The whistle trilled, and, focused on the sound, Tinker realized that it was two notes, close together, a shrill discord.

The monster shook its head as if the sound hurt and bounded away, heading for the bridge, so fast it seemed it teleported from place to place.

The whistler spread out great black wings, resolving all question of race. A tengu, the oni spies created by blending oni with crows. Tinker could guess which one—Riki. What she couldn't guess was why he had just saved them, or how.

"*Domi.*" Pony eclipsed the escaping tengu and his monstrous pursuer. He peered intently at her hands and then tugged at her clothing, examining her closely. "You are hurt."

"I am?"

"Yes." He produced a white linen handkerchief that he pressed to a painful area of her head. "You should sit."

She started to ask why, but sudden blackness rushed in, and she started to fall.

2: GO ASK ALICE

Tinker fell a long time in darkness.

She found herself at the edge of the woods near Lain's house, the great white domes of the Observatory gleaming in moonlight. The ironwood forest stood solemn as a cathedral before her. Something white flickered through the night woods, brightness in humanoid form. Like a moth, Tinker was drawn toward the light, entering the forest.

A woman darted ahead of her, wearing an elfin gown shimmering as if formed of fiber optics tapped to a searchlight—brightness weaving through the forest dimness. She was so brilliant white that it hurt to look at her. A red ribbon covered her eyes and trailed down the dress, bloodred against the white. On the ground, the ribbon snaked out into the distance.

It came to Tinker, knowledge seeping into her like oil into a rag, that she knew the woman and they were searching for someone. In the distance was a thumping noise, like an axe biting into wood.

"He knows the paths, the twisted way," the woman told Tinker while they searched for this mystery person. "You have to talk to him. He'll tell you how to go."

"We're looking in the wrong place," Tinker called.

"We fell down the hole and through the looking glass," the woman cried back. "He's here! You only have to look!"

Tinker scanned the woods and saw a dark figure flitting through the trees, keeping pace with them. It was a delicate-boned woman in a black mourning dress. A blindfold of black lace veiled her eyes. Tears ran unchecked down her face. At her feet were black hedgehogs, nosing about in the dead litter of the forest floor. In the trees surrounding Black and the hedgehogs was a multitude of crows. The birds flitted from limb to limb, calling "Lost! Lost!" in harsh voices.

"Black knows all about him." Tinker said. "Why don't we ask her?"

"She is lost in her grief," White breathed into Tinker's ear. "There is no thread between you. She has no voice that you will listen to."

The thumping noise came from the direction that they needed to head, speeding up until it sounded like helicopter rotors beating the air.

"Wait!" Tinker reached out to catch hold of White, to warn her. She missed, grabbing air. "The queen is coming. You've murdered time. It's always six o'clock now."

"We can't stand still!" White caught Tinker's hand and they were flying low, like on a hoverbike, dodging trees, the ground covered with a checkerboard design of black and red. "We have to run as fast as we can to keep in the same place. Soon we won't be able to run at all and then all will be lost!"

"Lost! Lost!" cried the crows and Black flew like a silent shadow on Tinker's other side. They had left the hedgehogs behind. The red ribbon of White's blindfold raced on ahead of them, coiling like a snake.

"He eats the fruit of the tree that walks." White stopped them at the edge of a clearing. The ribbon coiled into the clearing and its tip plunged into the ground. "Follow the tree to the house of ice and sip sweetly of the cream."

Feeling with blind fingers, White followed the ribbon, hand over hand, out into the clearing. The bare forest floor was black, and grew blacker still, until the woman was sheer white against void with red thread wrapped around her fingers. Tinker took hold of the thread and followed out into the darkness. Beyond the edge of the clearing, she started to float as if weightless. Tinker tried to grip tight to the red ribbon, but it was so thin that she lost track of it and started to fall upward. The woman caught hold of her, pulling her close, and wrapped the red thread tight around her fingers, making a cat's cradle. "There, no matter what, you can always find me with this."

Turning away, the woman pulled on the ribbon, and pearls started to pop out of the ground, strung on the thread. "It starts with a pearl necklace."

Tinker was drifting upward, faster and faster. Black and her crows flew up to meet her in a rustle of wings, crying, "Lost, lost."

Tinker opened her eyes to summer sky framed by oak leaves. Acorns clustered on the branches, nearly ready to fall. A cardinal sang its rain song someplace overhead.

With a slight rustle, Pony leaned over her, bruised and battered himself, worry in his eyes. "*Domi*, are you well?"

Tinker blinked back tears. "Yes, I'm fine." She sat up, trying to ignore the pain in her head. "How is everyone else?"

"Stormsong is hurt. We have called for help but we should start for the hospice in case it returns . . ."

"Its eyes are open," Stormsong said from where she lay on her side, a bloody bandage around the leg that the creature had bitten. "It's not coming back."

"What the hell does that mean?" Tinker asked.

"It means what it means," Stormsong groaned.

"There is no sign of the beast," Rainlily said.

"Okay," Tinker said only because they seemed to be waiting for her to say something. How did she end up in charge?

Almost in answer, a sudden roar of wind announced the arrival of Wolf Who Rules Wind, head of the Wind Clan, also known as her husband, Windwolf. Riding the winds with the Wind Clan's magic, he flew down out of the sky and landed on the barren no-man's-land of the Rim. He dressed in elfin splendor. His duster of cobalt-blue silk, hand-painted with a stylized white wolf, whipped out behind him like a banner. He was beautiful in the way only elves could be—tall, lean, and broad-shouldered with a face full of elegant sharp lines. With a word and gesture, he dismissed his magic. Released, the winds sighed away.

Beauty, power, and the ability to fly like Superman—what more could a girl want?

"Beloved." Windwolf knelt beside her and folded her into his arms. "What happened? Are you hurt? I felt you tap the clan's spell stones and pull a massive amount of power."

The "stones" were granite slabs inscribed with spells located on top of a vastly powerful ley line that the *domana* accessed remotely via their genome. Until Windwolf unleashed his rage on the oni, Tinker hadn't realized the power that the stones represented. In one blinding flash of summoned lightning, it suddenly became clear why the *domana* ruled the other elfin castes. Somehow, the monster had tapped and funneled the power through her.

"Oh, is that what the fuck it did to me?" And with that, she lost control of the tears she'd been keeping at bay. What was it about him that made her feel so safe in a way not even Pony could? She hugged him tightly, trusting he would make it right. As she wallowed in the luxury of being sheltered by the only force besides nature that seemed larger than herself, Windwolf turned his attention to Pony.

"Little Horse, what happened?" Windwolf's voice rumbled in his chest under her head, like contained thunder. "Is anyone hurt?"

"We were attacked by a very large creature." Pony went on to describe the fight in a few short sentences, ending with, "Stormsong took the brunt of the damage."

"We need to get her to the hospice." Tinker pulled free of Windwolf's hug, smeared the tears out of her eyes, and started for Stormsong. "The thing bit her in the leg."

Windwolf crossed to Stormsong in long strides, beating Tinker to the *sekasha's* side. The forest floor was annoyingly uneven; after stumbling slightly, Tinker slowed to baby steps. Pony hovered protectively close as if he expected her to pitch face first into the dead leaves. The big gray Rolls Royce they'd left on the other side of the valley and an ambulance had picked their way through the shattered streets to stop fifty-odd yards short of their location.

"Considering how fucked we were, I'm fine." Stormsong slapped Windwolf's hands away from the bloody bandage on her leg. "We didn't stop it—it just left."

Heat flushed over Tinker, and the sounds around her went muffled, as if someone had wrapped invisible wool around her head. It was dawning on her that she'd been stupid and nearly got them all killed. By returning to Stormsong, she'd pulled the other *sekasha* back to a fight that they should have lost. She should be dead right now. So fucking dead.

Stormsong glanced up at Tinker, frowned, and murmured something to Windwolf, giving him a slight push away from her. Windwolf looked up at Tinker and stood to sweep her off her feet and into his arms.

"Hey, I can walk!" Tinker cried.

"I know." He carried her toward the Rolls Royce. "I have seen you do it."

Tinker sighed at the nuances lost in the translation. This was how she ended up married to Windwolf—she accepted his betrothal gift without realizing he was proposing to her. "There is nothing wrong with my legs."

He eyed her bare legs draped over his arm. "No. There is not. They are very nice legs."

She studied him. All told, they had spent very little time with each other and she was still getting to know him. She was beginning to suspect, though, that he had a very subtle but strong sense of humor. "Are you teasing me?"

He said nothing but the corners of his eyes crinkled with a suppressed smile.

She smacked him lightly in the shoulder for teasing her. "You don't have to carry me!"

"But I like to."

"Windwolf," she whined.

He kissed her on her forehead. "You might think you are well, but you are in truth pale and wobbly. You have done what was needed. Let me care for you."

If she insisted on walking, she ran the risk of falling flat on her face. What harm could letting him carry her do, except to her pride? Like so often since he charged into her life, Windwolf left only bad choices for her to make in order to protect her sense of free will—and she was too smart to choose stupidity. Sighing, she lay her head on his shoulder and let him carry her.

He tucked her into the Rolls and slid in beside her. Pony got into the front, alongside the *sekasha* who was driving.

She noticed that her T-shirt was shredded over her stomach. Under the tattered material, five shallow claw marks cut across her abdomen; barely breaking the skin, the wounds were already crusted over with scabs. A fraction of an inch deeper, and she would have been gutted. She started to shake.

"All is well, you are fine," Windwolf murmured, holding her.

"I felt so helpless. There was nothing I could do to hurt it. I wish I could do the things you do."

"You can. I gave you that ability when I made you a Wind Clan *domana*."

"I know, I know, I have the genetic key to the Wind Clan spell stones." Which was how the monster sucked power through her. "What I don't know is *how* to use the spell stones. I want to learn."

"I was wrong not to teach you earlier." He took her hand. "I allowed myself to be distracted from my duties to you at Aum Renau; I should have started to teach you then."

"You'll teach me now?"

"Tomorrow we will start your lessons." He kissed her knuckles. "You will also have to learn how to use a sword."

"Shooting practice with a gun would probably be more useful."

"The sword is for your peers, not your enemies. Currently you have the queen's protection. No one can call insult on you or challenge you to a duel. But that protection will not last forever."

"*Pfft*, like random violence solves anything."

"True, it rarely does, but you need to know how to protect yourself and your beholden."

She made another noise of disgust. "What you elves—" She saw the look on his face and amended it. "—we elves call civilized. Can I still have the gun?"

"Yes, beloved, you may have the gun too. I will find comfort knowing you can defend yourself."

"Especially with a monster running around that sees me as some kind of power drink." She winced at her tone—he wasn't the one she was upset with.

"Reinforcements should be arriving soon, but until then Pittsburgh will not be safe."

"What reinforcements?"

"After you and Little Horse were kidnapped, I realized that there were more oni in the area than Sparrow previously led me to believe. I sent for reinforcements; the queen is sending troops via airship from Easternlands. They should arrive shortly. Unfortunately, this will pull the Fire Clan and probably the Stone Clan into the fight—which is why I'm thinking you should learn how to use a sword."

"Why is it a bad thing that other clans are going to help fight the oni? Isn't this everyone's problem?"

"We hold only what we can protect." Windwolf squeezed her hand; she wasn't sure if it was to comfort her or to seek comfort for himself. "By admitting that we need help, we have put our monopoly on Pittsburgh at risk. The other clans might want part of the city for services rendered in fixing this problem. The humans will fall under someone else's rule."

"You've got to be kidding! Why?"

"Because we cannot protect all of Pittsburgh from the oni. The crown will mediate a compromise."

"Couldn't your father, as head of the Wind Clan, have sent us help?"

"He has. He sent *domana* to Aum Renau and the other East Coast settlements. It is a great comfort to me to know that they are protected. The *domana* aren't that numerous, and the clans that can help are limited to those who have spell stones within range of Pittsburgh."

"This is all my fault," Tinker whispered.

"Hush, this battle is part of a war that started before even I was born."

She snuggled against him, logic failing to squash the guilty feeling inside of her. She was distracted, however, by something very hard under her. "Do you have something in your pocket? Or are you just happy to see me?"

"What? Oh, yes." Windwolf pulled a small fabric bundle out of his pants pocket. "This is for you."

"What's this?" Tinker eyed it tentatively. Accepting a similar package from Windwolf had indicated her acceptance of his marriage proposal—when she didn't realize the significance of his gift. She still had mixed feelings about being married to Windwolf. As a lover, Windwolf was all that she would want—warm, gentle, and caring wrapped in a sexy body—and she loved him deeply.

It was the whole marriage thing—having someone else's will and future joined to hers. They were building "their home" for "their people" and someday, maybe, "their children." Being the viceroy's wife, too, came with more responsibilities than she wanted; people were entrusting her with their lives. So far, the good outweighed the bad—but with elves "till death do us part" meant a very long time.

"Before the queen summoned me from Pittsburgh, I ordered clothes and jewelry to be made for you. I know that they are not of the style you might pick for yourself. It is important, though, that you look your best in front of the crown and the other clans."

"Okay." She pulled loose the bow and unwrapped the fabric. Inside were four small velvet pouches with drawstring pulls. She opened the first to the glitter of gems. "Oh!"

She gasped as she poured diamonds out into her palm. Over a foot of necklace studded with pea-sized diamonds. "Oh my! They're gorgeous!"

As she lifted them up, the afternoon sun prismed into a million tiny rainbows.

"They will look lovely against your skin." Windwolf dropped a kiss on her throat.

The second bag spilled rubies into her hand like fire, but as she lifted up the strand, it reminded her of the red ribbon in her dream. The third bag held a matching bracelet.

"They're beautiful," she said truthfully, but still put them away.

The fourth bag held a pearl necklace. She couldn't keep the dismay off her face.

"You don't like them?"

"I had a bad dream after the beast knocked me out. I was looking for something in a forest with this woman. She had a long red ribbon tied around her eyes and on the other end of it was a pearl necklace."

She'd wanted him to say, "It was just a dream," but instead he said, "Tell me all of your dream."

"Why?"

"Sometimes dreams are warnings. It is not wise to ignore them."

So she said, "It was just a dream." How could he rebuke her so easily with just his eyes? "I'm still me. I'm still mostly human—not elf. I would know by now if I had the ability to see the future."

"In elves it is carried by the female line; being that humans and elves can interbreed with fertile results, we must be very similar." He put away the pearl necklace. "It is the nature of magic to splinter things down to possibilities. Even humans without magic can see where the splintering will happen, and the possible outcomes. Humans call it an 'educated guess.' In the past, where magic would leak through natural gates from Elfhome to Earth, there were often temples with oracles predicting the future."

"So it doesn't matter if I'm mostly human or partly elf?"

"Tell me your dream." Windwolf ran the back of his hand lightly down her cheek.

So she described what she could remember. "Both women are someone I know but not really. Movie stars or something like that—I've only seen pictures of them."

"Both women wore blindfolds? The *intanyei seyosa* wears one when she's predicting. It helps block out things that would distract her from her visions, but also it is a badge of her office."

Tinker remembered then her one encounter with the queen's *intanyei seyosa*, Pure Radiance. The oracle had worn a white dress and red blindfold.

"So I'm dreaming that they're dreaming? That's very Escheresque."

Windwolf looked confused.

"Escher is a human artist that my grandfather liked; his pictures are all tricks of perspective."

"I see."

"Well, I don't. What does it mean?" She prodded the bags with a finger. "That you were going to give me jewelry? What is so dangerous about the necklaces?"

"Dreams are rarely straightforward. Most likely the necklaces represent something else."

"Like what?"

"I do not know, but it might be wise to find out."

3: NUTS AND BOLTS

Wolf spotted Wraith at the fringe of the Ghostlands when he flew back to Turtle Creek. He'd left his *domi* in the care of his household at Poppymeadow's enclave and returned to help deal with the beast that attacked her. He dropped down to land beside his First.

"I don't know what Storm Horse was thinking," Wraith growled in greeting. "How did he end up with all the babies?"

Little Horse had chosen the five youngest *sekasha* to make up the Hand that accompanied Tinker into Turtle Creek; not one of them was over three hundred. True, any death would have been grievous, but to lose the five youngest would have been a blow to the close-knit band of warriors.

"They are the ones my *domi* is most comfortable with." Wolf knew that Wraith was truly rattled if he was using the nickname, as some of the "babies" were in truth older than Wolf. His First Hand didn't like to remind him that he was impossibly young for his level of responsibilities.

"Oni, they could have handled," Wraith allowed and then handed a sheet of paper to Wolf. "But not an oni dragon. I'm amazed any of them are still alive."

Wolf recognized Rainlily's fluid hand in the drawing. The low-slung creature looked like a cross between a ferret and a snake. "An oni dragon? Are you sure?"

Wraith clicked his tongue. "It's much smaller than the one we fought when we closed the gate between Earth and Onihida, and the coloring is different. It might be just a less dangerous relative, like we have the wyvern cousins to our dragons, or perhaps a hatchling. It would explain how they survived."

The oni war had been shortly before Wolf was born. A Stone Clan trading expedition had discovered the way from Earth to Onihida by accident. When the survivors managed to return to Elfhome with their tale of capture and torture, the clans united to send a force to Earth to stop the oni spreading from Onihida to Earth, and then, possibly to Elfhome. Wraith Arrow and others of Wolf's First Hand had been part of the battle.

"Are oni dragons that dangerous?" Wolf folded the paper and tucked it away. He would have to let the Earth Interdimensional Agency know of this new threat if they couldn't kill the beast quickly. The EIA could best spread warnings through the humans.

"We lost two dozen *sekasha* in the caves to the beast. We couldn't hurt it. It could—" Wraith frowned as he searched for a word. "—*sidestep* through walls as if they didn't exist, and it called magic like you do."

"How did you kill it?"

"When the Stone Clan pulled down the gate and the connection between the worlds broke, its attack pattern totally changed. It dropped its shield and became like a mink in a chicken coop, stupid with bloodlust. We boxed it in so it couldn't turn and we hacked it to pieces."

"Maybe the oni were controlling it magically. Little Horse said that the tengu used a whistle to call it off them—perhaps the sound only triggered a controlling spell. Earth doesn't have magic."

"So their control over it vanished and we were fighting the true beast?"

Wolf nodded. "Perhaps."

"So the key is to kill the controller first."

"Perhaps." Wolf didn't want to fall into a wrong mind-set. He crouched beside the torn earth and spilt blood to find the monster's tracks. They were as long as his forearm, with five claw marks splayed like a hand. Pressed into the dirt at the center of one track was one of Tinker's omnipresent bolts, a bright point of polished aluminum glittering in the black earth. It must have fallen from her pocket during the fight. Wolf picked it out of the dirt, realizing for the first time the size of his beloved compared to what had attacked her. Gods above, sometimes he wished her sense of self-preservation matched her courage; she couldn't keep leaping into the void and swimming back. One of these times, the void was going to drink her down. He rolled the bolt around his palm to shake off the dirt, thinking he should talk to her about being more careful, only he didn't want to fall into the trap of becoming her teacher.

Wraith crouched beside Wolf, and stirred his fingers through the dirt. "*Domi* showed great courage in protecting Little Horse. She needs, though, someone who can steer her away from the dangers. Little Horse is lost at summer court."

From Wraith's tone, the *sekasha* also thought that Windwolf was too deep in the first throes of love to think clearly. Perhaps he was. "Are you volunteering?"

Wraith tilted his head. "Do you want me to?"

Wolf considered, tumbling the bolt through his fingers. Wraith was not the first to come forward in the last two days and let him know that they'd be willing to change allegiance to Tinker. He'd given them all permission to advance their case to Tinker since she needed at least four more sekasha to make a Hand. Wraith, though, was his First, and Wolf depended heavily on him. Without Sparrow, losing Wraith would cripple Wolf. "No. I need you. Others plan to offer, she will have plenty to choose from."

"Yes, but will they guide her?"

Do I want her guided? That was the true question. He'd benefited greatly by choosing *sekasha* who had served his grandfather, but they had brought subtle pressure to bear on him at all times. This conversation itself was a perfect example of their influence on him. Their persuasion extended out to the rest of the household, reinforcing the caste differences so that Wolf was always correctly above everyone. When the queen summoned Wolf to Aum Renau, he'd left Little Horse behind to guard over Tinker. The youngest of the *sekasha*, his blade brother had also been raised in a household where the caste lines had been allowed to blur. Little Horse would be open-minded, affectionate, and the least likely to try and change Tinker. Wolf had hated the necessity to make her elf in body—he didn't want to force her, even by subtle persuasion, to become elf in mind and habit.

No, I do not want her guided in the way that Wraith would.

He would speak with Tinker, but not point her toward the older *sekasha*. He would allow her and Little Horse to find those they were most comfortable with.

"On this, I will act." He let Wraith know that the conversation was closed, that he would not discuss it farther. He turned his attention back to the oni dragon.

The main fight area was a chaos of torn earth and blood. The *sekasha* might be able to read the course of events, but to him it was only churned earth. The bark of surrounding trees was gouged in the dragon's five-clawed pattern.

"It had *domi* pinned. Little Horse attempted to penetrate its shield." Wraith pointed at a spot on the ground, and at the nearest scored tree. "It leapt to that tree. Rainlily said that the tengu was on the bridge, so that tree there"—Wraith pointed to a distant tree with claw marks halfway up the towering trunk—"is the next set."

The leap meant the creature was stunningly powerful without magic.

"Let's see where the trail leads."

The railing of the bridge was scored deep by the dragon's claws. After that, however, the track became impossible to follow with the naked eye. The *sekasha* considered the bridge deck, scuffing it with their boots.

"Too much metal." Wraith voiced the *sekasha's* collective opinion.

Wolf nodded; he'd thought as much. Using magic to track was rarely possible in Pittsburgh with its omnipresent web of metal in the roads, the buildings, and the power lines overhead.

There was whistle from the rear guard, indicating the arrival of a friendly force. Still, the *a* around him went alert when a limo belonging to the EIA pulled to a stop at the far end of the bridge. The oni had infiltrated every level of the UN police force; they could no longer automatically assume the EIA was friendly.

With a cautiousness that made it clear that he understood his position, Director Derek Maynard got out of his limo and walked the rest of the distance to Wolf. Apparently Maynard had spent the morning dealing with humans, as he was in dressed in the dark solid suit that spoke of power among men. Wolf thought it might be the way they perceived color.

"Wolf Who Rules *ze Domou*." Over the years, Maynard had picked up much of the elfin body language. He projected politely constrained anger as he bowed elegantly.

"Director." Wolf used his title without his name to mildly rebuke him.

Maynard bowed his head slightly, acknowledging the censure. He paused for a minute, nostrils flared, before speaking. He looked worn and tired. Time wore Maynard down at an alarming rate; in twenty short years he had gone from a young man to middle-aged. Gazing at him, Wolf realized that in a few decades he'd lose his friend.

If I could have only made him an elf too. But no, that would have destroyed Maynard's value as a "human" representative.

"Windwolf." Maynard chose to continue in English, probably because it placed him in the less subservient role. "I wish you would have warned me about declaring the treaty void."

Wolf sighed, it was going to be one of those conversations. "You know the terms. Pittsburgh could exist as a separate entity only while it continued to return to Earth."

"You've said nothing in the last two days about voiding the treaty."

"And I haven't said anything about the sun setting, but it has and will."

"The sun setting does not cut me off at the knees."

Wolf glanced down at Maynard's legs, and confirmed that they were still intact. Ah, an English saying he hadn't heard before. "Derek, pretend I don't understand human politics."

"The treaty is between the humans and the elves." Maynard followed the human tendency to talk slowly and in short sentences in the face of confusion. It made the time to enlightenment agonizingly long, even for an elf. "But the treaty is the basis for many agreements between the United States and the United Nations. It makes Pittsburgh neutral territory controlled by a UN peacekeeper force—the EIA—for the duration of the treaty."

"Ah, with the treaty void, Pittsburgh reverts to control of the United States."

"Yes!"

"No."

"No?" Maynard looked confused.

"Pittsburgh now belongs to the Wind Clan, and I decide who will be my representative with the humans and I choose you."

Maynard took a deep breath as he pressed his palms together, prayerlike, in front of his mouth. He breathed out, took another breath. Windwolf was starting to wonder if he was praying. "Wolf, I thank you for your trust in me," Maynard said finally. "But for me to continue acting as director of the EIA, it would require me to disregard all human laws—and I cannot do that."

"There are no human laws anymore. Humans must obey elfin laws now."

"That's not acceptable. I know you're the viceroy, and as such Pittsburgh falls under your control, but the humans of Pittsburgh will not accept you unilaterally abolishing all human laws and rights."

"These were conditions agreed to by your own people."

"Well, shortsighted as it might have been, it was assumed that if something happened to the gate that Pittsburgh would return to Earth."

"Yes, it was." Wolf did not point out that humans were typically shortsighted, rarely looking past the next hundred years. "But we knew that sooner or later we would have to deal with humans wanting to or needing to remain on Elfhome."

"Yes, of course," Maynard said dryly. He gazed down at the blue paleness of the Ghostlands. "Is your *domi* sure that we're truly stranded? We're still a week before scheduled Shutdown."

"Something fell from orbit. She believes it to be the gate."

"But she could be wrong."

"It's unlikely."

"Let us say that we wait a week to be sure before calling the treaty null and void."

"A week will not make any difference."

"Ah, then it will be no problem." Maynard spread his hands and smiled as if Wolf had agreed.

In that moment, Wolf could see the tactfully charming young officer he had hand-selected out of the UN security force to act as the liaison between human and elf. Maynard had been so young back then. Wolf smiled sadly. "And if I agree to a week?"

"During this week, we draw up an interim treaty that basically extends the original treaty."

"No." Windwolf shook his head. "We could create an interim treaty but the original treaty can not stand. It makes humans too autonomous."

"Pittsburgh has existed as an independent state for thirty years."

"No, not Pittsburgh, humans. All elves belong to a household and to a clan. They hold a very specific position within our society. They are responsible to others, and others are responsible for them. It's the very foundation of our culture, and if humans are to be part of our world, then they must conform to our ways."

"You mean—you want humans to form households? Set up enclaves?"

"Yes. It's imperative. All of our laws are structured on the assumption that the people under our laws are part of our society. You can't be as independent as most humans are and still be part of us."

They searched late into the evening but found nothing more of the dragon. Storm clouds had gathered throughout the day, and as dusk became night, it started to rain. Unable to track the dragon farther, Wolf and his *sekasha* returned to the enclave. He checked first to see how his *domi* was doing. Tinker lay in the center of their shared bed, a dark curl of walnut on the cream satin sheets. Wolf paused beside the footboard to watch his beloved sleep. Despite everything, he found great comfort in seeing her back where she belonged, safe among the people who loved her.

A *saijin* flower sat on the night table, scenting the warm air with its narcotic fragrance. Little Horse slept in a chair beside the bed. The hospice healers had stripped off his wyvern armor; fresh bruises and healing spells overlaid the pale circles of bullet holes from two days ago.

I almost lost them both to the oni, Wolf thought and touched his blade brother's shoulder. "Little Horse."

The *sekasha* opened his eyes after a minute, rousing slowly. "Brother Wolf. I only meant to sit down for a moment." He looked drowsily to the flower beside him. "The *saijin* must have put me asleep."

The narcotic was starting to color Wolf's senses with a golden haze, so he opened the balcony doors to let in rain-damp air.

"Are you well?" Wolf took the other chair, waiting for Little Horse to wake up from his drugged sleep, wondering if he'd made a mistake pairing his blade brother with Tinker. They were both so young to go through so much.

"I'm bruised, that is all." Little Horse rubbed at his eyes. "My shields protected me."

"Good."

"I was thinking about the oni leader, Lord Tomtom, before I drifted off. He checked on our progress either at noon or at midnight. Some days he would make two inspections. It occurred to me that he was rotating between compounds, overseeing two or three of them."

"So the number of oni warriors in the area might be much greater than the sixty you counted?"

Little Horse nodded. "From what I observed, though, the warriors are like sea wargs." His blade brother named a mammal that gathered in colonies on the coast; the male animals fought to gather harems of females, and any cub left unprotected was usually killed and eaten by its own kind. "Command goes to the largest of the group and he rules by cruelty and fear. They fight among themselves, but I saw no weapon practice or drills. I believe that not one of their warriors would be a match for a *sekasha*."

"That is good to know." It backed what Maynard had told him at one point. Warned by Tinker, Maynard had begun to secretly sift through his people two months earlier. Using Tinker's description of "cruel and ruthless people with no sense of honor" he found the hidden oni fairly simple to find. So far intensive magical testing had proved his guesses correct.

Little Horse glanced toward the bed and a smile stole onto his face, making him seem younger still. "Despite their large size and savageness, she terrorized them."

Wolf laughed. Little Horse yawned widely, so Wolf stood up and pulled his blade brother to his feet. "Go to bed. The others can keep watch."

"Yes, Brother Wolf." Little Horse hugged him. It was good, Wolf decided, that he paired Tinker with his blade brother. They would protect each other's open and affectionate natures from the stoic older *sekasha*.

After steering Little Horse to his room, Wolf detoured to check on Singing Storm. He expected to find her sleeping when he cracked her door. She turned her head, though, and slit open her eyes. A smile took control of her face. Still she greeted him with a semiformal, "Wolf Who Rules."

He lowered the formality between them. It was her ability to see him as nothing more than a male that made him love her so. "How is my Discord?"

Her smile deepened. "Good and just got better."

"I'm glad." He leaned down and kissed her. She murmured her enjoyment, running her hands up his chest to tangle in his hair. She tasted candy sweet from her favorite gum.

"I've missed you," she whispered into his ear. She meant intimately, like this, because she had guarded over him every day for the last two months. Taking Tinker to be his *domi*, however, had meant an abrupt change in their relationship. They hadn't even had a chance to discuss it afterward.

"I'm sorry."

She nipped him on the earlobe in rebuke. "No matter who, if they were the right one, you would have wanted this."

"It was graceless." He had given her only a few hours warning of his intention to offer for Tinker. She knew him well enough to know that he would want a monogamous relationship as long as Tinker was willing to give him one.

"When did we start to care about grace? Wasn't that the whole point of leaving court, all the false elegance? I like that we're honest with one another—and I like her—which is not surprising since I like humans."

"She's an elf now," Wolf gently reminded her.

"In the body, but not in the mind. She speaks Low Elvish as if she was born to it, yes, but she doesn't know our ways, Wolf. If you don't have time to teach her, then get her a tutor."

Wolf found himself shaking his head. "No. I don't want a stranger trying to force her into court elegance."

"Are you afraid that she will lose all that makes her endearing to you?"

Only Discord would dare to say that to him—but then—that was another reason he loved her. She would risk annoying him to make him face what needed to be faced. For her, he sighed and considered the possibility.

"No," he said after thinking it through. "Yes, I love her humanity and I'll mourn it if she loses it completely, but she is so much more than that."

"Then have someone teach her. She nearly got us all killed today because she couldn't bear to sacrifice me."

He knew better than to argue with Discord on that but was pleased with Tinker's decision. It was Tinker's courage and ability to pull off the impossible that had initially attracted him to her, and he would have been deeply saddened to lose Singing Storm. "I'm trying to find a solution to this. I know she needs to be taught our customs, but I don't want her to necessarily conform."

"I never said anything about conforming." Discord nuzzled into his neck. "Conforming is for chickens."

He laughed into her short blue hair. "That's my Discord." He kissed her and drew away to consider her. From her hair to her boots, Discord challenged everything elfin. Yet of all his *sekasha*, she was the only one that had grown up at court and had high etiquette literally beaten into her. There was no one more knowledgeable, yet less likely, to force those skills on Tinker.

"What is it that you want of me?" she asked.

"You know me too well." He tugged on her rattail braid. "I want you to keep close to my *domi* and be there when she needs guidance."

"Pony is her First." Discord switched to English, a sign that she wanted to be bluntly truthful. "I'll be stomping all over his toes. I don't want to piss him off. He's one of the few that never said shit to me about being a mutt."

"Pony is not the type to put pride before duty. He loves Tinker, but he knows that he doesn't fully understand her. He hasn't spent enough time in Pittsburgh, away from our people . . ."

"Like me?" It was a point of sadness between them. For decades they had ignored all the little signs that they could not be more than *domou* and beholden. The fact that she would choose Pittsburgh over being with him had made clear that while they were good together, they were not right.

"Like you." Wolf took her hand, kissed it, and moved on. "Humans are still mysterious to him."

She thought for a moment and then returned to Elvish. "As long as it does not anger Storm Horse, I will be there for her."

4: ON GOSSAMER DEATH

The next morning, shortly after dawn, the oni made their first attack. Wolf heard a muffled roar and then the loud anguished wail of a wounded gossamer. Luckily, his people were already awake and ready. Only Tinker, having been drugged the night before, still slept.

"Have Poppymeadow lock down the enclave," Wolf told Little Horse. "I'm leaving you just with her guards and Singing Storm. Everyone else with me."

Wolf arrived at the airfield, though too late to scry the direction of the attack. All he could do was watch the gossamer die in the pale morning light. The great living airship wallowed on the ground, its translucent body undulating in pain. The remains of the gondola lay under it, crushed by the massive heaving body. The clear blood of the gossamer pooled on the ground, scenting the air with the ghost of ancient seas.

"We can't get close enough to heal the wound." The gossamer's navigator was weeping openly. "Even if we could, I doubt we could save her. It's a massive wound, and she's lost too much fluid. My poor baby."

The gossamer let out a long low breathy wail of pain.

"Did you see where it came from?" Wolf wasn't sure what "it" was because none of the crew had seen the attack clearly.

The navigator shook his head. "I felt it hit before I heard anything. She shuddered, and then started to go down, and I jumped clear."

"Here comes another one!" Wraith shouted as he pointed at some type of rocket flashing toward them.

Wolf flung up his widest shield, protecting the crew and *sekasha* surrounding him. "Stay close!"

The rocket struck his wind wall and exploded into a fireball that curved around them, following the edges of his shield. The deflected energy splashed back in a wave of pulverized earth, like a stone thrown into mud.

A piece of metal skimmed overhead and struck the gossamer. The shrapnel smashed the gossamer sideways, blasting through the nerve center of the creature. The airship gave one last agonizing wail and collapsed.

Wolf shifted carefully to maintain his shield and did a wind scry. The scrying followed the disturbance of the rocket path through the air, making it visible to him. It pointed back to a window a few houses down from the paparazzi's spy perch. The Rim had razed all the buildings between the airfield and the street at the first Startup, so he had an equally clear shot back at the sniper.

Wolf summoned a force strike and flung it along the scry. The power arrowed away, plowing a furrow in a straight line to the human structure. The force strike punched its way through the building, reducing the structure instantly to a cloud of dust and a pile of rubble strewn into the alley behind it.

"Have someone escort the crew to safety," Wolf told his First. "The rest, come with me."

Maintaining his shield forced him to move slowly toward the human buildings, following the rut carved out by the force strike. The dust expanded, shrouding the area as he crossed the no-man's-land of the Rim.

"Keep the winds close," Wraith murmured as they reached the street. "There may be more than one nest."

Wolf nodded his understanding. The *sekasha* activated their shields and moved out of his protection. The house had been two stories tall. It made a large hill of rubble, capped by the broken rooftop. If there were any survivors, they'd have to be dug out.

Maynard emerged out of the dust, followed by a score or more of his people in EIA uniforms. All of the EIA were spell-marked, verifying that they were human.

"Wolf Who Rules." Maynard bowed and signaled his people toward the rubble.

"Maynard." Wolf nudged his shield slightly so it wrapped Maynard in his protection.

"What happened?" Maynard eyed the rubble as his people started to sift through it.

Wolf indicated the dead airship with his eyes; maintaining his shields limited his ability to motion with his hands. "Someone fired on what is mine. I returned fire."

Maynard glanced at the distortion around them. "How long can you keep up your shields?"

"There is no reason for concern." The Wind Clan's spell stones rested on a powerful *fiutana* that provided unlimited magic. "My gossamer is dead, but my crew is safe. For that I am thankful."

A call came from the EIA digging through the rubble. Most of the roof had been shifted off. In the debris of the second floor was a female huddled under a sturdy table. She appeared human, as small and dark as Wolf's *domi*. Old bruises, like purple and yellow flowers, marked her face and arms; someone beat her on regular occasions.

She gazed at Wolf with fear. "Don't let them have me! We're like cockroaches to them! Razing this neighborhood is just the start of them stomping us out!"

The human workers moved reluctantly aside to let the *sekasha* claim her. Wraith took out his leatherbound spell case, slipped out a *biatau,* and pressed it to the female's arm.

She whimpered and one of the watching EIA said, "It doesn't hurt. We've all had it done to us."

The simple spell inscribed onto the paper of the *biatau* was merely the first of the spells that the EIA had been subjected to, but it was the quickest and easiest to use as a first screening process. The oni had relied on an optical disguise spell that let them appear human; the *biatau*, when activated, would shatter the illusion and allow their true form to show.

Wraith spoke the verbal command and the spell activated. There was, however, no change to the woman's appearance.

Maynard sighed deeply, as if he saw all the dangerous complications that the woman presented. "She's human."

"Unfortunately." Wolf motioned that the EIA should take her prisoner.

"Here's another one," Bladebite called.

The second person was a large male, badly hurt. Wraith took out another *biatau* with the same spell and used it on the male. There was a ripple of distortion and the male's features shifted slightly to a more feral looking face with short horns protruding from his forehead.

"Oni." Wraith growled out the word.

"He's badly hurt," Maynard said. "The prison has a medical ward. We can take him there."

Wraith jerked the oni up onto his knees.

"Wolf," Maynard said quickly and quietly. "We have protocols on how prisoners are to be treated. The Geneva Convention states that the wounded and sick shall be collected and cared for."

"We do not accede," Wolf said, "to your Geneva Convention."

In one clean motion, Wraith unsheathed his sword and beheaded the oni.

The woman shrieked and tried to launch herself toward the dead body.

"Wolf, you can't do this!" Maynard growled.

"It has been done," Wolf said.

Maynard shook his head. "The treaty, which the elves signed, states that you will adhere to the Geneva Convention in the treatment of prisoners."

"For human prisoners," Wolf said. "We will not take oni prisoners."

Maynard frowned. "That is the only option you're entertaining? A massacre of all the oni?"

"They breed like mice," Wolf said. "We do not fight for today, or this year, or even this century, but for this millennium—and to do so, we must be ruthless. If we leave a hundred alive, in a few years they will be several thousand in number, and in a thousand years, millions. We can not allow them to live, or they will crowd us out of our own home."

"You can't let the elves do this!" the woman wailed. "If we don't stop the elves, they'll turn on us next."

"It's their world." Maynard leveled his gaze and words at his watching men, aiming his words at them alone. "Not ours."

"It was their world!" the woman shouted. "We're stuck here now, so it's ours too."

There was a flaw in Maynard's logic. The old arguments that Maynard could have used to counter her were useless now. Her railing, unfortunately, could lead the humans to dangerous ground, so Wolf interceded.

"We are willing to share with humans. We do not wish to share with oni. A full contingent of royal troops is on its way to Pittsburgh. When they arrive here, their goal will be to find and kill every oni that ever set foot on Elfhome. My people have committed genocide before and have full plans to do it again. I strongly caution you not to put the human race between the royal troops and our enemy."

Whatever impact his words had, however, were lost when the woman suddenly looked past Wolf and shrieked. Wolf turned to see what she was focused on. One of the EIA workers had a small squirming creature in his arms. As the man neared, Wolf realized that the creature was a child, species so far undetermined, but human looking, perhaps four years old.

Wolf sighed. He had hoped it wouldn't come to this; that he would only have to deal with adult oni. Certainly among all of the elves, there were no children. In fact, he was fairly sure that—not counting his *domi*'s unusual status—Little Horse was the youngest elf in Pittsburgh. Unfortunately, when one could breed like mice, one did.

The name tag of the EIA worker holding the child read "U. D. Akavia."

"The child needs to be tested, Akavia," Wolf said.

Akavia's brown eyes went wide; he hadn't considered that the child was anything but what it appeared to be.

"No!" the woman sympathizer cried. "Don't give those monsters my baby!"

Akavia glanced to the woman and then down at the child whimpering in his arms. "She's just a little girl."

"We need to know if she is human or oni." Wolf tried to pose the statement in a nonthreatening way.

"She can't hurt anyone." Akavia covered the girl's small head with a protective hand. His eyes went past Wolf to the *sekasha* behind him.

Of course the human saw only the child, not the female that would be an adult in a decade, nor the army she could produce in the years to come. In truth, even to Wolf, she looked small and helpless.

"Let us test her," Wolf said. "If she is human, we will give her back."

Akavia's eyes narrowed in suspicion. "And if she's oni?"

Yes, Wolf thought as he scanned the hostile faces of the heavily armed EIA force that outnumbered his *sekasha*, that would be a problem.

He sensed the tension going through his *sekasha*, who were growing impatient. He had no doubt that his people would walk unscathed away from a fight with the EIA, but the EIA might not understand this, and he needed all the allies he could muster.

Maynard moved between Wolf and Akavia. Maynard's face set into hard lines, as if bracing himself for a fight. With Wolf or with his own people? "Let us test her."

He left unsaid: *Let us at least find out if we have cause to fight.* Wolf nodded. "That is acceptable."

"Uri David." Maynard motioned to Akavia. Wolf shifted his shields to include the EIA subordinate so Maynard could take the girl into his arms.

"Wraith." Wolf indicated that the *sekasha* was to hand Akavia the *biatau*.

Akavia placed the spell against the child's bruised and dusty arm. When the spell activated, there was no change to the girl's appearance. Relief went through the EIA.

"It proves nothing," Wraith growled. "It's probably mixed blood. The female has all but admitted that she's coupled with the monster."

Maynard's gaze skipped to Wraith and then came back to Wolf. *Please*, his eyes implored, *let her go.*

Wolf studied the child. She gazed at him with eyes as brown and innocent as his *domi*'s. He didn't want to kill this child. Wolf steeled himself and forced himself to remember that an oni wouldn't waver in killing an elfin child or a human child. His people counted on him to do the right thing, no matter how difficult the right thing might be.

How could he winnow the monster from the human?

"Little one, what's your name?" Wolf asked the girl.

"Zi." The girl pointed to the woman. "Mommy's sad."

"Yes, she is. So am I." Wolf let his face show his inner sorrow.

Zi considered him gravely, and then leaned out to pat him gently on the cheek. "Don't be sad. Everything will be a-okay."

Wolf threw out his hand to keep the *sekasha* from reacting. "She has compassion; oni don't have that capacity."

Wraith slowly took his hand from his sword hilt. "So human empathy is a dominant trait?"

"So it seems." Wolf gave the girl a slight smile. "Yes, Zi, everything will be A-okay."

5: TREE THAT WALKS

The dying echoes of thunder pulled Tinker out of the dark sludge of drugged sleep. She opened her eyes to see shadows moving across an unfamiliar ceiling.

Where am I?

For one panicked moment, she thought she was back in the oni compound with the kitsune projecting illusions into her mind. She fought her sheets to sit up, heart pounding, to scan the luxurious bedroom. *Saijin*-induced sleep still clung to her like thick mud, making it hard to think. It took Tinker a minute of comparing all the various places she had slept in the last two months to finally recognize the room. It was the bedroom she and Windwolf had shared a month ago at Poppymeadow's enclave. She remembered now the massive four-poster bed, the carved paneling, and the view to the courtyard orchard. The window stood open to a warm summer morning, letting in air sweet with ripening peaches. Dappled sunlight played across the walls and ceiling. Tinker flopped back into the decadent nest of satin sheets and down pillows, tempted to go back to sleep.

But if she did, she'd probably have another nightmare.

Her groan summoned Pony from his attached bedroom.

"Good morning, *domi*."

Eyes still closed, she grunted at him. "It's not fair to expect me to be polite before I'm fully awake. Where's Windwolf? Did he get back safely last night?"

"He was needed at the Faire Grounds this morning. He took everyone except Stormsong with him."

"How is Stormsong?"

"Her leg bothers her slightly, but she is whole. She is practicing in the swordhall."

That was good news.

Tinker heaved herself back up and rubbed a heavy crust of sleep from her eyes. "Gods, I hate *saijin*. It turns my brain to taffy. What's that for?"

That being one of the *sekasha*'s pistols. While the gun itself was of human make, the black tooled leather holster and belt were elfin. Pony laid it on the bed, a coil of dangerous black on the sea of cream.

"Wolf Who Rules wished you to have it."

Oh, yeah, I asked for a gun.

"It is specially made for the *sekasha*." Pony settled on the bed beside her. "Only parts of it are metal, and those are insulated with plastic, so they don't interfere with our shields. Once you learn magic, it will be important that you don't wear metal."

There was an elaborate system of wood buckles, D-rings, and ties to support the weight of the pistol on the hip without metal. In place of a metal snap, the belt maker had used a heavy plastic substitute.

"Is it loaded?"

"Not yet. I thought you would like to get comfortable with it first."

So they played with the gun. Taking it apart. Putting it together. Strapping on the holster (although it had a tendency to slide on her long silky nightgown). Drawing the pistol smoothly. Holding it with both hands to keep it steady. Aiming it. And finally, loading and unloading it.

"Wolf Who Rules wants you to start the basics of the sword fighting," Pony said. "It would be unwise for you to wear a sword until you are able to use it. Guns are simple. Point and pull the trigger."

"I'm fine with that." She had no interest in swords. They relied too much on brute force. At five foot nothing, it didn't matter how smart she was, she wasn't going to win a sword fight with an elf. "Okay. I think I'm ready to face the day."

"In that?" Pony indicated her current nightgown and holster outfit.

"I thought I'd start a new fashion statement." Nevertheless, she started to look for the clothes she'd had on the day before. She was going to have to do something about clothes. After being kidnapped twice, she was left with only one T-shirt and one pair of shorts. Everything else in her closet was elfin gowns.

Pony guessed what she was looking for. "They took your clothes to be cleaned."

"Oh no." She went to the window and looked out. Beyond the orchard wall was the kitchen garden and the clothes lines. Windwolf's household staff was hanging up the laundry. Her jeans dangled between several pairs of longer legged pants. Her T-shirt? Oh yes, that had been cut to ribbons by the dragon. "Oh pooh."

Well, she could wear a dress and just go clothes shopping. Of course she didn't have any cash in hand, nor did she ever receive the promised replacements for the ID that the oni stole the night she saved Windwolf's life. It could be sitting in her mailbox back at her loft—if the EIA had been so stupid as to mail it out after she was kidnapped by the oni. Oh gods, what if she'd been declared legally dead after the oni "staged" her death?

She did have Windwolf's entire household at hand. Surely one of the elves was savvy enough to go to the store and buy her clothes. She considered the elves in the garden washing clothes—by hand—in large wooden tubs. Okay, she had clothes at her loft.

Was it a good thing or a bad thing that she was now fashion aware enough to know that those clothes were too scruffy?

Tinker sighed. "I really don't want to run around Turtle Creek in a dress."

"*Domi*, I would rather wait until we could gather a Hand. It would not be wise for us to go alone."

Tinker wasn't getting the hang of the elfin "we" despite having had Pony at her side every moment for nearly two months. She was thinking of just trotting over by herself and seeing how much the Ghostlands had shrunk. Well, she supposed that could wait.

She used her walk-in closet as a dressing room, stripping out of the gun belt and her nightgown. She considered her informal gowns, called day dresses. She had bullied the staff into taking off the long sleeves, but the dresses still had bodices that accented her chest, tight waists, and flowing skirts. Her choices were sable brown, forest green, or jewel red, all in gleaming fairy silk that clung to her like wet paint. The red one, at least, had pockets and a shorter skirt. She had to admit that she looked fairly kicky with her new gun belt riding low on her hip. She added her polished black riding boots and the ruby jewelry that Windwolf had given her. She practiced drawing her pistol and pointed it at the mirror. "You looking at me? Uh? You looking at me?"

"No, *domi*, I cannot see you," Pony said from the other side of the closet door.

She laughed, holstering the pistol. "Did Windwolf find the monster that attacked me and kill it?"

"No."

"Okay." She came out of the closet. "Since we can't do anything about Turtle Creek, let's focus on the monster."

"*Domi*, I do not think we should go after the dragon alone."

"Dragon?"

"It was an oni dragon and very difficult to kill."

"Well, yeah, which is why I should figure out how to kill it. The oni probably have more than one. There has to be a way to take down its shields so anyone with a gun can kill it."

Pony looked at her nervously, as if he suspected she was going to hunt down the oni dragon and poke it with sticks.

Tinker felt the need to reassure him that she didn't have anything that radical in mind. "I want to start with Lain; she's a xenobiologist. When you've got a problem outside your field of specialty, you go to an expert."

A flatbed semi trailer sat parked in front of Lain's stately Victorian mansion. A yellow canvas tarp covered something lumpy. The xenobiologist stood on the trailer, leaning on her crutch, watching Tinker park the Rolls. Something about Lain's face made Tinker suspect that somehow the trailer was her fault.

"I thought you might turn up today," Lain said.

"Well, apparently I need a small army to go back to Turtle Creek, and Windwolf has all the *sekasha* today except Pony and Stormsong."

Said *sekasha* had already split up into Blade and Shield. Stormsong had moved off to scout the area as a Blade. Pony trailed behind Tinker, acting as Shield.

"So, I thought I'd come talk to you about the monster that attacked me yesterday," Tinker said. "The *sekasha* are saying it's an oni dragon."

"Ah." Lain made a sound of understanding. "I suppose I should thank you for your present."

"Present?" Tinker eyed the trailer apprehensively. What had she done now without realizing it?

Lain flipped up one corner of tarp to reveal limp willowy branches. "They told me that you sent it."

The black willow! "*He eats the fruit of the tree that walks.*" Tinker shivered as recognition crawled down her spine. It was just too weird having another part of her dream show up with her name attached to it. "I sent it?"

"That's what they told me," Lain said.

Tinker could remember finding the tree, but she—she didn't order this. Or had she? She turned to Pony. "Did I ask . . . ?" His look of concentration made her realize that she had been so rattled that she was still speaking English; she switched Elvish. "Did I ask to have the black willow brought here?"

"You said you would love to give it to Lain."

That apparently that had been enough of an order for Pony. Tinker really had to keep in mind that the *sekasha* took her word as law. While she had been smothered in attention, the elves had bound up the long limp branches and sturdy trunk-feet and hauled it to the Observatory. Once at Lain's, however, they'd abandoned it—trailer and all.

Lain had warned her once about elves bearing gifts. Tinker winced, realizing that she had become one of said elves.

"I'm sorry, Lain." She made sure she was speaking English, afraid that she might insult Pony for her own stupidity. "I didn't know they were going to bring it here and dump it on you."

"It's a matter of gift horses and teeth, I suppose." Laying her crutch down, Lain nimbly swung down off the trailer, her upper body muscles cording to make up for her weakened legs. On the ground, Lain reached up for her crutch, and then turned to rap Tinker smartly on the head with her knuckles. "Learn to think before you open that mouth of yours."

"Ow!" Tinker winced. "I'm bruised there."

"You are?" Lain tilted Tinker's head to examine her scalp, combing aside her short hair with gentle fingertips. "What from? That creature that attacked you?"

"Yeah."

Lain smelt as always of fresh earth and crushed herbs and greens. "Ah, you'll live." She rubbed the sore area lightly. "Give the nerve receptors something else to think about."

Tinker mewed out a noise of protest and pain at the treatment.

Lain held her at arm's length then and looked down over Tinker, shaking her head. "I never thought I'd see you in a dress. That's a beautiful color for you."

Tinker showed off her rubies and her pistol, making Lain laugh at the contrast. "Do you want the tree?"

"A fully intact specimen? Of course!" Lain let her quiet scientific glee with the black willow show. "I saw my first black willow my first Startup; they flew me in on an Air Force jet to look at the forest where Pittsburgh had been the night before. I didn't want to come; I was still wrapped up in being crippled. Then I saw that wall of green, all those ironwoods as tall as sequoias. Out of the forest came a black willow, probably seeking a ley line, and the ground shook when it moved. God, it was instant nirvana—an alien world coming to me when I could no longer go to it."

A hot heady mix of delight and embarrassment flushed through Tinker; she wanted to hear more about how thoughtful she been, yet she knew how little she had actually contributed toward getting the tree moved. "I thought you might like it."

"I love it! But not necessarily here." Lain motioned toward her house. "I'm not totally convinced that the willow is dead. It might be just dormant after a massive system shock. I'd rather not have it reviving on my doorstep."

The tree that walks . . . "Yeah, that might be a bad idea. I can get a truck and move the trailer . . . someplace."

"What would be best is storing it at near freezing temperatures. The cold will keep it dormant if it's still alive."

Tinker eyed the fifty-three-foot semi trailer. "Well, getting it off the trailer wouldn't be hard—I can get a crane to do that—but shoving it into something refrigerated—that's going to be hard."

"I have faith." Lain limped toward her house, calling back. "I know you'll be able to figure it out."

Ah, the disadvantages of being well-known.

Stormsong was on the porch. She flashed through an "all clear" signal and indicated that she hadn't been inside the house.

"Let us clear the house first, *domi,*" Pony said.

She wanted to whine, "It's just Lain's house." The *sekasha* had risked death for her, though, so she only sighed and sat down on the porch swing. "Can I have the willow cut up?"

"No," Lain said.

"I didn't think so. That would make life too simple." Tinker swung back and forth, the wind blowing up her skirt in a cooling breeze. "It would be easiest if we could keep the tree on the trailer and put it all into one large refrigerator. I could build one, but not quickly. Is there a large freezer unit that we can borrow?"

"There's Reinholds," Lain said.

"The ice cream factory?"

"I doubt they're using all their warehouses."

"That's true." The hundred-year-old company was one of the many Pittsburgh businesses that had survived being transplanted to another universe. Elves loved ice cream. Being stranded on Elfhome, however, limited Reinhold's production. Things such as sugar and chocolate all needed to be shipped in from Earth.

Pony reappeared at the door, and indicated with a nod and hand sign that the house was clean of menace. The *sekasha* took up guard at the doors, giving Tinker the privacy she was beginning to treasure so much.

It had been two months since Tinker had last been in Lain's house, the longest time in her life between visits. It was comforting to find it unchanged—large high-ceilinged rooms full of leather furniture, stained wood, leaded glass, and shadows.

Lain made a call to Reinholds to check on their freezer capacity. Apparently Reinholds shuffled her through various departments, as she repeated herself between long pauses. Tinker raided her fridge for breakfast. There were strawberries and fresh whipped cream, so Lain wasn't kidding when she had said that she'd expected Tinker to arrive.

The call ended with Lain hanging up with a sigh. "They have one large unit that has been shut down for some time. They're still trying to find someone that knows something about it; they'll call me back." She picked up the teakettle and limped to the sink to fill it. "You cut your hair again."

"Yeah, I cut it." It annoyed Tinker that her voice suddenly shook. When she had taken a razor to her hair, her oni guard had mistaken it for a suicide attempt; the following struggle came close to getting Pony killed. Immediately afterward, she had gone back to dipping circuit plates—it was stupid that tears now burned her eyes. She concentrated on stabbing a strawberry in the whipping cream.

"I know you hate it when people pry," Lain said quietly. "God knows, between myself, your grandfather, and that crazy half-elf Tooloo as role-models, it's no wonder you insist on keeping everyone at arm's length."

Tinker could guess where this was going. "I'm fine!"

Lain busied herself with teacups, the faint ring of china on china filling the silence between them. The teakettle started to rattle with a prewhistle boil. "God, I wish children came with instruction manuals. I only want to do what's best for you—but I don't know what that is. I never have."

"I'm fine." Tinker actually managed to keep her voice level this time.

The teakettle peeped, a final warning before a full scream. Lain turned off the fire and stood there a moment, watching the steam pour out of the shimmering pot. Taking a deep cleansing breath, she sighed it out and asked, "Lemon Lift or Constant Comment?"

"The Lemon Lift," Tinker said.

"The EIA made Turtle Creek off-limits when the fighting broke out." Lain moved the teacups carefully to the table, and changed the subject with equal deftness. "No one has been able to get down to look at these Ghostlands. What did you find?"

Tea was only a medium to transport honey, so while Tinker

coaxed it to maximum viscosity, she told Lain about what she found.

"Can you fix it?" Lain asked.

"I'm a genius—not a god. I don't even know what *it* is. But by the laws of thermodynamics, it should collapse. I had Pony score the trees around the edge. Once I can go back into the valley, I'll check on the rate at which it's decaying."

Tinker sipped her tea and then changed the subject. "What I really came here to talk to you about is the monster that attacked me. It's an oni dragon."

"There were warnings on the television last night and the radio this morning. Yet another beastie for us to worry about."

Tinker knew that she shouldn't feel responsible—but she did anyhow. She had made the Discontinuity that the dragon had passed through to get to Pittsburgh. "The dragon generates a magical shield that protects it. According to Pony and Stormsong, Windwolf's First Hand fought one of these things *nae hae*."

The elf phrase, meaning "too many years to count," dropped out of Tinker's mouth like she had been born to the concept of living forever. She found it a little disturbing. "Apparently the shield also protects it from magical weapons like spell arrows. They think Windwolf will be able to kill it—but he can't be everywhere at once. We need a more mundane way of dealing with the beastie."

"Do you know if it's a natural creature or a bioengineered one?" Lain took out her datapad and opened a new file to take notes.

"No. The oni didn't mention anything to me about the dragon, and the *sekasha* don't know. What's the difference?"

"The result of creatures evolving in an environment full of magic is they often can use magic to their own benefit. Take the black willow; it's mutated from a tree with all the standard limitations to a highly effective mobile predator. By and large, though, the bioengineered creatures tend to be more dangerous than the randomly mutated creatures."

"Like the wargs?" Tinker knew that the wolflike creatures had been created for war but now ranged wild in the forest surrounding Pittsburgh.

"Yes. The wargs not only have the frost breath, but they show no signs of aging or disease and their wounds heal at a speed that suggests a spell somehow encoded at the cellular level. They're massive, intelligent, and aggressive in nature."

"So the question is, how much did the oni dragons get in their DNA gift baskets?"

"Yes. But let's start with the basics. We've never encountered an Elfhome dragon—we only know that they exist because the elves keep telling us that they do, and that we really don't want to study them closely."

Tinker laughed at that comment.

"Is this dragon mammal or reptile?" Lain asked.

"I'm not sure. It had scales, but it also had some sort of weird mane. It was long, and lean, with a big square jaw." Tinker put her hands up to approximate the size of the head. "Short legs with big claws that it could pick things up with."

Lain got up to put the teakettle back on the stove. "Beware the Jabberwock, my son! The jaws that bite, the claws that catch!"

It took Tinker a moment to identify the quote, a poem out of *Alice Through the Looking Glass.*

"*We fell down the hole and through the looking glass.*"

The sudden connection with her dream was like a slap. White's face jolted into her mind again. With the addition of the book title, though, she remembered where she had seen White before.

"You know, I had the oddest dream about Boo-boo Knees."

Lain whipped around to face her. "Boo?"

"At least, I think it was Boo-boo."

"H-h-how do you know about Boo's nickname?"

"The picture. It has her name on the back of it."

"Which picture?"

"The one in the book." When Lain continued to stare at her in confusion, Tinker went to scan the bookcases until she found the book in question: *The Annotated Alice.* Complete in one book were both *Alice in Wonderland* and *Alice Through the Looking Glass and What She Found There,* with copious footnotes that explained layers upon layers of meaning in what seemed to be just a odd little children's story. Tinker had discovered the book when she was eight. Lain apparently had forgotten the photo tucked into the book, but Tinker hadn't.

It was an old two-dimensional color photo of a young woman with short purple hair. She hovered in midair, the Earth a brilliant blue moon behind her. She challenged the camera with a level brown-eyed gaze and a set jaw, as if she were annoyed with its presence. On her right temple was a sterile adhesive bandage. Written on the back was "Even in zero gravity, I find things to bang myself on. Love, Boo-boo Knees."

At the point Tinker had found it, she'd never seen a two-dimensional photograph; neither her grandfather or Lain were ones for personal pictures. From its limited perspective to the name of Boo-boo Knees, she'd found it fascinating. She stared at it until—ten years later—she could have drawn it from memory.

The picture was where she had carefully returned it, marking the place where one story ended and another started.

"Oh!" Lain took the photo. "I'd forgotten about that."

"Who is she?" *Why am I dreaming about her?* Tinker flipped through the book, remembering now forgotten passages echoing back from the dream. The tea party with the Mad Hatter murdering time, leaving his watch stuck at six o'clock. The checkerboard layout that they had flown over. Alice and the Red Queen hand in hand, like Tinker and White had been in the dream, racing to stay in place.

"That's Esme." Lain identified White as her younger sister.

"It is?" Tinker reclaimed the photo. She had always imagined Esme as a younger version of Lain, but Esme looked nothing like her. Come to think of it—Tinker had never seen a picture of Esme before, not even her official NASA mission photo.

"I'm not surprised you're dreaming of her," Lain was saying as Tinker continued to search the photo for the cause of her dreams. "You're bound to be upset about the gate and the colonists."

Was that the true reason? The dream seemed so real compared to the rest of her nightmares. She didn't know Boo-boo Knees was Lain's sister, and Lain had many retired astronauts as friends, so Tinker had had no reason to assume that this was a picture of a colonist. And why all the *Alice in Wonderland* references? Were they just reminders of where the photo was stored—or that the colonist had dropped into a mirror reflection of Earth? Certainly there was nothing to say that Earth had only two reflections: Elfhome and Onihida.

"Lost, lost," the crows had cried.

According to Riki, the first colony ship, the *Tianlong Hao,* was crewed entirely by tengu. If Black was a tengu female, that would explain the crows—but what about the hedgehogs? Tinker flipped through the book, found a picture of Alice with a flamingo and a hedgehog. The queen was screaming, "Off with his head!" Was this some oblique reference to the queen of the elves?

"Oh, this is going to give me a headache," Tinker murmured.

Down the hall, the phone rang. Lain gave her an odd, worried look and went to answer it.

Tinker found herself alone with the photograph of Lain's younger sister, looking defiantly out at her. "Why am I dreaming of you? I don't know where you are. I don't know how to save you. Hell, I don't even know how to save Pittsburgh."

Lain limped back into the kitchen. "That was Reinholds. The freezer in question is shut down because the compressor needs to be repaired. They said if I have someone repair the unit, we could store the tree there. They'll even throw in some free ice cream."

"He eats the fruit of the tree that walks," Tinker suddenly remembered all of what White—Esme—had said. *"Follow the tree to the house of ice and sip sweetly of the cream."*

"I'll go look at the compressor." Tinker kept hold of the book. She had a bad feeling she was going to reread the silly thing. "And see if I can fix it. I think I *have* to do this. Can you do me a favor in the meantime? See if you can find out anything about this oni dragon." Tinker described the magical shield that the dragon generated. "If we have to fight it again, I want to be able to hurt it."

6: LIVELY MAPLE FLAVOR

For years, Tinker had thought of herself as famous. The invention and mass production of the hoverbike made Tinker's name well-known even before she started to race. True, few people realized that the girl in the "Team Tinker" shirt *was* the famed inventor/racer; still, she often got a reaction when she introduced herself.

But she wasn't prepared for the welcome she received at the Reinholds' offices.

The receptionist looked up as Tinker and her bodyguards entered. "Can I help . . ." the woman started, and then her gaze shifted from Pony to Tinker, and her question ended in a high squeal that drew everyone's eyes. "Oh, my god! Oh, my god! It's the fairy princess!"

Tinker glanced over her shoulder, hoping that there would be a female in diaphanous white behind her. No such luck. "Pardon?"

"You're her!" The woman jumped up and down, hands to her mouth. "You're Tinker, the fairy princess!"

Other office people came forward. One woman had a slickie in hand, which she held out with a digital marker. "Can you autograph this for me, Vicereine?"

Vice-what? Tinker felt a smile creeping onto her face in response to all the brightly smiling people gathering around her. The slickie was titled, *Tinker, the New Fairy Princess.* The cover photo was of Tinker, a crown of flowers disguising her haphazard haircut, looking fey and surprisingly pretty.

"What the hell?" Tinker snatched the slickie from the woman. When in god's name was this taken? And by whom?

She thumbed the page key, flipping through the pictures and

text. The first half-dozen photographs were of Windwolf, taken across seasons and at various locations, looking studly as usual. The text listed out Windwolf's titles—viceroy, clan head for Westernlands, cousin to the queen—and added Prince Charming.

"Oh, gag me." She flipped on and found herself. It was a copy of the front cover. When was it taken? She couldn't remember any time appearing in public with a crown of flowers. The only time she had flowers in her hair like this was . . .

Oh, no! Oh, please, no. She frantically flipped on, hoping that she was wrong. Two more head shots, and then there it was—her in her nightgown, the one that looked like cream poured over her naked body. Oh, someone was so dead meat.

The morning after returning from the queen's court, she had breakfasted in the private garden courtyard of Poppymeadow's enclave. She had been alone with the female *sekasha*—and some pervert with telephoto lens. Thankfully, because of the distance involved, the photo was 2-D with limited pan and zoom features.

"Can you sign it, Vicereine?" the owner of the digital magazine asked.

"Sign?" Tinker slapped the slickie to her chest—she didn't even want to give it back.

The woman held out her marker. "Could you make it out to Jennifer Dunham?"

Tinker stared at the marker, wondering what to do. Certainly she couldn't ask her bodyguards—she suspected that they would not take the invasion of her privacy well. Not that the picture was all that indecent, but more that they had failed to protect her. She fumbled with getting the slickie back to its cover picture without flashing it at her bodyguards, scribbled her name in the corner, and thrust it back.

"I'm here about the broken freezer unit that Lain Shanske called about." Time to escape to something simple, understandable, and easily fixed. This freezer repair sounded like a good greasy project to let her forget all the big, unsolvable problems. "You said that if it was fixed, she could use it."

"That was me that she talked to." One man separated himself from the crowd. "Joseph Wojtowicz, you can call me Wojo, most people do. I'm the general manager here." Halfway through his handshake, he seemed to think he'd made a blunder in etiquette and bowed over her hand. "Yes, if you can get the unit working, she's more than welcome to it."

"Well, let's go see it." Tinker indicated that they should go out of the office, away from the crowd of people who were showing signs of producing cameras. "I want to see if it's actually big enough to hold the tree."

Thus they managed to escape, no picture taken, through the offices and to a backstreet. Stormsong led the way, moving through the maze of turns as if she worked at the offices. Pony trailed behind, keeping back the curious office staff with dark looks.

"I heard about the monster attacking you yesterday." Wojo didn't seem to notice her *sekasha*, focusing only on Tinker as they rounded a corner and took a short flight of cement steps up onto a loading dock. "Are you okay? It sounds like you had a nasty fight on your hands."

Gods, first Lain and now him. How many people had heard about the fight at Turtle Creek? "I'm fine."

"That's good! That's good! I knew your grandfather, Tim Bell. He was—" Wojo paused to consider a polite way to describe her grandfather. "—quite a character."

"Yeah, he was."

"This is it, here." He stopped before a large door padlocked shut. He pulled out a key ring and started to sort through the keys. "It was our main building before Startup. After that, it was so unpredictable that we only used it for overflow. Four years ago, we stopped being able to use it at all."

By Startup, he meant the first time Pittsburgh went to Elfhome. In typical fashion, Pittsburghers used Startup to mean that first time, and each consecutive time, after Shutdown returned Pittsburgh to Earth. Shutdown itself was a misnomer because the gate never fully shut down, only powered down sharply, a fact that she had counted on when she set out to destroy it. The oni could have stopped the resonance only by completely shutting off the orbital gate, something it wasn't designed to do easily. The poor crew that maintained the gate probably had no clue what was happening or how to stop it. Tinker tried not to think of the poor souls trying to save themselves before the gate shook itself to pieces. Had they abandoned the structure? Were there ships in orbit around Earth that could rescue them? Or had they, too, phased into space over Elfhome, doomed to rain down with the fiery pieces of the gate?

I've killed people, she thought with despair, *and I don't even know how many, or what race they belonged to.*

"Well, I'll be damned." Wojo turned away from the door, frowning at his key ring as if it had failed him. "None of these keys fit the lock. I guess the key was taken off this ring when we stopped using the building. I'll be right back."

Pony and Stormsong were conferring in whispers. Tinker caught enough to realize that Stormsong was translating for Pony. Was having her *sekasha* understand *everything* worth the convenience of not having to repeat herself?

A slight chiming caught Tinker's attention. Across the street sat a small shrine to a local ley god, its prayer bells ringing in the slight breeze.

The gods of the ley were all faces of the god of magic, Auhoya, the god of chaos and plenty. Tinker was never sure how he could be many different gods and yet still be one individual, but she'd learned that with gods, one didn't try to understand like one would with science. They were. Auhoya was shown always with a horn and a two edged-sword. She supposed in some ways, magic was a lot like science, used to make or destroy.

She clapped her hands to call the gods attention to her, bowed low, and added a silver dime to the hoarde already littering the shrine.

"Help me to make things right." Adding a second dime, she whispered, "Help me to never mess up this badly again."

"Tinker *ze domi*," someone said behind her, using the formal form of her title.

She turned and found Derek Maynard, head of the EIA, standing behind her. If Windwolf was prince of the Westernlands, then Director Maynard was prince of Pittsburgh. Certainly, there was a similarity in their appearance, as Maynard was elf-tall and elf-stylish. He kept his hair in a long, blond braid and wore a painted silk duster, and tall, polished boots. She noted that while he was primarily in white, his accents—earrings, waistcoat, and duster—were all Wind Clan blue.

"Maynard? You're about the last person I expected to run into here. Is the EIA out of ice cream?"

"I'm here to see you." Maynard bowed elegantly, weirding her out. For years she had been terrified of the EIA, and now its director was treating her like a princess.

"Me?" To her annoyance, the word came out as a squeak. Obviously, someone wasn't completely over her fear.

"I heard of the attack on you yesterday . . ."

"Hell, does everyone in Pittsburgh know about that?"

"Possibly. It made the newspaper. How are you feeling?"

"I wish people would stop asking."

"Forgiveness." He swept a critical gaze down over her, taking in her silk dress, black leather gun belt, and polished riding boots. "I am glad to see you well."

"You chased me down just to see how I was?"

"Yes." He motioned toward the shrine. "Did you convert after Windwolf made you an elf?"

"I was raised in the religion," she said. "My grandfather was an atheist or agnostic, depending on his mood. Tooloo often babysat me when I was a child; she thought if I wasn't watched over by human gods, I should be protected by elfin ones."

"Has anyone ever taught you about human religion?"

"Grandpa taught us to exchange Christmas presents, and Lain lights candles at Hanukkah."

"Lain Shanske? I take it that she's Jewish."

"By blood, although not totally by faith. It seems a weird compulsion that she fights, like she doesn't want to believe, saying she's not going to do Hanukkah, but at the last minute, she pulls out the candles and lights them."

Maynard nodded, as if Lain's behavior wasn't bizarre. "I understand."

"I don't. If you try to talk to her about the Jewish God—one minute she's saying that her god is the only true god, and the next minute, she'll be telling me that scientifically, her creation story is impossible. It's like she wants me to know her religion, but doesn't want me to believe it, because she doesn't believe it—but she does."

"Things that you're told as a child—your fear, your religion, your bigotry—become so much a part of you that's it hard to remove them when you grow to be an adult. Sometimes you don't realize such things are there until the moment of truth, and then they're suddenly as impossible to miss as a third arm, and as hard to cut off."

"You talk like you've been through it."

"There have been a few times when all I could do was kiss dirt and pray."

Stormsong scoffed, reminding Tinker that this wasn't a private conversation. On the heels of that, she remembered that this was the second most important person in Pittsburgh after Windwolf—and he had come looking for her.

"You didn't come here to ask me about my religion."

"Actually, in a way, I had," Maynard said. "You do realize that Pittsburgh's treaty with the elves is now null and void?"

"No. Why would it be void?"

"The basic underlying principle of the treaty is that Pittsburgh was a city of Earth only temporarily visiting Elfhome. Every article was written with the idea that humans would and could return to Earth."

"Shit! Okay, I didn't realize that." She frowned at him, wishing she wasn't so tired. Surely this conversation had to be making some kind of sense, but she was missing the connection. What did her religion have to do with the treaty?

"Little one." Stormsong took out a pack of Juicy Fruit gum and offered Tinker a piece. "He wants to know how human you are after everyone has had a chance to fuck your brain over for the last few months. He needs your help but he doesn't know if he can trust you."

Ooooh. Tinker took the gum to give herself a moment to think.

"Succinct as ever, Stormsong." Maynard also accepted a piece.

"That's why you love me." Stormsong stepped back out of the conversation, becoming elfin again.

The last time Tinker remembered talking with Maynard was before she'd been summoned by the queen. She'd warned him about the oni. Slowly unwrapping the gum, she tried to remember if she had seen Maynard after that. No, the oni had kidnapped her while she was on her way to see him. Yeah, she could see why he might be concerned she'd been somehow—damaged.

That still begged the question of what the hell he expected her to do in regard of negotiating a new treaty. As a business owner, she found all of the regulations set up in the original one to be baffling, perplexing, mystifying, bewildering . . . and any other word that meant *confusing*.

"Look, I can help with junkyards, hoverbike racing, and advanced physics." She sighed and put the gum in her mouth. For a moment the taste—not Juicy Fruit as she remembered but something similar, only a hundred times better—distracted her. It was like getting kicked in the mouth. "Wow." She checked the bright yellow wrapper in her hand. Oh yes, she was an elf now, and things tasted different.

Maynard was frowning, waiting for her to finish her point.

"Um—" What had she been saying? Oh yes, her areas of expertise. "But I've discovered that I know very little about anything else."

"You're Windwolf's *domi*."

"And this makes me an expert on—what? I don't know you well enough to discuss my sex life and quite frankly, the only place I get to see my husband is in bed."

"Whether you like it or not, *ze domi*, that makes you a player in

Pittsburgh. There are sixty thousands humans that need you on their side."

"Fine, I'm on their side. Rah, rah, rah! That still doesn't give me a clue on how to help. Fuck, I tried to help the elves and look at the mess I made. You can't screw up much more than Turtle Creek."

"A lot of elves see this as a win-win situation. If you had permanently returned Pittsburgh back to Earth, it would have been perfect."

"Some of us would have been pissed," Stormsong said.

Maynard gave Stormsong a look that begged her to be quiet.

"Look," Tinker said. "If shit hits the fan, I promise I will move heaven and earth to protect the people of this city, but I am not a political animal. At this point in time, I don't even want to try to tackle anything that can't be solved with basic number crunching."

Maynard was still gazing at Stormsong, but in a more intent fashion now. Stormsong wore an odd stunned look, like someone had hit her with a cattle prod.

"Stormsong?" Tinker scanned the area, looking for danger.

"You will," Stormsong murmured softly in a voice that put chills down Tinker's spine.

"I will *what*?" Tinker shivered off the feeling.

"Move heaven and earth to protect what you love," Stormsong whispered.

"What the hell does that mean?" Tinker asked.

Stormsong blinked and focused on Tinker. "Forgiveness, *ze domi*," she said in High Elvish, disappearing behind her most formal mask. "My ability is erratic and I'm untrained. I—I am not certain . . ."

"If that's the case, I'm satisfied." Maynard acted as if Stormsong had said something more understandable. "Forgiveness, *ze domi*, I must take my leave. *Nasadae*."

"*Nasadae*," Tinker echoed, mystified. What the fuck just happened? Maynard bowed his parting. Stormsong had gone into *sekasha* mode. And the conversation had been in English, so asking Pony would be pointless.

Wojo returned with the keys. "I see you've found the cause of all our problems." He indicated the shrine marking the ley line. "As soon as the magic seeped into the area after the first Startup, the whole unit went whacky. It was the weirdest thing I'd ever seen—including waking up the day before."

"Huh?" She was having trouble switching gears. *That's it, I won't fight any monsters today and will go to bed early.*

Wojo misunderstood her grunt of confusion. "I lived out in West View right on the Rim—almost didn't come with the rest of the city.

My place looked down on I-279. Every morning, I'd get up, have coffee, and check traffic out my back window. That first Startup, I looked out, and there was nothing but trees. I thought maybe I was dreaming. I actually went and took a cold shower before going back and looking again."

Tinker added a shower and maybe a nightcap to her "must get sleep" list—if she could find either.

"I never realized how noisy the highway was until afterward," Wojo continued blithely. "When the forest is still, it's absolute quiet, like the world is wrapped in cotton. And the wind through the trees—that green smell—I just love it."

Tinker bet Stormsong would know where to find booze and hot water.

"But between the wargs, the saurus, and the black willows, West View was just too isolated—I was way out past the scientist commune on Observatory Hill. It's all ironwood forest now. I have a nice place up on Mount Washington, beautiful view of the city, and it's much safer up there. And hell, with gas prices what they are, it makes sense to take the incline down the hill and take the light rail over."

"Yeah, yeah," Tinker agreed to shut him up and indicated the door. "Let's see what you have."

Wojo unlocked the padlock, freed it from the bolt, and opened the door.

Before her transformation, ley lines seemed nearly mystical—lines of force running like invisible rivers. The little shrines erected by the elves on strong ley lines served as the only warning for why the normal laws of physics would suddenly skew off in odd directions, as the chaos of magic was applied to the equation. "I hit a ley" embedded itself into the Pittsburgh language, blaming everything from acts of nature to bad judgment on the unseen presence.

But now, as a *domana*, she could see magic. The door swung open to reveal a room filled with the shimmer of power.

"Sweet gods," she breathed, earning a surprised look from Wojo and making the *sekasha* move closer to her.

The magic flowed at a purple on the far end of the visible spectrum, lighting the floor to such near-invisible intensity that it brought tears to her eyes. The high ceiling absorbed most of that light, so it stayed cloaked in shifting shadows. Heat spilled out of the room, flushing her to fever hot, and seconds later, the sense of lightness seeped up her legs, slowly filling her until she felt like she would float away.

"What?" Wojo asked.

"It's a very strong ley line," Tinker said.

Wojo made a slight surprised *hrumpf* to this.

She considered what she was wearing. An active spell with this much force behind it, snarled by something metal on her, could be deadly. She wasn't sure how dangerous this much latent magic might pose. "You might want to empty your pockets."

She pulled off her boots, emptied her pockets into them, and took off her gun belt. Since the *sekasha* caste couldn't sense magic, she told Pony and Stormsong, "This ley seems almost as strong as the spell stones."

"The shrine indicates a *fiutana*," Pony explained. "Like the one that the spell stones are built on."

"What's that?" Tinker asked.

Pony explained, "A single point where magic is much stronger than normal, welling up, like spring waters."

"If you're coming in," she told the two warriors, "strip off all metal. And I mean all."

The *sekasha* started paper, scissors, stone to see which was going in, and which would stay behind with the weapons.

There was a light switch by the door; Tinker cautiously flipped it on, but nothing happened.

"Lightbulbs pop as soon as you carry them into the room," Wojo explained, "so we stopped installing them."

"We need a light source shielded from magic." Tinker flipped the switch back to off. "I don't think even a plastic flashlight would work."

"No, they pop too." Wojo took out two spell lights and held out one to her. "These are safe, but you'll want to watch—they're really bright."

With this much magic around, that wasn't surprising.

She wrapped her hand tight around the cool glass orb before activating it. Her fingers gleamed dull red, her bones lines of darkness inside her skin. Carefully, she uncovered a fraction of the orb, and light shafted out a painfully brilliant white.

Stormsong won paper, scissors, stone and opted for coming inside. She ghosted into the room ahead of Tinker, her shields outlining her in blue brilliance, her wooden sword ready. Tinker waited for Stormsong to flash the "all clear" signal before entering the warehouse.

The cement floor was rough and warm under her stocking feet. She walked into the room, feeling like she should be wading. It lacked the resistance of water, but she could sense a current, a slow circular flow, and a depth.

Wojo followed, oblivious to magic. "This is the space. Is it big enough? If we can get the refrigerator unit to work?"

Tinker considered the loading dock, the wide door, and the large room. They would have to transfer the tree from the flatbed to something wheeled, then shift both back onto the flatbed to get the tree up to the loading dock height and still be able to shift it into the cooler. Given that they'd have to fit a forklift in to help with the transfer, it would be a tight fit, but certainly doable.

"Yeah, this will do." Of course they would have to drain off the massive excess of magic. Strong magic and heavy machinery did not mix well. "You had the cooling unit running for, what, ten years? I'm surprised you managed to keep it running that long."

"More like fourteen," Wojo said. "Your grandfather, actually, came over just after Startup and set us up so it worked fine for years. It didn't break down until after he died."

The machine room was off the back of the refrigerated room, through a regular-sized door in the insulated wall. The compressor itself was normal. The cement around it, however, had been inscribed with a spell. A section had overloaded, burning out a part of the spell. She'd never seen anything like it.

"My grandfather did this?" Tinker asked.

"Yes." Wojo nodded. "He heard about the trouble we were having and volunteered to fix it. We were a little skeptical. Back then, no one knew anything about working magic. People are picking magic up, but still, no one had a clue how to fix what he did when it broke."

Tinker's family had the edge that they were descended from an elf who had been trapped on Earth. Her father, Leonardo Dufae, developed his hyperphase gate based off the quantum nature of magic after studying the family's codex. It was the main reason Tinker had been able to build a gate when no one on Earth had yet figured out how to copy her father's work.

"Define *wacky*," Tinker asked.

"What?" Wojo said.

"You said that it went wacky after the first Startup."

"Ah, well, the compressor seemed to work like a pump. The magic was so thick that you could see it. It blew every lightbulb on the block. The forklifts kept burning out but then they'd skitter across the room, just inches off the floor. Loose paper would crawl up your leg like a kitten. It was just weird."

Yes, that fell under wacky. She knew that the electric forklifts had engines that could short to form a crude antigravity spell—it was what had given her the idea for hoverbikes. The loose paper was new. Perhaps they had something printed on them that had animated them.

"We finally just shut it down and gave all the ice cream to the queen's army." Wojo waved his hand to illustrate emptying out the vast storage area. "Kind of an icebreaker—pardon the pun. A thousand gallons of the cookie batter, chocolate fudge, and peanut butter. Luckily, the Chinese paid for the inventory loss and it hooked the elves on our ice cream."

Tinker sighed, combing her fingers back through her short hair. "Well, first I'll have to drain off the magic; by building a siphon that funnels magic to a storage unit. I have one set up for my electromagnet since a ley line runs through my scrapyard." She used to think of it as a strong ley line, but it was just a meandering stream compared to this torrent. "But that won't handle a flood like you're talking about."

"Whatever your grandfather did worked for years."

The question was—what had her grandfather done? To start from scratch would take time she didn't have, not with the black willow warming in the sun. Luckily, he had kept meticulous records on anything he ever worked on. "I'll go through his things and see if I can find a copy of the spell."

7: THINGS BETTER LEFT BURIED

-◦→⟫══○⟪══→◦-

The treaty between the elves and humans banned certain humans from Pittsburgh as it traveled back and forth between the worlds: criminals, the mentally insane, and orphans. When her grandfather had died, her cousin Oilcan had been seventeen and Tinker had just turned thirteen. Facing possible deportation, dealing with her grandfather's things had been the last thing on Tinker's mind. Truth be told, she'd run a little mad at the time, resisting Lain and Oilcan's attempts to have her move in with them. She had roamed the city, hiding from her grief, and sleeping wherever night found her. Terrified that she was going to lose the only world she'd ever known, she had drunk it down in huge swallows.

Only when Oilcan had turned eighteen, able to be her legal guardian, had they settled back into a normal life. With money from licensing her hoverbike design, she had set up her scrap yard business, moved into a loft, and laid claim to a sprawling garage between the two. Her grief, however, had been too fresh to deal with her grandfather's things; Oilcan and Nathan Czernowski had packed them up and stored them away in a room at the back of the garage.

Even now—looking at the small mountain of boxes, draped in plastic, smelling of age—it was tempting to just shut the door on the emotional land mines that the boxes might hold.

"*Domi*," Pony said quietly behind her. "What are we looking for here?"

"My grandfather created the spell at the ice cream factory. I need to find his notes on it so I can fix it quickly. I figure it's in one of these boxes."

Pony nodded, looking undaunted by the task. "How can we help?"

Backing out of the whole tree mess wasn't really an option; she already had too many people involved. The dust, however, was making her nose itch.

"Can you take these boxes out to the parking pad?" She waved toward the square of sunbaked cement. "After I look through a box, you can put it back."

The first box she opened was actually some of their old racing gear. Inside were a dozen of their FRS walkie-talkies, heavily shielded against magic. She'd upgraded the team to earbuds, and mothballed the handheld radios.

"Score!" she cried. "This is just what I wanted!"

"What are they?" Pony picked one up. "Phones?"

"Close. I want to make it so the Hands can communicate over distance better. These are a little bit clunky but they're easy to use." Oddly, Stormsong thought this was funny. She took the box, saying mysteriously, "This should be interesting."

Tinker supposed it could be worse. Her grandfather had been methodical in organizing his things. Oilcan kept everything carefully separated as he packed the boxes. Still she couldn't find anything filed under "Reinholds", "Refrigeration", "Ice Cream", or the type of compressor that Reinholds used.

"*Ze domi*," Stormsong murmured politely.

Tinker sighed. Random searching wasn't going to work. "What is it, Stormsong?"

"I want to thank you for yesterday."

"Yesterday?" Tinker found the Aa-Ak box and sat down beside it. "Can you put these boxes in alphabetical order?"

Stormsong started to rearrange the boxes, but switched to English, losing her polite mask. "Look, little one, you're a good kid—your heart is in the right place—so I guess I do have to thank you for that stupidity you pulled yesterday. If you hadn't come back, I'd be dead. But I had made my peace with that—being *sekasha* is all about choosing your life *and* your death—so don't ever pull that shit again. You really fucked up. When that thing hit you, you should have been so much dead meat—and that would have been a huge waste, because you are a good kid. The kind I would have been happy dying to protect—do you understand?"

Tinker blinked at her for moment, before finding her voice. "I thought I figured out a way to kill it."

"It wasn't your place to kill it."

"What? I lost at paper, scissors, stone?"

"You know what I hate about being a *sekasha*? It's the *domana*. We *sekasha* spend our lives learning the best way to handle any emergency. We train and train and train—and then have to kowtow to some *domana* who is just winging it because they've got the big guns. Do you know what? Just because you've got the big brains, or the kick-ass spells, doesn't mean you know everything. Next fight, shut the fuck up and do what you're told, or I'm going to bitch slap you."

It took Tinker a moment to find her voice. "You know, I think I like you better when you speak Elvish."

Stormsong laughed. "And I like you better when you speak English. You're more human."

Tinker controlled the urge to stick out her tongue. She deserved Stormsong's criticism because she had screwed up. Still, she suddenly felt like crying. Oh joy. The last few weeks had left her rubbed raw. Instead, she pushed the Aa-Ak box toward Stormsong, saying, "I'm done with this one," and moved on. At least, having had her say, Stormsong took the box away without comment.

Under "Birth" Tinker found birth certificates for everyone in the family but herself. She pulled Oilcan's and had Stormsong put it in the car. Under "Dufae" she found the original Dufae Codex carefully sealed in plastic. She'd only worked with the scanned copy that her father had made.

"Wow." That too she pulled out and had put in the Rolls to take home with her. The next box started with E's, and toward the back was a thick file folder marked simply "Esme." "What the hell?"

Tinker pried the file out of the box, flipped it open, and found Esme Shanske looking back. She ruffled quickly through the file. It was all information on Esme. NASA bios. Newspaper clippings. Photographs. It threw her into sudden and complete confusion.

"What are you doing here?" she asked Esme's photo. "I wasn't looking for you. What was I looking for?" She had to think a moment before remembering that she wanted to find her grandfather's notes on the spell at Reinholds so the walk-in freezer could function again so she could store the black willow. But why? "Why am I doing this again?"

Lain wanted the black willow (thus the whole reason it was salvaged in the first place) and it might revive—good reason to lock the tree in the cooler. The cooler was broken. She needed to fix it. They were all nice, sane, and logical links in a chain.

What made it all weird were her dreams and Esme popping up in odd places. It jarred hard with Tinker's orderly conception of reality. It pushed her into an uncomfortable feeling that the world wasn't as solid and fixed as she thought it was. She wanted to ignore it all, but Windwolf had said that it wasn't wise to ignore her dreams.

Perhaps if she dealt with them in a scientific manner, they wouldn't seem so—frighteningly weird.

She got her datapad and settled in the sun to write out what she remembered of the dream, and what had already materialized. The pearl necklace headed the list, since it was the first to appear. Second was the black willow and the ice cream. She considered the hedge-hogs of the dream and the flamingoes in the book's illustrations and decided her future might be decidedly weird.

And who was the Asian woman in black? She felt that the woman had to be tengu because of the crows. She had felt, however, that she knew the woman, just as she knew Esme. Perhaps she was another colonist, which was why the birds kept repeating, "Lost." Riki had told her that the first ship was crewed by tengu. Then it hit her—Riki lied about everything. She flopped back onto the sun warm cement and covered her eyes. Gods, what was she doing? Try-ing to apply logic to dream symbols was not going to work! So how was she going to figure out the future with only dreams and possible lies?

"*Domi.*" Pony's voice and the touch of his hand on her face yanked Tinker out of her nightmare. "Wake up."

Tinker opened her eyes and struggled awake. She lay on the warm, rough cement of the parking pad. Stormsong was doing a leisurely prowl in the alley. Pony knelt beside her, sheltering her from the sun. She groaned and rubbed at her eyes; they burned with un-shed tears.

"What is it?"

"You were having a nightmare."

She grunted and sat up, not wanting to fall back to sleep, per-chance to dream. Lately dreaming was a bitch. The oni had really force-fed her id some whoppers, not that her imagination really needed it, no thank you.

"*Domi?*" His dark eyes mirrored the concern in his murmured question. "Are you all right?"

"It was just a bad dream." She yawned so deep her face felt like it would split in half. "How can I sleep and wake up more tired?"

"You've only been asleep for a few minutes." He shifted so that he sat beside her. "Nor was it restful sleep."

"You're telling me." In her dreams, she hadn't been able to save him from being flayed of his tattoos. She leaned against his bare arm, his skin and tattoos wonderfully intact, glad for the opportunity to reassure herself without making a big deal of it. *Just a nightmare.*

He smelled wonderful. After weeks together, she knew his natural scent. He was wearing some kind of cologne, an enticing light musk. She felt the now familiar desire uncoil inside her. Gods, why did stress make her want to lick honey off his rock-hard abs? Was this some kind of weird primitive wiring—most of us are going off to be eaten by saber-toothed tigers, so let's fuck like crazy before the gene pool lessens? Or was she uniquely screwed up?

Every night with Pony among the oni had been a torture of temptation. There had been only one bed and she had been stupid enough to insist that they share it. She would lay awake, desperately wanting to reach out to him—to be held, to be made love to, to be taken care of. She managed to resist because of a little voice that reminded her that she would swap Pony for Windwolf in a heartbeat—that it was her husband she really wanted. There had been no way to kick Pony out of the bed without admitting how much she wanted him, so he and her secret temptation stayed.

Even now she fought the urge to plant little kisses on his bicep. *I'm a married woman. I'm married and I do love Windwolf.* She couldn't even imagine being married to Pony, although she wasn't sure why—he was to-die-for cute. Unfortunately, she could imagine having hot sex with him. She sighed as her curiosity stirred to wonder what running her tongue up the curve of his arm would taste like. *Now I've done it—it will eat me alive wondering . . .*

"*Domi*, what is it?"

Embarrassment burned through her. "N-n-nothing. I'm just tired. I haven't been sleeping well."

"Have you found what you needed?" he asked.

"No." She shook her head and yawned again. She saved her notes on the datapad and handed Esme's file to him. "Put this in the Rolls. I'll get back to work."

Luckily the information she was looking for was in the F's, under "Flux Compression Generator." *Huh?* Normally compressing a magnetic field would generate more amperes of current than a lightning bolt and cause an electromagnetic pulse. What in hell was her grandfather thinking? But there was no mistaking the Reinhold floor layout, and the accompanying notes on the spell. With the folder, it should be fairly simple to recreate her grandfather's spell.

She heard the scrape of boots on the cement behind her. The *sekasha* were probably bored to tears.

"This is what I was looking for." She got to her feet and brushed the dust from her skirt. She looked up and was startled to find the *sekasha* forming a wall of muscle between her and Nathan Czernowski. The sight of him put a tingle of nervousness through her. "Nathan? What are you doing here?"

"I saw the Rolls and figured that it had to be you."

"Yeah, it's me." She busied herself with the boxes as an excuse not to look at him, wondering why she felt so weird until she remembered where they'd left off. Last time she'd seen him, he—he—she didn't even want to assign a word to it.

Nathan had been like an older brother to her and Oilcan. He'd hung around the garage and scrap yard on his off hours, drinking beer with them, and shooting the breeze. On racing days, he acted as security for her pit. She knew all his sprawling family members, had attended their weddings and funerals and birthday parties. There wasn't another man in Pittsburgh that she would have let into her loft while she was dressed only in a towel. Nobody else she would have thought herself utterly safe with.

Then he'd held her down, torn off her towel, and tried to push into her.

In one terrifying second, he'd become a large, frightening stranger. She had never considered before how tall he was, how strong he was, or how easily he could do anything he wanted with her.

He hadn't actually done—it. He'd stopped. He seemed to be listening to her. She would never know if he actually would have gotten off her, and let her up, and gone back to the Nathan she knew, because Pony had come to her rescue.

A day later she'd been snatched up by the queen's Wyverns, dragged away to attend the royal court, and then kidnapped by the oni, where she witnessed true evil. She hadn't thought of Nathan once in all that time. She wasn't sure what she felt now.

"I heard about the monster—" Nathan started.

"You and all of Pittsburgh. I'm fine!"

"I see." Nathan gazed her wistfully. "You look beautiful."

"Thanks." She knew it was mostly the jewel red silk dress. She also knew that it clung to her like paint where it wasn't exposing vast amounts of skin. Suddenly she felt weirdly under-dressed.

They stood a moment in nervous silence. Finally, Nathan wet his lips and said, "I'm sorry. I went way over the line, and I'm—so—sorry."

She burned with sudden embarrassment; it was like being naked under him again. "I don't want to talk about it."

"No, I'm ashamed of what I did, and I want to apologize—though I know that really doesn't cut it." His voice grew husky with self-loathing. "I would have killed another man for doing it. That I was drunk and jealous excuses nothing."

"Nathan, I don't know how to deal with this."

"I just loved you so much. I still do. It kills me that I lost you. I just don't want you to hate me."

"I don't hate you," she whispered. "I'm pissed to hell at you. And I'm a little scared of you now. But I don't hate you."

At least she didn't think she did. He had stopped—that counted for something, didn't it? More than anything, she felt stupid for letting it happen. Everyone had told her that things wouldn't work out between her and Nathan—and she had ignored them.

They stood in awkward silence. It dawned on her that the *sekasha* were still between her and Nathan, a quiet angry presence. She realized that Pony must have told Stormsong who Nathan was and what he'd done, and embarrassment burned through her. Once again she was having her nose ground into the fact that she was being constantly watched. She pushed past the *sekasha* and Nathan, wondering how much detail had Pony told Stormsong. She could trust Pony with her life, but not her privacy; she wasn't even sure he understood the concept.

When she reached the Rolls, she was tempted to climb in and drive away, but that would mean leaving the storage room half unpacked. She dropped the file in the back of the car, beside the other things she'd set aside to take home. Nathan and the *sekasha* had trailed her out to the Rolls. Somehow, out in the alley, she felt more claustrophobic, their presence made unavoidable by the fact that they had followed her en masse.

"I have what I need," she told Pony and then realized she had said that already. "Everything else needs to be put back."

"Yes, *domi*." Pony signaled to Stormsong to return to the storage room; he remained with Tinker.

Nathan stayed too. His police cruiser sat behind the Rolls. For some reason the Pittsburgh police had doubled up and Bue Pedersen waited patiently for Nathan to finish.

"Bowman." Tinker nodded to Bue.

"Hiya, Tinker." Bue nodded back.

"They tell me that you're his *domi*." Nathan meant Windwolf.

"Yeah." She fiddled with the bracelet. She had no wedding ring to flash as proof. Elves apparently didn't go for those kinds of things.

"You know, everyone's going on and on as if you got married to him and you're a princess now, but Tooloo says that you're not his wife."

Her heart flipped in her chest. "What?"

"Tooloo says that Windwolf didn't marry you."

She stared at him dumbfounded for a minute before she thought to say, "And you believed her? Tooloo *lies*. You ask her five times in a row when her birthday is and she'll tell you a different date each time!"

He looked down at her bare fingers. "Then why was there no wedding? Why no ring?"

She tried to ignore the weird cartwheeling in her chest. "Nathan, it's not—they—they don't do things like we do."

He gave a cold bitter laugh. "Yeah, like changing someone's species without asking them."

"He asked!" she snapped. She just hadn't understood.

"Come on, Tink. I was there. You had no idea what he had done to you. You still don't know. You think you're married. Hell, half the city thinks you're married. But you're not."

She shook her head and clung to the one thing she knew for sure. "Tooloo lies about everything. She hates Windwolf. She's lying to you."

"Tink—"

"I don't have time for this bullshit! Stormsong, we're leaving! Just lock the door and come."

"The humans farm—grass?" Bladebite prodded the green rectangle of sod laid down in the palace clearing.

"Convenient, isn't it?" Wolf pointed out, although he suspected that his First Hand wouldn't see it as such.

"It's unnatural," Bladebite grumbled. "Grass already grows quickly—why would they want it to instantly appear?"

Wolf rubbed at his temple where a headache was starting to form. "Quickly," of course, was all a matter of perspective. The palace clearing was still a raw wound of earth from cutting down the ironwoods and tearing up the massive stumps. Until the dead gossamer could be removed from the faire grounds, the clearing would have to double as an airfield. Wolf knew his First Hand reflected what most elves would think of the sod. It couldn't be helped. After last night's rainfall, the clearing was turning into a pit of mud.

Wolf had delegated cleaning up the gossamer body to Wraith Arrow, an imperfect match of abilities and task, but currently the best he could hope for as Tinker had apparently found some project on the North Side that was taking up her time. Reports were drifting back, along with a box of walkie-talkies.

His First Hand viewed the devices with the same open suspicion as the sod. Luckily, while Wraith dealt with the gossamer, Cloud-walker filled the fifth position. The "baby" *sekasha* was cautiously prodding the buttons on the walkie-talkie.

While his Hands kept alert for trouble, Wolf focused on getting the clearing ready for the arrival of the queen's troops. The settlements on the East Coast reported that a dreadnaught had passed overhead, so it would be arriving soon.

"You're not going to take down the oaks—are you?" The human contractor pointed out the massive wind oaks. "That would be a crying shame."

Wolf hated the idea of cutting down the trees for a single day's use of the clearing. While the trees were spell-worked to be extremely long-lived, their acorns rarely sprouted hardy saplings, and thus the trees continued to be quite rare. Wolf had been sure that finding five so close to Pittsburgh was a sign of the gods' blessings. He had chosen the site because of the trees and planned to build the palace around them.

He paced the clearing, trying to remember the dreadnaught's size. Would there be room for it to land without taking down the trees? While he did, he wondered about the oni's attack. Why kill the gossamer? Thinking with a cold heart, he realized that it would have made more sense for the oni to attack Poppymeadow's in the middle of the night. The ley line through the enclaves wasn't strong enough to support aggressive defense spells. The rocket would have triggered the alarms, but Wolf wouldn't have been able to call his shields in time.

One would think that the oni would have realized by now that Wolf was their strongest adversary. But maybe he was overestimating their grasp on the situation. Taking himself out of the equation, he considered the question again. Why the gossamer? There had been a second gossamer in plain sight, waiting for mooring. True, that airship had fled the area and it would probably take hours for its navigator to coax the beast back to Pittsburgh. Perhaps the oni hoped to isolate Wolf by killing both his ships before he could react. Perhaps they didn't realize that he had already sent for support.

While the gossamer's death was a pity, he was glad that the oni attacked it and not the enclaves. He had lost two of his *sekasha* this century. He did not want to lose another.

Wolf became aware that the *sekasha* had stopped a human from approaching him while he was thinking. He focused on the man with pale eyes and a dark goatee. "What is it that you want?"

"I'm the city's coroner." The man took Wolf's question as permission to close the distance. Bladebite stopped the human with a straight arm and a cold look.

"I am not familiar with that word," Wolf said.

"I'm—I'm the one that deals with the dead."

"I see." Wolf signaled to his Hand to let the man advance. Sparrow had dealt with this man, since Wolf had been wounded the two times his people had been killed.

"Tim Covington." The coroner held out his hand to be shaken.

Wolf considered the offered hand. The other *domana* would not allow such contact—a broken finger would leave them helpless. Humans needed to be schooled in day-to-day manners—but was now the time to start? He decided that today, he would keep to human politeness and shook Covington's hand. At least the man introduced himself first, which would be correct for both races.

"Wolf Who Rules Wind."

"I was down the street, dealing with the oni bodies, and they said you were here."

"We only executed one oni."

Covington looked away, clearly disturbed. "They unearthed two more dead males when they brought in the backhoe."

"Why do you seek me out? I have no dead."

"I've been coroner for nearly ten years. I dealt with both Lightning Strike and Hawk Scream." Covington named the two fallen *sekasha*.

"They have been given up to the sky."

"Well, I prepared Sparrow but no one has come for her. The enclaves—they have no phones. I wasn't sure what to do."

Bladebite recognized Sparrow's English nickname. He spat on the ground in disgust.

"No one will come for Sparrow." Wolf turned back to pacing the clearing.

"What do you mean?" Covington fell in step with Wolf.

"Sparrow betrayed her clan. We will have nothing to do with her now. Deal with her body as if she was an oni."

Cloudwalker suddenly trotted up to them, looking concerned. "*Domou!* We have a problem."

"What is it?" Wolf cocked his fingers to call the winds.

Cloudwalker pointed to the oak trees. Humans had chained themselves to the massive trunks.

"How did they get there?" Wolf glanced around at the three Hands of *sekasha* scattered across the clearing.

Cloudwalker blushed with embarrassment. "We—we tested them and they were not oni. They had no weapons."

They did have a banner that read, "Save the oaks." Wolf had heard of this type of lunacy, but never seen it in action. How did they get organized so quickly?

"We did not realize that they were not part of the human work crew," Cloudwalker finished. "So we let them pass. What do you want us to do with them?"

Wolf didn't completely trust his *sekasha* to solve the problem without involving swords. He didn't want dead peaceful protesters. "Call Wraith Arrow—he has the EIA helping him. Have them send the police to arrest these humans."

Covington waited as if there was more he needed. Wolf turned to him.

"I'm not sure what to do with the oni," Covington continued their conversation. "Do you know their practices?"

"I am told that in times of plenty, they feed their dead to their hounds," Wolf said. "In times of famine, they eat both their dead and their dogs."

"I don't believe that's true. That's the kind of sick propaganda that always gets generated in a war."

"Elves do not lie." Wolf paused to consider the areas he had just paced off. He believed that the one section of the clearing was large enough for the dreadnaught to land easily, even in high winds. The other sections, however, were deceptively small—they should mark the areas in some manner.

"Everyone lies." Covington demonstrated in two words the humans' greatest strength and weakness. They were able to look at anything and see it as human. It gave them great ability to empathize but it also kept them from seeing others clearly.

"Our society is built on blind trust," Wolf said. "Lying is not an option for us."

But Covington couldn't see it. Perhaps it was too big for him to grasp. The need for truth came from everything from their immortality to their fragile memory, to the ancient roots of the clans, to the interdependency of their day to day lives. Tinker, though, seemed to understand it to her core.

"Treat Sparrow as you see fit." Wolf knew that Covington would be true to his human nature, and treat her with respect, but unknowingly consign the dead elf to the horrors of embalming fluid, a coffin, and a grave instead of open sky. "Ask the EIA what to do with the oni bodies. Be aware that there will be more. Many more."

Tinker's grandfather always said that you needed a plan for everything from baking a cake to total global domination. He taught her the minutia of project management along with experimental and mathematical procedure. Over the years, she had put the skill to good use, from starting a small salvage business at age fourteen, to thwarting the oni army with just her wits and one unarmed *sekasha*.

The truly wonderful thing about focusing on a complex project was there wasn't time to think of messy, extraneous details like elfin wedding customs. Just trying to drain the buildup of magic out of the cooler required creative scavenging for parts and guerilla raids across the city for workers. She designed four jury-rigged pumps that used electromagnets to siphon magic into steel drums of magnetized iron fillings. Unfortunately, the drums would slowly leak magic back out, so they would have to rotate them out, letting them sit someplace until inert. While the siphons were inside the cooler, she sat the drums outside, so whoever changed them didn't need to enter the locked room. The walls seemed solid enough—she would have to check the architectural drawings to be sure, but certainly reinforcing the door wouldn't hurt.

The more she considered safety procedures, the less sure she was this was a good idea. The project, however, was rampaging beyond her ability to stop it. The Reinholds employees were searching out drawings and adding bars to the door, the EIA was sending a tractor-trailer truck to Lain's, a dozen hastily drafted elves were gathering to help with the move, and she'd given out her promises like Halloween candy.

Why was she doing this again? Was her only reason some nonsense out of a dream? Or was she really focusing on the tree so she didn't have to consider that Tooloo was right?

Afraid that she'd fry any of her computer equipment, she had stuck to low-tech project management. Settling on the loading dock's edge, she wrote "*domi*" on her pad of paper and then slowly circled it again and again as her thoughts spun around the question.

Without question, she was Windwolf's *domi*—the queen herself had confirmed that. Tinker had assumed that *domi* meant "wife"; for a long time she simply translated it as "wife." Later, she had sensed that it didn't mean quite the same thing. And Windwolf never used the English word "wife" or for that matter, "married." He'd given her some beans, a brazier, and a *dau* mark. She rubbed at her *dau* between her eyebrows, feeling the slight difference in skin texture under the blue glyph. What the hell kind of wedding ceremony was that? And nothing else? Hell, when Nathan's cousin Benny had been married by the justice of the peace, they still had a wedding reception afterward. Surely the elves did *something* to celebrate a marriage—so why hadn't there been *something*?

If *domi* didn't mean "wife," what did it mean? When she had talked to Maynard two months ago about it, she'd gotten the impression it meant she was married, but now she couldn't recall the exact words that Maynard had used. What she remembered distinctly was how Maynard had been carefully trying to keep his balance on the fence between the humans and the elves. Had she heard only what she wanted to hear? Certainly it would make a neater package for Maynard if Windwolf had married Tinker instead of just carried her off to be a live-in prostitute.

Whispering in the bottom of her soul was a small voice that called her a glorified whore. She couldn't ignore the fact that the only thing she did with Windwolf was have sex. Great sex. Wives did more than that—didn't they? Nathan's mother and sisters went grocery shopping, cooked for their husbands, and cleaned up the dirty dishes but Lemonseed handled all that for Windwolf. Wives washed clothes—Nathan's sisters actually had long discussions on the best ways to get out stains. Dandelion, however, headed the laundry crew.

Without thinking about it, she started a decision tree, branching out "wife" and "whore." What difference did it make to *her*? She never worried about being a "good girl" but at the same time, she had always been contemptuous of women who were either too dumb or too lazy to do real work, using their bodies instead of their brain to make a living. Could she live with all of Pittsburgh knowing that she was a glorified whore?

Stormsong squatted down beside her, took the pencil from her hand, and scratched out "whore" and "wife" and wrote "lady." "That, *domi*, is the closest English word. It means 'one who rules.' It denotes a position within the clan that oversees households that have allegiance to them but are not directly part of their household."

"Like the enclaves?"

"Yes, all the enclaves of Pittsburgh owe fidelity to Wolf Who Rules. He chose people he thought could function as heads and supported the building of their households. It is a huge undertaking to convince people to leave their old households and shift to a new one.

To leave the Easternlands—to come to this wilderness—to settle beside the uneasy strangeness of Pittsburgh—" Stormsong shook her head and switched to English. "You have no fucking idea how much trust these people have in Wolf."

"So why did he choose me? And why do these people listen to me?"

"I think that he sees greatness in you and he loves you for it. And they trust him."

"So they don't really trust me?"

"Ah, we're elves. We need half a day to decide if we need to piss."

"So—I'm not married to him?"

Stormsong tilted her head side to side, squinting as she considered the two cultures. "The closest English word is 'married' but it's too—small—and common."

"So, it's grand and exotic—and there's no ceremony for it?"

Stormsong nodded. "Yup, that's about it."

A hoverbike turned into the alley with a sudden roar. Stormsong sprang to her feet, her hand going to her sword. Pony checked the female *sekasha* with a murmur of "*Nagarou*" identifying Tinker's cousin Oilcan as the sister's son of Tinker's father.

Oilcan swooped around the extra barrels and dropped down to land in front of the loading dock where Tinker sat.

"Hey!" Oilcan called as he killed his hoverbike's engine. "Wow! Look at you."

"Hey yourself!" Tinker tugged down her skirt, just in case she was flashing panty. Gods, she hated dresses. "Thanks for coming."

"Glad to help." He leaned against the chest-high dock. Wood sprites were what Tooloo had called them as kids—small, nut brown from head to bare toes, and fey in the way people used to think elves would look. Beneath his easy smile and summer stain of walnut, though, he seemed drawn.

"You okay?" She nudged him in the ribs with her toe.

"Me?" He scoffed. "I'm not the one being attacked by monsters every other day."

"Bleah." She poked him again to cover the guilty feeling of making him so worried about her. "It's like—what—nearly noon? And there's not a monster in sight."

"I'm glad you called." He pulled out a folded newspaper. "Otherwise I might have been worried. Did you see this?"

"This" was a full front-page story screaming "Princess Mauled." She hadn't seen a photographer yesterday when Windwolf carried her through the coach yard but apparently one had seen her. She flopped back onto the cement. "Oh, son of a turd."

Oilcan nudged against her foot, as if seeking the closeness they had just moments before. "I'm sorry, I shouldn't have shown it to you."

"You didn't take the picture." Lying down felt too good, like she could easily drift to sleep. She sat back up and held out her hand for the paper. "Let me see how bad it really is."

She looked small, helpless, and battered in Windwolf's arms, covered with an alarming amount of blood. The picture caption was "Viceroy Windwolf carries Vicereine Tinker to safety after she and her bodyguards were attacked by a large wild animal."

"What the hell is a vicereine?" she asked.

"Wife of the viceroy."

"Oh." There, she was married, the newspaper said so. "It still sounds weird."

"Vicereine?"

"All of it. Vicereine. Princess. Wife. Married. It seems unreal for some reason."

She scanned the story. It was odd that while it was she and the five elf warriors in the valley, all the information came from human sources. It listed her age and previous address, but only gave Stormsong's English name, not her full elfin one of *Linapavuata-watarou-bo-taeli* which meant Singing Storm Wind. And the *sekasha* were labeled "royal bodyguards." Was it because the reporter didn't speak Elvish, or was it because the elves didn't like to talk about themselves? She learned nothing except that the news had a very human slant. It was odd that she hadn't noticed before.

"Even after all this time, you don't feel married?" Oilcan asked. She made a rude noise and nudged him again in the ribs with her toe. "No. Not really. It doesn't help that Tooloo is spreading rumors that I'm not."

"She is? Why?"

"Who knows why that crazy half-elf does anything?" Tinker wasn't sure which was worse: that Tooloo was considered an expert on elfin culture, or that the people Tinker cared about most all shopped at Tooloo's general store. Her lies would spread out from McKees Rocks like a virus with an authenticity that the *Pittsburgh Post-Gazette* couldn't touch.

"Hell," she continued. "It was like three days before I even figured out that I was married—I don't even remember what I said when he proposed."

"Does he treat you well?" Oilcan asked. "Doesn't yell at you? Call you names? Try to make you feel stupid?"

She made the kick a little harder. "He's good to me. He treats me like a princess."

"Ow!" He danced away, laughing. "Okay, okay. I just don't want to see you hurt." He sobered, and added quietly. "My dad always waited until we were home alone."

His father had beaten his mother to death in a drunken rage. When Oilcan came to live with them, he was black-and-blue from head to knees, and flinched at a raised hand.

"Windwolf isn't like your dad." She tried not to be angry at the comparison; Oilcan was only worried about her. "If nothing else, he's a hell of a lot older than your dad."

"This is a good thing?"

Tinker clicked her tongue in an elfin shrug without thinking and then realized what she'd done. "The elves have been so much more patient than I could ever imagine being. Windwolf has moved his whole household to Pittsburgh to make me happy, because to them, living here for a couple decades is nothing."

"Good."

"Now, are you going to help me with this tree?" she asked.

"I'll think about it." He grinned impishly.

8: CALLING THE WIND

She had to learn not to be surprised when Windwolf popped up at odd times.

She was stretched out on the back room's floor, making a copy of her grandfather's spell. Her attempts with a camera had failed, the magical interference corrupting the digital image. After what it had done to the camera, she had decided against bringing in her datapad to scan it. Instead she had Reinholds find a roll of brown packaging paper. She had covered the floor with paper, and now was making a tracing by simply rubbing crayons lightly across the paper, pressing harder when she felt the depression of the spell tracings. Working with the damaged spell made her nervous, and her dress was driving her nuts, so she had stripped down to underwear and socks and Oilcan's T-shirt.

She'd worn the black crayon out, so she upended the box, spilling the rest of the crayons out onto the floor beside her. The array of colors splayed out on the floor shoved all other thoughts from her mind. She used to make magic pencils by mixing metal filings into melted crayons, pouring them into molds and then wrapping them with construction paper. The only bulk supply of crayons were the packs of sixty-four different shades, which she would separate into the eight basic colors: red, orange, yellow, green, blue, purple, black, and white. It got so she could look at a spray of crayons and see those eight—but she was seeing twelve now.

Since becoming an elf, she knew she saw the world slightly differently. Things she thought were beautiful had been suddenly nearly garish or clashed weirdly. This was the first time that she had proof that Windwolf had somehow changed her basic vision.

"There you are." Windwolf's voice came from above her.

She glanced up to find him standing beside her. "What are you doing here?"

"I was told that you were here, drawing pictures—mostly naked."

"*Pfft.*" She focused back on the paper, not sure how she felt about knowing that her vision had been changed. In a way, it was like getting glasses—right? "I only took my boots, bra, and dress off."

"I see."

She glanced over her shoulder at him and blushed at how he was looking at her. "Hey!"

He grinned and settled cross-legged besides her, resting his hand on the small of her back. "This is an odd beast."

It took her a moment to realize he meant the damaged spell, not her.

"Do you recognize it?"

"In a manner of speaking. It is not a whole spell." He studied the circuits. "This is only an outer shell—one that controls effects put out by another spell."

She had been focusing on the various subsections and hadn't realized that they didn't form a complete spell. Her knowledge of magic came solely from experimentation and her family's codex, which itself seemed to be an eclectic collection of spells.

"It's possible that this machine sets up a spell-like effect." Windwolf motioned to the compressor. "And this shell modifies that effect."

"Oh, yes. The heat exchanger could be acting like a spell."

"These are Stone Clan runes. See this symbol?" He traced one of the graceful lines. "This subsection has to do with gravitational force—which falls within earth magic."

"I didn't realize it was Stone Clan."

"Where did you learn it?" he asked.

"My family has a spell codex that's been handed down for generations."

"This means that your forefather was a Stone Clan *domana*."

"How can you be so sure?"

"Such spells are closely guarded. The clan's powers rest on the control of their element."

"Maybe he stole it." That appealed to her, a master thief as an ancestor.

"With your family's sense of honor, that is unlikely."

That pleased her more. She abandoned the tracing to roll over and smile up at him. "So my family is honorable, eh?"

He put his warm palm on her bare stomach to rub lazy circles there. "Very. It shows in everything you and your cousin do."

"Hmm." She enjoyed the moment, gazing up at him. The look in his eyes always made her melt inside. It still stunned her that someone could be directing such love toward her. How did she get so lucky? Of course her brain cared more about puzzles. "But I couldn't feel magic before you made me your *domi*."

Windwolf shook his head. "The magic sense is a recessive trait. It would have quickly vanished in the following generations of mating with humans."

"Would I be able to use their spell stones?"

"I doubt it very much." Windwolf shook his head. "Only part of that is ability, though; the rest is politics. Even if you somehow retained the needed genes, the Stone Clan will not train my *domi*."

"That's a bitch."

There was a slight noise and Windwolf glanced toward it. One of the *sekasha* who came with him, Bladebite, took up post by the door from the machine room into the warehouse. The pallets with the black willow filled the dim room now. The door out to summer was just a distant rectangle of light on the other side of the tree. For a moment, all of their attention was on the still tree. Thankfully, the siphons were working—she could sense no overflow of magic—and the tree remained dormant. She needed to finish up so they could kick on the compressor and take the refrigeration room down to freezing.

"I do not like you working close to that thing," Windwolf said. "The *sekasha* would not be able to kill it if it roused."

"I know. It usually takes dynamite and a bulldozer to take one down. But I think my dreams are saying that it's a key to protecting what we have."

"Dreams are hard to interpret."

"Yeah, yeah, I know. That's one thing I did learn with the whole pivot stuff—this dream stuff is counterintuitive. What feels like the wrong thing is sometimes the right thing."

The queen's oracle, Pure Radiance, had foreseen that Tinker would be the one person who could block the oni invasion of Elfhome—the pivot on which the future would turn. Oracles seemed to operate on the Heisenberg Uncertainty Principle; apparently telling Tinker how she was going to stop the oni would keep Tinker from doing it. Considering Chiyo's mind reading ability and Sparrow's betrayal, it was just as well that the oracle had been obscure. Thinking back, though, Pure Radiance must have known more than she told Tinker; having Tinker dragged to Aum Renau and kept there for three weeks allowed Tinker to strengthen her body, build a strong relationship with Pony, and learn skills she needed to kill Lord Tomtom, the leader of the oni.

Nevertheless, the key to stopping the oni had been doing what they wanted her to do—which seemed to completely defy logic.

"At least travel with a full Hand," Windwolf said. "Chose four more—any one of them would be proud to pledge to you."

"I don't want to take your people from you. Besides, didn't you say that once I took Pony that I couldn't set him aside without making him look bad? How could you give me yours without insulting them?"

"I cannot give them to you. They must offer themselves to you. It is their hearts, which I cannot rule, which you accept."

There were times she felt like the conversation had been run through a translator one too many times. "How can I just choose four at random? Wouldn't that be me asking and you giving?"

"They have let me know that if you need them, they would be willing to go. I have released all of them from their pledge so that they are free to go."

"All of them?"

Windwolf nodded. "With the exception of Wraith Arrow. I need him. You have gained much respect with the *sekasha*. And I am greatly pleased."

"Wow."

"What do you think of Stormsong? Do you fit with her?"

Fit with her? That was an interesting choice of words. Not "like her," which was what she expected Windwolf to ask. "She's a pistol. Sometimes it seems like she's two different people, depending on which tongue she's speaking."

"A language can govern your thoughts. You cannot think of something if you have no words for it. English is a richer language than Elvish, infused with countless other tongues over time. And in so many ways, English is freer. Elvish is layered heavily with politeness to enforce the laws of our society."

Tinker considered. Yes, politeness came more readily to her when she spoke Elvish. It was only when she was using the very formal, very polite High Elvish that she noticed—and then it was because it felt like being handcuffed into being nice.

"I like speaking English with you," Windwolf said. "I feel like I can just be me—the male that loves you, and not the lord and ruler of our household. That we show each other our true faces when we talk like this."

"Yeah, I noticed that when Stormsong drops into High Elvish, it's like she puts on a mask."

"We speak so little High Elvish here compared to court. My mother says that this rough country is making me uncouth—I'm too plainspoken after being around humans so long. She expects me to come home wrapped in bearskins."

She couldn't believe that anyone could think of him, and all his smooth elegance, as uncouth. "Oh, please."

"If you're determined, you can be eloquently insulting in High Elvish. Court makes an art out of it. I don't have the patience for that—which has earned me a label of boorish."

"Idiots, they deserve a bloody nose."

"My little savage." He pulled her into his arms and kissed her soundly. "I love you dearly—and don't ever lose your fierce heart— but please, pick no fights, not until you've learned to defend yourself."

She skirted promising him anything by kissing him.

"Are you done here?" he asked much later.

"With this part." Reluctantly she slipped out of his arms to lift up the paper that had been covering the spell. "I dug through my grandfather's things and found his notes on this project. I need to compare this to what he has and then fix it. I'll finish it up tomorrow."

"Good," Windwolf said. "There is much we have to do and things I want to do. For instance, I want to talk to you about what direction we're going with the computing center."

"The what?" she asked before remembering. When she had returned to the Pittsburgh area during Shutdown, she had realized that technology on Elfhome was nonexistent. From electrical power to Pittsburgh's limited Internet, everything went with the city when it returned to Earth. In a fit of panic, she'd razed ten acres of virgin forest and drafted a small army to start work on building infrastructure. Since she had been kidnapped only hours into the project, she hadn't even gotten the chance to ask belated permission, let alone finish it. "Oh. That. I wasn't sure—you know—if you even considered it a good idea."

"I think it's an excellent idea."

"I haven't even thought about it since that morning."

"You left quite detailed plans." He brushed his hand along her cheek. "I made a few changes and had it finished. I'd like to expand it, though we probably should wait until the oni have been dealt with."

"But Pittsburgh is kind of stuck here now. What's the point?"

"The point is that Pittsburgh, right or wrong, feels too human for elves to make technology their own. It's like our cooks in Poppymeadow's kitchen; they can cook there, but it's not their kitchen, so they bow out and eat whatever Poppymeadow's staff makes. The changes I made to the computing center were ways to make it more comfortable for our people to use."

"Wow, I never thought of that." In truth, she hadn't been thinking about anyone but herself that morning. "How long do you think we can keep this level of technology, though, without Earth?"

"Once the oni are dealt with, we will find a way back to Earth." Windwolf promised with his eyes.

"Pittsburgh is never going back. The only way to affect all of Pittsburgh is from orbit. Even if we managed to start a space program, we'd have to get the alignment perfect so the enclaves stay here, and then sending Pittsburgh to the right universe . . ." She shivered. "I don't want that kind of responsibility."

"You and I can shake the universe until we find a way." He kissed her brow. "But first things first. Come, get dressed, and let me teach you magic."

Much to her surprise, he took her to the wide-open field where they had been building the new viceroy's palace. Oddly, a gossamer was moored here instead of at the Faire Grounds. They pulled to the edge of the abandoned project and got out of the Rolls. The entire thirty acres had been covered with sod.

"Why here?" She swung up onto the gray Phantom's hood. The windswept woman of its hood ornament—the spirit of ecstasy— seemed so appropriate for the Wind Clan. She wondered if that was how Windwolf had ended up with the Rolls Royce.

"The spell stones represent massive power." Windwolf settled beside her on the hood. "Poppymeadow would probably be annoyed if you lost control of the winds in her orchard."

There was a typical Windwolf answer. Did he sidestep the real question on purpose or was he teasing her with his very dry humor or did they just simply have a fundamental miscommunication problem?

"You're going to teach me how to fly?"

"No," he said slowly. "You will learn how, someday, but not from me, not today."

Her disappointment must have showed, as he actually explained more.

"I have sent for a *sepana autanat*," Windwolf told her. "But arrangements must be made, and such things take time."

"A what?"

"He trains the clan children in magic." He paused to search out the English word. "A teacher."

"Oh." She'd had so few teachers in her life that the idea of a total stranger teaching her was unsettling. "Can't you just teach me yourself?"

"I wish I could, but there are things I don't remember of the early lessons. And there were so many silly learning games we played that even now I don't understand why we did them. I suspect that they were to teach focus and control."

"What kind of games?"

He gave an embarrassed smile. "You will laugh." He stood up, squared his shoulders, and closed his eyes. Taking a breath, he raised his hands to his head, and eyes still closed, splayed out his fingers like tree branches waving in a breeze. "Ironwood stand straight and tall." He dropped his hands slightly so his thumbs were now in his ears, and he flapped the hands. "Gossamer flies over all." Hands to nose this time. "Flutist plays upon his pipe. Cook checks to see if fruit is ripe." He touched index fingers together. "Around and around, goes the bee." He spun in place three times. "Yeah, yeah, yeah, yeah, yeah."

He clapped five times and launched into the song again, faster this time, and then again, faster still. Windwolf was right; she had to giggle at him. He was so regally beautiful, yet he purposely used a childish singsong voice as he wiggled his fingers, spun in place, and clapped his hands. After the third round, he collapsed beside her, laughing. "Well, you're supposed to do that faster and faster, until you're too dizzy."

"What is that supposed to teach you?"

"I don't know." He lay back onto the warm hood to watch the clouds roll overhead, considering. "I think—it might have been staying aware of where your body is regardless of what you're doing. That is very important in controlling magic. There is much for you to learn, and not all of it has to do with controlling the winds."

She scoffed at that understatement. "I thought I knew a lot about elves, about clans and everything, but I'm finding that I don't know anything at all. Like I didn't know each clan had their own spells."

Windwolf considered her for a moment, sadness gathering at the edges of his eyes. "Yes, there is so very much you need to learn. I suppose some history can not hurt, and probably help make sense of our people."

She had heard one long history lesson from Tooloo, but Tooloo tended to twist things to her own unique way of looking at things. "Yeah, it might help."

"In the beginning all elves were much like humans, as evidenced by the fact that we can still interbreed," Windwolf started. "Perhaps—there is a chance—that the first elves were humans, lost through the gateways from Earth to Elfhome—or maybe humans are the ones that became lost. We were tribes scattered, hither and yon, and in our homelands, we practiced the magic that was strongest. Back then, magic was considered holy, and those that used magic were our priests, and they were the first of the clan leaders."

This was different than what Tooloo had told her, in tone if not in fact.

"I don't understand," Tinker asked. "I thought all magic is the same. It's just a general force harnessed by the mechanics of a spell, right?"

"Yes and no. The Wind Clan spells have been refined for millennia, but they are based on certain natural properties. The Wind Clan, according to legends, started in the high steppe lands. For countless generations, those freeborn tribes used their magic, and were slowly changed by it. That's where the genetic stamp developed that allows you to key to one set of spell stones or another."

"But didn't the Skin Clan gather all those tribes together and force them to be the same?"

"They tried. They would conquer a tribe and do all they could to stamp out its culture. Burning temples. Killing the leaders, the scholars, and the priests. Skin Clan were ruthless masters, but we were not totally helpless. We managed to hide away some of our priests, keep them hidden for centuries. We formed secret societies that evolved into the clans. As slaves all we had to call our own was our life, our honor, and our pledge to protect and to serve. But those were weapons strong enough to overthrow the Skin Clan."

"So—since everything had to be kept secret—ceremonies like weddings were a big no-no?" If so, then her marriage to Windwolf made a lot more sense.

"Yes, we could not afford to be discovered. Simple words, whispered between two people, were all we could trust."

"How did the *domana* end up ruling?"

"The clan leaders realized that the only way we could win against the Skin Clan was to use their greatest abilities against them. Once the Skin Clan became immortal, they ordered all their bastards killed. We started to hide away healthy babies, offering up stillborn and deformed infants in their place. They were protected by the clan so that they could protect the clan."

Tooloo had told her a version of this, only somehow not as noble, not so desperate. Quick Blade, Windwolf's great-grandfather, had been one of the babies hidden away and had died fighting for his adopted clan's freedom.

"After we won the war with the Skin Clan, we suffered a thousand years of war among ourselves. Clan against clan. Caste against caste. Elf against elf. We had lived so long in slavery that we had no idea how to be free. It was the *sekasha* that held us together—they demanded that the clan structure be maintained when the other castes would have abandoned it."

"I would have thought it was the *domana* that kept the clans intact."

"The other castes feared that we would become cruel monsters like our fathers. The *sekasha* guard us—from harm and from ourselves. More than one *domana* has been put down by his own Hand."

"Why did *sekasha* want the *domana* in charge instead of just taking power themselves?"

It was as if Windwolf never considered the "why" of it. He frowned and thought for a minute. "I am not sure. It is the way they wanted it. Perhaps it was because with the *domana's* access to the spell stones, the *sekasha's* choices were limited to putting the *domana* in power, destroying the stones, or killing all the *domana*. While they are *sekasha* first, they are fiercely loyal to their clans. It is their nature to be so. And as such, it would go against their nature to weaken their clan."

"So the spell stones and the *domana* stayed."

Windwolf nodded. "And we have had what passes as peace for thousands of years—because of the *sekasha*."

Tinker glanced over to where Pony and Stormsong stood. Close enough to protect. Far enough away to give her and Windwolf a sense of privacy. Who was really in charge? On the surface, it would seem she was—but if she was—why was she stuck with *sekasha* watching her when she would rather be alone?

"In the Westernlands, the Wind Clan has only the spell stones at Aum Renau." Windwolf returned to his magic lesson. "On the other side of the ocean, there are other sets.

"What's the range of a set?"

"The stones can reach one *mei*; Pittsburgh is one-third *mei* from the coast."

It finally explained one mysterious elfin measurement. Unlike human measurements which were exact, the *mei* was said to be roughly a thousand human miles but subject to change. At Aum Renau, Windwolf had shown her how he cast a trigger spell. It set up a quantum level resonance between him and the spell stones, in essence a conduit for the magic to follow. Power *jumped* the distance. It had been his demonstration at Aum Renau that had given her the idea of how to destroy both gates. Magic, though, could be influenced by the moon's orbit and other factors, so the exact distance would be variable—which fit the quantum-based system.

The distance limit also explained why only two clans were coming to help them deal with the oni.

"So, the Stone Clan and Fire Clan each have a set of stones within a *mei*?"

"Yes."

"And spell stones from different clans can overlap." Tinker wanted to be sure she had it right.

"Yes. The *domana's* genetic key determines which one they pull from. The spells are slightly different. In the terms of battle, the Stone Clan is much weaker in attack, but they are superior in defense. Their specialty is mining, farming, and architecture."

Architecture was the forefather of engineering. It kind of made sense—her being Stone Clan and a genius in the hard science.

"Do we actually fight with them?"

"Yes and no. There has been no open warfare between the clans for two thousand years, not since the Fire Clan established the monarchy. To a human, that might seem like lasting peace, but my father saw battle as a young man, and our battles have merely become more covert. Fighting is limited to assassinations and formal duels."

The concept of elves wanting her dead was somewhat unnerving.

"You are under the queen's protection," Windwolf continued. "So you will be fairly safe from the other clans for the time being. I want to teach you, however, a shielding spell so you can defend yourself."

"Oh cool."

He laughed and distanced himself from the Rolls. "Have you been taught the rituals of prayer?"

She nodded.

"Good. First you must find your center, just as you do for a ritual." He stood straight and took a deep cleansing breath.

"Hold your fingers thus." He held out his right hand, thumb and index rigid, middle fingers cocked oddly.

She copied the position and he made minute changes to her fingers.

"Each finger has several degrees. *Laedin*." He tucked her index finger into a tight curl, and then, gliding his finger along the top of hers, showed her that there needed to be a straight line from the back of her hand to the knuckle. "*Sekasha*." He uncurled her finger to the second knuckle and corrected a slight tendency to bend at the first knuckle. "*Domana*." He had to hold her finger straight so she only bent the tip. "Full royal." This was a stiff finger.

"Bows to no one," Tinker said.

"Exactly. You must be careful with your hands. A broken finger can leave you defenseless.

"The first step is to call on the spell stones. You use a full suit—king and queen." These were thumb and pinkie held straight out. *"Domana, sekasha, laedin."*

Tinker laughed as she tried to get her fingers to cooperate.

"There are finger games you can play to get them to do this fluidly." He patiently corrected small mistakes in her hands. "In the base spells, correct positioning is not as vital, but later, a finger out of place will totally change the effect of your spell."

"This does get easier?"

"Yes, with practice.

"To call winds and cast the spells, you need to hold your hand before your mouth." He raised his hand to his mouth and demonstrated the desired distance and then dropped his hand to continue speaking. "Don't touch your face with your hand, but you should feel as if you're almost touching your nose. Also if you were to breathe out, like you were blowing out a candle, the center point of your breath would hit this center joint of your fingers."

"Okay." She held up her hand and found it was harder to not touch her nose than she thought.

"When I was little, my brothers and I would practice fighting with each other and in the heat of battle, sometimes we ended up punching ourselves in the nose."

Tinker laughed.

"Now, listen to the command to call the winds, and then to cancel." He raised his right hand to his mouth. "Daaaaaaaaaaaaaaaae."

Tinker felt the tremor in the air around Windwolf, like a pulse of a bass amplifier, first against her magic sense, and then against her skin.

Mentally, she knew that his body was taking the place of a written spell; his voice started the resonance that would establish a link between him and the spell stones, over three hundred miles away. Despite everything she knew, his summoning of power out of thin air somehow seemed more magical than any act she'd ever witnessed.

He dismissed the power with another gesture and spoken command.

"Now, you try it."

She felt the magic resonance deep in her bones, and then it bloomed around her, enveloping her. Carefully she dismissed it.

"Very good. Once you tap the stones, you are connected to them.

That means you need to immediately use the power, or dismiss it. Casting a spell that you hold, like a shield, keeps the connection open until you end the spell. Casting a spell like a force strike breaks the link immediately."

She nodded her understanding, trusting that when he taught her the various spells, he would tell which category they fell into.

"The shielding spell I'm going to teach you is the most basic of all the spells, but it is very powerful. With the power that the spell stones tap, it is nearly impenetrable."

"Nearly?"

"I do not know anything that could breach it, but I am afraid that *you* might find something—so I put in a cautionary note."

She stuck out her tongue at him. "You make me sound like a troublemaker."

"You do not make trouble—it finds you. And it is always sorry when it does."

She laughed. "Flattery will get you everywhere."

He kissed her then, making her melt against his body. They spent a few pleasant minutes kissing, and then he set her firmly down.

"You need to learn this, my love. You need to be able to protect yourself and your beholden."

"Yeah, I know. Teach away. I'm all ears."

"You summon the power and then shape it." He called forth the power, paused deliberately, and then changed the position of his hand and spoke a new command. The magic pulsing with potential changed, distorting the air around them so they stood inside a transparent sphere.

He held his stance. "Nothing can get in unless you allow it. It will last as long as you desire—but you must be careful with your movements." He moved slowly around to demonstrate the range of motion desired to maintain the shield. "Notice you must keep your hand in the correct position. If you shift your fingers or move your hand too quickly, you lose the connection for the shield."

He flapped his hands loosely and the shields vanished.

"Ugh!" Tinker cried. "It seems dangerously easy to lose your shield when you least want to."

"There are weaker shields that don't require you to hold your position. The *sekasha* spell, for example, allows them to continue fighting without disrupting their shield. The difference in strength is—" He paused to consider a comparison. "—an inch of steel versus a foot."

"Oooh. I see." That messed with her head. She had assumed that *sekasha* provided protection to the *domana* during battle—keeping them safe as they called down lightning and such. It seemed that the truth was that the *domana* were heavy tanks during fighting. They were able to take massive damage as well as deal it. It seemed that the *sekasha* must be for day-to-day life, allowing the *domana* to sleep and eat without fear.

Windwolf called up the shield again and this time showed her how to properly cancel the shield. "It is best for you to get into the habit of intentionally dropping the shield rather than just relaxing your position."

It seemed easy enough, once you got past bending your fingers into pretzels. Tinker managed to initialize the resonance conduit, trigger the shield spell, hold it for a minute, and then cancel the shield spell.

"What about air? If you keep up the shield, do you run out of air?"

"No. Air slowly leaches in, as does heat and cold. The shield will protect you for a period of time in fire, but eventually the heat and smoke will overcome you."

"Ah, good to know."

"Someone comes," Stormsong murmured softly, looking east.

The *sekasha* pulled in tight as they watched the eastern skyline.

"Listen," Wraith Arrow said.

After a moment, Tinker heard the low drone of engines in the distance.

"It has to be the dreadnaught," Windwolf said.

"They're coming," Tinker murmured, wondering who "they" might be.

"Yes." Windwolf tugged on her wrist. "We need to return to the enclave."

Tinker glanced at him in surprise. She would have thought they would stay to greet the newcomers.

"I am not sure who the queen has sent," Windwolf explained. "I want to look our best. Can you change quickly?"

She supposed it depended on your idea of quickly. "I think I can. What should I wear?"

"The bronze gown, please."

"That's not the most formal one I have."

He smiled warmly at her. "Yes, but I love to see you in it."

She blushed and tried not to worry about how she was going to get into the dress quickly.

As they got into the Rolls, a shadow passed overhead accompanied by the low rumble of large engines. A dreadnaught slid out from behind the hill to hover near the treeline. She'd forgotten how massive the blend of airship and armored helicopter was; it dwarfed the ironwoods, its four massive rotor blades beating a storm of leaves out into the meadow. Barrels of heavy guns bristled from the black hull, like the spiked hide of a river shark. The gossamer moored at the clearing stirred nervously in the presence of the large predator-like craft. As they watched, the mooring lines were cast off and the gossamer gave way to the dreadnaught.

The thumping of the rotors suddenly echoed into her memories of her dream. In the background, constantly, had been the same sound.

She shivered at the foreknowledge, and wondered what her dream had been trying to warn her of.

9: TRUE FLAME

At Poppymeadow's enclave, she discovered one of the *sekasha* had called ahead. Half the females of Windwolf's staff ambushed her at the door and hurried her to her room. She tried not to mind as they clucked and fussed over her, pulling her out of clothes, washing her face, neck, and hands, and pulling the formal gown over her head. Certainly she wouldn't be able to dress quickly without them, but their nervousness infected her.

At least she was confident about how she looked. The dress was a deep, rich, mottled bronze that looked lovely against her dusky skin. Over the bronze silk was another layer of fine, nearly invisible fabric with a green leaf design, so that when the bronze silk moved, it seemed like sunlight through forest leaves. Unfortunately, it still had long sleeves that ended in a fingerless glove arrangement and the dainty matching slippers.

"Oh please, can I wear boots?"

"You'll be outside, so the boots are appropriate," Lemonseed proclaimed, and her best suede ankle boots were produced, freshly brushed.

Tinker stepped into the boots, the females fastened the row of tiny hooks and eyes made of cling vine and ironwood down the back of the gown, and she was dressed.

Windwolf waited by the car, wearing the bronze tunic that matched her underdress and a duster of the leaf pattern of her overdress. His hair was unbound in a shimmering black cascade down his back.

"Where is your jewelry?" he asked.

"They wanted me to wear the diamonds." She held out both

necklaces. "But I thought the pearls would look better. I told them I'd let you pick."

"The pearls do look better." Windwolf took the diamond necklace and fastened it in place. "But the diamonds are for formal occasions such as this. The pearls would be for more intimate times, such as a private dinner party."

Sighing, she surrendered the pearls to Lemonseed for safekeeping. "We're just going out to the clearing and saying 'howdy,' aren't we?"

"We are greeting the queen's representatives who can strip us of everything if they deem us unable to protect what we hold. Appearance is everything."

"They can't *really* take everything—can they?"

"It is unlikely." Windwolf swept her into the Rolls. "Please, beloved, be on your best behavior. Keep to High Elvish—and forgive me, but speak as little as possible, since your High Elvish is still weak."

Great, the queen's representatives hadn't even landed and already she was being made to feel like a scruffy junkyard dog. Her annoyance must have shown on her face, because Windwolf took her hand.

"Beloved, please, promise me to keep that cutting wit of yours sheathed."

"I promise," she growled, but silently reserved the right to kick anyone who truly pissed her off.

Tinker could see why Windwolf had opted to dress first. True, the dreadnought had landed and its many gangplanks were lowered. There was, however, no sign of the queen's representatives. A sea of Fire Clan red moved around the ship as the queen's Wyverns secured the area with slow thoroughness. Their Rolls was checked at the entrance to the clearing where Wyverns had already erected a barrier. After their identities were verified, the Rolls was directed to a shimmering white tent of fairy silk. An ornate rug already carpeted the tent. Servants were setting up a teak folding table, richly carved chairs, a map chest, and a tea service.

Leave it to elves to do everything with elegance.

The queen's Wyverns were tall, with hair the color of fire pulled back and braided into a thick cord. Like the Wind Clan *sekasha*, they wore vests of wyvern-scale armor, and permanent spell tattoos scrolled down their arms; both were done in shades of red that matched their hair.

All of Windwolf's *sekasha* had come with them and formed two walls of blue in the sea of red. Seeing all the *sekasha* en masse, Tinker realized not only how much alike the Wyverns looked, but also how much the Wind Clan *sekasha*—slightly shorter with black hair—looked the same. Only Stormsong stood out with her short blue hair.

"Are the *sekasha* of the various clans separate families?" Tinker whispered to Windwolf as she held out a hand to him, so he could help her out of the car. Experience had taught her that the long skirts loved to wrap tight around her ankles as she got in and out of cars and carriages—she had nearly gone face-first into the dirt several times.

"Hmm?" Windwolf steadied her as she scrambled out.

"They look alike." Once out, she twitched her skirts back into place.

"The Skin Clan liked their *sekasha* to match—like coach horses. They would bioengineer a generation to suit them and then breed them one to another. They would kill all the children that didn't express the desired traits, weeding out stock until it bred true, like drowning litters of puppies when a mutt gets into a pure breed's kennel."

"That's horrible!"

"That's why we rebelled against them. Why we will have nothing to do with the oni who are so much like them."

"This one has the domana *genome?" Lord Tomtom had said when he held her prisoner. "Perhaps I'll get my own litter on her."* Tinker shivered as she remembered Tomtom's clinical gaze on her. No wonder the elves hated and feared the oni so much.

Alertness spread through the Wyverns, like ripples in a pool, moving outward. A figure in white and gold emerged from the dreadnaught. With the focus of every person on the field tight on him, the tall male strode across the meadow to join them at the tent. He wore a vest of gold scale, white leather pants, and a duster of white fairy silk that flared out behind him as he walked.

He ducked into the tent and nodded to Windwolf. "Viceroy."

Windwolf bowed. "Prince General."

Prince?   He had the queen's glorious beauty—the radiant white skin, the vivid blue eyes and oh-so-gold hair twisted into a *sekasha*-like braid.

Tinker carefully followed Windwolf's suit as to how low to bow. Not that she needed to worry, for the elf prince didn't even glance in her direction. The duster settled around him, revealing that it had a delicate white-on-white design of wyverns and flames.

"Well, it took a hundred and ten years." Surprisingly, the prince general used Low Elvish. He had a deep voice with a hint of rasp, as if he'd spent the day shouting. "But as I said, it was only a matter of time before you would be calling for help and then I would have to come save your sorry ass. Of course you never could do things small—you had to go find a nest of oni for me to wrestle."

Windwolf grinned hugely. "True!"

"Young pup!" The prince returned the smile and gave Windwolf a rough hug. "It is good to see you again. It has been too long."

"I have been busy."

"So I've heard."

"True Flame, this is my *domi*, my beloved Tinker of the Wind Clan. Beloved, Prince General True Flame of the Fire Clan."

The prince turned his vivid gaze onto her and his eyebrows arched up in surprise. "So this is your child-bride. They said she was little . . ."

"Spare her your razor truth, please, True. I love her dearly and do not wish to see her hurt."

True Flame snorted. "She better learn to guard her heart. Those vultures at court will rip her to shreds."

"I don't plan to take her to court . . ."

"Can we stop talking like I am not here?" Tinker matched True Flame's Low Elvish. A look from Windwolf told her that regardless of what True Flame did, she was expected to speak High Elvish.

"Certainly, cousin," True Flame said.

"Cousin?" Tinker glanced to Windwolf in confusion.

"My mother is the youngest daughter of Ashfall," Windwolf said, and then, seeing Tinker's blank look, added. "Ashfall was our first king."

True Flame gave Windwolf a look that clearly asked, *"She doesn't know that?"*

"Grandfather has been dead for *nae hae,*" Windwolf said.

"We've only had three rulers," True Flame said. "Ashfall, Halo Dust, and Soulful Ember."

"Yes, my knowledge of all things elfin is lacking," Tinker acknowledged and managed to bite down on "I'm sure, however, you're equally ignorant of buckyballs." *Be nice to the male who can take everything away from you,* she reminded herself, and managed to force her mouth into a slight smile. Thank gods, Windwolf seemed to be friends with him.

True Flame took in the weak smile and turned back to Windwolf with a slight look of distaste.

"Once you come to know her, True, you will see why I chose her."

True Flame clicked his tongue and waved toward the table. "Time will tell. Most of your choices continue to mystify me. Sit. Let us discuss this mess you're in."

He pulled a map from the chest and spread it on the table. It showed the city of Pittsburgh and the surrounding areas of Elfhome in detail.

"First, what is happening here?" True Flame pointed at Turtle Creek on the map. "The whole area seems—wrong."

Windwolf explained the events that had led to Tinker creating the Ghostlands.

True Flame looked at Tinker with slight surprise, sweeping a look down over her, before saying, "She's surprisingly destructive for her size."

"That's part of her appeal," Windwolf agreed.

She kicked Windwolf under the table, which earned her another warning look. She gave the look back at him. Being nice was one thing, having them gang up on her was another.

"Can the oni cross from their world to ours through this unstable area?" At least True Flame asked her directly.

"I don't know," Tinker said. "I need to study the area more. In theory, there should not be enough energy to keep it unstable."

"We think at least one creature has come through." Windwolf said. "My *domi* was attacked in the valley yesterday by what we believe is an oni dragon. It is unlikely that the oni could have smuggled such a creature across all the borders on Earth—so it stands to reason that it's a new arrival."

"Then we will have to wait until this area is secure"—True Flame tapped Turtle Creek on the map—"before you can continue your study."

"If the oni can come through, then we're in trouble," Tinker said. "They had an army poised to come through my pathway. With a few hours of study, I can—"

"Child, you will stay out of this valley until I give you leave," True Flame said.

"I am not a child," Tinker snapped.

"You have learned your *esva*?" True Flame asked.

Tinker didn't know the word. She glanced to Windwolf.

"No, she hasn't," Windwolf said quietly, as if holding in anger. "You know it takes years of study."

"A *domi* protects her warriors as they protect her," True Flame said. "Until we know the enemy's strength, we will not endanger any of our people by pushing them onto the front lines with a helpless child to protect."

Windwolf put a hand to her shoulder as if he expected her to say something rude. Tinker, however, found herself glancing at Stormsong and Pony standing with the Wind Clan's *sekasha*. She hadn't been able to protect her people—she'd nearly gotten them killed. She looked away, embarrassed by True Flame's correct reading, and that she had failed Pony and the others so completely.

True Flame took her silence as agreement and moved on. "Have you been able to determine any other oni stronghold?"

"Not yet. Tinker killed their leader, Lord Tomtom, but the size of their organization and the type of operations that they were carrying out suggested a number of subordinates, which we haven't identified or located."

True Flame grunted and signaled for tea to be poured. A servant moved forward to fill the delicate china tea bowls. After a month at Aum Renau, Tinker knew that talking was a no-no without Windwolf's glance in her direction; some elf bullshit about appreciating the act of being civilized. She distracted herself with the honey and milk. True Flame studied the map of the sprawling Earth city and expanse of Elfhome wilderness, ignoring the tea. Silence would rule until True Flame, as highest ranked person at the table, spoke.

"The oni weakness has always been their own savagery," he said finally. "To keep his underlings in check, an oni keeps his people weak and in disorder. There is no chain of command. Once you killed this Lord Tomtom, it was each dog for himself until one could emerge as strongest."

True Flame locked his gaze on Tinker. "Each elf knows who is above them, and who is beneath them, and that neither relationship is stronger than the other. Those who serve are to be protected, those who protect are to be served. We are not wild animals thinking only of ourselves, but a society that works only when we each know our position and act accordingly."

Tinker forced herself to sip her tea and chose her words carefully. "Having seen the oni up close, there is no need to convince me which is better."

She expected another angry look from Windwolf, but his eyes filled with sorrow, which only made her more uncomfortable than his annoyance would have. She focused on her tea instead.

"The rest of my force will be arriving on gossamers shortly," True Flame said. "I was afraid that you'd be overrun before they could arrive, so I came on ahead."

"Thank you," Windwolf said. "If my beloved's aim had not been true, all would have been lost before you arrived."

"Tonight, we can bivouac in this field, and tomorrow, we'll start securing the city." True Flame ran his hand over the great expanse of wilderness. "The Stone Clan is traveling under escort of my force. I will have no choice but to reward them for their service."

"I know that," Windwolf said in a carefully neutral tone.

It hurt to see him sit there and take it. She couldn't just sit there and watch him bow his head and have the Stone Clan swoop in to take what he had carved out of raw wilderness. "Wolf Who Rules didn't summon Pittsburgh here. And there was no way he could have kept the humans off Elfhome—not even killing every last human would have done that—because then there would have been retaliation. The door was open to the oni by no fault of his."

"I know that," True Flame said.

"Then why should he be punished and the Stone Clan rewarded? You claim that our society works because everyone works together. What benefit would the Stone Clan reap if the world was flooded by oni? Wolf Who Rules has put everything on the line—where is his reward?"

"Because it is the law of our people: you hold only what you can protect. It is the law that kept the peace for thousands of years."

"Beloved," Windwolf said quietly. "It is not as unfair as it seems. We are making a choice. Does the city fall to Stone Clan, who are honorable elves, or to oni?"

"I wouldn't turn over a—a—a—warg to the oni." That was an unfortunate choice of words as it reminded her of the warg at the oni camp and poor, poor—but hopefully dead—Chiyo. How could someone she hated trigger such remorse? One thing was certain—she cried much too easily lately. "This sucks," she snapped in English, wanting to blot the evidence of tears out of her eyes, but the damn fancy sleeves of her gown were in the way. She turned away from True Flame; she didn't want him to see her crying. Yeah, yeah, impress the elf on how grown up you are and bawl like a baby.

There was movement beside her and she realized Pony had moved up to her side. It took everything she had not to reach for him.

"If I may be excused." She hated that her voice shook. "I wish to go back to the enclave."

"You may go," True Flame said.

She reached for Pony's arm. He got her up and away smoothly, almost as if tears weren't blinding her. So much for appearances.

⋅⇥≡◑═⇤⋅

A full Hand peeled off to accompany her and Pony back to the enclave. Somehow, just having Pony there clearing a path to her bedroom refuge made it possible to blink back the tears and get herself under control. Still she was fumble-fingered with emotion as she tried to undo the hooks of her dress.

She finally gave up. "Can you undo me?"

Pony stood behind her and unhooked the tiny fasteners down the back of her dress. "*Domi*, do not be upset. True Flame can see that your heart is in the right place."

She groaned at the echo of what Stormsong had said to her. "They will put that on my gravestone. 'Here lies Tinker, her heart was in the right place, but her foot was in her mouth and god knows where her brain went.'"

He chuckled. "Usually we judge ourselves harsher than anyone else does."

It was a relief to let the dress slither down to the floor. She stepped out of the pool of silk and picked it up, not wanting it to be ruined. She had messed up enough things already today.

"So, Wolf Who Rules' mother is—" Tinker paused to recall the various words the elves used to denote relationships. This was made tricky because she wasn't sure if True Flame's mother or father was the connection. If True Flame was Soulful Ember's brother, then his father was King Halo Dust. What was the word for paternal aunt? "—father's sister to True Flame?"

"Yes. Longwind and Flame Heart formed an alliance of the Wind Clan and Fire Clan. Wolf Who Rules spent his doubles at court under the queen's care, learning the fire *esva*. It was there that he gained the favor of his royal cousins."

"What is that? *Esva*?" She hung up the dress and considered what was in the closet to wear—all elfin gowns and the sexy white nightgown that she didn't feel like wearing. She wanted the familiar comfort of cotton. Had her shorts dried yet?

"An *esva* is all the spells scribed into a clan's spell stones."

"Wait. Fire? Wolf Who Rules is Wind Clan."

"He is both. He is the only one of his family who can access both Clan's spell stones. It was expected that he would choose to be Fire Clan, but he chose Wind Clan instead."

"Why?" She found the T-shirt she had borrowed off of Oilcan and sniffed at it. It was a little stinky. She wondered when Oilcan had last washed it.

"I can guess it was because he was born and raised in the Wind

Clan," Pony said. "Such things are hard to ignore, but I cannot be sure. You will have to ask him."

The bedroom door opened and another of Windwolf's *sekasha*, Bladebite, stepped into the room. His gaze went down over Tinker; it was the heated calculating look a male gives a female. Suddenly the bra, underwear, and diamond necklace that had been plenty of clothes with Pony felt like nothing.

She clutched the T-shirt to her chest. "What is it, Bladebite?"

"It is time you finished your First Hand. I came to offer myself to you."

Oh shit. What should she do? She'd managed to screw up every single one of these encounters over the last two months, entering relationships with a careless "yes." After the look he'd given her, though, she didn't want to say yes—but would "no" be a deadly insult? She started to turn toward Pony, but Bladebite caught her arm, forcing her to look at him.

"This is between you and I, not him." Bladebite said. "You're making your preferences fairly clear to us all, but they're not wisely thought out. I have the experience you need. You should fill your Hand with strong males, not mutts like Singing Storm."

"What the hell is wrong with her?"

"Since you obviously have no taste for Galloping Storm Horse . . ." Bladebite used Pony's true elfin name.

"I love Pony," she snapped, and blushed red as she realized it was true. When did that happen? "Things have changed since we left Aum Renau. We've been through a lot together."

"And if a fruit is tempting, you take a bite when you're most hungry."

What the hell did that mean?

"I offer all of me to you," Bladebite continued. "Do you accept?"

"I—I—I," she stammered. *I don't know what the hell to say.* The bedroom's dressing mirror was behind Bladebite. She could see Pony; his jaw was clenched but he made no move to interfere. Apparently Bladebite was right—it was up to her to say yes or no. Her reflection reinforced that she was nearly naked, the glitter of diamonds the only thing visible besides the T-shirt clutched to her chest. She never thought of herself as short, either, until something like this forcibly reminded her that the elves were all a foot taller.

"I can't make that decision now," she finally managed to force out. "I'm upset and not thinking clearly."

"You don't need to think. Just accept me."

Not think?   Gods, he might as well be saying not breathe. "No." And then seeing the look on his face. "Not now. I'm too upset."

"We can't afford another spectacle—" Bladebite started.

But apparently she'd said the magic words. Pony's "on duty" light went on, and he shifted from behind Tinker to between her and Bladebite.

"Tinker *ze domi*" Pony used her most formal title and High Elvish, "said that she is upset and will decide later. Please, Bladebite, go."

The words were polite but Pony's tone was cold as steel.

Bladebite gaze locked with Pony's. For a moment, she was afraid that the older *sekasha* would draw his sword. He nodded though and bowed slightly to her. "Good night then, *ze domi*."

She started to shake when the door closed behind him.

"I am sorry, *domi*. Until you refused him, I could not act."

"Was I right to say no?"

"I am disappointed only in him. He has the years to know that you were upset and could not make such decisions."

She got dressed, annoyed that her hands still shook. Why was she veering all over the place emotionally? Maybe she was going to get her period. Usually she wasn't this hormonal, but she hadn't had one as an elf yet. Oh, she hoped that wasn't the case; thousands of years like this would drive her mad. How often did elves get periods? It had been over two months since her last one as a human. Oh gods, what if she was pregnant? Of course that made her feel weepy again.

"I need something to drink," she said. "Can you ask Poppymeadow to find us a bottle of—" What was that stuff called again? "Ouzo?" Wait, if she was pregnant, should she be drinking? And if she was just getting her period, what did elves use? Pads? Tampons? Magic? Hopefully a period only lasted the normal five days—surely even elves couldn't do—that—for more than a week. Damn it, when Windwolf made her an elf, he should have given her an owner's manual for her new body.

She fumbled with her necklace and failed to get it off. "Oh please, Pony, get this off me."

Pony undid the necklace. "I will get you something to eat and drink, and then perhaps you should take a nap. You have been through much lately, *domi*, and you are worn down."

"I want to practice magic." She needed to learn how to protect her people.

"It would be difficult and dangerous the way you are now."

She supposed that was true. "Okay, okay. Something to eat and a nap—and I need to talk to Stormsong about—female—things."

10: STORM WARNINGS

Wolf had watched his *domi* retreat with concern. He had expected her to be gnawing at the prince's ankles instead of breaking down into tears. He felt guilty for chiding her as he had. The oni must have affected her more deeply than he originally thought. He felt badly too that he had been pleased that she hadn't bedded Little Horse while they were prisoners together; he wanted her to himself as long as possible. Perhaps, if she had slept with Little Horse, she would have fared better.

At least she had turned to her beholden when she lost control of her emotions. As much as Wolf wished he could have taken her back to the enclave and comforted her, all of his people and the humans of Pittsburgh needed him to stay and deal with Prince True Flame.

Is this how the humans lived all their life? Having things that they desperately wanted to do—comfort their love ones, teach them what they needed to know—but with no time to do it? No wonder they seemed to rail at life so.

True Flame sat watching him, expression carefully neutral. "Being the pivot—" Wolf sighed and shook his head. "It has subjected her to extraordinarily difficult choices. She's only had hours to recover her center."

"This is recovered?"

"No, and it worries me."

True Flame glanced away, as if embarrassed by what he saw on Wolf's face. "Forgiveness, Wolf. We get along because we both have no need for empty politeness – but I remember now that politeness can render much needed gentleness to the soul. I will keep my sword sheathed from now on."

"Thank you."

"There will be nothing that I can do when the Stone Clan arrives except to remind them that she is under my sister's protection. She will have to interact with them, and they will take advantage of her."

Wolf nodded unhappily. "It will be like trying to keep wargs from the lambs at this point. I wish there was some way I could keep her safe until she has had time to heal from whatever the oni have done to her."

True Flame shook his head. "They'll arrive tomorrow with my troops. I can delay the *aumani* a day, on the pretense of giving them time to settle in."

"Thank you." In their current situation, a day was the most he could have hoped for. "Who have they sent?"

"Earth Son, Jewel Tear, and Forest Moss."

Wolf breathed out; the threesome was tailored for hostile opposition to him. He knew nothing of Forest Moss and thus could not foresee what danger lay there. Judging by the others, there was a good possibility, however, that this was an ancient member of the Stone Clan, to offset Wolf's youth. Earth Son's father was one of the three children of King Ashfall used to ally the strongest of the clans to the crown via marriage. Obviously Earth Son's inclusion was to eliminate Wolf's advantage with True Flame—at least in theory.

The Stone Clan had always misunderstood the nature of the alliance, and considered it a failure. The alliance had only produced Earth Son. While he showed his father's gene type in his height, his eyes, and his temper, his gene expression did not include attunement to the spell stones. Earth Son could not use the fire *esva*. When Earth Son came to court, he treated his Fire Clan cousins as strangers, and was regarded as such by them.

In comparison, Wolf's parents produced ten children, half of which inherited their mother's genome and pledged to the Fire Clan. Wolf grew up seeing the royal family as an extension of his own and when he went to court, he fell under his older brothers' and sisters'protection. Earth Son seemed to fail to understand the slight differences in their position. He only saw the younger elf being rewarded with favor he thought he was due, and held it against Wolf.

The Stone Clan could barely find a delegate more ill-suited to deal with Wolf—but they had managed. Wolf spent a decade at summer court, thinking he and Jewel Tear were soulmates, the other half of each other, and all the other lyrical nonsense you thought while blindly in love. A hundred years and meeting Tinker had taught him that he'd been wrong about the entire nature of love. He and Jewel

Tear had drifted apart soon after he came of age and his ambitions took him to the wilderness of the Westernlands. That the Stone Clan included her in the delegation probably meant he misjudged their relationship.

So these three were coming to his holdings and dealing with his people?

True Flame looked out at the sod-covered clearing and the dense forest of tower ironwoods beyond. "What in the god's name were you thinking of, leaving everything behind for this wilderness?"

"I was thinking of leaving everything behind for this wilderness."

"I've never understood why you're wasting yourself here."

"What would I be doing at court? Nothing has changed there since we last interacted with humans. We had completely stagnated. We had the same base of technology as the humans, and yet we didn't develop the car, or the computer, the telephone, or the camera."

"We have no need of them."

"It doesn't bother you that we sat completely still for hundreds of years while they raced ahead?"

"Less than three hundred years, pup. It passed like a lazy summer afternoon in my life."

Wolf clenched his jaw against this. He'd heard the like all his life from elves younger than True Flame's two thousand years. "Every agricultural advance since the days of poking holes in the ground with sharp sticks, we've stolen from the humans. The plow. Crop rotation. Fertilization. You're old enough to remember the great famines."

True Flame gave him a look that would have silenced him as a child.

Wolf refused to be rebuked. The events of the last three decades had proved him right. "It's as if we get locked into one mind-set— "this is how the world is," and can't conceive or desire something more. I tracked back all our advances while I was at court—"

"I've heard this theory of yours, Wolf."

"Have you? Have you really listened to my words and thought it through?"

"True, there were times of famine, and yes, we went to Earth and saw how to increase crop production and put those techniques to use. But we have lived in peace for thousands of years with all that we could want—why should we clutter up our lives with gadgets?"

Wolf sighed. "You never listened. Not to anything I ever said, did you? I told you over a hundred years ago that sooner or later, the humans would come to us. And I'm telling you now, it's only a matter of time before another race finds us."

✦═◉═✦

One instructional conversation with Stormsong, one stiff drink, one mystery meal of panfried wild game (what in gods' name had drumsticks that size?), and one short nap, and Tinker was feeling much better.

According to Stormsong, her emotional swings were from exhaustion. It would be a year before Tinker would need to worry about a period. Nor, Stormsong said as she poured a generous round of ouzo, could Tinker be pregnant. "Drink, eat, sleep," Stormsong repeated Pony's advice, only more succinctly.

It was fairly clear that *discussions* had taken place while Tinker was asleep. There was an undercurrent running through the *sekasha* and they were metaphorically tiptoeing around her as if she would break. She wasn't sure which was more annoying: that they felt that they needed to tiptoe, or that they were doing such a horribly obvious job at it. At least it kept Bladebite from hounding her, although he was clearly sulking.

Much to Tinker's disgust, Stormsong coaxed her out to the enclave's bathhouse. She went only because the enclave had no showers and the last time she done more than wallow in a sink was at the hospice. She was starting to stink even to herself. She thought she hated elfin bathing—the cold water prescrub gave new meaning to the word unpleasant—but when she discovered that the bathhouse was both communal and mixed sex, she decided to loathe elfin bathing. As far as she was concerned, if the gods wanted them naked, they wouldn't have invented clothing.

The bath at least was stunning, done in jewel-toned mosaics with marble columns and a great skylight of beveled glass. Minerals had been added to the hot water, so it was hazy to the point that it gave a small level of privacy. And the *sekasha* seemed well-practiced in using the towels to keep themselves discreet until the water covered them. Thankfully Bladebite didn't join them, though, surprisingly, Pony did. The eye candy of Pony covered only by steaming water, however, didn't outweigh the negative of being the shortest, darkest, smallest-breasted female present.

"Relax." Stormsong had proved to be naturally a pale-white blond—a fact Tinker hadn't really wanted to know. "We won't eat you."

"At least we won't." Rainlily smiled with a glance toward Pony.

Tinker stood up, realized that she was flashing them all, and sat back down to hide in the hazy water. "I am not amused."

Stormsong splashed Rainlily. "Shush, you."

"If we don't tease her," Rainlily said, "she'll think elves are just as prudish as humans. I've never understood how they can be so blatant with their sexual imagery, and yet in relationships with one another, they are so narrow-minded. As if a heart can hold only one love at a time, and you have to empty out one before there's room for another."

"Let her cope with one thing at a time." Pony watched Tinker with a worried gaze.

"I'm fine," she told him and wondered why she had to say that so often lately.

"One lover gets boring after thirty or forty years," Rainlily said. "It's like peanut butter on a spoon, it's really good, but with chocolate sometimes, it's even better."

Tinker knew that elves loved peanut butter as much as they loved Juicy Fruit gum and ice cream. Considering her experience with the gum, she really had to track down a jar of peanut butter.

Stormsong moaned at the suggestion of peanut butter and chocolate. She added, "Or peanut butter and strawberry jam on fresh bread."

"Peanut butter on toast." Sun Lance held up her hand as if she held a piece of toasted bread by its crust. "Where the bread is crunchy and the peanut butter is all hot and runny."

"Raisin bread toast." Tinker modified Sun Lance's suggestion to her favorite way to eat peanut butter before she became an elf.

"Peanut butter, pretzels, chocolate," Rainlily listed out, "and that marshmallow fluff all mixed together."

"Oh, that explains Cloudwalker and Moonshadow at the same time," Stormsong murmured.

"*Nyowr*," Rainlily growled with a smile, which was the Elvish version of a cat's meow.

"Peanut butter on apple slices," Sun Lance said.

"On a banana," Tinker said.

"On Skybolt," Rainlily said knowingly.

"Oh yes, that's nice," Stormsong agreed.

Tinker was going to need a scorecard to track the *sekasha's* relationships.

"Peanut butter ice cream," Pony said.

"Peanut butter ice cream!" The females all sighed.

"Unless *domi* takes another *sekasha*, though, then her options are limited." Rainlily pointed out. "There's Pony, and then there's Pony."

"That's still peanut butter and—" Stormsong thought a moment, before finishing. "—virgin honey."

Rainlily eyed Pony and smiled. "Definitely virgin honey."

Pony blushed and looked down.

"And Wolf Who Rules is peanut butter ice cream," Sun Lance said.

That triggered a chorus of agreement from the females. Tinker had one moment of feeling pleased that she married the prize male and then realization hit her like a two-by-four to the head. She gasped out in shock.

"*Domi*?" All four *sekasha* instantly reacted, moving toward her as they scanned the building for enemies.

"Windwolf! You've all slept with him?"

The female warriors exchanged glances.

"Well?" she pressed.

"Yes, *domi*," Stormsong said quietly. "But not since he's met you."

Was that really supposed to make her feel better? Well, giving it a moment to sink in, yes it did. She knew that Windwolf had to have had lovers before her—she just didn't expect to be naked in a tub with them at any point. There were two other female *sekasha*. Tinker supposed they were ex-lovers too. Windwolf's household numbered seventy-five—she didn't even know how many were female, but most of the sizeable kitchen staff was. The possible number staggered her. "Any females from the rest of the household?"

The *sekasha* blinked at her in surprise.

"No, *domi*, that wouldn't be proper." Was it a good thing or a bad that Stormsong was keeping to Elvish?

"Only the *sekasha* are *naekuna*," Pony explained.

"You're what?"

"*Naekuna*." Pony sat up slightly in the water to point at a tattoo on his hipbone. She blushed and looked away. "We can turn on and off our fertility."

"It is considered best if a *domi* and *domou* chooses among their beholden *sekasha* for their lovers." Stormsong had a similar tattoo on her hip. "The security of the household is not compromised and we're *naekuna*."

Tinker had one moment of relief until she realized that she had to interact with the five female *sekasha* on a daily basis. She stared at Stormsong, Sun Lance, and Rainlily, unsure how to cope with the sudden knowledge that these females had slept with Windwolf. They knew what a good lover he was—had probably helped him perfect his technique. What if—as the whole peanut butter conversation had suggested—Windwolf wanted variety? How did one deal with that?

The crushing weight of inevitability that you would have to share? With such drop-dead beautiful females no less?

Elves always were so focused on today. You couldn't get them to talk about the past. *Nae hae*, too many years to count, it happened long ago, why bother? The future was the future, why stress over it bearing down on you?

Given long enough time, the smallest probability became reality. Sooner or later, you would live through all the possible futures. Nor would the past really be a true indicator of the future as you worked through one unlikely chance to the next.

Did the elves wear blinders just to keep sane?

"Are you all right?" Pony asked.

"Um, let me get back to you about that."

"*Ze domou*." Wraith Arrow was operating at maximum respect now that the Fire Clan had arrived. Or more specifically, since the Wyverns had arrived. Wolf found himself wondering if perhaps the *sekasha* had chosen their king based on his Hands rather than his clan. "Forest Moss is one of those who traveled to Onihida when the pathway was found. He and the *sekasha*, Silver Vein in Stone, were the only two who managed to survive their capture by the oni."

At one time, certain caves and rock formations had created pathways that let a person walk from one world to the next. Anyone without the ability to detect a ley line could search closely for the pathway, even to the point of stepping in and out of worlds, and never find it. The dangers of traveling to Earth were great. The pathways themselves came and went like the tides of the ocean, apparently affected by the orbit of the moon. Earth had no magic, leaving the *domana* powerless and the *sekasha* without their shields. Still, all the clans sent out *domana* and their *sekasha* to barter silk and spices for steel and technology. To circumvent the dangers, the pathways were mapped out carefully, and traders crossed back to the safety of Elfhome as often as possible. In one remote area on Earth, a new pathway was discovered, and eagerly explored.

Unfortunately it was a pathway that led to Onihida. Of the twenty that went on the expedition, only two returned to Elfhome.

Wolf considered what he knew of that doomed expedition, which was very little since it happened before he was born. Unlike humans who seemed to be driven to chronicle their life and make it public, elves kept such things private. Everything he knew about the oni and Onihida came from questioning his First Hand. He had selected

Wraith Arrow and the others for their knowledge of the humans and Earth, not thinking he'd ever need their familiarity with the oni.

"So you've met him?" Wolf asked.

Wraith nodded. "They had tortured him, healed him, and then tortured him again. It broke his mind."

That was two hundred fifty years ago. Had Forest Moss recovered?

It made Wolf wonder about Tinker and her time with the oni. What had they done to her to change her so much? Wolf felt a wave of sadness and anger. His *domi* had been so brave, trusting, and strong.

Wraith continued his report. "Silver Vein did not look to Forest Moss. The Stone *domou* had a vanity Hand, which he lost. Last that I heard, he had not gained another Hand."

"He's coming here without *sekasha*?"

Wraith nodded.

What game was this? Why include someone who lacked the most basic abilities of building a household? Did this mean that the Stone Clan didn't intend to create holdings in Pittsburgh?

"I'm not sure you should be trying to call the spell stones." Stormsong was the only one who actually voiced the doubt all of them were clearly thinking as they followed her through the enclave's enclosed gardens.

"I'm fine," she said for what seemed the millionth time in the last three days.

"You spent a month working around the clock," Stormsong started. "And you haven't—"

"Shhh!" Tinker silenced her and worked to find her center. Getting her fingers into the full-suit position took a moment of concentration. Bringing her hand to her mouth, she vocalized the trigger word. The magic spilled around her, pulsing with potential. Carefully, she shifted her fingers to the shield position and spoke the trigger. The magic wrapped around her, distorting the air.

"Yes!" Without thinking, she threw up her hands in jubilation and the shield vanished. "Oops!"

The *sekasha* were too polite to comment. Finding her center was harder while burning with embarrassment. Her heart still leapt up when she called up her shield but she managed not to move this time. She held it for several minutes and then practiced at looking around, and then moving, without forgetting to maintain her hand positions.

"Okay," Tinker said. "Can I talk? Can you hear me?"

Pony grinned at her. "We can hear you. As long as you don't have your hands near your mouth, you can talk—but it's not always wise."

She dismissed the magic. Only after the power drained completely away did she celebrate. Laughing, she hugged Pony. "I did it!"

He surprised her by hugging her tightly back. "Yes, you did."

The walkie-talkie chirped and Stormsong answered with a "Yes? It is nothing—she is only practicing."

Tinker grimaced. She had forgotten Windwolf would notice her tapping the spell stones. "That's Wolf Who Rules?"

"Yes, *ze domi*," Stormsong said.

"Sorry, Windwolf!" Tinker called. "But I did it! I called the shields!"

Stormsong listened for a moment and then said, "He says, 'Very good,' and wants to know if you plan to continue practicing?"

"For a while." It occurred to her that the stones might only support one user. "That isn't a problem for him—is it?"

"No, *domi*." Pony answered the question. "Both of you can use the stones at the same time."

Stormsong listened and then said good-bye. "Wolf Who Rules merely wanted to be sure you were fine. Practice away, he said."

So she did until she momentarily forgot how to dispel the magic. When at last the magic washed away, Pony came and took her hands in his.

"Please, *domi*, go to bed. You can do more tomorrow."

Tinker woke from her nightmare to a dark bedroom. For a moment, she couldn't figure out where she was. She'd fallen asleep in so many places lately. She eyed the poster bed, wood paneling, and open window—oh yes—her bedroom at Poppymeadow's. Even awake, her dreams crowded in on her. She put out a hand and found Windwolf's comforting warmth. It was all she needed to push away the darkest memories.

Sighing, she snuggled up to her husband. This was one of the unexpected joys of being married, her secret treasure. She had never realized how lonely she was at night. Back in her loft, any light noise had her out of bed, and once awake, she often found herself getting dressed and wandering out into the sleeping city, in search of something she'd couldn't name or identify. Before Windwolf, if asked, she would have said she was perfectly happy—but if she had been, how could she be so much happier now?

She was just noticing something hard digging into her side, when she realized it was Pony beside her, not Windwolf. While Pony wore his loose pajamas, he slept on top of the blankets beside her, instead of under them with her. It was his sheathed *ejae* beneath her—she'd rolled on top of it when she cuddled up to him.

"Pony?" She tugged the sword out from under her, dropped it behind him. His presence confused her.

"What is it, *domi*?" he asked sleepily.

It took her another minute to sort through memories and dreams to know what reality should be. They weren't still prisoners of the oni and her husband *really* should be in bed with her. "Where's Windwolf?"

Pony rubbed at his face. "Hmmm? He's probably still with Prince True Flame. There was much to do before the troops arrived tomorrow."

"I had a bad dream about Windwolf. He couldn't see Lord Tom-tom. I could but the black willows were holding me—I couldn't move—couldn't warn him."

"Hush." Pony hugged her loosely. "Tomtom is dead. Wolf Who Rules is safe. It was only a dream—nothing more. Go back to sleep."

"What if the oni attacked?" She started to get up but he tightened his hold.

"No, no, Wolf would want you to sleep. You're exhausted, *domi*. You're going to make yourself sick if you do not sleep."

She groaned because she was so very tired but the nightmare pressed in on her. "I can't go back to sleep. Windwolf could be in trouble."

"He's fine."

"How do you know? We were asleep. He could be fighting for his life right now." Oh gods, she was turning into such a drama queen. *Go to bed, go to bed, go to bed*, she told herself, but she couldn't banish the memories.

"Oh, *domi*," Pony crooned. "When I was little and my mother was out with Longwind—Windwolf's father—I'd be worried just like you are now. And my father would say, 'Look at the clear sky, see the stars? If the Wind Clan fought tonight, the wind would throw clouds around, and lightning would be everywhere.'"

She relaxed onto his bare shoulder, gazing out the bedroom window at the peach trees beyond, standing still against a crystalline sky. "What did you do when it stormed?"

Pony chuckled, a good warm sound that did much to banish away her fears. "Ah, you've spotted the weakness in my father's ploy."

It puzzled her that his mother was out with Longwind when he was fighting until she realized that both of Pony's parents would have been *sekasha*. Pony's mother must be beholden to Windwolf's father.

"What is your mother like?" she asked.

"Otter Dance? She is *sekasha*," Pony said as if that explained everything. Perhaps it did. "We of the Wind Clan *sekasha* are known to be playful and lucky where the Fire Clan *sekasha* are considered hot tempered and rude. When we come together in large cities, we of the Wind Clan like to gamble and win, and the Fire Clan tends to lose and start fights. Almost every night ends in a brawl, everyone black-and-blue."

He smelt wonderful. His braid was undone and his hair was a cascade of black in the moonlight. As if it had a mind of its own, her hand drifted down over his chest, feeling the hard muscles under the silk shift.

"Hmmm," was all she managed as exhaustion—thankfully—was beating out desire.

"I do not know which my mother loves more: to gamble or brawl." Pony went on to expand on his mother's adventures in both, but she slipped back to sleep.

Tinker woke twice more that night. The second time was another nightmare, this of being chased by Foo lions through the ironwoods. Pony was there again to soothe away her fear. The third time was Windwolf finally returning home, but by then she could barely stir.

"How is she?" Windwolf whispered in the darkness.

"She woke twice with nightmares of oni." Pony's voice came from near the door.

The bed shifted with the changing of the guard.

"Thank you, Little Horse, for keeping her well."

"I wish I could do more," Pony whispered. "But I could not keep the dreams from her. May you have more luck than I. Good night, Brother Wolf."

11: PAPER SCISSORS STONE

"I would be happier if one of the other heads took them." Ginger Wine eyed the trucks arriving with the Stone Clan luggage.

Wolf nodded, staying silent. In truth, none of the heads of households wanted the Stone Clan taking up occupancy at their enclave. Ginger Wine, however, lost the decision because not only was she was the juniormost head, but her enclave was also the smallest, meaning she would put the smallest number of Wind Clan folk out when the Stone Clan turned her enclave into a temporary private residence. The households of the three incoming *domana* were reported to be fewer than forty people combined. Ginger Wine's enclave had fifty guest beds, thus a loss of only ten beds.

"I've never hosted someone from the Stone Clan before," Ginger Wine said. "I hope they eat our food. We don't have spices or the pans to cook Stone dishes, but I will not have them in my kitchens."

Wolf could not understand the fanaticism with which the enclaves defended their kitchens. He had had to settle several disputes between his own household and Poppymeadow's. He had learned, though, that there was only one correct answer. "If they will not eat, they will not eat."

Ginger Wine chewed on one knuckle, watching as the luggage was unloaded onto the pavement. The first trunks off, logically for a war zone, were the *sekasha's* secondary armor. Sword and bow cases followed. As Ginger Wine's people struggled to lift the shipping containers holding spell arrows, she murmured around her finger, "I want double my normal remuneration."

"Done."

Wolf had arranged to have his Rolls Royces ferry the Stone Clan *domana* from the palace clearing. The first pulled up in front of Ginger Wine's and a single male got out. As there were no *sekasha* attending the male, this had to be Forest Moss. Wolf couldn't tell if the male was pure Stone Clan genome. Forest Moss had the clan's compact build and dusky skin tone. His hair, though, fell shocking white against his dark skin. The lids of his left eye were sewn shut and concave, following the bone line of his skull, showing that the eye had been fully removed. Scars radiated around the empty socket, as if something thin and heated had been dragged from the edge of his face to just short of the eye. The scar at the corner of the eye, however, continued into his eye. After a score of near misses, that last one had burned out the eye.

The right side of Moss' face was smooth and whole, including the brown eye that glared at Wolf.

"Forest Moss on Stone." Moss gave a coldly precise bow.

"Wolf Who Rules Wind."

Moss' one good eye flicked over him and scanned the *sekasha*. Without the matching eye, Wolf found it difficult to read the male. "Yes, you are. And these are your lovelies. Very, very nice."

Wolf took the comment as a compliment and acknowledged it with a nod. There seemed, however, something more to it—like oil mixed in water, invisible until they separated.

"Otter Dance's son," Forest Moss said. "He comes of age this year, does he not?"

What did this battered soul want of Little Horse? "Yes."

"Tempered Steel." Forest Moss named Little Horse's paternal grandfather as he held up his left hand. He lifted his right hand, saying, "And Perfection." Who was Otter Dance's mother. He put his hands together and kissed his fingertips. "What a creature the Wind Clan has crafted."

It had been a mistake to respond to Forest Moss' first comment; Wolf would not repeat his mistake. While the *sekasha* could be ruthlessly practical, it was insulting to suggest anything but chance had brought the two most famous *sekasha* bloodlines together in one child.

Wolf gave him a hard stare, warning him not to continue on the subject.

"What a look! But I am mad. Such looks are seen only by my left eye." Forest Moss touched his ruined cheek to indicate his empty eye socket. He cocked his head, as something occurred to him. "The last thing I saw from this eye was Blossom Spring from Stone being drowned in the pisshole by her First, Granite. The oni had raped all the females from the start. The *sekasha* had their *naekuna* but the *domana*—" Forest Moss sighed and whispered. "Those mad dogs are so fertile they can even spawn themselves on us. Of course, a half-breed child would have given the oni access to the *domana* genome—so the *sekasha had* to act. The oni had taken Granite's arms and right leg, one bone at a time. They thought they had made him helpless, but still he managed to pin Blossom facedown in the sewage. She thrashed beneath him for so long—I would have thought drowning was faster. It was quiet. So very quiet. None of us daring to say a word until it was over. Shhhhh. Quiet as mice, lest the oni hear and realize that their rabid seed had taken and carry her off to bear their puppies."

Wolf steeled himself to keep from stepping back a step from the elf. Was Forest Moss as mad as he seemed, or was this an act to let him be as rude as he wanted? Or was the male deluding only himself, thinking that he was "acting"?

"What of your *domi*?" Forest Moss leaned close to whisper, his one eye bright. "Did those rabid beasts fuck her? Fill her up with their seed? Will there be puppies to drown in the pisspot?"

Wolf would not validate this conversation by explaining that Tinker would be infertile from her transformation long after the danger of pregnancy was past—regardless of what the oni did to her. "You will not speak of my *domi* again."

"I am not the one to fear. All your lovelies standing around you are the ones to fear. They hold our lives in their holy hands, judging every breath we take. They have to be strong because we're so weak. I fully expect that someday one of them will decide I'm too damaged to live."

"Hopefully soon."

Forest Moss laughed bitterly. "Yes, yes, actually, soon would be nice. I'm too afraid to do it myself. I am a coward, you know. Everyone knows. That's why I have no *sekasha*."

Ginger Wine had heard the whole exchange. A gracious host, she bowed elegantly and offered to escort Forest Moss to his room, but a tightness around her eyes meant she was keeping fury in check. Wolf's people might not know Tinker, but she was *his domi*, and they wouldn't take criticism of her lightly.

While he suspected the humans might blame Tinker for Pittsburgh being stranded, the elves always knew it was only a matter of time before the odd cycle of Shutdown and Startup would end. Humans never continued anything for long. As long as the Ghostlands didn't present them with more problems, most elves would see Tinker's solution as a good one.

Alertness went through his Hand, and Wolf turned to find Jewel Tear standing there.

She wore the deep green that always looked so beautiful on her. Her dark hair was braided with flowers and ribbons, most likely taking an hour to create. She had two spell spheres orbiting her. One cooled the air about her. The other sphere triggered favorite scent memories in those around her. The spheres always had made him leery. He knew that it was impossible for the spheres to collide with anything, but he always flinched when they got too near his head. Nor did it help that the one always made Jewel Tear smell like his blade mother, Otter Dance.

Around them the *sekasha* acknowledged each other's presence and waged their still and silent dominance battle. Not that it was much of a contest—Jewel had only been able to recruit a vanity hand of recent doubles. Against his First Hand, they were just babies.

"Wolf Who Rules Wind." Jewel Tear smiled warmly at him, and bowed lower than necessary, almost spilling her breasts out of her bodice.

"Jewel Tear on Stone." He bowed to her, wondering what her flagrant display meant. Was this strictly a personal invitation, however improper, or was the Stone Clan making use of her?

She stepped forward, rising up on her toes as if she meant to kiss him. He stopped her with a look. The spell spheres orbited them as she stood frozen in place.

"Wolf," she whimpered.

"You are not my *sekasha*, nor are you my *domi*."

"I should be!" She jerked her chin up and glared at him. "You asked me! I told you that I needed time to consider it. I finally make my decision, pack my household to join you here in the Westernlands, and I get your letter saying that you were taking a human—a human—as your *domi*."

"I gave you a hundred years. When I was at court last, thirty years ago, we did not even speak to one another."

"I—I was busy, as were you. And a letter? You could not come and tell me yourself?"

"There was no time." He wondered what she hoped to gain with this tactic. He would not break his vow to Tinker, no matter how guilty Jewel tried to make him feel. Because Jewel never responded, she had no legal recourse.

She reached out to neaten his sleeve. "We courted for years—that slow exquisite dance of passion. The boat rides on Mist Lake with the whiting of swans. The picnics in the autumn woods. The winter masquerades. We took the time that is proper, to learn each other, to know that we were right for each other. What do you know of this—this—female? How can you know anything?"

He knew even if he tried to explain how a lifetime of understanding could be distilled out of twenty-four hours, she would not believe him. The elves never did—with the exception of Little Horse. "I knew enough. This is not court, where you have eternity to decide, because nothing changes. I was willing to risk whatever may come because if I did not put out my hand, and take her then, she would have been lost to me forever."

"What of your commitment to me?"

Wolf controlled a flash of anger. "I waited. You did not answer. I moved on."

"I needed time to think!" she cried and then looked annoyed that she had raised her voice. "I thought you knew me well enough to understand my position. I do not have your resources as the son of the clan leader—a favored cousin to the queen. You would have been forgiven for taking a *domi* outside your clan. Both Wind and Fire want you merely because of the other clan's interest; Wind would never turn you out for the Fire to take in. I do not have your luxury. I had to consider long and hard my responsibilities to my household before committing to you. I couldn't risk not being able to support them if neither Wind nor Stone sponsored me."

"If you had come to me, told me your concerns, I could have done something to guarantee that you would always have Wind Clan sponsorship." Even as he said it, though, he knew that it was better that she hadn't. He had made a mistake in asking her to be his *domi*. When he brought her to the Westernlands, dismay had spread across her face when she realized they would spend the rest of their lives in the wilderness, far from court. It had opened his eyes; he had fooled himself about how well they suited each another. He'd been willing to honor that commitment a hundred years ago, even after that realization. Even as recently as thirty years ago, he might have still taken her as his *domi*. In the last two decades, though, he had considered himself released of his pledge.

Jewel tried to make it all seem his fault. "I was supposed to trust you to take care of me when you couldn't be bothered to explain anything to me? You would go off and leave me with no idea what you had planned, what you were doing, when you were going to come back."

"I trusted you to do what you needed to do. I thought you trusted me."

A look flashed across her face before being hidden away, but he knew her too well not to recognize it and could guess her thoughts. One thing you learned well at court was to trust no one. Not only did she not trust him, she thought him weak for expecting it.

But this left one question. "What made you finally decide?" he asked.

Her nostrils flared and she glanced away from him. "Things have not gone well for me. Some of my ventures failed, I had miscalculated the risks involved on one, and in trying to cover my losses, things— cascaded. I was forced to give up my holdings." Her voice dropped to a whisper. "My household was losing faith in me."

So coming to him was not an act of love but of desperation. It would also explain what she was doing here now—without holdings, she would lose her household and then her clan sponsorship. Jewel Tear was too proud and ambitious to live under someone else's rule. If she was that destitute, though, she wouldn't have the funds to set up a holding at Pittsburgh; it could only mean that the Stone Clan chose her and advanced her stake money.

Did the Stone Clan think that if something happened to Tinker, he would turn to Jewel Tear? How far were they willing to go to put their theory to the test? He knew Jewel well enough to know that she would let nothing stand in the way of her ambitions. That had been one of the things he loved about her.

Tinker wished the machine room didn't feel so much like a trap. Whoever designed the room had never considered that there would be anything as dangerous as the black willow between the back room and the front door. Being around the black willow made everyone nervous. There were no signs, however, of it reviving despite a full day of summer heat. Oilcan rotated the steel drums of metal filings, taking the ones saturated with magic to some place to drain, and replaced them with fresh drums. Tinker could see no overflow of magic. Still, the *sekasha* all kept their shields activated just to use up local ambient magic.

She had the old spell jackhammered out of place. She was now carefully prepping the site to lay down the new spell and cement it into place.

Stormsong settled beside her, her sheathed *ejae* across her knees, her shields a blue aura around her. "Do you mind if we talk?"

"Isn't that what we're doing?"

Stormsong gave a slight laugh, and then continued with great seriousness. "It's not my place to advise you. It should be Pony, as your only beholden, or Wraith Arrow, who is Windwolf's First, but—" Stormsong sighed and shook her head. "Wraith Arrow won't cross that line, and Pony—that boy has a serious case of hero worship for you."

"Pony?"

"You can do no wrong in his eyes. You know all, see all, understand all—which leaves you up the shit creek because you really don't and he won't tell you squat, because he thinks you already know."

"So you're going to tell me?"

"You'd rather walk around with your head up your ass and not know it?"

Tinker groaned. "What am I doing wrong *now*?"

"You need to choose four more *sekasha*, at minimum."

Tinker sighed. "Why? Things are working fine this way."

"No, they're not, and you're the only one that doesn't see that. For instance, Pony is just a baby to the rest of us."

"He's at least a hundred." She knew he was an adult, although just barely, like she had been as an eighteen-year-old human. Unfortunately, now she fell into a nebulous zone of being just barely adult for years and years.

"He just left the doubles this year." Meaning last year, he could use two numbers to indicate his age. "Only half of Windwolf's *sekasha* are in the triples—the rest are older."

"How old are you?" Tinker was fairly sure Stormsong was one of the younger *sekasha*. She was starting to be able to look at elves and see their age indicators. It was odd, to have her concept of Windwolf slowly change from "adult" to "her age" as her perception of all elves changed.

"I'm two hundred." Which made her Pony's age, because to the elves that hundred year difference barely counted.

"So we're all approximately the same age."

"You wish." Stormsong took out a pack of Juicy Fruit gum and offered her a stick. "Yeah, physically Pony and I are like human teenagers, but we've still had a hell of a lot longer than you to figure out people."

Tinker took the gum and let the taste explode in her mouth. "What's your point? Is Pony old or young?"

"That is my point." Stormsong took a piece for herself and put away the pack. "He's the youngest of the *sekasha*, but he's your First."

"Are you trying to confuse me?"

"Anything regarding you, Pony is in charge, but he's the youngest of the *sekasha*."

This was starting to make her head hurt. "Are you talking . . . seniority?"

"Seniority. Seniority." Stormsong took out a small dictionary, flipped through it, and read off the entry for *seniority*. "Precedence of position, especially precedence over others of the same rank by reason of a longer span of service."

"Oh that's not fair," Tinker complained. "You get a dictionary. I want one for Elvish."

"We don't have such things." Stormsong put away the dictionary. "They would be too useful."

Tinker had to put "Elvish dictionary" on her project list.

"Yes," Stormsong continued. "Pony needs seniority over those he commands, which he doesn't have because none of us are yours. What's more, when the bullets start to fly, we need to know which way to jump. Pony doesn't need to think. But the rest of us—we have pledged our lives to Windwolf; it's him we should be thinking of— but we know that only Pony is watching over you."

"I told Windwolf I'd think about this."

"Humans have a wonderful saying: *assume* is making an ass out of 'u' and me. Windwolf assumes that Pony will guide you in your choice, and Pony assumes that you know all."

"So you're doing it."

"Hell, someone has to."

"If it's Pony's job, shouldn't I just tell him that I don't know shit?"

Stormsong gave her a look that Tinker recognized from years of being a child genius.

"Oh gods," Tinker cried. "Don't look at me that way!"

"What way?"

"The 'what a clever little thing' look. It horrifies me how long I'm going to have to put up with that now that I'm an elf."

Stormsong laughed, and then lapsed into Low Elvish, sounding properly contrite. "Forgiveness, *domi*."

"Oh, speak English."

"Yes," Stormsong said in English. "You should talk to Pony, since those you hold need to work well with him. Let me give you pointers he might not think of—he is still new at this. Blind leading the blind and all that shit."

"You're not going to take 'later' as an answer?"

"Kid, how splattered with shit do you need to get before you realize it's hitting the fan? We're fuck deep in oni, Wyverns, and Stone Clan. Now is not the time to be worrying about chain of command."

Stormsong had a way of driving the point home with a sledge-hammer. Tinker just wished she wasn't the one being hammered. "Fine, point away."

"What all *sekasha* want is seniority. To be First. Failing that—in the First Hand." Top five, she meant. "Forever at the bottom is a bitch. Pony was wise to seize the chance to be your First once he saw what you were made of. You've proved yourself with keeping both Windwolf and Pony safe from the oni—that's what a good *domi* does—so all of us are willing to fill your Hand."

"But . . ." Tinker swore she could hear a "but" in there somehow.

"It would be best for all—" Stormsong paused and then added, "—in my opinion—that you don't choose from Windwolf's First Hand."

"Why not?"

"Most *domana* fill their First Hand with *sekasha* just breaking their doubles. The *domana* want the glory a Hand gives them, and the *sekasha* see it as a way to be in First Hand. We call it a vanity Hand. The thing is that most *domana* can't attract a Second Hand because not only is the incentive of being First gone, the *sekasha* of the Second Hand have to be willing to serve under the First Hand. Likewise the Third Hand knows that they will be junior to the First Hand and the Second. Adding into this is the personality of the *domana*: does the positive of being beholden to that *domana* outweigh the negative of not having seniority? Many *domana* can only hold vanity Hands."

"Okay." Tinker had assumed that all *domana* had multiple hands. Apparently not.

"Windwolf's grandfather, Howling, helped tear us away from the Skin Clan and form the monarchy that keeps the clans from waging endless war. When he was assassinated, his *sekasha* became Longwind's—but not as his First or Second, since those were already filled."

"Ouch." Tinker wondered how this related.

"Yes, it was a step down for them—but they saw it as fitting since they had failed Howling," Stormsong said. "Windwolf wanted his First Hand to advise him on setting up in this new land, setting up new towns and lines of trade, something he didn't think doubles could help him do. So he approached the *sekasha* of his grandfather's Hands and they accepted. It would make them First Hand again, but more importantly, they believed in him. Wolf Who Rules has always lived up to his name."

"So, the First Hand, they're all thousands of years old?"

"Yes."

"Okay." So maybe she wasn't so good at guessing age—none of the *sekasha* struck her as older than late twenties in human terms. Tinker finished setting the nonconductive pins that would hold the spell level. "Can you take down your shield? I'm going to set the compressor spell into place."

Tinker didn't want to risk brushing the spell tracing up against an active spell. Stormsong spoke the command that deactivated her shields. A slight pricking that Tinker hadn't really noticed vanished, making her aware by its absence that she had been feeling the active magic.

"Thanks." Tinker took the filigreed sections of the spell out of their protective packing and fit them into place.

Stormsong watched her for a few minutes before continuing her explanation. "It was his First Hand that let Windwolf pull a Second and Third Hand made up of triples and quads."

"So why—" Tinker paused to make sure all the pieces of the spell were stable and level. "Why shouldn't I take any of Windwolf's First? Wouldn't that help me, like it helped him?"

"It would help at a cost to Pony. There's no way he could be First to one of Windwolf's First Hand. Also, the First Hand are the ones that see you most as a child that needs firm guidance until you finish growing up. Lastly, they're all technophobes."

"Ick!" Tinker picked up her cordless soldering iron and started to tack together the pieces of the spell with careful, practiced solders.

"The younger *sekasha* won't bring you as much honor as those from Windwolf's First Hand but they'll be the ones that 'fit' with you best. When Pittsburgh appeared, Windwolf realized that he needed *sekasha* willing to learn technology—and that recent doubles would be the most open-minded. That's when he picked up his Fourth Hand."

"You don't think Pony will know that they'll fit best?"

Stormsong sighed. "Pony's mother, Otter Dance, is Windwolf's blade mother."

"His what?"

"Otter Dance is Longwind's favorite lover among his *sekasha*." Stormsong explained.

Tinker was missing the significance. "Pony is Windwolf's brother?"

"Genetically? no. But emotionally? yes, in a way."

"Oookay." Tinker wondered what Windwolf's mother felt about it. Did she see her husband having a lover as some kind of a betrayal? Or did the fact there was even a special name—*blade mother*—mean that it was somehow expected! Certainly Stormsong seemed to think this was nothing hugely remarkable.

"It has been assumed since Pony's birth that he'd look to Windwolf," Stormsong continued. "In my opinion—that assumption did what all assumptions do."

"Make an ass out of you and me?"

"Yes. Pony is fucking amazing, but neither Windwolf nor Pony seem to realize it. Windwolf still sees Pony as a child, and he's not!"

Tinker thought about Pony doing exercises up in their oni cell, wearing only his pants—chiseled muscles moving under silken skin dripping with sweat. "My husband needs his eyes checked."

Stormsong laughed. "I'm glad you snatched Pony up. As long as you don't do something to fuck him up, maybe he'll one day realize how special he is. Until then, he's going to overcompensate for what he sees as his own weakness. Pony might point you toward someone from the First Hand and then try to bow out—all in the name of doing right by you."

Tinker focused on the last of the solders, clenching her jaw in annoyance at Stormsong's comments about Pony and Windwolf. It felt wrong to hear anything negative about either one of them, like she was being disloyal. Really, what did she know about Stormsong other than she was one of Windwolf's trusted bodyguards? Besides the fact that she nearly died for Tinker?

Tinker sighed as she forced herself to consider that maybe Stormsong was right about all this—that it was vital she pick out four more guards immediately and that Pony needed a good slap upside the head. She found herself remembering that Pony had waited without comment for her to decide to accept Bladebite.

"Is Bladebite from Windwolf's First Hand?" Tinker tried to sound casual about it.

Stormsong nodded.

And if Tinker hadn't dodged the question, she would be stuck with Bladebite trying to control her. She sighed. "How do I tell Bladebite no?" Surely she didn't have to tell him "yes" just because he had offered. That would be a stupid system—but the elves never struck her as completely logical. "Can I tell him no?"

"You can say that you don't think you fit with him. That's copasetic."

Copasetic. Tinker shook her head, remembering the days immediately after she had become an elf—everything made more confused by the fact that Pony didn't speak English or understand the differences between the two cultures.

"When the queen called Windwolf to Aum Renau," Tinker said, "why didn't Windwolf leave you with me?"

"My mother is Pure Radiance and my father is the queen's First.

They have not seen me for a hundred years and wanted me there. Windwolf thought it unwise not to bring me."

Tinker stared at the elf in amazement. "The oracle and a Wyvern? What the hell are you doing with Wind Clan?"

"I had—issues—with court. Windwolf offered me a chance to escape all that and I jumped. Considering what my mother named me, she probably wasn't totally surprised."

Yes, Stormsong sounded more like a Wind Clan name than Fire Clan.

It occurred to Tinker then what "fit" was about. She felt comfortable sitting and talking with Stormsong. Annoying as the truth was, Tinker trusted her judgment. And it would be good to have someone who understood what it felt like to be the outsider.

"So," Tinker said to Stormsong. "Are you offering?"

Stormsong looked puzzled a moment, and then surprised. "To be yours?"

"Yeah. I—I think we work."

Stormsong blinked at her a few moments before standing, the scrape of her boots on the cement loud in the silence that fell between them.

"I can understand if you don't want to." Tinker busied herself checking the solders. All that was needed was to cement the spell into place, wait for the cement to cure, and the black willow could be safely stored indefinitely. Or at least, until she figured out what her dreams meant.

"I want to be honest with you." Stormsong paced the perimeter of the room in her long-legged stride. "But it's like opening a vein. It's a painful, messy thing to do."

Tinker lifted her hand to wave that off. "I don't think I can deal with painfully messy at the moment."

"You should know stuff like this before you ask. That was the whole point of the conversation. You have to make informed choices."

Tinker made a noise. "I've been doing fairly well lately blindly winging it through mass chaos."

Stormsong scoffed and then sighed. "I'm probably the most misbegotten mutt puppy ever born to the elves. Most people think my mother made a horrible mistake having me. I don't fit in anywhere."

"At least you stayed an elf, instead of jumping species like I did."

Stormsong laughed. "There have been times I wished I could. Just be human. Lose myself among them. But a hundred years of *sekasha* brainwashing made that impossible. I can't walk away from it. I tried, but I can't. I like being *sekasha* too much."

"Not to belittle your difficulties, but I really don't get the problem. You're a *sekasha*. I need *sekasha*. We work together well—at least I think we do. Or is it that you hate my guts?"

"I would die for you."

Tinker wished that people would stop saying that to her. "I'll take that as a 'no, I don't hate you' and frankly, I'd rather you didn't die. Now, *that's* painful and messy, and not just for you."

Stormsong laughed and then bowed low to Tinker. "Tinker *domi*, I would be honored to be yours. I will not disappoint you."

12: TEARS ON STONE

At first glance, Turtle Creek seemed the same to Tinker. Sunlight shafted through the Discontinuity in rays of blue. Mist rising off the chill gathered into banks of blue haze and then drifted out of the valley, existing momentarily as white clouds, before burning away in the summer heat. True, royal troops showed up as splashes of Fire Clan red—thus the lifting of the ban on Turtle Creek—but otherwise nothing seemed to have changed. It remained one big hole in reality.

Tinker led her Hand down into the valley to where they'd marked the trees. The first sapling they found had nine slashes in its bark—which should have meant it would be nine feet from the edge of the Discontinuity.

"That looks like only five feet to me." Tinker fingered the mark, wondering if someone might have added slashes after they left.

"Barely five." Pony pointed at the next tree along the edge of the blue.

The tree was marked with seven slashes but the blue came almost to its roots.

"This is bad." Tinker murmured.

"*Domi.*" Pony had moved on ahead and pointed now at a tree inside the effect.

She joined him at the edge of the blue; there were four slashes in the bark of the ghostly tree. "Shit, the Discontinuity has grown. How is that possible?" She motioned to the *sekasha* that they were leaving.

"Now what?" Stormsong asked.

"I'm going to need some equipment, then we're coming back."

Tinker scanned the valley with her camera's infrared attachment over the valley, watching the screen on her workpad instead of looking through the eyepiece. In one window, the video feed showed the thermal picture, and in other windows, programs reduced the images to mathematical models. At the center of the Ghostlands, she spotted a familiar circle.

"Something wrong, *domi*?" Pony asked.

She realized that she had gasped at her discovery. "Oh—this here—this looks like our gate. See, here is the ironwood ring and here is the ramp over the threshold."

"It is lying on its side?"

"Yes. The current probably toppled it, though I'm not sure what is causing the current. It might be simple—" Her Elvish failed her. Did they have a word for convection? "Heat rises and cold falls. Basic science. It's what makes the winds blow. I think this is the same thing on a microscale—like a pot boiling."

"Why not like a pond freezing?"

"I don't know. Perhaps because there's a pool of magic below this, heating the bottom, but it's losing massive amounts of energy before it hits the surface—thus the reason for the cold."

"Ah." Pony nodded like he understood.

"Do you see this point here? Right where the gate is lying. Can you shoot this arrow to that point?"

"With the line and weight attached?"

"Yes."

Pony considered for a moment. "Stormsong would be better."

Among the *sekasha*, Pony was considered the better archer. Her surprise must have shown as Pony waved over Stormsong and explained what Tinker wanted.

"When I have to make a shot, I do it with my eyes closed," Stormsong said. "I see where the arrow needs to be."

"Ooookay." Tinker handed her the end of the line.

Stormsong attached the line to an arrow, nocked it in her compound bow, pulled taut the string, and closed her eyes. For a moment she stood there, aiming blind, and then let loose the bowstring. The arrow soared straight and true as if it had nothing weighing it down or trailing behind. The reel whizzed as the line snaked out after the arrow, the numbers on the meter blurring as they counted up the feet. Near the point Tinker wanted, but not exactly, the arrow shot into the ghost ground of the Discontinuity. It appeared on Tinker's screen as a dot of red heat compared to the arctic cold of the land, too far to the right. The reel fell quiet and the line ran taut out into the Discontinuity.

Tinker sighed. "Close enough for horseshoes and discontinuities."

"It's where it has to be," Stormsong defended her shot.

"I'm trying to see how deep the Discontinuity runs. I figure it is deepest at the gate—it's close enough for that."

Tinker clicked on her mouse and the meter fed its number into the computer: 100 yards. Already the arrow chilled to blue, blending into the rest of the chilled landscape.

"Why does it matter how deep it is?" Pony asked as the reel started to click out as the arrow sank.

Tinker shrugged. "Because I don't know what else to do at the moment. I'm just fiddling around, poking at it until something comes to me."

"Will not the current affect this measurement?" Pony asked.

"Oh, damn." She muttered in English, and then dropped back to low Elvish. "Yes, it will." He was right. There was no way to know what was drift and what was the weighted end sinking. "I'll have to measure the drift and correct the measurements."

At least it gave her an excuse to reel in the arrow and try again to thread it through the heart of the gate. She flipped on the winch. The slack reeled in quickly but then the line went taut, and the winch slowed.

"Well, I'll be damned," Tinker said.

"What is it, *domi*?" Pony asked.

"The arrow hit something."

"The arrow went where it was needed," Stormsong repeated.

There were times Tinker really hated Elfhome—magic screwed with everything. "I didn't think anything would be solid enough to catch on the line."

"The line is solid."

"Yes, it is." She gasped as the implications dawned on her. "Pony, you're a genius. The line is solid."

"I cannot be that smart, *domi*, because I do not understand why that excites you."

"Well, it is an important observation. An object from this reality stays in this reality even after sinking into the Discontinuity."

"How is this important?"

"I do not know, but it is something I did not know before."

"Ah. I see."

The object appeared on the thermal scan, an oddly shaped mass of slightly lighter blue. By the naked eye, she could make out a boil of disturbance beyond where the line cut into the earth, creating a sharp V-shaped wake.

"It is big, whatever it is," Tinker said.

Pony unsheathed his sword.

"I doubt if it is anything living." Tinker backed up regardless. Gods knew what she was dragging in from between realities. "It is at—at . . ." She had to teach Pony English or learn more Elvish. What was Elvish for absolute zero? "It is frozen."

The thing hit shore. For a moment she thought it was a large turtle, and then the line kept reeling, rolling it. Long-fingered webbed hands and a vaguely human-looking face heaved out of the earth, rimmed with frost.

"Oh gods!" Tinker leapt back and the other *sekasha* drew their swords. The reel protested the sudden heavy load as the frozen body hit solid earth, the line vibrating. She killed the power before the line could snap. "Don't touch it!"

"I think it is dead." Pony had his sword at its throat just in case.

"The cold itself is dangerous. Don't touch it directly, but get it out."

Tinker kept her distance. The *sekasha* looped straps carefully around the outstretched limbs and hauled the thing out of the liquid earth. The creature was half Tinker's height and had a turtle shell, but also long scaly limbs and webbed feet and hands. Long straight black hair fringed a bare, depressed spot on a humanlike head, and its face was a weird cross of a chubby monkey's and a turtle's. It wore a harness of leather with various pointy things that could be weapons attached to it.

Pony pricked the creature with his sword, eyed the wound. "It does not bleed. It is indeed frozen."

"Ooookay," Tinker said. "It is probably safe to assume that it will stay dead, even if it thaws out."

"An elf would." Pony sheathed his sword.

"What do you think it is?" Tinker asked.

"It's a kappa." A voice called from above them.

Tinker and her Hand turned, looking upwards. Riki perched on branches of an ironwood, high overhead. He ducked back, behind the trunk, as the *sekasha* pulled out their pistols.

"Wait, don't fire," Tinker ordered. "Riki! Riki! What the hell is this?"

"I told you." He peered out around the trunk. "It's a kappa. Ugly little brats aren't they? In Japan, it's believed that they get their great strength from water in that brain depression and if you can trick them into bowing and spilling out the water, they have to return to the water realm to regain their strength."

Stormsong signed "Kill him?" in blade talk. Tinker signed back "Wait."

"It's an oni?" Tinker asked. "Or an animal?"

"That's a blurred line with the oni," Riki said. "I think you would call it oni—they're fairly clever in a homicidal way. The greater bloods made them by mixing animals with lesser bloods, just like Tomtom did with Chiyo. Legend has it that they used monkeys and turtles—a pretty sick mix, if you ask me."

"I didn't see any while we were making the gate."

"There aren't any in Pittsburgh. They're clever, but not enough to pass as a human."

"So you're saying it came through the gate?"

"The oni use them for special ops; they're strong swimmers and wrestlers."

Tinker looked back into the Discontinuity, the slow drift of blue mist. What were the oni up to? Were they just testing these strange waters to see where they led—or were they trying to salvage the gate?

Then again, was Riki telling the truth that there were no kappa in Pittsburgh?

"What are you doing here, Riki?"

"I need to talk to you."

"Talk? Talk about what? How can I even trust anything that comes out of that lying mouth of yours?"

"I'm sorry, Tinker, about everything that happened. I really am. I know you're pissed as hell at me, but I need to talk to you about the dragon."

"What dragon?"

"The one that attacked you. The one I pulled off you. The one that might have killed you and all your people if I hadn't called it."

"So it was a dragon?"

"Not an Elfhome dragon, but yes, a dragon."

"An Onihida dragon?"

"What does it matter where it's from? It's a freaking dragon. Can we just move on?"

"Just answer the fucking question!" she shouted at Riki. "It's rather simple. Was it an Onihida dragon?"

Riki paced the limb like an agitated crow. "For a long, long time dragons were worshipped as gods, both on Earth and Onihida. They lived in 'the heavens' and had great powers that they often used to help humans and tengu alike. All the legends about dragons go on about the heavens and traveling from to Onihida or Earth and back. What that mystical shit might have actually been talking about is travel between universes. So dragons may be native to Onihida—or might be from someplace else. I don't know."

If Riki had told her the truth about his childhood, he was raised on Earth and probably was less in tune with the mystical than she was. Not that she was particularly "in tune."

"The dragon cast an oni shield spell." She pointed out the flaw in Riki's "not from Onihida" logic.

"No, that's not oni magic, it's dragon magic. The oni true bloods figured out how to enslave dragons and stole their magic."

So he said—but how could she know if he was telling the truth? "Dragon magic? Oni magic? What's the difference?"

"Originally oni magic was only bioengineering, just like the elves."

"So the solid hologram stuff? Like your wings?"

"That's dragon magic."

"And the tengu? They're both oni and dragon magic?"

Riki did an angry little hop. "Tinker! I just want to ask you one simple question, not give you a history lesson."

"What do you want, Riki?"

"The dragon—when it attacked you—did it mark you with a symbol or tattoo or something like that?"

"Strange that you ask, but yeah, it put one right here." She half turned and patted her butt cheek. "It says, 'Kiss my ass.'"

Stormsong snickered.

"I know how pissed you must be, Tinker. Believe me, if this weren't important, I wouldn't come anywhere near you."

She scoffed at that. "What does this mark do?"

"So it marked you?" Judging by the excitement in his voice, it was very important to him.

Stormsong shoved Tinker suddenly behind her and activated her shields with a shout. At the movement, Riki jerked back out of sight. A second later, a bullet struck the tree trunk where Riki had been standing, ricocheted, and struck Stormsong's shield.

"Shields, *domi*." Pony triggered his own and pulled his sword.

Tinker felt a kick of magic from the west. She forced herself to find her center and cast the trigger spell. Her heart was pounding as the wind wrapped around her.

Sekasha emerged from the forest shadows; their wyvern armor and tattoos were the black of the Stone Clan. Five in all—a full Hand, the back two acting as Shields, which meant they had someone to guard. They halted some twenty feet off, tense and watchful.

"Lower your weapons," a female shouted in High Elvish.

"Lower yours! This is Wind Clan holding!" Tinker shouted angrily.

"It's a royal holding," The Stone Clan's *domi* came out from behind one of the ironwoods. "And you're conversing with the enemy."

The *domi* was short for an elf, several inches shorter than her *sekasha*, but willowy graceful as any other high-caste female Tinker had ever seen. She wore an emerald green underdress and an overdress with a forest of wildly branching trees over it. Her hair was gathered into elaborate braids, dark and rich as otter fur, twined with emerald ribbons and white flowers. Two small gleaming orbs circled around her, like tiny planets caught in her gravity.

"Yeah, I was talking to him." Tinker almost dropped her shield but then she realized that her *sekasha* hadn't put away their swords. "It's a good way to find out things you don't know. Like who are you?"

"Hmm, short and vulgar—you must be Wolf Who Rules' *domi*. What was your name again? Something unpronounceable."

"This is one of my issues from court," Stormsong murmured in English. "Lowest ranking introduces themselves first; it's a matter of honor. You outrank her, so she should go first. She's trying to provoke you since she can't call insult; you are still under the queen's protection."

"Fuck that. Who the hell is she?"

"Her name is Jewel Tear on Stone. She and the rest of the Stone Clan arrived this morning."

"Is she right about this being a royal holding now?"

"Unfortunately, yes."

"Shit!"

"You are talking to me, not her." Jewel Tear picked her way gracefully toward Tinker. Despite the sweltering heat and her long gown, there was no sweat on her creamy white skin. "You are Wolf Who Rules' *domi*? Tinkle? Thinker?"

Screw this. "Can you introduce us, Stormsong?"

"Me doing it would be a breach of etiquette and be considered extremely rude."

"Good. Do it."

Stormsong executed an elegant bow and said, "Jewel Tear on Stone, this is our Beloved Tinker of Wind."

Amazing how they all reacted as if she had slapped Jewel Tear. All the Stone Clan *sekasha* moved forward as if to attack.

"Hold," Jewel Tear snapped. She glared at Tinker for a moment, but then murmured, "You are such a rude little beast. I don't know if I should be flattered or horrified that Wolf Who Rules chose you after I cut him loose."

Tinker glanced to Stormsong, who nodded slightly, confirming that yes this was an old girlfriend of Windwolf's. Well, if it was a battle of wits that this bitch wanted, she'd come to the right place. "That proves what they say."

"Which is?"

"Only an idiot would turn down Wolf Who Rules."

"Your arrogance is only matched by your ignorance."

"I'd rather be unlearned than moronic—since it's so much easier to cure."

"When Prince True Flame learns of your treason, he will cure that arrogance too."

"I might have been talking to the tengu—but you let him get away." Tinker pointed out.

Jewel Tear spoke a spell and made a motion, and magic pulsed underfoot, pushing up through the ground, the low ferns, and then the trees to the very ends of the leaves. Tinker *felt* the ten *sekasha* standing around them, even Rainlily standing behind her. She and Jewel Tear *echoed* differently—their *domana* shields creating the change, or maybe their innate magical talents. Around them there were birds and animals unseen but now *sensed*.

She didn't, however, *feel* Riki—and by her angry look—neither did Jewel Tear.

"Horse piss!" Jewel Tear hissed quietly.

"I was trying to get as much information out of the tengu as I could." Tinker rubbed Jewel Tear's nose in it. Interestingly, the female didn't take it gracefully.

"The oni subverted you when they held you prisoner."

"No, they did not." Pony answered the charge. "I stand as witness to my *domi*: by my blood and my blade, she never bowed her will to them."

There was noise of something coming through the woods toward them. Jewel Tear triggered her sonar spell again and the forest was alive with *sekasha* moving toward them, and at least two other *domana*. Tinker was going to have to learn that spell.

"True Flame is coming. We'll see what he has to say."

A wave of red washed around them as Wyverns surrounded

them, and then, comfortingly, a tight knot of blue as True Flame and Windwolf entered the clearing. Jewel Tear dropped her shields, so Tinker followed suit.

True Flame glanced at the kappa all but forgotten on the ground, and then to Tinker and Jewel Tear. "What is going on here? Where did that kappa come from?"

"I pulled that out of the Ghostlands." Tinker stepped forward and gave it a slight kick to demonstrate it was frozen solid. "The Ghostlands must have instantly sucked the body heat out of it."

"She was talking with a tengu." Jewel Tear indicated the empty treetops.

"Yes, I was." Tinker saw no point in denying it. "We have a history together. He betrayed me to the oni and I beat the snot out of him for it. He found me and started the conversation."

"What did you speak about?" True Flame asked.

"I'm not sure what he wanted—they nearly killed me shooting at him."

Windwolf had moved between Jewel Tear and Tinker just as a *sekasha* would, his shields still up so he seemed to shimmer with anger. With Tinker's explanation, he took a step toward Jewel Tear. "How dare you?"

Jewel Tear jerked up her chin. "That was an unfortunate and unforeseeable accident. Forgiveness, Tinker *ze domi*."

Tinker nodded but Windwolf shook his head.

"If you harm my *domi*," Windwolf growled, "It will not be the Fire Clan that you'll be answering to."

"Wolf Who Rules—" True Flame snapped.

"I will not suffer future 'unfortunate' accidents. There will be no forgiveness."

True Flame studied Windwolf for a moment and then nodded. "That is your right."

Windwolf caught Tinker's hand. "Come." And he pulled her out of the clearing.

"Wait, my stuff."

"Leave it."

"No!" She jerked her hand free. "I'm not done here."

"You are for right now."

"No, no, no. I'm sick of this. Come here, go there, do this. My grandfather died five years ago, thank you, and I was happy making decisions for myself."

"These are royal holdings now." Windwolf swept a hand to take in the whole valley. "I cannot make her leave."

"So you're making me?" Tinker cried.

"Yes."

"No."

"Beloved. I do not trust her. I cannot stay here and watch over you now and I cannot make her leave."

As always, he seemed to cover all the options—leaving her no good choice but to do what he wanted.

This time she shook her head. "No. Again and again, you don't tell me enough to form my own options. All I know are your options and I'm not playing that anymore."

"Be reasonable."

"Reasonable? What is reasonable about taking the smartest person in this city and making them deaf and blind? I'm supposed to walk away from my work, leaving behind my currently irreplaceable equipment, because some female from the other side of the world is not playing nice in my backyard?"

"I told you that I cannot stay and I cannot make her leave."

"And those are the only options because they're the only ones you have thought of? You know, if I had a level playing field I could come up with options of my own."

"I do not have time to explain it all."

"Of course not. You never have time."

"Beloved . . ."

"Don't 'Beloved' me. Did you know that—until Pony told me, I didn't know the name of your mother? That I didn't know that you—and I—could use Fire Clan spell stones? I don't even know when I'm going to have a period! I'm stuck in this stranger's body and no one tells me diddly. And when did I agree to be called Beloved Tinker? I think I should at least be able to pick out my own name."

Windwolf looked stunned at her outburst and after a moment, said quietly, "Your name is . . . short."

"Tinker isn't my real name. My real name is Alexander Graham Bell."

"It is? I did not know that."

"Score one for me."

"Beloved—Tinker—Alexan . . . der?" He floundered for a moment. "Isn't that considered a male name?"

"I can hold my own with Jewel Tear. I'm not done here, and I'm not leaving my stuff."

"No, you cannot hold your own." Windwolf caught her by her shoulders. "Do not ever think that you can. Only you can sense her magic—so it is possible for her to attack you without your *sekasha* knowing it. She could make a tree fall, the ground give way, dozens of little ways that you *do not know*."

"You really think she would try to kill me?"

"Yes."

"Any one of us," Stormsong added in English, "can make a bullet ricochet and hit a target. The tengu was a convenient excuse."

Tinker turned to her and saw in her eyes that none of her *sekasha* took the event as an accident. They hadn't relaxed until Windwolf and True Flame appeared.

"But why?" she asked.

"Because the Stone Clan stands to gain much if you are dead and I'm distracted. Because she is a self-centered, ambitious bitch."

That was unnerving. Tinker kicked at the dirt, not wanting to leave, hating that once again she was bowing to his limited options. "Can we can get True Flame to order her out of the area?"

"No, we must let her try and fix this valley."

Tinker laughed. "With what?"

"Magic."

She doubted that greatly, but she was up against the wall of her own ignorance. "I'm the one that made this mess. I'll be the one that fixes it."

"That is quite possible. Stone Clan, however, has assured True Flame that they can quickly fix the Ghostlands, while you said you needed to study it further. Everyone knows that you were being realistic—but True Flame had to believe the Stone Clan or it would be an insult to them."

"God forbid he insults them." Tinker growled and looked back toward the Discontinuity's edge and her abandoned equipment.

"*Domi*, I will bring your things," Stormsong offered. "I am not totally ignorant of these computer things."

Since Stormsong could manage the Rolls Royce and the walkie-talkie, she should be able to disconnect the equipment and carry it back to the enclave unharmed. Tinker sighed and nodded. "Okay. Thank you."

Windwolf signaled that Cloudwalker would accompany Stormsong, and the two *sekasha* moved off.

"There is so much I need to know," Tinker said to him. "And if we're really going to be husband and wife—you need to take the time for me. How do you expect me to trust you when you keep throwing me in the pool to sink or swim?"

He sighed deeply and scrubbed his hands over his face. "I want to be there for you—protect you—but I can't. It's killing me that you're in the water and floundering—but the only other option I have is to lock you away someplace safe, and that would only kill you faster. The only thing that has kept me sane so far is knowing that you're actually very good at finding your own way out of the water."

After seeing his *domi* safely back to Poppymeadow's, Wolf went in search of Earth Son to lodge his complaint. He found Earth Son at the palace clearing, pacing it out as if he planned to claim the piece of land for himself. Apparently the Stone Clan *domana* had expected the *aumani* as soon as they arrived in Pittsburgh; Earth Son wore a full tunic of rich green silk and a gold burnt velvet duster with a stone horse pattern. Like Jewel, he had a spell orb keeping him cool in the muggy Pittsburgh summer.

Wolf closed the distance between them. "Earth Son, I will have a word with you."

Earth Son had inherited his father's height, so he was slightly taller than Wolf. He tried to use it to look down on Wolf, but then ruined the effect by doing a sketchy bow. "Wolf Who Rules."

Wolf was too angry to acknowledge the veiled insult of Earth Son's greeting. "Has the Stone Clan all run mad? We do not know the number of the oni forces, and the way between our worlds is not fully shut, and you're already asking for a clan war."

"Us?" Earth Son feigned confusion.

"I may be young, but I spent my doubles at court. I recognize power maneuvering when I see it."

"You are seeing things that are not there—like your so-called oni." Earth Son's First, Thorne Scratch, tried to silence her *domou* with a hand on his shoulder. Earth Son flicked the female *sekasha's* hand away. "I have been out for hours doing scrys." He waved toward the forest beyond the clearing. "And found nothing remotely resembling an oni. 'I can see the shadows of the oni on the wall,' is that not what you said at court? Apparently that's all that you've seen—shadows! You're jumping at phantoms if you ask me."

Wolf didn't even bother with magic. He stepped forward and caught Earth Son by the throat. "Listen, you little turd, my *domi* is under the queen's protection, which means you are not to attack her. But if you can't get that through that rock skull of yours, then understand this—if she is hurt in any way, I will hunt you down and tear out your throat."

"You would not dare," Earth Son managed to whisper.

"I started with nothing here. I can do it again. If my *domi* is killed, I will let the crown strip me bare to have my revenge. Do not think our royal cousin will protect you either—after you shit all over the queen's commands, True Flame will not stop me."

"I cannot be held accountable for what that the others—"

"You are clan head for this area and I will hold you responsible."

"Forest Moss is mad!"

"If you didn't want the disadvantages that the mad one brings with him, you shouldn't have chosen him."

"I didn't choose him."

Earth Son's Hand looked relieved as the clearing filled with Wyverns.

"Wolf." True Flame followed on the wash of red. "Let him go."

Wolf released Earth Son, turning over this new piece of information. He knew that Earth Son did not have considerable standing in the Stone Clan, but he thought that Earth Son would have at least been party to picking out the clan *domana* that would be under him. Now that Wolf had talked with Forest Moss and Jewel Tear and learned their situations, their inclusion seemed less a personal attack on the Wind Clan, and more a statement of the Stone Clan's assessment of Pittsburgh. They had sent two of their most disposable *domana*. Or was the count three?

In the clans, birth did not guarantee rank. It was acknowledged, though, that children of the clan leaders learned much from observing their parents. Genetically, too, the leaders were the best that the clans had to offer. True, barring accident or assassination, it was unlikely clan heads would ever change—but as his mother's only child, Earth Son was a likely future leader. Then again, he had arrived with only one Hand. Was he escort for the other two, or fellow exile? If the latter, what had Earth Son done to be sent to Pittsburgh?

"I did nearly a hundred scrys," Earth Son reported to True Flame while he rubbed his throat. "There's no oni here."

"The oni are savage but not stupid," Wolf snapped. "Acting quickly is not to their advantage. They are hiding themselves well and waiting for the best time to strike."

Earth Son scoffed at this. "If that was the case, they should have struck while you were here alone, with even your voice turned against you."

"They tried. They failed." Wolf did not mention how near the assassination had come to succeeding. The brutal attack killed one of his *sekasha*, damaged one of his hands, and stranded him deep in Pittsburgh's territory just as it returned to Earth. If not for Tinker, the plot would have succeeded. "If the Ghostlands can be used to their advantage, they will wait for reinforcements."

"Wolf is right," True Flame said. "That they managed to stay hidden for nearly thirty years shows that they have patience. No matter what happens, we need you to ferret them out."

13: IGNORE THAT MAN BEHIND THE CURTAIN

-⋆-▷═◁-⋆-

Tinker sat high up on a towering cross, clinging to the crossbrace. Black was sitting at the very end of the crossbrace, sobbing quietly. The delicate-boned woman wore a puffy black mourning gown and a crown. Lying beside her was a long wand with a star attached to it. Her host of crows sailed overhead, cawing, "Lost, Lost!"

With a flurry of wings, Riki perched on the tip of the brace between Tinker and Black. He was wearing an odd red outfit. "There's no shame in being afraid of heights. Most people are."

"Oh, go away, monkey boy," she snapped.

"I'm not a flying monkey," the tengu said. "I gave that up. You melted the witch, so I got out of my no-compete contract. I'm working strictly as a freelance crow. The health benefits suck, but I make my own hours."

Tinker pointed to the sobbing Black. "Why is she crying?"

"She gave her heart to the Tin Man but she lost him," Riki told her. "Not even the wizard can fix that."

"Hey!" On the ground, Esme gazed up at them, wearing blue checked overalls and red ruby boots. "You can't get down. Your not smart enough. You're head is full of straw."

"I'll figure a way down," Tinker shouted back.

"Falling will work," Riki said.

And Tinker was falling.

The dream seemed to hiccup and she was safe on the ground then. Esme had a wicker basket and a little black dog. Pony was there, his hair loose and curly as a mane, whiskers, cat ears and tail to finish the cat look. Oilcan too, looking like he was made out of metal.

"You have Black's heart?" Tinker asked Oilcan.

"I have no heart." He thumped on his chest and it echoed.

"That was a different tin man." Esme butted between the two of them. "We need to find the wizard! Only he can solve all our problems."

"I can take you to the wizard." Oilcan squeaked as he moved his arm to point down a yellow brick road that led into a dark forest of black willows. "But we don't need to hurry, it's only six o'clock."

"We've murdered time." Esme took out a pocket watch. It seemed to be coated with butter. "It's always six o'clock—we have to run to stay in the same place."

"We will have to go through the trees." Pony's cat tail danced nervously behind him.

"I don't know if that's smart," Tinker said.

"Of course you don't, you have straw for brains." Esme picked straw out of Tinker's head to prove her point. "Look! See!" She held out the straw as evidence. "We have to get to the wizard. He's the only one who can give you brains so you can solve this problem."

"But the road ended with the tree," Tinker pointed out as they crept forward, clinging to one another.

"It's not the tree," Esme said. "It's the fruit."

The trees turned, their gnarled faces looking at them with wooden eyes. They were black willow trees but there were apples—red and tempting—in their branches.

"You need the fruit." Esme pushed Tinker hard toward the trees.

The trees plucked the apples from their branches and flung them like hard rain at Tinker.

⊷≡◉≡⊷

Tinker flailed her way out of her sheets to sit up in bed. It was very early morning by the pale light in the window—the birds hadn't yet started to stir. Windwolf was awake though, and dressing.

"I didn't mean to wake you." He came to kiss her. His shirt was still unbuttoned, and she burrowed into his warmth.

"I had another dream about Black, Esme, and the black willow."

"Esme?"

"I figured out who White was—she's Lain's sister."

"Ah, the one in white—you're dreaming that she's dreaming." He wrapped his arms around her, kissing her hair.

"Hm? Oh, yes, the Escher thing." Gods, it felt so right to be held by him.

"Have you talked to Stormsong?"

"Yeah. She—we fit."

He tipped her head back to gaze intently into her face. "You've accepted her? To be your beholden?"

She gave a tiny nod. It sounded like some kind of wedding vow. Was this what elf society was all about—getting married again and again, only without sex? "Yes. To be mine."

Windwolf gave her his smile that warmed her to her toes. "I release her to you. But—"

"But?"

"But that is not what I meant. You should talk to Stormsong about your dreams. She has some training in *yatanyai*. She might be able to help you determine what they mean."

"She does?"

"It was thought she would be an *intanyei seyosa* but in the end, she had too much of her father's temperament." Windwolf kissed Tinker again and slipped out of her hold. "I need to go. True Flame expects me. Why don't you go back to sleep?"

She eyed the bed. She was still tired, but to sleep would most likely mean another dream.

"I'll send Pony to you." Windwolf buttoned up his shirt.

"I'd rather have you." She settled back into the warm softness.

Windwolf smiled. "I am glad of that, but alas, you cannot have me, so you must make do with Pony."

Did he really know what that sounded like in English? She curled into ball and resolved to be asleep before Pony joined her. And she was.

Another day, another dress. She really had to do something about clothing. She picked out the Wind Clan blue dress and had the staff add pockets to it while she ate. Breakfast proved that Windwolf's household was still intent on mothering the life out of her. They stacked the garden table with plates of pastries, omelets, and fresh fruit. Tinker eyed the collection of dishes with slight dismay.

"If they keep this up, they're going to make me fat," Tinker complained.

"Eat." Stormsong pointed at a bench, indicating that she was to sit. "You and Pony have both lost weight since Aum Renau."

Pony nodded, acknowledging that this was the truth. "You should eat."

"*Pft.*" Tinker began loading a plate. "Fine, but you both have to eat too."

A sign of their "fit," they ate at first in companionable silence, then drifted into a conversation about which of the *sekasha* would work well with them. Of Windwolf's four Hands, they came up with a list of seven possible candidates to fill the three open positions of Tinker's First Hand.

"We can spend a few days pairing with others to see who works best with you." Pony meant Tinker. "Windwolf chose all of his *sekasha* so we work well together, and we've had years to learn each other's ways."

"What are your plans for today?" Stormsong asked. "Are we finished with that tree?"

"I don't know," Tinker whined. "I had another dream about it. Windwolf said I should talk to you about my dreams."

"You dream?" Stormsong said.

"I don't want to believe that I do," Tinker said, "but things keep showing up out of my dreams."

"Dreams are important," Stormsong said. "They let you see the future."

"Oh gods help me if this is my future," Tinker muttered.

"Tell me this dream," Stormsong said.

"Well, I had a couple, and they're all centering around two people, and the tree." Tinker explained the first dream and then the discovery of Esme's identity, and then last night's dream, ending with, "And I don't have a clue where all *that* weirdness came from."

Stormsong cocked her blue head with a faint disbelieving look on her face. "It sounds like *The Wizard of Oz*."

"What's that?" Tinker asked.

"It's a movie," Stormsong said.

Tinker had never heard of such a movie. "What's it about?"

"It's about—It's about—It's odd." Stormsong said. "Maybe you should just see it."

Since Tooloo rented videos, Tinker gave her a call.

"I'm looking for *The Wizard of Oz*."

"Well, follow the yellow brick road," Tooloo said and hung up.

Somehow, Tinker had totally forgotten how maddening it was to deal with Tooloo. She hit redial, and explained, "I'm looking for the movie called *The Wizard of Oz*."

"You should have said so in the first place."

"Can you set it aside? I'll be by to pick it up." And while she was there, she'd find out why Tooloo had lied to Nathan.

"No, you won't," Tooloo said.

Amazing that someone can give you an instant headache over the phone. "Yes, I will."

"You can come but the movie won't be here."

"Oh, did someone else rent it?"

"No."

"Tooloo!" Tinker whined. "This is so simple—why can't I rent the movie if no one has it?"

"I never had it."

"You didn't?" Tinker asked.

"It was fifty years old when the first Shutdown hit, and I couldn't stand it after having to watch it every year for thirty years running."

Should she even ask *why* Tooloo had to watch it every year? No, that would only make her head hurt more. "So that's a 'no'?"

"Yes," and Tooloo hung up.

Tinker sat drumming her fingers as she considered her phone. Should she call Tooloo back and try to find out why Tooloo was telling people she wasn't married to Windwolf? Go and visit the crazy half-elf in person? She suspected that even if she could understand the logic behind Tooloo's action, she wouldn't be able to change it so the half-elf would stop.

She decided to focus on her dream. Where had she seen the movie? Her grandfather thought movies were a waste of time, so that left Lain.

"I don't have that movie," Lain stated when Tinker called and asked.

"Are you sure?"

"Yes, I'm sure. Esme insisted that we watch it every year after Thanksgiving. God knows why they picked Thanksgiving. It always gave me nightmares. I would be quite happy never to see that stupid movie again."

"Esme liked it?"

"She always identified too much with Dorothy, though she never understood why Dorothy wanted to go back home. Esme would go on and on about how if she were Dorothy, she would stay in Oz, which would make my mother cry. Every Thanksgiving we would have this huge family fight about watching it; Esme would win, Mother would cry, and I'd have nightmares."

They said their good-byes like polite people and Tinker hung up. Where had she seen this movie?

She called Oilcan. She never watched a movie alone, so he most likely had seen it with her. "Hey, I'm trying to remember something. Did you see *The Wizard of Oz* with me?"

"The what?"

"It's a movie called *The Wizard of Oz*. It's about Dorothy who goes to Oz." That much of the story Tinker had gathered from Lain, although she wasn't clear where Oz was. Africa?

"It's not ringing any bells."

She sighed. "If I track this down, do you want to watch with us?"

"A movie night? Cool. Sure. Meet you at your loft?"

She hadn't considered where to watch the movie once she found it. She suddenly realized it had been two months since she'd been home to her loft. Weirder yet, she didn't want to go—as in "don't want to go to the dentist because it would hurt" way. Why the hell did she feel that way? Her system made Oilcan's look like a toy, which was why they always used her place. But she was cringing at the thought of doing movie night at her loft.

"Tink?" Oilcan asked.

This was stupid—it was her home. "Yeah, my place."

"See you later then."

"Later."

She slumped forward onto the table, resting her cheek on its smooth surface. Three phone calls, she hadn't yet stirred out of the garden, and already she was emotionally raw and tired. Damn, she wished she could get a good night's sleep. Her exhaustion felt like it was teaming up with all her problems, conspiring to keep her off balance.

"*Domi*," Stormsong said quietly. "When I saw the movie, I rented it from Eide's."

At least something was working out in her life.

Eide's Entertainment was an institution in Pittsburgh, down on Penn Avenue in the Strip District. Established in the 1970s as a comicbook store, it had been one of the many landmarks that somehow not only survived but also flourished when transplanted to Elfhome. It was a mecca of human culture, which not only humans but also elves went on pilgrimage to. Tinker and Oilcan would always hit the shop once immediately after Startup to see what was new, and then several times a month to see what used music and videos were brought in by other customers. Besides music, videos, and comic books, the store was a treasure trove of collectible items: non-sport cards, magazines, Big Little Books, pulps, and out of print books.

Ralph raised his hand to them as they entered. "Hey, Lina, long time no see. I've got that Nirvana CD you wanted in the back."

It wasn't until Stormsong touched hands with Ralph in a rocker's version of a handshake that Tinker realized he had been talking to Stormsong. Lina? Ah yes, *Linapavuata*, which was Elvish for "singing." Ralph looked past the elf, saw Tinker.

"Tinker-tiki!" Ralph used Tinker's racing nickname, which meant "Baby Tinker," "Look at you!" He ran a finger over Tinker's ear point, making her burn with embarrassment. "Like the ear job. Love the dress. You're looking *fine*."

Pony slapped Ralph's hand away and reached for his blade, but Stormsong kept him from drawing his *ejae*.

"Their ways are not ours," Stormsong murmured in High Elvish to Pony, and then dropped to Low Elvish to continue. "Ralph, this is Galloping Storm Horse on Wind, he looks to Tinker *ze domi*—and she is *very* off-limits now."

"Forgiveness." Ralph bowed and used passable Low Elvish. "Does that make you Tinker of the Storms?"

"Beloved Tinker of Wind," Pony corrected Ralph with a growl.

Ralph glanced to Stormsong and read something on her face that made him decide to flee. "Let me go get that CD."

Tinker turned to Pony, who was still glaring after Ralph. "What was that about?"

"He should show you respect," Pony said.

Stormsong clarified in English. " 'Baby Tinker' is disrespectful, nor should he have touched you."

"I've known him for years!" Tinker stuck with Low Elvish. She didn't want to cut Pony out of the conversation. "Oilcan and I go to his parties. Tinker-tiki is what all the elves call me."

"Used to call you," Pony said. "No elf would be so impolite as to use it now."

"Only because they fear you would call insult," Stormsong implied, with a glance, that Pony would use his blade in dealing with anyone who insulted Tinker.

"Like—kill them?" Tinker asked.

"We have the right to mete out punishment as we see fit," Pony explained. "By the blood and the sword."

Oh boy. The little things people don't tell her. "You can't just whack the head off anyone that pisses you off!"

"If the insult is severe, yes, we can," Pony said. "*Sekasha* are divine warriors, who answer only to the gods."

"We have the right," Stormsong said. "Our training guides us not to take the options allowed to us."

"Look, if I'm insulted, I'll punch the guy myself. As far as I'm concerned, you guys are just here for oni and monsters with sharp teeth."

"Yes, *domi*." Stormsong gave an elaborate bow.

Pony looked unhappy but echoed, "Yes, *domi*."

Which didn't make Tinker happy, because she felt like she was somehow the bad guy for not letting them lop off heads right and left. Worse, she *knew* it was all really Windwolf's fault because her life gotten weird the exact second that he entered it. Suddenly she was very annoyed with him, but didn't want to be, which made her grumpier. She tried to ignore the whole confusing swarm of emotions and thumped over to the video rental section. The *sekasha* and stinging feelings, unfortunately, followed close behind.

She'd never actually rented a video from Eide's before and their categories confused her. There seemed to be two of every category. "Why two?"

"These are bootleg copies with subtitles in Low Elvish." Stormsong pointed out a sign in Elvish that Tinker had missed because a male elfin customer stood in front of it, flipping through the anime.

The elf noticed Stormsong with widening eyes, bowed low, and moved off with a low murmured, "Forgiveness."

"The other elves—they're afraid of you?" Tinker noticed that all the elves in the store covertly watched the *sekasha* and had cleared out of their path.

"If they do not know us, yes," Stormsong spoke quietly so her words wouldn't carry. "You are one that sleeps in the nest of dragons. You do not know how rare we are—or how dangerous."

"What makes you so special?"

"The Skin Clan did; they created the perfect warrior."

Tinker was afraid to ask how this gave them the right to preform indiscriminate head-lopping, so she focused on why they were here— to rent *The Wizard of Oz*. Knowing that Pony would be watching the movie with her, Tinker scanned only the translated videos. Unlike the originals in their glossy colorful boxes, the translated videos had plain white covers with Low Elvish printed onto the spines. She pulled out one at random and studied it. The movie was *The Wedding Singer* which had been translated to *The Party Singer*. Was it a bad translation or was there actually no Elvish word for wedding? How could the elves exist without the most basic of life ceremonies?

Tinker put the movie back, and scanned the shelves.

Stormsong had been searching too, and now pulled out a box and handed it to Tinker. "This is it."

The translator hadn't even tried to find Elvish to match the words *Wizard* and *Oz*. Instead, the title was phonetically spelled out.

Tinker turned and found Tommy Chang leaning against the end of the DVD rack, watching her with his dangerous cool. He was wearing a black tank top that showed off the definition in his muscled arms, a corded leather bracelet, and his signature bandana.

Tommy organized raves, the cockfights in Chinatown, and the hover-bike races—the last being how she knew him best.

"Hi, Tommy." Somehow, the normal greeting sounded dorky. Something about his zenlike menace made her feel like a complete techno geek. If she didn't watch it, she ended up overcompensating around him.

He lifted his chin in acknowledgement. "I wasn't sure if they'd let you out." He glanced toward Pony. "They keep you on a short leash. In a dress, even."

"Piss off." That was a record.

"Aren't we touchy now we're an elf?"

"Excuse me, but I've had one fucked-over month."

"So I heard." And then, surprisingly, he added. "Glad you're still breathing."

"Thanks."

"You still going to ride for Team Tinker?"

She felt a flash of guilt as she realized that she hadn't thought about racing in months. Last she had heard Oilcan had taken over the riding. "How is my team doing?"

"It's been Team Big Sky's season since," he lifted a finger to indicate her appearance, "the whole elf thing."

That made sense. Oilcan was heavier than she was, had a different center of gravity, and was less aggressive on the turns. Team Banzai would have lost their edge when the oni stole Czerneda's custom-made Delta. That left John Montana, captain of Team Big Sky, with the only other Delta in the racing circuit, and his half brother, Blue Sky, a good match to her build and skills.

"So—you going back to riding?" Tommy asked.

"I don't know. A lot of shit has hit the fan that I need to deal with before I can think about that."

A flash of Wyvern red outside made Tommy look toward the store windows. "Yup, a lot of shit."

Her loft smelled of garbage. Months ago—a lifetime ago—she, Oilcan, and Pony had eaten, washed dishes, left trash in the can to be taken out, left, and never come back. Stormsong was too polite to say anything, carefully sticking to Low Elvish. Even after they'd opened the windows and let in the cool evening air, the place depressed Tinker with its ugliness. She had lived alone at human speed, always too busy cramming in what was important to her to deal with beautifying where she lived. Most of her furniture was battered, mismatched, used stuff that she had picked up cheap. The couch had been clawed by someone else's cats, the leather recliner was cracking with age, and the coffee table was scrap metal she'd welded together and topped with a piece of glass. The walls had been painted dark green by the loft's last occupant—not that you could see a whole lot of the color as her cinderblock and lumber bookshelves covered most of the walls and overflowed with her books. She had nothing beautiful—everything was just serviceable and in need of a good cleaning.

She knew it could be made pretty. She had time now, if she wanted to take it. The place could be cleaned, painted, and furnished. She could even hire carpenters to make her bookcases and kitchen cabinets. There was no room, though, for all the people in her life now. The place was for one busy person who was barely there or a married couple with no interests outside of each other. Windwolf would never fit—his life was too big—and she didn't want to live without him. Without Pony. And of late, not without Stormsong either.

She didn't fit into her old life anymore. This wasn't her home anymore, and it saddened her for reasons she couldn't understand. Perching on the couch's overstuffed arm, she tried to cheer herself up with an inventory of what had replaced her old life. A stud muffin of a husband with wads of cash who was crazy in love with her. A luxurious room at the best enclave. Fantastic food for every meal. A best friend who was even now sitting beside her on the couch, eyeing her with concern.

"What is wrong?" Pony asked quietly.

"I think I'm homesick," she whispered and leaned her forehead against his shoulder. "Look at this place. It's a dump. And I miss it. Isn't that the stupidest thing you've ever heard?"

He pulled her into his lap and held her in his arms. "It is not stupid. It only means you lived with joy here, and it is sorrowful to put joyful things aside."

"Bleah." She sniffed away tears that wanted to fall. "I was lonely, I just never let myself know how much. I made the computers all talk, just so I felt like someone else was here."

"You can grieve for something lost, even if it was not perfect."

The front door opened and Oilcan walked in. "Hey," he announced, not noticing that he had started Stormsong to attention. He balanced boxes and a carton of bottles. "I didn't think you would have anything to eat here, so I brought food." He settled the various boxes onto the coffee table. "Hey, what's with the sad face?"

"I'm just tired." She didn't want him to know how lonely she had been, or think that she was unhappy with her life now. "I've been having all these bad dreams. It's put me on edge. It's like I've been rubbed down to all nerves."

"Ah, yeah, that can happen." Oilcan had suffered from horrible nightmares when he first had come to Pittsburgh. For that first year, she'd climbed into his bed late at night, armed with boxes of tissues, to get him to stop crying. It was one of the reasons she led and he followed despite the fact he was four years older.

"Scrunches?" He asked her if she needed to be held, just as she had once asked him.

"Pony has it covered." She leaned against Pony. "What's in the boxes?"

"Chicken satay with peanut sauce." He lifted up the first lid to show off the skewers of marinated chicken. "Curry puffs, fried shumai, Thai roll, Pad Thai noodles, and Drunken Chicken."

He went into the kitchen to collect dishes and silverware.

"We'll get fat eating all this." She helped herself to one of the Thai rolls, dipping it in the sweet chili sauce. He must have come straight from the Thai place because the thin fried wrapper was still piping hot.

"Feed the body, feed the soul, you sleep better." Oilcan handed her one of the plates and found room for the others on the crowded table.

"Feed on spirits," Stormsong added as she examined the bottles of alcohol. "Hard cider, vodka coolers, and beer?"

"Beer is for me. Figured I'd bring a mix for you guys."

"These are good." Stormsong handed a cooler to Tinker. "The cider carries less of a punch, so Pony and I should stick to those."

"Ah, leave the hard drinking to me." Tinker twisted off the top. Half a cooler, a curry puff, and a plate of pad Thai noodle later, she realized that the rubbed-raw feeling had vanished, and the loft felt like home again.

Tooloo had mentioned that the movie was old, but Tinker was still surprised when it started in only sepia tones. Dorothy was a whiny, stupid, spoiled brat who was clueless on how to manage a rat-sized dog. When Tinker had been Dorothy's age, she had been an orphan and running her own business. Esme identified with this girl? That didn't bode well.

The Earth the movie showed was flat, dusty, and featureless. Tinker was with Esme—why would anyone pine for that?

"Is that what Earth is like?" Pony asked.

"I don't know—I've never been to Earth." Tinker groaned at yet another stupid thing that the girl did. "I'm not sure I can take a full ninety minutes of this."

"It—changes," Stormsong said.

And change it did as a tornado sucked the house up into the air and plopped it down in glorious color. Dorothy's dress turned out to be blue checked and she acquired glittering red high heels that they called "slippers," the source of Esme's overalls and red boots in Tinker's dream.

It took Tinker several minutes to realize how Glinda the Good Witch worked into her dream. "That's Black. She had the wand and the crown. And she was crying."

"I think I would cry if I was stuck in a dress like that," Stormsong said.

Tinker had to agree with that assessment. Tiny little people in weird clothes surrounded Dorothy and talked in rhyming singsong voices.

"Oh, this is so weird," Tinker whispered.

"Does this make more sense in English?" Pony asked.

"No, not really," she told him. "Do they ever stop singing?"

"Not much," Stormsong said as the munchkins escorted Dorothy to the edge of town and waved cheerfully good-bye.

"Oh, of course they're happy to see her go; she's a cold-blooded killer," Tinker groused as Dorothy discovered a talking scarecrow. "Oh gods, they're singing again."

Dorothy and Scarecrow found the apple trees that threw fruit, and then the Tin Man, whose first word was "oilcan." Tinker huddled against Pony, growing disquieted.

"What is it, *domi*?" Pony asked.

"How did I know? I didn't see this movie before, but so many things are just like my dream."

"Maybe we did see it and forgot," Oilcan said.

"Something this weird?" Tinker asked. "And we both forgot?"

Pony's lion showed up next. Tinker scowled at the screen. It annoyed her that she didn't understand how she had dreamed this movie—and that her dream self had cast Pony in such a cowardly character. "All these people are dysfunctional, delusional idiots."

Finally the foursome plus dog found the wizard, who turned out to be a fraud.

"What was this dream trying to tell me?" Tinker asked.

"I am not sure," Stormsong said. "Normally an untrained dreamer borrows symbols uncontrollably—and this movie is rife with them. Everything from the Abandoned Child archetype to Crossing the Return Threshold."

"Huh?" The only threshold crossing Tinker knew about related to chaos theory.

"Dream mumbo jumbo." Stormsong waved a hand toward the television screen.

The wizard/fraud had produced a hot air balloon, and was saying good-bye. ". . . am about to embark upon a hazardous and technically unexplainable journey to the outer stratosphere."

"Dorothy is taking a heroic journey," Stormsong continued. "She crosses two thresholds, one out of the protected realm of her childhood, and the other completes her journey, by returning to Kansas. If you were familiar with this movie, I would say you were seeking to move past your old identity and claim one that reflects growth. The tornado could be a symbol of the awakening of sexuality, especially suppressed desire."

Tinker resisted the sudden urge to shift out of Pony's arms. "I didn't dream about the tornado."

"Yeah, well, the odd thing is that you're not familiar with the movie. So the question is: Where is the symbolism coming from?"

"Don't look at me!" Tinker closed her eyes and rested her head on Pony's shoulder. "So, what should I do next?"

"Tell me your last dream again."

"I'm up high with Riki and he's a flying monkey. He's got the whole costume, and I'm the scarecrow. Riki talks about me melting the witch and setting him free. Then I'm on the ground, and Esme is there as Dorothy, Pony was the lion, and Oilcan was the Tin Man."

The movie was obviously drawing to a close as Dorothy tried to convince people that her journey had been real.

"We wanted to go to the wizard," Tinker said. "But the road ends with the black willows, but they're also the trees in the movie that throw their apples. Esme keeps saying we need the fruit. I don't know. Do black willows even have fruit?"

Thankfully the movie was over and the credits rolled.

"I am not sure," Stormsong said slowly, "but I think, *domi*, finding out more about this Esme would be best."

"I'm going to have to talk to Lain about a lot of things." She went to her phone mumbling, "Fruit. Esme. Flying monkeys. Yellow brick roads. Munchkins."

She got Lain's simple unnamed AI. "It's Tinker."

"Tinker," Lain's recorded voice came on. "I'm going to be spending the next few days at Reinholds with the black willow. If you need me, you can find me there."

Tinker hung up without leaving a message. Sighing, she considered her home network. She should take it out before someone broke in and stole it. Pushing back from her desk, she lazily spun in her chair, scanning her loft. "I should really—you know—move out."

Oilcan glanced around, bobbing his head in agreement. "Yeah, unless you get divorced, I don't see you living here again. Well, I've got to go. I still have those last drums on the flatbed. I need to go dump them with the rest."

"See ya." She continued to spin, thinking of what she needed for the move. A truck. Boxes. People. As she considered how many boxes and how many people, she realized how little she really needed to move. Her computer. Her books. Her underwear. Most of her clothes were ratty hand-me-downs of Oilcan's, or too oil-stained to wear around the elves. Her battered furniture, her unmatched dishes, and all her other sundry things were just odds and ends she had picked up over time and weren't worth keeping. She could have a yard sale. She could make up a flyer and put an ad in the newspaper. They would need a way to tag all her stuff, a cash box with a starter kit of change, a tent in case it rained. They could sell hot dogs and sauerkraut to raise more money—except she didn't need money. Hell, a yard sale was a stupid idea.

She spun in her chair as plans came to mind and proved unneeded. And where would she move her stuff to? She supposed the computer could live in her bedroom at the enclave, but what about all her books? Her jury-rigged bookcases would clash horribly with the elegant hand-carved furniture. She could probably get bookcases. Snap her fingers. Make it so. But where would she put them?

Windwolf didn't fit into her life, but did she fit into his either?

She bumped into something and stopped spinning.

Stormsong stood beside her, looking down at her. "You're going to make yourself sick doing that."

"Pshaw." She stood up and toppled over.

Pony caught her and carefully put her back into the chair.

"I wish you guys wouldn't hover," Tinker snarled as they stood over her.

Pony crouched down so he was now eye level with her. "You are still upset."

She sighed and leaned her forehead on his shoulder. "I don't like being like this. This isn't me. I feel like I'm living without my skin. Everything hurts."

He put his arms around her and eased her into his lap. "*Domi*, I have been with you every day for some time now. I have seen you happy and relaxed. I have seen you bored. I have seen you snarling into the face of the enemy. And you were always yourself until two days ago. Something has changed."

"Do you think the oni dragon did something more to me than just draw magic through me?"

He considered for a few minutes, and then shook his head. "I do not know, *domi*."

"How do we check?" She asked.

He and Stormsong exchanged looks.

"Let's go to the hospice," Stormsong said. "And have them check you."

The hospice people poked and prodded and did various spells on her and shook their heads and sent her home feeling even more unbalanced. Her beholden fended off Windwolf's household, else she probably would have been doused again with *saijin* and put to bed. Ironically, the only place she had to retreat to was her bedroom, which didn't feel like home.

"There's no me in this room!" She paced on the bed just to get as tall as the *sekasha*. "This is not a room I live in. I need a computer. And a television. Internet connection! Is it any wonder that I feel like I'm going nuts when the most mechanical item in this suite is the toilet? Hell, I don't know even where to find my stuff! Where is my datapad? Where's—where's—shit, I don't even own anything anymore!"

The *sekasha* nodded, wisely saying nothing, probably thinking she was insane.

"I mean, how am I supposed to do anything? I know I have stuff. I had you put stuff in the car to bring home. Where did it go?"

"I will find it," Stormsong said and went off to search. While Tinker was still pacing the bed, she returned with the MP3 player Riki had left for her at Turtle Creek, the Dufae Codex, her grandfather's files on the flux spells and Esme, and a bottle of ouzo. Of course everything had been cleaned and given lovely linen binders tied with silk ribbons. Elves!

Tinker settled down with the file and a glass of ouzo. Smart female Stormsong. Must keep her. She tossed the player onto the nightstand where she might remember to take it to Oilcan, dropped the codex and the flux folder onto the floor, and opened up Esme's file. As she noticed earlier, the file contained general public information.

NASA bios. Newspaper clippings. Interspersed into it, though, was detailed personal information. One paper was a genealogy chart of Esme's parents going back a dozen generations on both sides. Another set of papers chronicled medical histories for family members. Another sheet claimed to be account numbers for a Swiss bank account. Tinker weeded these unique papers out, wondering how and why her grandfather had such information on Lain's sister. Lain herself, she could understand. But Esme?

Last item in the file was an unlabeled manila envelope. She opened it up to find a photo of her father and Black wrapped in each other's arms, looking blissfully happy.

"Who the hell?" Tinker flipped the picture but the back was blank.

"What is it?"

"This is Black." Without her blindfold or hands covering her face, Black was clearly a tengu. She had Riki's black hair, blue eyes, and beaklike nose.

"This is Oilcan?" Stormsong pointed to Leo.

"No, my father." Tinker looked in the envelope to see what else was inside.

There was a handwritten note stating:

Two can play this silence game. I'm not going to let you pressure me into leaving her just so you can have grandkids. I've made a deposit at a sperm bank, just in case things change. I don't know what else I can do to make you happy. The next step is yours. If you don't call, this is the last you'll hear of me.

The attached form noted that Leonardo Da Vinci Dufae had deposited sperm to be held in cryo-storage for his personal use.

The last sheet of paper in the file was a form from a fertility clinic on Earth. Tinker read over it three times before its full import hit her. It was a record of her conception.

Esme Shenske was her mother.

She was still shaking when she found Lain at Reinholds. The xenobiologist was dressed in winter clothing and running the slim willow limbs through a machine. She glanced up as Tinker stormed into the big freezer.

"What is it, dear?" Lain paused to pluck something off the limb and place it in a jar.

"Look at this! Look!" Tinker thrust the form into Lain's hands.

Lain took the paper, scanned it, and said quietly. "Oh."

"Oh? Oh? That's all you have to say?"

"I'm not sure what to say."

Something about Lain's tone, the lack of surprise, her uneasiness got through, and after a stunned moment, Tinker cried, "You knew!"

"Yes, I knew."

"You've known all along!"

"Yes."

"How could you lie to me all this time? I thought you . . ." She swallowed down the word "loved," terrified to have to hear it denied. ". . . cared for me."

"I love you. I have wanted to tell you about Esme for so very long, but you have to understand, I couldn't."

"Couldn't?"

Lain sighed and her breath misted in the freezing cold. "You don't know everything. There's so much that I had to keep from you."

"What the hell does that mean?"

"It means what it means." Lain busied herself labeling the jar; the contents wriggled like worms. "Don't come storming in here all hurt and emotional about something that can't be changed."

"You could have told me!"

"No, I couldn't have," Lain said.

"*Tinker, my sister is your mother.* See how easy!" And then cause and effect kicked in. "Oh my gods, you're my aunt."

"Yes, I am."

"But what about those tests you did to show Oilcan and I were still related? You used your own DNA as a comparison."

"I didn't use my own. I used a stored test result. I wanted to make it clear that you and Oilcan are still cousins."

Tinker could only stare, feeling betrayed.

"Oh, put the hurt eyes away. I have been here for you, loving you as much as humanly possible. What does it matter that you called me Lain instead of Aunt Lain? I have always given you the care I would give my niece, no matter what you or anyone else might know." Lain snorted with disgust. "I always thought that Esme was a result of lavish parenting until you came along—daily I've been stunned to realize it was all actually genetic."

"That hurts," Tinker snapped.

"What does?"

"That you could look at me and see my mother and never share that with me."

"Nothing about your birth and life has been cut-and-dried. I suppose that was one reason I wasn't that surprised when—out of the blue—you changed species."

A sound of hurt forced itself out of Tinker, and Lain came to fold her into a hug.

"Oh ladybug, I'm sorry, but I did my best."

"Can we get out of here and talk? It's very creepy and cold."

"Oh, love." Lain sighed, rubbing Tinker on her back. "This is the only time I'm actually going to be able to do this."

Tinker pulled out of her hold. "What are you doing that's so damn important?"

"I'm justifying all your hard work at preserving this." Lain gave her a hard look that meant that she thought Tinker was acting spoiled. "I'm scanning the structure of living limbs before this thing wakes up."

"What are these?" Tinker picked up one of the jars. Inside, small reddish-brown capsules had broken open, spilling out tiny, hairy green seedlike things, all wriggling like worms.

"Those are its seeds," Lain said. "It's possible that the Ghostlands somehow drained the tree of magic and made it inactive. It hasn't accumulated enough to wake, but the seeds need less magic."

"Seeds—are—fruit, aren't they?"

"Yes, dear." Lain focused on the limbs.

Okay, I have the fruit. Now what? Tinker eyed the seeds as they wriggled about. "I think—"

"Yes?"

"I think—Esme is trying to drive me nuts."

"Ah, that means you're family."

Tinker shoved the jar at Pony to keep while she continued her argument. "Why didn't you tell me? Why did you and Grandpa keep it a secret? Why Esme? Was she in love with my father?"

"I never knew why Esme did any of the things she did. She certainly never explained herself. I don't think she ever knew your father. I didn't think she knew your grandfather and yet—somehow—they managed to create you. She called me from a roadside pay phone right before she left Earth. She told me that she'd hidden clues to her greatest treasure in my house the last time she had visited but wouldn't say anything more. She kept repeating, 'The evil empire might be listening, and I don't want them to have it,' like she was some type of rebel spy."

"Huh?" Tinker felt as if the conversation had just veered around a blind corner. "What evil empire?"

"That's what we called our family; the empire of evil. Our stepfather was Ming the Merciless, his son was Crown Prince Kiss Butt, and our half brothers were Flying Monkeys Four and Five."

Tinker fought to ignore the sudden intrusion of *The Wizard of Oz* into the conversation. "I was her greatest treasure?"

"Yes." Lain went back to examining the limbs. "Although I'm stunned that she had the maturity to recognize that. I was expecting something more trivial like her diary, or bearer bonds she'd stolen off our stepfather. But no, it was a copy of that form, and your grandfather's address, and a note saying, 'Watch over my child. Don't tell the empire of evil—or a world away won't be far enough.' No please, no thank you, no why she had done it."

"So you're not happy that I was born?"

"Don't you twist that into something personal. I thought—and still think—it was horribly selfish and irresponsible of her, as if a child needed no more care than a dandelion seed. Throw it to the wind and hope for the best." Lain made a sound of disgust. "Which is so like Esme."

"I don't understand, though, why didn't you tell me?"

"I didn't think it was wise to trust such a secret to a child. Could you have kept it from Oilcan?"

"Oilcan wouldn't have told anyone."

"Tooloo?"

Tinker looked away. Yes, she would have trusted Tooloo, but who knew what Tooloo would have done with the information. Just look at what the half-elf was doing now—spreading lies about her not being married. "You could have told me when Grandpa died."

"Yes, I could have, but I didn't." Lain found another wriggling bundle and dropped it into a specimen jar. "My family are takers. If there's something they want, they have the money and power to take it. No one can stand against them for very long. They go above, around, and sometimes through people to get what they want."

"But—but—what does that have to do with not telling me about Esme?"

"Until you met Windwolf and had seen the kind of power he wields, I don't think that you could have possibly understood our family. One word to the wrong person, and they could have snatched you back to Earth, and nothing that you, your grandfather, or even I could have done would have stopped them."

14: A PARTING OF WAYS

Tinker fled the freezing cold of Reinholds and stumbled out into the baking heat of the summer evening. Oh gods, could her life get any more fucked over? Everyone she thought she knew was turning into total strangers. Tooloo was telling everyone she wasn't married, Lain was her aunt, and her grandfather had lied and lied and lied. He had always told her that her mother was dead at the time of her conception and that her egg had been stored at the same donor bank as her father's sperm. He maintained that he randomly selected the egg from a vast list of anonymous donors. He took the truth to his grave, not breathing one word that she had living family as close as Lain. He died and left her and Oilcan with no one to turn to. She'd gone nearly mad with fear and grief, and he had lied about everything, and then left them all alone.

"*Domi*, where are we going?" Pony asked quietly beside her.

She blinked and paid attention for the first time to where they were. They were walking up Ohio River Boulevard, halfway to McKees Rocks Bridge. The two Rolls Royces followed slowly behind her, effectively blocking traffic—not that there was any on this lonely stretch of road late in the evening. "I don't know. How the hell am I supposed to know. What day is it? I never know what day it is anymore. Do you know how long it's been since I've seen a calendar? Thursday I destroyed the world and Friday I slept. Saturday we moved to the enclave and slept some more. Sunday a dragon used me for a straw. Monday I was on the front cover of the newspaper. Tuesday I got another person to follow along behind me and ask me impossible questions and I dreamed about my mother—who may or may not be dead—and this mystery person, Black. Wednesday. Today is Wednesday."

"If you say it is," Pony murmured.

"Tomorrow is Thursday. Thursday is the day I take scrap metal to the steel mill. They cut me a check. I drive downtown, deposit the check except for fifty bucks. I stop at Jenny Lee Bakery in Market Square and pick up a dozen chocolate thumbprint cookies. Thursdays the thumbprints are fresh. I head back to work and put in a few hours paying bills and filling orders. I cut Oilcan his paycheck and give it to him so he can go to the bank before it closes. We get together with Nathan and Bowman and some of the other cops at the Church Brew Works in the Strip. I get the pierogies or the pizza or the buffalo wings—I like being flexible—and try expensive beer. I liked beer. Now it just tastes like piss."

As if she'd summoned him, a Pittsburgh police cruiser pulled over on the other side of the road slightly ahead of her and Nathan got out.

"Tinker?" He came across the four lanes toward her. "What the hell are you doing?"

"How the hell am I supposed to know? I was never an elf before. I was never in charge of anyone. People left me alone. I could go all day without seeing anyone but Oilcan or you. I cooked my own food. Washed my own clothes. It's not like I blow up the world every day."

Nathan walked backward, staying a few feet ahead of her, scanning the bodyguards and the Rolls Royces. "Are you," he asked quietly, "trying to go home?"

"I don't know." And she didn't. She was nearly to the intersection where she could continue on Ohio River Boulevard or cross over the McKees Rocks Bridge or head up to Lain's house—not that Lain was home—but really, she had not a clue which direction she was going to go . . . although she was starting to suspect that it would be straight through, staying on Ohio River Boulevard until it hit the Rim.

"Do you want me to take you home? Or to Oilcan's? Lain's? Tooloo's? I can take you to a woman's shelter if you want. I am a cop; you can trust me to help you if you need help."

She made a rude noise. "How do you know who you can trust? How do you know when people are telling you the truth?"

"Tinker, I'm sorry about that—I know that doesn't forgive anything—but I'm sorry. I really thought you felt something for me. I thought that was why you said you wanted to go out on a date. But it's just like I offered a kid candy; I talked about dating and of course, you were curious. I should have known what you're like with something new. You don't stop until you know everything."

She hit the intersection and needed to make a choice. She nearly went straight through, but then realized that it was getting dark, and none of the streetlights worked out that way. She veered left, almost decided on going across the bridge, but realized that going to her loft would be depressing, and she didn't want to talk to Tooloo, not now, she'd probably strangle the crazy half-elf. She continued looping to the left. Nathan had a good idea; she should go talk to Oilcan. But that seemed silly, since the shortest way to Oilcan's was the way she'd come. Of the four ways out of the intersection, however, only going to Lain's house remained, and she didn't want to go there either.

She kept walking, now distinctly making a full circle in the center of the road. The Rolls Royces halted at the intersection, silver ghosts in the twilight. Pony ground to a halt behind her, watching her with a faintly worried look.

"Tinker, are you all right?" Nathan asked.

"Do I look all right? Seriously? I don't think so. Something has definitely come loose. But can they find out what's wrong? Nope. Can't do that."

"Tink." Nathan caught her by the wrist. "If you're not feeling right, walking around in the night isn't going to solve anything. Let me take you to Lain."

"No!" She tried to tug her hand free. "I don't want to see her. She lied to me!"

Nathan ignored her attempts to get loose, pulling her toward his police cruiser. "Then let me take you to your cousin."

"Pony!" Tinker cried, turning to the *sekasha*.

She saw the blur of the *ejae's* blade and was only registering its meaning when Nathan's lifeblood sprayed across her face. His hand tightened a moment on her wrist, and then his fingers went limp. She stared numbly as his hand slipped off her and his body crumbled to the ground with a heavy thud.

With the strength of a black hole, Nathan's body dragged her gaze down to it. He lay on his side, his wide shoulders canted back so she could see the thick column of his neck. The skin up to the sword cut was unblemished white, and then his neck stopped abruptly in a meaty collar of muscle, bone, and gaping pipes. Blood still fountained rhythmically from a severed artery.

She opened her mouth but couldn't form any words. She dropped to her knees beside Nathan and touched him—felt the warmth and solidity of his body. His heart still pounded, wild and frantic, pumping out his blood with lessening force until it shuddered to a stop.

What just happened? Nathan can't be dead—he was just talking to me.

She looked up to Pony and saw he had drawn his sword. Blood dripped from his blade. She whimpered, realizing she had cried out to Pony and he'd reacted as he'd been trained. She had gotten Nathan killed.

An oddly shaped object on the ground behind Pony caught her eye, and she gazed at it for a minute, puzzled, until she realized it was the back of Nathan's severed head.

She had killed Nathan.

A sound struggled up out of her chest. She pushed a hand against her mouth to keep it in and felt a sticky wetness on her face. She jerked her hand away from her face, stared at the blood covering her hand, and a loud, wordless keen forced its way out of her. Once free, it would not stop. She knelt there, wailing, as her stained hands fluttered about her as if they were trying to escape the sudden brutal reality.

"*Domi*." Pony crouched beside her, gathering her into his arms. "Tinker *domi*."

She rocked in his arms, keening, holding out her stained hands so he could see the blood on them. Anguish, dark and wild as floodwaters, poured into her.

Pony picked her up. Tears blinded her and she slipped into black swirling hurt, losing sense of everything but guilt and grief. Fear tainted the dark pain; she couldn't stop wailing. It was as if she'd been pushed out of her own body by the raw distress. Only Pony's warm, strong presence kept her from falling into complete panic. Slowly she became aware that he had carried her back to the Rolls, and they had driven back to the enclave. Voices of Lemonseed and others of the household came out of the darkness that she seemed to be trapped in.

When Pony sat her down and let her go, Tinker cried out and reached blindly for him.

"I am here, *domi*." He pressed close to her as he tenderly washed the blood from her face. "I will not leave you. Nothing could take me from you."

They were in the bathroom of her suite at Poppymeadow's. He'd stripped off his sharp-edged wyvern armor. She wrapped her arms and legs around him, clinging to him.

"*Domi. Domi*," Pony crooned. "*Domi*, please, stop crying."

She tried to push out words, but they came out strangled cries.

"*Domi*, please." Pony carried her into the bedroom and sat on the edge of the bed. "If I'm to understand you, you have to speak Elvish."

"I am!" She wailed, and choked out the words, "I—I wa-wa-want Windwolf," as if they were huge boulders. She needed him there, now, holding her, comforting her, making love to her, to drive away the pain.

"*Domi*, Stormsong is looking for him." Pony wiped the tears from her face. "We do not know if he will be able to come." The thought of being alone threatened to submerge her into anguish. "Oh, *domi*, please don't cry."

She buried her face in Pony's hair and breathed in his spicy musk scent, warmed by his body. She felt the play of his muscles under his fine cotton undershirt. Desire, suddenly monstrous in strength, surged through her. This time she didn't even try to resist, terrified of falling back into the dark gnawing pain. She abandoned herself to her need and kissed Pony.

He shifted his head up, giving her full access to his mouth. He tasted of cinnamon. She fumbled with his clothes, wanting to feel him, to anchor herself. The undershirt tore under her desperation, parting to reveal the chiseled lines of his body. He pulled the tattered cloth out of the way, giving her access to his warm skin and hard muscle.

While in the oni cell, she'd been so good, keeping her eyes and hands on a tight leash. Now, she nuzzled down his body to every point she'd resisted, sought out the parts of him that she had only caught glimpses of. He moaned as she freed him from his clothes and savored all his velvet hardness with her mouth.

He reached for her, pulled her up to his mouth, kissed her deeply. He rolled them so she was under him. His body eclipsed the rest of the world, blotting out everything else, so that all she could think of was him. His broad shoulders moving downward. His strong calloused hands sliding up her dress. His soft hair falling free of his braid to pour over her stomach like silk. His mouth on her, coaxing her into pleasure.

She came, gripping him tightly as her climax roared through her. It burned away the overpowering grief and pain that had been threatening to swamp her. Letting go of Pony, she slumped back into the sheets, feeling empty and fragile as a broken eggshell.

Worry filled Pony's dark eyes as he moved up to lean over her. His erection pressed against her, seeking her entrance. There was a quiet little voice, though, in the back of her head, saying it was time to stop this, that she'd already taken it too far.

"Pony," she whispered.

He froze. "*Domi*?"

She swallowed and stroked his check with a trembling hand. "I don't think," she whispered, "it would be wise to go farther."

"I never thought this was wise." He slid sideways so he was no longer pressed against her opening.

She laughed but her laughter broke in the middle and became a sob. "Oh, Pony, he loved me and I killed him."

"Oh, *domi*, please don't cry."

"I have to. If I try to keep it in, I'll just go under again." It still hurt, but it wasn't the drowning flood of pain.

She was still crying when the door opened and Windwolf walked into the bedroom.

"Windwolf!" She pushed at Pony so she could get up.

Windwolf's eyes widened at the sight of her on the bed with Pony. He shouted a command, summoning wind magic. It spilled into the room, the potential glittering at the edge of her teary vision.

Pony was jerked backward off her and thrown across the room. His shields flared seconds before he hit the wall with a crash—elaborate inlaid paneling splintering under him. He landed on the floor, coiled to spring, one of his swords miraculously in his hand.

"No!" Tinker leapt between Windwolf and Pony. Sword aside, she could guess which one was the more dangerous of the two. "Stop it, Windwolf! Don't hurt him! He did nothing wrong."

"It doesn't look like *nothing* to me." Windwolf glared furiously at the *sekasha*. "Did he hurt you?"

"No!"

"Why are you crying then?"

"I killed Nathan!"

Windwolf went still and quiet, gazing down at her. "You did?" he finally asked.

"Yes," Tinker said.

"No, she did not," Pony murmured. "I killed him, as is my right."

"He only did what I told him to do!" she cried and realized that, in the same manner, Pony had made love to her. He had thought it unwise, but he had done what she asked of him.

Oh gods, she had made love with Pony.

"Oh, shit," she sniffed. "I think I'm going to cry again. I'm sorry, Windwolf. I didn't realize Pony would do anything I told him. *Anything*. That he trusted me to do the wise thing—not the stupid. This is all my fault."

Windwolf sighed and glanced at Pony. "Leave us."

"*Domnae*." Pony used the nonpossessive form, bowing slightly to Windwolf, but didn't otherwise move.

"Pony," Tinker murmured in Elvish. "Go, I need to talk to Wolf Who Rules alone."

Pony sheathed his sword and bowed out of the room.

That left her alone with her husband, wrapped in Windwolf's silence.

He reached for her and she flinched back. "I would never," he said huskily without dropping his arm, "strike you."

She closed the distance between them and allowed him to take her in a loose embrace. "I'm sorry. I was so hurt and confused. I've been through so much lately. Do you know that there's a slickie out there with pictures of me in my nightgown? That when I get attacked, it makes headlines in the newspaper? That women scream when they see me?"

He said nothing for several minutes and then whispered into her hair. "Are you unhappy being my *domi*?"

She hugged him then, suddenly afraid of losing him. "It's just—it's just . . ." she sobbed. "When humans get married there's a ring, and a church, and people throw rice at you and you get your picture next to the obituaries, and there's just the two of you, together, all the time, and nobody else to get in the middle and confuse things. There's no oni or royal princes or dragons or nudie pictures!"

"Beloved," he said after a minute of silence. "I'm not sure if that's a yes or a no."

"Exactly!"

He considered another minute and picked her up and carried her to the bed.

"I'm sorry," she cried. "I'm sorry. I've broken us."

"We are not broken." Windwolf eased her down and lay carefully beside her. "You are hurt and need healing—that's all."

Tinker was trying to write her full elfin name in the sand of the enclave's garden. She knew the runes but any time she went to scribe them out, the letters would creep and crawl oddly.

"You're dreaming," Stormsong stood beside her, a ghost of sky blue. "Those kinds of things never work. The part of your mind that processes them is asleep. You need dream runes. I could write what you want."

"No, no, I have to be able to do this. I'm the only one that can do this."

"Are you sure?"

"Yes, I'm sure."

Something moved in the darkness of the garden around them.

Stormsong activated her shields and they enveloped both of them, brilliant pale blue that was nearly white. "Go away. You're not wanted here."

"Give her to us." Esme prowled the darkness. She was the color of old blood. Black stood weeping in the woods with her host of crows oddly silent—only a rustle of many wings in the night. "We need her. We murdered time and now it's always six o'clock."

"No. I won't let you have her."

"You're not stopping us." Esme pressed a dark hand to the gleaming shell of Stormsong's shield, the light shafting through her spread fingers like solid spears. "You might be able to keep them out, but not me."

"You're hurting her!" Fear filtered into Stormsong's voice. "Leave her alone."

Esme moved counterclockwise around them, trailing her hand across the shield's radiance, a dark mote on pale brilliance. "There is too much to lose to worry about hurting her."

"Go away," Stormsong growled.

Esme had made a complete circle around them, testing the boundaries of Stormsong's protection. They stood as odd mirror reflections of each other—hair short and spiked—red, dark to the point of almost black versus blue paled to nearly white.

"I won't let you in," Stormsong said.

"We don't have time for this!" Esme balled up her hand into a tight fist of blackness, and punched into the light.

Stormsong's shield failed like a candle snuffed. Tinker fell into darkness.

"... *focusfocusfocus* ..." she whispered into the black.

A world snapped into being around her, but she ignored it to focus on the control panel in front of her. She punched a set of keys, ones she had practiced until her hands ached. Even as she entered the codes, and the world jerked hard to the right, alarms screamed to life.

She hit the intercom pad. "All hands suit up! Suit up!" She shouted, knowing what was coming. "Brace for impact!"

She looked up and found she hadn't seen the full truth. Instead of one colony ship looming in the great blackness of space, the feed from the front cameras showed several ships colliding together—heaving, twisting, and buckling. For a moment, she could only stare—stunned. Compartments of the ships were collapsing like crushed soda cans— their atmosphere spraying out in plumes of instantly freezing gushers.

She wasn't able to stop it. It was going to happen anyhow.

"We're going to hit! We're going to hit!" Alan Voecks screamed those hated words that had haunted her nightmares for months.

Something cartwheeled toward them, jetted on a haze of frozen oxygen. As it grew larger, she realized it was a human—without a space suit. There was time to recognize the face—Nicole Pinder of the *Anhe Hao*—before the body hit the camera. That screen went to static . . .

Tinker bolted out of the dream. She was tight in Stormsong's arms, panting from the remnants of her terror. "Oh gods! Oh gods!"

"It is over." Stormsong rubbed her back soothingly. "You are safe with us."

"Something went wrong," Tinker cried. "That's what they've been trying to tell me. Something went wrong."

"Well?" Windwolf spoke from the foot of the bed.

Tinker sat up to discover the room was full of silent people, all watching her sleep. In addition to Windwolf and Pony, Wraith Arrow and Bladebite stood guard. "What the hell?"

"There are other dreamers," Stormsong said, as if answering a question Tinker had missed. "One seems to be *domi's* mother. The others might not be able to reach *domi* alone, but her mother's blood connection is giving them all access to *domi*. *Domi's* mother is quite strong but untrained and with the morals of a snake; she does not care that what she's doing is hurting *domi*. They are crowding into *domi's* dreams, leaving her unable to cope with her own nightmares."

"Why now?" Windwolf asked. "It's been eighteen years."

"It might be that becoming an elf awakened latent abilities in *domi*," Stormsong said. "Or it might be something that happened when the dragon pulled magic through her at the edge of the Ghost-lands. I can't stop them. United as they are, they are too strong. Something must be done or they will drive the *domi* mad."

"Will giving her *saijin* help?" Windwolf asked.

"Please, not *saijin*," Tinker whimpered. "I hate that stuff. The oni forced it on me."

Windwolf gave her a look full of raw grief.

"No, *saijin* will only make things worse," Stormsong said. "Now she can wake up from the nightmare, breaking its hold on her. Drugged, she would be trapped in her dreams."

"Oh please," Tinker cried. "Not that."

"There are some drugs," Stormsong said, "that she can take for a limited time that will keep her from dreaming completely. Someone more trained and gifted in dreaming would know better what to do."

"I like the idea of not dreaming." Tinker crawled across the bed to Windwolf, who took her into his lap.

"You need to dream," Stormsong said. "Dreams are how your mind heals you from emotional harm. The oni rode you hard, but you were able to heal yourself each night and stay strong. Your mother is raping the very core of you. She will destroy you if we don't stop this."

"Can we use some other terms for this?" Tinker asked. "Something nonsexual? This is my mother we're talking about. Ick."

"Find what she needs for now," Windwolf ordered. "I will send for a dreamer."

15: STICKS AND STONES

Wolf made time the next morning to pray at the enclave's shrine. Last night, he'd had the hospice deliver drugs for Tinker and sent a message to the *intanyei seyosa* caste in the Easternlands, but now there was nothing more he could do for his *domi* except pray. It filled him with helpless rage that the ones tormenting her were so far outside his reach. He had thought the time he spent wounded and helpless in Tinker's care was the worst possible torment, but this was far, far worse. Even when she had been held captive, there had at least been something he could do, the illusion of making a difference. Now he could only watch as the female he loved slowly went mad.

Worse, he could not even stay with her and comfort her. He needed to attend the formal negotiations between the clans. For the sake of everyone who counted on him, he needed to be centered and calm when he wanted to be raging at the universe. At least he had the comfort of knowing that his *domi* was in the care of Little Horse and Discord, who both loved her well, and they were supported by the rest of his household. He prayed to the gods that they too lend their aid to his *domi*.

Maynard was waiting outside the enclave when Wolf headed to the *aumani*. "We need to talk," Maynard said in greeting.

"I do not have time." Wolf headed down the street toward Ginger Wine's enclave. It had been decided before the Stone Clan arrived that Ginger Wine's public dining area would be considered neutral ground for the three clans. At that time he had liked the idea of keeping the sanctity of Poppymeadow's—now he wished he could stay close to Tinker, even though she was still sleeping.

"I have a dead cop missing a head on Ohio River Boulevard," Maynard continued in English, falling in step with Wolf. "And people are saying they saw a lot of *sekasha* in the area before he died. Tell me that this isn't what it sounds like. My people are scared enough without your people killing cops."

Wolf gritted his teeth to control his anger. Lashing out at his ally would not help the situation any. "You have a dead rapist missing a head."

"How could he have raped her? She doesn't go anywhere without her *sekasha*. Do you know how bad this looks?"

"It was after I transformed her. I left Tinker at my hunting lodge with a full Hand to guard her, but somehow, she ended up back in Pittsburgh with only Galloping Storm Horse." It put Little Horse in a difficult position as there was no way for him to communicate with the rest of the Hand, short of driving back to the remote lodge. "Your police officer forced his way into Tinker's home, stripped her nude, pinned her down, and tried to enter her."

Maynard looked like Wolf had just handed him a poisonous snake. "Tinker says that Czernowski forced her?"

"My blade brother does not know many English words, but he does know 'no' and 'stop' and 'don't.' My *domi* was threatening to gouge out Czernowski's eyes when Storm Horse intervened."

"Oh, fuck," Maynard whispered and then sighed. "That was two months ago. Why did they kill him yesterday?"

"The *domana* are forbidden to take lovers outside their caste other than their *sekasha*. I made Tinker *domana* caste because it was the only way we could be together. It also means she is now strictly off-limits to humans. Czernowski would not keep his distance. He stated at the photographer's that he would take Tinker back. Last night, he attempted to pull her into his car."

Czernowski's intentions might have been innocent, but he had crossed the line of Little Horse's patience. Wolf could sympathize only with Little Horse. His blade brother, seeing Tinker spiraling downward, had been given the opportunity to take action—had been given a way to make at least one thing right—had been given a target. In the light of Tinker's imbalance, Czernowski's death had been inevitable.

"Stupid fucking idiot," Maynard growled, but it wasn't clear who he meant. Wolf chose to believe he meant Czernowski. "This was the last thing we needed, Wolf. My people are not going to trust yours after this."

"Did they truly trust us before?"

Maynard glanced away and ignored the question, which meant

the answer was "no." "Which one of your people killed Czernowski?"

"*Sekasha* are exempt from all laws except the ones of their own making."

"So you're not going to tell me?"

"There is no need for you to know."

"What am I supposed to tell the police? Czernowski's family?"

"What is done is done and cannot be undone," Wolf said. "I have other problems to attend."

Maynard acknowledged the dismissal with a hard look but took himself away.

Ginger Wine intercepted Wolf in her front gardens, bowing low. "What is wrong?"

Ginger Wine's face tightened and she glanced down the garden path. There were only her own *laedin* caste guards in sight. "These," she hissed in English, "conceited, pompous, arrogant Stone Clan pigs—that is what is wrong. I should have asked for four times my normal fee, instead of twice. The way they eat, you'd think they were hollow."

"I cannot do anything about arrogance and gluttony. Have they done anything wrong?"

She let out her breath in a long sigh, and then stood nudging a rock in the garden path. "It is just everything is—off; nothing seems right. Everyone is tripping over one another, plates are being dropped, laundry is being mislaid, and they eat and eat and eat." She looked pleadingly up to Wolf. "Everyone is frightened of them. We've lived so long with just you and your *sekasha*, I actually forgot how the world really is, what it is to live in fear."

"Do you want them out?"

She looked away, chewing on her bottom lip. Finally she shook her head. "No. Things are not that bad—perhaps it will settle down after another day or two—once we grow used to them." She laid her hand on Wolf's arm. "Please, *domou*, get rid of these oni so we can go back to our comfortable life."

He patted her hand. "We will work hard to resolve this quickly."

Ginger Wine gave Wolf a tight smile. "Thank you. Please, let me show you to the dining room."

As they entered the elegant dining room, there was a crash from the far kitchens, followed by loud sobbing. Ginger Wine sighed, begged his pardon, and hurried off toward the kitchen. A large round table with six chairs stood in the center of the room. All the extra tables had been cleared away, leaving the space bare and echoing.

While only five *domana* were attending, there would be fifteen *sekasha* and a server from each clan.

Wolf considered the sixth chair. Tinker should attend the meeting, but she was in no mental state to do so. He ordered a chair to be removed. Unfortunately, Jewel Tear arrived as the chair was being carried out.

"Your *domi* is not attending?" Jewel Tear managed to put malice into the innocent words.

"No." Wolf warned her with a look that he did not wish to discuss it further.

True Flame arrived with a shifting of the *sekasha* and a new contest of rank between them. "So this is where we will be?"

"Yes, Your Highness." Jewel Tear appropriated the role of hostess. She bowed low, displaying her charms to the prince.

True Flame recognized her with a slight cold nod. Wolf's cousin never had approved of Jewel Tear. It had been a source of bitterness between him and Wolf, even afterward, as it had been hard to acknowledge that his cousin had been right all along. Wolf could only hope that his decisions with Jewel Tear wouldn't now taint True Flame's opinion of Tinker.

True Flame glanced at the table and then to Wolf. "Five chairs?"

"My *domi* will not be able to attend." Wolf wished Jewel Tear weren't standing there, reminding True Flame of his bad choices in the past. "She is—" He found himself at a loss for words. What was Tinker? "—not herself."

"An interesting choice of words," Jewel Tear murmured.

Wolf ignored her.

Earth Son arrived with Forest Moss in tow. They made their bows to True Flame.

All parties gathered, they settled at the table to start the *aumani*, a formal meeting of clans.

Windwolf was sure that if they captured any oni and needed to torture information out of them, an *aumani* would be perfect for it. He sat across from Earth Son, studiously ignoring the servants as they laid out the elaborate table settings. Between the Skin Clan's love of elaborate power icons, and the thousands of years during which the clans had needed to conduct meetings in secrecy, elves had had the use of symbology beaten almost out of them. There had to be some deep buried need left in them that seeped out at times like this. How else explain the pure white table runner, the scattering of blood-red roses, the black ceramic place settings, and the glasses of sapphire blue? The lit candle. The smoking incense. The polished pebble. All the colors and the elements of three Clans were subtly present on the table.

They sat in reflective silence until the servers withdrew from the table. True Flame sipped his tea, opening the meeting. They drank, waiting for him to speak.

"So that we can all be of one mind," True Flame broke the silence, "Wolf Who Rules Wind, tell us our past."

Wolf recounted the last few weeks since the meeting of the three clans at Aum Renau. Knowing that he would lose face with True Flame for holding back information, he tried to be as thorough as possible in Tinker's kidnapping, Lord Tomtom's killing, and the discovery of Sparrow's treachery.

"And what of the Ghostlands?" Earth Son asked when Wolf came to an end. "Is your *domi's* gate still functioning?"

"Perhaps," Wolf admitted. "Something is keeping Turtle Creek unstable."

"Stupidity upon stupidity," Jewel Tear scoffed. "She shouldn't have built them a gate."

"I defy you," Windwolf said, "unarmed and captive of a ruthless enemy, to do better."

"Defy, there's an interesting concept, indicating lack of cooperation," Earth Son said.

"Yes," Jewel Tear said. "I wouldn't have cooperated."

"She cooperated because it's now in her nature to be cooperative," Forest Moss said. "Wolf Who Rules remade her and blessed her with our mothers' curse—to be yielding. Why else would we need the *sekasha* to guard over us? We cannot stand against anything, especially our own nature. How can you, sitting there with never a moment of stark helpless fear in your lives understand? Our mothers were bred to lie on their backs, spread their legs, and not whimper too loudly—unless their masters liked it when they screamed. If it wasn't for the steel of our fathers' ambition, we would be cattle in the field."

"You may count yourself one of the cattle, but I do not," Earth Son said.

"Yes, yes, let us not listen to the one that has been under the heated blade. No, he did not have his eyes forced open to the truth just before one was seared out," Forest Moss spat. "You cannot hope to understand what it is like. To lie there unable to move as they ready the tools of your destruction. The first time, oh, you can be so very brave because you don't know what is coming; everything in your imagination is just a pale shadow of the pain. It's the second time and the third, when you've been so well taught, that the very smell of hot metal makes your heart race. You see the torch only once, right before they strap you down, but the hiss of the gas flame haunts your nightmares for years to come. You lay there, listening to the invisible dance of their preparations, the scrape of boots, the rattle of the cutting blades in a metal tray, the creak of tightening leather restraints, and there's nothing, nothing you can do."

"She wasn't tortured," Earth Son pointed out.

"Clever female knew the truth," Forest Moss said. "The truth you're refusing to see."

"If she didn't do something the gate in orbit would remain functional," Windwolf reminded the others. "The gate we couldn't shut down. Yes, the result poses a threat, but it is now in *our* realm, where *we* can deal with it ourselves."

"We will solve this problem you caused," Earth Son said. "Damn these humans and their gate."

"We can't blame this on them," Wolf said. "We elves went to Onihida and led the oni to Earth. If we hadn't done that, none of this would have happened."

He did not bother to point out that it was the Stone Clan who had gone to Onihida.

Earth Son countered it as if he had made the statement aloud. "The humans built the gate in orbit."

Wolf shook his head. "The oni stranded on Earth used the humans to build the gate—and manipulated them to keep it functioning."

"Why are you defending them?" Earth Son snapped. "It's unlikely that they're all innocent in this."

"Yes, some might be guilty," Wolf allowed. "But not all of them."

Earth Son waved the truth away. "Bah, they're just as bad as the oni—breeding like mice."

"Fie, fie," Forest Moss whispered. "We were all blind beings even before the oni burned out our eyes. Why should such arrogant fools as we listen to the warnings of the human natives? Of course the cave was a mystical place with mysterious goings and monstrous comings. What importance to us that humans were forever losing their way to other worlds and rarely coming back? What did it matter that we recognized nothing of ourselves in their stories?"

"Oh, please, shut him up," Jewel Tear hissed.

"Oh! Oh!" Forest Moss leapt to his feet and wailed, waving his hands over his head. "It's all so ugly! No, no, who cares if perchance we might learn something important? We must close our ears to this wailing of a madman!"

"Forest Moss!" True Flame snapped. "Sit!"

The male sat so abruptly that Wolf wondered if the outburst had been yet another example of Forest Moss using his reputation of being mad.

"Does anything he has to say have any relevance to what we need to do here?" Jewel Tear asked. "It seems to me that our task is simple. Do findings to track down the oni nests and burn them out. Instead we are sitting here constantly being distracted by the mad one's ramblings. By his own account, he was shortsighted in his venture. So he was caught and tortured—but all that hinges on one gross error; on the first moment of discovery, his party have fought their way clear and returned to the pathway."

"I had dealt with discovery by humans many times," Forest Moss said. "A show of power, a few trinkets, and we would be safe enough to pass on. How was I to know that the oni were monsters under the skin?"

"I'm trying to determine what the Stone Clan brings to the table," True Flame said. "And what they will come away with."

Earth Son made an opening bid. "Since the Wind Clan is demonstrating that it cannot hold the Westernlands, we will take them over."

Wolf shook his head and begain to tick off his strong points. "We are providing access to the fire *esva*. Without our assistance, you would have to deal with the oni and a dragon with only defensive spells."

"You can't withhold the fire *esva* the crown," Earth Son stated.

Was he being naïve, or clumsy in his attempt to undermine the Wind Clan's position?

"I did not suggest that." Wolf used small words. "I'm only pointing out that we are providing attack spells on two fronts, plus my four Hands, and ten enclaves. The Wind Clan can hold its own here—the same cannot be said of the Stone Clan."

"Yet you called for help."

"Because we did not know then—nor do we know now—the strength of the oni," Wolf stated. "We would rather give up some part of our holdings than give the oni a stronghold here."

"Which the crown sees as a strength, not a weakness," True Flame said. "We are limiting the amount awarded to Stone Clan. The area in question will be Pittsburgh and the surrounding land. Excluded will be the enclaves owned by the Wind Clan households."

"We want both virgin land and that from Earth," Earth Son said.

"And I want the *sekasha*, Galloping Storm Horse on Wind," Forest Moss said.

Startled silence went through the room.

"Never," Wolf snarled.

"If you release him, he can serve me," Moss pressed on.

"He looks to my *domi*," Wolf said. "He is her First. She also holds Singing Storm on Wind."

"That cross-caste mistake?" Moss made a sound of disgust. "Your *domi* can release Galloping Storm Horse and keep the mutt."

"She will not release him." Wolf was sure of this. "She loves him dearly. The oni captured him because they knew he would be an effective whipping boy for her. All that she did was to protect him."

"It is a simple thing—" Forest Moss started.

The two Stone Clan Firsts, Thorne Scratch and Tiger Eye, and True Flame's First, Red Knife, stepped forward to loom over their *domana*'s shoulders. Wolf felt Wraith Arrow behind him, joining the other Firsts at the table.

"This is not for you to discuss," Red Knife said quietly. "No beholding will be broken in this manner."

Earth Son coughed and carried on. "We're asking for a hundred thousand *sen* of virgin land for each of us, plus half of the city, to be awarded immediately."

The land, ultimately, Wolf did not care about. The three hundred thousand *sen* was a small price to pay for the safety of his people—and perhaps all of Elfhome. He did not want, however, to put humans under the care of the Stone Clan. He shook his head. "I granted the humans an extension of their treaty to work out issues among themselves. I think at this time it would be unwise to start procedures on dividing up the city."

"Who gave you the authority to agree to that?" Earth Son asked.

True Flame glanced at Earth Son. "As viceroy, it was in his authority to do so. But I must ask, on what basis?"

"We're not entirely sure that the orbital gate no longer functions. If my *domi* failed to destroy it and only damaged it, it is possible Pittsburgh will return to Earth."

"Yes, dividing the city could be premature," True Flame said. "How soon will we know?"

"Shutdown was scheduled for two days from now at midnight," Wolf said. "But if the gate is only damaged, then the humans might delay Shutdown for weeks. Without communication with Earth, it is impossible to know."

"Are we truly going to wait for something that may never happen?" Earth Son asked.

"We are elves, we have time," Wolf said.

"Most convenient for the Wind Clan," Earth Son said.

"We will wait three days, and then speak again on dividing the city." True Flame took out maps of the area. "Let us discuss virgin land."

16: LITTLE MONKEY BRAIN

After a long, long cottony warm sleep, Tinker was able to view the last few days with a saner eye. Thinking of Nathan threatened to drag her back to the painful void of grief, so she considered the last dream with Esme and Black. Obviously, something had gone drastically wrong with Esme, but what did her mother think Tinker could do for her? Esme was in space—someplace—in another universe, far, far away. And who was Black? The tengu woman obviously had been on Earth to meet Tinker's father, but where was she now? Why was Tinker dreaming about her in conjunction with Esme? Was it because Black was a tengu colonist and on one of the ships that Esme crashed into?

The dreams of Alice and Dorothy—little girls lost far from home—held a sad irony; Esme thought Dorothy should stay in Oz—but obviously that wasn't what she wanted for herself now. So what did she want from Tinker? Even if Esme's ship had crashed, that would have taken place eighteen years ago, shortly before Tinker was born.

In the movie the yellow brick road started when Dorothy crashed the house into Oz—bringing a stain of sepia on a world of lush color. The Discontinuity appeared as a stain of blue. Tinker's nightmares had gotten out of hand the same day that the Ghostlands had formed—even if the first one with Esme and Black had come two days later. The first dream had been *Alice in Wonderland*, the second *The Wizard of Oz*, and the last was Esme going through the hyperphase gate; little girls crashing into other worlds.

Tinker sprawled in the enclave garden, watching the sun shift through the tree branches. As usual, she had a full Hand standing around, doing nothing but watching her think. They shifted to full alert as someone came through the gate into this private area. Lemonseed carried in a tray of tea and cookies—midmorning snack. Tinker started to sit up but Lemonseed *tsked* at her and crouched beside her to lay out a mini picnic. Exquisite china bowls of pale tea. Little perfect cookies. A platter of rich rosewood. A small square of printed silk.

Esme wasn't the only girl who fell into another world.

"Can you have lunch packed?" Tinker knew that the enclave's staff most likely had the meal half-finished. "We're going out."

"Yes, *domi*." Lemonseed bowed and left to make it so.

"Where are we going?" Stormsong asked.

We? How did it get to this point that she was so comfortable with having all these people in her life? No, she guessed she wasn't really at ease—but the edges of her discomfort were wearing away. Like the fact that she could strip in front of Pony without thinking. That it took Lemonseed's arrival to remind her that an entire staff of nearly a hundred people were poised around her—waiting for her to do something. Anything. Be the *domi*. Save the world again.

"The scrap yard," she told Stormsong but thought "Home."

She drained the tea to be polite, gathered up the cookies, and went to change.

Two newspapers, still neatly folded and bagged, lay in the driveway of the scrap yard. She picked them up on her way in, wondering why Oilcan hadn't brought them in. Tinker expected to find her cousin at work and was both relieved and disappointed that he wasn't. She didn't know how he would take Nathan's death. To her, it was a dark well of guilt and grief with a crumbling edge. She was trying to keep her distance just so she could keep functioning. Ironically, she was fairly sure she could deal with Oilcan being angry at her more than she could help him with his grief.

"You know—I just don't get it," Stormsong said as Tinker was puttering around her workshop, trying to get back into being herself.

"Get what?" Tinker asked.

"This place, you, and Windwolf—it just doesn't—doesn't make sense."

"Yeah, I've never understood why he fell in love with someone like me."

"I do. You can go toe to toe with him. It's this place that doesn't make sense. You two are too big for something like this."

"Big?"

"With your abilities—why did you limit yourself to this tiny corner of the world?"

That sounded like Lain—who had always pushed for her to go to college, leave Pittsburgh, do something more with her life. She thought her plans were big enough, but it suddenly dawned on her that they were plans she laid out when she was thirteen. They seemed huge when she was a child—certainly they were larger than what other people planned—but yes, she'd grown to fit, and then the limits started to chafe. Had Lain seen a truth that she herself was blind to?

She veered from that line of thinking and distracted herself by poking at her insecurities. "I think it's fairly obvious what attracted Windwolf to me: I look like Jewel Tear. She's his perfect woman. And I can't measure up to that—elegance."

"No. You only think that because you've never met Otter Dance."

"Pony's mother?"

"Ever notice that Pony is the shortest of the *sekasha*? Otter Dance is half Stone Clan *sekasha*."

Tinker turned to look at Pony standing beside Cloudwalker; he was half a head shorter yet wider in the shoulders and deeper in the chest than Cloudwalker. Pony was the most compact elf she'd ever met until the Stone Clan arrived. Now that she looked at him, she could see points of similarity. His eyes were brown where everyone else's were blue. The shape of his face was different.

"You mean we—Jewel Tear and I—look like Otter Dance?"

"To know Otter Dance is to love her. Personalitywise, you're much more like Otter Dance than Jewel Tear could ever pretend to be—and she did try."

Tinker wasn't sure how to feel about that. She cleared her iboard. She needed a project—something big and complex—to keep from thinking about Nathan and all the messy bits of her life. Something that would help keep Pittsburgh safe from the elves, the oni—and the dragon. Oh gods, in all the chaos she'd forgotten about the dragon. There was a worthwhile project, especially since she hadn't collected enough data on the Ghostlands yet.

She called up an animation program and created a quick rough model of the dragon, using a ferret body, a male lion's head, and a snakeskin to cover the frame. Dragging the dragon model out onto the iboard, she let it gallop across the white screen. There had been a spell painted onto the dragon's hide. She wasn't sure what the spell did. Was it how the dragon raised its shield or was it what the oni were using to control the dragon? It seemed to her that the wild waving of the mane might have triggered the shields—much like the *do-mana* hand gestures triggered theirs.

"What do you think?" she asked Pony. "How did the dragon raise its shield?"

Pony put his hands to his head and wriggled his fingers. "Its mane."

Stormsong and the others who had been in the valley with her that morning nodded in agreement.

Okay, so the mane worked like *domana* fingers. She paused the dragon, added a "shield" effect to her model, and restarted the animation. "Next question is—does anything breach the shield?"

"Our shields do not stop light and air, because we must see and breathe," Pony said. "There is a limit to the force they can absorb. They will take a hundred shots fired in a hundred heartbeats, but not a hundred fired in one heartbeat."

"So light and air." Tinker opened a window in the corner of the iboard and noted this.

"Spell arrows don't affect the dragon," Cloudwalker reminded her.

Tinker wrote: *Different frequency of light?* And then thinking of Pony driving his sword point through the shield, she added, *Speed of kinetic weapon?*

"Pony, can I see your sword?"

He drew his sword and held it out to her to examine. "Careful, *domi*, it is very sharp."

She knew that the *ejae* had magically tempered ironwood blades, but she had never examined them closely before. It was a single length of rich cherry colored wood with a bone guard. The very tip came to a fine point. There was no sign of the spell that had created the blade, which she supposed was necessary since the *sekasha* used their swords while their shield spells were active. The surface area of its tip was smaller than a bullet; if they both struck at the same speed, the *ejae* would have a greater PSI. Pony's slow push through the dragon's shield might indicate speed was more important than force.

She wasn't sure how they could use a "slow" weapon against the dragon. It would be unlikely that the beastie would ever stand still like that again. She considered a giant glue trap, sleep gas, and mega stun guns. They all had their drawbacks from "what do you use as bait?" to "would it do anything but just piss the dragon off?" That got her wondering about what would affect the dragon once they got past its shields. Where were its vital organs? Would poison necessarily kill it? Elves couldn't tolerate some of the food humans ate in abundance. The inverse could be true—what was poisonous for Elfhome creatures might not hurt the dragon.

Maybe the stupid dream was telling her that she needed to melt the dragon with a bucket of water. Waterjets had jet speeds around Mach 3 and could cut through several inches of steel. She didn't have any in her junkyard, but perhaps she could salvage one and modify it. . . .

The *sekasha* were rubbing off on her. She really liked the simple "hit it with a big gun" solution. Too bad they couldn't simply make the shield go away so "a big gun" was a safe bet.

Her stomach growled. She realized that she had spent hours in front of the iboard.

"What time is it?" Maybe she should take a break to eat the packed lunch.

"I'm not sure. That clock is broken." Stormsong pointed to an old alarm clock that Tinker had dismantled to use in a project.

We've murdered time, it's always six o'clock.

Wait—wasn't that a line from *Alice in Wonderland*? During the tea party, didn't they talk about time not working for them? She sorted through the things she brought from the enclave, found the book, and flipped through it. Under the drawing of the Mad Hatter, there was a footnote that caught her eye.

Arthur Stanley Eddington, as well as less distinguished writers on relativity theory, have compared the Mad Tea Party, where it is always six o'clock, with that portion of De Sitter's model of the cosmos in which time stands eternally still. (See Chapter 10 of Eddington's *Space Time and Gravitation*.)

"Oh shit." Tinker took out her datapad and pulled up her father's plans on the gate.

"Shit?" Pony asked.

"Excrement," Stormsong translated. "It's a curse."

"Shit," Pony echoed.

"That aside, what did you figure out?" Stormsong asked.

"I made a huge mistake in the variable for time on the gate equations. And if I did it—I bet the oni did too. These plans, as they stand—all the spaceships would have arrived at the same moment. That's why they collided."

"When did they go to?" Pony asked.

"I think . . . that they were *held in time* until the gate was destroyed. They finished their journey—all five ships—three days ago."

"Your mother found herself in great danger and you're her only link to home," Stormsong murmured.

"Yeah, at which point, she started to hound me with nightmares." Tinker tugged at her hair. "But what the hell am I supposed to do? I mean, the good news is that obviously she's alive—for now. The gods only know *where* she is. She could be on the other side of the galaxy. And which galaxy? This one? Earth's? Onihida? We're talking a mind-boggling large haystack to lose a needle in. Even if she was in space over Elfhome, *what* am I to do? What could I *possibly* do?"

"Forget the egotistical she-snake," Stormsong said. "You have pressing duties here. Her problems are not your concern."

"But why then, do things keep turning up? Like the pearl necklace, the black willow, and Reinholds? The dreams relate to me and my world, somehow. Don't they?"

Tinker saw a troubled look spread across Stormsong's face before the *sekasha* turned away, hiding her unease.

"Oh, don't do that!" Tinker picked up the morning's newspaper, still tightly folded in its bag, and aimed a smack at Stormsong's back.

Stormsong caught the newspaper before it connected and gave her a hard look.

"I need help here." Tinker jerked the newspaper free. "This is part of the whole working together. I need to know what you know about dreaming."

Stormsong sighed. "That is a wound I don't like to dig into. Everyone assumed that my mother had some great vision when she conceived me—and no one invested more in that myth than I did. But I did not have the talent or the patience for it. I was too much my father. I like solving problems with a sword. And I don't like feeling like I'm failing you."

Tinker fussed with getting the newspaper out of its bag so she didn't have to face Stormsong's pain. "You're not failing me."

Speaking of failing someone, the newspaper's headline was "Policeman Slain."

Nathan's body was draped with a white cloth in the island of light on the black river of night highway. *Nathan Czernowski, age 28, found beheaded on Ohio River Boulevard.* She stood there clutching the newspaper as faintness swept through her. How could seeing it in print make it more real than seeing his body lying in front of her?

Stormsong continued, "As you're finding out the hard way, dreamers can join for a gestalt effect, but unless they share *nuenae*, the resulting dream is conflicted."

Tinker pulled her attention away from the newspaper. "What?"

"Dreams are maps for the future." Stormsong held out her right hand. "If the dreamers share *nuenae*—" Stormsong pressed her hands, matching up the fingers. "Then the two maps overlaid remain easy to understand. But if the dreamers don't share *nuenae*—" Stormsong shifted her hands so her fingers crosshatched. "There is a conflict. It becomes difficult, if not impossible, to tell which element belongs to which *nuenae*. The pearl necklace was from your *nuenae*. *The Wizard of Oz*, is from your mother's."

"*Nuenae* being . . . ?"

Stormsong pursed her lips. "*Nuenae* reflects goals and desires. Among elves, it is one's clan and household. I'm not sure humans can share *nuenae* like elves can. Humans are more—self-centered."

The newspaper screamed at how self-centered Tinker had been.

"So, Esme, Black, and I are operating at cross-purposes." Tinker folded the accusing headline away and went to stuff it in the recycling bin. "And my dreams may or may not have anything to do with helping with the mess we're in."

"Yes, there is no telling. At least, I can't, not with my abilities. Wolf has sent for help from my mother's people. They might be able to determine something since they share our foci in regards to the oni."

"Whereas my mother could care less."

"Exactly."

As Tinker dropped the paper into the recycling bin, the top newspaper caught her eye. The headline read: "Viceroy's Guard Kill Three Snipers, Gossamer Slain." She lifted out the paper.

When did this happen?

The paper was dated Tuesday. Tuesday? Wasn't she awake on Tuesday? Yes, she was—she had spent Tuesday at Reinholds—why hadn't anyone told her? The paper also reported that the EIA had declared martial law, that the treaty had been temporarily extended until Sunday, and the elves had plans to screen everyone living in Chinatown. How had she missed all this? She dug through the pile of papers, uncovering growing chaos that she had been oblivious to. Wednesday's paper had stories on the lockdown of the city by the royal elfin troops, a wave of arrests of suspected human sympathizers, the execution of more disguised oni, and the start of a rationing system as fears of the Pittsburgh dollar collapsing triggered massive stockpiling. Above the headline was an extra banner proclaiming, "Four Days to Treaty End."

Four days? Was that today?

The other unread paper was dated Friday. She had lost at least a day to drugged sleep. The top banner read, "Two Days to Treaty End." The Pittsburgh police had called a "blue flu" strike when the EIA closed Nathan's murder case.

Oh, gods, what a mess.

"What day is this?" she asked Stormsong. "Did I sleep through Saturday too?"

"It is Friday," Stormsong said.

"*Domi*," Pony said from the door. "It is the lone one."

Lone one?

The *sekasha* escorted in Tooloo, who must have walked up the hill from her store. Tinker stared at her with new eyes. Not that the female had changed; Tooloo was as she had always been Tinker's entire life. There were no new creases in the face full of wrinkles. Her silver hair still reached her ankles. Tinker even recognized her faded, purple silk gown and battered high-top tennis shoes—Tooloo had been wearing them when Tinker and Pony helped her milk her cows two months ago.

Only now Tinker realized how odd it was for an elf in a world of elves to live alone. What clan and caste had she been born into? Why wasn't she part of a household? Was it because she was a half-elf? If she was half human, born and raised on Earth, how could she be so fluent in High Elvish, and know all things arcane? If she was a full-blooded elf, trapped on Earth when the pathways were dismantled, why hadn't she gone back to her people? Three centuries was a short time for elves.

Tinker doubted if Tooloo would tell her if she asked. Tooloo had always refused to be known. She went by an obvious nickname, neither human nor elfin in origin. Not once, in the eighteen years that Tinker had known her, had she ever mentioned her parents. She would not commit to an age, the length of time she had lived on Earth, or even a favorite color.

Tooloo squirmed in Cloudwalker's hold. "Oh, you murderous little thing! You had to satisfy that little monkey brain of yours. I told you, starve the beast called curiosity—but nooo, you had to play with Czernowski and now you've killed him."

Tinker felt sad as she realized she'd lost yet another part of her life. "I didn't mean for Nathan to get killed."

"Oh, you didn't mean to! Do you think those threadbare words will heal his family, grieving over his headless body?"

"I'm sorry it happened." Tinker swallowed down on the pain that the words caused her. "I—I wasn't paying attention when I should have been—and I'm so sorry—but there's nothing I can do. I was wrong. I should have listened to you from the very start—but I didn't see where all this was going to lead."

"*Pawgh*, this is all Windwolf's fault—killing my bright wee human and making a dirty Skin Clan scumbag in her image." Tooloo spat.

"This has nothing to do with Windwolf making me an elf."

"Does it? My wee one never had such superciliousness of power."

"Supercil-*whatis?*"

Tooloo glanced at Pony standing behind Tinker. "Giving you *sekasha* is like giving an elephant rollerskates—stupid, ridiculous, and dangerous."

Tooloo could say what she wanted about her, but now she was going too far to include the *sekasha* too.

"Yes, I killed Nathan," Tinker said, "but I'm not the only one to blame. I'm a stupid clueless little girl, but you've lived with humans for over two hundred years—you knew exactly how Nathan would react if—" And then it dawned on Tinker and she gasped with horror. "Oh sweet gods, you wanted him to think I was a whore! You deliberately misled him! You evil she-goat!"

Tooloo slapped her hard across the face, enough to make stars dance in her vision.

Tinker heard the *sekasha* draw their blades and threw out her hands to keep Nathan's death from repeating. "No! No! Don't you dare hurt her!" Once she was sure that she was obeyed, she turned back to the stranger who raised her. "Why? Why did you do that to Nathan? You had to see it coming!"

"Because nothing else would have slapped you out of wallowing in your own piss. The city is about to run with blood unless you do something. Czernowski was the sacrificial lamb to save this city."

"I was trying to! I don't know how!"

"Use that little monkey brain of yours! The elves are about to march all over this city with jackboots. I've lived with humans for hundreds of years. They are good, compassionate people. I lived through the America's Revolutionary War, its Civil War, the fight for women's suffrage, and the struggle for civil rights—and all those advancements for equality among humans are about to be flushed down the crapper. It's already started—they're searching through Chinatown, dragging people out of their homes, and testing them and killing them where they stand."

Tinker glanced to Stormsong since the rant had been in English. Stormsong nodded in confirmation. "Why didn't anyone tell me?"

"You've been too fragile."

She couldn't trust Tooloo's version of this; the "lone one" kept whatever truths she had to herself. Nor, as much as she loved them, could she count on the elves in her life to understand what it was to be human. Tinker gathered up the newspapers; she needed their human-biased facts. And Maynard—she needed to talk to Maynard.

Red was becoming a predominant color in Pittsburgh, like an early autumn. They encountered four roadblocks on the way to the EIA offices, all manned by *laedin* caste Fire Clan soldiers.

"If True Flame has this many warriors, why do we need the Stone Clan?" Tinker had let Pony drive, but she hung over the front seat to talk to him and Stormsong. The backseat was crowded with the other three *sekasha*.

"Stone Clan magic can find individuals in a wilderness and things hidden in the ground," Pony told her.

"It's like calling in bloodhounds," Stormsong said in English.

Tinker remembered the sonarlike spell that Jewel Tear had used. Yes, that should make finding the oni hidden in the forest easier. She wondered how the Stone Clan would fare, though, in the steel-riddled city.

"And if you cannot solve the problem with the Ghostlands," Cloudwalker added. "They should be able to. They closed the natural pathways after the first invasion."

Stormsong made a rude noise. "There is a difference between collapsing caves and dealing with whatever is wrong with the Ghostlands."

"The Ghostlands should collapse on their own." Tinker was growing less sure of that—she would have expected the rate of decay to be faster. This morning marked the fourth day since she had reduced Turtle Creek to chaos. Now there was something not everyone could claim: *I reduced a square mile of land into pure chaos.* It made her sound like a small atomic warhead—"someone dropped a Tinker on us!"

The EIA offices directed her back across the Allegheny River to Chinatown. There she found Maynard overseeing the testing of the Chinese population. A mix of *laedin* caste soldiers and Wyverns were systematically emptying a house, putting the occupants into a line to be tested by the EIA. As she approached, it became clear that the process was hampered by the fact that most of the elves and many of the Chinese didn't speak English. East Ohio Street was a cacophony of shouted instructions, crying, and pleading. The coroner van—identified by bold letters—stood at the far end of the street. Blood scented the hot summer air. And for one dizzy moment, she was back on Ohio River Boulevard, splattered with Nathan's blood.

"*Domi*, are you all right?" Pony murmured into her ear as he supported her by the arm. He'd activated his shields at some point and they now spilled down over her.

She nodded and pulled out of his hold.

"It is clear!" One of the Wyverns came out of a nearby building shouting in High Elvish.

There was a pulse of magic, and she *felt* the house, from the pipes underneath it to the tip of the chimneys. There wasn't anyone inside. Apparently that was the point. On some unheard command, the Wyverns moved down to the next building. Annoyingly, because of her height, Tinker couldn't see through the crowd to spot the Stone Clan *domana* directing the search.

"Is Jewel Tear here?" she asked Stormsong, who could see over the heads of most of the humans.

Stormsong shook her head. "It is the mad one, Forest Moss."

"Oh, joy," Tinker muttered. "Where is Maynard?"

"This way." Stormsong started forward.

Tinker thought they would have to push their way through the crowd, but as they approached the humans and elves, the crowd parted as if shoved by an invisible wedge. In the human faces there was a mix of fear and hope. They wanted her to be one of them but were afraid she was wholly an elf.

The crowd was avoiding a section of sidewalk. As Tinker drew even with it, she saw that it was covered with congealing blood, thick with black flies. As the *sekasha* brushed past, some of the flies rose in fat, heavy buzzing. The rest continued to feed.

"I want this to stop," Tinker whispered to Stormsong, dreading her answer.

"This is by order of the crown," Stormsong said. "There is nothing you can do to stop it."

Maynard saw Stormsong first and then scanned downward to find Tinker. "What are you doing here?"

"I want to talk to you about this stuff." Tinker waved the newspaper at Maynard.

"I'm busy at the moment. Why don't you get your husband to explain it to you?"

"Because you're here. I have the power to pin you down and make you explain it to me. And you'll use words I can understand."

Maynard glanced at the paper. "What don't you understand? That article is fairly clear."

"What can I do?"

He gave her a long unreadable look before saying, "I'm not sure. Windwolf bought us some time, but without proof that the gate is in orbit and possibly repairable, that time runs out Sunday."

Figures, after everything she had gone through to destroy the gate, she now had to save it.

"So," Tinker said, "if I can prove the damn thing is still up there, would that help?"

Maynard's eyes widened in surprise. "You think you can do that?"

It was tempting to say yes, but she had to be honest. "I don't know. I can try. It's a fucking discontinuity in Turtle Creek, across at least two or three universes. If Earth is one of those universes, there might be a way to use the Ghostlands to communicate."

"The elves are keeping everyone away from the Ghostlands," Maynard said. "The scientists at the commune are ready to storm the place for a chance to study it."

"Keep them away from it," Tinker said. "At least until we can make sure the Fire Clan and the Stone Clan don't kill them on sight."

Maynard looked away, as if to hide what he thought. When he turned back, his face was back to its carefully neutral—nearly elfin—facade.

"What do you fucking want from me?" Tinker cried. "I was raised in a junkyard!"

"You're the only one in a position to understand fully what it is to be human," Maynard said, "and still be able to do anything about this situation."

"But I don't know what to do."

"I know you don't," Maynard said but didn't add anything more—which would have been a big help.

There was a pulse from Forest Moss and this time the building wasn't empty. She—and Forest Moss—picked up two people still inside on the second floor. A shout went up. Tinker turned to see the Wyverns swarm in through the door of a tiny secondhand shop. Like flashbulbs going off, she felt spells flaring the small rooms into brilliance, one after another. The Wyverns quickly worked their way to the room with the hidden couple.

"Oh, no." Tinker started for the store.

Stormsong pulled her short. "They are only killing oni."

Was that supposed to make it better? Much as she hated the kitsune, she didn't want to see Chiyo beheaded. She didn't want Riki dead any more than she wanted Nathan hurt.

"We can't go in there—it would be asking for a fight." Stormsong kept hold of her. "One we cannot win. Wait. Please."

Much as she wanted to protect the strangers, she couldn't bear the thought of sacrificing her *sekasha*.

Tinker nodded numbly and pulled out of Stormsong's hold. "Let's get closer."

She lost sight of the storefront beyond the wall of backs. This time her *sekasha* had to clear a path, pushing people aside to make what they thought was a wide enough path for her. Maybe if she was an elephant.

The Wyverns muscled out only one person. They dragged him to a white-haired elf, announcing, "We killed one inside—it tried to run. This one is spell-marked, but it was with an oni."

It was Tommy Chang.

"Kill him," the male *domana* said.

"No!" Tinker plunged forward, forced her way through the towering Wyverns to Tommy's side. "Don't hurt him!"

The white-haired elf turned and Tinker gasped at the damage done to his face.

"Ah, what honest horror!" the half-blinded elf said. "You must be the child-bride. Not much to you—how did you come out in one piece?"

"Because they underestimated me." Tinker tugged Tommy's arm out of the Wyvern's hold. "Look, he's been tested. He's not oni."

"He might be mixed blood," said the half-blinded elf.

"Who gives a flying fuck?" Tinker snarled in English.

"*Domi*," Stormsong murmured behind her.

"He's not one of them." Tinker switched back to High Elvish.

"How do you know?" Forest Moss asked. "From what I hear, the tengu fooled you."

She was not going to let them kill someone she knew. She stared at Tommy, trying to remember something that would prove he was what she thought he was—to herself as much as to them. Maddeningly, he said nothing in his own defense, just stood there, wrapped in his bulletproof cool. Didn't he know that no one was sword-proof?

True, she'd trusted Riki blindly, but she hadn't known oni existed, and had awarded him the trust she gave all strangers. Her world had been a different place not so long ago.

"I know because—" she started in order to stall them. Because she'd known Tommy half her life. His family had owned a restaurant in Oakland since before Startup. He'd been a driving force organizing the hoverbike racing, and most summers she saw him on a weekly basis. He wasn't a stranger. She wouldn't immediately say he was "good" people. He had a temper and a reputation of being ruthless when it came to business; that didn't make him any more evil than she was. She suspected the elves wouldn't accept those facts as a good argument for his humanity. Riki had proved her judgment was flawed.

What could she say as proof that these elves would accept? They were growing impatient for her answer.

"Because—" And then unexpectedly, Riki provided the answer. "Because when the tengu came looking for me, he didn't know where to find me."

That puzzled them, which was fine, as she needed to cram a lot into this argument to make it sound.

"Two years ago, Tommy bought a custom Delta hoverbike off me. He needed to write a check, and there were the pink slips—forms to show transfer of ownership for tax reasons. I told him my human name, which was Alexander Graham Bell." Which of course had triggered a round of teasing from Tommy, and occasionally afterward, he'd called her "Tinker Bell." "I even told him why I was called that." In truth, she had been trying to stem the teasing with a sympathy play since Tommy's mother had also been murdered. "And that my father was the man who invented the orbital gate. I told him—he didn't tell the oni."

That seemed to buy it for the Wyverns. They released their hold on Tommy.

Magic suddenly flared across her senses, like a gasoline pool catching flame. Tinker spun around but there was nothing to see. Forest Moss made a motion, and she turned to watch him call on the Stone Clan Spell Stones and use the magic to trigger his shields. Around them, the Wyverns and her Hand went alert.

"What was that? Did you feel that?" she asked Forest Moss.

"It was a spell breaking." Forest Moss cocked the fingers of his left hand and brought them to his mouth. "Ssssstada."

The spell Forest Moss triggered was a variation of the ground radar. A long, narrow wedge of power formed from the male elf to the river's edge. He shifted his right hand, and the wedge swept northward through Chinatown. At the heart of Chinatown, he hit an intense writhing of power.

"How odd," Forest Moss said.

"What is that?" Tinker noted that Tommy, being smart, had vanished while they had been distracted.

Forest Moss gave her an odd look. "It's a ley scry. It lets me see recent and active disturbances in the ley lines. I don't know what it was

supposed to do, but a spell was just violently altered, and it's now acting as a pump on a *fiutana*."

"Oh shit. The black willow."

The great doors of the refrigerated warehouse stood open to the
summer heat. Magic flowed down over the loading dock in a purple
haze of potential. Tinker cautiously pulled the Rolls around, trying to
angle the car so they could see into the cave darkness, but the dock
was too high, and the door, facing the afternoon eastern sky, was cave
dark. Tinker flicked on the headlights, but even the high beams failed
to illuminate the interior.

"I want a closer look." Tinker put the Rolls into park. She wished
she could leave the engine running, but it would be a mistake with
this much free magic in the area.

She got out and the *sekasha* followed. Magic flooded over her, hot
and fast. The heat tossed the chimes on the ley shrine, making them
jangle in shrill alarm. A smell like burnt cinnamon mixed with a taste
like heated honey. The invisible brilliance hinted at by the shimmering purple made her eyes water.

"Be careful." She blinked away tears. "The magic is all around us."

"Even we can see that." Stormsong's shields outlined her in hard,
blue radiance. "Your shields, *domi*."

Yeah, now would be a good time for that.

Tinker set up a resonance with the spell stones and then triggered her shield spell. Once the winds were wrapped around her, she
waded up the steps, making sure that she didn't disturb the spell by
gesturing.

The padlock had been cut off with a bolt cutter. Her spell hadn't
failed; someone had broken in and sabotaged it.

Violet sparkled and shifted in the black of the warehouse, casting
patterns of shadows and near light. Tinker couldn't see anything that
looked like the black willow. Stormsong tried the lights, but the
switch had no effect.

"The flood would have popped the lightbulbs." There was no
way Tinker was going in there blind. "Do we have a light?"

"Yes." Pony took out a spell light, closed his left hand tight
around the glass orb, and activated it. He played a thin beam of
searchlight intensity over the room.

They had left the black willow tied down on pallets. The restraints now lay in tatters. Splinters of wood marked the pallets' destruction. The forklift sat upended like a child's toy. Dead leaves rode

convection currents, dancing across the cement floor with a thin, dry skittering noise.

"Where is it?" Tinker whispered.

"I don't see it." Pony's eyes swept the room again.

"Neither do I." Tinker glanced back to the street. Where was Forest Moss? That ground radar thing would come in handy just about now. "Let's turn off the compressor and at least stop this flood."

They moved through the warehouse to the back room. The small windowless room was empty of trees, with only the purring compressor to wreak havoc. A crowbar lay across the metal tracings of her spell, encircled with charring. Odd distortions wavered around the compressor.

Cursing, she started for the breaker box.

"*Domi*, no!" Stormsong caught her shoulder and stilled her. "Stay here at the door. Let Cloudwalker do it."

"The willow isn't in here." Tinker nevertheless stayed at the door as Stormsong asked while Cloudwalker crossed to the breaker box and cut the power to the compressor. "See, no dan—"

Her only warning was the ominous rustle of leaves, and then the forklift struck her shield from behind. She yelped, spinning around to see the forklift rebound back across the warehouse.

"Shields!" Stormsong shouted.

Tinker had let her shields drop in her surprise. She fumbled through the resonance setup as Pony's narrow light played off the suddenly close wizened "face" of the black willow. They had to have walked straight past it, somehow blind to it. It filled the warehouse now, blocking them from the door. It lifted a root-foot and replanted it with a booming sound that shook the floor. Its branches rattled as it blindly felt the confines of the room. A dozen of it's arms encountered the upended forklift, scooped it up again, and flung it at her.

Tinker snapped through the shield spell, already wincing, as the forklift sailed toward her. At the last second the winds wrapped tight around her and the forklift struck the distortion's edge.

"Shit!" Tinker swore as the forklift bounced back across the warehouse to wedge itself sidewises in the far door. "There's no other door, right?"

"No, *domi*," Pony said.

Tinker wasn't sure whether to be amazed or annoyed that Pony sounded so calm, as if she could pull doorways out of her butt. "Oh damn, oh damn, oh damn. Okay, I know I'm smarter than this tree."

The black willow lifted another root-foot and shook the world as it planted it back down, a few yards closer to them, instantly pulverizing the cement floor, digging roots down into the building's footing.

"But I have some doubts," Tinker admitted, "that brains are going to win over brawn this time."

What did she have to work with? She scanned the room of bare concrete block as the willow stomped ponderously closer. Crowbar. *Boom!* Compressor. Five *sekasha*. Five *ejae*. *Boom!* Circuit breaker box.

"Stormsong, what do you know about electricity?" Tinker asked the most tech-savvy of her Hand.

"Nothing useful," Stormsong said.

Boom!

"Nothing?" Tinker squeaked.

"It lives in a box in the wall." Stormsong detailed what she knew. "It goes away if you don't pay for it."

Boom!

Right—nothing useful. Scratch having Stormsong rig an electrical weapon. Just as well, good chance they'd just electrocute themselves.

The black willow stretched out its hundreds of whipping branches to scrabble at her shield. Tinker forced herself to scan the room again, and ignore the massive creature trying to reach her.

"The roof! It's only plywood and rubber. See if you can cut through."

The tree found the gap between the top of the tall doorway and her shield. The thin branches pushed through the space, caught hold of the doorjamb, and started to pull.

"Oh, shit!" Tinker cried. "If it makes the door larger, I'm not going to be able to hold it! It's coming in!"

There was a pulse of magic from Forest Moss, instantly defining the Stone Clan elf with Wyverns out by the Rolls, and themselves, pinned inside by the black willow.

"Forest Moss!" Tinker shouted. "Get it off us!"

The concrete walls buckled under the strain, tearing free to leave sawtooth openings, exposing twisted and snapped rebar. The branches flung the debris against the back wall of the warehouse like mad shovels.

"Forest Moss, get it—"

And suddenly the branches wrapped around her, cocooning her shield in living wicker, and lifted her off the ground.

"*Domi!*" Pony shouted.

The black willow heaved her up. Its branches creaked as it tried to crush her shields down.

Oh please hold! Oh please hold!

A dark orifice opened in the crook where its main limbs branched from it's massive trunk. As the tree tried to stuff her into the fleshy maw, she realized what the opening was.

They have mouths! I wonder if Lain knows that. Oh shit, it's trying to eat me!

Luckily the diameter of her shielding was larger than its mouth. It was trying to fit a golf ball into a beer bottle. She held still and silent, afraid to disrupt her shields. Smell of burnt cinnamon and honey filled her senses, and her vision blurred—the tree fading slightly—even as it repeatedly jammed her up against its mouth.

It has some kind of hallucinogen—that's how we missed it, she thought.

And then the tree flung her through the wall.

The street beyond was a flicker of brightness, and then she plowed through a confusion of small, dim, dusty rooms of an abandoned office building beyond. She felt Forest Moss track her through the building. His power flashed ahead of her, surged through the next building in her flight path, and locked down on all the load-bearing supports.

The white-haired shit was going to pull the building down on her! She'd be buried alive—shields or not!

Dropping her shields, she made a desperate grab for a battered steel desk as she flew over it. She missed the edge and left five contrails across its dusty top. A floor to ceiling window stood beyond the desk. She smashed through the window into open sky.

I'm going to die.

And then Riki caught her, wrapping strong arms around her, and labored upward in a loud rustle of black wings.

"Riki!" She clung to the tengu, heart thudding like a motor about to shake itself apart. Yeah, yeah, she was still pissed at him. She'd let him know that—after he put her down safely.

17: A MURDER OF CROWS

"Stop squirming or I might drop you," Riki growled through teeth gritted with the effort of carrying Tinker aloft.

She glanced down and went still in shock at being dangled midair forty feet up and climbing. "Shouldn't we be going down?"

"Down is good for you—very bad for me."

"Damn it, Riki, my people need me. Put me down!" Tinker found herself gripping his arms so he couldn't just drop her.

"There are so many things wrong with that statement that I don't have breath to explain it all."

Movement at the window she'd smashed out of caught her eye, and with relief she saw Cloudwalker pointing up at her. Moments later Pony and the others joined him at the opening.

"Oh, thank gods," Tinker breathed.

Riki rose above the roofline. The crown of the black willow bristled in the street beyond. Its booming footsteps echoed up from the canyon of buildings. She felt a great surge of magic and a massive fireball suddenly engulfed the tree. Whoa! Apparently Prince True Flame had arrived. No wonder the tengu didn't want to land.

Riki dipped down behind the next building, out of sight of her Hand. Black smoke billowed behind them. He flew straight west—as the saying went, as the crow flies—faster than a man could run despite being weighed down by her. When he reached the Ohio River, he turned and followed its course.

Where the hell was he taking her? It occurred to her that he couldn't have been just passing by and caught her by luck.

"You planned this! You knew if you screwed with my spell, I'd come to fix it."

"Would you believe this had nothing to do with you?"

"No."

"Believe it not, the world does not revolve around Tinker the Great."

How far could Riki fly? Could he keep up this speed, or had that been a sprint? And what did he want with her?

She tried to form a plan to escape. Riki, though, wouldn't underestimate her—he knew her too well. Of all the people in Pittsburgh, he could match wits with her. Her first thought was to force him to drop her into the river. The large dark form of a river shark swimming under the water, following their passage, killed that plan. They followed the Ohio around its gentle bends, and Pittsburgh vanished behind the swell of the surrounding hills. Once the city was out of sight, Riki climbed the steep hill that once was Bellevue and crossed the Rim. There he dove into the ironwoods. The forest canopy rushed toward them, seeming to her a solid wall of green. Riki, though, flicked through openings she hadn't seen, darting through slender upper branches to finally land on a thick bough, close to the massive trunk.

The moment they landed, Tinker twisted in his hold and swung at him hard as she could, aiming for his beaklike nose.

"God damn it!" He caught her hand and twisted her arm painfully up behind her back. He leaned his weight against her, pinning her to the trunk. "Just hold still!"

Cheek pressed to the rough gray bark, Tinker saw for the first time how far up the tree they stood—the forest floor lay a hundred feet below. Normally she didn't mind heights—only normally she wasn't this high up with an enemy spy. She stopped struggling, fear trying to climb up out of her stomach. She swallowed down on it— she had to keep her head.

Riki grabbed her right wrist, caught hold of her left, and bound both hands behind her with a thin plastic strap. Once she was bound helpless, he turned her around. He wore war paint—streaks of black under his vivid blue eyes and shock of black hair. His shirt was cut on the same loose lines as the muscle shirt he wore often during her captivity by the oni, made of glossy black scale armor. On his feet, with their odd birdlike toes, he wore silver tips that looked razor-sharp.

"What do you want?" She was pleased she didn't sound as scared as she was.

"I'm not going to hurt you."

"Somehow I don't believe you." She wriggled slightly to indicate her tied wrists. It made her teeter alarmingly on the branch, so she carefully scrunched down until she straddled the thick limb. There, perfectly safe. Ha!

Riki watched her with a cocked head. "There's no shame in being afraid of heights. Most people are."

She stared at him with shock. That was exactly what he said in her dream—wasn't it? She glanced downward and felt déjà vu; they'd been up high in her nightmare.

"What do you want?" she asked. "Are you going to turn me over to the oni again?"

"No. When you killed Lord Tomtom, we tengu managed to break free of the oni."

"*I gave that up. You melted the witch, so I got out of my no-compete contract.*"

This was seriously weird.

"Riki, who is the wizard of Oz?"

"Huh?"

"I had a dream and you were in it."

"And you and you and you too," Riki quoted the movie.

"Oh good, at least you know the source. In my dream, I was trying to get to the wizard of Oz."

"Oookay, and I thought I was deep in left field. Oh this is sad."

"Do have any idea who he might be?"

"The wizard?" Riki pulled a pack of cigarettes out of his back pocket, tapped out a cigarette, lit it, and took a deep drag. "Hmmm, in the movie the wizard was the traveling performer that Dorothy met when she ran away from home. Chances are, then, he's someone you've met but don't recognize now."

Taking another drag, Riki vented the smoke out of his nose in twin columns as he thought. "His nature is changing; some perceive him as great and powerful, others see him as foolish, but he's the only character that fully understood both Kansas and Oz. Most likely, you're looking for someone with great knowledge, but his intelligence is disguised somehow." Riki gazed off into the forest, eyes unfocused, thinking. "Like Dorothy, he's a traveler between worlds, just as lost . . ."

Riki's eyes snapped back in focus. "Impatience. He's your wizard."

"Who?"

"Impatience. The dragon that you fought at Turtle Creek."

She tried to fit the name of "Impatience" with the countless jagged teeth and massive snaky body.

"See, intelligence disguised." Riki waved his cigarette, reminding her of the astronomer postdocs when they went into lecture mode.

"Legends say that a dragon has a body and a spirit, and you can encounter the one without the other. Usually in the old stories, the dragons send their spirits out to cross great distances—but while they're doing it, it's a very unwise thing to approach their bodies. The lights are on, but no one's home."

"Running on autopilot?"

"Let's just say that there's more than one story about someone getting their head bitten off while a dragon's spirit is absent."

She remembered the impression that intelligence filled the dragon's eyes—its surprise at having a hand clamped into its mouth. "So you're saying the dragon was unconscious at the time he attacked me."

"Probably."

That would certainly explain how she'd managed to walk away with nothing more than a sore hand. "So where is this dragon now?"

"Even if I knew that, I wouldn't tell you. I want Impatience for the tengu. That's what I was doing at Reinholds. The oni had set a trap for it, using the fountain as a lure."

"The oni?"

"Impatience was one of two dragons the oni had waiting on Onihida for the invasion. The other is Malice, who is much bigger. Somehow Impatience managed to slip the oni's hold on him and escape."

"So, on top of the royal troops and the oni, we have an unaligned dragon running loose in Pittsburgh."

"Well, a party is only fun if you invite lots of interesting people."

She stuck her tongue out at him. "How do you plan to find Impatience?"

"I don't know. *You* apparently have to follow the yellow brick road."

In her dream, though, the road ended with the tree. This was going to drive her mad. In the silence between them, she heard a slight noise from Riki's hip pocket. He frowned, slipped out a cell phone, and answered it with a cautious, "Hello?"

As he listened, his caution changed to worry. "You're where? Jesus Christ, what are you doing there? Oh fuck. Yes I said that, what do you expect me to say? No—don't—don't . . ." Riki sighed. "Put your cousin on. No, no, not Joey! Keiko." Riki waited a moment until the phone could be traded off on the other side of the conversation. "Yeah, I'm here. What's going on?"

Riki listened for several minutes, grimacing as if what he heard pained him. "I'll be there in a few minutes. Hang tight." Riki tucked away his phone. "Change of plans."

"You're letting me go?"

"Sorry." He actually managed to look it. "I'll never have this chance again. I can't throw it away." He pulled out a silk scarf and tied it over her eyes. "I don't want you to know where we're going." He took firm hold of her and jerked her off her feet. "This time, don't wriggle so much."

She felt him leap, knew that he'd left the safety of the tree, and nearly screamed at the knowledge. His wings rustled out, caught the air, and they swooped upward.

Fifteen or twenty minutes later, Riki dove down and wove through light and shadows to land again. Numb from dangling, her legs folded under her. Riki lowered her down to a prone position and then knelt behind her, panting with exertion.

Their landing site seemed too flat to be a tree branch but it swayed slightly with the rustling of the wind.

"Damn it, Riki, where are we?"

Riki tugged down her blindfold. She lay just inside the door of a tiny cabin; only eight-foot square, it would have been claustrophobic if it had actually contained furniture.

"We're at a cote," he panted. "Emergency shelter."

The cabin seemed to be made of scrap lumber. The one small round window letting in light held glass, and the high ceiling bristled with nails, indicating that the roof was shingled, so the cabin was weatherproofed.

"Stay put." He stepped past her to pull something off a set of shelves on the back wall. "There's no safe way down to the ground. I'll be back."

Cabin, hell, it was a tree house. Under any other circumstance, she would have been entranced with the notion.

Riki took a deep breath and stepped backward out the door, spreading his black wings.

"Stay," he repeated and flapped away.

Not trusting his word, she struggled to her feet and went to the door. The view straight down made her step backward quickly. It was a place strictly for birds. If her hands weren't bound behind her back, she could get to the massive branch just outside the door, but there was nowhere to go from there. The tree was too wide, and the lowest branch too far from the ground to allow climbing down. She could see nothing but virgin forest through both the door and window, not even a glimpse of sun or river to give a clue which direction they had flown.

The cote was cunningly made. A brace along the back wall provided the one anchor point so the stress of the shifting tree could not tear the room apart. The front of the cabin rested on a beam yoked over side branches. A loft bed nearly doubled the floor space. A generous overhang meant the front door could hang open even during a rain shower to let in light without the weather. The outside of the cabin had been painted gray and black in a pattern that mimicked ironwood bark.

She kicked shut the door but the latch was too high for her to shift with her hands bound.

The shelves on the back wall were stocked with survival gear: warm clothing and blankets in plastic bags, extra plastic bags, rolls of duct tape, a serious first aid kit, ammo for guns, flashlights, two box knives, waterproof matches, bottled spring water, a water purifier kit, a small cooler filled with power bars and military rations, and even a roll of toilet paper. Judging by the shape of the bag, Riki had taken a set of clothes with him.

She fumbled with one of the box knives, blindly sawing at the plastic strap binding her wrists. The blade kept slipping, nicking her wrists, before she finally managed to cut through. She bandaged her wrists, looking at what she had to work with. A rope ladder from strips of blanket, reinforced with the duct tape? Or perhaps she should just try to jump Riki and take his cell phone. No, he'd gone to meet someone, so he could return with others.

As if the thought summoned the tengu, Riki kicked the door open. She snatched up the box knife and spun around to face Riki as he dropped in through the doorway. He wasn't alone. He had a child with him—a little boy in an oversized black hooded sweatshirt.

"Riki!" She started toward him, angry at the tengu, and afraid for the boy.

Riki looked up, saw the knife in her hand, and his face went cold. She had always suspected that the tengu treated her with kid gloves. Suddenly, it was as if a stranger was looking at her, one who would hurt her if she took another step forward.

She stopped, and reached out with her empty hand. "Don't hurt him."

Still tight in Riki's hold, the boy glanced over his shoulder at her, and blinked in surprise. He had the tengu's coarse straight black hair, electric blue eyes, and sharp features—though his nose wasn't so nearly beaklike as Riki's. "Oh, hello," the tengu boy said with no fear in his voice. "I'm Joey. Joey Shoji. Who are you?"

With a rustle of wings, two slightly older tengu children crowded the doorway. Wearing blue jeans and torn T-shirts, they would have seemed like human children except for the way they clung to the sides of the doorway with birdlike feet, fanning the air with black wings. The girl looked thirteen and sported the black war paint and sharp spurs that Riki wore. The boy was younger—eleven? Ten? Both had Riki's dark wild hair and sharp features.

"Hey, what's a girl doing here?" the boy asked in English and hopped into the cote.

The girl scowled and remained hovering at the door. "She's an elf—the fairy princess."

"What's an elf?" Joey asked.

"She's still a girl elf, Keiko," the boy insisted.

"What's an elf?" Joey asked again.

"It means I have pointed ears." Tinker tapped on her left ear. She used it as a distraction to put the knife on the shelves as casually as she could. The two younger kids studied her ear, but Riki and Keiko's eyes followed the knife.

The coldness left Riki's face, but he still watched her carefully. "This is Mickey and Keiko." He released the littlest one. "And Joey. They're my younger cousins."

"Should we really be telling her our names?" Keiko asked. "What's she doing here?"

Joey pulled off the adult-sized sweatshirt he was drowning in. Underneath he had a ragged T-shirt like the other two—the back torn open to reveal the elaborate spell tattooed from shoulder to waistline, in black. "Look, look, I have wings too!"

He spoke a word, and magic poured through the tracings, making them shimmer like fresh ink. The air hazed around him, and the wings unfolded out of the distortion, at first holographic in appearance, ghosts of crow wings hovering behind him, fully extended. Then they solidified into reality, skin and bone merged into his musculature of his back, glistening black feathers, all correctly proportioned for his thin, child's body.

"Wow," Tinker said. "Those are cool."

Keiko hopped into the cote to catch hold of Joey and pull him away from Tinker, giving her a dark distrusting look.

Riki said something in the harsh oni tongue that made the younger tengu look at Tinker with surprise.

"Her?" Keiko cried. "No way!"

Riki shrugged, making his wings rustle. "She's the one that killed Lord Tomtom. The dragon went to her. I have to check."

"Wait," Tinker said. "This is all about the tattoo you think the dragon put on me?"

"Yes." Riki nodded.

"Are you nuts?" Tinker said.

"No, just desperate. Please, take off your dress."

"Oh, you have to be kidding." Tinker took a step back and realized how crowded the tiny cabin had just gotten with tengu wings. "I am not taking off my dress in front of all of you."

Riki touched Joey's shoulder. "Wings, Joey. Keiko and Mickey, you too."

The boys spoke spell commands and their wings vanished. Riki picked them up, one at a time, and swung them up to the loft bed. They sat on the edge, dangling down their three-toed feet until Riki said, "Nyah, nyah, all the way up. Quiet little birds."

Keiko crossed her arms, flared out her wings, and leveled a hostile look at Riki. "I'm a warrior."

Riki glared at the tengu girl until the girl added something in oni. "A witness? Yes, I guess you're right."

"Yeah, I'm supposed to act as if that's better?" Tinker asked.

"Take off your dress, let me look at you, and if you don't have the mark, I'll let you go."

Tinker scoffed. "Yeah, sure."

"I promise," Riki said.

Like that was worth anything.

"Don't be such a chickenshit!" Keiko said.

Riki slapped the tengu girl on the back of the head. "Hey, you're not helping. Would you want to take off your clothes in front of strangers?"

Keiko blushed and stuck out her tongue at her cousin.

Riki returned his attention to Tinker. "Come on. Just do it quick and it'll be over."

"I don't have any mark."

Riki's face went neutral, all emotion draining out, leaving only resolve.

Tinker considered whether she wanted her dress forcibly taken off. There wasn't any running away, and while Keiko was young, the tengu girl was as tall as she was. Probably if Tinker tried calling the winds she'd end up in a wrestling match before she got the spell off. "Fine. I'll take it off."

She struggled out of her dress, and as she feared, the bra had to go.

"It would be over her heart, wouldn't it?" Keiko looked as uncomfortable with Tinker's nudity as Tinker felt.

"It should." Riki took Tinker's hands and examined her arms carefully, even to the point of undoing the bandages and peering under them. It wasn't as bad as Tinker feared. She realized it was the kids' presence; she trusted Riki not to do anything with them there—watching. Hopefully she was right.

"Okay," Riki finally said. "You can get dressed."

"Does she have it? Does she have it?" Mickey called from the loft.

"No." Riki glanced down at Keiko. "Can you make it to the near cote without stopping? It's going to be dark and we'll need to move quietly and fast."

Keiko screwed up her face, torn between saying yes and admitting the truth. Finally she hunched her shoulders, looked away, and said, "No."

Riki tousled the girl's short black hair. "It's better that you tell the truth now. I'll take Joey and then come back to guide you two. Rest up."

"What about her?" Keiko asked, and then added quietly. "You promised her."

If it wasn't her freedom they were talking about, it would have been funny to see Riki realize how screwed he was. He could start to ferry the kids back home, but it would leave her alone with at least two of them. Taking her home meant all three kids would be alone for a much longer time—perhaps a very long time if he ran into trouble with the elves. He looked at her in sudden panic.

She sighed and waved her hand. "Take care of them first."

"Promise me that you won't hurt them."

She laughed. "Who is going to protect me from them?"

A wry smile came and went. "I'm trusting you two to behave. Understand?"

"Yes, Riki," Mickey said.

Keiko nodded, watching Tinker.

"Joey?" Riki motioned to the littlest tengu and the boy flung himself out of the loft into Riki's arms. "Ooomph! Settle down, you little monster. Here, sweatshirt on first." Riki knelt and pulled the sweatshirt onto the boy. "Remember, once we leave, no talking. Quiet little birds."

Joey mimed locking his mouth and throwing away the key.

"Good boy." Riki picked up the child and gave them a worried look. "Remember there are oni in the woods. Keep it down and no lights."

"Quiet little birds," Mickey said.

Riki wavered at the door, Joey clinging to his neck. "Tinker—I love them as much as you love Oilcan. Everything I've done has been for them. Please just—just wait for me to get back."

The tengu kids took the loft bed and Tinker settled by the door, her back to the wall so she could keep an eye on them. Keiko continued to stare at her. Mickey swung his legs. Dusk fell on the forest and darkness crawled into the cabin.

"How far does Riki have to go?"

Mickey started to say something but Keiko poked him.

"We're not allowed to say."

"What are you doing so far away anyhow?"

"Joey just got his wings," Mickey said. "We were on his first long flight and got cut off by a troop of oni moving through the area. We tried to go around them and got lost. When we hit the city's edge, Keiko said we should call Riki. I'm the one that remembered the number."

"Then all you would do was cry," Keiko said.

Mickey pulled up his legs, curling into himself.

Keiko gave him a look of remorse and then swung down. She rummaged through the shelves and then handed up a bottle of water and a power bar to her younger cousin. "Here. You can have the last chocolate one."

Keiko put a second bottle and bar up beside Mickey. Wordlessly, she left an offering of food and water for Tinker down on the floor, carefully staying outside of Tinker's reach, and then swung back to the loft.

Tinker hadn't had a power bar as an elf—she expected something tasteless. She was surprised how good it tasted. "Oh, these are yummy."

Mickey nodded in agreement, made instantly happy by Keiko's offering. "I didn't think elves could speak English."

Keiko pinched Mickey.

"Ow! What?"

"Don't display how ignorant you are. She was a human until the viceroy turned her into an elf a few months ago."

Mickey looked at Tinker, recognition dawning on him. "Oh, she's the Dufae girl?"

"Yes," Keiko said.

Fear filled Mickey's face.

"Why are you scared of me?" Tinker asked.

"We know what Riki had to do to you," Mickey whispered. "How he had to turn you over to the oni."

"Riki didn't want us to come to Elfhome," Keiko said. "He said that either the elves would find us, or the oni would. Better stay on Earth where we were at least free. But the oni came to our house and took Joey hostage. Riki sent us on ahead to be with our aunt, but he stayed to work for the oni—to try and get Joey back."

"He never told me about you."

"If he told you, then the kitsune would know, and then the oni would know. He couldn't tell you the truth about anything—or he'd put us in danger."

"You hate the tengu now—don't you?" Mickey whispered.

A few days ago, Tinker probably would have said yes. She knew that when she found the MP3 player, she'd been angry enough to beat Riki to a pulp again. Now, with the dead in Chinatown, and the children looking at her in fear, she couldn't hate all the innocent strangers. "No."

Keiko scoffed, disbelieving. "I'd never forgive anyone that did that to me."

"I saw what Lord Tomtom did to those that failed him—and it scared the living shit out of me." She shuddered with the memory of the torture; the flash of bright blades and white of bone stripped clean of flesh. "I was willing to do almost anything to keep the knives away from me."

"So you forgive Riki?"

There was something about the darkness that demanded honesty. "I'm still angry at him. But I was with the oni for nearly a month—I can understand why he did it and don't think I can hate him for it. He took my shit and never complained, and when he could, he protected me."

There was a sudden roar outside and a hoverbike—lift engines at full—popped up and landed on the massive branch outside the door. Its headlight flooded the room with stark white blinding light.

Tinker stood and called magic, wrapping the wind around her.

"Tinker *domi!*" Stormsong's voice came out of the light.

"Stormsong?" Tinker squinted into the glare.

The headlight snapped off. Stormsong sat on a custom Delta Tinker had done for a charity auction last year. Somehow Stormsong had managed to land and balance on the branch—it was going to take work to get it down in one piece. In her right hand the *sekasha* held a shotgun resting across the handlebars and trained at the cabin door.

"How the hell did you find me?" Tinker asked.

"I closed my eyes and went where I was needed." Stormsong glanced beyond Tinker to the kids. "They're tengu."

Tinker realized that her being safe meant the kids were now in danger. "I promised that they wouldn't be hurt."

"That was a silly thing to do," Stormsong said.

"They're just kids." Tinker moved to protect them with her shield.

"Kids grow up," Stormsong said.

Tinker shook her head. "I can't let you hurt them. I promised."

"Yes, Tinker *ze domi*," Stormsong said in High Tongue.

Tinker released the winds. The kids huddled against the back corner of the loft bed.

"We won't hurt you," she told them, "but I need to leave."

"Hey," Keiko called. She pulled off a necklace and scrambled forward to dangle it out to Tinker. "Take this. It will protect you."

"From what?"

"Tengu."

Tinker looped the necklace over her neck and picked her way out onto the branch. "How the hell did you get a hoverbike the whole way up here? I know the lift engine can't do a hundred feet straight up—or down."

"Flying blind." Stormsong uncocked her shotgun and holstered it. "Hang tight to me—this is going to be tricky. And you might want to close your eyes."

Tinker clung tight to Stormsong, trying to let her trust of the bodyguard override her knowledge of the hoverbike's limitations. Stormsong didn't even turn on the bike's headlight, just raced the bike's engine and then tipped them over the edge. A squeak of fear leapt up Tinker's throat—followed by her heart—as they nose-dived. They hit a lower branch that cracked under the lift drive and suddenly they were corkscrewing madly. She gripped Stormsong tight. She felt more than saw the blur of tree trunks and branches as they kissed off them. Seconds later they straightened out and roared through the darkness—Pony on a second hoverbike waiting on the ground running alongside them.

"Thank you," Stormsong called back.

"What for? You rescued me."

"Yes, but you trusted me to do my job."

18: SEEK YOU

The *sekasha* suggested a bath and bed, but Tinker didn't want to unwind and take it easy. Things in Pittsburgh were bad, and getting worse, and like it or not, she was one of the few people who had the power to fix things. The only question was how.

She placated the *sekasha* by agreeing to dinner and took her datapad with her to the enclave's private dining hall. Maynard thought that opening a line of communication with Earth would be key. Yeah, right, just phone home. Riki had said that the dragon was the wizard of Oz, and implied that dragons understood how to move from world to world. She didn't know where the dragon was, however, and from the sounds of it, both the oni and tengu were searching hard for it. Follow the yellow brick road? What road? Ohio River Boulevard? I-279? The last lead she had was the black willow tree and last she saw of that, it was flambé.

Wait, she had seeds from the black willow. At least, she thought she did. She had Windwolf's staff track the small jar down, and the MP3 player. Watching the seeds wriggle in the glass, she listened to the songs recorded on the player. It was one of Oilcan's favorite elf rock groups, playing a collection of songs that her cousin had written for them. If you didn't know Oilcan, the songs seemed to be about lost lovers. Tinker knew that they were about his mother. Odd how the words could stay the same but knowledge changed the meaning.

Tinker laid her head on the table and remembered Riki in another light.

Pony ran his hand across her back, a delicious feeling that uncoiled a sudden deep need. On the heels of that, like cracking open a bottle full of dark storm winds, a confusing wash of emotions.

"Don't do that." Tinker shifted away from his touch and tried to cork the bottle. She was too fragile for that.

"Have I hurt you?" Pony asked.

She shook her head.

"All day, you have avoided me as if I had. I need to understand—what have I done wrong? We are not fitting this way."

She had? She hadn't even been aware of it. "It's not you. It's me. I-I've so totally—" Unfortunately there wasn't an Elvish match for "fucked up," so she stuck in the English, "everything and everyone."

"Fuck," Pony repeated the English curse. "Can you teach me that?"

"No!" She realized he meant the word's meaning, not the actual action. "It means intercourse." And once she saw the confusion in Pony's face as he tried to plug in the meaning into her sentence, she added, "It's a curse word generally meaning—well—anything you want it to mean. It's one of the more versatile words we have."

"How do you conjugate it?"

"Fuck, fucking, fucked when used as a verb. It can be used as a noun, indicate a person, place, or thing, generally derogatory." This was not the conversation she thought she'd be having with Pony this evening. "It could also be combined—creatively—with other words. Fuckhead. Fuck off. Fuckwad."

"I'm starting to understand a little more about human fascination with sex."

"Besides the fact that it's so damn fun?"

"What is damn?"

"Pony!"

"I feel that it is time that I learned English."

She felt a pang of guilt knowing that Pony hadn't understood any of Nathan's last words, that he had only seen her struggling in Nathan's hold and her cry for help. "Yes, that would be good."

"Why do you feel this way? That you have 'fucked up'? You have done the best you can against very difficult situations."

"Pittsburgh is stuck here on Elfhome. Nathan is dead. Half the people I know probably hate my guts now. I'm not sure even Oilcan or Lain will ever want to see me again. I cheated on my husband, and seduced you! How is that 'the best'? Gods forbid if I had done my worst!"

He reached out and pulled her back, into his lap.

"Pony." She wriggled, trying to escape him.

"*Domi*," he whispered into her hair, his lips brushing the tips of her ears, sending a shiver of want through her. "Have I no will of my own? Am I your puppet?"

She stared into his dark eyes and felt cold dread take hold. "I don't want to talk about this."

"Because if you're in control, I am not to blame for my actions?"

"Pony, please."

"And if I am not under your control, does that make me a terrifying stranger? Someone that you do not know?"

She clung to him then, afraid that he would slip away from her. "Please, Pony, you're the only thing sane about my life right now."

"You are being unfair to both of us to say that what happened was only by your hand. I am not your puppet. You did not act alone. You can not be solely responsible."

"You do what I tell you to do. I told you I wanted sex and you gave it to me."

"I choose to do what you tell me." He took her hand and nuzzled her wrist. "I was pleased that you trusted me enough to turn to me and to stop when you changed your mind."

"I'm just supposed to use you? Get off and then throw you across the room? Like you're some kind of—" She was going to say "vibrator" but elves didn't have a word for battery-operated sex toys. Nor did she want to hurt him more by being crude. "—substitute for my husband?"

"That is what I am. I am to be here for you when Wolf cannot be."

"But—But— And you're okay with that?"

"I have lived my entire life knowing that as a *sekasha*, if I became a *domi's* beholden, she might take me to bed. And I knew, when I offered myself to you, that meant all of me. My life is yours. My love is yours. And I have watched you fight the demon spawn themselves to keep me from harm. Nothing happened yesterday that I did not know might happen, that I wanted to stop, and that I am sorry about—except the part about being thrown across the room."

If he thought this was going to make her feel better, he was wrong. She felt worse, and struggled to keep from showing it. Obviously she sucked at it as sadness filled his eyes.

"I did not realize until Stormsong explained that humans are so—singular—with their love. It is not our way." Pony used the inclusive "our," meaning that they both belonged to it: she was one of them. "That is why we *sekasha* are *naekuna*; so you can turn to us if you need us."

"Oh, Pony, I might have the body of an elf, but in here—" She tapped her temple. "I'm still a human. I can't commit to one person—heart and soul—and then take another one to bed, without feeling like I'm doing something wrong. I just can't."

"I know." He said it with quiet acceptance in his voice, and then nothing more. After a minute, she leaned against him and soaked in his calmness. It still felt wrong to stay so close, so intimate with him when she was married to Windwolf. Her logical side, though, was starting to recognize what Pony must know—that while she was emotionally fully human now, that in a hundred years or so, she would slowly grow to be elf inside as well as out. And to elves—a hundred years was a very short time.

Well, sitting wallowing in her own pain wasn't going to help Pittsburgh. Time to pull rabbits out of her butt. How could she communicate across realities when Earth wouldn't have a receiver for her transmitter? She'd already tested Turtle Creek for radio waves, and nothing recognizable was coming through. She entertained the idea of linking two phones together with a phone line and tossing one into the Discontinuity. No, a phone would sink like the gate had. So would messages in bottles.

She sighed and slid out of Pony's lap. "Time to get busy. I need to do some modeling."

Communication with Earth was a simple science problem. What was happening in Pittsburgh was a vast sociological problem that she didn't know how to solve. She didn't even know where she stood in regards to it. How far did her responsibility extend? Were the elves right in hunting down all the oni and killing them? The scientist in her could see the simple logic of it. Both races were immortal, only the oni were prolific and the elves weren't. If the elves did nothing, the oni would win eventually by default. Morally, genocide was wrong—but did the elves have a choice? It wasn't like the gods had put both races on one world. The oni had invaded, which put them in the wrong. It would be stupid to put them in the right simply because they failed to kill the elves first.

And what about the tengu, who seemed to be a race separate from the oni and on Elfhome against their will? What was her responsibility to them? Riki had betrayed her, but if the tengu children were telling the truth, he had been forced to choose between her and his cousins. She knew she would move the world to protect Oilcan; how could she hold Riki's betrayal against him when that meant putting the children in danger?

And how many tengu were there on Elfhome? Would she be protecting Riki, the three kids and the unnamed "aunt" or were there more? A dozen? A hundred?

Where did her responsibility begin and end? Could she protect all the humans and the tengu too? Or to keep the humans safe, would she have to ignore what was morally right?

And under it all was the dark suspicion that she didn't really have the power to protect anything, despite what Tooloo might think. True Flame thought she was a useless child. The Stone Clan was trying to kill her. Windwolf had lent her his power, but if she took a stand against him, would he take it back?

When Wolf asked Tinker to be his *domi*, he'd suspected that she would be able to lead. Certainly, when she spoke, people obeyed. She didn't seem to be aware that she had the quality, but the day she saved his life, everyone listened to her without quarreling. Time and time again since then there had been satisfying—although usually mystifying—proof that he was right about her. He found his *domi* deep in another mysterious project in the middle of the Westinghouse Bridge, overlooking the Ghostlands.

"What is this?" Wolf pointed to a large cylindrical machine beside his *domi*.

"This is an Imperial searchlight." Tinker patted the three-foot-tall light fixture. "It uses a Xenon 4,000-watt bulb to output 155,000 lumens. They say that the output is visible at distances of more than twenty kilometers."

Wolf eyed the wires snaking away to either end of the bridge. "Do you have more than one?"

"Three. I tried to get four, but these babies are hard to find in Pittsburgh—and a bitch to move. They weigh nearly two hundred pounds and then you need almost four hundred pounds of ballast so they don't tip over. I put the other two on either hill to get maximum spread."

Tinker settled at the table at the center of the bridge. "I've got them tied together to this control board. I'm trying to track down a manual on—" She paused to eye her screen closely. "Ah, there, Morse code."

Wolf crouched beside her. "You're going to use the light to communicate?"

She smiled and leaned down to touch her forehead to his. "Exactly. By the composition of the buildings inside the Ghostlands, it's clear that Earth is one of the dimensions intersected by this Discontinuity. The blue shift of the area seems to indicate that certain wavelengths of light are being absorbed and only the blue is reflecting back to us."

"So other wavelengths are traveling on through to the other dimensions?"

"I think so. If we communicate with Earth, we might be able to get them to help. I'm just a little worried that no one on their end will be paying attention—this will only work in the middle of the night."

"They're missing a city with sixty thousands souls. They're paying attention."

"Well—there is that." She kissed him and went back to work.

"Have you considered that the oni will see this too?"

"Yes, I know, that's a flaw in the plan. We'll have to consider any communication from another world as suspect."

He considered this problem as she typed. "It is unfortunate that the EIA had been compromised. Maynard might have had a way to verify any communication from the UN as authentic."

"Hmmm, hadn't considered that angle. Human agencies that have security protocols. Wait—I wonder—what happened to those NSA agents?"

"The human agents that tried to kidnap you?"

His tone made her glance at him and giggle. "Oh, don't look like that. They only wanted to protect me from the oni. They actually were nice, once they stopped trying to drag me back to Earth."

"Maynard will know where they are, if they are in Pittsburgh."

She took out a cell phone and made it beep repeatedly. "I would have never dreamed of having the God of Pittsburgh's phone number in my address book."

"He is not God of Pittsburgh. He is our servant."

"Somehow I doubt that he sees it that way." Her face changed as the call went through. "Oh, hi, yeah, this is Tinker. Say, do you know what happened to the NSA agents? Briggs and Durrack? Really?" She listened for a minute. "Oh cool! Can you send them out to Turtle Creek? I need them out here. Thanks."

As she hung up, Wolf wondered what Maynard made of the phone call. It was a perfect example, though, of his *domi's* leadership skills. She saw the need and did what was needed to fill it without guidance from him. All she needed was the authority of her title. And she probably did not realize how rare the ability was.

"They didn't leave last Shutdown, so they're stuck here." Tinker relayed what she learned. "They've been working with him. Apparently when they kidnapped me, he put them through a detailed background check. They're among the few people in Pittsburgh he could trust to be who they said they were. He was using them to weed through the EIA's databases to find altered files and recover the original data."

Her walkie-talkie beeped and one of the work crews reported in that the other two searchlights were in place and pointed down into the valley. The walkie-talkies tickled him to no end. That was what he wanted for his people—the ease of communication that humans had.

Tinker glanced up into the night sky. Dark lay full on the land and the stars gleamed brilliant overhead. "What do you think? Is it dark enough?"

"It will not get any darker without clouds."

"These lights are about two hundred times brighter than a normal lightbulb," Tinker warned him. "You shouldn't look directly at them when they're on. Okay, let's see if it works." Tinker radioed the other two units with "Turn them on."

The three beams of light cut brilliant down into the valley. Midway the light shifted to blue, somewhat muted, but still dazzling in the pitch darkness.

"Hmm, that's a good sign," Tinker murmured.

"Did you plan tonight because of the lack of moon?" Wolf asked.

"I'd love to say yes, but actually we just got lucky." Tinker clicked her keyboard, activating her program. The searchlights started to flash. "I've written a short script in Morse code—C-Q-C-Q-C-Q-D-E-S-1-K—and interspersed it with three minutes of darkness."

"What does that mean?"

"This manual says it means 'calling any station, this is designation station one, listening.' I'm not sure if that's totally correct Morse, but I figure it's close enough for horseshoes."

She saw his smile, and her eyes widened as she realized what she'd said, and then she smiled too. He'd asked her to be his *domi* after playing horseshoes with her.

The searchlights snapped off, plunging them into darkness, and Tinker slid down into his lap.

"Did you—" Tinker whispered to him. "Did you have lovers other than Jewel Tear—and the *sekasha*?"

"A few. Not many. I had my insane idea of coming to the Westernlands and establishing a holding here."

She made a small unhappy sound.

"If I had known you were in my future, I would have waited," he whispered. "Think, this way I came to you a skilled lover. This way one of us knew how it was done."

"I can build a hyperphase jump gate, I'm sure I could have figured sex out. Insert Tab M into Slot F. Repeat until done."

Windwolf laughed. "You delight me."

"Good. You delight me too."

They stole several minutes for themselves. With much regret, Wolf focused back on their many problems. "I think we'd better strengthen our position." he said. "We're going to stir the oni up doing this."

"Oh! I hadn't considered that," Tinker said.

He was learning that his *domi* became so fixated on a puzzle that she ignored the outside world. It meant that she could lock all of her brilliance onto finding a solution, but it left her open to being blindsided.

He kissed her brow and reluctantly left her to make the valley safe for her.

Despite their rocky start, Tinker actually liked the NSA agents. They arrived in a sleek grey sedan so out of place in Pittsburgh that it didn't need the D.C. plates to identify it as out of town. Nobody drove new cars because the parts were too hard to find, and no one knew how to service them. Corg Durrack and Hannah Briggs got out of the car cautiously, as if they were trying not to spook the heavily armed elves.

Both NSA agents, though, looked like they could hold their own with the *sekasha*.

The tall, leggy Briggs wore a clingy black outfit that looked like wet paint, and slid in and out of the shadows with feline grace. A Batman utility belt with small mystery packs had been added to her ensemble, slung low on her hips, holstering her exotic long-barreled handgun. Tinker couldn't tell if Briggs was now flaunting her weapon, or just displaying the one that was impossible to conceal.

Corg Durrack had a boyish face and the body of a comic book hero. He carried his usual peace offering of a white wax-paper bag, which he held out Tinker with a grin. "Your favorite."

"I'll be the judge." Tinker opened to the bag to find her favorite cookies—chocolate frosting thumbprint cookies from Jenny Lee. "This is spooky. How did you know?"

"It's our job to know." Durrack winked.

Briggs scoffed at this, and drifted back into the darkness.

"So what's our little mad scientist up to now?" Durrack settled down beside Tinker's chair where Windwolf had been a short time before. The searchlight flashed the work area with brightness as it cycled through the short message.

Tinker stuck her tongue out at him. "You know, I thought Maynard kicked you two out of Pittsburgh months ago."

"You were only the top of our to-do list. It took twenty-four hours of negotiations, but we stayed in this mud hole after the last Shutdown."

She laughed at the look of disgust on Durrack's face. "You don't like our fair city?"

"This isn't our world and the elves seem determined to remind us of that every chance they get. Besides, it's like getting stuck in a time warp; Pittsburgh is missing a lot of the simple conveniences of home. The television sucks here. And I would kill for Starbucks."

"Starbucks?" Tinker said. "Sounds Elvish. Who is he?"

Durrack gave her an odd look.

"What else is on your to-do list?" Tinker asked.

"Little of this, little of that," Durrack said. "Gather intelligence."

"In Pittsburgh?"

"You're got five or six races stuffed under one roof, it makes for lots of secrets floating around."

"How do you get six?"

Corg ticked them off on his fingers. "The elves, the humans, the oni, the tengu, the mixed bloods, and now a dragon—which the tengu say is a sentient being."

The searchlight fell dark, dropping them into blackness.

Tinker wasn't sure why, but she found it annoying that the NSA had apparently talked to the tengu about the dragon. "I didn't know you were so friendly with the tengu."

"Politics has nothing to do with friendship." Durrack's voice came out of the darkness. "It's doing whatever you have to do to protect what's yours. Pittsburgh might be under UN control, but its people are Americans and it's our duty to protect them."

"You realize the tengu lie."

"Everyone lies."

"The elves don't. They see it as dishonorable."

"They might not lie, but they dance around the truth. Like yesterday, during that little encounter you had with the tree. You analyze the events and it's fairly clear that the Stone Clan tried to kill you. Forest Moss withheld his support until you were captured by the tree, and the building you should have landed in collapsed for no apparent reason."

"I know."

"He made elegant excuses about why he was so slow, but it was all bullshit. He wanted that tree to kill you."

"I know. You don't have to rub it in."

"Are they trying to keep you from building another gate? If there is a way to travel back and forth between Pittsburgh and Earth, the treaty stays intact."

She hadn't considered that as the reason why the Stone Clan

wanted her eliminated. "Nothing I could build would transport the entire city."

"At this point, I'd take a trapdoor back to Earth."

Tinker laughed. "And I'm not sure I can really build a gate that works right. Look at the mess I made with this one."

The searchlight flared on, bathing the Discontinuity with brilliance.

"Is it getting bigger?" Durrack asked.

Tinker nodded. "And oni are coming through it."

"Yeah, I saw the kappa you pulled out. The oni are sick puppies to warp their people into monsters like that. You know, the more I find out about the oni, the more I think the elves are right in wiping them out. The problem is collateral damage."

"I don't think the tengu are all that bad." Tinker whispered what she hadn't had the courage to say to Windwolf.

"The tengu aren't oni," Durrack said. "They were mountain tribes of humans living on Onihida, descendants of people that ended up there by mistake. The story goes that half of them were killed on a battlefield trying to resist the oni, and the greater bloods that defeated them merged the survivors with the carrion crows that had been feeding on their fathers and brothers. Twisted little tale, isn't it?"

"But it is true?"

"Their DNA supports the claim."

The searchlight finished its cycle and dropped them into silent darkness.

If the story was true, then the tengu had been screwed from the very start, the moment their ancestors lost their way and fell from Earth.

"I'm going to do everything I can to protect the humans of Pittsburgh," Tinker said. "But I don't know what I can do for the tengu."

"From what I've seen, there's not much anyone can do for the tengu."

"How long are we going to do this?" Durrack asked an hour later, when darkness fell over them yet again.

"Until the lightbulbs burn out, my husband loses his patience, I figure out something better—or they answer us."

"Want to bet which happens first?"

"My bet is that they answer us, or the bulbs burn out. The lifespan of these bulbs are rated at a thousand hours, but there's no telling how many hours they have left."

"And there are no replacement bulbs?" Durrack guessed.

"Nope, not unless Earth can sling them through the Ghost-lands."

"Are we going to be able to tell if they're answering us?"

"I have a collection of detecting devices aimed at the valley to catch heat, light, sound, and motion."

"Where are you aiming the spotlights?"

"At the buildings. I'm not sure if the air over the valley is part of the Discontinuity, so I'm not positive if light passing through it will be visible in another dimension. The buildings though, will either reflect the light or absorb it, which in theory makes them visible on all dimensions—but I could be wrong."

"This just seems so basic. If it could work, then Earth should have—"

Blue slashed upward, out of the darkness, pulsing in the rhythm of Morse code.

"They're responding!" Tinker scrambled to kill her transmission program. Her detectors were already translating the flashes.

Calling S1, this is S2, listening.

"It's Earth!" she said.

"You don't know that. Here." Durrack nudged her away from the keyboard. "This is where I come in—remember?"

The searchlights flashed quickly through code and then went dark.

"What are you saying?" Tinker asked.

"I'm requesting verification. It might take them a while to dig someone up who can answer . . . or they might have someone standing by. Fort Meade isn't that far from the Pittsburgh border."

The valley went dark and then a reply blazed back.

"Someone standing by?" Tinker asked.

"No, they want to know if Pittsburgh is safe on Elfhome."

"Depends on your definition of safe."

Durrack laughed and typed. "I'm repeating my request. Never give info unless you're sure of who is listening."

"Most likely the oni on Onihida can see this."

"Exactly."

Wolf returned to his *domi* to find her looking unhappy.

"What is it?"

"We've verified we're talking to Earth. The gate is gone, just like we thought. Pittsburgh is stranded."

"You are still communicating?"

"We're comparing notes—seeing if we can use the Ghostlands to our advantage, or close it up somehow. From the sounds of it, though, Earth is still fighting over who has jurisdiction."

A runner from Poppymeadow's threaded his way through the *sekasha* to hold out a piece of paper. "A distant voice came from Aum Renau, relayed from court."

Wolf took the folded paper, opened it, and read the five English words within: *Follow the yellow brick road.* He frowned at the message and flipped the paper over, hoping for more. No. That was it.

"What does it say?" Tinker asked.

He handed it to her. "It's from Pure Radiance. I sent word to the *intanyei seyosa* caste asking for help with your dreams. I don't understand this."

"Follow the yellow brick road? Follow the yellow brick road? Just point the sucker out and I will. So far, I haven't found any road—bricked yellow or otherwise—figuratively, literally, allegorically."

"You understand her message?"

"No!" She sighed deeply. "But it looks like I have to figure it out."

19: SNAKES, SNAILS, AND PUPPY-DOG TAILS

Tinker kicked the blackened remains of the willow tree. It had died on the waterfront, leaving a burnt trail from the warehouse. Several buildings along its path had scorch marks where the burning tree had brushed up against them while staggering toward the river.

"Okay, let's take it from the top. We're off to see the wizard, the wonderful wizard of Oz."

"Because?" Pony asked.

"Because—because—because—because." Tinker didn't know. Did she ever know?

"Because of the wonderful things he does," Stormsong deadpanned.

Tinker glared at her. "In the dream, the yellow brick road led to the willow trees." She gave the tree another kick. "Which threw apples at us. Esme told me to follow the fruit to find the wizard—which is the dragon."

She followed the black path of soot and cinders back toward the warehouse. "Lain gave me one of the seeds, but I couldn't figure out anything interesting with it. Most of the times it doesn't even wriggle. So obviously fruit is something else. Whatever it is, it will lead us to the dragon. The dragon is the desired end product—not the fruit."

"I am not sure it would be wise to face the dragon again," Pony said. "We barely survived the last fight."

"I know, I know, I know. Riki did say that it needs magic to become sentient, and once it used me to tap the spell stones, it—" She paused. "Wait. Riki said that the oni messed with the spell to trap the dragon. What if the 'fruit' is just magic?"

"In the movie," Stormsong said. "The apples were gathered up by Dorothy, the Scarecrow, and the Tin Man."

"No, the Tin Man came in during the apple scene, Dorothy was picking—" Tinker stopped with sudden realization. "Oh, gods, Oilcan! He was hauling the overflow cans away—when was the last time anyone saw him?"

"The day we watched the movie," Pony said. "Wednesday."

Neither Oilcan nor the flatbed had been at the junkyard on Friday. He had left two days of newspapers in the drive. Feeling sick, she fumbled with her phone, picking his number from her address book. His phone rang three times and dropped to voice mail. Trying not to panic, she called the scrap yard and then his apartment, getting only voice mail. Where had he taken the barrels? Had he said? No, just that he had to dump them. Where could he have taken them? They had gone through nearly a hundred barrels before she got the spell repaired—a massive pool of magic to dump haphazardly, but Pittsburgh had lots of big empty places. Still, the barrels and the steel filings represented a good bit of money once the magic leached out—so he would probably leave them on land that they owned. That left one place—the barn.

She dialed the land line to the barn. She expected his machine to pick up after three rings, but it continued ringing. She clung to the phone, whispering, "Oh, please answer."

On the twelfth ring, the phone clattered off the hook, and Oilcan said breathlessly, "Yeah?"

"Oh, thank gods, are you all right?"

"I'm fine. What's wrong?"

She laughed, not even sure where to start on that question. "Did you take the barrels from Reinholds to the barn?"

"Yeah, they're here."

"Look, I think you're in a lot of danger. I want you to leave the barn."

"What's going on, Tink?"

"It's all rather complicated. I think my dreams are telling me to trap the dragon and do something with it."

"Trap it?"

"Yeah, the barrels are the fruit." That sounded sane! "Look, you're in danger there. Just go home and let me deal with it."

There was only silence from Oilcan.

"Are you okay?" Tinker asked again.

"I'm kind of in the middle of something. You know—I don't want to mess with the flow. Why don't you come out and we'll talk about what has gone down since Wednesday?"

Wednesday. Nathan died Wednesday. Did Oilcan know? If he didn't, she didn't want to tell him over the phone—not that she really wanted to tell him face to face, either.

"Okay, I'll see you in a couple of minutes."

Oilcan used a barn deep in the South Hills as a retreat. Just as she tinkered on machines, he played with art. It was a side of him that few people saw, as he seemed to think it revealed too much of his soul. Sometimes he welded bits and pieces taken from the scrap yard into mechanical ogres, other times he painted dark and abstract murals. Those he kept at his retreat and only friends got to see. She knew he kept journals with poetry that he never showed anyone, not even her. The only form of his art that he shared was music he composed, a fusion of traditional elfin music with snarling, angry human rock, which he didn't perform but sold to local bands under the penname of Orphan.

Art wasn't something that Tinker had patience for. She liked computer logic of true or false, knowing if something worked or didn't with a flip of a switch or a turn of a key. She could help Oilcan animate his ogres, but she could never see why the sculpture had to take a certain form, or move in a certain way, or make a certain sound. She couldn't perceive what made one piece "right" despite how many times Oilcan tried to explain it.

It was midmorning when they drove up the driveway lined with wild lilac bushes. The flatbed was parked in the apple orchard, its bed littered with fallen apples. Across the road, the magic gleamed purple in the shadows of the tractor shed, stuffed full with the barrels.

Tinker had debated bringing two Hands with her. She wanted a small army between her and the dragon, but in the end, she decided that if Oilcan was fine, then most likely she was wrong about the barrels. Certainly, it was a stretch in logic to get from the black willow to the barn.

"Not that there's any real logic involved in this," she complained as she parked the Rolls away from both apples and magic. It had been easier to drive than constantly interrupt her thoughts to give directions. "It would be simpler to believe that the oni drove me stark raving mad than all this dream hocus pocus."

"You are not mad." Pony got out, taking point.

"My mother would have not directed us to 'follow the yellow brick road' if you were only mad." Stormsong kept close to Tinker as they headed for the large barn doors.

Denial, the most misshapen of Oilcan's animated ogres, lurched out of the lilacs. It moaned out its low recording of "nooo, nooo, nooo," as it wrung its crooked arms around its deformed head. Instantly her guard had all weapons out and leveled at the mechanical sculpture.

"Whoa, whoa, whoa!" Tinker cried. "Don't shoot it!"

"What is it, *domi*?" Pony kept his machine gun trained on it.

"It's a sculpture," she said.

Denial folded back down, stretching out a third hand to grasp in their direction. The guards backed up, unnerved by the thing as its recording changed to a wordless keening.

"It does not look like art to me." Pony reluctantly slung his gun onto his back and motioned to the others to stand down.

"Well," Tinker admitted, "sometimes it doesn't seem that much like art to me, either, but that's what it is."

She pointed out the motion sensor by the door; Pony had tripped it as he moved ahead of her. "That activates it, though, that's new. I wonder . . ."

The big door rolled open, and Oilcan called, "Hey!" in greeting.

"Hey," she said back. "What's with Denial?"

"Just using him as a doorbell." He eyed the guards with their hands still riding their weapons. "Can—can we leave them here? I don't want them shooting anything by mistake."

Considering what else he had in the way of art, Tinker didn't blame him. She held up a hand to her *sekasha*. "Stay."

The *sekasha* peered into the barn. The back door was rolled the full way open, flooding the cluttered floor with light. They didn't look happy, but stayed put outside while Oilcan rolled the door shut.

"You really have to leave." Tinker followed him through the clutter. From the looks of it, he'd been camping out here for the last few days. "This might be a total long shot, but it's really dangerous here if I'm right. What did you do to your answering machine?"

Oilcan glanced down at the dissembled unit, the parts carefully arrayed on a blank canvas like a piece of art. "Ah, it got taken apart. What are you going to do with the dragon?"

She groaned as she hadn't considered that far ahead. "Gods if I know! He's the wizard of Oz."

"And that means?"

"Riki—Riki wove this whole theory that sounded so right about the dragon being the wizard, but it just hit me—Riki lied and lied about so much. Yeah, so his reasons were good, but he has this history of twisting things to suit his goals."

Thinking of Riki, she pulled the player out of her pocket. "Here. Riki says he's sorry."

As Oilcan stood looking at the player, the oni dragon snaked out of the shadows to stop beside Oilcan. Its eyes gleamed in the dimness, its mane flowing like a bundle of snakes.

"*Yanananam mmmoooootaaaa summbaaaa radadada*," the dragon said with a deep breathy voice, the words rumbling against her skin like the purr of a big engine. "*Aaaaah huuu ha*."

"Oh shit!" Tinker jerked back, fumbling for the pistol on her hip.

"It's okay!" Oilcan held up his hands to ward off her action. "He won't hurt you. He's friendly."

"Friendly?"

"Yeah, see?" Oilcan patted the huge head butting up against him. "He scared the shit out of me. But he talked, and, well, I listened."

She backed up regardless, wanting distance between her and it. "You can understand it?"

"Actually—no."

"*Mmmananan pooooo kaaa*."

It was weird to watch such a huge thing speaking, but there was no mistaking the rumble of syllables and consonants for anything but language.

"So you have no idea what's it's saying."

"No." Oilcan shrugged with a sheepish grin. "Sorry. But come here, look at this."

After the surprise of the dragon, Tinker wasn't sure she wanted to see what else he had to show her. Oilcan walked down the stone steps to what used to be the milking stalls. The dragon glanced back and forth between her and Oilcan. Apparently realizing that they were all to follow Oilcan, it finally bounded after him. Despite its short legs, and ferretlike humping run, its gait remained fluid.

"We've been working at communicating," Oilcan was saying. "We finally resorted to drawing. It's been—educational."

In the back was a little dragon nest complete with rumpled blankets, a barrel of drinking water, and a large dog dish of well-chewed bones. Drawings covered the walls. She recognized Oilcan's hand in the ones done in chalk. Scratched into the wall, the dragon's pictures were fluid and elegant and incomprehensible.

"Educational? Really?" she asked after several minutes of trying to understand the alien pictograms.

"It's just so different how he sees the world. Here—" He pointed out his map of Pittsburgh, with the two rivers converging to make the Ohio River, and the many skyscrapers and bridges. "After I drew this, he made this."

Less stylistic than the other dragon drawings, it was a series of wavering lines, some lightly etched and others deeply gouged. She studied it for a moment, keenly aware of the huge monster shifting beside them. It seemed completely random, but she trusted Oilcan's intelligence. If he said this meant something, it did. If the dragon recognized Oilcan's Pittsburgh—was this how he saw the city? It was the deep pit on the north side, roughly at the location of Reinholds that triggered the recognition. "He's drawn the ley lines."

"Yes. I think it was the magic in the barrels that drew him here." Oilcan pointed out a blank area of the wall. "And look at this."

"At wh—?"

The dragon nosed her aside—jolting her heart into a fierce pounding—and raised a long, sharp claw to the wall. In a nerve-grating rasp, it lightly sketched a dot at the center of Turtle Creek and radial lines outward, carefully linking the radials up to existing ley lines. The dragon glanced up at her, making sure she was watching, and then flattened its great paw and smudged away the dot and lines, creating the same blank space.

"There's no magic," she whispered.

"Tooloo has always said the dragons can't exist without magic." Oilcan absently scratched the dragon's jaw, getting a deep purrlike rumble from it.

"So as long as we keep him saturated in magic, he's safe."

"Yeah."

Tinker thought of the barrels stacked in the tractor shed. They represented a huge pool of magic, but a leaky one, draining away. "He can't stay here, then. I have no idea how long the magic will last from the barrels, but it's an artificial environment. Sooner or later, it's going to be drained."

"Yeah, I know."

"Oilcan! This isn't some stray dog. Look what I found, Grandpa, can I keep it? It didn't work with the warg puppy."

"This isn't a warg, this is an intelligent being that can talk, and create art, and communicate. Look!" He pointed out a set of small pictures. "It has a written language!"

"How do you know? That could be—be—anything!"

He gave her an annoyed look. "Did it or did it not just communicate something meaningful to you?"

She sighed. "Yes."

The *sekasha* were going to just love this.

"What?" Stormsong asked for about the third time in a row when Tinker updated the *sekasha* on the current plan.

"We need to move the dragon to the scrap yard. It's got a strong ley line running through it, so the dragon will stay sentient there. But the flatbed is a double clutch manual transmission, so if none of you can drive manual, then I'm going to have to—"

Stormsong caught her by the hand, dragged her to the side of the barn into the old apple orchard.

"Hey, hey, hey, what are you doing?" Tinker cried.

"What am I doing?" Stormsong snatched up an apple and flung it at Tinker. "What am I doing?"

The apple smacked the barn wall, blossoming into a flower of rotten sweetness unnervingly close to Tinker's head.

"What fucking part of that don't you understand?" Tinker shouted at her.

"You—are—too—trusting!" Stormsong flung apples to emphasize her words—one apple per word. They whizzed past Tinker so closely she felt their passage. "And—too—slow—at—putting—up—your—shields."

There was now a halo of spattered fruit outlining Tinker.

"I get the point! I get the point!" Tinker called up her shield. "See, shield! Happy?"

"Happy?" Stormsong snorted, picked an apple from the tree instead of the ground, and polished it against her black jeans until it gleamed with promise. "Here!" She tossed the apple in a lazy arc toward Tinker.

Tinker moved her hands to catch the apple and her shield vanished.

"You're—too—trusting!"

The first apple hit Tinker in the shoulder in a painful splatter. The second and third were intercepted midair by other apples so that they exploded in front of her, spraying her with apple bits.

"Stop it." Pony had another apple ready. Part of Tinker was impressed that he could knock apples out of the air—the other part wanted to know where the hell he was for the first volley. "She is the *domi*. She leads us."

"She's going to get herself killed!" Stormsong growled.

"What she says is true," Pony said. "The dragon cannot stay here. The truck is the only vehicle that will carry it. She and Oilcan are the only ones who know how to drive it—and he will be focused on keeping the creature calm. The fewer people we involve in moving the beast, the less likely the oni will learn that we have it."

"How can you support this plan?"

"The *domana's* self-centered creativity is why we chose to obey them. We need their drive. Trust her, she will make it work."

"Or die trying," Stormsong muttered. "This is insanity."

"Is it? We have the Scarecrow." Pony pointed at Tinker and then tapped his chest. "The Lion. The Tin Man." He pointed at Oilcan's metal sculpture. "And the apple trees." He held up the apple in his hand. "And the apples being thrown at the Scarecrow."

Stormsong's eyes went wide.

"There, see!" Tinker cried. "It's crazy with a purpose."

"And that is supposed to make me feel better?" Stormsong snarled. "What are you going to do with the dragon now that you've found him?"

Tinker held up her finger, indicating they were to wait, and pulled out her datapad. "Give me a few minutes. I've been keeping notes on the dreams. Offhand, I don't remember anything. Wait—how about this—Esme said, 'He knows the paths, the twisted way, the garden path. You have to talk to him. He'll tell you the way.'"

"The way? To where?"

"Obviously where I need to go."

It was like having a *very* large, hyperactive five-year-old in her workshop. The dragon flowed in and out of the various rooms of the trailer, carrying on a running commentary in its rumbling voice, as it examined everything with its massive but manipulative paws. After rescuing her scanner, their radio base, and antique CD player, Tinker realized what had happened to Oilcan's answering machine and started to fear.

"Okay, okay, I think first thing in communicating would be—to—get a record of what it's saying." She snatched her camera from the dragon before he could disassemble it. She flipped out her tripod, snapped the camera to it, and caught Cloudwalker by the hand and dragged him to the camera. "Here, keep the dragon—the dragon's image—in this little window." Great, she was actually dealing with two groups of technology-challenged people. "And we'll build a dictionary of his words."

"I was trying to do that." Oilcan distracted the dragon from her computer systems with a flashlight. "But usually it's hard to tell where one word starts and another ends."

"... *mmmenananannaaaaaaapooooookaaaammmmammamamy-*

yyyyyaaanananammmmoooo . . ." The dragon rumbled while clicking the flashlight on and off, and then disassembled it and sniffed at the batteries.

"Yeah, I can hear that." Tinker had microphones planted in the offices so she could trigger her computers without a headset. "Sparks, are you active?"

"Yes, boss," her office AI answered.

"Filter audio pickup into separate voiceprints and put it up on the workshop screen."

"Okay, boss."

As she had hoped, Impatience's ramblings easily divided out. "Sparks, record this track." She tapped the bass rumbles of the dragon's voice. "Convert to phonetics and indicate all pauses and breaks."

Impatience stuffed the batteries back into the casing, screwed on the lid, and tried the switch. When the flashlight didn't light, the dragon took it back apart and eyed the pieces carefully. Apparently it had spotted the "this way up" diagram stamped on the plastic as it eyed the batteries closely, repacked them into the casing and turned it on. This time it was rewarded with a beam of light. "*Huuhuuhuuhu-uhuuhuuhuuhuuhuuhuuhuu.*"

One word down.

"Okay." Tinker pulled up the recordings she had made of Turtle Creek and directed them to her largest monitor. "Since I don't have a clue how I'm supposed to help my mother, let's see what he has to say about my biggest problem: the Ghostlands."

The great Westinghouse Bridge had fallen. The Ghostlands had lapped up against the centermost support column and toppled it. Two of its four great arching spans now lay in ruins on the valley floor, slowly leeching to blue. The remaining two spans would soon follow.

Wolf gazed down at the ruin, trying to not let dismay overtake him. "There's nothing you can do?"

Jewel Tear glared at the valley as if it personally defied her. "Not in time. At the rate it's expanding, it will involve the main river shortly."

She meant the Monongahela River, which flowed past the mouth of the Turtle Creek.

"The creek froze solid," Wolf said. "You don't think the river will freeze?"

"If I understand this correctly, the worlds are mirror images."

Jewel pointed out at the river. "Where there is a river here, there is one on Onihida?"

"Yes."

"I can't predict what will happen when the force of the river meets this, but what I fear is that the oni can make use of it. As they are now, the Ghostlands are a deathtrap. The forces are funneling downward, like the pit of an ant lion. The river might allow the oni to pass unchecked through the Ghostlands."

"How soon?"

"Only a few more days." She turned away from the Ghostlands and him. "Something has to be done. They say your *domi* can work miracles. Since this is her fault, it would be good for her to fix her mistake."

Yes, he needed to talk to Tinker. He had faith that once she was given opportunity to study the situation, she would find a solution. He had brought a second Hand just so he could have one of the *sekasha* "babies" along to operate the walkie-talkie.

"Find out where *domi* is," Wolf said to Wraith and turned back to Jewel Tear. "I want Stone Clan to keep their distance from my *domi*. After what happened with the black willow, I do not trust any of you near her."

Jewel Tear looked away, giving a slight huff of indignation, but didn't deny the implication that they meant Tinker harm.

Wraith came back with unease clear on his face. Wolf bowed his leave-taking and headed for his Rolls.

"What is it?" Wolf asked Wraith once they were out of the Stone Clan's hearing.

"*Domi* is at the scrap yard. The dragon is there."

Wolf's heart leapt at the news. "She's fighting the dragon?"

"No. Apparently, she's—talking—to it."

"No, I'm not talking to it," Tinker said with much disgust in her voice. She smelled of apples, butter, and sugar, and her face had mysterious streaks of color paste on it—but otherwise she looked unharmed. "It's giving me math lessons—and I think my head is going to explode."

"Math lessons?" There were times he wondered if his English wasn't as strong as he thought it was.

His *domi's* workshop was normally ordered chaos, but it now looked like a storm front had passed through it. The digital wall boards were covered with elaborate designs and fluid pictures. Printouts were tacked to bare walls, extending the boards to each side and up onto the ceiling. A television cycled through pictures of the Ghostlands. Machines either half built or partially disassembled covered all the table surfaces and the floor was littered with magazines, engine parts, and chewed tires.

The only sign of the dragon itself was its long tail sticking out from behind the worktable, thumping against the floor with a force that shook the entire trailer.

"I think it's math." Tinker tugged at her hair as if she wanted to tear it out. "Whoever said math is the universal language should be hunted down and shot. Or maybe they thought that sentient creatures wouldn't have the attention span of a gnat."

"So you're safe with it?"

Tinker glanced toward Stormsong instead of the dragon for some reason. "I—don't know. It seems playful as a puppy, but it has sharp teeth—lots of them—in a big mouth."

Wolf shifted sideways until he could see around the table. Tinker's *nagarou*, Oilcan, and the dragon stared at a television screen while they manipulated something in their hands. On the television screen, a small human female in a skimpy red dress fought a tall muscle-bound creature with energetic kicks and punches. The fight ended abruptly with the words "Winner" flashing on the screen and the female bouncing around cheerfully. Oilcan groaned and slumped to one side.

"He—he learns fast." Tinker shook her head. "I've never met anyone that intimidated me with their intellect before—but I always thought that the person that did would be more—"

"Human?"

Tinker waved her hand, as if trying to sift out a better word, and then nodded. "I suppose that would work. The language is a huge barrier to understanding what's he's trying to explain to me."

"Have you learned anything useful?"

"This was educational." Tinker caught Wolf's arm and pulled him to the kitchen. On the counter was an odd sculpture. A rainbow of creamy paste whirled upward like a tornado with paper plates dividing the various colors. It was supported by a silvery aluminum plate, which had been balanced on a base of soda cans.

The paste was the source of the color streaks on Tinker's face, and the smell of butter and sugar. Wolf smeared some off her face. "And this is . . . ?"

"Frosting. Long story. Doesn't matter anymore. This—" Tinker pointed to the structure. "I think this is a model of the Ghostlands. Look, he's sculpted the frosting into a Roy G. Biv spectrum and at each color shift there's a universe marker—the paper plates. Well—at least I think that's what they are."

Tinker took out a camera from her dress pocket, and flipped up the screen. "I filmed it all." She played a minute of the dragon building the sculpture, rumbling in a low steady tone. "What we need is someone that speaks dragon. But, until then—" She folded the camera back up and stuffed it into her dress pocket. "This is what I think it's trying to tell me. Look, can you see down into the middle of this? He made a big production of dropping a lug nut down into there, and did a lot of pointing and talking. He took it out and dropped it a couple of times. And then the math started. I think—he's trying—maybe—to say that my gate is still active."

"Can you stop the Ghostlands from expanding?"

"If I can figure out a way to remove my gate, yes, I think it might close the Ghostlands completely. What I think is happening is this." She dragged him to the whiteboard.

Tinker swept her hand across dragon writing and the English words "save: yes no" appeared. She touched the "yes" and the board went white. Drawing a straight horizonal line, she turned to him. "This is Turtle Creek before the chaos started. According to Stormsong, when you originally surveyed this area a hundred years ago, there was a *fiutana* here." She added a large purple oval under the line. "Now, Lord Tomtom talked about protective spells that the oni had cloaking their compound, so I think this is why the oni were based here—which also might indicate where their other camps are and why you can't find them."

Yes, that would explain much. "If the other springs in the area are cloaked, then we know that the oni are using them. Look for what is missing instead of what is there."

"Huh? Oh, yes, that would work. Now, my gate was here." She drew in a black circle above the line, and then added a second black circle at the bottom of the board. "And that's the gate in orbit. I set up a resonance between then." The resonance was represented by a wavy line connecting the two black circles that ran through the heart of the purple oval. "I think what Impatience is telling me is that along this line, a discontinuity emerged, which immediately affected the land under my gate."

She turned and typed on a keyboard. The television, which had been cycling pictures of Turtle Creek, stopped on a blur of blue. "This is thermal readings of the Discontinuity. It's hard to see, but this area here—" She tapped a circle at the heart of the screen. "That's the same size and shape as my gate, lying on its side."

Tinker turned back to the whiteboard, and drew a series of black circles stacked inside the pool of purple. "See, as it sinks, the area affected by the gate would expand." She stepped back from the board, gazing at it. "I'm not a hundred percent sure this is an accurate model, but it explains why the effect is growing."

"Even though the gate in orbit was destroyed?"

"Each gate was designed to operate independently."

"So if we remove the gate, the Discontinuity will heal?"

Tinker sighed. "I don't know. If I'm right, and we can get the gate out, it will at least stop the Ghostlands from growing."

Wolf considered what Jewel Tear claimed about the current forces working in the valley. "That would be good enough for now. We need to do something quickly."

"Well, I'm not getting anything done here." She picked up various items and slipped them into her pocket. "I can get to work on the retrieval now."

20: FOLLOW THE YELLOW BRICK ROAD

Stone Clan chose to wait until the next morning to protest Wind Clan's actions. Wolf wasn't sure why they had delayed, so he stood and listened to Earth Son rant on about protocol and etiquette.

"Wind Clan is insulting us at every step. Look." Earth Son pointed up the tall ironwood scaffolding to where Tinker stood, overseeing the installation of her scrap yard crane. Little Horse was up in the scaffolding with her, but the rest of her Hand were keeping to the ground. "Wind Clan's *domi* hasn't come down to hear our complaints."

Wolf made a show of glancing around. "We did not know this was to be a formal *aumani*. I see the rock, but where is the incense and the flame?"

Wolf surprised True Flame into a smile, but the prince caught himself and gave him a hard look.

"Do we need to call an *aumani?*" True Flame's look warned him not to make light of it.

Wolf spread his hands to show that he didn't know. "Jewel Tear came to me and stated that the Stone Clan could not solve this problem before—"

"It was not her place to make that decision!" Earth Son snapped. "I will say when the Stone Clan can or cannot do something."

Wolf glanced at Jewel Tear but she had her court mask on, letting none of her emotions show. There was no way to judge if this was an honest miscommunication within the Stone Clan, or a contrived situation. If it was the latter, then politically it had been a mistake to act.

Wolf would have to salvage the situation by forcing True Flame to disregard political protocol for the sake of military imperative. "If the information she gave us was accurate, then what is important is that the oni are prevented from using the Ghostlands—"

"Are you saying that I'm lying?" Earth Son seemed eager for Wolf to slander him.

Wolf considered Earth Son for a minute. Was he that blind to the dangers that they were facing? "I'm saying that there are tens of thousands of oni and an oni dragon on the other side of the Ghostlands, and it would be good to keep them there."

Earth Son waved that concern aside. "Your untrained *domi* and her Hand survived the first dragon."

"Do not mistake that creature for a true oni dragon." True Flame had studied Impatience at Tinker's workshop. The prince pointed out that not only was the "dragon" much smaller than the creatures he had fought; it also had one more digit per foot.

Tinker theorized that since the spell painted onto Impatience's scales had been washed or rubbed away, the dragon might be free from the oni's control. Regardless, they still didn't know how to cage or effectively fight the beast. All options weighed, it was decided to leave the creature in Oilcan's care as an ally instead of treating it as a foe. According to the tengu, however, and confirmed by some mysterious means by the NSA agents, there was a second, larger dragon by the name of Malice still on Onihida. Plans to update the Stone Clan on the dragons, however, had been waylaid by Earth Son's attack on Tinker's operation.

Wolf pushed the conversation back to the military implications. "Jewel Tear stated that if the Ghostlands expand to the river, there will be a shift in forces that will allow the oni to push their army through."

Jewel Tear's mask slipped and she gave him a look of pure hatred.

Earth Son scoffed. "They'll be pinned between the river and the Ghostlands. With five *domana*, seventy *sekasha*, the dreadnaught, and the royal troops, we can easily deal with the oni as they emerge . . ."

True Flame lost his patience. "If the oni send a dragon across first, we will be too engaged with it to block the oni. We will do whatever it takes to close the Ghostlands before anything more can come through."

Earth Son recognized that he was treading on an edge with the prince and retreated with, "I am not saying we ignore the Ghostlands. I am saying that this is a Stone Clan specialty—"

"Are you being hampered by the Wind Clan *domi*?" True Flame snapped. "She will not be using magic, since, as you pointed out, she is untrained."

Earth Son smoothed his face to court mask to consider his options. Finally he said, "No, we will not be hampered."

True Flame nodded and turned to Wolf. "Have you found the maps?"

"Yes. There are four possible sites not counting the *fiutana* that was located here and the one at the icehouse."

"What maps?" Earth Son growled.

"My *domi* believes that the oni are camping on *fiutana*. I had my people pull up the original survey maps for this area, showing the *fiutana*."

"Have you scryed out any *fiutana*?" True Flame asked Earth Son.

"No."

They waited for Earth Son to elaborate, but he didn't.

Behind them were shouts and the crack of splintering wood.

Wolf turned to see a massive oni dragon surge up out of the Ghostlands. It shouldered aside the scaffolding, shattering it to pieces. Tinker and Little Horse were falling from their high perch. Little Horse had been near the ladder and was falling with the tumble of heavy timbers. Tinker, though, had been far out at the end of the boom, over the liquid blue.

"No!" Wolf shouted as a call on the Wind Clan spell stones thrummed across his senses.

Tinker hit the ground, sending up a spray of blue, and then sank down into the ground. Ripples spread out from where she disappeared. And then all sense of her vanished. The Ghostland went smooth and her call on the stones broke off abruptly.

"Wolf!" Stormsong struggled with Little Horse, who had fallen to the "shore" of the Ghostlands and was now trying to fling himself into the blue. "Stop him! He'll only die! She's gone already."

Wolf gasped, feeling her words stab through him. No, Tinker couldn't be gone.

The dragon scrambled out of the blue, clawing up the shore with feet as large as the Rolls Royce. It shook dirt from its massive head, growling low and loud as thunder. Its seemingly endless body heaved up out of the chaos.

"Wolf!" Stormsong had Little Horse pinned, but it left her vulnerable to the dragon now turning its attention to the small figures at its feet.

Wolf called the wind. The dragon's head whipped toward him as if it sensed the magic gathering around Wolf. He aimed a force strike on the dragon and flung the spell at the beast. As the magic arrowed at the dragon, it crouched low and its mane lifted. A shield effect shimmered into existence. The force strike slammed into the shield and was swallowed up.

Jewel Tear flung up a force wall between the dragon and the elves, curving it to include Stormsong and Little Horse. A fire strike from True Flame hit the dragon's shield; the blaze curled harmless around it.

The dragon sprang away, landing among the rubble of the fallen bridge.

Wolf started to summon lightning when it leaped again, landing this time on the far section of the bridge still standing, high above the valley. A third leap took it out of sight.

Since the call-lightning spell took both hands, he couldn't cast a scrying spell.

Beside him, Jewel Tear cast a ground scry. "It took flight. I can't track it through the air."

True Flame cast his more inclusive, weaker scry of flame. "It's out of your range already, Wolf."

Wolf locked his jaw against a growl of impatience, forcing himself to remain silent as he canceled the lightning call. The spell was too dangerous to leave in a potential state. The power neutralized, he started to call the winds to fly after the dragon.

True Flame caught Wolf's wrist, stilling his hand. "No, I will not allow you to fight it alone. It's too dangerous."

"It killed my *domi!*" Wolf snarled.

"No." Stormsong dragged Little Horse up to Wolf, as if she was afraid to let the young *sekasha* go. "*Domi*'s on the yellow brick road." Stormsong's eyes were soft and dreamy. "She's talked to the wizard. She's gone now to steal the flying broomstick from the witch and the flying monkeys."

Tinker fell into the cold blue air. She shouted the trigger to her shields seconds before plunging into the dark blue mass of out-of-phase ground. The blue deepened to midnight black, and then all sensation fell away, as if she had no longer had a body. Was she dead? She had felt the shields form around her in a flood of magic, and the deepening cold of the Ghostlands, but now she sensed nothing.

Suddenly, something hit her from her left. Startled, she lost her shields, and she smacked into a flat, hard surface and then slid *down* it, to land hard on something perpendicular to whatever she had struck. Pain shot up from her left leg. She lay panting in darkness. The air was hot, dry, and tainted with smoke. Nearby, water gurgled through unseen pipes. A distant hammering was muffled as if carried through a thick wall.

What had she hit first? Sliding her hand along the smooth floor, she found a right angle that rose up in a wall of steel. But how did she hit a wall sideways when she'd been falling down?

And where was she now?

She sat up and pain jolted up her leg again. Wincing, she felt down to her ankle and discovered that she was bleeding. "Shit." And then she remembered—she hadn't been alone on the scaffolding. She searched the area around her with blind hands. "Pony! Oh, gods, Pony!"

There was a loud, metal clank and then the squeal of hinges as a door opened somewhere out in the darkness. Someone was coming. It dawned on her that that might not be a good thing; the Ghostlands had been the oni compound. She groped at her side and found her pistol.

A flashlight flicked on some fifty feet away, its light a solid beam in smoky air. As it swept the room, her eyes adjusted, and she made out the figure of a being standing in the open doorway. The shock of hair, the sharp beak of a nose, and the tall lean body suggested a tengu.

She covered her mouth and nose to muffle her breathing.

The tengu moved toward her, shining his flashlight onto pieces of equipment on either side of the room—large tanks, pipes, pumps, and pieces of computer monitoring stations.

Go away, go away, go away, she thought hard at him.

The tengu paused at one of the monitoring stations, checking the gauges there, and then moved to the second one. Grunting at what he found, he turned and ran his light high along the back wall. The beam swept over her head, moved on, stopped, and returned to a point a few feet above her.

Gripping her pistol tight, she glanced up to see what caught the tengu's attention. A smear of fresh blood led down to her.

Don't look. Just move on. There's nothing here to see.

Inexorable, the light slid downward to shine on her.

Squinting against the brilliance, she pointed her pistol at the tengu. "That's far enough."

"Well, well." The tengu spoke English with a heavy accent, the flashlight obscuring his features. "You're what's down here making so much noise."

"Where is Pony? What have you done to him?"

Confusion filled the tengu's voice. "We don't have any ponies here."

"Where am I?"

"You don't know?"

"Answer me, damn it!"

"Water storage."

That explained the tanks, pipes, and liquid sounds. "Okay, you're going to walk me out of here."

"Walk?" He closed the distance between and crouched down in front of her, twisting the flashlight's base so it became a lantern, bathing them both in soft light. He was an older version of Riki, from the electric blue eyes under thick unruly black hair to the birdlike cock of his head. "Walk where?"

She tried to hold the gun steady but reaction from her fall was setting in, making her tremble. "Out of this place."

"You—you want to go outside?"

"Yes."

"Where exactly do you think we are?" He seemed more puzzled than alarmed, ignoring her gun to search her eyes.

"Water storage."

"Which is . . . where?"

"What is so hard to understand about this? I've got a gun and I'm willing use it. You either get me out, or I'll shoot you."

"Okay, okay, my English, it's good but not perfect. I don't understand what you want, princess."

"Oh, please, don't call me that; technically I am not a princess."

"Ooookay." He acted like this was a hard concept to wrap his brain around. "What should I call you?"

"Tinker. Of the Wind Clan."

"I'm Jin Wong."

Tinker knew she had heard the name before, but she couldn't place it. "Jin, I want to go home, and you're going to take me."

He sighed and shook his head. "I'm sorry, Tinker, but you're going to need to give me the gun before I can take you anywhere."

"Like hell."

"You're hurt."

"I'm fine." And she scrambled to her feet to prove it. When she tried to put weight on her left foot, though, pain jolted up her ankle.

Jin had stood with her—as to be expected, he was at least a foot taller than she was. He wore a dark polo shirt with his name embroidered over his heart, dark nylon pants, and white socks, all stained with soot, oil, and blood. He stepped to her as she sagged back against the wall, hissing against the sudden agony.

"Don't touch me." She stopped him by raising the pistol.

"I'm not going to hurt you."

"Are all you tengu liars at birth?"

"No," he said after a moment of surprised silence. "Our mothers give us lying lessons so we can tell when someone is lying."

He looked down at her foot to indicate what he thought she was lying about.

"My ankle is just twisted," Tinker snapped.

"Just to point out the obvious, if you shoot me, you're going to have to crawl out of here." He held out his hand. "And I'm not going to let you out of this room with the gun. So just give me the pistol, and I'll do what you want."

"I give you my gun and you'll turn me over to the oni."

"There are no oni here."

"Liar."

"We lie, but tengu still have honor. I give you my word—you won't be harmed."

They stood there at an impasse, half in shadows, the gun growing heavy in her hand. She had fought to the death before, but she'd never shot someone in cold blood. She wasn't sure she could actually do it and live with herself afterward—certainly not after exchanging names and carrying on a civil conversation.

"I'm so screwed." Sighing, she unloaded the pistol, pocketed the clip, checked the chamber, and handed him the empty gun.

"I'll take care of you." He tucked the pistol between two pipes near the ceiling, way out of her reach. "I promise."

"Bleah." She wished she could believe him. Had Riki broken his word? Or had he actually never given her any promises, knowing full well that he couldn't keep them? She couldn't remember.

Jin produced sterile bandages out of his pocket and dealt with the shallow, bleeding cut on her ankle. He slipped an arm around her, then helped her up. As he supported her, they headed toward the door.

The room was a maze of tanks and pipes, gurgling ominously. At the end of the room, they stepped through a low steel door, reminiscent of old submarine movies, and into another low-ceilinged room of mystery machines. What the hell did the oni have buried under Pittsburgh? She seethed with anger that Riki hadn't warned her about this.

"What the hell is this place, anyway?" she asked.

"This is life support."

She scoffed at that. Life support made it sound like a damn spaceship.

At the far end of the room, she could see there was a narrow, tall window. It gave her pause. Who put a window in an underground area? She forced Jin to detour through the equipment to look out it. At first she only saw night sky, above and below them, which confused her more. When had she fallen? It was midmorning—wasn't it? And how do you fall *into* the ground and end up above it? The stars were more brilliant than she had ever seen them. And they seemed to be moving—which really meant she was.

A planet rose on the horizon, filling it completely.

She'd seen enough photos of Earth from orbit to recognize the luminescent blue swirled with gleaming white clouds. The sight of it punched the air out of her; she stood gasping, like a fish finding itself out of water, trying to get her breath back. The planet rose, filling the window, evidence that the ship she was on was rotating to maintain artificial gravity.

"No—we can't be—this isn't possible. This is a trick. I can't be in space. I was in Pittsburgh. You don't fall in Pittsburgh and land in orbit." She couldn't be in space. Could she? "You don't fall in Pittsburgh and land in orbit," she whispered again. But she hadn't fallen to ground, but into the Discontinuity—who knew what all was tied into that knot of realities? "Oh gods, where am I?"

"Apparently quite lost." Jin tightened his hold on her, as if he expected her to collapse. Considering how weak she suddenly felt, it was probably a good idea.

"*Lost! Lost!*" *cried the crows in her dreams.*

She realized where she must be. She had fallen straight to Esme. "You're part of the tengu crew of the *Tianlong Hao*."

"I was the captain."

"Was?"

"This is the *Dahe Hao*." Jin leaned over her shoulder to tap on the window, drawing her attention back outside. "There's the *Tianlong Hao*."

The ship had continued to rotate and a vast debris field of broken ships slid into view. The great long cylindrical ships were shattered to pieces. Parts were folded like soda cans. The space around them hazed and glittering from frozen moisture and oxygen trapped in the same orbit as the ships. The bodies of astronauts tumbled in among the litter.

She covered her mouth to keep in a cry of dismay. Still her shock came out in low whimpers.

"The *Dahe* managed to rescue most of my crew minutes after the accident," Jin said quietly. "We saved crew from the *Zhenghe Hao* and the *Anhe Hao*, but the *Minghe Hao* reentered before we could get to it, along with parts of what we think was the gate."

"Jin!" A female voice called from beyond an open hatch. "Did you find what the hell made the loud bang?"

"Yes!" Jin shouted. "We somehow picked up a visitor."

"What kind of visitor?" the female snapped.

"The gun-waving elfin kind," Jin shouted.

"Have you fucking flipped?" The female voice drew closer. "An elf?"

"Yes, an elf," Jin called.

"Jin." There was something familiar about the female's voice. "There were no elves on any of the crew lists."

Jin cocked his head at Tinker and made a slight noise of discovery. "You did fall from Pittsburgh."

A purple-haired woman appeared at the door and Tinker recognized her. It was Esme. She hadn't changed from when Lain's photo had been taken, with the tiny exception of the bandage on her forehead. On her temple was a pink line of recently healed flesh. Like Jin, she was marked with soot, blood, and exhaustion.

"Well, I'll be fucked." Esme had Lain's voice, only slightly more raspy, as if she had shouted her throat raw. "Well, it's about time you got your scrawny ass up here."

"You had a gun-waving elf princess on order?" Jin asked.

"Not exactly. I had a dream. And you were there." Esme pointed at Jin and then Tinker. "And you."

"I'm starting to understand the appeal of Kansas," Tinker grumbled.

Jin looked at Tinker in surprise. "You forgot your little dog."

"I'm Dorothy," Esme corrected him. "She's the Scarecrow. So, how the hell did you get here?"

"I fell," Tinker said.

"Down the rabbit hole?" Esme asked.

"More or less," Tinker said.

"Great, you can get us out of this fucking mess," Esme asked.

Tinker could only laugh bitterly. "I'm not even sure *where* I am, let alone how to get out. What planet is that? Elfhome? Onihida?"

Esme glanced at Jin with narrowing eyes. "Onihida?"

"The tengu homeworld," Tinker said. "Or don't *you* know about the tengu?"

"We've covered that little speed bump," Esme said dryly, still looking at Jin. Then she shrugged. "All things considered, finding out that half the crew isn't human is just all part of the weirdness."

"It doesn't matter which planet it is," Jin said. "We've lost all our shuttles in the crash. We can't land. Normally that wouldn't be a problem, the ship is designed to support its crew for decades—but we've got the survivors of four ships onboard."

"I think its Elfhome." Esme turned back to Tinker. "At least, Pittsburgh is down there. Every now and then, we pick up an FM station." Esme named a couple of Pittsburgh radio stations. "It sounds like a fucking war has broken out."

"More or less," Tinker said.

"Oh joy." Esme indicated that they should start in the direction she had come from. "Hopefully you have something other than straw in that head of yours, because I've got a mess for you to fix."

"Aren't you supposed to be the expert?" Tinker let Jin pick her up and carry her. All the little speed bumps, as Esme would put it, had finally gotten the best of her.

"Yes, I am." Esme led them through the next section of the ship. Smoke hazed the air here, and red lights flashed unattended. "But you're the Scarecrow."

"What the hell does that mean?" Tinker asked.

"It means what it means." Esme opened a hatch, stepped through, and closed it after Jin. The light was dim in this section, but the air was clean. The floor was cluttered with crew sleeping. At a glance, at least half of the sleepers were wounded. "All fucking logic went out the window about seven days ago."

Stormsong had said the same thing when her dreaming powers had told her that Impatience was no longer a danger to them. Esme sounded like she was operating on the same skewed logic—she wanted Tinker to fix the mess that the colonists were in because the dreams said she would.

Oh great, yet another group of people expecting me to pull rabbits out of my hat.

For the first time in her life, Tinker felt intimidated by a piece of hardware. She knew that a spaceship was a delicate balance of systems, a spiderweb pretending to be a simple tin can, with the lives of everyone inside dependent on it. "Look, I really don't know a whole lot about spaceships."

"I'll use terms you can understand," Esme said. "My ship is sinking and I can't bail fast enough."

"Okay," Tinker said. "Exactly how does a spaceship 'sink'?"

"The jump did something to my computers." Esme stopped beside a workstation with a monitor showing static. The front panel had already been pulled, and the boards inside gleamed softly with magic. "I'm getting—all sorts of weird errors—and I'm starting to lose systems completely."

"Well, doh." Tinker dug through her pockets until she found a length of wire and her screwdriver set. "Magic is causing your systems to crash."

"Magic?" Esme echoed, looking mystified.

Tinker realized that none of the colonists could see the magic. "That's Elfhome and this universe has magic. Your computer systems aren't shielded for it."

"Oh fuck, it is blindingly obvious, isn't it?" Esme pressed her palm to her forehead, took a deep breath, and let it out. "I should have thought of that when I started to dream true again. Okay. This system controls my engines. Right after the crash, I pulled into what should have been a stable orbit and started up the rotation that allows for the artificial gravity. We're drifting, though. If I don't correct our orbit, we're going to enter the planet's atmosphere—and my ship is not designed to survive re-entry."

"Okay." Tinker took the lantern from Jin and started to strip it for parts. "We need to first siphon off the magic, and then create shielding for the system. Here's what I need . . ."

Tinker had never worked with astronauts before and was amazed how quickly they learned. While Esme had fired the positioning jets to stop the ship's rotation and pulled them back into a stable orbit, Jin drafted a team of people to drain excess magic from the computer equipment. Despite Esme's "you're the Scarecrow" statements, everyone seemed hesitant about Tinker actually working with the ship's systems. After Tinker trained the astronauts, she found herself in a supervisory-only position. She floated in place, stranded by the lack of gravity, with an ice pack strapped to her ankle.

For some reason—whether it was because Tinker had missed the event, or because she was the ultimate outsider as an elf, or because she had magically appeared—the astronauts started to tell her their stories. They had gone through a harrowing experience, filled with confusion, death, lucky chances, small miracles, and a great deal of heroics. At the core of it all was Esme, riding roughshod over rules and logic, ruthless in purpose, making one lucky guess after another. Esme, everyone agreed, forged a miracle, salvaging what should have been complete disaster.

Even Esme opened up to Tinker when they found themselves alone together. "One summer, while I was in college, I went to visit my older sister on Elfhome. Two months on another world—it seemed like an exotic vacation. Then the dreams started—like I had some third eye that had been forced open and I was made to see. Some of what I had to do was so very clear, like changing my master's degree to astrophysics and applying to NASA. Some of it was—blind faith—that it would matter. Somehow."

"I hate to tell you this, but I have no idea how to help you beyond this."

"This buys me time, which is what I needed most, Scarecrow." Esme scowled at her screens. "It gives me a chance to figure out what the fuck to do next."

"Don't call me Scarecrow. I rented the movie and watched it. Everyone in that movie was a dysfunctional idiot."

"You didn't read the books? The Scarecrow is the wisest being in Oz and rules the kingdom after the wizard and Dorothy leave."

Tinker found the news vaguely disturbing. "That doesn't help."

"It's like flying blind in the clouds—you have to have faith in what instruments tell you. The dreams told me that I needed you. Things are still iffy—but I have a chance now to make everything right."

Tinker was torn between relief and annoyance that Esme seemed to think Tinker's part was done. She didn't want to be responsible for all the astronauts, but she didn't want to be stuck in space either. She didn't know what else to do. She couldn't even stay decent. Without gravity to constrain it, the skirt of Tinker's red silk dress developed a life of its own, determined to show off her panties as often as possible. Still, she had hoped they had gotten past all the dream bullshit. She hated not having an obvious direction to go, a clear-cut problem to solve. The path here had been so convoluted, the clues so obscure, that she would never have guessed where it was taking her. She supposed that she could only do everything she could imagine, and hope that one of them was the right thing.

Sighing, Tinker nudged one of the magic sinks. "These are just makeshift. They'll fill quickly and then leak. We'll have to burn off the magic until we can create a large, permanent storage tank."

"How do we do burn it?" Esme asked.

"You burn it off by doing spells," Tinker explained. "It can be used to create heat, light, cool things off, do healing—"

"Healing?" Jin seized hold of the word, proving that her "private" conversation with Esme had been just an illusion.

Tinker pulled out her datapad and made sure it worked. "Well, I have spells for healing but I don't know much about—"

Jin didn't let Tinker finish. He scooped her up and they flew through the ship as if Jin had wings. "We've got so many wounded that we've wiped out the *Dahe*'s supplies. Most of the medical supplies on the other ships were destroyed."

"I really don't know much about healing," Tinker finally managed to finish her statement.

"We're desperate. Some of our people—we can't do any more for them."

"Are they tengu?" Tinker asked.

He stopped and looked down at her. "You won't help us?"

"I didn't say that—although a 'please' would go a long way. It makes a difference what spells I use. Some won't work on humans—but they might work on tengu."

"Please, help my people. I beg you. They're dying."

She felt shame and anger at the same time that he would think she would let a wounded person die merely because of some biological difference she could barely see. "I'll do what I can. I just don't know how much that will be."

The infirmary was a tiny cramped place stained with blood, filled with people hooked to machines. The beds were more like cocoons with nylon bags holding the patients flat. Jin paused at the first bed to gaze at a blond man lying there.

"What happened to Chan Way Kay?"

"Sorry, Jin, we lost her," a man said from back of the room.

"This is Wai Sze Wong." Jin turned Tinker's attention to the patient to her other side. "She's tengu."

Wai Sze was Black from Tinker's dream. More a sparrow than a crow, she was a little female with delicate wrists and fingers. Massive bruising on Wai Sze ran the range from deep purple to pale yellow. Apparently they had run out of surgical tape, as black electrical tape held splints on Wai Sze's left arm and leg in place. The monitors on her showed an unsteady heartbeat.

Tinker gasped in the shock of recognition and the extent of Wai Sze's injuries. "I—I—can only guess at how to help her."

"So guess." Jin gave her a look that spoke of trust and confidence. "We have done all we can, and she's only getting worse. If you can't save her, then we're going to lose her."

Tinker sighed and tried to think. Riki had recuperated quickly from the savage beating Tinker had given him, so the tengu probably had recuperative powers similar to the elves'. Tinker had saved Windwolf's life with a spell that focused magic into his natural healing powers. The ambient level of the ship, while enough to wreak havoc on the unshielded computer systems, was actually quite low. If the tengu's ability was close enough to the elves', the same spell might save Wai Sze. She searched the memory of her datapad and found that she did have the spell downloaded.

"Do you have transferable circuit paper?" Tinker asked.

Jin nodded.

"Okay," Tinker said. "I need the first magic sink we set up, some power leads, and a computer connection so I can print on the circuit paper."

One of these days she had to learn bio magic. She hated gambling with people's lives. Hopefully today wasn't going to be the day that she guessed wrong.

She explained to the doctor how she needed Wai Sze prepped while Jin sent people off to fetch the sinks and leads, and then Jin took her to print off the spell.

"If this spell works, we can use it on all the tengu." She explained to Jin how it focused magic on the tengu's natural abilities. "But it's useless on humans. For them, I'll need to see if there is a spell for their specific injury in my codex. It will be a much slower process."

"Let's save the spell onto this system; that way, if Wai Sze shows improvement, I can come back and print off more spells while you start working with the humans."

When they returned, they found Wai Sze stripped bare to her waist. Burning with embarrassment, Tinker peeled the protective sheet from the circuit paper and pressed the spell to Wai Sze's small chest as Jin watched her intently. It required a lot of fiddling to make sure it was smoothed down over the hills and valleys of Wai Sze's breasts. On the female's hip was a tattoo of a lion overlaying the Leo star constellation, Leo's heart—the star Regulus—a blaze of blue-white in its chest. Tinker used it to change the subject. "She's a Leo?"

"Hmm? Oh, that, no, it's for Gracie's husband, Leo. He got a tattoo for her in the same place, a little bird."

Gracie was obviously the Americanization of Wai Sze's name. Leo was the name of Tinker's father, killed by the tengu before she was born. "He's a tengu?"

"No, Leo was human. He was my college roommate at MIT—and my best friend for many years."

"Was?"

Jin glanced at her sharply. Whatever he saw on her face made his hard look softened. "Leo and Gracie were like Romeo and Juliet. They fell madly in love at first sight. Their families didn't want them to be together. They got secretly married. And it all ended in senseless tragedy. Leo was killed in an accident, and for the last five years, Gracie has been suicidal with grief. Crows mate for life."

"Leo's family didn't want him to marry her?" Tinker asked. "They knew she was tengu?"

"No. We were Chinese—that was enough."

Yes, that would have been enough. Much as she loved her grandfather, she knew the truth of his bigotry. She had been wondering why she dreamed of Gracie. Now she could only remember how the little tengu female had endlessly wept in her dreams.

Tinker had taped the leads to the power-distributor ring of the spell and hooked the other ends to the battery. "You check to make sure all the metal is clear of the spell. It would distort the effect of the spell, which could be deadly. The activation word is pronounced this way."

Jin listened closely, and then nodded as the outer ring powered up, casting a glowing sphere over the rest of the spell. The healing spell itself kicked in, the timing cycle ring clicking quickly clockwise as the magic flowed through the spell in a steady rhythm. "How long before we can tell if it's going to work?"

Tinker shrugged. "On an elf, I could tell immediately."

As they watched, color flushed back into Gracie's face and her breathing grew deeper. The machines monitoring her health verified that her heart was stabilizing.

Jin clapped his hands, just like an elf would, to summon the attention of the gods to him, and then whispered a prayer. Tinker floated in place, gazing at the female who would have been her mother, if everything had gone differently. Had it been chance that put Gracie on the same ship as Esme—or some dream-inspired plan of Tinker's real mother?

Jin finished his prayer and turned to Tinker. "Thank you. Truly you must have been sent by the gods to us."

"No, just the wizard of Oz."

21: NO PLACE LIKE HOME

Wolf was ready to kill something. They should have been reacting quickly, but instead they stalled with negotiations. Wolf had demanded that one of the Stone Clan return to the enclaves to guard the noncombatants. Earth Son assigned the task to Jewel Tear but then tried to maneuver True Flame into qualifying it as a failure on Wolf's part to protect the enclaves.

"I can choose to protect the enclaves," Wolf said, "and leave you to face the dragon."

"We will have the dreadnaught," Earth Son pointed out.

"No, we won't," True Flame snapped. "Human weapons can't pierce the dragon shielding. The dreadnaught is good at spotting and attacking ground troops. It would be an aerial banquet table for the dragon."

"We should travel light," True Flame continued. "One Hand each. The fewer we have to protect, the better."

Wolf let Wraith choose which of his *sekasha* would remain. Wolf drew Little Horse and Stormsong aside; of the *sekasha* returning to the enclaves, they were the ones best suited to interacting with humans. "Call Maynard. Let him know what his people might be facing. They need to know that their weapons won't work on this."

Even as Jewel Tear and the extra *sekasha* left, Earth Son was still arguing against True Flame's decision. "We should wait until it comes to us. Running around looking for it will only weaken our position."

Wolf scoffed at this idea. "Sit here on our hands while it does what it will to the city?"

"Property damage can be fixed later," Earth Son said.

"And what of the humans?" Wolf said.

Earth Son had the gall to say, "I do not know why you fuss so. They are short-lived anyhow."

"I think we should go and be the heroes." Forest Moss struck a heroic pose. "Females are attracted to males of action."

"What females?" Earth Son cried.

"Poor Earth Son, I might have one blind eye—" Forest Moss tapped his cheek under his ruined eye and then reached out to tap both of Earth Son's. "—but apparently you have two."

Earth Son slapped away Moss' hand. "I am not blind."

"Then you must see that this city is filled with fertile young females? There are so few *domana* females, and they are a choosy lot. The law prevents us from taking lovers outside our own caste who are not *sekasha* with *naekuna*, and the *sekasha* frown on us making another caste into *domana*—that would be too much like our Skin Clan fathers. Would not the *sane* plan be to follow Wolf Who Rules' path, winnow out the perfect female from the thousands and thousands of humans, and make her elfin?"

"No!" Earth Son flinched back from the mad one. "Are you capable of even recognizing sanity?"

Forest Moss thought a moment and then shrugged. "The sad truth is: I am not sure. But neither am I sure I care. I have found a certain freedom in madness. Ah, but it is oh so lonely. I do not wish to be alone anymore. Unfortunately, I have fallen into a paradox. As *domana*, I cannot attract a household without *sekasha*, but the *sekasha* no longer trust me. I failed to protect what was mine. What a small mistake led to my downfall, and I did not make it alone. At our first encounter with the oni, despite their displays of friendship, we should have fought. One miscalculation and all was lost. Lost forever."

"I fell in love," Windwolf stated coldly. "Do not mistake my honest passion for calculated convenience."

Forest Moss made little flicking motions with his hand. "Feh, feh, I will love her. She will, after all, win me what I wish for the most. I tried to show my responsibility and leadership by holding dogs and monkeys, and small birds. Surely keeping safe such fragile packages of life shows some ability to protect? Alas, no elf has offered themselves into my keeping."

"And this mad plan would bring you respect?" Earth Son looked puzzled.

"Beloved Tinker holds two *sekasha*. I'm told that she lacks a full Hand merely due to the limits of time. Even the renowned Bladebite offered to her. Surely there is another female of the same caliber in this city."

"No," Windwolf growled. "My *domi* is a rare and treasured find."

Forest Moss refused to be distracted from his plan. "Ah, well, I will have to settle for some lesser gem then. Let us be off. There are dragons to kill, and females to impress."

With the elder Stone Clan male strutting off, Earth Son had no choice but to agree to go after the dragon. It made sense now that Forest Moss had tried to use the *aumani* to gain Little Horse. Although young, Little Horse's bloodlines meant young *sekasha* would be willing to look to him as First. There was some sound reasoning to that—as well as this current plan of Forest Moss. Both, however, were equally distasteful.

Hopefully Malice would cut short Forest Moss's plan.

Tinker spent hours in the infirmary, choosing spells out of the Dufae Codex, modifying them to work with the batteries, printing them off, and casting them. She was learning that she wasn't cut out to be a doctor; having to touch strangers so intimately was still unnerving.

Being weightless was at once a joy and a constant reminder that she wasn't on Elfhome. What had happened when she fell into the Ghostlands? Pony had been up on the scaffolding with her. Had he fallen into the deadly cold and died? Or had he fallen through, like her, and was now lost on another world, or out in space? The possibilities terrified her. She wouldn't allow herself to even consider what that might have happened to Windwolf. There was, however, the dreadful knowledge that Windwolf would put himself between Malice and Pittsburgh, and continue until either he or Malice was dead. She had to get back and help Windwolf—somehow.

The largest drawback to being weightless was that you didn't fall down when you fell asleep. One moment she was drifting in a niche, waiting for some crew to move past, trying to think of a weapon that could kill Malice. The next she was wondering if there was enough black willow left to make lively maple-flavored ice cream. Dragons, Oilcan was telling her over the phone, had a weakness for sweets.

"You're going to have to make it." She became aware that she had made the phone from two tin cans and a long string of red thread strung between them. The thread vibrated as they talked, a blur of red, resonating to their voices. Resonation was the key to everything. "It's really easy to make. Just follow Grandpa's recipe."

She realized then that the ice cream had been what they needed all along—but she had taken the recipe with her. While she considered this, she drifted through the wall of the spaceship. Space, it turned out, was all sticky, sweet black treacle. Here was all the molasses they would want. She could make the ice cream out of this—only how did she get it back to Pittsburgh? Fling it from orbit? No, no, it would all burn up before it hit Pittsburgh.

"*Domi*?"

Tinker looked up. Stormsong was drifting toward her, a flowing angel of hazy gleaming white. The *sekasha* had one hand on the red thread and was following it to Tinker's tin-can phone. "Stormsong, I'm stuck in the treacle."

"No, you aren't." Stormsong held out her hand and Tinker caught hold of it. It felt warm and intangible as a sunbeam. "Remember."

"Remember what?" Tinker cried as Stormsong hazed to a nebulous gleaming form.

"There's no place like home," Stormsong whispered, brilliant now.

Tinker blinked against the brilliance. Stormsong had transformed to a shimmering ghost of Impatience. She clung to some of his snaky mane.

"*Sssssaaaammmmmmmaaananana*." Impatience's voice rumbled against her skin.

A loud gasp made Tinker turn her head. Jin floated a few feet away, gazing at her with amazement. They were back in the infirmary, the wall beside her lumpy and cold and the smell of smoke and blood omnipresent.

Am I still sleeping? Tinker looked back at Impatience.

"*Huuhuuhuuhuuhuuhuu*," Impatience rumbled and faded away.

Jin drifted toward her, his eyes still wide as he gazed at her. "Remember what?"

Tinker scrubbed at her face. Was she awake or still asleep? Her right hand felt warmer than her left—like she had held it over a open flame. "There's no place like home."

"That's it?"

Dragons have a weakness for sweets and space is treacle? "Maybe." Tinker realized that she was awake now—yet somehow Jin had experienced part of her dream. "Did you hear Stormsong?"

"The dragon's name is Stormsong? That doesn't sound like a dragon name."

Was pinching yourself an accurate test to see if you're awake? If it was, then she was awake. "You *saw* the dragon?"

Jin nodded. "And I heard it. It said, 'Remember.' "

"You understood what it said?"

"I'm Providence's child."

"You're what?"

Jin cocked his head in his birdlike inspection of her. "You walk with the dragons but don't know their way?"

"No."

Jin crossed to her side and settled beside her. "Providence is the guardian spirit of the tengu. Each generation a tengu child is born with the mark of Providence upon him." The tengu undid his shirt buttons to expose his chest. Over his heart was a red birthmark that looked like the flowing outline of a dragon. "We're taught the language of the dragons."

A whole mysterious part of her life suddenly made sense. "This is what he was looking for."

"The dragon?"

"No, Riki. He kidnapped me and made me strip. He wanted to know if Impatience marked me but he didn't tell me what the mark was for."

"Who is Riki?" Jin asked.

"A tengu—stuck between a rock and a hard place. Apparently he tried to stay out of oni control, but they took his younger cousin, Joey, hostage. It put us on opposite sides, which is too bad, because I think we could have been good friends."

Jin reached out and touched the necklace Keiko had given her. She'd forgotten she was even still wearing it. "Did he give you that?"

"No, his younger cousin Keiko did. She said it would protect me from tengu."

"It will." He tugged it out of her neckline so it laid overtop. "But you've got to keep it out where it can be seen. That way we can tell you're under the protection of the Chosen blood."

"The what?"

"I'm the Chosen one. The spiritual leader of my people. I decide the path for my people and they follow me. Riki and his cousins are all my nieces and nephews. In my absence, my people are turning to them."

"Which made them targets for the oni wanting to control the tengu."

Jin nodded.

Having experienced people turning to her for leadership, Tinker felt sudden sympathy for Riki. "One thing I don't get. These people are astronauts and still buy 'the chosen one' bullshit?"

"When you're born a mythical creature, you tend to have a different mind-set on these things."

"Wait—so—all this colonization—going back to Onihida stupidity was your idea?"

Jin looked away. For a moment, Tinker thought he wouldn't answer, but he sighed, and said, "We're half bird—we can't breed with humans—not without magic. Yes, a couple hundred of us came to Earth before the elves destroyed the pathway, but it wasn't a big enough gene pool. For generations we've been careful not to interbreed, but we were coming to a dead end. We had to find some way to get back to Onihida and the rest of our tribe. You have no idea what it's like to see genocide bearing down on you."

"If Riki was looking for a chosen one, then that means the tengu don't have a leader."

"It seems like it."

Tinker yawned. "When this is all over, I think I'm going to sleep for a week. Are we going to get gravity back?"

"We did another course correction, but it seems like something is pulling us down toward the planet. It's already pulled all the debris into reentry. We're not spinning up this time to save fuel."

"So—if we don't do anything, eventually the ship will be pulled out of orbit?"

"It seems like it."

Tinker groaned. She didn't want to deal with dreams! "No place like home—that's what Dorothy says to get home. The stupidity was that she had the means to get home the entire time; she just didn't know it. I have no idea how that Glinda bitch gets away with being the 'good' witch. What do I have on me?"

She unloaded her pockets, letting the items float in orbit around her. Although the dress had limited pocket space, she still managed to fit a large amount of stuff into them. Not only did she have her datapad, she also had her camera with the recording of Impatience trying to teach her—something.

"Oh my, these could be my ruby slippers!"

Tracking Malice proved difficult, despite his size. The massive dragon leaped and bounded and shifted through buildings like he was a ghost, leaving a shattered trail. Wolf chafed at the slower speeds that others traveled, but True Flame would not relent, and Wolf had to acknowledge that the older elf had battle experience, whereas he did not.

The trail led up the Monongahela River valley to beyond the Rim, and then disappeared without a trace.

"There is something wrong here," Wraith whispered to Wolf as his Hand gathered close. "Smell the blood?"

Wolf gazed at the still, boulder-strewn forest around them. There was a slight blurring to the trees, as if a mist hazed the air. He would not have noticed it if the *sekasha* hadn't called his attention to it. Pulling out a survey map for the area, he confirmed his suspicions.

"I think this might be an oni encampment, covered by an illusion."

The sekasha pulled their *ejae*, readying themselves for a possible ambush.

Forest Moss did a ground scry, took a few steps, and repeated it several times until he stopped beside an ironwood sapling. "Wolf Who Rules, break this tree."

Wolf aimed a force strike at the sapling and unleashed it.

The sapling vanished when the leading edge of his blow struck it. A tall square stone, inscribed with spells, replaced the sapling for a heartbeat before disintegrating into rubble. An oni camp sprang into being around them. The boulders changed into rough cabins. Mossy logs became well-gnawed humanoid carcasses. Blood soaked the ground and everywhere were dragon tracks.

"All the magic flowed toward the sapling." Forest Moss nudged the remains of the crude oni spell stone.

The *sekasha* moved out to search the cabins.

"Malice has wallowed in magic and feasted on oni." True Flame used his sword tip to point out that the skulls were horned. "Maybe it slipped its bonds, like the little one did."

"There were no spell markings on Malice." Wolf wondered too the significance of the dragon's name. Tinker had called Impatience "hyper." If the dragon's names reflected a personality, perhaps one named Malice needed no prodding to wreak havoc.

"I am not sure what the other beast is, but there is no mistake here, this is an oni dragon." True Flame pointed out a four-toed print in the dirt. "The little beast has five claws like the hand of an elf."

Red Knife reported for the *sekasha*, saying that the cabins were empty of oni and any evidence of what they planned. "There were, though, a hundred oni here only hours ago."

"It is a good thing that we delayed, then." Earth Son earned a sharp look from even his First, Thorne Scratch. "We would have had to face both oni and the dragon at the same time."

Instead both had vanished away after having time to lay cooperative plans.

The dragon tracks led down to the river.

Earth Son made a sound of disgust, eyeing muddy water. "None of us will be able to track it in that."

"If Malice was sent by the oni on Onihida to distract us, then he will circle back to the city and attack." Wolf was glad that Jewel Tear was protecting the enclaves. While the Stone Clan was weak on attack spells, they had the strongest defensive spells. "We should return."

Tinker and Jin found a working computer station and with some jury-rigging managed to get her state-of-art camera interfaced with the two-decade-old systems.

"I recorded about six hours so this is going to take a while." Tinker started the playback.

". . . *we'll build a dictionary of his words*," her recorded voice started out the recording. Cloudwalker had been filming the dragon but had trouble tracking it as it moved through the scrap yard's offices.

"Riki says the dragon's name is Impatience," Tinker said, "but Riki has lied to me—a lot."

Jin attention was on the recording. He said nothing but he frowned slightly at this.

". . . *mmmenananannaaaaaaapoooookaaaammmammamam-yyyyyyaaanananammmmoooo . . .*" Impatience rambled on the recording.

"I'm not familiar with the name." Jin paused the recording after another minute of the dragon's monologue. "Dragons usually use a lot of words to say anything. Like 'a pleasantly warm but not too warm, sunny, cloudless time of the day that isn't dawn but the sun hasn't quite reached its zenith' for 'good morning'. It is considered rude to get to the point too quickly. When you talk to a dragon, you're supposed to elaborate as much as possible."

"Dragon Etiquette 101?" Tinker asked.

"Historically, rude tengu are dragon snacks. This dragon, however, is being very to the point. He might come across as impatient to other dragons, which would explain his name."

"So you understand him."

"Yes, so far he's said, 'What is this object? Oh, this moves. Ah, it makes light. I wonder how. This part twists. What are these? I see. It does not work without those. Why does it not make light? Have I broken it? It seemed as if it was supposed to come apart. A diagram. I must have them backward. Ha, ha, ha.'"

"Yeah, I got the laughing part."

A female astronaut flew into the cabin with tengu grace, "Wai Sze is awake and wants to see the Scarecrow."

The tiny tengu woman was awake and looking surprisingly well compared to how awful she had been before. She gasped as Tinker swam into the infirmary. "Oh my, you *are* here! Oh, look at you! You're so beautiful."

Tinker blushed. As a female elf in a deep jewel-red silk dress in zero gee, she was attracting a lot of attention from the crew. "It's the dress."

"Ah, yes, it not so practical in space, is it, my dear? Xiao Chen, can you find her something to wear?"

Xiao Chen had been the crew member who summoned them to Gracie's side. The tengu female nodded, cocking her head to study Tinker's size before moving off, graceful as a bird in flight.

Jin looked at Tinker as if noticing the silk flowing around her for the first time and then smiled. "I don't know. It's good for morale. At least with the guys."

Tinker smacked him and found herself floating backward.

He laughed, and caught Tinker before she could hit something. "I am only joking."

"Shoo, shoo!" Gracie waved Jin away. "I want to talk to her without your noisy squawking."

Jin smiled fondly at his cousin and flew away.

Gracie held out her unbroken hand to Tinker. "Let me look at you." Gracie had tears in her eyes, which Tinker expected, but not the brilliant smile that the fragile tengu bestowed on her. Tinker found herself smiling back. "You've got Leo's eyes and his smile."

"Yeah, I guess. The patented Dufae face."

"I'm so happy to see it. It hurt so much that I hadn't been able to give Leo a baby. It made losing him all the more horrible. He was a wonderful, wonderful man and he was utterly gone."

It occurred to Tinker for the first time how awful to lose your husband—never see him again—and a sudden fear took root in her. What if she couldn't get back to Windwolf? What if she never saw him again?

"There, there, my love." Gracie wiped Tinker's tears away. "We'll get you back to him somehow."

"Yeah, I know, we're working on it." Tinker sniffed.

"Let me see your leg. I know Jin, he probably didn't think to clean that cut. He might be Dalai Lama of the crows, but he's hopeless with first aid."

Gracie deftly took off the bandage, gently cleaned the wound and applied an antiseptic, and rebandaged the cut.

"Are you a medic?" Tinker asked her.

"I'm the ship's xenobiologist," Gracie said.

"You're kidding."

Gracie looked up in surprise, and Tinker found herself talking about Lain, and then about Esme. "Have you told her? I don't think she's realized who you are yet."

Tinker shook her head. "Right now, it's all too weird. I don't even want to think about it. Besides, I'm kind of ticked at her. Not about leaving me. About everyone having to lie to me about it because—I don't know—some strange family stuff. I didn't know the truth for eighteen years. She can go on not knowing for a couple of days. I'll tell her later."

Xiao Chen flew into the area, carrying a set of clothes. "These should fit our Scarecrow."

"I don't know if I like that nickname." Tinker took the clothes and drifted awkwardly as she checked the pant size against her waist.

Xiao Chen laughed. "I am sorry. For so long, we did not know your name, just that you were the Scarecrow."

"Did you tell everyone about your dream?" Tinker asked Gracie.

Xiao Chen, though, answered. "All of us that slept that night shared Wai Sze's dream—that is her ability. She is our dream crow."

"In some ways, we are more bird than human," Gracie said.

"Can you see the future?" Tinker asked "How am I going to get us out of this mess?"

Gracie shook her head. "Where one person can determine the future, the way is clear, but we're in a tangle of possibilities. Many people can push the future one way or another. This is a time when everyone will determine the end."

Since there were no private places, Tinker turned her back and they pretended to ignore her, talking in Chinese, as she changed. She tried not to feel like they were talking about her. Certainly with the ship falling out of orbit, they had plenty of things to discuss. At least with the dress on, she was able to change panties and pull on her pants without flashing them. The pants were a little loose, but Xiao Chen had included a length of nylon cord to serve as a belt.

Tinker turned back around and pulled on the knotted cord.

"I look the part of the scarecrow now."

The tengu laughed.

"I've been greedy." Gracie reached out and squeezed Tinker's hand. "I've kept you here too long. Thank you for letting me see you."

Tinker hugged her good-bye and returned to the task of finding out how to get them back home to Windwolf.

⋯⋙◯⋘⋯

Impatience, it turned out, had been trying to teach her a spell. It incorporated math, something that Elvish spells didn't do, and used magic to manipulate time and space. It took everything she knew and pushed it in a new direction using an entirely new symbol set. Jin translated the words and then, later, the number system that Impatience used but looked mystified by most of what he was saying.

"You understand this?" Jin asked.

"Yes, yes. The roots of elfin magic are here, but taken to another order of understanding. This is recognizing the quantum nature of magic and its effects *across* boundaries of realities. My god, I really screwed up. I never considered that I could warp the fabric of space and time on this kind of scale."

"What?" Jin cried in surprise. "*You* made this mess?"

"I had help. Okay, here's what happened." She found a marker in her pocket and drew a planet on the nearest wall. "The oni forced me to build a downsized gate on Elfhome. I set up a resonance between my gate and the orbital gate." She drew both gates in their proper positions and the wavy resonance line between them. "Now, Leo's gate was flawed. The time coordinate was never set." She drew the ships entering the orbital gate. "So the default time coordinate became the moment of the gate's destruction—or around midnight Eastern standard time, seven—eight days ago."

She had totally lost track of time since she landed on the spaceship. What day was it now?

Jin understood the result. "Thus the collision."

"Yeah. Old news. This is the important part—all the ships, when they passed through the gate, must have picked up the resonance signature." She drew a ship on the other side of the gate, labeled it *Dahe Hao,* and continued the wavy line to it. "As long as there are objects in orbit, the resonance will continue, which is why the Discontinuity hasn't collapsed. It's because of this link, that when I fell into the Ghostlands, I ended up onboard. For every action, though, there is an equal and opposite reaction. Basically the power spike originates here on Elfhome and travels in this direction—" She drew an arrow parallel to the wavy line through the planet. "—the multiuniverse is trying to drag the *Dahe Hao* back along this line." She drew a second arrow from the ship running beside the resonance path toward the planet. "Again, as long as the Discontinuity continues, the *Dahe Hao* will be affected by this force."

She turned and was startled to find her audience had grown from Jin to about twenty crew members. "Um, well, this isn't all bad. We can use this force to our advantage. The entire ship and everyone on it is keyed to *this* location." She underlined Turtle Creek. "Now, if you look at this section of the text . . ." She pointed to the screen. "This is a spell. It creates a sphere of hyperphase. All we need to do is cast this spell which will step the ship into hyperphase and follow the line of force back to Pittsburgh."

"That's *all?*" Esme said.

Tinker turned back and found her audience had grown again. Esme and another twenty crew members crowded the small area. "My biggest concern is power. If the amount of magic we feed into the spell is too small, it will just punch a hole in the middle of the ship. We need enough power that we can guarantee that the entire ship goes. Even if we think we have sufficient magic, we probably should gather everyone close to the spell, and close all the hatches between the sections of the ship."

"What we've collected isn't enough?" Esme asked.

"I don't think so, and access time on it is slow. The spell is set up to mimic how the dragons cast magic with their mane. With elf magic, there's a timing ring around the spell that controls the power coming in. It gives the magic a slow steady burn. This spell takes all the free magic and converts it in one burst." Tinker sketched the ship and put an "X" at roughly the center of the ship. "It's kind of like dropping a stone into a pool of water. Splash!" She drew in the initial impact in a large circle around the "X". "That's the rock hitting the surface. There seems to be some resulting ripples in the fabric of space." She added larger circles around the first, and then shaded in the space between the circles. "I'm not sure what the ripples will do, but I can't imagine the delay factor will be good for the structural integrity of the ship."

"In other words," Jin sought to clarify what she said, "part of the ship returns to Pittsburgh seconds before the next section goes?"

"Yes. Leo's gate, however flawed, did transfer all the ship to the same second. These ripples would have a different time coordinate, so probably we're looking at pieces of the ship arriving in Pittsburgh—unless we hit it with a damn big rock."

"So where do we get it?"

"I don't know. If we could tap the spring under Turtle Creek, that would work, but I don't see any evidence that power is seeping through."

There was no sign of Malice in Oakland when Wolf and the others returned to the enclaves. Maynard had set up a command center in the building across the street from Poppymeadow's. He and the NSA agents had set up lookout posts across the city, linked by radio.

"Unless it can go invisible, it hasn't appeared in the city yet." Maynard tapped three points on the map. "Between the Cathedral of Learning, the USX building, and Mount Washington, we can see for miles—and Stormsong said that this thing was huge."

Wolf nodded. "Unfortunately, it will be dark soon."

Someone was hammering upstairs. The hammering stopped, and something large moved overhead accompanied by an odd rhythmic clicking noise.

Wolf cocked his head, trying to place the sound. "What is that?"

Stormsong glanced toward Earth Son standing in the street, just outside the open door, and lowered her voice. "*Domi's nagarou* brought the little dragon, so the humans can see what we're fighting."

Interesting how one afternoon could change your perspective on size.

Maynard had caught Stormsong's caution and spoke quietly in English. "Briggs and Durrack are seeing what works against it."

Wolf couldn't decide if this was ingenious or unwise. He found the stairs leading up to the one large open room taking up the entire second story. The windows had been boarded shut and mattresses leaned against the walls. The dragon and others were in the far corner, standing around a computer set up on the floor. While Oilcan and Durrack were focused on the screen, Briggs and Little Horse and Cloudwalker were standing back and watching the dragon.

All beings—dragon, humans, and elves—looked up when he arrived with his Hand.

"*Domou.*" Little Horse acknowledged his arrival.

"What are you doing here?" Wolf thought he had sent his blade brother back to the enclaves.

"There is nothing I can do for *domi*, but she would want her *nagarou* safe. Surely, the oni will try and take back the little dragon."

Wolf glanced at his *domi's nagarou*. There was so much of Tinker in Oilcan's appearance that it hurt—her mouth, her eyes, and her haphazard haircut. In the hectic last two months, Wolf had not spoken once to the young man. Wolf realized now that Tinker was Oilcan's only family; he was now quite alone. Wolf could not imagine it; an elf only found himself alone if he was exiled from his clan. Clans were so vast that natural disaster could lay low entire households and families and there would still be someone left to be responsible for the orphans.

Wolf had been lax toward Oilcan because he was an adult—if he had been an elf, Oilcan would have chosen a clan that superseded all family responsibilities. That had been wrong of Wolf. Even if he lifted Tinker out of her species, it did not completely free her of her culture's obligations—and as her *domou*, her responsibilities were his own. But beyond that, it been wrong of him to be a stranger to the one human that Tinker loved as much as life.

Oilcan cautiously separated himself from the dragon, as if he didn't fully trust either the dragon or the warriors from either race. "Wolf Who Rules." Oilcan gave a proper bow. "I heard about Malice on the scanner," he said in High Tongue. Sorrow filled his eyes as he spoke, and then was firmly put aside. "I thought we might learn something from Impatience."

"Thank you, *nagarou*. That was wise of you." Wolf dropped to Low Elvish, and put a hand to the young man's shoulder.

A smile flashed over Oilcan's face, then vanished as he sighed. "Unfortunately, most of what we've found out so far isn't good."

"I did not expect anything else. What have we found out?"

"Well, there was a question if Impatience and Malice are both really dragons, given their size and various other differences. From what we've pieced together, we think they are. In Chinese mythology, the four-claw dragons are considered common dragons but the imperial dragon has five claws. We think the variations are racial instead of species differences, and possibly represent political differences too."

"Tengu worship five-claws—they—compassionate guardians of tengu in past," Durrack spoke very rough low Elvish. "Four-claws—they have bad reputation—they work with the oni without being enslaved. Malice is not enslaved."

"Now, the dragon can't maintain its shields all the time." Oilcan patted Impatience on the head, showing that the little dragon's shields were currently down. "It takes them approximately thirty seconds to raise their shields."

Durrack abandoned Low Elvish, to add in English, "If we could catch Malice completely unaware, a sniper might be able to take him out with a well-placed bullet. But once his shield goes up, things get tricky."

Oilcan murmured a translation to Little Horse and Cloudwalker, and then added in Elvish, "The shields, while they use ambient magic, are very efficient and translate all kinetic energy—including the motion of the dragon's body—somehow into magic. Bullets, rockets, baseballs—" Oilcan nudged a ball on the floor that they apparently had been using in their experiments. "—anything you can throw at them—will only make them stronger."

"And they can keep the shields up while they phase through walls." Durrack patted a wooden partition erected next to him. Impatience took this as a request to demonstrate his phasing abilities. His mane lifted up and he shimmered into a ghostly haze and leapt through the wall and returned.

"Good boy!" Oilcan produced a large gumball from his pocket and gave it to the dragon, who chewed it with obvious relish. "We believe your lightning will cross the barrier because it's composed of a different type of energy particle."

"Electricity works." Durrack lifted up half a cattle prod. "We established that."

Impatience snatched the cattle prod out of the NSA agent's hand and phased it into the wall. When the little dragon let go, the cattle prod remained as part of the wall. The other half, Wolf noticed, was already part of the wall. Apparently the little dragon didn't like that test.

"As a one shot deal, pepper spray will work." Durrack picked up an aerosol can. "Of course, it only annoys the hell out of them, and then the dragon changes its shields so that gas won't penetrate."

"I'm stunned you are all still alive." Wolf realized that Impatience had to be remarkably forgiving to put up with these experiments.

"We talked first," Oilcan said.

Briggs scoffed, "We drew pictures and did a lot of pantomime."

"He seems to understand what's going on," Oilcan said. "He seems to hate both Malice and the oni, but he's made it clear that he can't beat Malice in a fight."

"How do oni enslave the dragons in the first place? Do the tengu say?"

Durrack shook his head. "No."

Wolf wondered if this was the truth. While he trusted Oilcan to be as forthright as Tinker, the NSA clearly saw themselves as separate powers, with all that implied.

After the accident, and the various course corrections, the *Dahe Hao*'s low orbit didn't put them within range of the Wind Clan spell stones at Aum Renau. After discussing their fuel situation and the reliability of their engines, they decided to look for stones elsewhere within a *mei*. The spell stones were large enough and distinctive enough that the pattern recognition software found several sets. It was impossible to distinguish which clan the stones belonged to, but they found four grouped together in the place the crew nicknamed Giza.

"There are four major clans—Wind, Fire, Water, Stone—so I think it's a safe bet that it's one set for each major clan." At least, Tinker hoped it was. She knew there were lesser clans, but she didn't know anything about them. "At this speed, though, we're already out of range, so I'll have to wait until next orbit to check."

"You've got about an hour and a half then." Esme murmured a curse as something flashed red on her monitor. "But we're drifting again. We're going to have to do another course correction."

"Try and keep us in this orbit," Tinker said. "A *mei* is only a thousand miles, give or take a couple hundred miles. If we drop much closer to the equator, we'll be out of range."

Tinker then retreated to work on printing out the spell. Jin tracked her down a short time later.

"Gracie wanted to be sure you got something to eat." Jin held out a container.

"*Pft.*" Tinker waved away the offering. "If I eat, I'll have to figure out how you go to the bathroom up here, and I figure that's not going to be a pleasant activity."

Jin laughed, still holding out the cup-sized container. "You have to eat."

"What is it?"

"Cream of tomato soup."

"Oh! My favorite." She took the container and found that it was warm. As she snapped it open and sipped the rich creamy broth, Jin swung up to perch across from her.

"It was your father's favorite too." Jin sipped his own soup. "I can see Leo in you. Hear him in the way you talk. It makes me happy."

"Why?"

"Leo was my best friend for many years. I'm glad that in a way, he is living on through you."

"If he was such a good friend, why did you kill him?"

She expected him to deny it, but he only gazed at her, sorrow filling his eyes.

"I—I made a mistake. We never told Leo that we were tengu. And he never told us—at least, not until it was too late—that he was elfin. We kept our secrets from one another, and in the end, it killed Leo."

"I don't understand," Tinker said.

"Leo and I met at MIT. We both had radical ideas, ones that made us unpopular. We believed that magic existed—that there were other realms that could be visited via magical portals. Of course, we had the proof in our very blood, but we never told anyone that, not even each other." Jin sighed, shaking his head. "It seems so obvious now. Dufae. How did we miss it?"

"What really happened? My grandfather never told me the details."

"When Leo showed us his gate design, a possibility opened up to us. A paradise for the tengu. It became the flock dream, a bright promise at the end of a path through dark woods full of unseen danger. To be able to choose one's mate out of love, and not a carefully ordered breeding plan. To be able to fly. To walk under the sun in our true form, and not to be always hidden. I went to the kitsune, who are powerful in the Chinese government, and talked to them about funding. They involved other parties. It was dangerous, I know, but I thought I understood all the factors. What I didn't know was that Leo was an elf—that he knew exactly what the oni were—and that he wouldn't cooperate with them."

"Halfway through the meeting with the investors, Leo just freaked. He told them that he would never help the oni build a gate. And worse, he told them why. As much as the elves feared the oni, the oni of Earth feared the elves. He stormed out of the meeting. I went after him. We were arguing—" Jin fell silent for a minute. "It happened so fast. One moment he was standing beside me on the street corner, arguing with me, and the next he was dead in the middle of the road.

Jin sighed. "I wasn't driving the car. I didn't push him out into its path. But I brought death to him. And I can only say I'm sorry. And I truly am. I loved him like a brother."

All Tinker could imagine was Nathan out on the road, his blood on her. Oh gods, she didn't want to cry again. She squeezed her eyes tight on the sudden burn of tears. "How do you deal with knowing that you fucked up so bad? That you killed someone who loved you? Who trusted you?"

"Accept the truth of what happened, and then forgive yourself. They would if they could."

She laughed bitterly. "Why would they?"

"Because they loved you."

She pressed the palms of her hands into her eyes, and struggled to get back in control of herself. The truth of what happened? The truth was that she had ignored all the warning signs with Nathan. She had to pay attention, think about the consequences of her actions. Like now—she was desperately trying to get back to Pittsburgh, but what if she was totally wrong? With sudden terror, she saw the implications of her actions. She was taking *Dahe Hao* to Pittsburgh. She might be saving the human crew, but she was dooming the tengu crew to genocide.

"I'm worried about what will happen to the tengu when we reach Pittsburgh. The elves are killing people that they just suspect are oni. And I know they *will* see tengu as oni."

"You still don't think of yourself as one of them?"

"No, not really. Wait—how do you know?"

"For the last week, all we've dreamed about is you—all the weird twists and turns your life has taken." Jin picked up the camera. Cloudwalker had had trouble tracking the hyperactive dragon through the trailer and caught her and Pony in the viewfinder instead. "We've seen what you've done to keep your *sekasha* safe."

"You know everything?" She wondered if this was why she had been having such horrible nightmares lately.

"Enough. Your fight with the Foo dogs. Your transformation from a human. Your fight with the oni lord." Jin played a few seconds of recording as Pony acknowledged one of her requests with a slight bow. "This is just proof of what we already knew. You're the Wind Clan *domi*, guarded by a Hand of *sekasha*, one of which is another dreamer."

"Her name is Stormsong."

"You told me."

"I don't know what to do about this," Tinker admitted. "If we don't do the spell, I don't think anyone will survive. If we do the spell, then you end up in the mess in Pittsburgh."

Jin reached out and tapped Tinker's forehead, reminding her of the *dau* marked onto her forehead. "You have the power to protect us. You could make us part of your household. We could be yours, as these *sekasha* are yours."

"Mine?" Tinker squeaked. "Why would you want that?"

"Because we trust you more than we trust the oni."

That wasn't saying much.

"I don't know if that would work," Tinker said. "The elves make a big thing about beholding. The *sekasha* promise to serve in exchange for protection. That everyone fits into society—someone above them responsible for them, but they are answerable to."

"It seems fairly simple. I will promise that the tengu will obey you and you promise to protect us."

"You're serious? You would listen to what I told you to do?"

Jin nodded.

"Are you sure your crew is okay with obeying some snot-nosed kid?"

"Leo's daughter who talks with dragons? Yes, I am sure."

She opened her mouth and then closed it, reminding herself to think about implications and complications this time. She supposed that the tengu could make up a household like Poppymeadow's, where the crew would be under Jin and the tengu captain would be under her, yet they wouldn't be directly part of her household. She wished that she knew more about how the enclaves worked, but she suspected that they were like all things elfin, where an exchange of promises were enough to bind both parties. But how would the tengu fit into her life? There was a terror deep inside her, one she didn't want to look at closely, that if she promised the tengu to protect them, it would have to be against the people that she loved the most. What would she do if Windwolf refused to acknowledge her claim on the tengu? She didn't want to think about Windwolf systematically killing the tengu she had gotten to know. She didn't want him to be the type of person who could do it. Yet she couldn't stop thinking of Nathan dead in the road because she was married to Windwolf. Of the bloody streets of Chinatown. Of Tommy Chang within moments of being cut down.

If she committed to the tengu, then she might have to fight even Windwolf to keep them safe. *I can't. I can't.*

She pressed trembling hands to her mouth. But if she didn't protect them, who would? How could she stand aside and let them be killed and do nothing to save them? "I'll do my best to protect you, but you have to remember to do what I say, or I won't have the power to stop the elves from killing you all."

"I promise. You will have the obedience of the tengu."

Her life had so many strings attached that she felt like a puppet.

"Hey! Scarecrow!" Esme called over the ship's intercom. "We're getting close to your mark in five minutes!"

Tinker swam back to the bridge, blinking on the salt burning in her eyes.

"Two minutes," Esme announced.

They waited in tense silence, bathed in the soft earthshine.

"In ten," Esme said quietly.

Tinker made sure she had her fingers in the correct position.

"We're in range."

Tinker brought her hand to her mouth and said the trigger word. Nothing happened. Her heart jolted with the sudden spike of fear. "Daaaaaaae." Still nothing. She checked her finger positions and carefully announced the trigger word. Zip. "Daaae. Daaaaae. Dae. Daaaaaaae."

"And we're out of range," Esme said.

"Oh, fuck," Tinker said.

"Just checking—it didn't work?" Jin asked.

"No." Tinker rubbed the heels of her hand into her eyes.

"Well, you better think of something else, Scarecrow," Esme said. "We only have fuel for one more burn."

"How's it going?" the tengu Ushi asked. Tinker was finding that while the humans treated her with slight condescension after the initial novelty wore off, the tengu regarded her with an odd mix of awe and affection. The ratio of worship versus familial warmth seemed to be dependent on how well they had known her father. Either way, they kept seeking her out, wanting to know if she was comfortable, or needed anything. It was driving her to distraction.

"I'm still thinking." Thinking she needed to find a hiding place. "We're at about two hundred miles above Elfhome's surface, crossing over spell stones in Giza around eighteen miles per second. The reach of the spell stones are one *mei*, which is approximately one thousand miles, which means that theoretically we're within their reach for about a minute and a half."

"Why are they important?"

"They're a source of a lot of magic. If I could pull on them, then I could use the magic to trigger the spell."

She covered her eyes to think. Apparently Ushi took the cue that he was distracting her; when she opened her eyes again, he was gone. Too bad all her problems didn't solve themselves so neatly.

Why couldn't she call the spell stones? They were in range, for more than a minute, nearly two, and a call took less than one. Something had to be interfering with the call. Was it that there wasn't enough ambient magic to fuel the initial call? Tinker ran her hand across the wall of the ship, focusing on her magic sense. She could feel the latent magic. It was as strong as a ley line, but with a strange texture. It was like the difference between silk and wool. Magic on Elfhome flowed, smooth and quick. The magic here buzzed with static. If the call was supposed to be resonance of magic across the DNA signature of the *domana*, then perhaps that chaotic nature of the magic on the ship was creating too much static for that call.

Perhaps if she could filter the background magic to one frequency—oh, gods—how the hell did she do that? She groaned and pulled at her hair. The *sekasha* had magic stored in the beads woven into their hair, which guaranteed that if they were in a magic-poor area, they still could trigger their shields and have a few minutes of protection. She never had examined them but knew in essence that they were metal balls, insulated with glass, that acted like her power sinks. She believed that storing the magic in a "clean" enough medium would reduce the static. So, she should be able to use a sink just like they used the beads. The problem probably would be eliminating the background magic so only the stored magic was active.

Wait, if she modified the Reinholds spell based on Impatience's theorems, she might be able to trigger a magic equivalent to a wide-scale electromagnetic pulse. It would basically clean the slate. The danger would be that, if the pulse worked, not only on the magic wavelength but also included the electronics of the ship, she could accidentally kill all the computers maintaining the ship's life support. That would be bad.

But if she wiped out the buildup, and then used one shielded source to do a call on the Wind Clan spell stones—would that be enough magic to trigger the jump? It might. Too bad she couldn't pull from a second set . . .

Or could she? She had felt the Stone Clan magic. She had watched Forest Moss call on the Stone Clan's spell stones. Did she remember the hand positions and vocalization? Yes, she was sure.

She was nearly quivering now with possibilities. If she could pull on both stones at once—wait—*at once*—that kind of meant at the same moment. Since the vocalization was different she couldn't do both. She wished she could pace. She thought better pacing. She settled for bouncing between the walls, flying through the air.

"Whoa, whoa, whoa!" Jin suddenly caught her, and brought her to a stand still. "You're going to hurt yourself doing that."

"I can't say two things at once! I suspect that the genetic key equates to vibrations in the quantum nature of magic—and I'm at a loss as to how to test that theory. There isn't time for me to invent a device that can sample how the magic interplays with matter at the molecular level, or the equipment we would need to recreate that resonance. And according to my last dream, resonance was the key to everything. And if getting home isn't the full ball of wax—"

"Shhh." Jin put his finger to his lips.

She frowned at him and then put her finger over his lips. "Do that again."

"Tinker, listen."

"No, do the 'shhh' thing again."

"Shhhh," Jin repeated and then said, with her finger still in place,

"We're picking up the radio from Pittsburgh again. They say that Malice is attacking Oakland."

"I need to get home. And I think I know how."

True Flame drew Wolf aside to speak quietly with him. "You and I have the only attack spells that have a hope of hurting Malice. We need to pair off with the Stone Clan. They'll provide defense while we focus on attack. Which do you want? Forest Moss or Earth Son?"

The mad one or the male who hated him? Both had good cause to see him dead. If they were wise, they would hold their political maneuverings until after the dragon was dead. Where Forest Moss lacked sanity, Earth Son lacked political savvy; Wolf did not think either was rational enough for wisdom. While he trusted Jewel Tear to defend the enclaves, he was not sure he could entrust their safety to the males.

"I would rather not stake my life—and the lives of my people—on the Stone Clan." Wolf spoke the blunt truth.

"I realize that," True Flame said. "But we will need both hands for our most powerful attack spells, which means no shield."

"In that case, I don't want to take *Sekasha* into this battle. I do not want to leave them at the mercy of the Stone Clan."

True Flame nodded. "That would be wise."

"I'll take Earth Son." When faced with two evils, Wolf would rather deal with the known.

When True Flame announced the pairing, Earth Son shook his head.

"I do not like this pairing," Earth Son said. "Forest Moss will go with Wolf."

"You will go with Wolf," True Flame said.

"As clan head I should be with you," Earth Son said.

"I have given the choice of partners to Wolf since he is in disadvantage," True Flame said. "We don't have time for this. You are to pair with Wolf."

Thorne Scratch stepped forward to murmur in Earth Son's ear. The Stone Clan *domou* cast a dark look at his First and then smoothed his face to the unreadable court mask. Wolf wondered what Thorne had to say to Earth Son.

"Fine, I will pair with Wolf Who Rules," Earth Son said. "But my mewling infant of a cousin, I swear that was the last time that you'll twist matters to get an unfair advantage."

The wind shifted, blowing hard from the east. Clouds boiled over

Oakland as weather fronts collided. Wolf could sense something alter the wind flow.

"I think the dragon is coming." Wolf motioned that the non-*domana* should retreat to the enclaves.

"Wolf." Stormsong held out something. "This goes in your ear. It's like the walkie-talkie but smaller. *Nagarou* wanted you to have it. You should be able to use it without it interfering with your magic—I tested it with my shield."

Wolf took the small bud of plastic. "How does it—"

Stormsong fitted it into Wolf's ear. "*Nagarou* has gone to act as a spotter with the NSA. He is in the cathedral. He will talk to you."

"Windwolf, this is Oilcan," the young man stated calmly in Wolf's ear. "The dragon is in southeast Oakland, at the intersection of Bates Street and Boulevard of the Allies. It seems to be leveling houses."

Which meant it was less than a mile away.

Wolf did a wide range scry and caught the passage of something large in that area. Earth Son finished his spell and as he shook his head, Wolf lost the scry on the dragon.

"This way." Wolf started to walk. Forbes Avenue was a major street in Oakland, with multiple lanes leading from the downtown out to the Rim. The EIA had stopped traffic in the city, erecting barriers. To his right, at the center of its lush lawn, was the towering Cathedral of Learning with Oilcan at its summit. To his left was the massive stone Carnegie museum.

"Tell me how to get to Bates," Wolf said.

"Go through that parking lot on your left." Oilcan started into the directions.

True Flame indicated that he would continue down Forbes Avenue, following his scry.

The boil of clouds had darkened to angry grey, with streaks of black where thunderheads were starting to build. When Wolf reached the top of Bates Street and looked down the hill it climbed, he saw that the shield around the massive dragon created a miasma that was forming the clouds. He understood now why the humans thought his lightning would be able to strike—it was perfect lightning weather. Cloaked by his shields, Malice moved within the misty darkness, showing only flashes of himself.

"Call your shields," Wolf told Earth Son. "Keep him back, otherwise the lightning will arc to us."

Remember, you can't trust Earth Son, Wolf thought to himself, and called on the winds in order to summon his lightning.

The darkness shifted, as if Malice had turned, and the gleam of his eyes appeared in the miasma and then vanished.

"He's shifting to your right." Oilcan's voice was flat with the effort to keep the information concise. "He stopped just around the corner, behind the brick house."

Wolf didn't know how Oilcan could tell from his perch above the miasma, but Wolf knew the humans had their ways. Magic thrummed around him, ready to be used. He shifted through his call-lightning spell. His right hand primed the clouds as his left hand readied the ground. Magic flooded the street on a hot wave of air that flared out his duster. The hairs on his arms lifted as the magic shifted into potential. He felt it reach critical point and he brought his hands together, aiming the channel through which the lightning would run. The faint leader flashed downward out of the belly of the clouds, and then the return stroke leapt from behind the brick, up to meet the leader with a deafening clap of thunder. The blinding column of light flared the dark miasma to white haze, and the thunder rumbled as the stroke climbed up into the sky.

Malice roared in pain and anger. The lightning licked the sky, as leader and return stroke danced back and forth over the open channel.

"He's coming at you!" Oilcan said.

"Keep him back!" Wolf shouted at Earth Son and started another call.

Earth Son locked into place, both hands set into shields. He was holding a force wall set half a block around them and another shield wrapped tight around himself. The lightning flared again and again. Wolf could feel the thunder in his bones. Malice stepped *through* the brick house, coiling like a ghost snake. His eyes gleamed bloodred. Down Malice's left flank was a massive smoking wound.

Wolf felt twin spikes of magic flash through the area and a moment later a fire strike bloomed around the ghost Malice. The dragon ignored the flames, rushing toward Earth Son's force wall. Wolf focused on the growing potential, waiting for it to hit the critical point. He could only cast the spell, though, if Earth Son kept the dragon at a distance.

The lightning died and darkness closed in around them.

"He's through your shield!" Oilcan cried. "He's through your shield!"

Malice must have stepped through Earth Son's shield the same way he had walked through the house. There was no time for Wolf to change spells.

"Earth Son, cover me, damn you!"

In the dark, the ghost Malice was a presence felt, not seen or heard, bearing down on him. A fire flare went off, lighting the area. Malice loomed over them, transparent as smoke. As the dragon snapped into solid form, a shield wrapped around Wolf. Forest Moss was protecting him.

The dragon struck Wolf. The shield held, but the ground underneath didn't. The pavement under Wolf's feet lifted, and he was airborne.

He had a dozen heartbeats to realize that Forest Moss had lost track of him. He had no protection. And then he smashed down through the skylight roof at the museum. He tumbled painfully downwards through the building. Unseen layers broke under him, as if he was falling through a house of cards. He landed hard on a marble floor, surrounded by construction materials.

"Windwolf! Windwolf!" Oilcan shouted over the radio. "He's still after you! Can you hear me! Malice is coming for you!"

Gasping for breath he tried to get up. Pain shot up from Wolf's right hand. Hissing, he looked down and found his fingers bent at impossible angles. He cursed, hunching over his hand. He could attack or defend, but not both now.

"Windwolf?" Oilcan called to him again.

"I hear you."

"The oni are attacking the dreadnaught."

Wolf cursed. "Get a message to True Flame. Tell him to deal with the oni. I'll keep Malice busy."

A backup source of magic was shielded, the spells were printed off and floated in place, the computers were turned off, and the crew was gathered around her. Tinker cast the magical magnetic pulse spell and it flashed through her like a cold wind, leaving her feeling strangely empty. With sudden panic, she realized that her body might be a living computer.

Oh gods, I hope that didn't destroy my ability to call the stones!

Esme powered up the workstation beside her. "Well, it didn't kill our computers. We're coming up to spell stone range in two minutes."

Tinker triggered the first spell that pumped the filtered stored magic out. It was a relief to feel the magic start to pool around her feet. Tinker had told the astronauts that she needed silence, and they had taken her seriously. They watched now, silent, fearful. More than one had their eyes closed, and lips moving in prayer.

Esme indicated that they were at the one-minute mark.

Tinker made sure her fingers on both hands were in the correct position, and then stood, waiting.

Esme held up her fingers then and counted the last ten seconds down silently. When she nodded, Jin—with Tinker's right hand nearly touching his mouth—and Xiao Chen—on Tinker's left—pronounced the activation words for the Wind and Stone Clans.

Magic flooded through the connection. Tinker let it run for thirty seconds by Esme's silent count. She could feel the purity of it, but the edges were starting to tangle, caught by the magnetic field of the ship. She dropped her hands and the tengu went silent.

The activation word for the dragon spell was simple. She spoke it into the tense silence.

The universe went dark and formless.

It wasn't the sense of falling that she always felt during Startup and Shutdown. This was like death. All Tinker could feel was growing terror that she had just pulled her greatest fuckup. She had killed herself and all the astronauts. Then light and sound and gravity returned, tumbling Tinker and the others into a pile of bodies. The "floor" now formed walls up to the matching bulkhead ceiling. They untangled themselves, laughing with relief.

"It worked." By the tone of her voice, Xiao Chen hadn't expected it to.

Tinker wanted to say, "Of course," but the way her life had been going, the mind boggled as to all the ways it might have screwed up. "We're on a planet, but which one?"

Esme glanced upward to the window far over their heads. "Don't know yet."

"We landed well." Jin headed up the ladder. Tinker followed.

"That was not a landing," Esme called after them.

"We're on the ground," Tinker said. "Engines down, bridge up. That's good enough for me."

"You do realize that this ship is nearly a half mile long?" Esme said.

Oops.

Jin reached the window. He turned his head this way and that, studying the view intently, before announcing. "Trees. Nothing but trees."

"It's not Onihida or Earth then," Tinker said. "I hope it's Elfhome, or we ended up someplace totally new."

"That was the point of the colonization program as far as the humans were concerned," someone said from below.

"There's an airlock at midsection." Jin kept climbing upward. "We might be able to get a better view."

Tinker only gave the window a passing glance. The trees looked like ironwoods but it was difficult to tell. They were ten or twenty feet above the canopy. If this was Turtle Creek, then she had just erected the tallest structure in Pittsburgh—for however long it remained standing.

The airlock opened to summer dusk. There was a narrow ledge that wrapped around the ship. Tinker carefully picked her way around and found what she most wanted to see—Pittsburgh. Clouds boiled over Oakland, but no lightning flashed from them. Was that a good sign or bad? Had Malice killed Windwolf?

They had "landed" in Turtle Creek, neatly replacing the Ghostlands with the massive bulk of the ship's engines. The *Dahe Hao* would have taken out the center section of the Westinghouse Bridge if it hadn't already fallen. The remaining spans of the bridge butted up against the side of the ship just ten feet down from the ridge she stood on.

And like one of her impossible dreams, Pony stood on the bridge, looking up at her. He lifted up his arms and motioned for her to jump to him. Relief flooded through her like a weakness. Her legs started to buckle, so she leapt to him.

Pony caught her and pulled her close. "*Domi.*"

"Oh, Pony, I was so scared that you were killed." She hugged him tightly, burying her face into the warmth of his neck, smelling his scent.

"I thought I lost you." His voice was husky with emotion.

She kissed him on the strong line of his jaw. He turned his head and captured her mouth with his and kissed her deeply. He tasted of the enclave peaches; the sweetness poured through her like warm honey; she clung to him, letting the feeling push out the fear and worry.

Tinker realized that Stormsong was beside her. She burned with sudden embarrassment at the way she was acting. Knowing that neither elf would see it as wrong didn't help.

She broke the kiss but couldn't bring herself to let go of Pony. With one hand, she reached out to Stormsong to pull her into a three-way huddle. "And you too. I was worried sick about both of you."

"What? I don't get a kiss?" Stormsong teased.

Tinker laughed and kissed her quickly on the lips. Then holding them close, she whispered. "Is Windwolf all right? Where is he? What's happened?"

"We can not get close enough to the museum to look for Wolf,"

Pony said. "Malice, though, appears to be searching for something, so we think that Wolf has eluded him."

"The oni have stolen the dreadnaught and taken it down river," Stormsong said. "Our greatest fear has been that while Malice kept us busy, the oni would push an army through the Ghostlands."

"Well, I stopped that." Tinker gave a weak laugh.

As Pony and Stormsong updated her, Cloudwalker, Rainlily, and Little Egret joined them at the end of the bridge. She greeted them with hugs. It felt good to be surrounded by her people.

The *sekasha* shifted to face crew members picking their way around the edge of the ship. It was Esme with Jin and a handful of the tengu crew members.

"It's okay. I've taken the tengu as my beholden."

"Are you sure that's wise?" Pony asked.

"Yes." She took a deep cleansing breath. She pressed her palms to her eyes and considered current obstacles and possible tools. If Malice was hunting Windwolf, then they would have to hunt Malice. The EMP spell that she had used to clear the ship should work on Malice. They needed, however, a big gun to take advantage of it—a very big gun. She could think of only one place they could get such a gun. "Okay, we're going to need the dreadnaught."

"What's a dreadnaught?" Jin asked.

"I suppose you could call it an attack helicopter on steroids," Tinker said. "It's more a flying fortress. It's armed with a variety of heavy guns, from machine guns to cannons, and can carry a large number of troops into any location. The elves built them with magic in mind—so they're very low tech, and thus extremely clunky."

"And you want us to take it out?" Jin asked.

"No," Tinker said. "We need it to take on Malice."

"Take it over?" Stormsong said. "Are you fucking insane?"

She held up her hands to ward off Stormsong's objections. "While we were at Aum Renau, I got inside of the dreadnaughts. I think it was part of me being the pivot—they didn't know what I would need to stop the oni, so they told me anything I wanted to know—full access to everything."

"Yes," Stormsong hissed, her eyes going soft and vague. "The pivot keeps turning until the door is fully shut."

Tinker shivered. "Oh, that creeps me out. I took detailed notes and I scanned them into my datapad – I was thinking of making a few for the Wind Clan."

"You would," Jin murmured.

"The big question is—do we have anyone that knows how to fire the guns?" Tinker expected that they would need to track down some the Fire Clan crew. Surprisingly, all the *sekasha* pointed to themselves.

"We were all taught how when we were in Aum Renau," Pony explained. "After you showed an interest in the airship."

"They didn't miss a trick with me being the pivot, did they? How the hell did I miss—never mind, don't answer that."

"We will need a pilot," Stormsong said. "The oni killed the dreadnaught's crew."

"How close is it to Earth's aircraft?" Esme had worked her way down to the bridge. She spoke Elvish, which surprised Tinker and also made her realize that Jin had been speaking it too.

"The controls are modeled after a helicopter's," Tinker said.

"I'm your pilot then." Esme noted Tinker's surprise. "I'm the best fucking pilot you're going to find. It's the magic. On Elfhome, I can fly blindfolded." Tinker remembered Stormsong's ability with the hoverbike and realized that Esme probably had the same type of talent. "Taking over controls midair might be tricky—but should be a piece of cake compared to some of the NASA simulations."

"You know," Durrack called out of the gathering twilight, announcing the NSA's arrival. "We're going to have to reclassify you to 'force of nature.'"

"Oh good," Tinker said. "We're going to do an assault on the dreadnaught and we could use your help."

Briggs laughed as she joined Durrack. "And she's not even trying to be scary."

Tinker kept losing count of their numbers. They would need a tengu to get every non-tengu up to the dreadnaught while it was in flight. The problem was that she kept forgetting to count herself, or she added herself to both elves and humans. It was really starting to bug her.

"Eighteen," she hissed to herself. "Nine tengu and nine people without wings."

While the elves and the NSA agents arranged transportation and weapons, and the *sekasha* magical supplies, she and the ship tengu gathered high-tech gear.

"I found the dreadnaught," Durrack called as Jin winged her down to the bridge. Dusk was deepening into night. "The oni took it downriver to Shippensport and took over the nuclear power plant."

"Without power, the humans will be crippled." Pony pointed out the logic of the oni's attack.

As if we didn't have enough to worry about. "Did they damage the nuclear plant?"

"No, they haven't. They just took it off the grid. EIA has dispatched a team to take it back, but they don't have any way to fight Malice. They're leaving him to us."

"Did you find everything?" Getting a nod, she motioned toward the yellow delivery truck that the NSA had produced. "Let's go."

Malice cocked his head, as if listening carefully.

Suddenly there was a massive boom, loud beyond description. A shock wave of air suddenly blasted through the streets, and a moment later, there was an echo under foot.

What was that? Wolf wondered.

Someone looped an arm under Wolf's and pulled him to his feet.

"Shhhh," a male hissed, and then added in English. "Don't use magic."

The male was an Asian human. He tucked in under Wolf's arm, supporting him.

As Malice crashed loudly through the rubble, the man guided Wolf backward, unhurried. Malice scanned the room, swinging his head back and forth, as if searching for them without seeing them. What magic was this that the man had?

A cold chill went down Wolf's back as he realized that the male's ears were furred and pointed like a cat's. This was an oni like Lord Tomtom. Judging by Malice's seemingly blind search, the oni was keeping the dragon from seeing them. But why was the oni helping Wolf?

Malice stilled and the oni froze in place. The dragon cocked its head again as if listening closely. The oni male tightened his hold on Wolf as if worried that Wolf could act. Wolf, however, was under no illusions as to how useless his magic was at the moment.

The great beast grumbled, its voice like thunder, and it sniffed deeply. The massive head turned toward them and Malice stared long at where they stood. The oni stared back, gripping Wolf tightly.

Was the dragon truly fooled, or was Wolf the one being deceived? It was an uncomfortable thought—as was the awareness that the oni had hold of his good hand, making him totally helpless.

Malice stalked forward, muttering deeply. The dragon stopped again, now only a dozen paces from them. Malice rumbled out, seemingly in disgust; its breath washed over them. The oni pulled a container of red powder out of his pocket, and silently emptied it onto the floor. Malice sniffed deeply again, forming runnels in the dust at their feet breathing in the red powder. The dragon flung back its head, gave a series of deep coughing roars, and shuffled back suddenly, away from them.

The oni jerked Wolf backward and they hurried to a staircase at the corner of the room, and down the steps into darkness. Behind them, Malice smashed loudly, roaring, but Wolf couldn't tell in which direction the dragon was heading—after them or away. In the complete darkness, they made a series of quick turns. Either the oni could see in the darkness or was running blind with one hand on the wall.

"What is that red powder?" Wolf asked.

"Cayenne pepper."

They turned again, and the black gave way. A grate stood half-open to a dimly lit tunnel crowded by three pipes thick around as an elf. The oni pulled Wolf into the tunnel and shut the grate.

"This way," the oni male said.

The floor was curved, making walking difficult. A hundred feet down, the tunnel joined another. Wolf knew that they couldn't be inside the museum anymore.

"What is this place?" Wolf asked.

"You ask a lot of questions."

"I like knowing where I stand."

"Yeah, nice when you can get it." The oni kept walking. "These are the old steam tunnels that used to heat all of Oakland."

"Who are you?"

"My name is my own to have," the oni said.

"That makes it awkward to thank you."

The oni paused to look at him. Finally, he said, "You can call me Tommy."

"Tommy," Wolf bowed. "Thank you."

Tommy grunted as if surprised.

"You are Lord Tomtom's son?" Wolf asked.

Tommy started down the tunnel without seeing if Wolf followed. "His bastard. Don't think that you did a disfavor to me by killing him. Quite the opposite. I would have killed him myself if I thought I could have gotten away with it."

"I see."

"No, you don't. You have no idea. He raped my mother just to see if he could get a human pregnant. It took him months to get her knocked up, and he kept her tied to the bedpost the entire time. Even after I was born, he'd come to our place and beat the snot out of both of us and rape her again, just because he could."

"Is that why you helped me?"

Tommy glanced at Wolf, ears laid back. At the next intersection, he paused to ask quietly, "What am I?"

"You? You're an oni."

"The fuck I am. I'm a human."

"Your father—"

"Was a sadist pig." Tommy stalked off. "So my good, kind, beat-to-death mother doesn't count, even though she contributed half my genes, gave birth to me, and raised me to be a man? A human man. I'm *not* one of them. Not that that means shit to you elves."

Wolf had never considered that the half-oni would think of themselves as human. How could he refute the difference that mind-set made in a person? Making Tinker an elf had not changed her basically human outlook. If the half-oni had the capacity for human compassion, then it had to be logical that they could be revolted by the oni's lack of it.

"It means something to me," Wolf told Tommy.

Tommy stared at him again, as if trying to see into the inner workings of his mind. Perhaps he could. "We know that the plan is to kill all of us mixed-bloods alongside of the oni, but we're more willing to gamble on you elves being humane than the oni."

How ironic, that both sides were looking for humanity in the other.

"We don't want to be their slaves," Tommy continued. "We've had thirty years of that shit."

"Then why didn't you leave? There's a whole planet for you 'humans' to go to."

Tommy made a sound of disgust. "It's all so black-and-white to you elves? I don't get how you can live so long and not realize the world is full of grey. We didn't leave because we couldn't."

"Why couldn't you?"

"You can't just walk out at Shutdown. The UN has fences and guards and you have to have the right papers or they throw you in prison. And even if you get past the guards, you need a birth certificate and social security numbers and high school diplomas to live in the United States. And you need money, or you're out on the street and starving."

"And you don't have these things?"

"The oni are masters of keeping power to themselves. They've got all the paperwork. They try to keep us from learning how to speak and read English. They know how much money we're making, and they'll beat us half to death if they even suspect we're trying to keep a little on the side. We don't know how many oni there are in Pittsburgh—who is a disguised oni and who isn't—so we can't even turn to the humans for help. The oni spy on us as much as they spy on you."

Wolf wasn't sure if Tommy was telling him the truth, but certainly it would explain how the oni kept control of the half-breeds. He could see ways around the oni enslavement—until he remembered that all the half-oni would have been born and raised in the oni control. A child could be kept ignorant, molded into believing it was helpless.

Tommy stopped him with a hand on his shoulder. The half-oni's ears twitched. Wolf caught an echo of harsh voices. He would have to accept it as real.

"There are oni ahead of us," Tommy whispered. "We can't go this way. I can only cloud their sight and they have noses like dogs."

Wolf nodded, and followed Tommy back to a tunnel they'd passed before. They went through a maze of turns and up a flight of stairs to go through another grate into a basement stacked high with cardboard boxes. The labels indicated that the boxes once held cans of food. Just as Wolf wondered whether they still contained their original contents, Tommy opened a door and the smell of cooking food flooded over them.

Beyond the door was a large kitchen filled with Asians. A low right-angled counter divided the kitchen off from the restaurant's dining room. The long leg into the dining room was a bakery display case filled with buns and breads.

"What are you doing here, Tommy?" one of the cooks, an old man, asked in Mandarin as he took a tray of buns from the oven. "Bringing him here?"

"The oni are in the steam tunnels," Tommy answered in the same tongue.

"Ugh!" the old man grunted. "You'll get us all killed."

Wolf looked at the crowded kitchen. "These are all mixed bloods?"

"No." Tommy wove through the cooks. "These are all humans. That was my great-uncle."

A herd of children galloped into the kitchen from a back room. Some could pass as human—might even be fully human—but mixed in were children with horns and tails. With cries of dismay, in ones and twos, the adults yanked the children out of Wolf's path, leaving only one child standing alone.

The little female looked up at him fearlessly and he knew her. Zi.

"Hi." She cocked her head, puzzled by his presence. She had a cookie in either hand. She held one up to him. "Do you want a cookie?" And when he hesitated, she added, "I didn't drop it or anything."

"Thank you." Wolf took the cookie with his left hand and bowed slightly to her. "That is very nice of you."

"Come on." Tommy caught him by the left wrist, and said in rough Low Elvish, "If oni find you here—they kill everyone."

"What is she doing here?" Wolf resisted being moved. He had demanded that the little female be kept away from people that would poison her against elves.

"No one else would take her. The humans are afraid of the oni and the oni don't give a shit. Look at me, I'm Lord Tomtom's son, and even I don't get a disguise to protect me."

Wolf scanned the kitchen, seeing this time that the children were in the arms of only small-framed, battered women. There were only two males, men made fragile by time. They used Mandarin in their fearful cries, and it was Chinese written on the signs posted around the room. The Skin Clan had used this kind of slavery—transporting women out of their homelands to places they couldn't speak the language and then tied them down with children.

He understood now Tommy's hate. It was the same hate that had fueled the genocide of the Skin Clan.

Tommy suddenly pushed him back against the wall. "Stay still! I don't have my father's talent—I can't mask a moving object from multiple watchers. They will kill *everyone* if they find you here!" He glanced to his uncle. "Mask the scent!"

The uncle opened the fridge, took out a container, and flung the contents on the grill. An eye-watering reek filled the air. "Onions! Pepper!"

While some of the women quickly herded the children upstairs, others took out knives and attacked onions and bright red peppers. Tommy's focus was on the door. Moments later, it opened, and oni warriors crowded into the restaurant. There were a dozen large, red-haired, horned males. They had war paint on their faces and carried machine guns and swords. They snarled in Oni, wrinkling up their noses against the assault of smell.

The leader was the tallest among them. He set four of the warriors to watch the street and barked orders to the others. Three warriors raided the bakery counter. The rest moved into the kitchen and back rooms. The leader picked out a female, shoved her face down onto one of the tables, tore away her skirt, and forced himself into her with brutal casualness. The woman pressed knuckles into her mouth, stifling whimpers. No one else appeared even to notice, but Tommy locked down hard on Wolf's good arm.

The bakery raiders stuffed their mouths and pockets and then flung the buns to other warriors.

Outside, a deep roar from Malice echoed up the street.

"He sounds hungry." The leader spoke Mandarin so that the humans could understand. "He's probably looking for something to eat."

The warriors bayed with laughter and gestured at the frightened women. "We can feed him one of these fat sluts. That one looks like it has a fat ass."

The leader finished with the woman he was raping and slapped her buttocks. "Yes, a nice fat ass."

Their hunger satisfied, the warriors pelted each other with bread. The leader barked an order. The warriors gathered again at the front of the restaurant. The last one out of the back room, though, was carrying a whimpering, squirming Zi.

"Look what they have." The warrior held the little female out by the back of her shirt.

The leader took her by her throat. He turned and shook the child at the human like rag doll. "What is this doing here?"

"The EIA—" Uncle stuttered. "They imprisoned her crazy mother."

The leader grunted. "If the elves find this here, they'll know that this place belongs to us."

"We'll move her." Uncle held out his arms but moved no closer to the warriors.

Without word or warning the oni leader broke Zi's neck.

Everyone had told Wolf about the oni savageness—but he hadn't comprehended it fully until too late. He gasped out in shock as the oni leader dropped the child's limp body onto the floor.

"Malice is coming. Throw this out onto the street for him to eat."

Wolf breathed in and anger burned through him like fire. Nothing mattered but to see these monsters dead. He jerked his arm free of Tommy, summoned a force strike and slammed it into the back of the oni leader. The front of the restaurant exploded out as the strike drove the oni male across the street. He made a bloody star on the far building. The warriors scrambled for cover, pulling out their machine guns.

"Hold still, you stupid elf fuck!" Tommy growled.

Wolf braced himself as he flicked through a fire burst. The oni bullets chewed through the other side of the restaurant. Apparently between Wolf's sudden attack and Tommy clouding their minds, the oni were disoriented as to where Wolf was really standing. The fire burst went off, igniting three of the oni into columns of flame.

Wolf slammed a force strike at the last oni. A second bloody star joined the first.

"What the fuck was that?" Tommy screamed. "She was dead! This does nothing but make you feel better! All those women and children are now dead because you had to be a hero!"

Someone as young as the half-oni couldn't understand that to be immortal was to have forever to regret. Wolf knew if he had let the oni walk away unpunished, he would not be able to live with himself. But Tommy was right. He had brought danger down on the rest—the human mothers and half-oni children.

"I'll see that they're safe until this is done."

"Yeah, that will make the kids safe! Until you kill them for no other reason than their mothers were raped by the wrong species."

"I give you my word—they will not be harmed."

Tommy caught himself from saying anything else, and stood, fists balled, panting.

"Windwolf?" Oilcan murmured in Wolf's ear. "If you're the one that just took out the Changs' restaurant, Malice is coming your way."

Wolf glanced out into the street where the oni still burned like massive candles. "Malice is coming. Get the others. We need to move to someplace safe."

Tommy's cat ears flicked. "Oh fuck. He is coming." Tommy went off to gather the women and children.

Wolf gazed again the wreckage he was leaving behind. Tinker was rubbing off on him.

22: END OF THE RAINBOW

Briggs drove while the rest of them sat in the back. Tinker had grabbed a flex screen from the ship and now spread it out on the floor. Downloading the dreadnaught's layout and defenses, they planned the assault.

"The dreadnaught's biggest weakness is that it wasn't built with an aerial attack in mind. It's like a turtle, with lots of service hatches down in through its shell. Also it tends to be blind in the butt. I was going to fix that with a turret on top."

"Prince True Flame said that it was useless for fighting the dragon because it couldn't defend against from attacks from above," Pony said.

"That's true," Tinker said. "So we're going to have to kill Malice before he has a chance to close."

"Oh, fun," Esme muttered.

"But the airship is vulnerable to the tengu," Tinker said. "I think if we fly up behind it, we can approach it unseen—but it leaves a very choppy wake."

"We can handle it, *domi*." Jin waved off the worry.

Domi. That drove her commitment to them home and left her a little breathless. *I'm responsible for them—and I'm taking them straight into danger.* But what recourse did she have? Just as the elves were not about to let the oni live, the oni couldn't leave any of the elves alive either.

"We need three things." Tinker forced herself to focus on the plan and not how badly it might end. "We need to keep the ship in the air, pick where it goes, and fire the cannons. So, that means we need to secure the fore and aft engine compartments, the cannon turrets, and the bridge."

Pony gazed at the plan for a moment, and then pointed to the access hatch nearest to the rear, which opened to the aft engine compartment. "We'll enter here. Once we've secured it, we'll break into teams. These tengu are good with machines—yes?" Getting a nod from Tinker, Pony continued. "There are three doors to this area including the hatch, so Little Egret and four tengu will stay."

Jin assigned Xiao Chen and three of the other tengu to the aft team.

"The rest of us will then move to the fore engine compartment and take it." Pony traced a route across the top of the airship to the forwardmost service hatch. "Four doors open to this area, but we'll control what's beyond these two doors. Rainlily and four of the tengu will hold this position. We split here. *Domi* and Cloudwalker will take the bridge with Esme, Jin, and Durrack—which should be lightly manned and will have only one door not controlled by us. Stormsong and Briggs will come with me. We'll take the main cannon turret— which will be heavily manned."

Tinker explained how she planned to kill Malice. "Now when this spell goes off, you're going to lose your shields and it might take a minute or two before a normal level of magic is restored," she warned her Hand. "Your beads should be protected from the spell effects, so if you save the power in them, you can recast your shields immediately."

The *sekasha* nodded, indicating that they understood.

Durrack pressed his hand to his ear and listened to it intently. "Okay. Understand." He knocked on the partition to the driver's cabin. "Briggs? Where are we?"

"Nearly to McKees Rocks Bridge," Briggs answered.

"The dreadnaught is here." Durrack tapped the map just down-river of Neville's Island, and then ran a finger up the Ohio River toward Pittsburgh. "They're following the river."

"If we're carrying others, we won't be able to climb fast," Jin said. "We should start high, like at the edge of a cliff or on top of a building."

"They'll come over the bridge," Pony pointed to the bridge. "We can wait on the supports. The bridge will give us cover, and then the tengu can take us aloft."

"That will work," Jin said.

Nearly a mile and a half long, the McKees Rocks Bridge stretched across the wide, flat Ohio River valley in a complex string of structures—more a chain of bridges than one single bridge. The part that actually sat above the river was a seven hundred feet long trussed-arch bridge. On each side of the elegant steel curve were two massive stone pylons. They hid the truck in the shadows of the western pylon.

The cloudy night was on their side—it cloaked them in darkness.

"I hear it." Jin put out a hand to Tinker. "I'll take you up."

The other eight tengu paired off with the humans and elves.

It was a short spring up to the arching steel. They crouched down, tucking themselves in the crossbeams.

The roar of the dreadnaught grew louder.

"There! See it?" Jin whispered.

Twin searchlights appeared in the distance, slashing downwards; the cockpit was a pale gleam between them. The dreadnaught moved up the broad valley, keeping between the hills that flanked the Ohio River. The searchlights played back and forth in a narrow arc, directly in front of the airship.

Durrack glanced upriver toward the darkened city and then back to the oncoming dreadnaught. "They're probably following the river because it's the most recognizable landmark they can see with the power out."

"Lucky for us," Jin said. "They're going slow so they don't hit anything. That will make it easier for us to get to it."

In the dark, the true size of the dreadnaught was lost. It was a wedge of darkness behind the searchlights' brilliance. They crouched in the bridge's shadows as the gleaming spots moved across the shimmer of the water, encountered the bridge, and played up and over the network of steel struts. Tinker held still, heart hammering, trying not to think about the machine gun cannons. Her luck on this kind of thing had been so bad lately.

The cockpit slid overhead, and the belly of the dreadnaught followed, the air throbbing. Ushi with Pony leapt upward, the rustle of his black wings spreading lost under the rumble of the dreadnaught's engines. As he took his first downstroke, Xiao Chen with Stormsong vaulted after him. Niu and Zan rose together. Tinker lost sight of them in the dreadnaught's eclipse.

Jin took hold of Tinker and murmured, "Hang on." And then they were airborne.

Amazingly, in some strange heart-stopping manner, winging upward was fun. In her flights with Riki, she had been so concerned about their end destination that she never noticed the thrill of flying. Did it say something about her that as long as she knew where they were going, she could enjoy the ride?

Jin landed them between Ushi and Xiao Chen.

"I think I envy you," Stormsong murmured to Xiao Chen.

Tinker smothered a laugh, and whispered. "Yeah, once you get used to it, it's fairly cool."

"It's wood!" Jin whispered, running his hand over the hull's surface.

"Of course," Tinker whispered. "These are elves."

Her Hand activated their shields. Pony asked a question with blade talk. Getting a nod from the others, he opened the hatch and the *sekasha* dropped down into the dim engine room.

She had never seen the elves really fighting before. Not a full Hand against hordes, unconcerned for her protection because she was safe behind her own shield. She hadn't expected it to be so beautiful. Their swordplay became a fluid dance, the oni seeming like paper cutouts instead of real opponents. The dreadnaught, though, was buzzing like a kicked beehive, and they had spread themselves thin.

On the bridge, Tinker used her shield to back the oni warriors away from the door. Cloudwalker slipped around her on the right and Durrack went left.

"Don't shoot any of the instruments!" Tinker had her pistol out, but was afraid to fire. She rarely hit what she aimed at and all the controls were vital to their success.

"I—don't—miss." Durrack picked his shots with deliberation. "Someone get the pilot before he crashes us!"

Two warriors blocked Tinker.

"Esme, the pilot." Jin spun on one heel and kicked one of the warriors out of Tinker's path. Tinker edged sideways, covering Esme as her mother scrambled into the low cockpit.

The ship banked hard to the left, rushing toward the hills that lined the valley, Esme struggled with the oni pilot.

"Tinker!" Esme cried. "We need to lift! Pull up on the collective."

Dropping her shield, Tinker scrambled into the cockpit and grabbed hold of the collective control stick and pulled up. The engines roared louder and they started to climb.

"Tinker!" Jin shouted warning, and she ducked instinctively.

Bullets sprayed the windshield just over her head. A dozen bullet holes reduced the Plexiglas to a haze of cracked glass.

The oni pilot kicked Tinker backward. She hit the cracked windshield; it held for a moment then gave way. She screamed, flailing, and caught hold of the pilot's leg as she fell. Her weight jerked him half out the cockpit. He grabbed the edge of the cockpit before he fell the whole way out. They dangled far above the last mile of I-279 before it ended at the Rim, the oni pilot holding onto the airship and Tinker onto his leg.

"Jin!" Esme shouted, struggling to keep the airship aloft and reach for the oni pilot at the same time. "I can't reach her!"

Jin shouted; his words resonated against Tinker's senses with magic.

The oni pilot clawed at the edge of cockpit, trying to pull himself up. He grasped the windshield wiper and started to pull himself up.

The wiper snapped and he fell—and Tinker with him.

Tinker screamed and Esme, staring down at her, cried out in dismay.

Then someone caught Tinker's wrist, and she was jerked hard in both directions.

"Let go of him!" Keiko cried, flapping madly. "I can't catch you both; we'll all fall."

"No! No! No!" the pilot wailed, dangling upside down by Tinker's grip on his leg. But she wasn't strong enough to hold his weight by one hand. He slipped out of her hold and plunged downward again. The clouds had slid away and moonlight gleamed silver on the pavement below. The pilot dwindled to doll size but still hit the road with a loud carrying thud, a sudden burst of wet on the grey pavement.

"Shit, shit, shit!" Keiko cried as they continued to slowly fall. "You're still too heavy."

Xiao Chen swooped down and tried to intercept them.

Keiko hissed in anger, bringing up her razor-sheathed feet. "She's charmed by the Chosen's blood. She's not to be hurt!"

"You heard her," Riki glided in. "She's charmed by my line!"

"It's only Xiao—" Tinker yelped as Keiko suddenly passed her to Riki in a mid-air fling.

"I got you," Riki said it as if this was supposed to be comforting. "Keiko!"

The tengu female was heading for the airship. "I was called! He's here! He called!"

"Keiko!" Riki shouted, chasing after the teenager. "Wait! Damn it, Tinker, who is on that dreadnaught?"

"Your uncle Jin."

"That's not possi—" Riki gasped as they swept back in through the shattered windshield and he saw Jin. "Uncle Jin?"

Jin reached out and pulled Tinker out of Riki's hold. "Are you okay?"

"I'm fine." Tinker fought the need to cling to Riki, or Jin. *I'm safe inside. I'm safe inside.*

"What the hell is going on? Where did you come from?" Riki gazed in stunned amazement at the tengu, elves, and humans.

"We got her. She's safe." Durrack had found the speaker tubes to the gun turret and engine rooms. Cloudwalker and Keiko were holding the door that boomed with the oni's attempts to break it down. "Tinker, your cousin says that Malice has Windwolf pinned down in Oakland. If you don't want to be a widow, we better get going."

It took Tinker a second to realize that Durrack had received the last part via his earbud radio and not the speakertube.

"What?" Riki cried. "You're taking on Malice? Are you nuts?"

"I've got a plan." Tinker wondered if that sounded remotely reassuring. She couldn't stop trembling. *Yeah, yeah, I'm fine.* "Do we have the guns?" she asked.

"The Storms are holding the guns." Durrack meant Storm Horse and Stormsong.

Tinker hugged herself, panting, trying to remember said plan. She was missing something important. "Oilcan? Wait? Where's Impatience? I don't want to take him out with this spell—he'll revert to a wild animal and kill anyone near him."

"He's in the cathedral with your cousin," Durrack said.

"Okay, I *really* don't want Impatience in the spell range then." Tinker thought a moment. "Tell Oilcan to put distance between him and Impatience—just to be on the safe side. Esme, let's do a strafing run on Malice."

"And NASA thought it covered all possible flight simulations." Esme banked the ship hard back toward the city.

Clouds continued to clear, and the city resolved out of the darkness. Their shadow ran on ahead of them. Esme climbed out of the river valley, and crested over the Hill District to the flat plain of Oakland.

"Where is Malice?" Tinker asked Durrack.

"See that dark cloud?" Durrack pointed at a billow of darkness that looked like smoke. "That's him."

"Oh, good, he's at least a half mile from the cathedral." Tinker started to unload her bag, setting up for the spell. "Let's get his attention. Esme, get ready to run. Pony, can you hear me?"

"Yes, *domi*."

"Shoot Malice with one of the cannons. He's going to come fast, so get ready with the other cannon. Fire the second cannon when my spell takes your shield down."

"Yes, *domi*," Pony said.

Esme had edged sideways so that they hung over Fifth Avenue where it spilled down the hill toward the flood plain of Uptown. The cannon thundered, deafening at close range. The shell whistled away. It hit the edge of the miasma and the black deepened. Something stirred in the darkness. Massive eyes gleamed at the heart of the cloud and then Malice uncoiled and lifted from the ground.

"Here he comes!" Tinker cried.

Esme scuttled the airship backward, roaring out over Uptown, keeping the cannons pointed toward the onrushing dragon. "Come on, come on."

Suddenly Malice dove into the ground.

"Where the fuck did he go?" Esme cried.

"He's phased!" Durrack shouted. "He can move through solid objects!"

"Oh, you've got to be shitting me!" Esme flung the airship forward and they raced up Fifth Avenue, into the heart of Oakland.

"Where are you going?" Tinker cried.

"You said run." Esme put all power into forward motion, tilting the airship to fit down the narrow space of Fifth Avenue. They lost something—hopefully not vital—as they took out one of the red lights over the street.

"Not this way!" Tinker cried, pointing at the towering cathedral that stood over Oakland, where Oilcan was with Impatience.

"It had to be this way!" Esme snapped.

Tinker looked behind them. Malice rose out of the ground where they would have been if they had continued toward Uptown. "Okay, this is good."

"He'll come after us," Esme said. "Trust me. When you run, it's like you put out a sign that says 'free lunch.' It's an easy way to make even the smartest ones get stupid."

Perhaps she was right; Malice was giving chase, coiling through the air like a snake in water. Esme banked around the curve of the Hill, nearly clipping the tops of houses.

"It's like trying to drag race in a Volkswagen," Esme complained.

Tinker had been watching the cathedral dwindle behind them. She realized now that they were heading into Downtown, the most densely populated area in Pittsburgh.

"No, not this way either!" Tinker pointed away from the city. "I don't want to open fire in the middle of the city!"

"I don't either," Esme said as they skimmed across the Veterans

Bridge and ducked into the forest of skyscrapers. "But we need time for me to get turned around and face him."

They wove through the tall buildings, the gleam of the cockpit reflecting in the glass walls as they streaked by.

"Okay, keep going west." Tinker pointed out west just in case Esme didn't know. "After you get out of the city, try to get Malice south of us, up against Mount Washington. It's a blank slate. We can open fire on him there."

Esme suddenly squeaked in surprise and banked hard to the right. A moment later Malice came *through* a skyscraper and fire jetted out of his mouth. The night went bright with the flame, the light reflecting off the canyon of glass around them.

"Oh shit!" Esme banked again, somehow dodging both the flame and the PPG tower. She clipped the side of the Fifth Avenue Place. "Oh shit—we lost our front right props." She fought the ship to keep it from careening out of control. "No one said anything about him breathing fire!"

"He's a dragon," Jin said. "That's what they do!"

"We've got a fire up here!" one of the tengu shouted from the front engine room.

"We're running out of city," Durrack warned.

"I know, I know, I know." Tinker was loath to open fire in the city, but if Malice took the airship down, they'd lose the guns and then they'd all die. Point Park was going to have to do. "Get ready, people!"

Esme wrenched the airship about as they roared over the empty expanse of the park. Malice flew at them. Tinker watched him come, spell in hand, waiting for him to get clear of the city.

When he cleared the highway dividing the city from the park, she cast the spell.

The coldness flashed over her. The wings vanished from the tengu's backs. Cloudwalker's shield winked out. The miasma of Malice's shield vanished and he fell, twisting madly as he plunged out of the sky. The cannon roared. The shell caught him in the left eye, blasting his head backward.

"I'm losing it!" Esme shouted as the dreadnaught slid sideways toward the massive Fort Pitt Bridge. "We're going down!" Tinker called for her shields and nothing happened. The ambient magic in the area hadn't recovered from the flux spell yet. "Oh shit."

And then they hit the bridge.

⊷⊜⊷

Wolf braced himself for the worst. He had trusted that Tinker would somehow kill the dragon, but he was afraid she had leapt one too many times into the void. As he hurried toward the downed dreadnaught, his fears only deepened. The airship had struck the first span of the twin-decked bridge and then crashed into the Mononga-hela River. The crumpled wreckage lay half in and half out of the wa-ter. Human emergency crews gathered on the shore and on the water, trucks and boats with bright flashing lights.

Wolf pushed through the tightest knot of people to find Little Egret lying unconscious on the pavement. A pair of soaked tengu were giving the young *sekasha* CPR. As he watched, Little Egret coughed and sputtered weakly back to life. Oilcan had told him that the astronaut tengu were helping Tinker kill the dragon. He assumed that these two were part of that crew.

"Where's Tinker?" Wolf asked the two tengu.

"We were in the aft engine room." The tengu female indicated the submerged section of the dreadnaught and then made a vague motion at the part smashed up against the bridge. "She was in the cockpit."

He left a healer from the hospice with Little Egret and moved on, working his way around the airship. One section was still burning, and the humans were frantically trying to douse the flames. Wolf caught snatches of their conversations that focused on the live ammo still on board the ship.

There was a body under a white sheet. He paused to draw aside the sheet. A male tengu, badly burned.

Little Horse, Discord, and Briggs were on the other side of the wreckage. They worked with the Pittsburgh fire fighters and more tengu, hacking at the splintered wood hull.

"*Domi* was on the bridge with Cloudwalker." Little Horse hacked at a section of the hull with his *ejae*. "Rainlily took in too much smoke, but she got out without being burned. Two of the tengu with her were not so lucky. You were hurt?"

Wolf held up his spell-covered hand, careful not to flex. "Just this but it's healing." Wolf glanced over at a row of dead bodies covered with sheets. "How many tengu did you take with you?"

"Those are oni." Discord was favoring the leg bitten by the dragon earlier in the week. "Most we killed taking the dreadnaught."

Blood on the pavement showed that there had been fighting after the crash too.

A cry went up and people were lifted free of the wreckage. A tengu male and female, both young, faces painted for war. They were battered but alive.

"Were they with you or against you?" Wolf asked.

"They caught *domi* when she was knocked from the dreadnaught," Little Horse said.

"*Domi* promised that all tengu would be under her protection," Discord added.

"All?" Wolf indicated that the war-painted tengu were not to be harmed. "How many does that include?"

Discord shrugged and then gave a wry smile. "I do not think *domi* bothered to find out."

More survivors were lifted out. Durrack, a woman, and another pair of tengu, these from the spaceship.

"I can see shielding!" Little Horse cried. "Cloudwalker has his shield up!"

"He and *domi* should be the only ones left," Discord said.

They cut carefully through the shattered wood and broken instruments to the young *sekasha*. Despite his shield, he'd been knocked unconscious. He still protected Tinker, however, in his loose hold. Wraith leaned into the hole they had cut and whispered to Tinker the word to deactivate Cloudwalker's shields, which needed to be spoken close to the *sekasha*'s heart. It felt like eternity before the hurt and dazed Tinker understood what was wanted of her and the shimmering blue of the shields vanished.

The healers from the hospice cast spells to make sure they could be safely moved, then the two were lifted carefully out of the womb of twisted wreckage. Only then could Wolf hold Tinker in his arms and reassure himself that she had emerged once again safely out of the void. She seemed so small and fragile without her normal vibrant personality.

"Oh, thank gods, I was so worried about you," she murmured as if it had been him in the airship. "The others?"

"Your Hand is safe." He spared her the news of the dead tengu.

She cried in dismay at the extent of the damage to the airship. "Oh, I crashed True Flame's dreadnaught! He's going to be angry."

"He will not care. It is a thing. All things wear out—just usually not in such a spectacular fashion."

Tinker groaned.

"Do not worry, beloved. He will only be concerned that you and yours are safe and that the dragon is dead."

Tinker whimpered against his shoulder. "Windwolf, I've made the tengu mine."

"So I've heard."

"Please, don't hurt them. I promised them that they will be safe."

"They are safe."

"You won't hurt them?"

"I will protect them for you." He kissed her carefully. "Rest."

True Flame and the Stone Clan were arriving, so he reluctantly, gave Tinker over to the healers and the protection of her beholden.

True Flame stopped on the edge of the roadway where he could see the dead dragon, the crashed dreadnaught, and in the distance, like an exclamation mark in the weak morning sky, the towering spaceship.

"You were right, Wolf."

"I was?"

"She's surprisingly destructive for one so small. I am starting to see why you love her so—she is the right size for you."

"Yes, she is."

A shout caught his attention. Little Horse and Wraith Arrow were holding the Stone Clan *sekasha* back from the tengu.

"What's going on here?" True Flame stalked down to the river's edge.

"These tengu are still alive." Earth Son stood behind his First, Thorne Scratch. He pointed at the battered and soaked tengu who had given Little Egret CPR.

"Yes," Wolf noticed that the Wyverns were watching. A whispered discussion was being passed through their ranks. "And they are staying that way. My *domi* has taken the tengu as beholden."

"They are oni," Earth Son snapped. "We must eliminate the monsters before they can breed to dangerous numbers."

"The tengu and the half-oni are no different than the elves," Wolf pitched his argument to True Flame and the silent *sekasha*. "We were created by the Skin Clan, as they were created by the oni. They are turning on the oni as we turned on the Skin Clan. Yes, the oni are as evil as the Skin Clan—but we merely need to look at ourselves to know that good can come from evil."

"Tengu flock together." Forest Moss drifted into the conversation, his tone light, as if he was discussing clouds. Wolf could not tell how the mad one felt on the issue. "Their loyalty to one another will supersede any claim that they make to you. If you act against one of their brethren, they will turn on you."

"Tinker *ze domi* holds all the tengu," the astronaut tengu named Jin said.

True Flame looked at Jin. "All? How many are all?"

The war-painted male stepped forward, apparently speaking for the Elfhome-based tengu. "We don't have a full count. It has been too dangerous to count, lest the oni ever found out what we were doing."

"Which was?" Wolf asked.

"We hoped to be free here on Elfhome," Riki said. "So in the last twenty-eight years, all of the tengu of Earth and Onihida have come to Elfhome."

"All?" True Flame glanced over the ten living tengu. "Are we speaking hundreds? Thousands? Millions?"

"Several thousand." Riki glanced to Jin to see if he should be more specific and got a nod. "We believe around twenty thousand."

Which meant they greatly outnumbered the oni now trapped on Elfhome.

True Flame turned to Wolf. "How does your *domi* possibly think she could hold all of them?"

"Through me," Jin said, "I am Jin Wong. I am the heart and soul and voice of the tengu. I speak, and all will listen."

"I doubt this greatly," True Flame said.

Jin raised his hands and gave out a call toward the east. It resonated with magic, as if his voice alone triggered some spell. He turned to the north and called. He faced the west and called. Even as he faced the south and called, a rustle of wings announced the arrival of a great flock of tengu. The sky went dark with the crow-black feathers. Warriors all, faces painted, and feet sheathed in sharpened steel. They carried guns holstered on their hips. They settled silently on the bridge trusses, the tops of buildings, and streetlights.

When the last tengu went still, Jin called again, magic pulsing out from him. It echoed off the buildings and the hillside across the river. He turned, gazing at them, as if he too were stunned by the massive numbers of them. "I am Jin Wong! I have returned to our people!"

And the tengu flock shouted back, "Jin! Jin! Jin!"

Jin raised his hands and the flock fell silent. "We are entering into an alliance with the elves. We are taking Tinker *ze domi* as our protector. Under her, I hope that for the first time our people will live in peace, security, and prosperity."

The flock roared in approval, a deafening sound that washed over them. Jin raised his hand, commanding silence, and received instant obedience.

"Jin offered his people," Wolf said in the silence. "*Domi* offered her protection. Such an oath, once made, no other person can break."

"This is true," True Flame said.

Earth Son had cast his shield, encompassing only him and his *sekasha*. "She can't hold them. This is preposterous."

"They fit the model of a household with Jin as the head," Wolf said.

"Only clan heads can hold that many people," Earth Son said. "And she is nothing but a—"

"She is my *domi* and we are the clan heads of the Westernlands," Wolf growled. "Forest Moss is right. You are blind. Tinker has closed the Ghostlands." Wolf pointed to Malice's massive body. "She killed the dragon that four of us could not harm. She has made a peace with a force that we didn't even know existed. Do not assign her your limitations. We can hold the tengu."

"They are monsters!" Earth Son shouted.

Wolf shook his head. "They were once human, forced into their shape by cruel masters. They have fought beside my *domi* to kill the dragon. They have protected my youngest *sekasha* from harm."

"You are a traitor to your people," Earth Son spat the accusation and then looked to True Flame, as if challenging the prince to refute it.

True Flame said nothing, waiting to see the outcome of the debate.

Wolf directed his argument to the Wyvern and the Stone Clan *sekasha* because he knew that his Hands had already decided on the issue—they wouldn't have defended the tengu otherwise. But their decision was based on their trust in him. The others would need convincing. "My people are those that offer me their loyalty, be they elfin, human, tengu, or half-blooded oni. It is my duty as *domana* to extend protection to those weaker than I am."

"It is our duty to keep our race pure," Earth Son said.

"That is our Skin Clan forefathers speaking. Kill the misbegotten children. Eliminate the unwanted genetic line. Ignore trust, obedience, loyalty, and love in the search for perfection. It was the Skin Clan's way, but it is not ours."

"This is insanity. They breed like mice. All of them do. The oni and the humans. This is our world. If we don't eliminate them, they will overwhelm us."

"If they offer their loyalty and we give them our protection—do they not become one of us? They do not lessen us—they make us greater."

Earth Son worked his mouth for a minute, and then finally cried. "No! No, no, no! They are filthy lying creatures. I am Stone Clan head of the Westernlands, and I say that the Stone Clan will never accept this!"

"I do not care what the Stone Clan accepts." Wolf cocked his fingers, wondering if Earth Son would be as stupid as to actually start a fight with all the tengu assembled. Since Earth Son was holding shields, he could strike quickly. "Know this—the tengu are Wind Clan now. I will protect them."

Earth Son made a motion. It was a start of a spell. What spell Wolf would never know. Wolf snapped his hand up to summon the winds, even though he would be too late to block the attack. Thorne Scratch reacted first. With deliberate calm, she struck out and beheaded Earth Son. His lifeblood sprayed his Hand, but none moved against their First. They watch impassively as his body toppled to the ground.

"We will not follow the path of the Skin Clan." Thorne Scratch cleaned the blood from her *ejae*.

Red Knife, True Flame's First, nodded. "Those that offer loyalty will be protected."

Jewel Tear gazed down at Earth Son's body. "As temporary Stone Clan head of the Westernlands, I recognize that non-elfin can be beholden."

23: PEACE

Tinker woke slowly. She had been dreaming, but for once, it was a pleasant dream of the new viceroy palace being complete. She had walked from room to room to room, marveling that all this was hers. Theirs.

When she opened her eyes, she knew instantly she was in her own bed at Poppymeadow's because Windwolf lay beside her, his black hair poured like silk across the cream satin sheets. Contentment poured through her like warm honey. She snuggled closer to him. For once the taffy thickness of the *saijin*-induced sleep didn't seem threatening. If she was with Windwolf, then everything was right with the world.

And then with sudden dark coldness, she remembered the tengu. She had promised to protect them but then had let the elves drug her. What had she been thinking of? The elves would have only seen the tengu as enemies.

She sat up, hands to her mouth to hold in the cries of dismay. What had happened after she was carried away? Were Jin, Grace, Xiao Chen, and all the others already dead?

"Beloved?" Windwolf sat up beside her.

"Oh gods, I failed them! I promised Jin I would protect the tengu! I failed them."

"You did not. You are my *domi*. Your promises are mine. I protected them. It was, after all, the right thing to do."

She knew, in a way she wouldn't have known a week ago, what she had asked of him, and how different he had to be from other elves to understand. There been a secret fear hiding inside her that he wouldn't understand, that instead of being a powerful protector, he would be in truth a ruthless killer. That cold knot of fear dissolved.

"Oh, thank you!" She hugged him tight. She didn't need anything else but to be in his arms and hear his heart beating. She snuggled closer, wanting to drown in the *saijin*-laced honey contentment. She never wanted to let him go; never wanted to risk losing him forever again.

"It was the least I could do after you solved that small dragon problem I had." He said it with complete seriousness, but there was laughter in his eyes.

She laughed, tangling her fingers in his hair and pulling him down to kiss her. She delighted in his taste, the feel of his hands on her, finding the hem of her nightgown to slide up her bare skin.

"I love you," she murmured. "I'm never letting you go."

His gaze went serious and deep. "I am going nowhere, my love."

Only later, after a proper renewal of their relationship, did she think about another small dragon problem.

"What happened with Impatience when we did the flux spell? Is Oilcan okay?"

"He is fine." Windwolf smoothed away her fear. "Your spell did not affect the little dragon. And the tengu have been quite useful already. With their help, we had a long discussion with Impatience about creating a pathway to Earth. The question is where to put it."

"What about the Squirrel Hill tunnels? They go nowhere now."

Windwolf considered for a moment and then nodded. "Yes, that would be expedient."

Using the tunnels would open four travel lanes between Elfhome and Earth and yet be easily controlled. "Wow."

"I told you, beloved, you and I would shake the universe until we found a way."

EPILOGUE: CUP OF JOYS

Elves may live forever, but their memories do not. Every elfin child is taught that any special memory has to be polished bright and carefully stored away at the end of a day, else it will slip away and soon be forgotten. The eve of Memory was past, but Wolf wanted to share the ceremony with his *domi*—even if somewhat belatedly. They had time now. He wanted her to know how to save the memories of all that had happened in the last few days, the good along with the bad.

Wolf settled before the altar of Nheoya, god of longevity. His beloved sat down beside him.

Tinker took a deep breath and let it out in a deep, heartfelt sigh. "This is going to be like being dragged through thorns—there's so much I regret. So many ways I've fucked up."

"This is not to punish yourself, beloved. Nothing is gained from that. The worth comes from reflecting on the events—removed from the passion that blinded you at the time—and learning from the mistakes."

"Easier said than done."

"Think of it as something that has happened to someone else—the person that you used to be and not the person you are now."

She nodded and lit the candle of memory. Together, they clapped to call the god's attention to them and bestowed their gifts of silver on the altar. They sat in companionable silence, waiting to reach perfect calmness before starting the ceremony. Wolf reached his center quickly, but waited until Tinker was ready to pick up the cup of tears and taste the bitter memories.

He allowed himself to reflect on his failure with Jewel Tear and the bitter things she had to say to him. There was some truth in what she had to say. He had allowed silence to create a gulf between his heart and hers, so that their dreams took different forms. He would have to remember this, remind himself to keep his heart open to his beloved, so that they could share their dreams.

Dawn was breaking, and the cups of tears were drained, so they set aside their bitter memories. As light spilled into the temple, they lifted the cups of joys.

All Wolf's new moments of happiness centered on Tinker. They were scattered through his days, bright like diamonds. As he took them out, played them close, and stored them away, he found a pattern to them. In every occasion, he had known he had at last found the one who could not only understand his vision, but see possibilities that he hadn't considered, and had the ability to make them real. He found at the root of it all a loneliness he hadn't allowed himself to acknowledge, an awareness that he had been totally alone while surrounded by people, an emptiness now completely filled.

"Are you okay?" Tinker asked him in English.

He smiled. He had told her that he felt most free speaking English, and by her answering look, she remembered. "Yes, I am very content at this moment."

"Good. So am I." But then unease seeped into her eyes.

"What is it, beloved?"

"You probably have someplace to go, something you need to do."

He held out his hand to her, and she took it, interlacing their fingers. "What I need is to sit here with my *domi* and talk about what we want to do next."

The End

ABOUT THE AUTHOR

Born in 1963, Wen Spencer grew up on the family farm in Evans City, Pennsylvnia. Not ones to be typical, her family raised mink, ring-neck pheasants, Shetland ponies, quail, geese, turkeys, rabbits, German sheperds, Labrador retrievers, and Christmas trees. Graduating from the University of Pittsburgh with a degree in Information Science, Wen worked various jobs from Aluminum Expediting to Medical Research and Museum Renovation. Having lived in Pittsburgh's neighborhoods of Oakland, Bloomfield, Bellevue, Avalon and Ben Avon for almost twenty years, it seemed only natural to set her science fiction novels there. She has written three novels—*Alien Taste* (which received a four-star review from *Romantic Times*), *Tainted Trail* and *Bitter Waters*—which combine private eye and science fiction genres with striking success.